EVERY FAMILY HAS ITS LITTLE SECRETS.

continued ...

KAREN ROSE

CLOSER THAN YOU THINK

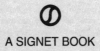

A SIGNET BOOK

SIGNET
Published by the Penguin Group
Penguin Group (USA) LLC, 375 Hudson Street,
New York, New York 10014

USA | Canada | UK | Ireland | Australia | New Zealand | India | South Africa | China
penguin.com
A Penguin Random House Company

Published by Signet, an imprint of New American Library,
a division of Penguin Group (USA) LLC

First American Printing, February 2015

Copyright © Karen Hafer, 2015

Ⓟ REGISTERED TRADEMARK — MARCA REGISTRADA

ISBN 978-0-451-46673-0

Printed in the United States of America
10   9   8   7

PUBLISHER'S NOTE
This is a work of fiction. Names, characters, places, and incidents either are the
product of the author's imagination or are used fictitiously, and any resemblance
to actual persons, living or dead, business establishments, events, or locales is
entirely coincidental.

To my readers all over the world.
You make it possible for me to have the coolest job ever.

To my wonderful family and friends, for your support
during this difficult year. I love you all more than I can say.

As always, to Martin, for loving me just the way that I am.
You are my heart.

ACKNOWLEDGMENTS

Marc Conterato, for answering my medical questions when you probably have much better things to do!

Cheryl Wilson, Christine Feehan, Susan Edwards, and Kathy Firzlaff, for welcoming me into your writing group. Writing with you has been my anchor. Cheryl, you were unequivocally right—I should have joined you guys a lot sooner!

Terri Bolyard, Kay Conterato, and Sonie Lasker, for helping me brainstorm when I got stuck and for encouraging me through this year.

Mandy Kersey, for taking care of all the barn details so that I could write this book and for going with me to the hospital even though you knew it was going to make you queasy.

Caitlin Longstreet, for being everything I've needed you to be and more.

Denise Pizzo, for getting me back in the writing chair (and keeping me there).

Claire Zion, Vicki Mellor, and Robin Rue, for your ongoing encouragement and for allowing me to tell my stories the way the characters tell them to me.

Martin Hafer, for loving me, for taking care of our family, and for supporting my dreams. You are the very best.

As always, all mistakes are my own.

Prologue

Oh God. Corinne fought the sudden wave of nausea, contracting her body into the fetal position. *Wine. Too much wine. This is the worst hangover ever.*

But . . . *Wait. No. Can't be.* A sliver of clarity returning, she shook her head, swallowing a moan when the room tilted. *Haven't had a drink in two years.*

The flu. Dammit. She'd had the damn flu shot. She lifted her hands to rub her eyes, but —

Tied. Realization rushed in. She gave her arms a panicked jerk, shooting pain up through her shoulders. Her hands were tied. Behind her back.

The room wasn't dark. *I'm blindfolded.* She lurched to one side, heard the clank of a chain before her movement was abruptly checked.

Terror crashed through her, filling her mind. *Tied. Chained. Blindfolded.*

A scream rose in her throat but came out a rusty croak. Her throat was dry as dust, her lips cracked. *Not a hangover. Drugged. I was drugged.*

How? When? Who would have? Who could have? What had they done to her? She drew a breath, tried to calm herself. Breathed deeply. *Think, Corinne. Think hard.*

The musty odor of the room burned her nose, making her sneeze violently, sending her head spinning again. She clenched her teeth. Rode the nausea through.

She listened, but there was nothing. She heard nothing. No wind. No music. No voices.

Okay. Okay. This sucks. This really sucks. Calm down. Think. Think.

She forced her arms to relax, felt the chain go slack. She moved her fingers, her toes. Straightened her spine, careful not to make any more sudden movements.

She was on a bed. A mattress. With a sheet. And a pillow. Slowly she rubbed her cheek over the pillow. Rough. The room was musty, but the pillow smelled clean.

A sudden creak had Corinne freezing. The door opened, letting in a cold draft. And the smell of lemons. And the beginning of a shrill scream, muffled by the quick closing of the door.

Who was screaming? *Who is here?* And then Corinne remembered. *Last night.* Walking back to the dorm. From the library. With Arianna. They'd walked together because it was late.

Oh God. Ari is here, too. She's screaming. Somebody has her and they're hurting her. They're hurting her. They'll hurt me next.

"You're awake." It was a girl's voice, shocking Corinne out of her panic. The girl sounded young. Not a little girl. Not an adult. A teenager, maybe. She sounded . . . hesitant. "I've been worried about you," the girl added.

Corinne could hear the girl's feet shuffle against the floor. *Count her steps.* One, two . . . four, five . . . eight, nine, ten. *Ten steps to the door.*

"Who are you?" Corinne whispered, her throat so dry it burned. "Why?"

The mattress shifted. Just a little. The girl was small. Cool hands cupped Corinne's face. "You had a fever," the girl said. "It's better now. Are you thirsty?"

Corinne nodded. "Please. Water."

"Of course," the girl said agreeably. A cup was placed against Corinne's lips. A metal cup. Not glass. Glass could be broken, used as a weapon, but that wasn't going to happen here.

The water trickled down Corinne's throat, and she gulped greedily. "More."

"Later," the girl said, gently laying her head back on the pillow. "You've been very sick."

"Who are you? Uncover my eyes."

"I can't. I'm sorry." The girl actually sounded sorry.

"Why not?" Corinne asked, trying to keep the panic from filling her voice.

"I just can't. I'm allowed to take care of you. I'm not allowed to take off your blindfold."

Panic won, and Corinne lunged, rattling her chains. *Who the hell are you?*

The mattress abruptly shifted as the girl jumped off the bed. "Nobody," she whispered. "I'm nobody." Footsteps shuffled, the girl moving away. "I'll come back later with some soup."

"Wait. *Please.* Please don't go. Where am I?"

A slight hesitation before the resigned answer. "Home."

"No. This is *not* my home. I live in the dorm. King's College."

"I don't know about your college. This is ... home. My home. And yours. For now."

For now? Oh God. "But where are we?"

"I don't know." Said simply. Truthfully.

"Can you help me get away?"

"No. No." The girl's tone became adamant with fear. "I can't."

But she wanted to. Corinne could hear it in her voice. Or she wanted so badly to hear it that she told herself it was there. Either way, she needed this girl on her side.

"All right," Corinne said softly. "Can you tell me your name?"

Another long hesitation. "I have to go." The door opened. Ari's screams filled the air.

"Please. What's happening to my friend? Her name is Arianna. *What's happening to her?*"

The girl's answer was quiet, spoken with a dull finality that had fresh terror clawing its way up Corinne's throat. "He's teaching her."

"Teaching her what?"

"What she needs to know," the girl said. "I'm very sorry."

The door closed. Corinne waited a few seconds. "Hello? Are you there? *Please.*"

But the girl was gone and Corinne was alone in the dark.

Chapter One

"It's only a house." Dr. Faith Corcoran gripped her steering wheel, willing herself to look at the house in question as she slowed her Jeep to a crawl. "Just four walls and some floors."

She drove past, eyes stubbornly pointed forward. She didn't need to see. She knew exactly what it looked like. She knew that it was three stories of gray brick and hewn stone. That it had fifty-two windows and a square central tower that pointed straight to heaven. She knew that the foyer floor was Italian marble, that the wide staircase had an elegantly curved banister made out of mahogany, and that the chandelier in the dining room could sparkle like a million diamonds. She knew the house top to bottom.

And she also knew that it wasn't the four walls and floors that she really feared, but what lay beneath them. *Twelve steps and a basement.*

She did a U-turn and stopped the Jeep in front of the house. Her heart was beating faster, she thought clinically. "That's a normal physiological response. It's just stress. It will pass."

As the words slipped out, she wondered who she was trying to convince. The dread had been steadily building with every mile she'd driven the past two days. By the time she crossed the river into Cincinnati, it had become a physical pain in her chest. Thirty minutes later, she was close to hyperventilating, which was both ridiculous and unacceptable.

"For God's sake, grow the hell up," she snapped, killing the engine and yanking her keys from the ignition. She leapt from the Jeep, angry when her knees wobbled. Angry that, after all this time, the thought of the house could make her feel like she was nine years old.

You are not *nine. You are a thirty-two-year-old adult who has survived multiple attempts on your life. You are* not *afraid of an old house.*

Drawing strength from her anger, Faith lifted her eyes, looking at the place directly for the first time in twenty-three years. It looked . . . *Not that different,* she thought, drawing an easier breath. *It's old and massive. Oppressive.* It was more than a little run-down, yet still imposing.

It looked old because it *was* old. The house had stood on O'Bannion land for more than a hundred and fifty years, a testament to a way of life long gone. The three stories of brick and stone loomed large and dark, the tower demanding that all visitors look up.

Faith obeyed, of course. As a child, she'd never been able to resist the tower. That hadn't changed. Nor had the tower. It maintained its solitary dignity, even with its windows boarded up.

All fifty-two windows were boarded up, in fact, because the O'Bannion house had been abandoned twenty-three years ago. And it showed.

The brick stood, weathered but intact, but the gingerbread woodwork she'd once loved was faded and cracked. The porch sagged, the glass of the front door covered with decades of grime.

Gingerly, she picked her way across the patchy grass to the front gate. The fence was wrought iron. Old-fashioned. Built to last, like the house itself. The hinges were rusty, but the gate swung open. The sidewalk was cracked, allowing weeds to flourish.

Faith took a moment to calm her racing heart before testing the first step up to the porch.

No, not the porch. The veranda. Her grandmother had always called it "the veranda" because it wrapped around the entire house. They used to sit out there and sip lemonade, she and Gran. *And Mama, too.* Before, of course. Afterward . . . there was no lemonade.

There was no anything. For a long time, there was absolutely nothing.

Faith swallowed hard against the acrid taste that filled her mouth, but the memory of her mother remained. *Don't think about her. Think about Gran and how she loved this old place. She'd be so sad to see it like this.*

But, of course, Gran never would see it again, because she was dead. *Which is why I'm here.* The house and all it contained now belonged to Faith. Whether she wanted it or not.

"You don't have to live here," she told herself. "Just sell the property and go . . ."

Go where? Not back to Miami, that was for damn sure. *You're just running away.*

Well, yeah. Duh. Of course she'd run away. Any sensible person would run if she'd been stalked for the past year by a homicidal ex-con who'd nearly killed her once before.

Some had said that she shouldn't be surprised she'd been stalked, that by doing therapy with scum-of-the-earth sex offenders, she'd put herself in harm's way. Some even had said she cared more about the criminals than the victims.

Those people were wrong. None of them knew what she'd done to keep the offenders from hurting anyone else. What she'd risked.

Peter Combs had attacked her four years ago because he'd believed that her "snitching" to his probation officer about missed therapy sessions had sent his reoffending ass to prison. Faith shuddered to think of what he would have done had he known the truth back then, that her role in his reincarceration had been far more than marking him absent. But given the cat-and-mouse game he'd played with her in the year following his release, the fact that his stalking had escalated to attempted murder four times now . . . Maybe he did know. Maybe he'd figured it out.

Slipping her hand into the pocket of her jacket, Faith's fingers brushed the cold barrel of the Walther PK380 she hadn't left her Miami apartment without in almost four years. Miami PD hadn't been any help at all, so she'd taken her safety into her own hands.

She was sensible. Prepared. But still scared. *I'm so tired of being afraid.*

Suddenly aware that she'd dropped her gaze to her feet, she defiantly lifted her chin to look up at the house. Yeah, she'd run, all right. She'd run to the one place she feared almost as much as the place she'd left behind. Which sounded about as crazy now as it had when she'd fled Miami two days ago. But it had been her only choice. *No one else will die because of me.*

She'd packed the Jeep with as many of her possessions as she could make fit and left everything else behind, including her career as a mental-health therapist and the name under which she'd built it. A legal name change, sealed by the court for confidentiality, had ensured that Faith Frye was no more.

Faith Corcoran was a clean slate. She was starting fresh. No one she'd left behind in Miami—friend or foe—knew about this house. No one knew her grandmother had died, so no one could tell Peter Combs. He would never think to look for her here.

She even had a new job—a sensible job in the HR department of a bank in downtown Cincinnati. She would have coworkers who wore conservative suits and stared at spreadsheets. She would make an actual living wage and receive benefits for the very first time. But the most valuable benefit would be the bank's security, just in case her efforts to lose Faith Frye hadn't been quite good enough.

Lightly, she touched her throat. Although the wound had healed long ago, the scar remained, a permanent illustration of what the man who hunted her was capable of doing. But at least she'd lived. Gordon hadn't been so fortunate.

Guilt and grief welled up in equal measures, choking her. *I'm so sorry, Gordon.* Her former boss had had the bad luck to be standing next to her when the bullets started to fly—bullets meant for her. Now his wife was a widow, his children fatherless.

She couldn't bring Gordon back. But she could do everything in her power to make sure it never happened again. If Combs couldn't find her, he couldn't hurt her or anyone else. Her grandmother's passing had presented her with a place to run to when she'd needed it most.

The house was a gift. That it was also her oldest nightmare

couldn't stop her from accepting it. Forcing her feet to move, she marched up the remaining two steps to the front door, dug the key from her pocket, and went to open the door.

But the key wouldn't open the lock. After the third try, it finally sank in that the key didn't fit. Her grandmother's attorney had given her the wrong key.

She couldn't have gone inside if she'd wanted to. Not today, anyway. The relief that geysered up inside her made her a little ashamed. *You're a coward, Faith.*

It was just a delay of one day, she reasoned. Tomorrow she would get the right key, but for the moment her inability to enter bolstered her courage.

Peeking through the dirty glass on the front door, she saw a room full of furniture, draped in sheets. Her grandmother had taken only a few favorite pieces when she'd left the house for a townhouse in the city twenty-three years ago. The rest she'd left to Faith.

The thought of unveiling the furnishings elicited the first spark of excitement Faith had felt in a long time. Many of the items were museum-quality, or so her mother had told her on many occasions. *This will all be mine someday, Faith, and when I die it'll be yours, so pay attention. This is your legacy and it's high time you learned to appreciate it.*

The memory of her mother's voice doused her excitement. She could recall the fear that had filled her at her mother's words as if it were yesterday. *But I don't want my legacy,* she'd replied. *Not if it makes you die, Mama.*

An affectionate tug on her pigtail: *Silly girl, I'm not going anywhere for years and years. You'll be Gran's age before this place is yours.*

And in her eight-year-old eyes, Gran was already ancient. *Then I have lots of time to learn about my legacy, don't I?* She'd hidden her relief with a roll of her eyes, she remembered. She'd also remembered being far more interested in the golden retriever that belonged to the cook's son than in the silver teapot in her mother's hands. *Can I go outside and play? Pleeeease?*

An exasperated sigh had escaped her mother's lips. *Fine. Just don't get dirty. Your father will be back soon with the car and we'll head home. But next time we're here, young lady . . .* Her mother had shaken her finger at her with a smile. *We do teapots, 101.*

But the next time Faith had come to this house there had been no talk of teapots or anything else that was happy. Her mother was gone, leaving her life irrevocably changed.

Faith ruthlessly shoved the memory from her mind. Dwelling on the past would make her crazy. She had enough problems in the present without dredging up old hurts.

Except . . . this was a hurt that needed dredging. And then purging. She hadn't been back to this place since that last horrible day. Never told her mother how angry she was. She'd never told anyone. She'd covered up her rage and hurt and fear and moved forward. Or so she'd told herself, but here she was, twenty-three years later. Still hurting. Still angry. And still afraid.

Time to deal, Faith. Do it now. Resolute, she walked around the house before she could change her mind, not realizing that she was holding her breath until it came rushing out.

There it was, off in the corner of the backyard. *A respectable distance from the house,* as Gran had always said. Someone had kept it tidy all these years, pulling the weeds, cutting the grass around the wrought-iron fence, fashioned in the same style as the one bordering the front. The historical society, Faith remembered. Gran's attorney had told her that the local historical society paid for the upkeep because the O'Bannion cemetery was a historic landmark.

Her family was buried here, all the way back to Zeke O'Bannion, who'd died at the Battle of Shiloh in 1862. She knew who rested here, remembered all of their stories, because, unlike silver teapots, she'd found their stories riveting. They'd been real people, lived real lives. Like a faithful dog, she'd followed her mother whenever she visited the graves, helping her pull weeds, hanging on her every word as she talked about their ancestors.

Faith pushed at the gate, frowning when it refused to budge. A glance down revealed the issue—a padlock. Her grandmother's attorney hadn't given her any other keys, so she walked around the fence until she came to the most recent headstone, carved in black marble.

It was a double stone, the inscription on the left weathered over twenty-three years. *Tobias William O'Bannion.* Faith remembered her grandfather as a stern, severe man who'd attended Mass every single day of his life. *Probably to confess losing his temper,* she thought wryly. He'd had a wicked one.

The inscription on the other side of the black marble was crisp and new. *Barbara Agnes Corcoran O'Bannion. Beloved wife, mother, grandmother. Philanthropist.*

Most of that was true. Gran had been a strong supporter of a number of charities. And Tobias had loved her in his own way. *I loved her.* Enough, in fact, to have taken her name.

Most of her children had loved her. Faith's mother's younger brother Jordan had taken care of Gran uncomplainingly until she'd drawn her last breath. Faith's mother had been devoted to Gran, although Faith wasn't sure how much of her devotion had been love. And the jury was out on Jeremy, her grandmother's only other living child. He was . . . estranged.

Faith's grandmother had been quietly laid to rest next to her grandfather in a very private service with only her priest and Faith's uncle Jordan in attendance, in accordance with her grandmother's wishes. Faith thought it was likely due to the fact that Tobias's funeral had become a bitter battleground that had shattered the O'Bannion family.

And her own little family as well, she thought as she moved past the next five headstones, all children of Barbara and Tobias who had not survived into adulthood. She stopped at the sixth headstone. Its design was identical to that of her grandparents', the inscription as weathered as Tobias's. Not surprising since they'd been bought and carved at the same time.

One side, her father's, was mercifully blank. The other bore a terrible lie.

MARGARET O'BANNION SULLIVAN
BELOVED WIFE AND MOTHER

"Hello, Mother," Faith murmured. "It's been a while."

A high-pitched scream floated across the air as if in response. Startled, Faith did a three-sixty, looking for the source, but saw nothing. No one had followed her, of that she'd made certain. There was nothing like being stalked to teach a woman to be careful.

No one was here. It was just Faith, the house, and the

fifty acres of fallow farmland that was all that remained of the O'Bannion family holdings. She patted the pocket of her jacket, calmed by the presence of her gun. "It was a dog howling," she said firmly. "That's all."

Or it could simply have been her mind playing tricks, echoing the scream from her nightmares. *Twelve steps and a basement.* Sometimes she woke from the nightmare to find herself screaming for real—which had scared the hell out of her ex-husband, a fact that gave Faith a level of satisfaction that was admittedly immature. Officer Charlie Frye deserved a hell of a lot more than a start in the night for what he'd done.

Her mother had done so much worse to her dad. "Dad deserved a hell of a lot better than what you did to him. So did I. I still do." She hesitated, then spat the words out. "I have hated you for twenty-three years. I *lied* for you. I lied to Dad so that he'd never know what you did. So if you meant to hurt him, you failed. If you meant to hurt me, then congratulations. You hit the bull's-eye."

It suddenly occurred to her that her best revenge might be to live as her mother had always expected to—as mistress of the manor. It was almost enough to make Faith smile, but the memory of her father's devastation made her angry all over again.

The thought of her father brought to mind the promise she'd made. Reluctantly, she snapped a photo of Margaret's headstone with her phone and texted it to her dad. He'd made a pilgrimage to her grave every few years, but a recent stroke had him housebound. Faith had promised him the photo so he'd know for sure that her grave was okay.

Got here safely, she typed. *All is well. Mama's grave is—*

Her finger paused as she searched for the right words, rejecting all the wrong ones that would be sure to hurt her father, who still believed the inscription to be true. "Well cared for" was honest, she decided, so she typed it. *Will call from the hotel.*

She didn't dare call now. Standing here, looking at her mother's headstone . . . She wouldn't be able to keep the bitterness from her voice. Swallowing hard, she hit SEND, then she turned back to her Jeep with a sigh. If she couldn't get into the house, there was nothing more to be accomplished here today. She'd hit the Walmart near her hotel to buy some cleaning supplies and turn in early. She had a busy day tomorrow.

Mt. Carmel, Ohio
Sunday, November 2, 6:05 p.m.

His hand froze, midstrike, as the light in the ceiling began to flash. *What the hell?*

The alarm. Someone was outside.

"Fuck," he bit out. It couldn't be the caretaker. He'd mown the grass a few days before. It was a trespasser. Rage bubbled up, threatening to break free. Someone had the nerve to trespass here? To interrupt him *now*?

He glanced down at the young woman on his table. Her mouth was open, her breath sawing in and out of her lungs, her expression one of desperation. It had taken him two fucking days to get her to this point. After fighting him tooth and nail, she'd finally begun to scream.

She had the most remarkable threshold for pain. He'd be able to play with her for a long, long time. But not right now. Someone had trespassed and needed to be dealt with.

If he was lucky, it was someone who was lost, looking for directions. When they realized the house was abandoned, they'd leave. If not . . .

He smiled. He'd have another playmate.

He put the knife aside, several feet away. Just in case. The woman on his table had proven to be smart and strong. A little too smart and strong for his liking, but he'd soon fix that. The moment his captives' wills broke, the moment they realized that no one would come to save them, that he was their master for as long as he chose . . . He smiled. *That* was satisfaction.

Closing the door behind him, he left the torture room and went to his office. Powering up his laptop, he brought up the cameras, expecting to see a salesman or someone stranded—

He stared at the monitor, shock rendering him motionless for several long seconds.

It can't be. It simply can't be. But it was. It was *her*. She was *here*. Standing at the cemetery fence. Staring at the grave markers, her face as cold as ice.

How can she be here? He'd seen the news reports, the

pictures of her little blue Prius, twisted and smashed. She could not have walked away from that. *I know I killed her.*

"Fuck," he whispered. Obviously, he had not. The girl had more lives than a damn cat.

Go, finish the job. But first he had to make sure she was alone. He switched to the camera out front and got another jolt. A Jeep Cherokee, bright red. Filled with boxes.

She'd already bought a new car, but at least there were no other passengers. *Good.* He'd take care of her once and for all. He'd have to catch her unaware because the bitch carried a gun. He couldn't allow her the opportunity to use it. *She's all alone out there. Kill her now.*

He switched back to the cemetery camera, then cursed again. She had a cell phone out, taking a picture. He ran to the stairs, taking them two at a time. Skidded to a stop at the back door and peered through the gap between the boards that covered its window.

His heart sank. She was typing into the phone, giving it a final tap.

She'd sent a text. She'd texted a damn photo.

Somebody would know she'd been here. He couldn't kill her now. Not here. *Never here.* Disappointment mixed with his panic. He couldn't risk it. Couldn't risk the law coming around, poking into his business. Or even worse, the press.

Find her and kill her, but not here. He edged his way to the front room, peered out the window. His pulse pounding in his head, he watched her get in the Jeep and drive away.

Part of him wanted to jump in his van and follow her. To kill her now.

But he made himself slow down and think. He liked to plan. To know exactly what he'd do at every phase of a hunt. At the moment he was too rattled—and anyone would be, seeing her at the cemetery like that. He'd been so sure he'd killed her. But she was obviously quite alive.

That would soon be remedied.

He drew a deep breath. He was calming down now. More in control. This was better. A rattled man made mistakes. Mistakes drew attention, requiring even more drastic cleanup. This he had learned the hard way.

He'd find her easily enough. He'd followed her long enough to know her preference in hotels—and Faith was even more of a creature of habit than he was. Although she'd surprised him with the Jeep. A red one, even. That didn't seem to be her style, but perhaps she'd been forced to be less choosy when her old car had become a pile of twisted metal.

How she'd walked away from the wreck was a detail that she would divulge before he killed her. Because he *would* kill her. He'd find her and lure her someplace else and *end* her, once and for all. Nobody could come looking for her here, to this place. *My place.* Nobody could know. They'd spoil everything. Everything he'd built. Everything he treasured.

They'll take my things. My things. That would not happen. *Think carefully. Plan.*

Flinching at a sudden pain in his hand, he looked down to realize he was holding his keys in a white-knuckled fist. He was more rattled than he'd thought.

Which was . . . normal, he supposed. But ultimately unnecessary. *She's just a woman, just like all the others.* Easily overpowered. When he found her, she'd be sorry she'd threatened him.

Except . . . Faith wasn't easily overpowered. He'd tried to kill her too many times. She'd become careful, aloof. Now she never allowed herself to be unprotected. So he'd just have to work a little harder to lure her to a place of his choosing. *And if you don't manage to lure her far enough away? If she comes back here? If she tries to come in?*

Then he'd have to kill her here, which might bring the cops. *They'll take my things.*

He drew a deep breath, let it out. Refused to allow the panic to overwhelm him. He would not lose his things. If he had to, he'd move them. All of them.

Nobody will ever take my things again. Not now. Not ever.

Mt. Carmel, Ohio
Sunday, November 2, 6:20 p.m.

Once Faith had reached the paved road, she began dictating a new to-do list into her phone. Her lists had helped her stay sane, enabling her to accomplish everything she'd needed to do to leave Miami as Faith Corcoran, leaving Faith Frye behind, in an insanely short period of time.

She'd learned the magic of lists after her mother died

and her father began turning to the bottle for comfort. She'd had to run their little household back then, and she'd been only nine years old. Lists were her salvation.

Tomorrow, she'd contact her grandmother's attorney to get the correct house key and then call the utilities to have the power and water turned on. She'd need a landline, too, because cell service was spotty out—

Oh no. Her heart sank as she realized what she'd forgotten. *Cell service. Dammit.* She stared at the phone she held clutched in her hand. She'd changed her name, her address, her driver's license and credit cards, but she hadn't changed her cell phone number.

Irritation swept through her. How the hell had she forgotten about her phone? Not only was it still in her old name, it was a damn homing signal.

She stopped the Jeep in the middle of the road and pulled the chip from the phone. She'd get a new one tomorrow. An untraceable one, just like some of her former ex-con clients carried.

Then, once she got all her ducks in a row, she'd return to the house to begin what was sure to be a massive cleanup job. *Correction. It's not "the" house. It's "your" house. Get used to saying it and going inside next time will be a lot easier.*

Relax. You left Peter Combs in Miami. No one is stalking you. No one is trying to kill you. There's nothing to be afraid of here.

Mt. Carmel, Ohio
Sunday, November 2, 10:15 pm.

Arianna Escobar came to with a gasp, then held her breath, listening hard. She heard nothing. If *he* was in the room with her, he was holding his breath as well. She waited until she could hold her breath no longer. Air rushed out, and with it, a moan. She'd tried so hard to suppress the moans.

He loved her moans, she'd learned. He loved her agonized screams even more.

At the beginning she'd been determined to give him neither. To give him no satisfaction.

But he'd hurt her. A whimper escaped her pursed lips. With knives and . . . Another whimper escaped. She'd gritted her teeth and bitten her tongue until she couldn't take the pain another second more. She'd screamed then, delighting him.

She'd screamed and screamed until her throat was raw. And then he'd abruptly stopped, backing away with a muttered oath. He'd left. She'd heard the door close. When had that been? She didn't know. She could only see a bit of light through the edges of her blindfold. She thought she'd seen lights flashing overhead just before he stopped and swore.

He'll be back. He always came back. At first she'd prayed that someone would save her. But no one had. Now she prayed for death to come quickly.

It didn't seem like that was his plan. Whoever he was. He seemed intent on stretching this out. On making it "last." He'd said so several times. That he needed to "make it last."

But worst of all, she didn't know if he had Corinne, too. The last thing she remembered was him shoving Corinne into the back of a van, but Arianna had heard no other screams since waking. Only her own.

Please let Corinne have gotten away. But she didn't think her friend had escaped. Corinne had been limp when he'd thrown her in the back of that van. Like she was dead already.

The door closed quietly and she tensed. *Lemons.* She smelled lemons. It was the girl. Again.

"Help me," Arianna begged, her voice raspy and broken. "Please, help me."

A damp towel patted her cheeks, cleaning up what was probably sweat and blood. And tears. Arianna had shed all three.

"I'm sorry," the girl whispered. "I'm so sorry."

Arianna tugged the rope again. "Untie me. Please. I'll get you out, too. I promise."

The girl drew in a slow breath, still blotting Arianna's face. "I can't ever leave."

"Who says? I'll take you with me. Please. You're my only hope."

"I'm sorry." The girl's hands froze, and in the silence that followed, Arianna heard footsteps.

The door opened. Arianna heard the girl's breathing accelerate. "I w-was only c-c-cleaning her," the girl stammered out. "Like you told me to."

There was a loud crack, his hand slapping the girl's face. "You've been talking to her. I told you not to talk to her. I told you not to talk to any of them, but you dare disobey me. Get an empty box from the kitchen and pack my things. Yours, too."

The girl didn't say anything. Arianna didn't breathe. *He's leaving? Why?*

But that didn't matter. What mattered was that he'd have to cut her free from the table if he moved her. *That'll be my chance to escape.*

The girl's footsteps shuffled across the floor, then the door closed quietly. Arianna could hear him approaching. She braced herself, expecting the slap, but it still hurt when it came. Her jaw ached, her cheek burned. But she didn't cry out.

"Did you beg her for help?" he asked silkily. "Did you ask her to untie you? She won't help you, you know. She wouldn't know how. You are stuck here. Forever. Or until I kill you."

Gritting her teeth, Arianna waited for the next assault, but he moved away. A moment later she heard the sound of metal clanking. *Knives,* she thought. *He's packing up his knives, putting them into a box.* There was a loud, flat clang. The lid of the box being slammed down? *Yes. Like a toolbox.*

The door slammed and he was gone. Arianna let the air seep out of her lungs. She didn't know what had just happened, or why, but she knew she had a chance now. She'd survive, she vowed. She'd break free, find Corinne, and they'd get the hell out of this nightmare.

Mt. Carmel, Ohio
Sunday, November 2, 10:25 p.m.

He slammed the door to his torture room, pissed as hell. "Roza! Where the fuck are you?"

The blanket that covered her doorway was pushed aside, and the girl came out into the hall. "I'm here," she said quietly.

"I told you to pack my things. What're you doing back there?"

She hesitated. Dropped her gaze. "You told me to pack my things, too."

That he had, he had to admit. It wasn't like it would take her long. She owned maybe four things. "Okay. Fine. Get back to it." But she didn't move. "Well? What's the problem now?"

She flinched. "Wh-wh-what about Mama?"

He stared down at her. She was skinny, but she'd grown taller. Rounder in places she hadn't been round before. He'd noticed. "What about her?"

She glanced down the dark hall that led to her little room. "I can't just . . . leave her here."

He shook his head. He'd known she was stupid, but she'd really surprised him. "You can't take her with you. That's just disgusting. She's not prepared or anything. She's probably a pile of rotting goo by now." The kid's mother had died when he'd been away last year, and by the time he'd returned she'd buried the bitch all by herself. The body had already started to rot, so he'd left it alone. No matter. Time had not been kind to the woman. He wouldn't have wanted to preserve her face anyway.

He knew that the kid was attached to her mother's grave. She talked to it, slept next to it. That he could understand. But taking the remains with her? The child was not right.

"I left a take-out bag in the kitchen." It had grown cold as he'd driven around town, looking for Faith's red Jeep. "Warm it for me. If you eat even one bite, I'll know. I weighed it."

"All right," she whispered.

That was better. He'd let her have too much freedom. She'd been talking to his captives when he wasn't around. He'd been too easy on her since her mother's death. He'd have to clamp down, show her the meaning of respect. "When you're done with my dinner, I want everything washed down with bleach. Every wall, every inch of the floor. If I see one dry surface . . ."

He'd beat the tar out of her. He was in the mood to do some major violence. God help the child if she got in his way. It was handy that he had Arianna Escobar. She would take the full brunt of his frustration tonight. Arianna thought she was so tough. She thought she'd had the worst of him. She hadn't seen anything yet.

He hadn't been able to find Faith. He'd looked everywhere that she'd ever gone while visiting the old bag who'd left this place to her, but he hadn't seen her red Jeep in any of the places he'd looked. *I should have followed her. I should have shot her tires out and stopped her from leaving.* He was a damn good shot. If only he'd had his rifle loaded.

But he hadn't. And had he stopped her, she might have called 911 before he could get to her. That was *all* he needed.

As long as she was alive, that she'd enter the house was a given. She'd explore it and then she'd sell it. He'd have Realtors underfoot all day long, poking around. *Touching my things.* He had to find her before she got the opportunity to enter. He wanted her dead, but on his own terms, because once she was gone, he'd buy the house himself.

He'd already set the plan in motion, goddammit, so she needed to be gone *soon*.

He went to his office, closed the door, pulled the desk away from the wall, and pried off the cover to his hidey-hole. He had dozens of these hiding places. Some he'd built, but most had come with the house. These old Victorian houses had nooks and crannies galore, and he had made good use of them.

He pulled a lockbox from the wall and set it carefully on his desk. It had grown heavy over the years. It held his most treasured collection. This would be the one thing he'd take if he had to make a quick escape.

It was the one thing that could bury him were it found. He unlocked the box and lifted the lid. It was filled with memories—cell phones and wallets and driver's licenses. Hair bows and earrings, necklaces and rings. Photographs, car keys, and cans of pepper spray—never used by their owners because he'd been far too quick. He even had a deputy sheriff's badge.

Deputy Susan Simpson had been her name. She'd been a feisty one. Tall and buxom and much stronger than she'd looked. But she'd bent to his will eventually, just like the rest. She'd been a real treat, had lasted weeks before she'd finally given up and died. He'd been able to work out an amazing amount of rage and stress on that one.

He was under a far greater strain now than he'd been when he'd taken Deputy Simpson. It had been worse when he'd targeted Corinne Longstreet on Friday night. He'd been watching her for weeks, waiting for just the right time. Friday had been that time. All because of Faith.

On Friday night, he'd been completely wound up. He'd

driven straight to King's College. He'd been tired and hadn't been thinking properly and had nearly made a mistake that might have cost him everything.

He'd waited for the two women to separate at the fork in the path. Arianna had gone off to her dorm, leaving Corinne alone and vulnerable. Nabbing her had been a piece of cake. But he hadn't been expecting Arianna to return, to leap to Corinne's defense. That he'd managed to take Arianna before she'd had a chance to call 911 had been a bit of cosmic good fortune.

He didn't want to have to kill either of them now. He wasn't done with them, not by a long shot. He wanted to stay put. Wanted to have his fun. To work out his frustration. He needed to vent somehow. He was on edge.

All because of Faith Frye. Why hadn't she died like a normal person any of the times he'd tried to kill her? He could feel the agitation growing inside him, spreading into his brain. If he let it go too far, he'd do something inadvisable. Spontaneous. And then he'd get caught. It was inevitable. So he never allowed the agitation to go too far.

By the time he'd finished with Arianna, he'd be calm, cool, and collected once again.

He'd find Faith Frye and he'd kill her. His troubles would be far from over, but at least they would be far less immediate.

He picked a hotel key card from the lockbox and frowned. He couldn't remember who'd brought this key card, but it didn't really matter right now. What mattered was that Faith possessed one of these. She'd be in a hotel somewhere. It might take a while, but he'd find her, even if he had to call every hotel in the tristate area.

On his cell phone, he searched for the hotel chain that Faith always used. Such a creature of habit. He dialed the first location. "I'd like Faith Frye's room, please."

"Could you spell that, please?" the hotel clerk asked pleasantly.

"Frye. F-R-Y-E."

"Are you sure she's staying here? We don't have her in our computer."

It would have been too easy for him to find her on the first try. "I could have sworn she said she was staying at this hotel. I'm sorry to have troubled you. Thank you."

He repeated the call with every location in that hotel chain in the tri-state area with no luck. He was becoming frustrated again when the girl knocked softly. He flung open the door with a silent snarl to find her standing with a tray in her hands. His supper. He'd nearly forgotten.

Her eyes were down, her arms trembling from the weight of the tray and probably fear. He grabbed the tray. "Do not *spy* on me, girl."

She kept her eyes down. "I wasn't. I'm sorry."

"Go to your room. You can wash my tray tomorrow. Go. *Now*. I'm busy." He slammed the door and ate his dinner while he looked up more hotels. He'd have to take a break soon. He was becoming too snippy with the desk clerks. He'd be too memorable if he called them the names that were hovering on the tip of his tongue.

He pushed his empty plate away and went back to his torture room. He'd vent some of his rage on Arianna before his next set of calls. He'd keep at it all night if he had to, calling every hotel in town until her found her.

Cincinnati, Ohio
Monday, November 3, 2:45 a.m.

"No, no, no, don't make me! Please don't make me!" Faith screamed as she had a million times before, but no one ever heard. No one ever helped. She stood on the very edge, staring down into the blackness that filled her with dread. She knew what was down there. She wouldn't go there again.

It was always her own treacherous feet that moved, hovering over the blackness . . . lowering until . . . they hit a step. One. She grabbed the banister, wrapped her arms around it, and held on for dear life, but still her feet moved, dragging her down another step. Two.

Crazy. Three. I'm crazy. Four. I'm losing my mind. Five. Six. No, no, no. Please. She moaned now, but it never made any difference. Her feet kept going down. Seven, eight. Nine.

Ten. Eleven. Twelve. That was all. Now run! But she was always frozen.

Don't look. She clenched her eyes shut as her body pivoted against her will. Don't. Look. She knew what she'd see. Don't open your eyes. But her eyes always opened.

One red Ked. Just one, swaying gently, bright white shoe-

laces lazily dragging through the dirt. Don't look up. Do. Not.
Look. Up. But her chin lifted and—

Faith bolted upright in bed, the air sawing in and out of her lungs, her ears ringing with her own scream. One hand reached for the lamp on the nightstand, the other for the gun under her pillow. She squinted at the light, her mind desperately scrambling to establish her location.

She was in a hotel. In Cincinnati. Surrounded by boxes and suitcases. She was all right. She was all alone. The breath shuddered out of her body, now violently trembling.

The shrill ring of the hotel phone broke the silence and, numbly, she reached for it. "Yes?" she asked, her voice raspy and raw from the screaming.

"Dr. Corcoran, are you all right? One of the guests on your floor reported hearing a scream."

Her cheeks heated in humiliation. "I'm fine," she lied. "I had a bad dream. I'm sorry I bothered the other guests."

Faith replaced the phone in the cradle, then got out of bed and turned on the television, keeping the sound low while she found the box containing her Xbox and unpacked its contents.

A few minutes later she was settling on the floor, game controller in hand, picking up the game where she'd left off the last time she had the nightmare.

"It's time to kill us some zombies," she murmured, because trying to sleep after the nightmare was an exercise in futility. This she'd learned twenty-three very long years ago.

Chapter Two

Cincinnati, Ohio
Monday, November 3, 8:45 a.m.

She'd wised up, he thought, watching Faith take a ticket at the entrance to a parking garage near Fountain Square. All the attempts he'd made on her life had made her careful.

Good for her. Bad for me. He'd finally found her in a long-term-stay hotel with valet parking, which had kept her Jeep out of his sight. He'd waited all night until she reappeared. Once he caught her, she'd pay for the sleepless nights she'd caused.

She'd finally come through the hotel's front door an hour ago, dressed to the nines in an emerald green suit and matching heels. At first he'd assumed she was going to see her attorney, but she hadn't. Instead, she'd driven into the heart of downtown. Where she was still being careful. The parking garage she'd chosen had cameras at the entrance. Probably on every floor.

It was centrally located on one of the busiest blocks in the city, so she could walk to her destination, losing herself among the pedestrians. He was unlikely to catch her alone, but that was okay. He wasn't going to kill her here anyway— it would be insanity to even consider it. He was biding his time until he could lure her to an isolated spot. One that was *not* near his basement.

He followed her into the garage, unconcerned with the

camera that snapped his picture when he took a ticket from the machine. His face was disguised, and no one could link him to the Tennessee license plates on his van. The plates had been taken off a car driven by a drifter who'd decided that because the O'Bannions had abandoned their house, he could use it as his personal hotel. That had been a bad decision. The drifter hadn't lasted nearly as long as the woman currently tied to his table. He'd screamed like a little girl at the first slice of the knife.

The memory made him eager to return to Arianna. *Patience.* He'd be able to enjoy his newest guests once he took care of Faith. Now that he'd located her, he wouldn't have to take the drastic step of evacuating the house.

He slowly rounded a corner in the garage, pretending to look for a space when he was really looking for Faith's red Jeep. Instead, he saw Faith's red hair.

There she was in her vivid green suit, a dark coat draped over one arm, crossing the garage right in front of him. She dropped her keys, then bent over to pick them up, and he had to stem the urge to gun his engine. She was the perfect target. *End her. Now.*

But that would be beyond stupid. The garage was busy this time of the morning. He probably wouldn't make it to the street before the cops were on his tail. She couldn't just disappear like the others. The cops would search all the places she'd recently been. Which included the cemetery and the house. *So stick to the plan.* She wasn't worth risking everything.

He parked the van and, getting out slowly, made a show of gripping his cane as he closed the door. Shuffling with his back hunched, he knew he looked every day of ninety. A full beard covered his face, spectacles covered his eyes, and a hat covered his head. And, as always, gloves covered his hands. He'd never left a fingerprint he hadn't meant to leave.

When he got to the Jeep, he dropped a pen so that it rolled under her fender. He lowered himself to one knee, pressing a hand to his back for the benefit of anyone who might be watching, now or later. As he picked up the pen, he took the tracking device he'd brought from his coat pocket and slipped it under the fender.

There. His phone would beep when she moved the Jeep.

He didn't care where she went while in the city. He wanted to know when she left the city to head his way. Because he had to kill her before she came back to the house.

Miami, Florida
Monday, November 3, 9:30 a.m.

Detective Catalina Vega placed the cup of *colada* on her boss's desk and waited for the aroma to get his attention. The Cuban espresso was his weakness, and the shop in Cat's neighborhood made the very best.

Lieutenant Neil Davies drew a deep, appreciative breath before looking up from his computer screen, his expression wary. "What do you want, Vega?"

She flashed a grin as she put two smaller plastic cups on his desk and filled them with the thick, sweet brew. "What I always want. A promotion, a new ride, a swank office like yours."

Davies leaned back in his chair, looking around his "swank" office. It was barely larger than a coat closet, one side of his desk piled high with folders, each one an unsolved homicide.

"Then I'd say you're even crazier than I am," he said mildly. He tossed back the shot of espresso, then held the cup out for more. "What *else* do you want?"

"This." She laid a photograph on his desk.

"This is a wrecked car," he said slowly. "Why do you want a wrecked car?"

"Because that's the Prius that caused that four-car pileup on I-75 yesterday morning."

His gaze jerked up to meet hers. "I take it you're telling me that it wasn't an accident."

"No, it was not. The garage techs found that both the steering and brakes had been tampered with. Either one would have resulted in an accident, but both together . . ." She lifted a shoulder. "The car crossed the median, plowed into ongoing traffic, hit three cars as it spun out, then got slammed by a semi. The driver of the Prius died at the scene, her son died later. Four of the injured are in serious condition, the other two are critical."

Davies sighed. "It's a tragedy, Cat, but not our case. Traffic Homicide is handling this. Why are you even involved? Let them do their jobs. You have your own caseload."

"Hear me out. Traffic already talked with the driver's family. She'd bought the car only the day before. The title hadn't been changed over yet. The previous owner was Faith Frye."

"I know her name. Where did I read it?"

"In my report on the Shue homicide." She ran her finger down the stack of folders on his desk, pulling out the one she wanted and handing it to him. "Gordon Shue was the director of a women's crisis center. They counseled victims of rape, incest, and various cases of domestic violence. Four weeks ago he was shot in the chest as he was leaving his office, then again in the head. The woman standing next to him was his employee, Dr. Faith Frye."

He sat back again, his eyes narrowing. "You've got my attention now. Go on."

"Frye gave me several leads on Shue's killer—initially all of them were husbands or partners of their clients. I remember her touching a wicked-looking scar on her throat when she said it, and so later I checked up on her. Four years ago she was attacked by one of her own clients—a sex offender on probation. He slit her throat. She almost died."

"Social work can be a dangerous business," Davies said quietly.

The lieutenant's wife was a social worker and he worried about her constantly, Cat knew. "I think your wife knows how to defend herself better than most."

"I know she does, because I taught her how." Davies closed the Shue file. "So how did Frye go from being a homicide witness to having her old car tampered with?"

"My search yielded more than the throat-slitting incident. Peter Combs, the guy who almost killed her? After he was paroled, he began stalking her. For a year."

"Did she report it?"

Vega nodded soberly. "Thirty times."

Davies's brows shot up. "Holy shit. Did she think she was the target and not Shue?"

"Not at first. Not until she claimed that Combs had tried again."

"She *claimed*? You didn't believe her?"

"I did actually, but there was no evidence her stalker had made any attempts on her life other than the one he went to jail for four years ago. I couldn't even prove he still lives in Miami. There was nothing connecting Peter Combs to the murder of Gordon Shue. Not until now."

"There's still nothing connecting Frye's stalker to Shue's killer, or the car for that matter," Davies pointed out. "Even if this tampering was targeted at her, you're assuming her stalker did it. And even if you're right, it doesn't mean that Shue's bullet had her name on it. But you are right that someone did something to that car for a reason. You've found a good place to start with that one. Go ahead."

Cat took the photo back. "Thanks, sir."

He gave her a small nod, then pointed at the cup on his desk. "What about the *colada*?"

"My gift to you. *Salud*."

Mt. Carmel, Ohio
Monday, November 3, 2:45 p.m.

Arianna lay on the table, teeth gritted, every muscle tensed as she waited for the next slice of his knife. He'd come to her whistling. So damn happy. He'd been gone for hours, but now he was back and in high spirits. Whatever had rattled him enough to tell the girl to pack was no longer a threat. Apparently they weren't leaving. There would be no escape.

He'd whistled all the time he'd unpacked his knives. Whistled all the time he'd used those knives. On her. Not a single slice deep enough to kill. All deep enough to hurt like hell. Each one slicing away a little bit more of her hope. *I'm going to die here. Alone.*

And then, abruptly, he froze, snarling a curse. Through the blindfold Arianna saw the strobing light, just as she had before. And, just like he had before, he went ballistic.

"Sonofa*bitch*," he growled. "She can't be back. The phone didn't beep. It was supposed to goddamn beep. I should have stayed and watched her." She heard the pounding of his feet, then the tapping of computer keys, followed by another vicious curse. "Fuck. *Fuck her*."

Hope rose anew. Someone *was* coming.

He ran to the door, threw it open. "Roza!" he bellowed. "Come here. Now!"

Shuffling footsteps. "Yes?"

"Bandage her. I don't want her bleeding everywhere. When you're done, get the bleach and spray down this room. Then put the box of your things at the bottom of the stairs."

Yes! They're leaving after all! Arianna wanted to sing. Somebody had scared him again. *He'll have to untie me when he moves me. That will be my only chance.* She flexed her fingers, hoping he wasn't watching. She'd been tied for so long that her muscles were stiff. But she was stronger than she looked. *I can take him. I have to.*

She heard the clinking of glass. "Give her this first," he ordered. "Fill the glass to this line. No more. No less. Make sure she swallows every drop. When you're done, give the other one the same amount. Don't fuck it up, girl, or I'll beat you till you can't see. I'll be back."

Of course he would, Arianna thought as the door slammed. *But I'll be ready.* Whatever he'd told the girl to make her swallow, she'd spit out. She would not let this opportunity to escape slip through her fingers.

Mt. Carmel, Ohio
Monday, November 3, 2:48 p.m.

He ran up the stairs, his happy mood gone. *The power company.* Faith had called the goddamn power company. A fucking meter reader was standing at the back of the house.

He burst out of the basement and slowed his pace, creeping out of sight of the windows until he got to the kitchen door. Carefully, he unlocked it and eased it open, gratified when he heard no hinges creak. He kept them well-oiled for a reason.

He'd slipped from the house more than once to catch a trespasser unaware. The trespassers never knew what had hit them, and neither would the meter reader. Palming his pistol, he dropped into a crouch when he reached the back corner, leaning forward far enough to catch sight of the intruder.

He could see the name "Ken Beatty" written clearly on the man's ID tag. Ken stood at the meter, studying it with an annoyed frown. *Of course he's noticed.* Ken would have to be blind not to note the discrepancy between the actual meter reading and what the power company had on file.

He'd been stealing power for quite some time. Ken would report him if he wasn't stopped, so he pointed the pistol at the man's leg. Abruptly, Ken looked up, his eyes growing alarmed.

Goddammit. Ken took off at a run, but along with a beer gut, he had a serious limp.

Luckily, I have neither. Sprinting, he reached the man as he rounded the east corner. He fired once, and Ken went down, clutching his thigh with a shriek of pain.

"Okay, okay," the man babbled. "So you're stealing power. No biggie. I won't tell, I promise. I'll pretend I was never here."

"Too late," he said. "I saw you make a call on your cell when you arrived. I have to assume that was to inform your boss of your whereabouts." Ignoring Ken's pleas for mercy, he rapped the man's head with the butt of his pistol and then lowered his now-limp body to the ground.

Now for the hard part. He shoved his pistol into his waistband, grabbed handfuls of the man's jacket, and gave a mighty tug. As soon as he'd hidden Ken in the basement, he'd use the guy's cell to text his boss that he'd finished connecting the power and was headed to his next appointment. Then he'd drive the power company's truck back into the city and abandon it near a bar. Everyone would believe Mr. Beer Gut had stopped for a brewski or two.

Halfway across the back of the house he took a breather, releasing the man's jacket, letting the body slump to the ground. He straightened his back, his lungs working overtime.

Damn, but this guy was heavy. *Now I remember why I stick to women. They're half his weight.* And there was the little bonus of the sex, he thought with a smirk. Stretching his arms to the sky, he turned his head until he felt his neck crack, providing a little relief.

He'd bent down to grab the man's jacket again when he caught the movement from the corner of his eye. He turned to see Ken's hand emerging from his pocket, clutching a black aerosol can.

Understanding dawned a split second too late. *"No!"* He reached to knock the can out of the man's hand, but pepper spray already filled the air, burning his eyes, mouth, and nose. "Fucking sonofabitch!" His voice was a high-pitched screech. He couldn't help it. The pain was excruciating. *Hot pokers in my eyes.* "You motherfucking sonofabitch!"

He staggered back, tears streaming down his face. The pain . . .

The bastard wasn't unconscious at all. He was playing possum, biding his time until he could hit me with that damn pepper spray. He panted, unable to get enough air. His lungs were swelling up, closing in. He gasped like a landed trout but couldn't draw a full breath.

He needed to kill this meter-reading motherfucker so that he couldn't get away.

He could barely make out the man's form through the rivers flowing out of his eyes. *He's moving. On his knees.* The bastard was on his knees, dragging himself . . . *Toward me. The idiot doesn't even have the sense to run away.*

He took a few steps backward, pulling the gun from his waistband and blinking hard to try to clear his eyes. Without warning, Ken launched himself, throwing beefy arms around his legs, taking him down. His head hit the ground so hard he almost missed the jab in his leg. Like a bee sting, but worse. He slapped at his leg, dislodging something plastic.

He brought it close to his burning eyes. *Not a syringe,* he thought. *It's a dart.*

"You stuck me with a *dart*?" he demanded. "What the hell is wrong with you? Who the hell carries *darts*?"

"What the hell is wrong with *me*?" Ken cried. "What the hell is wrong with *you*? Are you insane?" He rolled away, scrabbling to his hands and knees. *Now* he had the sense to crawl away, trying to escape.

That could not be allowed to happen. He came to his feet, stumbling after the blurry blob that was moving alarmingly fast. He aimed for the blob and fired. Ken screamed, but kept moving—so he kept firing. Finally, the blob stopped, inches from the corner of the house.

Mt. Carmel, Ohio
Monday, November 3, 2:55 p.m.

Please, God, Arianna prayed. *Please let him help us, who-ever he is.*

She could hear the girl, who she now knew was named Roza, shuffling across the floor, but she passed the table, stopping on the other side of the room. "What is 'Earl P and L'?" Roza asked.

Under her blindfold Arianna blinked in surprise. "The power company. Why?"

"Because there's a sign on a truck outside that says that. There's a man up there, with tools. And *he's* afraid." Something was different. A hardness in her tone that hadn't been there before.

Arianna felt the girl's hand, cold and bony against her arm. Then . . . tugging. Tugging and the rough sound of the rope being cut. Arianna was afraid to breathe, afraid she was imagining this, but she wasn't. Roza was cutting her free.

Holding her breath, Arianna said nothing, afraid of making Roza change her mind. But she didn't, and soon Arianna's other hand was free. Tearing the blindfold from her face, she gritted her teeth and struggled to sit up while the girl cut the ropes at her ankles.

Arianna blinked hard, squinting against the bright overhead lights to get her first glimpse of the girl, who looked as young as she sounded. Maybe twelve years old. Her dark hair was tangled, her skin almost white. Like she'd never seen the sun.

Then she noticed that in the corner there was a laptop whose screen was divided into six areas, like in the security office of a department store. He had cameras, Arianna realized. One of the six partitions held the video of a man wearing a jacket that read EARL POWER AND LIGHT across the back. That picture was from a camera to the outside.

Arianna's heart sank. He'd come to read the meter. He hadn't come to help them.

He doesn't know we're here.

She had to get his attention. Shoving back the panic, she scanned the room, looking for something to use to make some noise. Instead, she saw walls lined with shelves, and on the shelves were jars filled with liquid. The countertop was also covered with the jars. All contained dark brown liquid. Some had . . . things floating in them. Arianna gagged.

"Don't throw up," Roza snapped, briskly rubbing Arianna's feet, forcing circulation. "There are some stairs that go up. There's a door at the top. That's all I can do for you. Go."

"Thank you." Arianna reached out her hand. "Let's go."

A beat of silence passed, then the girl shook her head. "No," she whispered. "I can't go."

"Why not?" Arianna whispered back desperately. "Who does he have that you love?"

Saying nothing, Roza grabbed Arianna's arms and slid her off the table. The moment Arianna's feet hit the floor, they felt as if they were being stung by a thousand bees. "Who?" she repeated through clenched teeth. "Who does he have that you love?"

"My mother. You need to go. Get help. Get Faith Frye."

"Why? Who is she?"

"I don't know, but he's trying to find her. He hates her."

"What about my friend? Is she here?"

"Yes. But she's chained and I don't have the key. I can't get it. I'm sorry."

"But I can't leave her here. He'll kill her."

"If he catches you trying to free her, he'll kill you both. Now go."

Arianna got to the door of the room where she'd been held and took a look back to find Roza holding a bottle made of dark brown glass. "Where is my friend?"

"You have to go," Roza said urgently. She twisted the lid off the bottle, brought it to her mouth, and drank it all.

"What are you doing?" Arianna cried, horrified.

"I can't leave. You can. I'll tell him you escaped, but he'll know I cut your ropes. If you don't kill him, he'll beat me. I don't want to be awake for it. Now go. I have to finish cleaning so he thinks I obeyed him. *Go.*"

Arianna stumbled out of the room, the smell of bleach burning her nose. There were the stairs. And three other doors. Where was Corinne? Arianna was heading for the first door when the sound of a gunshot made her stop in her tracks.

He'd had a gun the night he'd taken her and Corinne. *He shot me with it. Now he's killed the meter reader.* There wouldn't be anyone else to come and help them.

Run. Get help. Before he kills us all. She started up the stairs, tears rising in her throat. *I'm sorry, Corinne. I'll be back for you. I promise.*

Mt. Carmel, Ohio
Monday, November 3, 2:59 p.m.

He knelt beside the well in the back, pumping water to keep flushing his eyes until he could blink without screaming.

He sagged against the cold iron of the pump, breathing hard. *Goddamn asshole meter reader. Goddamn asshole Faith Frye for calling the power company to start with.* Where was she? All he needed was for her to show up right now when he was incapacitated.

His hands trembled as he took his cell phone from his pocket. He was tired. *So damn tired.* His arms felt like they weighed six hundred pounds. Each. And his vision was still blurry.

Squinting at his phone's screen, he brought up the app that monitored the tracking device he'd put on Faith's Jeep. It hadn't moved. At least one thing was going as he'd planned.

He pushed himself to his feet, forced himself to walk over to Ken's body. He looked dead enough. *But I'm taking no chances,* he thought. *Fool me twice, shame on me.*

He grabbed a handful of the meter reader's hair with one hand and shoved his gun to the base of the man's skull with the other. He pulled the trigger, putting a final bullet in Ken's brain. Then he found Ken's cell phone and figured out which contact was his boss.

Finished with the last house. Feeling sick. Going home early. He hit SEND. *There.* It was done. Now he had to get this sonofabitch into the basement and clean up the mess.

He tried to stand, but his head spun. His knees wobbled. There was a roaring in his head.

No. That was an engine. "Whatza fuck?" His words were coming out slowly. Slurred. He'd felt like this only once before, when he was being anesthetized for surgery.

Shit. The dart. Ken had tranqued him. He heard the sound of the engine roaring again and forced himself to crawl around the back corner of the house so that he could see the road.

The power company truck was driving away. Someone had escaped his basement. He could see a vague shape in the driver's seat. Too tall for Roza, too dark for Corinne Longstreet.

Arianna Escobar had gotten away. *Get her. Stop her.* But his body would no longer cooperate. *So tired. Dammit.* His arms gave out. His chest hit the ground hard, knocking the wind out of him. *Fuuuck,* he thought bitterly as his eyelids lowered and everything went dark.

Chapter Three

Faith's fingers tightened on her steering wheel as she exited the interstate, the blaring noise of traffic giving way to a restless kind of quiet. The bumper-to-bumper traffic and miles of golden arches were suddenly gone, and now there were only trees. As far as the eye could see.

After a day of constant activity—introductions, paperwork, greetings from new coworkers, calls to utilities and locksmiths, and, importantly, the lunchtime purchase of a new untraceable cell phone—the respite should have been welcome. But it wasn't.

Because now, in the quiet, she could finally hear what her mind had been muttering all day. *Twelve steps and a basement.* The feeling of impending doom had hovered over her since she'd woken from the nightmare, but it was growing exponentially with every mile she drove, until it was all she could do to maintain her direction. Everything within her screamed for her to *turn around and run.*

Which was both ludicrous and humiliating. Twelve steps and an empty basement should not have the power to control her actions. She wouldn't let it.

Besides, she had an appointment with the locksmith, and it would be rude to stand him up. The lawyer had told her that the key he'd given her was the only one he'd had, so she'd called a locksmith to come open the door and make her a new one. Soon she'd have a key. She'd go into that house and march straight down those basement stairs.

Or . . . *Maybe I'll save the basement for later.* There was certainly more than enough to do on the first floor to make it livable. Or maybe she'd wait until the contractor came to check the foundations, pipes, and wiring and let him go down there first. *I like that idea much better.*

Because she had self-delusion and denial down to art forms. And self-distraction, she thought, switching on the radio. Country music poured from the speaker, the Jeep's stereo still connected to her iPod from the trip up from Miami. Her playlist had kept her awake on the long drive, giving her something to focus on besides what she was running from—and what she was running to.

She sighed when a new song started to play, a Tim McGraw tune she recognized from its intro, about all the things a man accomplished once he found out he was dying. The words hit far too close to home. She started to skip it, but made herself stop and listen.

Had her boss not been standing next to her that day, she'd have taken those bullets to her chest and head. *And I'd be dead.* Had Combs been successful any of the other times he'd tried to kill her, she'd be dead. If he managed to find her, she still might die.

She hadn't told her father she loved him in too many weeks.

She hadn't called him from the hotel the night before as she'd promised in her text. She'd put off dialing until it was too late to call, resorting to e-mail instead. Just as she had every night for several weeks. Not because she didn't want to talk to him, but because she did. Too much.

She needed the comfort of his voice but was afraid he'd hear the fear in hers and know she was hiding something. Which, of course, she was. She'd been hiding all kinds of things from him, the least of which was that she'd quit her old job, found a new one, changed her name, sold her Prius, and driven fifteen hundred miles with her belongings in the back of her new Jeep.

She'd e-mailed him that she was going to Cincinnati as she'd packed up the Jeep. He'd assumed that her trip was to prepare the house for sale, not to get it ready to live in.

She'd let him believe what he wanted, but now he needed to know the truth. At least as much of it as she could share without scaring him, quite literally, to death. His heart was not strong enough to know everything.

Steeling her spine, Faith instructed the Jeep's voice-activated system to dial her father's home, the song pausing itself mid-chorus as the phone started to dial.

She slipped the hands-free earpiece over her ear, as was her habit. She'd survived one bad car accident because she'd been religious about keeping both hands on the wheel. Plus, the earpiece allowed her to keep her phone in her pocket, so that she always knew where it was.

At the moment, her new cell was in her right pocket, her gun in the left. She kept both on her person at all times, in the event she needed either quickly. The precious seconds it would take to find them in her purse could mean the difference between life and death.

This she'd learned the hard way, her boss paying the price.

"Which we will not think about right now," she muttered as her dad's phone began to ring.

"Hello?" Her stepmother answered warily, which was to be expected. The number on the caller ID would be a strange one.

"Ya wanna buy some encyclopedias, lady?" Faith teased, hoping to break any ice that had formed because she hadn't called in so long.

"Faith?" Lily shuddered out a breath that sounded like a sob. "Oh God. Oh God. I'm so glad you finally called. I've been trying to call you for hours. What number is this?"

Panic grabbed Faith by the throat. "What's wrong with Dad?" she demanded.

"Nothing. But only because I got to the phone before he could, every time it's rung today." Her stepmother drew a deep breath. "First, are *you* all right?"

"Yes. What's happened, Lily?"

"That's what I want to know," Lily whispered fiercely. "What number are you calling from? Why haven't you answered your cell phone all afternoon? Why is a detective trying to find you? I've been trying to reach you. *For hours.*"

Guilt swamped her. "I got a new phone on my lunch break. I was calling to give you my number. Who was asking for me?"

A beat of silence. "What happened to the old number, Faith?" Lily asked, quietly now.

"It didn't transfer over." Because Faith hadn't wanted it to. "Who's been calling for me?"

"A detective from Miami PD. I tried calling your home phone, but all I got was a recording saying the number was no longer in service. Your old cell kept going straight to voice mail. I must have left ten messages. I tried your hotel, and the phone in your room just rang. Where are you? Why are the police looking for you? What the hell is going on here?"

"I don't know," Faith said truthfully. "What was the name of the detective?"

"I have it written down. . . . Vega. Detective Catalina Vega."

"Okay. I know her. Did she leave a message?"

"Yeah, that you should call her. What is going on?"

That was a good question. Best case, Vega had called to make sure she was okay. Worst case, to tell her that the man who'd made her life a living hell was headed north. That Vega had found it urgent enough to call her stepmother did not bode well.

"I'm still in Ohio. Didn't Dad get the photo I texted? The one of my mother's grave?"

"Yes, he did, and don't you try to distract me, Faith. Who is Detective Vega and why is she—" A pause, then a whispered oath. "Your dad's coming. We'll finish this later."

"Lily?" Faith could hear her father in the background, sounding slightly slurred and short of breath. "Is that Faith on the phone?"

"Yes, it sure is," Lily said brightly. "I'll put her on the speaker."

"Faith? How are you, darlin'?" Her father's voice had been shaky ever since his stroke, but his love came through as strong as ever.

Relief washed over her in a warm wave, and her shoulders sagged in relief. She hadn't realized just how much she'd needed to hear his voice. "I'm fine, Dad. How are you?"

"Better now. I got your picture of your mama's grave. Thank you, sweetheart." He cleared his throat. "Did you talk to the Realtor?"

"Well, not exactly. I changed my mind, Dad. I don't know if I'll sell the house after all."

There was a long pause, and Faith visualized her father and Lily frowning at each other. "Why not, honey?" her father asked carefully.

"Because I'm thinking of living in it." There. She'd said it. "If it's livable."

Another pause, even longer. "But ... I don't understand," her father said.

"Neither do I," Lily added, a tad more sharply. "What about your job, Faith?"

"I quit. Wait, hear me out," she said over their startled protests. "The crisis center lost most of its funding." After its director was shot to death outside the center's front door. "I'd been thinking of moving on anyway and, well, it seemed time, so I resigned." She'd quit because she hadn't wanted anyone else at the women's crisis center to be hit by a bullet meant for her, but her dad didn't need to know that. "I didn't have any real ties to Miami."

"Because that snake of a husband of yours turned all your friends against you," her father growled. "If I could, I'd kick his ass up his throat and through his teeth."

The thought nearly made her smile. But though her ex had committed a multitude of sins, that hadn't been one of them. "They weren't really my friends, Dad. They were Charlie's friends from the force, from before we got married. He didn't turn them against me. If they'd been my friends, they would have stuck with me."

"Well, I'd still like to kick his ass," her father grumbled. "For the things I know he did do."

Like divorcing her to marry his pregnant girlfriend. But that was done and over now. Faith had moved on, mostly. Her father, not so much.

"So, about this move to Ohio," Lily said, changing the subject before Faith's father started in on a well-worn anti-Charlie rant. "What do you plan to do with yourself?"

"I've got a new job, a really great one with HR at one of the banks up here. And I'll fix up the house. Make some friends. What normal people do."

"Do you need any money, Faith?" her father asked. "We can spare a little."

Faith swallowed hard. He and Lily were living on his GI

pension. They had nothing to spare. But that he'd offer was no surprise. That was the kind of man he'd always been and just one of the reasons why she loved him.

"No, Dad. I'm okay. My new job pays great. And I'll probably sell most of the land. I don't need fifty acres. Once that money comes in, I'll be sittin' pretty." She'd even be able to send some home to them, but she'd never say that to her father. Richard Sullivan had a huge heart—and a sense of pride to match. Faith would quietly address the checks to Lily, who'd bank them just as quietly. Her father would never know.

"But . . ." Her father's voice trailed off. "You worked so hard to become a psychologist. And now you're going to count *money*?"

"No, Dad, I'm not a teller. I'm working in the HR department. That's Human Resources."

"Doing what?" Lily asked.

"Evaluating the employees, especially those who are on the list for advancement to management. The bank wants to identify employees with sociopathic tendencies." Identifying sociopaths was one of Faith's specialties. It was vaguely ironic that she'd be searching for them at the same time she was hiding from them. Or at least from one in particular. "It's a new approach to preventing embezzlement."

"But, honey . . ." He sounded disappointed. "For as long as I can remember, you wanted to help people. Make a difference."

She'd prepared for his concern, not his disapproval, and it stung. She *had* made a difference. For *years* she'd made a difference, and it had almost gotten her killed. It *had* gotten Gordon killed. Which he totally did not need to know. Faith opened her mouth, then closed it.

Lily intervened in a soft murmur. "Richard. She's helped so many victims already."

"But—"

"Richard," Lily said more firmly. "It's her life. Let her live it."

"But a *bank*, Lily?" he whispered, as though he'd forgotten Faith could hear them. "Since when has she been concerned with *money*?"

Ah. It was the *money* that bothered him the most. Her father had once studied for the priesthood and had been pre-

pared to take a vow of poverty. Money had been one of the
few things she could remember her parents arguing about.
The O'Bannions had had wealth and Margaret O'Bannion
Sullivan had wanted her share of it, but Faith's father would
have walked over hot coals before taking a dime.

Her father wasn't upset that she'd moved to Ohio. He
was upset that she was working for a *bank*. She wondered
how he'd feel if he knew the truth—that the armed security
guards in the lobby had made her feel safer going to work
than she'd felt in the entire ten years she'd counseled victims of sexual assault.

"The job at the bank's not forever, Dad," she said gently.
"It's just until I can figure out what to do with my life. I'm
kind of at a crossroads. Looking for a change. But I need to
pay the bills while I figure things out."

"Of course you do," he said firmly, his disapproval, if not
gone, at least hidden for the time being. "But, honey, if
you're at a crossroads, you should come home. You could
live here, with me and Lily." His voice became wheedling.
"We have a new neighbor who would be perfect for you.
He's handsome, and I've told him all about you."

Faith's response was a strangled groan. *"Dad."*

"Richard!" Lily exclaimed. "Leave her be. She's got to
find her own way."

"Her *own* way is too damn *far* away," he grumbled.
"What if she meets some guy? How will I grill him? On
Skype? Hell, I don't look half as threatening on Skype."

Faith smiled, the first time she'd done so in more than
four weeks. "I'm not meeting any men, but if I do and it's
serious, I'll bring him home so that you can give him the full
treatment."

"Promise?"

Her smile faltered, her eyes stinging, and she was suddenly,
fiercely glad they weren't on Skype. She injected a bright note
into her voice and hoped she'd pulled it off. "I promise."

The long pause told her she had not. "You'll call me if
you need me?" he asked.

"I just did," she said softly. "I love you, Dad."

"I love you, too, baby," he whispered. He cleared his
throat. "Call me again, please. Soon. The sound of your
voice is so much nicer than all those texts and e-mails."

Faith swallowed hard. "I will, Dad. I promise. I have to

hang up now. I'm at the curvy part of the road. I need to concentrate on driving."

"I don't like you being all alone in that big house," he said, making one last-ditch effort to keep her on the line. "It's in the middle of nowhere, and anybody could break in and hurt you."

"Maybe," Lily interjected quietly, "you'd feel better if Faith had an alarm system installed."

"It would cost too much," her father said. "She doesn't have money to spend on an alarm."

"Actually, it already has one. Gran's attorney said they put one in years ago because they'd had some squatters." Faith didn't mention her gun. Her father didn't like guns.

"I'd feel better if you got a dog," he said. "A big dog. With big teeth."

"I'll think about it," Faith said, surprised to realize how appealing the idea was. A dog would make coming home to an empty house a lot less lonely. "I really have to go now. I love you both." She tapped her earpiece to hang up before he could offer any new worries or before Lily could finish the interrogation she'd started.

Tim McGraw's voice took over her speakers once again, but she turned the volume down a little so that she could think.

Calling Detective Vega would have to wait until she got to the house. She didn't have the number for Miami PD programmed into her new phone, so she'd have to Google it.

A glance at the clock on her dash had her grimacing. Traffic had made her a few minutes late. The locksmith was probably there already, but she wasn't about to speed on these curves. She hoped the man wouldn't leave without—

The animal came out of nowhere, hurling itself into her path. A *big* animal. Faith slammed on the brakes and wrenched the wheel to the left to avoid it—just as the road curved again.

Before she could adjust, her tires slipped off the edge of the road, propelling her down the embankment. Panic gripped her as trees flew by and she desperately pumped the brake.

And then what she'd glimpsed sank in. Long, dark hair. An outstretched arm. Fingers. Flesh, covered with blood. *Oh my God. Not an animal.*

It had been a girl. Naked. In the middle of the road.

Mt. Carmel, Ohio
Monday, November 3, 5:02 p.m.

There was a buzzing in his ears.

"Hey. Hey, buddy. Are you okay?"

He blinked, growling when someone shook his shoulder. His head hurt and he was woozy. He was also lying on the ground outside. *What the hell?* Memory returned in a rush. The trespasser, the guy from the power company. *Ken.* The bastard who'd tranqued him. *The dead bastard whose body was still lying out in plain view around back.*

And the girl. Arianna. She was gone.

Shit. She was gone. *I have to find her. I have to get her back. She'll tell. She'll ruin everything.* He tried to sit up, but someone pushed him back down.

"Don't move." A man. Older, by the sound of his voice. "You've been in an accident. I saw your truck crashed up the road. How'd you get all the way down here? Well, you're lucky I came by. Nobody lives here yet. Name's Tommy Dilman, by the way. I'll call 911."

The hell you will. Forcing his eyes open, he saw Dilman kneeling beside him, pulling a cell phone from the pocket of his coveralls. Fury poured through him, giving him the strength to grab the phone from Dilman's hand and throw it as hard as he could.

"Hey!" Dilman protested. "What the hell is wrong with you, buddy?"

He waited until Dilman had turned to retrieve the phone, then lunged to his feet and leaped, bringing the older man down in a tangle of limbs. Stunned, Dilman lay on his back staring up.

He didn't know what the old man was doing here. All he knew was that he was not calling 911, nor was he leaving here alive. He drew his switchblade from his pocket and plunged it into Dilman's throat. Warm blood spurted all over his hands as the old man struggled like a fish on a hook. A minute later, the guy wasn't moving at all.

He rolled off Dilman's body and looked up at the sky. It was getting dark. He'd been out for a couple of hours at least. Plenty long enough for Arianna to get away, goddammit.

She'd escaped in the power company's truck. But how had she escaped the basement? She never could have untied her ropes. And yet she was free.

He thought of Roza, bending over Arianna, talking to her, and his fists clenched. *The ungrateful little bitch. She cut Arianna loose. I'll beat her half to death, and if she sasses me, I'll beat her the rest of the way.* At least Roza hadn't freed Corinne Longstreet. He had the only key to the shackles. Arianna was the real threat. *She could be in the next town by now. Getting help.*

Wait. The tranq-induced fog in his mind was beginning to clear. What had the old man said? *I saw your truck crashed up the road.* Dilman had thought he worked for the power company, that he'd wrecked the truck.

At least Arianna hadn't gotten far. Pushing to his feet, he staggered for a few steps, finally getting his balance. Damn, he had a mess on his hands. Dilman was lying in a pool of his own blood, and Ken's hand was visible at the back corner of the house. It was good that Dilman hadn't seen the hand and investigated. He would have known the real meter reader was dead.

But now I have two bodies to hide. Sonofabitch.

He made his way behind the house to the old carriage house where he hid his van. He backed it out, keeping to the gravel road. Gravel was a wonderful material. It showed little evidence that it had been driven over and could be raked so that it looked perfectly undisturbed. None of the caretakers who'd come to cut the grass had ever suspected he'd been there.

Parked in front of the house was the old man's car. On the door was a magnetic sign. DILMAN'S LOCK AND KEY. The guy was a locksmith.

He ground his teeth in rage. Faith had been a busy girl today. First calling the power company and then a locksmith. That bitch would have locked him out. Kept him from what he'd claimed as his own. What he'd created. What he'd collected.

He drew a breath, calming himself. First order of business was to retrieve Arianna. Then he'd dispose of the two bodies. Then he'd find Faith and finish what he'd started. And when he was all done? He'd punish Roza severely and pick up where he'd left off with Arianna.

Mt. Carmel, Ohio
Monday, November 3, 5:05 p.m.

Faith lifted her head when the Jeep stopped moving.

Tim McGraw was singing the closing strains of his song, the sound surreal in the absolute quiet. She touched her brow bone, her fingers coming away sticky. *I'm bleeding.*

And something smelled bad. The airbag, she realized. The passenger-side airbag had deployed. She'd managed to turn the steering wheel as she'd gone down the embankment, so that she'd hit the first line of trees broadside rather than head-on. The Jeep must have bounced and slid the rest of the way a lot more gently, because she now rested hood-first against a tree and the driver's airbag was still intact.

She turned off the ignition and sat motionless for a moment, just breathing. Her memory reengaged with a jolt.

"*Oh my God.* The girl." There'd been a girl. She'd been . . . naked. Naked? How could she have been naked? *Did I hit her? Oh God, please let her be okay. Please.*

Panicked, Faith groped at the Jeep's door, needing a minute to remember how it opened. *You're in shock.* It didn't matter. All that mattered was finding the girl. *What if I killed her?*

The door made a horrible sound as she shoved at it with her shoulder, but it finally opened and Faith stumbled out, falling to her knees. *911. Call them.* She needed her phone. *Where is it?* She had one. She'd just been on it, talking to her father. *But with the hands-free.* She tapped her ear. The earpiece was still there. Good.

She'd put the phone in her coat pocket when she'd left the office. She patted her pockets, finding her gun in the left, and her phone in the right. Hands shaking, she tried to dial, but smeared blood all over the phone's screen. She wiped her hand on her skirt and tried again, finally dialing the three numbers.

"This is 911. What is your emergency?"

Faith tried to stand, but fell back to her knees. Stifling what would have been a shrill scream of pain, she dropped her phone back into her pocket and started to crawl. "There was a girl in the road. I swerved. Hit a tree."

"Are you injured?"

"Yeah." She blinked when her eyes burned, then realized it was blood in her eyes. She swiped at her forehead with her sleeve. "Cut my head."

"I need you to stay still, ma'am. You could have other injuries. What is your name?"

"Faith. Faith F—" *Frye*, she'd almost said. But that wasn't true anymore, was it? She blinked hard, making herself think. "Faith Corcoran." She started crawling again, up the steep embankment, whimpering when she slid back a few feet. If she wasn't careful, she could tumble all the way down. She wasn't going to look. She already knew it was steep.

"Stay put, Faith. I've sent help. They'll be there in a few minutes."

"I can't. There was a girl. In the road." She dug her fingers into the dirt and kept climbing. "She was hurt. I didn't hit her. I swear I didn't." Her fingers touched asphalt, and she dragged herself up the final foot of embankment and on to the road. There she was. The girl. "I see her."

"The girl?" the operator asked carefully, as if Faith were delusional.

"No," Faith snarled. "Frosty the damn snowman. Of course the girl. But . . . she's not moving."

She dragged herself to where the girl lay. She'd been right. The girl had no clothes. Which allowed Faith to see every oozing wound on her body. *Jesus, Mary, and Joseph.*

"Dear God. Who did this to you, honey?" she whispered.

"Faith?" the operator asked. "Are you still there?"

"I'm here. With the girl. She's all bloody. Her face is bruised. And cut. She's . . . naked. Someone's cut her, all over." Wiping her bloody hand on her skirt, Faith pressed her fingers to the girl's neck, relieved when she felt a pulse, though it was faint. "She's alive, but barely. I can hardly get a pulse. She's nonresponsive."

"Can you describe her?"

"Young. High school, maybe. Long, dark hair, past her shoulders. She appears Hispanic. Tall. Five-nine or so." The setting sun had cast the road in shadow, but the gash in the girl's thigh was big and bad enough to be easily visible. "She may have been shot in the leg. Maybe in the arm, too, but there's too much blood to tell." Faith struggled out of her coat and spread it over the girl, her own body sagging from the exertion.

Pushing the edge of her coat to the middle of the girl's

leg, she exposed the wound, then leaned closer, frowning. "Looks like somebody did a patch job on the bullet hole, but it busted open." She took off her scarf, balled it up, and pressed it to the girl's wound. "I'm putting pressure on the wound in her leg. She's lost a lot of blood. Tell whoever's coming to hurry."

"They'll be there in a few minutes. What about you? How's your head?"

"It hurts," she said tersely. "And I'm tired."

"Don't sleep yet. Stay on the phone with me."

"I've had a concussion before. I know the drill." Squinting into the growing darkness, Faith searched for any sign of whoever might have dumped the girl there, but she saw nothing but trees. Whoever had left her was gone. Or hiding.

That they might come back to finish what they'd started was not impossible. "They won't get at you again," she whispered to the girl, who made no sign that she was aware of anything that was happening. Her loss of consciousness might be a mercy in this situation. "They'll have to go through me first."

Taking her gun from the pocket of her coat, Faith staggered to her feet. Standing in place, she turned a slow circle, watching for any threat. All the while she prayed that the Mount Carmel cops responded faster than the Miami cops she'd known.

Mt. Carmel, Ohio
Monday, November 3, 5:20 p.m.

Arianna couldn't have gotten far. It was getting dark, so he switched on the van's high beams, driving slowly, scanning the trees along the roadway. Within minutes the wrecked power company truck came into view. Arianna had crashed into a tree. The hood was a crushed mess.

Even better. If she was hurt, she might still be in the truck. Leaving the van on the road, he jogged to the wreck. *She's there. She's got to be there.*

But she wasn't. The truck's cab was empty. He clenched his teeth so hard that a sharp pain streaked up his neck into his skull. She'd escaped. Again.

Relax. There's blood all over the seat. This isn't so bad. Bleeding like she was, she had to be around here somewhere. He looked around the truck, careful not to touch it. His fingerprints weren't in anyone's system, and he planned to keep it that way.

He walked slowly through the trees, following the trail she'd left in the dirt as she'd dragged herself forward. He had to give her some credit. She had guts and spirit.

He so looked forward to breaking her.

He'd rounded a curve in the road when he heard sirens, and his heart simply stopped.

No. No, no, no. He crept closer and silently cursed when he saw the flashing blue lights up ahead. It was a squad car. A fucking squad car.

There was a body in the road, covered by a black wool coat. The body had long black hair. Arianna Escobar. Maybe she was dead. *Please let her be dead.*

The siren belonged to an ambulance, which came to a screeching halt next to the cruiser. A paramedic raced to her side and was waving his partner to hurry with a stretcher. When they rolled her away, her face was uncovered, an oxygen mask pressed to it.

Dammit. She's alive.

A second ambulance drove up as the first was driving away. Why two ambulances?

This paramedic went to the squad car, leaned into the open rear passenger door, and helped someone out. Someone with dark red hair wearing a green suit.

His eyes narrowed. *Faith.* She'd called the power company. She'd called a locksmith. She'd been on her way to his house. She'd found Arianna.

Panic tried to choke him, but ruthlessly he pushed it back. He couldn't panic now. He needed to get back to the house. *Get rid of the evidence.*

He backed away, careful not to disturb a single leaf, and when he was out of sight, he ran to his van. He barely pressed his foot to the accelerator, wanting to draw no attention to himself.

That the cops would connect the girl to the power company's truck and the truck to the O'Bannion house was a given. There were no other houses around. How much time did he have to get away? Unknown.

He had to hurry and hope they'd knock, find no one home, and go away.

But he knew that wouldn't be the case. Not with Faith there. Fury simmered in his gut. He was going to lose everything. Because *she* had come back. *I should have killed her when I had the chance.* And he'd tried, but the bitch simply wouldn't die.

Arianna was a setback, but not a complete disaster. Even if she lived, she couldn't identify him. She'd been blindfolded the entire time, except for when she was running to the meter reader's truck. There were a few seconds when he'd begun to chase her. If she'd looked in the rearview mirror . . .

Unlikely, he told himself harshly. It was only a few seconds and she'd been distraught.

He turned into the gravel drive and pulled the van around to the back. He had two dead bodies outside and two live ones inside. The two live ones would be dead soon enough. Corinne Longstreet was now excess baggage. A liability. Once Arianna was identified, people would start looking here for Corinne. He needed to get her out of here and dead and buried ASAP.

And the child? She'd better be very, very contrite. Showing even an iota of spirit meant that she was too dangerous to be retrained. Which meant he'd have to kill her, too.

Mt. Carmel, Ohio
Monday, November 3, 5:30 p.m.

You will not throw up. Sitting in the back of the ambulance with a blanket wrapped around her shoulders, Faith had been repeating the same phrase for twenty minutes. She didn't know if it was helping, but at least it wasn't hurting. She hadn't been sick all over the crime scene. Yet.

She'd held it together until the cops had arrived, but the moment they'd taken over, her adrenaline crashed. Nausea and uncontrollable shaking had commenced, accompanied by the playback loop in her mind.

Gunshots, screams. Blood on her hands. Gordon's sightless eyes staring up at her. She kept telling herself that this was different. That the girl she'd found would live.

The first ambulance had rushed the teenager to one of the hospitals downtown. Faith would soon follow, but at a much more sedate pace. The EMT had advised her to have her head checked out by the ER, but Faith wasn't sure she could ride in a moving vehicle just yet.

Besides, the detectives investigating the girl's assault would be arriving soon. She knew they'd want a full report. The thought of which made her want to turn tail and run.

They'll ask questions about you, too. They'll find out who you really are. Or were.

If they asked, she'd answer honestly. Although she might get lucky. The detectives might keep their questions focused on the girl she'd found in the road and leave her alone.

And if they do find out who you were? Well, maybe it wouldn't be so bad. She knew not all cops were like Charlie and his friends. Some were like Catalina Vega, who'd believed her when she'd reported being stalked and terrorized by Peter Combs. Unfortunately, Vega was in the minority. Most of the cops who'd taken her reports had treated her like she'd deserved what she'd gotten from Combs. When he'd escalated from stalking to attempted murder, they'd thought she was making it up, that she was desperate for attention. Unstable, even. The latter had likely been encouraged by her ex-husband's trash talk, though she'd never been able to prove it. Even if that had been true, they still should've done their jobs, but they hadn't. *And so here I am. Forced to flee and start all over again.*

So while not all cops were like Charlie and his friends, she really wasn't in the mood to take the chance. She didn't need their "help" and didn't trust their motives.

The EMT came around the back of the ambulance to check on her. "How are you feeling?"

"Okay." Her head still throbbed, but the nausea was abating. "How's my Jeep?"

"I'm no mechanic, but it doesn't look good, ma'am. I'm sure the detectives can give you a better idea. This is probably them now."

Faith peered around the ambulance's open door to see a black SUV rolling to a stop. The driver's-side door opened and—

Holy hell. Faith's eyes widened, her headache momentarily forgotten. It was a man. A really big man. Over six feet tall and broad-shouldered, he seemed to dwarf his vehicle. But it wasn't his size that had her staring.

He was ... different. She blinked hard, thinking she must

have hit her head harder than she'd thought. But when she opened her eyes, he was still there, standing next to his SUV, doing a visual scan of the scene from behind the darkest wraparound sunglasses she'd ever seen.

His hair appeared to be white. Not the white-blond that came from the sun, but the snow-white that came with age, even though he looked no older than she was. It was cut short, the ends kicking up haphazardly all over his head, like a churned-up frozen sea. In stark contrast, his face was a warm bronze, broken only by the white goatee that framed an unsmiling mouth.

And the pièce de résistance, the unbuttoned black leather trenchcoat that hugged his shoulders like a glove, the tails whipping in the wind. He looked like he'd stepped out of an action movie.

If she hadn't been in pain, she might have thought she was dreaming. Of course, she had hit her head, so hallucinations were still a possibility.

"I think I might get that CAT scan after all," she murmured.

The EMT huffed a strained chuckle. "Maybe I'll join you."

"He's . . . real, then?"

"Yes, ma'am. He is most definitely real."

Chapter Four

Special Agent Deacon Novak got out of his SUV, blinking rapidly against the sudden blast of cold air. They'd have a hard frost tonight. The victim had been discovered just in time.

A few more hours and she would have succumbed to exposure—if she hadn't bled to death first. The young woman had been beaten, stabbed, shot, and then dumped in the middle of nowhere on the side of a road that did not appear to have been used in years.

Deacon had almost forgotten that places this isolated still existed so close to the city. The crowded Cincinnati suburb where he'd grown up was less than fifteen miles from here, but it felt more like a hundred. Here the houses were few and far between, where those in his neighborhood were so close together that he'd needed only to open a window to talk to the cousin who'd lived right next door.

Here, there was no one to witness a young girl being dumped like garbage. In his neighborhood there'd always been self-appointed sentries watching from lace-curtained windows, making sure that all the kids' mothers knew every move they made.

They still did, in fact. The sentries had grown old, but they still watched the neighborhood with eagle eyes, still reporting misbehaviors. Deacon knew this because he and his sister, Dani, were now on the receiving end of their reports.

Their younger brother had fallen in with a very bad crowd, and Aunt Tammy, who'd raised Greg from an infant after their mother died, was at the end of her rope. Which was why Deacon had come home—not just for a vacation or a holiday, but permanently. There were details to work out, but it was nothing he and Dani hadn't been able to handle.

Until this afternoon. *God.* Greg had gotten into trouble at school *again,* and what had started as a conversation nearly escalated into a brawl. The angry, ugly words that Deacon and his brother had shouted at each other still echoed in his mind. Deacon didn't often lose his temper, but somehow Greg managed to push every single one of his buttons with a simple smirk.

Deacon didn't think he'd yelled so much in years, maybe ever. Not that it had done any good. Greg had simply turned down his hearing aid, which had made Deacon see red.

He was glad the victim had been discovered for her sake, of course, but also for his own, because the call to the crime scene had forced him to walk away from his brother before he'd done something unforgivable. He'd seriously wanted to slap the smirk off the kid's face. He didn't think he'd have done it, but the very idea that he'd been tempted left him rattled.

He couldn't afford to be rattled. He had a job to do. He pushed his guilt and worry aside. His focus had to be on the young woman who'd been assaulted and left to die.

Out here no one watched through lace curtains. Whoever had left the victim had counted on that. Had counted on the fact that there were trees as far as the eye could see on either side of the pitted and potholed road. That beyond the trees to the south ran a lonely stretch of the Ohio River, miles away from the bars and restaurants of the Cincinnati riverfront.

That the victim had been discovered at all seemed like a miracle.

Deacon found miracles suspicious. The initial report stated that the victim had been found by a woman who'd swerved to avoid her, wrecking her vehicle. But there didn't seem to be any good reason for anyone to be on this road. It was too cold for most hikers and campers, and deer season hadn't started yet. He hoped the first responders hadn't let the woman leave. He had a few questions for her.

One of the local cops had strung yellow crime-scene tape across the road. Ducking under it, Deacon started toward the flashing lights of the two sheriff's department cruisers, parked on either side of an ambulance whose back doors stood open, revealing the woman sitting inside.

Red was his first impression. Dark red hair the color of Bordeaux framed a pale but pretty face. Her cheek was smudged with blood, her forehead bandaged.

Not the victim. He knew she was already on her way to the trauma unit in Cincinnati.

This, then, had to be the Good Samaritan. About thirty years old, she sat huddled under a brown blanket. Her green skirt stopped an inch above the bandages that covered her knees. She wore thick white socks on her feet, leaving her lower legs bare.

Very nice legs, in fact. Shapely calves that he would have had to be blind not to notice. Deacon had issues with his eyes, but impaired vision had never been one of them.

The woman's deer-in-the-headlights expression might have simply been leftover shock, but as her gaze was focused on him, Deacon doubted it. He got that reaction a lot.

"Hold it right there, buster."

Deacon stopped abruptly when a uniformed officer blocked his path. The officer eyed him with a mixture of incredulity, fascination, and contempt. Another reaction that Deacon got a lot.

"You can't come through here, buddy," the officer said. "Please get back in your vehicle and go back the way you came."

I'm not your buddy, friend, leapt to the tip of Deacon's tongue, but he bit it back. Going for his badge with one hand, he took off his wraparound glasses with the other and fought not to squint at the intense glare of the setting sun. Leveling the officer an unamused stare, he gave the guy a few seconds to react. *Wait for it, wait for it. . . .*

The officer didn't disappoint, flinching when his eyes met Deacon's. "What the f—"

"Special Agent Novak, FBI," Deacon interrupted, showing his badge. "Update, please."

The officer's eyes narrowed as he scanned Deacon from head to toe. "Nice contacts, asshole, but Halloween's over. Now move along and take your fake ID with you."

Dammit. I really hate Halloween. Deacon had come to depend on that flinch. Had spent years honing the image he projected, maximizing the window of distraction his slightly-less-than-normal irises offered. But Halloween ruined his rhythm, totally axing his advantage.

Now all he had left was his bubbling personality. *Shit.*

"Officer," he said, lowering his voice to a menacing growl. "I do not have time for this. Who's lead here?"

"I am." The dry reply came from an older uniform. "Deputy, get back to your post." When the younger officer was gone, the older man leaned forward to study Deacon's badge, then straightened to meet his eyes. No flinch. Just a disbelieving blink from which the sheriff recovered quickly. "Sorry about that, Agent Novak. I'm Sheriff Palmer. We, uh, don't get many FBI agents around here." *And none that look like you,* went loudly unsaid. "I have to admit that I'm surprised to see you. I called CPD, not the FBI."

"I work a joint task force with CPD—MCES, the Major Case Enforcement Squad. We cover homicide, abduction, and assault." Deacon had joined the newly formed squad the month before. CPD wanted an FBI member with joint-task-force experience, and Deacon had needed to come home, so his transfer from the Baltimore field office to Cincinnati had been a mutually beneficial one. "What's the status here?"

"We responded to the 911 at five fourteen p.m., eight minutes after it was called in. The victim was lying in the road, bleeding. Her face was bruised, and she had a bullet hole in one thigh and stab wounds all over her torso. Deep enough to hurt, but not enough to kill."

"Her abductor was playing with her," Deacon murmured, stowing his anger.

"Yeah. We haven't found any ID around the scene. No clothes either, or personal effects."

"Did she at any point regain consciousness?"

"No. When we got here, she was unresponsive. She was nude, but the woman who found her covered her with her own coat. She was also standing guard over the girl." Palmer lifted one eyebrow. "With a fully loaded .380."

Surprised, Deacon turned to check the woman out more thoroughly. She was watching him, the stunned look gone from her eyes. Now he saw only intelligence. And a guarded calculation that put him on alert. "Was it her gun?" he asked Palmer.

"She said it was, and based on her grip and stance, I'd say she knows exactly how to use it. When I bagged it, she didn't argue."

"Had she seen anyone around the girl? Anyone coming or going?"

"She said she hadn't, but she might have been in shock. When I asked for her weapon, she handed it over—then collapsed. Not a faint, but like her legs wouldn't hold her up anymore."

"Is she hurt?"

"Cuts and bruises on her hands and knees and a nasty gash on her head. She said she swerved to keep from hitting the victim, went down that embankment. This way."

Feeling the woman's watchful gaze as he walked away, Deacon followed the sheriff to the edge of the road. For a moment he stood there and gaped. He'd expected a small wreck. He hadn't expected this. A red Jeep rested on some trees halfway down the embankment, looking like it had been hit in the side with a wrecking ball. The embankment was not only treacherously steep, but rocky as well.

He looked back in disbelief at the Good Sam. "She climbed up *here* from down *there*?"

The sheriff shrugged. "Unless she has wings or stashed a helicopter, she climbed."

"Was anyone with her?"

"She says no. I checked it out myself once we'd secured the scene up here. I didn't see any other footprints, and there's no one else in the vehicle. I have to admit that the climb back up was a challenge. I asked her about it, and she said she used to wall-climb at the gym."

"Interesting." Deacon noted the tire tracks and broken trees that showed the Jeep's path down the embankment. The tracks were pointed head-on to the trees at first, but a wide swath of disturbed dirt indicated that she'd turned a tight circle at the last moment, slamming into the trees from

the side. It wasn't a move that many people could have accomplished, especially under stress. The Good Sam had serious driving skills.

He pulled a pair of binoculars from his pocket. The fading light made it hard to focus, but he was able to make out
the Jeep's Florida plates, making him doubly suspicious as
to why she'd been here to begin with, on a road that didn't
even show up on the map as having a name.

He turned to study the skid marks. "She tried to stop."

"She claims she wasn't speeding," Palmer said. "Skid
marks appear consistent with that."

The thick marks started about twenty feet from where
an evidence marker sat in the middle of the road. "That's
where you found the victim?"

"Yes." Palmer pulled a small digital camera from his
pocket. "I took pictures before the medics transported
her."

Deacon clicked through the photos, grimacing at the
girl's wounds. He'd seen worse, but not by much.

"I'll need copies of these, please," he said.

"I've already uploaded them to our server. I can e-mail
them to you."

"That'd be great, thanks." Sweeping the tail of his leather
trenchcoat to one side, Deacon crouched beside the marker.
It was a move that had become second nature over the
years. He and his coat had been together a long time.

The asphalt had dark, wet patches. "She bled a lot," Deacon murmured.

"Woulda bled more, but the Good Sam did some decent
first aid. Applied pressure to the wound with her scarf."

It seemed their Good Sam had all kinds of skills. "What's
the Sam's name?"

"Faith Corcoran. Says her ID is in her handbag, still in
the Jeep. We don't get many out-of-towners this far out.
Seemed a little odd that she'd be here at the same time as
the girl."

"And toting a .380, no less," Deacon said dryly.

A slight nod. "The thought crossed my mind," was the
sheriff's equally dry reply.

Deacon came to his feet and carefully walked to the
other side of the road, his eyes on the pavement. There was

a smeared path, dark and wet, that stretched from the marker to the shoulder opposite the side the Jeep had gone down. "The victim came this way."

"Crawled from the shoulder where they dumped her. She had dirt on her hands and knees."

Deacon dug his Maglite from his coat pocket and, aiming the beam at the shoulder, started walking away from the scene into the setting sun.

"We didn't see any signs of tire treads on the shoulder or in the grass," the sheriff said. "Whoever dumped her stayed on the road."

"They might have, but she didn't," Deacon said, focusing his light on the grass at the shoulder's edge. "There's blood here."

"Where?" the sheriff demanded, then propped his fists on his hips as he looked at the illuminated grass. "I'll be damned. Those eyes of yours function just fine, Agent Novak."

"They do, indeed," Deacon murmured. People sometimes wondered if his unique eyes had impaired—or enhanced—vision, but they didn't. He had a sensitivity to bright light, but other than that his eyesight was only average, though he'd taught himself to notice changes in color and texture. "I think the victim came from the woods."

He paused at the sound of approaching vehicles. A few seconds later, the CSU van came around the bend, followed by a sedan that looked like his partner's. But Detective Scarlett Bishop was supposed to be at the hospital with the victim. Unless the victim could no longer give a statement.

Shit. Please don't let that girl be dead.

"Now that CSU is here, they can set up lights. Excuse me, Sheriff." Briskly, Deacon walked toward the sedan, slowing as he passed the Good Sam in the ambulance. She'd been leaning forward so that she could see around the ambulance doors, watching him. Now she sat back so that her face was in the shadows. She appeared to be worried.

That wasn't good. His attention swung back to the sedan, his eyes narrowing in confusion. The person who emerged was not Bishop.

Cincinnati, Ohio
Monday, November 3, 5:45 p.m.

Detective Scarlett Bishop stood against the wall of the ER cubicle, watching the trauma team prepare the victim for surgery. The rape kit had been positive, which hadn't really surprised anyone, since she'd been found nude.

Locking her gaze on the victim's face, Scarlett looked for any sign of consciousness, but there was nothing. She'd tried to talk to the girl three times already, with no success.

The nurse standing at the victim's head stepped away, and Scarlett slipped into the vacated space to try again, leaning close to the young woman's battered face. "Sweetheart," she said, quietly but urgently, "I need you to wake up, just for a minute."

"We're moving her in less than a minute, Detective," the doctor warned.

"Okay, okay." It would be easier if she knew the girl's name. "Honey, please, wake up." Scarlett let her desperation come through her voice. "I need to know your name."

The victim's eyelids fluttered, and Scarlett sucked in a breath. "Faith," the girl whispered.

"Detective, we're moving her."

Scarlett shot the doctor a silent plea for a few more seconds. "Your name is Faith?"

The young woman shook her head weakly. "No. Need faith."

Oh no. Scarlett's voice softened. "You want me to call a priest?"

The girl's jaw clenched infinitesimally. "No. Faith. Fry."

"All right," Scarlett soothed, although she had no idea what the young woman meant. Or even if she spoke English. It sounded almost like she was saying *fith fry*. Fish fry? No, that couldn't be right. "Who did this to you?"

Tears filled her dark brown eyes. "Krin. Krin."

One of the monitors started to beep, and the team flew into action.

"BP's dropping," a nurse said. "She's going into V-fib."

"That's it, Detective!" the doctor snapped, issuing a string of orders to the team as they pulled the stretcher out of the bay and rushed it to the elevator.

Scarlett pulled out her phone, dialing her lieutenant's info man as she walked to the ER's exit. "Crandall, this is Bishop. Can you check the missing-persons list for anyone named Faith? She's five-ten, dark hair to her shoulders, possibly Hispanic."

"Just a second," Crandall said, his keyboard clacking in the background. "No. We have a Fawn and a Fiona. No Faith."

"I knew that was too good to be true," she muttered. "I ran a check based on the medics' description before I came over here and came up empty. I was hoping for something new."

"How long ago was that?"

"Twenty-five minutes or so. Why?"

"Because there is a new report, uploaded fifteen minutes ago. Arianna Escobar, seventeen years old. She fits your description and was last seen on her campus at King's College, where she's a freshman. I have a photo. Hold on. I'll send it to your phone."

Scarlett ran to her car and was buckling herself in when the photo came through. It took her a moment to find any similarity between the girl in the photo and the victim she'd just seen. "Man, the bastard did a number on her face. It's hard to tell if it's the same girl. I think it is. Who filed the report?"

"Her roommate, Lauren Goodwin. She's in Harrison dorm. I'll send her cell number to your phone."

"Thanks, Crandall. Let Isenberg know I'm headed to the college, if you don't mind."

"She'll want to know the girl's status."

"They were charging the paddles when they rushed her into surgery," she said, trying to ignore the twinge of guilt. If she hadn't kept the girl talking ... And she hadn't even gotten anything useful for having risked the girl's life. "Cross your fingers."

"I'll pray."

"Yeah," Scarlett said flatly. "You do that, too. I'll call when I have something." She hung up, annoyed with herself for having snapped at Crandall, but the whole prayer thing rubbed her wrong. It didn't seem fair that some people's prayers were answered and others' weren't.

Let it go, Scar. Her phone buzzed, a text from Crandall

with a phone number for Arianna's roommate. *Thx*, she texted back and then dialed Lauren's number.

Mt. Carmel, Ohio
Monday, November 3, 6:10 p.m.

When his partner didn't emerge from the vehicle, Deacon was surprised, but he was shocked when he saw Adam Kimble get out instead. Adam had been part of Isenberg's Homicide Unit prior to the formation of MCES, when he'd moved to Personal Crimes—CPD's euphemism for sex crimes. The more delicate term didn't diminish the ugliness that the PC squad dealt with on a daily basis. It seemed to have taken its toll on Adam.

The man who now scanned the crime scene with a hardened expression was a far cry from the boy who'd grown up in the house next door to Deacon's. Their mothers had been sisters who'd given birth to their sons only two months apart. Best friends from the time they could crawl, Adam had been Deacon's partner in their childhood adventures—the ones that had had the neighborhood sentries reporting to their mothers. In school Adam had defended Deacon and his sister from the bullies who had hassled them for their unusual appearance. Deacon had been too scrawny to fight back then. When his growth spurt had finally hit, it was Adam who'd taught him how to use his new muscle to defend himself. His cousin had been there for him during the most traumatic events of his life.

Even the fact that Deacon was with MCES was Adam's doing. When Greg's behavior had become so serious that Deacon needed to come home, Adam had not only made sure his cousin got the heads-up on the new task force, but had personally and enthusiastically recommended him to MCES leader, Lieutenant Lynda Isenberg, who was now Deacon's boss.

But then something had changed—and whatever it was, it was epic and sudden. Adam had completely avoided him since he'd arrived from Baltimore. Deacon didn't take it personally, though. Instead, he worried, because Adam was completely avoiding everyone, including his mother, Deacon's aunt Tammy.

Based on Adam's current scowl, whatever was bothering him had taken a turn for the worse.

Oh no. Deacon remembered his aunt's pale face as he'd fought with Greg. *Not again.* Aunt Tammy's heart attack had been the catalyst for Deacon coming home. "Is your mom okay?"

Adam's body seemed to still, an oddly menacing sight. "Why wouldn't she be?"

"Because we upset her. Greg and I. We were arguing and it got kind of ... intense."

Adam shook his head. His shoulders relaxed, but his expression remained dark and closed. "She's okay, as far as I know. Why were you arguing?"

"Greg's getting suspended again for fighting. Same old," Deacon said with a shrug.

"Goddamn idiot kid," Adam spat. "He's gonna kill her, Deacon. One of these days—"

Deacon held up a hand to stop Adam's tirade. "I have two more rooms to paint, and then Dani can move in." The house he and his sister had bought together had been a fixer-upper, because it was all they could afford. Deacon had spent much of his free time doing repairs, but he was almost finished now, and pretty proud of his work, actually. "Dani and I are coordinating our shifts so that one of us is always home with him. We'll have him out of Aunt Tammy's by the end of the week." He hesitated. "If your mom's okay, then why are you here?"

Adam's lip curled. "Our boss sent me."

Our boss? Deacon's eyes widened. "You're in MCES? Since when?"

"Since an hour ago." The words were spat out in a show of temper that had Deacon backing away.

"I take it that this wasn't your idea," Deacon said cautiously.

Adam's jaw clenched so tightly that Deacon was surprised his teeth didn't crack. "Still the boy genius, I see. No. It wasn't my idea, but I'm here and I'm all yours. Lucky you."

O-kay. "What about Bishop?"

"Don't worry. She's still your partner. Think of me as the water boy."

"The water boy," Deacon repeated, feeling as if he'd been sideswiped. Isenberg had some explaining to do. "Tanaka," he called to the leader of CSU, who was getting his gear from the van. "Come here and I'll bring you both up to speed. We need to hurry. The light's nearly gone."

"I have spotlights," Vince Tanaka said when he'd joined them. A veteran crime-scene analyst, he was very good at his job. "My tech's setting them up by the marker in the road."

"Not yet." Deacon pointed to the shoulder where he'd seen the blood. "Over there first. I think she came from those trees."

"I thought she was dumped," Adam said with a frown.

"She may have been, but I found blood on the grass." Deacon quickly filled them in. "I want her path traced. Mark every blade of grass that she dragged herself across. The sheriff took photos when he got here. He said he'd e-mail them to us. He also bagged and tagged the Good Sam's coat and gun."

Tanaka blinked. "The Good Sam was armed?"

"Apparently so. Make sure she gets a receipt for her things."

"Will do." Tanaka headed toward the shoulder, leaving Deacon and his cousin alone.

Deacon searched Adam's angry face, wanting to dig deeper, to find out what the hell was wrong, but this wasn't the time. "Look," he whispered, "I don't know what your issue is or what happened to land you on my team, but you need to deal with it on your own time. The girl is the priority. Can you do that?"

Adam flinched, then nodded. "Yeah," he said quietly. "I can handle that."

"Handle" wasn't the word Deacon had used. That Adam had used it . . . *Isenberg has a lot of explaining to do.*

"Thank you," Deacon said. "I'll get a statement from the Good Sam. I want you to see what's down there." He pointed in the direction from which the girl had come. The direction in which the Good Sam had been headed. "Do it on foot. Take one of Tanaka's techs with you to sweep for evidence."

Adam gave him a terse nod. "I'll be back soon."

Deacon turned his attention to the woman sitting in the

back of the ambulance. Faith Corcoran. She'd been watching him the entire time he'd been talking with Adam and Tanaka. Now she swallowed hard, fear flickering across her face, troubling him. He wanted her off guard, not afraid.

He'd taken two steps toward the ambulance when his cell phone buzzed in his pocket. A glance at the caller ID had him backing up, out of Corcoran's earshot. It was Lieutenant Lynda Isenberg, his boss. *Oh, wait. Excuse me. "Our" boss.*

"When did you plan to tell me about Adam?" he demanded, forgoing the pleasantries.

Isenberg's voice was level, as usual. "Twenty minutes ago, but I had to take two other calls. Kimble's officially part of your team." A slight hesitation. "Keep an eye on him."

"You'll tell me why later?"

"No," she said in a way that brooked no argument. "I'm calling now because I have new information regarding your case. Bishop's ID'd your vic. Her name is Arianna Escobar, and she's a seventeen-year-old freshman at King's College. Her roommate reported her missing yesterday, but the cop who took the report figured Arianna was off partying. Lauren Goodwin, the roommate, kept pushing and finally got campus security to view the tapes this afternoon. They show that Arianna left the library at eleven on Friday night with another student, Corinne Longstreet, who also appears to be missing. I've added her to the missing-persons database."

Deacon muttered a curse. "Can you send me the profiles on both girls?"

"They've already been sent to your phone. Corinne's a sophomore, but she's older than her classmates. She's twenty-six years old, five-six, about a hundred and thirty pounds, blond hair."

"Thanks. Does Bishop have a feel for whether Corinne's a victim or if she's involved in the abduction?"

"She's not sure. Arianna tried to say Corinne's name when Bishop asked her who'd taken her. But she was crying, too, so she might have been trying to tell Bishop that Corinne was in trouble."

"Did Arianna say anything else?"

"Bishop thinks she was saying 'fish fry,'" Isenberg said flatly. "She has no idea what that means. The victim's roommate was equally puzzled."

"Okay. We'll assume that Corinne Longstreet is a victim until we learn differently. Adam's tracing Arianna's path. I'll have him search for signs of Corinne also. The local sheriff seems sharp, and he knows the area. I'll ask him to organize a search party."

"I'll send you as much manpower as I can spare," Isenberg said. "If the sheriff doesn't have access to search dogs, let me know. I'll get some out there."

"Good, thanks." Deacon eyed the woman in the ambulance, whose gaze had followed every move he'd made. She was biting her lip, her face shadowed with concern. "Do me a favor, Boss. Run a check on a woman named Faith Corcoran. She has Florida plates." He recited the plate number, which he'd committed to memory earlier. Good thing, too. It was now too dark to see the Jeep, much less its plate.

"Okay. Why am I running a check on her?"

"She's the Good Sam who discovered Arianna, but this road is way off the beaten path and she's acting twitchy. I want to know why she's here at the same time Arianna turned up."

"Did she hit the girl?"

"No. The skid marks show she swerved off the road about twenty feet from where the girl was found, so that's not it."

"Maybe she's in shock."

"She might have been, but she's not anymore. My gut says she's nervous about something."

"I have to admit that your gut's proven pretty reliable so far," Isenberg said grudgingly. "I'll put Crandall on it. He'll text you with whatever he can dig up."

If it was accessible online, Crandall would find it. "Thank you. I'll keep you—"

"I'm not finished yet. The ER did a rape kit on the Escobar girl and it came up positive."

"Shit," Deacon whispered. He wasn't surprised, but he always hoped it wouldn't be the case.

"I know. Doctor found evidence of previous abuse, too. Arianna's been in the foster system for years. Because of this, and because she's under eighteen, we've called in social services and they've recommended a kid shrink. Dr. Meredith Fallon. Bishop's still at the college, but she'll head back to the hospital when the girl gets out of surgery. That's all I have for you right now. Keep me up to speed with what you find."

"I will." Deacon hung up, his gaze zeroing in on Faith Corcoran, who'd bent her head wearily when he'd whispered his oath over Arianna's rape as if she'd understood, even though she couldn't have heard a word that Isenberg had said.

What did she know? Where had she come from? Why was she here, and why was she carrying a gun? *Faith Corcoran, I think it's time we were formally introduced.*

Chapter Five

The white-haired cop had been all over the crime scene, talking to everyone on the ground. *Except for me,* Faith thought, although she'd had his attention off and on the entire time. He'd studied her as if she were a bug in a jar.

Which was ironic, actually. *Of the two of us, he is totally the not-normal one.* What with his white hair, that leather coat, and those ultra-dark wraparound sunglasses.

He was definitely in charge here. Everyone he talked to followed his orders. Although that one other agent had looked really angry. And that first deputy's initial reaction to him still had her puzzled. And a little nervous.

More than nervous, actually. She was trembling. She hadn't been able to hear much of what he'd said, but she'd watched his mouth as he'd said it. He had a nice mouth, and the thin white goatee that surrounded it set it off, making it even easier to see. She'd been staring at him when she'd realized his lips were carefully enunciating a familiar set of letters and numbers.

He'd called in the Jeep's license plates. *He suspects.*

Suspects what? You haven't done anything wrong. Besides, he wasn't going to find anything. She'd changed her name on all of her documents.

And if he digs deeper? Finds Dr. Faith Frye? Places a few

calls to Miami? Her relocation effort would end up being a big waste of time. Once one Miami PD cop knew, they'd all know. Cops were the biggest gossips she knew. Once Miami PD knew, it wouldn't be long before her new address "leaked out." And then the nightmare would start up all over again.

She'd know soon enough, she thought, her pulse racing even faster as he closed the distance between them. When he stopped, he was close to where she sat. *Too close.* Far too close.

"Ms. Corcoran? I'm Special Agent Novak with the FBI."

In a moment of panic, she fell back into old habits, dropping her gaze to the inch of asphalt that was all that separated her thick wool socks from his shiny black wingtips. He was so close that she could feel the heat of him. Hear the flapping of his leather trenchcoat in the wind as he towered over her, looking down.

He's trying to intimidate me. It was working. *Stop this. You are better than this. You have done nothing wrong. Look him in the eye and tell him to move the hell back.*

She lifted her chin to speak, but the movement reminded her all too quickly why she was still sitting in the back of an ambulance. She slammed her eyes shut as a wave of nausea smacked her hard. She heard a soft moan and realized that it had come from her mouth.

You will not throw up on his shiny shoes. You will not.

"You're the EMT?" he asked, startling her. She had nearly forgotten about the medic.

"Yes. I'm Jefferies, Mount Carmel Fire and Rescue."

"How is she?"

"*She* is fine," Faith said, keeping her head down and her eyes closed. "And perfectly able to speak for herself."

"Glad to hear it," Novak said levelly. "Jefferies, I'd like to speak to Ms. Corcoran before she's transported. Can you give us a few minutes?"

"Sure," Jefferies said. "I got reports to do. But Ms. Corcoran should be seen in the ER. The contusion on her forehead needs to be sutured. Her hands may also need attention."

"May? You mean you don't know?"

"She wouldn't let me touch them," Jefferies said, sounding slightly defensive.

A slight pause. "And . . . why not?"

"I was afraid I might have picked up evidence from the girl's skin when I touched her," Faith answered. "The sheriff already bagged my coat because I covered her up with it, but I thought your forensics guys might want to swab my hands."

"I see," Novak said. "Anything else, Jefferies?"

"Not that I know of. Just tell me when you're done."

Faith winced as the ambulance shuddered at the impact of the driver's-side door closing, even though the EMT had shut it softly. "Any word on the girl's condition?" she asked.

"She's still in surgery. Do you have any other injuries that you wouldn't let the EMT see?"

Novak's voice had subtly shifted. Now low and deep, it had a hypnotic quality that made her feel calm at first—and then annoyed at the realization that she'd been affected so easily by a vocal technique that she herself had used on countless clients over the years. Someone had obviously trained him well. It made her wonder how he sounded when he was being himself.

"My head's a little sore," she said. "My hands and knees are scraped. I'm really quite fine."

"You don't look really quite fine," Novak said in that same soothing voice. "You look a little green around the gills."

"I've had better days," she allowed. *I've also had much worse.* "But I haven't thrown up on your shoes. Not yet, anyway. But I'd hurry if I were you. Those shoes look new."

He chuckled, surprising her. "Not new. Just well cared for. Can you look at me?"

"Why?"

"Because I like to see the eyes of the witnesses I interview. Please."

She remembered the deputy's flinch and wondered if Novak had a scar she hadn't been close enough to see. She knew how it felt when people stared, then looked away. That had happened often when the scar on her throat had been raw.

"It would help if you weren't quite so tall," she said. "Looking that far up makes me sick."

She heard the muted squeak of soft leather. "Better?" he asked.

Opening her eyes, she found that not only had he leaned down, knees slightly bent, but he'd also leaned in, taking up even more of her personal space. Or maybe it was simply that he was a big man. His thighs were the size of tree trunks and looked just as solid. His shoulders completely blocked her view.

"Ms. Corcoran?" he prompted.

Dr. Corcoran, she wanted to correct, but did not, focusing instead on her rapidly escalating pulse. *Don't flinch if he has a scar.* She lifted her chin. "Please back up. You're—"

Her mouth stopped working as her gaze focused on his eyes.

Oh my God. His eyes. They were . . . mesmerizing.

She'd met individuals with different-color eyes. She'd met individuals with one bicolored iris. But she'd never seen eyes like Special Agent Novak's. Deep brown and bright blue they were, but both of them. Each iris half-brown, half-blue, the vivid colors pixelating, then blending where they met in the middle.

"Oh," she breathed, unable to break her stare. "How . . . beautiful."

He went perfectly still, and for a long moment they stared at each other.

He broke away first, straightening to his full height. From where she sat, she found herself staring at his midsection, his eyes no longer in her view. For a moment she felt strangely bereft.

Until she realized what she'd said. *Out loud, even.* Her face flaming, she cleared her throat. "I'm sorry. I was just . . . I mean, I wasn't . . ." She sighed. "What would you like to know?"

"Tell me what happened." His voice had gone flat. Expressionless.

Great. She'd managed to offend him, even when she'd tried not to. "Well, I was driving home, or to what will be my home anyway. All of a sudden she was just *there.* I don't know where she came from."

"I thought she was lying in the road."

Faith forced herself to concentrate on the girl instead of Novak, who stood as rigid as a statue. "I don't think so. I know it sounds crazy, but it was almost like she jumped in front of my car."

"What happened after you saw her?"

That he hadn't said that she *wasn't* crazy didn't escape Faith's notice. "I slammed on my brakes and swerved. Went down the embankment and hit a tree. I got out of my Jeep, called 911, then went to the girl. I took her pulse, did some basic first aid."

Returning to his crouch, he carefully took her left hand. "Where did you touch her?"

His hand was large and warm. His whole body radiated heat. She had to fight the urge to lean in to him, just enough to take the edge off her chill. She wondered what he'd do if she tried.

Not that it mattered. She hadn't leaned on a man in four years, and she wasn't going to start now. Especially with a cop. No matter how mesmerizing his eyes.

"On her throat to take her pulse and around the wound on her leg. She was bleeding from what looked like a bullet wound, and I used my scarf to stanch the flow, but I was careful not to directly touch the open wound." She shrugged. "You can never tell who's clean these days. Better safe than sorry."

Still holding her left hand, he reached for her right, turning both palms up. "But your hands are covered in her blood."

"Not hers," Faith said. "It's mine. I cut my hands when I crawled up the embankment."

"Why?"

"There were sharp rocks in the dirt. Or broken glass, maybe from my Jeep's windows."

"No, I mean why did you crawl up the embankment?"

She frowned at him. "Because she was hurt. I couldn't leave her there, lying in the road."

He was studying her with an intensity that made her feel . . . exposed. A part of her wanted to close her eyes again, to hide from his scrutiny, but another, bolder, nearly forgotten part of her didn't back down. She locked on to those amazing eyes and didn't look away.

Novak rose abruptly. "Sergeant Tanaka! Come here, please. Bring your collection kit."

A forty-something man of Asian descent hurried over, carrying a tackle box. "What is it?"

"Ms. Corcoran, this is Sergeant Tanaka. He leads our

crime-scene unit. This is Ms. Corcoran. She has refused medical attention because she touched the victim and wanted to protect any evidence. Can you process her hands so that the EMT can take care of her wounds?"

Tanaka regarded her curiously. "Of course." He transferred the grime from her hands to evidence bags, swabbing the blood and scraping under her nails, apologizing when she winced.

Novak stepped back far enough to give Tanaka room to work. Far enough that Faith could see him without having to crane her neck to look up.

Far enough that he was no longer crowding her space, allowing her to breathe normally again. He'd dropped his gaze to his phone, leaving her free to study his face without the distraction of his eyes staring back. He was a handsome man in a stark, startling, action-hero kind of way. He'd never be ignored, that was for sure. If his white hair and remarkable eyes didn't do enough to set him apart, the black leather coat and the sci-fi wraparound sunglasses he'd worn earlier would certainly do the trick.

Which made Faith wonder why he would make himself so instantly recognizable. So completely unforgettable. So visible.

The thought of being so visible bothered Faith more than she wanted to admit. She'd spent most of her life trying to be *in*visible, but Novak was as far from invisible as a person could be.

"Thanks," he said to Tanaka when the sergeant had finished with her hands. "I'll interview Ms. Corcoran so that she can get the medical care she needs, then catch up with Kimble." When Tanaka was gone, Novak dropped into a low crouch so that Faith could look down at him. "I'll make this as quick as I can. You said you were driving home?"

"Yes. To what will be my home."

His brows bunched slightly. "On this road?"

He continued to use the soothing voice, but his eyes had gone sharp, setting off an alarm in Faith's head. "Yes, on this road."

"I just checked the map on my phone, and this road dead-ends about a mile from here. There are no houses between here and there. Just a cemetery. Are you planning to build?"

Huh. Now, there was a suggestion she hadn't considered. She'd inherited fifty acres of land along with the house. She could sell forty-nine of those acres and build one hell of a house on the acre she kept. Except that building a new house seemed a poor use of the money the sale of the acreage would bring. Her dad might need that money.

Hell, I *might need the money if I have to run again.*

"No," she said, adopting the same soothing tone, taking satisfaction in watching his eyes flicker in surprise. "I don't intend to build, and yes, there *is* a house at the end of the road. The map doesn't show it since it doesn't have a traditional address. It never has, as far as I know. But it's visible in Google Earth, a big, old, abandoned house with a cemetery in the backyard."

His head tilted slightly, his interest piqued. "Abandoned? For how long?"

"Twenty-three years."

"Who owns it?"

She drew a breath. "I do. Now."

"You bought it?"

This was getting too personal. "I don't see how that's your business," she said coolly.

"Humor me, then. I could find out through the public record, but you could save me some time by telling me. Time I could use to find out who brutalized that young woman and left her out here to die," he added, as a parent might when trying to make a child feel guilty.

It worked. Faith looked away, appropriately chastised. And aware that the deed in the public record might still list her as Faith Frye. Her attorney in Miami had filed for the name change several days ago but had told her it could take a week or more to update. "My grandmother owned the house but hadn't lived there for twenty-three years. She died a month ago and left the house to me."

"It's sat empty all this time? Really? That's hard to believe."

"Oh, she had people go in and tidy up from time to time, but from what I saw yesterday, it looks pretty much as it always did. The grounds are kept up by the historical society, on account of the cemetery being a landmark. Why all the questions about the house?"

"Just getting the lay of the land," he said mildly. "You'd been armed with a gun when the sheriff arrived."

She blinked, startled at the topic change and now back on her guard. "Yes."

"Why?"

She blinked again, this time in disbelief. "Why? Seriously? Maybe because I was alone, my Jeep wrecked, stranded on a deserted road with an unconscious victim of a violent assault? That girl was left there by someone, Agent Novak. If that someone had stuck around, I wasn't going to give him the opportunity to hurt her again. Or me."

"That's sensible, of course. But why did you have a gun to begin with, Ms. Corcoran?"

So I can shoot my sonofabitch stalker if he manages to track me here, she thought, but had the presence of mind not to say it aloud. If she ever did shoot the sonofabitch stalker, she didn't want anyone claiming she'd done so with premeditation. "A lot of women carry weapons."

"True enough. But most of the civilian women I know carry them in their purse. You left your purse in your car, yet you had your gun handy."

That he'd noticed shouldn't have rattled her, but it did. "I don't carry it in my purse."

"In a shoulder holster, then?"

"No."

He narrowed his eyes, clearly frustrated. "You're going to make me work for this, aren't you? Fine. Why did you have your gun so handy, Ms. Corcoran? Did you bring it from your Jeep on purpose, expecting to need it? Did you perhaps see more than you're admitting?"

It was her turn to blink in surprise. *Holy hell. He thinks I'm lying.* Which she was not. She had simply withheld personal information that he did not need to know. There was a difference.

"No," she said firmly. "I did not expect to need my gun. It was in my coat pocket, if you must know. I didn't see anyone except the girl, just like I told you. I'm not lying."

He stared at her. "You carry a gun in your coat pocket? Why in God's name would you do something so dangerous?"

She glared back, irritated. "I'm not stupid, Agent Novak.

I don't carry it in my pocket unprotected. I have a pocket holster."

"Why?" he asked again, his urgency mounting.

She feigned nonchalance, hoping to ratchet his intensity down a bit. He was making her nervous again. "Because shoulder holsters chafe."

Abruptly, he rose from his crouch, simultaneously leaning in to her space until they were eye to eye, their noses nearly touching. "Why do you carry a gun in your pocket, Faith?" he demanded, his voice rich with an authority that crushed her defenses as if they'd never been.

"So I can get to it when I need it," she blurted out, then clamped her lips together. *Goddammit.* She hadn't meant to say that.

He was really good, she had to give him that. He'd known how to push her buttons. For a minute there, she was a teenager, cowering in the confessional while her grandmother's priest thundered at her from the other side.

Novak had immediately stilled at her answer. "But *why* do you need it?" he asked quietly.

None of your damn business, was on the tip of Faith's tongue, but she was saved from having to respond by the approach of the agent who'd been talking with Novak earlier. The angry one.

"Agent Novak, I need to talk to you. *Now.*"

"Excuse me, Ms. Corcoran," Novak said. He and the angry agent stepped several feet away, speaking too quietly for her to overhear and turning so that she couldn't see their faces.

Faith closed her eyes. This evening was shot to hell. By the time she made it through the ER, it would be time to sleep. There would be no going into the house for her tonight, either.

Oh no. She grimaced. *The locksmith.* He had to still be at the house. He would have come back this way if he'd gotten tired of waiting, and no other vehicles had approached from the direction of the house since she'd hit the tree.

She was frankly surprised that he had waited so long. Maybe he'd never shown up. Or maybe he had and was charging her by the hour. *Wouldn't that be just my luck?*

She patted her pockets, looking for her phone so that she could call him, then remembered it had been in her coat pocket. *That's just perfect.* The sheriff had bagged her coat since it had touched the girl, so they now had her cell phone, too.

Novak and the angry agent parted ways, the other man heading toward the sedan parked behind the CSU van. Novak returned to the ambulance, knocking on the driver's window.

"Jefferies, I need to leave for a few minutes. Can you please take care of Ms. Corcoran's hands while I'm gone?" Without waiting for a reply, he took off at a jog for the sedan and jumped in the passenger seat before Faith could ask about her phone.

The sedan squeezed past the ambulance and disappeared from view, headed in the direction of the house. The other agent must have found evidence on the animals who'd dumped the girl, she thought. Her locksmith troubles were nothing in comparison. If the locksmith had actually shown up, he'd eventually grow tired of waiting and would come back this way. Until then, all she could do was stay here until Novak released her from the scene.

"You ready, Ms. Corcoran?" Jefferies asked.

Faith held out her hands with a sigh. "As I'll ever be."

Mt. Carmel, Ohio
Monday, November 3, 6:40 p.m.

Deacon successfully fought the urge to look over his shoulder. He knew Faith Corcoran was in good hands with the EMT. But he was still reluctant to leave her alone.

Which was ridiculous. She was surrounded by armed cops. She was not in danger, nor was she helpless. She'd climbed a rocky hillside to save a girl she didn't know and had stood watch over that girl, gun in hand.

A gun she carried because she was frightened of something. Or someone.

"What's with the Good Sam?" Adam asked. "What did she say to you?"

Beautiful. She'd said his eyes were beautiful. He could count on one hand the number of times that had happened in his life. The word had hit him hard when she'd whispered it, left him momentarily speechless.

Deacon was accustomed to the reactions of others. The flinches. The avid, clinical curiosity. Sometimes even suspicion. Over the years he'd learned either to ignore people or to manipulate their initial surprise to suit his own agenda.

But Faith had called him "beautiful."

Adam smacked his shoulder. "Hey. What the hell's wrong with you?"

Deacon cleared his throat, rewinding his brain to remember Adam's question. "She said that she was on her way home when the girl jumped in front of her."

"And?" Adam prompted. "There's more. I can see it on your face. What else?"

"She's hiding something. She's definitely afraid."

"Of what?"

"I don't know. She wouldn't tell me. All I could get is that she carries a gun in her pocket so she'll have it if she needs it. But she didn't hurt Arianna Escobar."

"And . . . you're sure about that?" Adam asked carefully.

Deacon started to say yes, then frowned. Was he really? He'd found her suspicious enough to ask his boss to run a background check. Before she'd called him beautiful.

Had he been that easy to distract? *I guess so.* It was a little humiliating, actually.

"Why?" he asked, unsettled. "What did you find? Any sign of Corinne Longstreet?"

"No, but I traced the Escobar girl's trail to a utility truck crashed into a tree, around the next curve. Hell of a coincidence."

Dread building, Deacon kept his gaze on the trees. That the other crashed truck was a coincidence, that Faith Corcoran really was a valiant protector was what he wanted to be true. But what he wanted rarely mattered. What mattered was finding who'd assaulted Arianna—and determining what had happened to Corinne Longstreet.

Adam stopped the car, and Deacon swore. Down a slight hill was a truck with a dented hood, its front right tire hovering about six inches off the ground. The vehicle had struck a young tree, snapping it in half, and was now suspended on the broken trunk.

On the side of the utility truck a cartoon nobleman balanced one booted toe on the tip of a lightning bolt. "Earl

Power and Light," Deacon murmured. "Arianna's trail ends there?"

Adam nodded. "The driver's seat is covered with blood. It hasn't completely dried. Tanaka's tech is down there, taking blood samples. He found woman-sized bloody handprints on the door and the other side of the truck. He typed the blood and said it matches what was on the road. He also found a hair that's the same length and color as Arianna's, but none that match the description of the second girl."

"So Arianna was driving the truck. We have to assume that she used it to get away from whoever abducted and assaulted her. Have you contacted the power company?"

Another nod. "They sent a man out here this afternoon to turn the power on in an old house at the end of the road. Guess who phoned in the request?"

"Faith Corcoran."

"Yep. Earl Power said that they hadn't heard from the tech since a little after three, when he texted that he'd turned the power on and that he was sick and heading home early. He's not in the truck or anywhere around it."

"And he never made it home?"

"Still waiting to hear. His boss called his cell while I waited. Went straight to voice mail. I ran a check, but the driver's clean. Ken Beatty's a family man. Never late, always finishes the job. The fact that he texted that he was sick was unusual."

"Corcoran said she was on her way to the house that she'd inherited from her grandmother, who died last month. A big, old, abandoned house with a cemetery in the backyard. It stands to reason that she called the power company for innocent reasons. Like, to turn on her power."

Adam met his eyes. "I still don't like the coincidence."

"Neither do I," Deacon murmured. "The house is the only one around for miles, has been abandoned for twenty-odd years, and doesn't show up on the map."

Adam scowled. "Perfect place to hide while you torture some teenagers."

"That's what I'm thinking. Take me back to the scene. I'll find out what Corcoran knows about the power company employee and the truck. I'll get her permission to do a search of the house. You take one of the deputies and check out the house. Coordinate your search with Sheriff Palmer. He and his men know this area far better than we do."

Adam turned the sedan around. "What do you think about her now?"

"I still don't believe she hurt Arianna. She called 911, waited for them to come. It doesn't make sense that she'd do that if she was up to anything nefarious. But I still think she's hiding something big." They were halfway back when Deacon's cell phone buzzed. "This is Novak."

"It's Crandall. Isenberg said you wanted a background on the Corcoran woman."

New dread piled atop the lump in Deacon's stomach. "Yeah. And?" He put the phone on speaker so Adam could hear. "What's on her record?"

"She doesn't have one. No speeding tickets, parking tickets, nothing. And I literally mean she's got *nothing*. She applied for her driver's license less than a week ago, and the Miami address she listed is an attorney's office, but I couldn't find an employment history or a phone number. It's like she popped up out of frickin' nowhere."

"Shit." Deacon pinched the bridge of his nose. He felt a massive headache coming on.

"You knew she was hiding something," Adam said. "Sounds like she's someone who needed to disappear, become someone new."

"Which might explain her nervousness." *I hope.* "Crandall, call Tanaka and get the serial number on her gun. Let me know if it's linked to any crimes. I don't want her walking away until we get to the bottom of all this, but right now I don't have anything to hold her on."

"On it. I'll let you know when I have something."

"Make it quick," he said as they rolled to a stop next to the ambulance. Faith was still sitting in the back, but her hands were now heavily bandaged. "Looks like the EMT has patched her up. Her next stop is the ER, and then she's in the wind."

Mt. Carmel, Ohio
Monday, November 3, 7:05 p.m.

Faith stared at Agent Novak when he stopped in front of her. The angry agent's sedan had returned, staying still only long enough for Novak to hop out and for a uniformed officer to take his place. Then it was gone again, back in the same direction. Toward the house.

"What's going on here?" she asked. "What did you find?"

"Are your hands better?" he asked, ignoring her questions.

"Can I have my phone back?" she asked, ignoring his.

"I don't have it."

"The sheriff does. He bagged it along with my gun. I expect that you'll hold on to the gun for a while, but I need my phone."

"I'll see what I can do. Is there anyone I can call for you in the meantime?"

Something was very wrong. His eyes had grown suspicious. He knew. He had to know. *The jig's up. You might as well just tell him.* But still she hesitated. She saw suspicion, but none of the contempt she'd come to expect from cops. She hated the thought of putting it there.

"No, because I don't know the number I want to call. It's in my phone."

"Who do you need to call, Ms. Corcoran?"

It was clear that she wasn't getting her phone back anytime soon. *Be careful. Answer only the questions asked.* "If you must know, I need to call the locksmith who's waiting for me at my grandmother's house to tell him I'm not coming."

He frowned slightly. "A locksmith? Why?"

"Because the key my grandmother's attorney gave me doesn't fit, and he told me he doesn't have another one," she said, her patience thinning. "And it's only smart to change the locks anyway. The house is a hundred and fifty years old. My cell phone, please?"

"You'll get your phone back, but I have a few questions first. When was the last time you were in the house?"

She narrowed her eyes at him. "Why?"

"Please, Ms. Corcoran, just answer my question."

She regarded him with the same suspicion with which he regarded her. "I was *at* the house yesterday. I haven't been *in* it in twenty-three years."

"You never entered it yesterday?"

She frowned. "I said the key didn't fit. That's why I called the locksmith. What's going on here? What did you and that other agent find?"

"You said you were meeting the locksmith," he said, once again ignoring her question. "Did you arrange for anyone else to go to the house?"

Realization dawned sharply. *This isn't about me at all.* She'd been paranoid. Selfish, even. *This is about the girl.* "What does my grandmother's house have to do with the girl? Do you think she was in there?"

He bent his knees until his eyes met hers. "Please. Did you call anyone else?"

"Yes. I called a lot of people. My to-do list is stored in my phone, but let me think. I called a septic service, a Realtor, and the trash-collection service. And a contractor, too."

"Why?"

"Because the house has been unoccupied for twenty-three years. I need to be sure it's still even livable."

"Sensible. Anyone else?"

She thought hard, ticking off her list in her mind. "The locksmith, which I already said, and ... Oh, of course. I called the power company to turn on the electricity. They said they'd send someone today." A flicker in his eyes told her that was the answer he'd wanted. "Why are you asking me these questions, Agent Novak?"

"Who was scheduled to be there today?"

"Just the power company and the locksmith. *Why?*"

"I need to look inside the house. Do I have your permission?"

Her eyes widened. "You *do* think the girl was there!"

"It's possible," he admitted. "So, we can search?"

"What does this have to do with the power company?"

His jaw tightened impatiently. "I'm wasting time here. Do I have your permission or not? Because if I don't, I'll get a warrant."

"I know you're looking for who hurt the girl, so yes, you can search. But only if I'm present when you do."

"No. Not possible."

His immediate, intractable reply raised the hackles on the back of her neck. Searching the house was about the girl. But keeping Faith away ... that was personal. As personal as all those questions about her gun. When a cop got personal, it never ended well.

"If you want my permission, take me with you. Otherwise, get a warrant."

His eyes narrowed, making him appear menacing. "Why?"

"Because I don't trust cops," she said flatly, more than a little unnerved. "Call me jaded, call me a bitch, call me anything you want. That's the condition. The sooner you agree, the sooner you're in the house and not standing here wasting time arguing with me."

He gave a single, sharp nod. "Come with me, then." He straightened and looked over at the EMT. "I'll see that she gets to the hospital for any additional care she requires. You can go."

"Are you all right with this, Ms. Corcoran?" Jefferies asked cautiously.

"I am. It's okay. Help me down if you would." Jefferies helped Faith out of the ambulance, shaking his head when she tried to give him the blanket.

"Keep it for now," he said. "It's cold out here."

Novak took her arm as the ambulance pulled away from the scene. "I may have a jacket in my vehicle," he said, his tone less aggressive. "I should have looked when I first got here. I'm sorry." He frowned at the thick wool socks on her feet. "Where are your shoes?"

"The sheriff found them down there." She pointed down the embankment. "But they're trashed. I had a pair of sneakers in the gym bag on the front seat of the Jeep, but that side is so crushed, I doubt you'll find them without cutting off the door. I'm okay to walk like this. It's not that far."

He was staring in that bug-in-a-jar way again. "You climbed the embankment barefoot?"

She shrugged. "Adrenaline, I guess. I didn't realize I'd lost my shoes until after I'd called 911 and my feet started to get cold and my stockings were ripped up. The sheriff gave me these socks. He swore they were clean," she added wryly because he was looking at her too intensely. "Are we going to stand here and talk about footwear or go to the house?"

He gave her a final searching look before guiding her to his SUV, one hand spread lightly on her back, steadying her when her knees threatened to buckle. His body threw off heat like a furnace, tempting her once more to lean in to him.

It would be so nice to lean on someone, for just a little while. But that someone would never be a cop. No matter how warm he was. Or how good he smelled. Holding her back straighter, she politely refused his offer to help her up into the seat.

Pride kept her going, giving her the energy to buckle up. But pride petered out under a wave of exhaustion as soon as she heard her seat belt click. They'd walked less than fifty feet and she felt like she'd walked a mile.

"Are you all right?" Novak asked quietly. He was standing in her open door, crowding her.

"Not really, but I'll let you know if I feel like I'm going to throw up."

"I'd appreciate it." He closed her door gently, opening and closing the tailgate, then his own door the same way. He handed her a flannel-lined Windbreaker, one that screamed FBI in giant white letters across the back. "It's clean," he said, then abruptly leaned over her lap to retrieve a bottle of pain reliever from the glove box. He pulled a bottle of water from the car's cup holder. "Does your head still hurt?"

Like an army was marching through it, wearing spikes on their boots. "Yes."

The sudden ringing of his phone made her flinch. "Sorry," he said. "I'll turn it down." He handed her the bottles, then answered his phone. "What do you have for me, Crandall?"

He cranked the engine, then froze, his fingers still holding the key. His jaw tightened. "Are you sure?" He glanced over at Faith, held her gaze. She wanted to look away, but forced herself not to. Not breaking eye contact, he leaned back in his seat. If he'd studied her like a bug in a jar before, he was dissecting her now. And not approving of what he found inside.

Yep. He knows, all right.

"Well." He let out a long breath. "Not what I expected, but thanks for digging it up," he said. "Can you e-mail me the files? Then call Detective Kimble and fill him in. I'm not able to do so at the moment." He dropped his phone in his pocket and tilted his head meaningfully, as if waiting for her to speak.

Faith said nothing. He'd come to his own conclusions, no matter what she said.

"All right, then," he said, ending the standoff. "I'll go first." A long pause. "Dr. Frye."

She sighed wearily. "I thought I'd changed everything. What did I miss?"

"Your gun registration. It still lists you as Dr. Faith Frye, PhD."

She glared at him. "Dammit. I changed that, too."

"You may have submitted the paperwork, but the computer hadn't caught up."

"Goddamn computers," she muttered.

"Speaking of computers, our data guru could find no record of you changing your name. We know you changed your driver's license and credit cards within the last week, but there's no official record in the system of a name change."

"That's something, at least," she said grimly.

His brows crunched, making him appear very threatening. "Do you think this is a *joke*?"

Faith laughed at the very notion. "No, I don't. I truly don't."

"You listed your profession on your gun registration as mental-health therapist. Is that true?"

"Yes."

"So you really are a therapist to sex offenders?" he asked, sounding so very disappointed.

Don't you dare look down, girl. You have nothing to be ashamed of. She forced herself to meet his disappointed gaze. "I was. I'm not anymore."

"Why not?"

None of your damn business. "I needed a change."

"You seem to have changed quite a lot in a short time."

"Is there a question in there anywhere, Agent Novak, or are you just wasting time?"

He clenched his teeth so hard that a muscle in his cheek twitched. "Since we couldn't find a record of your name change, should I assume the court record was sealed?"

"Yes, you should," she snapped, at the end of her patience. "Which *should* indicate that I proved my need for privacy to a judge."

"Why?"

She smiled at him, feeling no mirth of any kind. "You mean your Internet guru didn't find any of the thirty complaints I filed with Miami PD? How good can he be?"

He frowned. "Thirty complaints? Against whom?"

Part of her wanted to tell him to fuck himself. But a bigger, more exhausted part just wanted this day to be over. "Tell your guru to look up Peter Combs."

"I will, but in the interest of my time, which really belongs to the girl you found, tell me what he'll find."

"Combs is a sex offender who attacked me with a knife."

There was a flicker of recognition in his eyes, followed by that expression of grave disappointment again. "Our guru found an article on Combs's trial. He summarized it for me."

Her lips twisted bitterly. She knew which article he meant. "I'll bet he did."

"Peter Combs was found guilty. He got prison time."

Not enough. Forever wouldn't have been enough. "He got out early." She'd tried for a nonchalant tone, but her voice trembled. *Dammit.*

Novak blinked. That obviously hadn't been in his guru's report. "And he stalked you? You asked for help thirty times?"

I'm not doing this again. I can't. She turned to look out the window. "Aren't you supposed to be searching my grandmother's house?"

"Dr. Frye, why did Peter Combs attack you with a knife?"

Hot, rancid breath on her cheek, the bite of his knife against her throat. The rasp of his voice against her ear. "You ruined my life, bitch, so I'm taking yours. But first I'll make you sorry you ever crossed me. Before I'm through with you, you'll wish you'd never been born."

She swallowed back the bile that burned her throat. Then she turned to face Novak, for no other reason than to reassure herself that it was him sitting beside her and not the man whose voice she would never forget.

From his expression, his Internet guru had been very thorough. Novak knew what Peter Combs had claimed in court. Under oath. What every cop she'd known was all too willing to believe. *Make that every cop plus one FBI special agent.* Because Novak's wish that she deny it was written all over his oddly compelling face.

"You know," she said with a calm that she did not feel, "I went to a lot of trouble to change my name, so I'd appreciate it if you'd use it. Now, do you want to see my grandmother's house or not? If yes, then drive. If no, then let me go and get a damn warrant."

He regarded her in stony silence as the seconds ticked by. Then threw her a curveball. "Dr. *Corcoran*, where were you on Friday evening, between the hours of ten and midnight?"

Faith blinked. "Am I a *suspect*?" she demanded, appalled that she was on the verge of tears.

He leaned over the center console, until his face was inches from hers. Close enough that she could once again feel the warmth of his body, smell the tang of his aftershave.

Don't you let him see you cry. Focus. All she could see was his eyes. They weren't truly split down the middle. His left eye was more blue than brown, his right more brown than blue.

"I don't know who or what you are yet," he admitted quietly. "But at least I'll know what you *aren't* if you can tell me where you were on Friday night. So please, Faith. Just tell me."

The supplication in his tone convinced her to answer. "I was in a hotel room in Miami." Her voice trembled again, but at least she'd willed the tears away. "Packing. To come here."

He exhaled on a relieved sigh. "Do you have *anybody* who can confirm that?"

She wasn't sure if his relief was genuine or if he was playing her, trying to lull her into a false sense of security. *But for what purpose?*

Hell if she knew. Who knew what went on in cops' minds, anyway? After nine years of being married to Charlie, Faith still hadn't a clue. She'd been trained to analyze human behavior, but most cops didn't behave remotely like humans.

"I have a receipt from a gas station near South Beach," she said. "It should still be in my purse. I bought gas around ten Friday night at a well-lit station with good security. I'm sure they'll be more than happy to provide you with video proof."

"Thank you," he said simply. He returned to his seat and put the car in drive. They hadn't gone ten feet before his cell phone rang again. "What do you have?" he said without greeting. He listened, whispered a vicious curse, then punched the accelerator. "She's with me. Wouldn't allow the search without her being present. . . . Yes, I talked to Crandall, and yes, he gave me the information. . . . She says she was in Miami. She has a receipt from a gas station. . . . We'll get the store's video to verify." Then he sighed. "True enough. We're on our way."

"What's true enough?" she asked when he'd ended the call.

"That your presence in Miami doesn't mean you aren't somehow involved."

Involved in what? Faith opened her mouth to protest, but the road curved, revealing a flash of white in Novak's headlights. It was a truck with a coat of arms painted on its side, its front end crashed into a tree. Then the road curved again and it was gone.

"That truck," she said slowly. "It wasn't there yesterday."

"No, I don't suppose it was," Novak said evenly. "Arianna Escobar's blood all over the driver's seat was still wet."

"Arianna Escobar?"

"The girl you found on the road. That's her name."

Faith stared at him. "How did her blood get on the truck's seat?" Her brain finally clicked into gear. "Are you saying that she was in that truck? That she was *driving* that truck?"

"In the absence of DNA analysis of the blood, I can only say that it's likely."

"Oh my God," Faith whispered as the pieces fell into place. The coat of arms . . . It was the logo of Earl Power and Light, the power company she'd called to turn on her electricity. "That truck was at my house today. Where's the driver? What happened to the driver?"

Novak just looked at her, waiting, and her horror doubled.

"You think I know?" Still he said nothing, and her heart began to pound in her chest, in her head, until it was all she could hear. "I called them to turn on my electricity. That's all, I swear."

She looked away, breathed through her nose. Tried to calm herself. *They think I know. They think I'm involved in whatever happened to the electric guy.*

And in whatever had happened to Arianna Escobar. She looked up, saw that Novak's odd eyes were filled with concern. And apprehension.

"Oh my God." It was a hoarse whisper that she couldn't have held back had she tried. She lifted her hands to her mouth, the bandages rough against her lips. "I tried to save her. I didn't hurt her. I couldn't hurt her."

Novak rubbed his forehead. "Dammit. I really want to believe you. Let's see what the house has to say."

Trembling, Faith lowered her hands to her lap and focused her gaze on the darkness of the trees that lined the road. The house had always had a great deal to say, she thought. And for the past twenty-three years, none of it had been good.

Chapter Six

Just in time. He dragged one last limb across the entrance to the dirt road, then straightened with a grimace. No one driving down this stretch of highway would notice the entrance unless they were looking for it. The other end of the road emerged in the woods, a fair distance from the house in the opposite direction to the road that led to the interstate. He'd already hidden that entrance, but he didn't think it would stay hidden. Not for long.

Because of Faith. That motherfucking little bitch. She'd ruined everything. *Brought the cops to my door. I wish I'd killed her when I had the chance.*

But he hadn't, and now through the trees he caught strobing flashes of blue—a cruiser had pulled up in front of his house. *My house.* That the bitch's name was on the deed didn't matter. He'd fixed it up. He'd called it home.

He hadn't been able to clean it all up—inside or outside. Hadn't been able to get rid of the power tech's blood. Or the locksmith's.

And he hadn't been able to move all his treasures out of the house. He'd only had time to rescue a small portion of his collection. He'd hidden the rest where no one would ever think to look. Now he needed to make himself scarce.

The only consolation was that he'd left nothing of himself behind. No DNA. No prints. He always wore gloves and Roza cleaned religiously.

Looking both ways to be sure no one was coming, he walked back to the van he'd left idling on the shoulder, curbing the urge to check the cargo in the back. They'd still be there, either too drugged or too dead to run away. He briefly considered tossing them all in the river, but decided against it. Not here, anyway. With nothing to weigh them down, they'd float and be discovered.

Headlights off, he pulled out onto Kellogg Avenue, heading east, the river now only a stone's throw away. Kellogg ran parallel to and below the steep embankment from where all the cruisers had gathered. He could take the river road east all the way to West Virginia if he wanted, but he had a different destination in mind. He crept along without his lights, waiting until he'd rounded the bend and was out of sight of the cruisers above before turning his headlights on.

When his cargo was safely buried, he'd make Faith sorry she'd ever left Miami.

Mt. Carmel, Ohio
Monday, November 3, 7:35 p.m.

Deacon parked behind Adam's sedan. The house was *huge*, an imposing structure that would have been perfect for the Addams Family. It certainly wasn't a house that seemed to fit the woman who stared out the window of his SUV, her bandaged hands lightly folded in her lap.

She hadn't moved a muscle, yet her body vibrated with tension. Which was to be expected, Deacon thought. He had all but accused her of a terrible crime. She wasn't involved. He knew it in his gut. But she kept too many secrets. Her arrival was too coincidental. And her newly discovered past appeared to be far from pristine.

Crandall's call had rocked him. Dr. Faith Frye, therapist. *To sex offenders.* Deacon had dealt with her breed before, the bleeding hearts who believed that the monsters who raped children could be rehabilitated. They were as bad as defense attorneys. Maybe even worse. At least defense attorneys could claim to be defending the accused's constitutional rights.

*Sex offenders cannot be rehabilitated, and any therapist
who believes they can is*—

Deacon reeled himself back in before he disintegrated
into a mental rant. Faith Frye had paid for her association
with child rapists, and paid dearly. One of her clients had
attacked her, then stalked her after his prison release.

She'd submitted thirty complaints to Miami PD in the
last year. That she'd changed her name and relocated a
thousand miles away was understandable. That she wouldn't
have needed to if she'd chosen a different client population
was undeniable.

But even after hearing her admit to her profession, he
couldn't believe everything Crandall had told him. Couldn't
believe Peter Combs's stated reason for attacking her with
a knife. Couldn't believe Combs's claims that she'd cheated
on him, that she'd been having an affair with him.

That was simply . . . vile. *And if it is true?* It couldn't be.
You just don't want it to be.

Still, he knew that Faith Frye or Corcoran—or whatever
she called herself—wasn't involved in whatever had brought
Arianna Escobar to this place. The woman who'd bloodied
her hands, knees, and feet to help a girl would never be in
league with those who'd abused her.

Four years ago or now. He simply could not believe it.

"This is your house," he said quietly.

"Yeah, I know," she said bitterly. "Beautiful, ain't it?"

Interesting. When she'd called his eyes "beautiful," she'd
been awed. But when she used the same word for the house,
he heard hatred. "Don't you like it?" he asked.

"No."

"Why not?"

A slight hesitation. "I was here when I was told that my
mother had died. I was here when they buried her."

"So you have bad memories of the house? Then why did
you decide to live in it?"

"It seemed like a good idea at the time," she said crypti-
cally. "What are they looking for?" she asked, pointing to
ten arcing beams of light moving methodically away from
the house.

"The other victim," he said, needing to see her reaction.

She swung her head to stare at him, new horror in her
eyes. "There were *two* girls?"

"Yes. Arianna Escobar and her friend Corinne Longstreet. They disappeared from their college campus Friday night."

"Oh my God. And you think they were in my grandmother's house?"

"Possibly."

Her hand flew up to cover her mouth. "The locksmith. Have you found him?"

"Not to my knowledge. Do you have any other keys to the house?"

She shook her head. "The only key I had didn't fit the front door. I told you that already. I got it from my grandmother's attorney, and when I told him it didn't work, he said it was the only key she'd given him. That's why I called the locksmith."

He believed her. "Let me see what's what. Then we'll talk some more. Stay here, please."

She nodded slowly, reminding Deacon of a porcelain doll. Only her head moved, every other muscle and every feature on her face frozen. "Of course," she murmured, shaken.

From the corner of his eye he saw Adam coming across the front lawn, urgency in his step.

"I'll be back," Deacon said. He rushed through the antique wrought-iron gate that Adam held open. "What do we have?"

"Nothing good, for the victims or for us. We have signs of a fight and gunfire. On the side of the house and at the back corner. CSU found two bullets embedded in the wall and four casings."

"More casings than bullets," Deacon said. "Some of his bullets could still be in his victims, then. Arianna has a bullet wound in her leg. Was the bullet still in it when Faith found her?"

"No clue. You want me to find out?"

"Later. We'll get Bishop to ask the ER doc. What else?"

"This." Adam held out a sixteen-inch-long tube and a dart. "Found it in back of the house along with a can of bear Mace. Tanaka searched the Earl Power truck and found another tube about six feet long and a case filled with more darts. I called the power tech's boss, who said that Ken Beatty was mauled by a dog a few years ago. He had no knowledge that his employee carried tranquilizer darts, but he wasn't surprised."

"Then the power tech fought back," Deacon murmured. "What else?"

"Someone drove a van from the driveway on the west side of the house across the grass. Stopped three times. Once at the kitchen door, once in the back, and once at the side. There are signs of a body being dragged across the back of the house, but only halfway. The trail stops at the same place the van stopped."

"He put the body in the van. Can CSU estimate the body's size?"

"Only that whoever it was, was big."

"Corinne Longstreet is five-six, a hundred thirty pounds."

Adam shook his head. "We're talking two-fifty big. Like Ken Beatty, the Earl Power tech. Plus, the meter's back there and there's blood spatter along the back wall."

"Shit. I was afraid of that. What about the third van stop?"

"A lot of blood on the grass. Enough that the person probably bled out. No casings found."

"Any trail from the blood on the grass to the power meter?"

"No, none. We're talking two separate victims. Likely shed at different times. The blood on the grass isn't fully dry. The blood found around the power meter is."

"So two victims. We've got Arianna Escobar and Ken Beatty. We also still have a possible locksmith and Corinne Longstreet unaccounted for. I have a bad feeling about the van's first stop. He may have taken Corinne away through the side door, but let's get inside and see what we find." Deacon started for the house's front door, but Adam held him back.

"Wait. What possible locksmith?" Adam asked.

"Faith said she called the power company to turn on her electricity and a locksmith to change the lock on the front door. The key she'd been given didn't fit. Which makes sense if someone has been using her house to hide his victims. If it were me, the first thing I'd do is change the locks so nobody could come in and catch me."

Adam gave him a hard look. "Faith?"

"That's her name, yes."

"You mean you believe her story?"

"Yes. She's still hiding something, but I don't believe she hurt Arianna."

"Even after everything that Crandall told you about changing her name?"

Adam's tone had taken on an ugly, troubling edge. "I confronted her about the name change. She admitted it."

"*After* you confronted her. She didn't offer it up. Did Crandall tell you about her trial?"

"Faith Corcoran wasn't on trial, Adam," Deacon said. "She was the victim. It was the sex offender who attacked her with a knife who was on trial."

"The sex offender she was sleeping with," Adam shot back, no longer hiding his contempt.

Deacon fought back the sudden surge of anger that took him by surprise. "Or so claimed the sex offender. Since when do we believe the word of a scumbag over a public servant? Crandall didn't say that anyone believed him. There was never an indictment because there was no evidence to support it."

Adam shrugged, his eyes harsh and angry. "Where there's smoke . . ."

"There's fire?" asked a voice from behind them.

Both Deacon and Adam turned to see Faith standing on the other side of the gate, her bandaged hands looking like white mittens as she clutched the iron bars. Her pale cheeks bore two streaks of crimson, her chin trembled. But her eyes flashed fury.

Standing there, her red hair tumbled around her shoulders . . . *She looks like a flame.*

Adam was regarding her steadily. "You have to admit that we have a remarkable set of coincidences here, Dr. Frye."

"It's Corcoran," she corrected crisply. "I thought you were going into the house."

Deacon gave Adam a stand-down look. "We're about to, aren't we, Detective Kimble?"

"We'll need a warrant unless she gives us permission to break the door down. The key in her purse didn't fit."

Deacon barely contained his surprise. "You tried it already?"

"After she gave you permission to search, I had one of

Tanaka's guys get her purse from the Jeep. She's telling the truth about the key not fitting."

The look Faith shot Deacon was like a jagged blade. "*This* is why I don't trust cops. You were supposed to search only if I was present. If you need to break the door down, then do it. Better yet, *I'll* do it." She pushed open the gate, but Deacon grabbed it to stop her.

"Dr. Corcoran, wait. Faith," he added when she continued to push the gate. "You don't have any shoes. Stay here." When she didn't listen, he hardened his voice. "*Stop.* That's not a request."

She was vibrating with fury. "You agreed that I'd go with you."

"That was before we found evidence of a gunfight around back," he snapped. That got her attention, thank God. She took a step back, her eyes wide with shock. "We don't know what we'll find inside," he said more gently. "I have to focus on finding the second girl. I can't be worrying about your safety."

"Okay." She swallowed hard. "Have you found the power company man or the locksmith? They were here because I called them. I . . . I'm responsible for them. For their safety."

Adam smiled, but it wasn't pleasant. "You are very good, Dr. Frye. I almost believe you."

"Detective," Deacon warned.

"No, Agent Novak," she said, "it's quite all right. I'm accustomed to the innuendo. And familiar with the whole good-cop bad-cop routine, so don't waste your efforts. I'll ask again—did you find those two men?"

"No," Deacon told her, unwilling to say any more. Not because he didn't trust her, but because she already looked so devastated. "We're wasting time. Corinne might still be alive. Do I have to have an officer escort you back to the SUV?"

"No." She took a step back. "I'll go. Just find the other girl."

"Thank you. Detective, let's go." He started walking, relieved when Adam cooperated. But then he heard his cousin muttering under his breath.

" 'Just find the other girl,' " Adam mimicked.

Deacon grabbed his arm, yanking him to a halt. "What the hell is wrong with you?"

"What's wrong with *me*? I'm not the one drooling over a possible suspect."

Deacon stared at the man who seemed like such a stranger. "I am not drooling. And she's not a suspect. Not yet, anyway. At this point she is a witness."

"She aids sex offenders. And guess what, *Agent Novak*? The girl she found was raped."

Deacon went still. "I know Arianna was raped," he murmured. "But just because Corcoran counseled offenders does not make her a suspect."

Adam shook his head. "She shacked up with a rapist. How do you know she didn't know the girl was there? That she's not covering for a new *lover*?"

Deacon grimaced at the instant picture his mind conjured, pushing it away before it could stick there. "Because she called 911. Because she guarded the girl."

"With the gun she just happened to have with her?"

"The gun she carries because she's been stalked."

Adam's mouth twisted in disgust. "What did she say that made you drink her Kool-Aid?"

Beautiful. She'd called his eyes beautiful.

But that wasn't why he believed her story. *Though it sure doesn't hurt, does it?*

"At this point, she is not a suspect," he said evenly. "And until we determine that she is, you will show her respect. Got it, Detective?"

"Got it, Special Agent Novak," Adam said coldly. "I'm yours to command."

Deacon hesitated, not trusting the Adam who stood before him. "I need you focused," he whispered. "Not jumping to conclusions based on the unsubstantiated testimony of a convicted sex offender. I need you to help me find Corinne Longstreet. Are you with me?"

"Totally," Adam said coldly.

Hoping he was making the right choice, Deacon motioned him to follow. "Then come on."

Miami, Florida
Monday, November 3, 7:35 p.m.

Detective Catalina Vega leaned against the doorframe of Davies's office, waiting impatiently for her boss to finish his call. He took one look at her and motioned her to come in.

"I have to go," he said into the phone. "Something's come up here. I'll see you at home. Love you, too."

Hearing Davies talk to his wife so tenderly always made Cat both wistful and hopeful at the same time. She'd all but accepted that she could either be a cop or have a normal, healthy relationship, but not both. And then Davies had found his CiCi. Somehow they made it work.

Davies started cleaning off his desk, locking up his files. "What do you have?"

"Not Faith Frye, that's for damn sure. I can't find her anywhere. She's disappeared." Cat crossed his office, holding her phone so that he could see the photo on her screen. "I started with her last-known residence this morning. This is it. Or what's left of it."

Davies frowned at the burned shell of a building. "What the hell? When did that happen?"

"Thursday night. Faith wasn't there at the time. Her super hadn't seen her in at least a week, but said he'd seen her car parked in the lot outside as recently as Saturday morning. I traced her through her credit cards to a hotel downtown, where she stayed for one night, then a second hotel where she stayed one night, and so on, and then . . . nothing. Since Saturday there's been no trace of her, no more credit card charges. She cleaned out her bank accounts and quit her job."

"She's on the run."

"I hope so. I've been trying to get a lead on where she'd go. I've called her cell and home phone. Both go straight to voice mail. Her coworkers said that while she wasn't unfriendly, she didn't have any close relationships at the office. After Shue was killed, she became withdrawn. Kept to herself. Wouldn't walk or go out to lunch with them. Came in early, left late. Alone."

"She was afraid they'd be in danger. Caught in the cross-fire, like Shue."

Cat nodded. "That's what I think, too. None of her coworkers were shocked when she quit because she transitioned all her clients to the other counselors first. Nobody was left hanging."

"Even the offenders?"

"She hadn't been working with offenders anymore. She left that job after Combs's attack and went to work in Shue's organization, where her client list was all victims. The woman in the cubicle next to Faith's said that she came in one morning, cleaned out her desk, tendered her resignation, and walked out without drama. She hasn't contacted any of the other agencies in town looking for work. I called her parents' house in Savannah, but according to Lily Sullivan, her stepmother, Faith wasn't there. Lily would only tell me that she'd pass on the message that I'd called. I asked to speak to Faith's father, but according to Lily, he's too ill to come to the phone. She said that talking to a Miami cop would upset him."

"Why?"

"Because Faith was married to one—Charlie Frye, a uniform out of Central District. I didn't realize she was Charlie's ex when I talked to her about Shue's murder." Cat made a face. "I knew Charlie before he married Faith. Actually went out with him a few times. He's not . . . a modern man."

Davies's brows shot up. "He likes 'em barefoot and pregnant?"

"Well, his new wife *is* pregnant for the third time in four years, but I got the sense that she wanted to be, so that's good for her."

"You met her?"

"Today, when I visited Charlie to find out if he'd seen Faith. The new wife seems to like being a homemaker, which, again, is great if that's her choice. And to be fair, Charlie was clear when we dated that was what he wanted in a wife, which is why we only went out twice. I was surprised to find out Faith had married him at all, much less stayed with him for nine years."

"*Had* Charlie Frye seen her?" Davies asked pointedly, bringing her back to topic.

"No, not since their divorce. He said that he knew Combs had stalked her for a year, but didn't seem torn up about it. Said she'd danced with the devil and was now paying her due."

"I assume he meant her alleged affair with Combs," Davies said. "I looked her up after you left this morning," he added when she blinked in surprise. "I read the report on her attack four years ago and the transcripts from Combs's trial. The ex-husband believed Combs?"

"Yeah, he did. He wouldn't say why. But that's not why they got divorced. Combs didn't accuse her of anything until the trial started. She'd already filed for divorce by then because Charlie had been cheating with the current wife."

"A real winner. But surely her family isn't judging all of us by Charlie."

"I don't know. Lily wouldn't say more even when I told her it was urgent. I'm pretty sure she knows where Faith is. I didn't tell her why I was asking. I wanted to keep the details of the Prius tampering under wraps as long as I could. But then CSU found this on the Prius."

Cat put the plastic evidence bag on Davies's now-spotless desk. He picked it up, his eyes narrowing on the small electronic device. "He was tracking her."

"CSU says the tracker was put there after the fire. There's evidence of soot underneath."

Davies's face darkened. "He was trying to flush her out of her apartment."

"And when she wasn't there, he tagged her car, tracked it, and not realizing she'd sold it, cut a few hoses. But the new owner and her son died instead, and two kids are left without a mother. He's not going to stop, sir. Faith's in danger, wherever she is. And so is anyone around her."

"So you were right. Her stalking reports were true. All thirty of them," he said angrily. "Why was she ignored?"

"That may be why her stepmother was so chilly. I think Charlie stirred the pot. I talked to a few of the officers who took the stalking reports, and they said Charlie told them she was a head case. Not to waste resources on her. Her work with the offenders made it an easy sell."

Davies closed his eyes. "And now we have three dead and a missing victim because the boys in blue stuck together."

"And her parents aren't talking to us for the same reason. If they don't know where she is . . . She's been missing for a few days now, sir."

He opened his eyes, his gaze grim. "Call her stepmother

and explain how things really are. If she still won't tell you where Faith is, then put both of her parents in protective custody until she talks. But find Faith Frye."

Mt. Carmel, Ohio
Monday, November 3, 7:45 p.m.

Deacon took the porch steps cautiously. They were solid enough, the porch itself wide and gracious. Using a crowbar, Adam pried the door open.

"High or low?" he asked.

"High," Deacon said, and Adam dropped into a crouch. Deacon opened the door and they crept in, scanning the room. "Holy hell," he whispered.

It had once been grand, with high ceilings and a curving staircase. Now the wallpaper was peeling, and all the furniture was covered with sheets. The room looked old and sad and lonely.

Deacon took a pair of shoe covers from his pocket and slipped them on. Behind him, he heard Adam doing the same. They went from room to room, finding nothing and no one. No disturbed dust. No sign that anyone had been here in a very long time.

Until they reached the kitchen. The appliances and the table and chairs were vintage seventies and, like everything else, appeared undisturbed. But the grime on the floor had been wiped away—in a path that started at the steel door that opened to the side yard and ended at an older interior door that appeared to be made of solid wood with an old-fashioned keyhole.

Deacon tugged on the doorknob, surprised when it gave way easily. Not even a creak as the hinges were well-oiled. "The basement," he mouthed soundlessly, looking down a flight of stairs that disappeared into darkness. Or not, he amended when he saw the pulse of red light that repeated every few seconds. They'd triggered some kind of silent alarm.

He started down, the beam of his light revealing red handprints on the walls. And on the steps. The handprints were fresh and the same size as the prints he'd seen on the wrecked power company truck.

Arianna had been here. Had clung to the wall for support as she climbed these stairs. They crept downward, stopping at the bottom to get their bearings. They were standing in a long, narrow hallway that ran the breadth of the house. There was a door at one end and doors on both sides. The smell of lemon floor cleaner hung heavy in the air. Someone had tidied up.

Deacon pointed to Adam, sending him to the left. He himself went to the right and opened the first door, flinching when the smell of pure bleach hit him like a brick. His Maglite illuminated cabinet doors that hung open, their shelves bare. In the middle of the room stood a steel table with channels around the periphery for catching blood. It was the same kind of table they used in the morgue. Ropes hung from all four corners.

Arianna had been tortured here. He was sure of it.

Where was Corinne? He shined his light into the corners but saw no one.

The next room was a kitchenette, with a small refrigerator, an oven, and a microwave. A drop-leaf table big enough for only two was pushed against the wall. It appeared to be antique, likely taken from upstairs. He checked cabinets, inside the oven. Nothing. Bracing himself, he opened the freezer, afraid of what he'd find.

He blinked, surprised. Frozen pizzas were stacked neatly in three columns, each box precisely even with the others. The refrigerator held a two-liter bottle of diet cola, a few bottles of water, and some packets of ketchup. In the trash can he found a smashed carryout container. He lifted it gingerly and sniffed. Fresh garbage. Perhaps a day old, maybe two.

He backed out of the kitchen, met Adam in the narrow hall.

"Anyone?" Deacon whispered.

Adam shook his head. "No one. Alive or dead."

"I found the torture room, but it's been emptied out and sprayed down with bleach. The kitchen has a freezer stocked with pizzas."

"I found an office, also emptied. And a cell."

Deacon followed him into another small room with a single cot. A few inches above the cot, a chain was bolted into the wall. At the end of the chain were shackles. They'd been unlocked.

Adam pointed his light at two strands of hair caught in the cot's metal frame. Blond. Like Corinne Longstreet. She'd been here and they'd missed her.

Deacon went back into the hall, where a shadow flickered at the edge of his peripheral vision. A dark blanket hung from the ceiling. Once again he braced himself for what he'd find. He pulled the blanket aside. Once again he blinked.

It was a tunnel dug into the earthen wall. Deacon took a cautious step forward, checking to make sure the earthen ceiling would hold, then glanced over his shoulder. Adam was right behind him.

They had to crouch because the tunnel was only about five feet eight inches high and got lower until they came to a small cave, barely five by eight and perhaps five feet high.

He swept his light across the cave, revealing a blanket that lay neatly on the floor, a pillow at one end. Another blanket was folded at the other end. And in the middle was a box.

"Somebody lived here," he whispered.

"Go check it out," Adam whispered back. "I'll go back to the hall and stand watch. I don't want to be cornered in here if he's waiting for us."

"Agreed." Crouching as far down as he could go, Deacon swept the bottom hem of his coat up under his arm and duckwalked across the dirt floor until he could see into the box.

It held a sad array of items: a hairbrush that was missing a third of its bristles; a very faded pair of jeans with multiple patches, and two T-shirts, also neatly folded; a metal cup and plate; a worn toothbrush; and a round plastic disk the size of a pie pan with a domed lid. The tag in the T-shirt said that it was a woman's size small.

He touched the domed lid of the disk, flinching when the inside of the box was suddenly filled with dim illumination. A night-light. Whoever had bunked down in this little cave had at least had a little light. He turned it off and backed out under the blanket, gradually straightening until he'd returned to where Adam waited none too patiently.

"Well?" he demanded.

"Whoever lived there wore a woman's size small," Deacon said. "The box was nearly empty, but it looked like someone was packing. Let's let CSU do their thing down here. I want to know exactly what Faith knows about her house."

Eastern Kentucky
Monday, November 3, 7:45 p.m.

Corinne woke with a gasp, her body aching, her head pounding. Yet numb. Fuzzy. Again.

He'd drugged her. Again. She remembered now. He'd done it himself this time, not sending the young girl in to do his dirty work. He'd been in a hurry, so frantic that she'd hoped they were about to be found.

It was still dark. *Still blindfolded.* Her hands were bound, this time behind her back. She gave a tentative tug, stifling a cry when her wrists burned like fire. He'd tied her with rope so tightly that she'd never get free.

No. You will not panic. She drew a deep breath through her nose, trying to calm her racing heart. *Oh no. Oh God.*

The odor was all too familiar. Blood. Sweat. Death. *Ari.* The memory of her friend's screams echoed in her head. *Oh God, please don't let it be Arianna.*

The floor bumped up, and she gritted her teeth for the inevitable landing. She was in a vehicle. A moving vehicle. Not a truck. Probably a van. She was being taken away.

She bit her tongue to keep from whimpering. *Someone* was driving the vehicle. If whoever that was thought she was still out cold, her chances were better. *Better than what?*

Better than dead, she told herself sternly and made herself remember the voice of her boot-camp instructor. *Pull yourself together, soldier. Figure this out.* She could do this. She had to.

First thing—she needed to see. The blindfold was . . . She lengthened her jaw, feeling the skin around her eyes go taut. Duct tape. *Just wonderful.*

She needed something rigid to scrape against the edge of the tape. She turned her head, smooth, cold metal against her cheek. That wouldn't help at all.

She rolled her head the other way, hit something hard. It moved a fraction of an inch. Rocked actually, pressing back on her face even as she placed the sensation, the odor.

A boot. And from the weight, a large one. A man's boot.

Was he a prisoner, too? Was he even alive? *What if it's his blood I smell?* Bile burned her throat. *What if he's dead?*

Worse, what if he was a guard and conscious? *He'll know I'm awake. And if I'm still blindfolded and bound when this van stops, I'll be at the driver's mercy.*

She had to take the risk. "Hello?" she whispered. Nada. Nothing. Drugged or dead.

She bit back a curse. *Stay calm. Figure this out.* She brushed her cheek across the boot and breathed a sigh of relief. It was a lace-up boot. There'd be ridges around the laces.

She prayed they'd be rigid and sharp enough to give her a hard edge. Using her body to rock her head, she scraped the tape across the boot. It might work. It had to.

Mt. Carmel, Ohio
Monday, November 3, 8:30 p.m.

Without her cell phone, Faith had no idea how long Novak and Kimble had been inside the house. But it seemed like too long for them to have found nothing.

That the obnoxious Detective Kimble hadn't been able to make her key fit gave her comfort. At least she wasn't crazy. Somehow the events of the evening before seemed wavy in her mind. Like when she woke from a dream and wasn't sure if she was still in the dream or in real life.

She'd walked around the house. Had seen no one. Had heard no one. Except . . . *Oh no.*

She closed her eyes, suddenly ill again. She'd heard a scream. She'd told herself it was a dog howling. Or all in her mind. But it had been real.

"Oh God," she whispered. It had been Arianna Escobar, crying out for help. Screaming in pain. Faith remembered every one of the girl's wounds clearly. She'd been tortured.

And I walked away.

She pressed down her horror. *Novak needs to know.* She started to get out of the SUV, then remembered his "not a request." He seemed to be her ally at the moment. She didn't want to piss him off, too. She kept the door open but remained in her seat.

A few minutes later, the front door of the house opened and Novak and Kimble headed straight for her. Faith's heart sank when she looked at their faces. Grim. Angry. Frustrated.

She got out of the SUV, biting back a wince when her feet protested.

"Did you find her?" she asked before they could say anything. "The other girl?"

"No," Novak said. But he'd found something else. She could see it in his face. "We need to ask you some more questions about this house."

"Okay," she said, "but first I need to tell you something. When I was here yesterday, I heard something. I think it was a scream."

Novak frowned. "Why didn't you mention this before?"

"I didn't think of it until you were in the house and I'd started to calm down. And because, at the time, I'd convinced myself I hadn't really heard it."

Kimble stepped closer, hemming her in. "What did you hear, exactly?"

She leaned back, putting space between them. "I'm not sure. It was getting dark and it was just a soft sound. I told myself it was a dog or maybe a coyote howling. Or that I had simply imagined it." She searched the men's faces. "But I didn't, did I?"

"No," Novak said quietly. "I don't think you did."

She slumped into the SUV's seat. "Arianna was in there. I walked away. I left her there."

Novak's grim expression softened a fraction. "Did you know she was in there, Faith?"

"No! I would have called the police, just like I did when I found her on the road."

"Then you couldn't have helped her. But you can help her now by showing me where you were when you heard it."

"Of course." She accepted the hand he offered to help her to her feet, wincing when her soles prickled like pins and needles. "What did you find in the house?"

"We'll get to that," he said. "Adam, did Tanaka's tech find any shoes in the Jeep?"

Kimble glanced at Faith's feet, confused. "I don't think so. What happened to her shoes?"

"She lost them climbing the embankment to get to the girl."

Kimble's eyes shot up to hers, now narrowed. "You climbed that hill in your bare feet?"

"Yes," she said simply. "My sneakers were in a gym bag."

Kimble nodded thoughtfully. "That they found. Wait a minute." He opened the trunk of his sedan and rummaged around. When he returned, he was holding her sneakers.

Novak dropped into a crouch, sweeping his coat out of the way with a flourish that seemed more of a reflex, then stunned her by lifting her foot and slipping on the shoe.

"You don't have to do that," she protested.

Novak didn't respond. He tied the laces and did the same with the other foot with a gentleness that surprised her. "Can you walk on your own?"

She wanted to say no, wanted to lean on him. But his compassion might be part of his good-cop persona and that she wanted no part of. "I think so."

"Then take us through what happened yesterday, from the moment you arrived."

She started to walk. "I parked where your SUV is now, got out of my car, went to the front door. My key didn't work. I almost left then, but I needed to see the cemetery."

"Why?" Novak asked.

"Because I'd promised my father I'd send him a photo."

"Of a cemetery?" Kimble asked, incredulous.

"My mother is buried here. My father used to come on the day of her death every few years, but he had a stroke a year ago and can't travel anymore."

"When did your mother die?" Novak asked.

"Twenty-three years ago," she said, managing to sound neutral. She hoped.

"Oh." Novak packed a lot of understanding into the single syllable. "So you were here the day she died, you attended her burial, then you never came back? Not until yesterday?"

"Yes." They reached the cemetery fence. "I tried to get in yesterday," she said, "but the gate was padlocked and I didn't have a key. My grandmother's attorney didn't have it, either. The local historical society cares for the area around the cemetery. They probably locked it."

"Okay, so where were you when you heard the scream?" Novak asked.

She led them to where she'd been standing. "Right here. That's my mother's grave."

Novak shined his flashlight on Margaret's headstone, then flicked the beam over the others, stopping at the stone identical to her mother's. "'Barbara Agnes Corcoran O'Bannion.' You took your grandmother's maiden name?"

"My maiden name would make me too easy to find. Not that it matters now."

Novak moved his light to the other side of the headstone and made a surprised noise. "Your grandfather died only two days before your mother."

"We'd come up for his funeral, me and Dad and my mother. Dad and I went home alone."

"What happened?" Novak asked.

"Car accident," she said tersely.

"You didn't live here?" Kimble asked.

"No. We lived in Savannah. After my grandfather died, nobody lived here. Gran moved to the city because she didn't walk well and couldn't live out here in the country by herself."

"What time did you hear the scream?" Novak asked.

"About five thirty. The sun was starting to go down."

"When did you arrive?" Kimble asked.

"Maybe twenty minutes earlier. I sat outside for a while, trying to make myself go in."

Novak glanced at her curiously. "Why?"

"Because . . . I don't have the best memories of this house."

"And yet you came here when you needed to disappear," he noted.

She felt like he'd figured something out that she'd wanted to keep secret. "Yes."

"Okay," Novak said. "When did you leave Miami?"

"Saturday, a little after noon. I stopped for the night in Atlanta, then came straight here."

"Did anyone know you were coming?"

"Only my father and stepmother knew I was coming here. I suppose anyone who saw me packing up the Jeep knew I was going somewhere, but I didn't tell anyone else."

"Not even your grandmother's attorney?"

"He didn't know I was in town until I called him today to ask for the key. Why?"

Kimble jumped in. "We'll get to that. What did you do after you heard the scream?"

"I texted a picture of my mother's headstone to my dad because he'd asked me to. Then I left, went to Walmart, checked in to my hotel, unloaded my Jeep, and went to bed."

"And today?" Novak asked.

"I went to work downtown. At Schipper Bank."

Both men looked surprised, but it was Kimble who spoke. "You're a psychologist who treats sex offenders," he said, his contempt clear. "Why are you working in a bank?"

She stifled a weary sigh. "I'd appreciate it if you could confine your questions to this case. And then let me go on my way." She lifted her bandaged hands. "I still need to get to the ER."

Novak's odd eyes flickered with what seemed like genuine distress. Or maybe she just wanted it to be genuine. He played the good cop so very well. "We'll make this as brief as possible," he said. "While at work, you called your grandmother's attorney, the power company, the locksmith, and various other service people. Did you have contact with anyone else?"

"Coworkers, yes. But about the house, no."

"Does anyone else have access to the house?" Kimble pressed.

"Not that I know of. Neither of my uncles wanted it. Not to live in, anyway." She blew out a breath. "Uncle Jordan needs to know what's happening here. Whatever 'this' is."

"Wait." Kimble held up his hand. "You have uncles?"

"Yes, two of them. Twins, actually. Jordan and Jeremy."

"Do they live here? In Mount Carmel?" Novak asked.

"Oh no." The very thought was downright ludicrous. "Jordan lives in a townhouse in Mount Adams. I don't think he's been out here since he moved my grandmother in with him, except for the day she was buried. Jeremy lives on an estate in Indian Hill." Less than fifteen miles from her grandmother, yet he'd never once come to make things right.

Kimble's brows rose. "They're your mother's brothers and they didn't inherit the house?"

"No, my grandmother left the townhouse in Mount Adams to Uncle Jordan. She left the house and the property out here to me."

"Nothing to Uncle Jeremy?" Kimble asked.

"No," she said, suppressing a grimace. "Jeremy and my grandmother were never on the best of terms. Not in my memory, anyway. They've been estranged since my grandfather died."

"Why?" Novak asked curiously.

Faith hesitated. "My grandmother didn't approve of Jeremy's sexual preferences."

Novak tilted his head. "That can mean a whole lot of things."

"In this case it means he's gay." Not a lie but not the whole truth. Her uncle was bisexual, preferring his partners to be youthful. And pretty.

So pretty was what he'd said to her, looking at her, touching her in ways that had made her uncomfortable even then. A thought inserted itself into her mind, one that made her sick to even consider. Jeremy had had access to the house at one time. He could have easily changed the locks. Could he have done this—kidnapped and tortured Arianna and her friend?

Instantly, she rejected the idea. It simply didn't make any sense. She realized that she'd dropped her eyes to her feet. When she looked up, she saw that both men had picked up on her distress. Kimble was coldly assessing, but Novak's eyes flashed fury.

"What?" Novak demanded.

Faith shook her head. "Nothing. I'm sure it was nothing." But she heard the doubt in her own voice. Novak heard it, too.

"What did he do to you?" Novak's tone was so close to a growl that Faith took a step back.

"Nothing," she insisted. "That's the truth. He'd say I was pretty. Would touch my hair. He was . . . a little creepy," she allowed, "and my father never trusted him. Dad made my mother promise to never leave me alone with him. My mother thought he was being silly, but she did promise him."

"So he never touched you because he never had the opportunity," Kimble said.

"Possibly. But you have to remember that this was the early nineties, and I grew up in a very strict Catholic family," she said, feeling the need to defend her uncle. With the hindsight of adulthood, she'd never been certain that her father had been right about Jeremy. "Being gay was often considered interchangeable with being a pedophile. I can tell you that he's never been accused of anything." Not outside of her own family, anyway.

"And you know this how?" Kimble asked sarcastically.

Her chin lifted. "Because I checked."

Novak's white brows shot up in surprise. "Why? When?"

"Several times. Most recently, about a year ago. As for why, the memory worried at me. I couldn't allow someone to be hurt because I didn't want to air the family laundry. I gave a discreet heads-up to a social worker I knew from school. Her police contact kept an eye out, but there was never even a wisp of smoke. And you can't arrest someone on suspicion alone."

"No, you can't," Novak murmured. "Do you have contact information for your uncles?"

"I have Jordan's home and cell numbers, but nothing for Jeremy. You might find him at work. He's a professor at the med school. He teaches surgery, last I heard." Faith shifted her feet, which had started to throb. "If you're finished with your questions, I'd like to sit down."

"We're finished for now," Novak said. "I'll find someone to take you to the ER."

For now. He hadn't said it threateningly, just factually, but it sounded threatening just the same. She turned away from the cemetery fence to head back to the house, but it was pitch-black and she missed a dip in the ground. Her stiff knees buckled and with a cry she went down.

But not all the way down. Strong hands caught her around the waist, Novak hauling her back up as if she weighed no more than a child. For a moment they stood there, the fingers of both his hands spread wide against her rib cage.

God, he smells good. Like cedar and clean leather.

"Are you all right?" Novak asked quietly, his mouth so close to her ear that she shivered.

"Yes." She swallowed. "I just tripped."

"We shouldn't have had you standing out there so long." He released her, pulling his hands away a little more slowly than he should have, so that it was almost a caress.

Faith shivered again, then stepped forward, putting some distance between them.

"Let me help you, Ms. Corcoran," Novak said, startling her when he took her elbow in a firm but gentle grip. "The ground is rough and I know you're hurting."

She really was, so this time she let him assist her, absorbing the pleasant warmth of his hand on her elbow through the fabric of the jacket she wore. "Thank you."

Through all of this Kimble had said not a word, but he fell into step with them on her other side. Faith almost laughed. *Does he think I'm gonna run for it?*

The three of them walked slowly back to the front of the house, which was now far busier than it had been before. Several more police cars had arrived along with the CSU van. New spotlights had been set up in the front and around the far side, bathing the property in bright, white light. Whatever they'd found, it was big. And very, very bad.

"What did you find in the house, Agent Novak?" Faith asked quietly.

But before Novak could answer, Kimble took her other elbow in a grip that made her wince. "What do you *think* we found, Dr. Frye?" he asked smoothly. Mockingly.

Something inside her snapped. *Sonofabitch still thinks I'm involved.*

"Detective," Novak said sharply as Faith yanked her arms free, first from Novak's gentle grip, then from Kimble's punishing one.

She stepped back a pace so that she could see Kimble's face. His lips quirked in a smirk that she knew was intended to make her angrier, to make her say things she'd regret. He'd be disappointed. She'd had too much experience with his kind of bad cop.

"What I *think*, Detective Kimble," she said calmly but coldly, "is that you'll find yourself in need of your PBO rep if you touch me like that again."

Anger flashed in his dark eyes. "Are you threatening me, Dr. Frye?"

"No more than you just did to me. The difference is, I didn't leave bruises." She thought she saw a flicker of uncertainty in his expression, quickly masked. "And if you think I won't file charges against you because I'm trying to stay under a stalker's radar, you're wrong."

"I think it's a fair question, Dr. Frye," Kimble said, not backing down a whit. "It is, after all, your house and your family member who you so skillfully threw under the bus."

"Adam," Novak hissed. "That is enough."

Faith ground her teeth, tired of them both. "Detective,

you're laying the bad cop on a little too thick. Kudos to you, Agent Novak. You've played the good cop to perfection. I've told you both what I know. I don't expect you to believe me." She shook her head, willing back the angry tears that were trying to climb up her throat. "I didn't want to find that girl. I didn't want any of this. All I wanted was to be left alone."

"Dr. Corcoran," Novak began in the soothing tone she no longer found comforting.

She sliced her bandaged hand through the air to cut him off. "Save it, Novak. The voice won't work with me. I suggest you put your energy into figuring out where the bad guys went and how they snuck several vehicles, two grown men, and a young woman past a legion of cops."

Novak frowned. "What do you mean, several vehicles?"

"You found the Earl Power and Light truck, but what about the vehicle the locksmith was driving? Have you found that? No? I didn't think so," she said as the two men stared at her. "Unless the locksmith stood me up, he would have arrived minutes before I found the girl. He didn't leave, nor did anyone else. Whoever took Arianna also had transportation. Therefore, unless they were all beamed up by Scotty, the abductor hid one vehicle, then took two men and a woman away from here by a different road, which to my knowledge doesn't exist."

"You're assuming we believe you when you say that they didn't pass your way," Kimble said. "Even if that's true, they might have left here before you arrived."

Ignoring him, Faith met Novak's gaze. "You said the girl's blood was still wet in the Earl Power truck. Do you truly believe her abductor would have passed by that wrecked truck and not stopped to find her? That he'd let her live? You found her trail of blood easily enough. Don't you think her abductor could have as well?"

Novak opened his mouth, but his reply was cut off by someone calling his name. A woman had broken away from the pack of CSU techs and was headed their way. She was about the same height as Faith, but sturdier. Curvier. That she was a cop would have been obvious even without the telltale bulge under her arm, just from the way she carried herself.

"I thought you were at the hospital," Novak said when she stopped in front of them.

The woman's jet-black hair shone blue under the lights, and her black eyes were sharp enough to cut straight through to the bone. "I was, but they sedated her. She won't wake up for hours. I left a uniform standing guard outside her room." She cocked her head toward Faith. "This your Good Sam?"

"Yes," Kimble answered. "This is Dr. Faith Frye. She found the girl. She owns the house."

Faith clenched her teeth. "It's Dr. Corcoran."

"It's good to meet you, Doctor. I'm Detective Bishop. You might have saved Arianna's life tonight. I'm sure she'll thank you when she wakes up."

Faith wasn't sure if the woman was mocking her, baiting her, or sincerely thanking her, but something was off. "I hope she does wake up."

"Gentlemen," Bishop said, "may I talk to you for a moment? Alone?"

Faith waved Novak away. "You don't need to escort me. I'll escort myself."

"I'll get you that ride to the ER in a moment," Novak promised as she turned to walk away.

The three cops waited until Faith was in the SUV before Bishop held up her cell phone and the three of them leaned in, listening. Bishop hit a button on her phone and they listened again.

Perplexed and grim, the three cops walked to the SUV and formed a tight semicircle around Faith's open door. Caging her in. It was a cop thing and Faith hated it.

Novak was the first to speak. "Dr. Corcoran, when you called 911, you said that Arianna Escobar was unconscious."

Faith rose to her feet, forcing the Three Musketeers to step back. She did it so that she could breathe but pretended that her goal was to defend her space. "That's right. At least I thought she was. I'm not that kind of a doctor, obviously. But she didn't respond to anything I said. Why?"

"What did you say to her?" Kimble asked harshly. "Exactly?"

"I don't remember *exactly*. I was hurt, too. Something like, 'Are you okay?' *Why?*"

"Faith, had you ever met her before?" Novak asked. "Was there any way the two of you had crossed paths in the past?"

New panic settled over her. "No," she said, resisting the urge to press her hand against her chest. Her heart was beating so hard it hurt. "Before tonight I'd never seen her before. *Why?*"

"Because she knows you," Novak said, and her gaze snapped back up to meet his.

For a moment Faith thought she'd misheard, but the three cops stood there, waiting for an answer. She cleared her throat, but her voice was weak and faint. "Excuse me?"

Novak nodded. "She regained consciousness briefly as she was being prepped for surgery. She told Detective Bishop to 'find Faith.'"

"I thought she meant faith in God," Bishop said. "I asked her if I could call her a priest or a minister. She grabbed my hand and said, 'No. Faith Frye.' Now I realize that she meant you."

"But how . . . ?" Faith sagged into the seat, light-headed. "I told the 911 operator who I was. Arianna had to have heard me then."

Novak shook his head. "No, you didn't. We just listened to the 911 call. You gave your name as Faith Corcoran, not Frye."

Faith glanced up at him. Novak looked even more troubled. "How could she know me?"

"Yeah," Kimble said, his lip curling. "How *could* she know you?"

"I don't know. The only answer that makes sense is that she heard my name during her captivity." A violent shiver jerked her body. "Which means that whoever took her knows who I am."

"That makes perfect sense, Dr. Corcoran," Kimble said, and she could feel the heat from his body as he leaned in closer. "I guess the million-dollar question is, how do you know *him*?"

Chapter Seven

"That's enough," Deacon ordered. Faith was perched on the edge of his passenger sheet, hunched over, shaking like a leaf. "Back off and let her breathe."

Bishop's eyes had narrowed at Adam in concern. Scarlett Bishop was a sharp cop. She and Deacon had achieved a comfortable rhythm in the short month they'd worked together, able to wordlessly communicate as if they'd been partners for years. Adam was the wild card tonight.

Adam straightened more slowly, a direct challenge in his eyes. "She knows who's behind this. This"—he gestured to Faith's trembling form with contempt—"is all an act."

Deacon didn't think so. He didn't want to think so, anyway. But he didn't think there was anything he could say that would convince Adam to reconsider, and more to the point, he owed it to Arianna and Corinne to be sure.

"It may very well be. But until we know that for sure, Dr. Corcoran will remain a witness. And I think she's right about at least one thing. Arianna's abductor wouldn't have let her live if he'd escaped via the road. Which means there must be another way out of here. There's a trail or something. We need to find it. And we need to find out if that locksmith did make it out here, because he sure as hell is not here now. Nor is his vehicle. So we have too much to do, Detective Kimble, to waste time berating a witness."

"Whose name the victim knew," Adam said through clenched teeth.

Deacon had seen the shock flatten Faith's face when she heard the news. He believed it was genuine. "Yes. Which makes her too valuable a resource to frighten to death."

Faith's dark red head lifted until she met his eyes and it was like a punch to the gut. She was pale, drawn, and every bit as furious as Adam, but coldly so. "Very nicely done, Agent Novak," she said quietly. "I couldn't have handled me better myself."

Deacon kept his sigh inside. She might have actually trusted him before Adam ruined it. She sure as hell didn't trust him now. "If you'll excuse us for a moment, Dr. Corcoran. We'll be right back." He walked away, hands shoved in his pockets—whether to keep himself from touching her or from beating the shit out of his cousin, he wasn't certain.

He led Adam and Bishop through the gate and to the front porch. Adam appeared to have managed to calm himself somewhat. Bishop was watching Adam cautiously.

"I heard you got booted out of Personal Crimes because you lost it," she said, "which I didn't want to believe, but that little display convinced me."

Adam looked away, a dark flush staining his cheeks. "I'm sorry. I may have overreacted."

"Y'think?" Deacon kept his voice down, but he didn't try to contain his frustration. "You're goddamn right you overreacted. Now we'll be lucky if she tells us anything."

"It's an act, Deacon. I know it."

"If it is, she's damn good," Deacon snapped. "Too good to tell you anything she doesn't want you to know. I don't think she was bluffing when she threatened to file charges. *You hurt her*, Adam. This isn't like you. What the hell is wrong with you?"

Adam's jaw tightened. "Do you agree that she knows something she's not telling?"

Deacon looked across the front yard to where Faith sat watching them. If looks could kill, the three of them would be pushing up daisies. "I think she knows lots of stuff she's not telling. But I don't believe she is behind this."

Adam huffed his derision. "I knew you'd say that. She's leading you on, man. Pretty face, a twitch of the ass—they're all the same. I hate to see you falling for her act, like a fish on a damn hook. Although I gotta admit, she's prettier than most." He met Deacon's eyes. "Way prettier than Brandi ever was, but I would've thought that experience would have cured you for life."

For a moment Deacon could only stare at him, stunned that Adam had even gone there. Then a blast of fury and hurt burned away his shock and he realized his hands had become fists. Thankfully, they were still in his pockets where no one could see.

Bishop intervened with a low whistle and brisk words. "Gentlemen, I'm about to choke on all this testosterone, so tone it down so we can discuss our next steps."

"The priority is finding the person who tortured Arianna," Deacon said, "who may have killed two men and may still have Corinne, and who somehow got them out of here without anyone noticing. Adam, your next step is to find out how he did that."

Adam jerked a nod. "Yes, *sir*."

"Oh, for God's sake." With a shake of his head, Deacon turned to Bishop. "Go back to King's College and find out everything you can about these two women. Search their dorm rooms, talk to their friends. Isenberg said she'd get the security footage from the college. Find out where they disappeared from and secure the scene. Call me if you need backup."

"And Corcoran?" Bishop asked. "What about her?"

"She's a key to this. I just don't know how. She went to a lot of trouble to hide from an ex-con sex offender who was stalking her in Miami. I can't believe it's a coincidence that Arianna was held in her house just as Corcoran was relocating."

Bishop's brows went up. "You think our perp is her stalker?"

"It's a possibility we can't ignore. She's either lying about knowing Arianna, or she's a victim, too. I'll take her to the ER, try to get her to talk to me again while we wait for a doctor to see her. While she's being tended to, I'll contact Miami PD and check out her stalker story. I'll also contact the two uncles and invite them in for a chat." He turned back to Adam. "While you're searching for the other way out, talk to the local cops. Find out if there are any gangs or weird kids in the high school who hung out here. Give Tanaka any help he needs in the basement. I will be back as soon as I can. Are we square?"

The muscles in Adam's cheek tightened as he clenched his teeth. "Yeah."

"I'll call you from King's College campus," Bishop said. She'd been assessing Faith as Deacon gave Adam his orders. "I'm not sure about her, Novak. Be careful."

"I will, thanks."

Deacon waited until Bishop was gone before turning back to Adam. "Don't," he snapped when Adam opened his mouth to speak. "I'm not interested in anything you have to say right now. All I want is for you to do your goddamn job. Can you manage that, Detective?"

Adam swallowed hard. "Yeah."

"Good. One more thing. If you ever throw my past back in my face again, you'll find yourself regretting teaching me to fight. Got it?"

Anger roiled in Adam's eyes, but he nodded again. "I shouldn't have said what I did. Not in front of Bishop, at least."

"*Not in front of Bishop?* Hell, you shouldn't have said it at all! What the fuck is wrong with you?" Deacon held up his hand when Adam started to answer. "No. I don't really want to know. Just keep your shit together or—" He stopped himself before he went too far.

"Or?" Adam asked far too calmly.

"Or I'll request that you be reassigned. Again. I don't have time for drama queens."

Adam's lips curved, but it was not a friendly smile. "This from the king of drama queens himself. You with your hair and your coat. You're a walking freak show, Deacon."

Deacon flinched. That was the thing about family, he thought. They knew exactly where to stab for maximum damage. He just never would have expected Adam to be doing the stabbing.

"Low blow, Adam," he said quietly. "Effective, though."

Adam closed his eyes. "I'm sorry. I shouldn't have said that. You know I don't think it."

Deacon swallowed hard. It had been a long time since

anyone had really gotten under his skin, but it had happened twice tonight. Too bad that Faith's "beautiful" didn't even begin to cancel out Adam's "freak show." He had to clear his throat before he could speak.

"I may be a walking freak show, but I do my job. That's all I want from you. Just do your damn job." He walked away, unable to look at his cousin's face for another second.

But the face waiting for him in the SUV was no more welcoming than Adam's had been. Faith Corcoran might know lots of things, but at the top of the list—at least for the moment—was that she despised him. Deacon couldn't really blame her.

He got into the SUV and cranked the engine. "Buckle up, Dr. Corcoran."

She didn't move. "I thought you were going to find someone to take me to the ER."

"I did. Me. Buckle up."

She pivoted in her seat, holding her bandaged hands out to him, her dark red brows arched in sarcastic challenge. "Aren't you going to cuff me?"

Deacon exhaled wearily, closing his eyes as he sagged back into his seat. "Hell." He pinched the bridge of his nose to quell his rising headache. "No, I am not going to cuff you. I just want to do my job, Faith. Now, please buckle up."

He heard the sound of her seat belt fastening. When he opened his eyes, her hands were folded in her lap and she was watching him uncertainly, her anger appearing to have subsided.

"What?" he asked, not caring that she heard the exhaustion in his voice.

"Look, I know you have a job to do. I appreciate the urgency in finding the missing girl. You're busy. So busy that you don't have to waste your time babysitting me. Any uniform can take me to the ER. I . . ." She glanced down at her hands, then looked up, her jaw set resolutely. "I promise not to run. So you don't have to drive me."

While her side of the SUV was illuminated by CSU's spotlights, his was not, allowing him to study her from the shadows. He wondered if Adam wasn't right in accusing him of allowing himself to be influenced by a pretty face and a twitching ass. Because, although she hadn't twitched her ass once, Deacon would have had to have been a dead man not to notice that it was round and ... very nice. Especially since it was all he'd been able to see in the moment when she'd stumbled while walking away from the cemetery.

Although he'd studied her face enough, too. It was a face that, even bandaged and streaked with grime, was lovely. But, now, in this moment, it was her eyes that captured his full attention. Deep green like a forest in the summer, they held none of the forest's tranquility. Her gaze was unflinching but turbulent. The hands folded in her lap trembled.

"Are you afraid of me, Dr. Corcoran?"

He didn't want her to be, and that bothered him. If Adam was right and she was complicit in any of this, then she was a terrible person and any fear that Deacon could engender would only push her to talk to him sooner. If she was completely innocent, her emotional well-being was not his problem.

But he wanted it to be, and that bothered him even more. He'd known agents who'd gotten involved with women during an investigation. With a few notable exceptions, it rarely ended well. He needed to stay focused. Objective. He needed to stop worrying about Faith Corcoran's feelings. But he found himself holding his breath for her answer.

A slight frown wrinkled her forehead. "I don't know. I don't trust you, but I don't think I'm afraid of you. Should I be?"

It wasn't what he'd wanted to hear, but it was a step in the right direction. He cocked his eyebrows as if he didn't care what she'd answered. "If you don't trust me, then it's pointless for me to answer that question."

"Fair enough." She swallowed hard. "*Am* I a suspect, Agent Novak?"

The little quiver in her voice was like a punch in his gut. If Adam was right and she was faking this, then she was scary good. "I don't want to think so," he said honestly.

"Then ... what am I?"

He considered his answer carefully. "I think you're connected, which could be different from involved. I think you're telling the truth, but I don't think you've told me all of the truth."

"Fair enough." She sounded as exhausted as he had. "What exactly do you want to know?"

He hid his surprise behind a slow blink. "I'm not sure. I wasn't expecting you to offer."

"I wasn't expecting Arianna Escobar to know my name. I think I am connected, if by nothing more than my owner-ship of this damn house." She practically spat the last two words. "I'll help you as much as I can, but I'd like your promise on one thing."

"Depends on what that one thing is."

"If I do become a suspect, you'll tell me, so that I can get an attorney and protect myself."

He shook his head, surprised at the intensity of his re-gret. "I can't make that promise. If you become a suspect, my responsibility is to the victims. Not to you."

She dropped her gaze to her hands, letting out a quiet breath. "Fair enough," she said again, very quietly. "Can you at least recommend a decent defense attorney?"

He gritted his teeth in disappointment. She was lawyer-ing up. Finding out what she knew was going to take hours longer, hours Corinne Longstreet might not have. But Dea-con found he couldn't blame her. She'd been viciously at-tacked by a client who'd later vilified her during his trial, accusing her of sleeping with him. And if she was telling the truth, that same client had stalked her and thirty complaints to the local PD hadn't kept her safe.

In her place, Deacon thought, *I'd lawyer up, too.* He'd certainly urge his own sister to do so.

"I'm new to the task force here, so I don't know many defense attorneys in this area yet. But I know a good one back in Baltimore. I can ask him if he can recommend any-one here."

"Thank you. Well, then, let's go. The quicker I get stitched up, the quicker I can answer your questions and then get back to my hotel for a shower, some clean clothes, and a decent night's sleep. I only hope that whatever I know is something you can use."

He frowned, unsure that he'd heard her correctly, his mind having tripped over the unexpected image of her in the shower. Unexpected, but not entirely unwelcome. He scrambled to regain his focus. "I don't think you'll find a local attorney all that quickly."

"I know. I'll talk to you without one."

This time he was unable to hide his surprise. "Why?"

"Because Arianna didn't ask to be assaulted. I can't erase her trauma any more than I could for any of the girls who came through my office over the years. But if I can help you find her friend, I want to do that. I'm not involved. I know that. I'm going to have to trust the system even if I can't trust you."

Deacon's chest tightened as a host of emotions slammed into him. Respect. Pride. And an overwhelming need to protect her from the very system she trusted more than him.

Adam might be right. She might be using him, lying to him to save her own skin. But Deacon didn't think so. He also was pretty sure he shouldn't say what he was about to say, but if she wasn't lying, she deserved what little he could guarantee. "I can't promise to protect you if I believe you're a suspect," he said, "but I do promise that I'll listen to what you have to say and make no assumptions based simply on your background."

One side of her mouth lifted. "Pretty words, Agent Novak, but we all make assumptions. It's part of being human. I'll just have to hope that I'm not making a big mistake."

He hoped that she wasn't, either. "And if you are?"

Unexpectedly, she unbuckled her seat belt and leaned forward, wincing as she reached up to turn on the dome light. Then she leaned over the center console, tilting her face up toward his. "Look at me, please," she said.

"Why?" he asked, Adam's cruel barb still ringing in his ears.

"Because I like to see the eyes of people who've made me a promise."

Deacon forced himself to hold his expression rigid while he waited for her to flinch. But there was no flinch. Instead, she searched his face with a strange mix of keen discernment and vulnerability. Finally, she sat back, still watching him, saying nothing.

She was using her silence to create a vacuum intended to make him uncomfortable enough that he spoke first. He knew this because he routinely used the same ploy. But damned if it didn't work. He cocked his brows, forcing the nonchalance that he normally faked so easily. "So, what's the verdict, Doc?"

Her gaze didn't falter, but sharpened, as if detecting the mask he'd assumed. "I'm willing to try not to make assumptions simply based on your background, either."

"Which means what, exactly?"

"It means I still don't trust you, but I am willing to entertain the notion that just because you play the good cop so well doesn't mean you aren't one."

"And if I'm not?"

She shrugged self-consciously. "Then it won't be the first time I took a risk and had it bite me in the ass. Take me to the ER, Agent Novak, and on the way you can ask me what you will."

He pulled away from the line of cars in front of her house, suddenly annoyed with himself. He prided himself on reading people, but she was a shrink and he couldn't let himself forget that fact. In matters of reading people and manipulation, they were on equal footing.

"Not on the way. I'll wait until we get there before I ask you anything."

"Why?" she asked, her confusion sounding genuine. "I thought you'd be in a hurry. The clock is ticking, and Arianna's friend is still out there."

"That's true, but I like to see the eyes of the people I'm interviewing," he said, intentionally rephrasing her earlier words. He glanced at her in time to see her slight flinch but wouldn't allow himself to feel any pity. If she was involved, he needed to know. She needed to pay. If not, her hurt feelings would have to be acceptable collateral damage.

"Fair enough," she murmured, sucking in a sharp, pained breath when he hit a pothole in the driveway, reminding him that, involved or not, she had been injured and she had to be hurting.

He flicked a switch on his dashboard. "I turned on your seat warmer," he said. "It might provide some relief from the bumpy roads. I'll get you there as painlessly as I can."

Her eyes slid shut. "Thank you, Agent Novak."

Eastern Kentucky
Monday, November 3, 9:15 p.m.

Yes! Corinne's face was raw and bleeding, but she didn't care. She'd finally succeeded in working a corner of the damn duct tape free.

But she was tired. And her back hurt. And her hands and shoulders. She'd wondered how long she could go without her meds before the symptoms started to flare. *About this long, however long this has been*. She still had no idea how long she'd been gone.

She scooted down a few inches, caterpillar style, then turned her head to press that one little corner of loosened duct tape against the boot. She couldn't think of the person wearing it. Who was probably dead.

Focus, Corinne. Do this thing now. She tested the bond between the tape and the boot, felt her skin burn as the tape tugged. Too hard and she might lose the grip. Too fast and she might draw the attention of the driver.

Although she now thought they were closed off from the driver. She'd heard no breathing or coughing. No radio. Just the hum of the road and the occasional clatter when they hit a bump. But she couldn't take a chance that he might see her in his rearview mirror, so she rolled gently, pulling the tape off of her face a little bit at a time. *Slow and steady, girl.*

She freed one eye enough for her to open it and see. She blinked rapidly, her eyes dry. It was dark. She could vaguely see the man who lay beside her, the man who wore the boots. But just his legs and his stomach. She couldn't see his face yet. She wasn't sure she wanted to.

Pull . . . Slowly. Yes. Finally, both eyes were free. She gave one last hard, jerking pull, the tape peeling off the man's boot and hanging limply from her hairline.

She'd done it. She could see. But now that she could see, she had to look. She didn't want to. But she had to know. If Arianna was still alive, she had to get her out of here.

Yeah, right. You can't even help yourself. Fat lot of help you'll be to Ari.

Stop it. Just stop it. She'd been strong once. She'd be strong again. Or she'd die.

She lifted her chin, sliding the back of her skull along the floor, looking directly behind her, and felt a surge of intense relief. She'd been right. They were in a cargo van with no window to the driver. The relief was short-lived, though, because there was no window to the outside world, so there would be no signaling for help.

Drawing a breath, she pulled her upper body off the floor, supporting herself on one very sore elbow. Her joints were starting to swell. To lock up.

Damn Wegener's disease. The Army doctors thought it had always been lurking within her but had been triggered by an infection. Within months she'd gone from a healthy soldier to an ex-soldier with a medical discharge who couldn't get out of bed without help. But after three years of treatment, she'd finally gotten it under control. Friday had been a good day. No headache. Low pain. Good movement.

And then some asshole went and grabbed me. Without her meds, she'd be in pain within hours. Within a day or two she wouldn't be able to function. *So hurry up. Get out of here.*

It was dark inside the van, the only light coming in through a gap at the door's hinge. It was white light and it strobed with an almost hypnotic frequency.

Streetlights, she thought. The sliver of light flashed on the face of the man with the boots.

Corinne squinted, then the breath she was holding came out in a horrified rush. There was a bullet hole in his head and his face was battered. But she forced herself to look at the rest of him, if for no other reason than to find some tool to cut the ropes that bound her hands.

He wore a heavy jacket with EARL P&L stitched in the fabric above his heart. Earl was the power company. He must have come to the house. *Poor guy. Wrong place, wrong time.* Even in this light she could see that the fabric covering his torso was darker than the rest. As were his knees. He'd bled profusely from what looked like multiple gunshot wounds.

Her captor had capped the man's knees, probably to keep him from running away. *How brave,* she thought with a spurt of fury. She grabbed on to the fury, fanned it higher, used it as fuel. She'd need every ounce of energy she could get.

She twisted at the waist to see what was on her right and let out a quiet sigh. An old man. He was dead, too, his throat slit. Her captor used both guns and knives. *Good to know.*

She'd figured it was just the three of them in the back until her eyes spied something pale. Skin. She stretched her body until she could see over the old man, and her heart skipped a beat. It was a girl. It had to be the girl who'd washed her.

The one who'd refused to help her. The one who'd called that hellhole "home." She was tiny, inches shorter than Corinne. She appeared to be about ten or eleven years old and didn't look like she'd ever had a full meal, her hair matted and dirty. But she didn't look dead, at least.

But where was Arianna? Corinne twisted one way and then another, scanning the corners of the van. But there was no Arianna. A wail filled her throat and mercilessly she forced it back.

He killed her. He killed her and left her behind. But . . . why bring the men? Why not leave them behind, too? Corinne felt the first tendril of hope. Maybe Arianna had escaped.

I need to escape, too. I need to find her. She had to find something to cut the rope around her wrists. The old man was closer, so she searched him first, hoping to find something sharp. Twisting so that she could reach him with her hands tied behind her back, she fumbled for his pocket, nearly weeping with relief when her fingers closed awkwardly over a penknife.

God, give me enough time and strength to cut through this rope. I'll do anything you say for the rest of my life. Which, if her prayers went unanswered, wasn't going to be all that long.

Cincinnati, Ohio
Monday, November 3, 9:55 p.m.

Faith woke with a start, smelling cedar and hearing the sound of a man's deep voice.

Her eyes flew open, and she felt a moment of disoriented panic. She lunged forward, only to bounce back against her seat, held firmly in place by her seat belt. The subsequent twinge of pain shooting down her lower back cleared the fog. *Oh yeah. I hit a tree.*

And she'd found the girl. *Arianna.* A chill of dread chased the pain. *She knows me.*

She turned her head to find Novak on his cell phone, the glare of oncoming traffic making his white hair look even whiter against his tanned skin. Making her wonder if that was his natural coloring or if he worshipped the sun. Which wasn't relevant.

He was a cop. *A dangerous kind of cop,* she thought. One who made her want to trust him.

And she had trusted him, far more than she'd expected.

Or she must have been more tired than she'd thought, because she'd fallen asleep on the way to the ER. They were back in the city already, and the last thing she remembered was being on the interstate.

"Thanks for getting back to me so quickly," he was saying quietly to the caller. "Are you on tonight?" The answer must not have been the one he wanted because his mouth firmed in frustration. "I forgot," he murmured. "I'm sorry. *Can* you be on tonight?" His frown faded into relief. "Thanks. I'll owe you one. . . . Okay, whatever. More than one. I need you to check out a witness. She got banged up in a car wreck tonight. . . . Sutures. Maybe a concussion."

I do not have a concussion, Faith wanted to snap, but she didn't because his expression suddenly tensed as he listened.

"Tell him I'll talk to him in the morning before he goes to school. And tell him to leave his homework on the kitchen table and to make sure he shows his work. Thanks, Dani."

Faith frowned. School? Did he have a son? A wife? Or maybe a girlfriend? And who was Danny? A babysitter? No, because whoever he was, he was coming to the hospital to suture her head, so he must be a medical doctor. Novak's lover? Was Novak gay?

And? So what if he is? It didn't matter, of course. Nor was it any of her business.

Novak had been listening to Danny and now sighed wearily. "No, it's okay. I'll go. You've gone all the other times, so it's my turn. . . . No, don't tell him. Let him think you'll show up. We have to keep him off balance or we're done for before we even get started." The corners of his mouth turned up wryly at something Danny had said, making Faith stare.

Novak was a handsome man, but when he smiled he was devastating.

"You know that I know the place," he said, amusement lacing his tone. Then his white brows shot up. "*She's* still there? No way in hell. I thought she'd be dead by now. I guess only the good *do* die young." He glanced at Faith, his face stiffening when he saw that she was awake. "I need to go, Dani. See you soon." He slipped his phone into his pocket. "Sorry about that."

Faith knew she should keep her mouth shut, but there

was something about the way he'd smiled that made her a fool. She wanted to know if he had a son. And a wife. *Because I'm curious, nothing more.* "Whose homework will you check?"

He hesitated, then shrugged. "My brother's. He's a freshman in high school."

Not his son. Her eyes widened as she did the math. "Wow. Your mother must have been surprised. There are quite a few years between you." His brother would be only fourteen or fifteen, and Novak appeared to be in his early to mid-thirties.

Another smile bent his lips, this one rueful but equally devastating. "She was."

"I take it that your brother is in trouble?"

Novak sighed. "For fighting and being a rebellious pain in the ass."

"Most teenagers are rebellious," she said mildly.

A growl rumbled deep in his throat. "Most don't get suspended from school twice in as many months."

His side of the conversation started to make sense. "You're going to the principal's office?"

"Yeah. And not looking forward to it."

She bit back a smile. "Spent a lot of time there, huh?"

He slid her a wary glance. "Quantify 'a lot.'"

She chuckled, charmed in spite of her best intentions. "If I have to quantify it, that answers my question." But then something he'd said to Danny sank in. "Did you go to the same school as your brother?" she asked sharply.

He'd smiled at her chuckle, but his expression now smoothed to one of bland curiosity. "Why would you think that?"

Again he'd avoided her question, giving her the answer. Disappointment rose to clog her throat. She'd really hoped he'd be different. *You, Faith, are an idiot.* "Maybe because the same principal is still there? You know, if you didn't want to give me the name of a defense attorney, you could have just said so. You didn't have to tell me you were new and didn't know any. God. I keep hoping I'm wrong, but you guys really are all the same. You lie about the small things and then wonder why people don't trust you with their lives."

He was quiet for a long moment, then finally blew out a breath. "I didn't lie to you. I did grow up in Cincinnati—in

Norwood, actually, then later we lived in Clifton. Google me if you need verification. I went all-state in track my senior year of high school and there was a write-up in the paper. You should find it in the archive. But then I went away to college, and I didn't come back except for holidays and birthdays. I joined the Bureau after graduation and worked all over the country before getting transferred back here a month ago. I said I was new in my job. From a professional networking standpoint, I'm new to the area. I meant no deception."

"I see." More than she'd expected to. There was a roughness in his voice when he'd answered, making her wonder why a young man would leave home never to return except for holidays and birthdays. And there was a desperate relief deep in her gut. She hadn't merely hoped he'd be different. She'd *wanted* him to be different. And she wasn't sure what to do with that realization. "I apologize, Agent Novak."

"It's all right." One white brow lifted as he stopped at a red light and looked over at her. "I can understand your assumption based on my background."

Well, hell. Her cheeks heated, and from the twitch of his lips, he'd noticed. "Touché," she said. "For the record, I was wrong. I'm sorry."

His demeanor changed, his odd eyes growing intense, and Faith didn't think she could look away if she tried. "Thank you. And, for the record, I have not lied to you once all evening."

She met his gaze with a challenge. "But you have withheld truths. Like what you really found in my grandmother's basement. Which I would still very much like to know."

"I know you would," he said quietly. "And I'll tell you what I can, when I can. You've withheld truths as well. I suspect it was to guard your personal safety."

Faith swallowed hard, thinking of her old boss, of his blood on her hands, both literally and figuratively. Of her father, whose heart could not withstand the stress of knowing the danger that had stalked her. Of all the people in her old apartment building who'd been lucky to escape the fire with their lives. "And that of others."

He frowned at that, but then the light turned green, and he returned his attention to traffic. "You've discovered other young women near death recently?"

"No. But I do seem to be a magnet for violence."

"You will tell me about this violence," he said sternly.

It was not a request, but she wasn't offended. Lives were at stake, just as they'd been in Miami. "Of course." They turned a corner, and the bright lights of the hospital came into view, reminding her of the phone conversation she'd overheard. "Who is Danny, and why did you ask him to come in to stitch me up when it's his night off?"

"*Her* night off. Danika is an attending at Cincinnati General."

Her. Danika was a woman. Which wasn't a big deal. Except he'd been here only a month and had no professional network.

"How long have you known *her*?" she asked carefully.

The hint of a smile played over his lips. "Oh, we go way back, to when I lived here before. Don't worry. She's a very good doctor."

Faith was horrified to feel a spurt of jealousy and quashed it before it could gain any appreciable ground. "I never meant to imply otherwise. But I am surprised to be getting such preferential treatment. I figured I'd be triaged and would sit and wait for two or three hours."

Novak's lips firmed to a hard line. "We don't have two or three hours. We need to find Corinne Longstreet before she ends up like Arianna. Or worse."

Assuming she hadn't already, Faith thought sadly. "Or worse," she murmured.

"Dani's not sure how much faster she can get you through, but she'll do her best. She can't treat you if there are any life-threatening cases ahead of you, but she's not on staff tonight, so she can see you sooner than the other doctors." He guided the SUV into the ER's parking lot. "Let's get you into a private exam room, then we'll talk."

"A private exam room? Not the waiting room?"

"That's the plan. I don't know how long this will take, but I didn't think it was prudent to have you sitting in the waiting room for hours. Arianna is at the same hospital, and I know there will be reporters around. It won't take them long to get wind of what's going on out at your house. We've got it lit up like the surface of the damn sun. One of them sees you with me, puts two and two together, then all of a sudden you're front-page news. I don't think having your picture online is the best way to stay under your stalker's radar."

The air rushed from her lungs at the thought of Peter Combs knowing where she was. "No, it's not." She gave Novak a long, considering stare. "Thank you. I didn't expect this."

"Expect what?"

She shrugged uncomfortably. "Thoughtfulness from a cop. You're being very kind."

"I get something out of it, too. A private area also ensures that we can talk without being overheard." He switched off the ignition, then sat back in his seat to give her a probing, troubled look. "Miami's a big city. You must have known *some* decent cops."

He'd shared a few personal details about himself. It wouldn't hurt her to do the same. "I'd thought the one I married was."

Novak went still, his eyes growing hard, his jaw tight. "Did he hurt you?"

"Not the way you're thinking," she said quickly. "He wasn't a violent man. But our divorce was less than civil, and trash-talking me to his friends on the force must've made him feel a lot better because he did it often."

Novak studied her in the way he had at the beginning of the evening, like she was on display in a specimen jar. She now suspected it was a way for him to put the subject of his questions on edge. "Is that why you don't trust cops?"

"It's one reason."

"I can't wait to hear the others," he said dryly. He got out of the SUV and came around to her side, opening her door and extending a hand. "You've got to be feeling sore from the impact with the tree," he said. "I don't want you to fall again. Let me help you."

Gingerly, she took his hand, not expecting the gentleness of his grip. It was something about Novak that surprised her every time, that he could be so gentle. He let her go as soon as her feet were solidly on the ground but stayed close enough to steady her if she stumbled. Though not so close that he sent her into a panic.

He was a quick study.

"Thank . . ." The words died on her lips. He was staring at her throat, his jaw gone even tighter than it had been before. She knew what he was looking at. The cowled collar of her sweater had shifted when she'd exited his vehicle, exposing the scar Peter Combs had left behind. Suddenly self-conscious and annoyed to be so, she pulled a lock of her hair forward to cover the scar.

"No," he said, regret thickening his voice. Carefully, he hooked his finger through the lock of hair and pulled it back over her shoulder. "Don't hide it. I'm sorry, Faith. I hate it when people stare at me, and I just did the same to you."

"It's all right," she said, and meant it. "I'm used to it by now."

"So am I, but that doesn't mean I like it. Peter Combs did that to you?"

She pulled the lock of hair back to cover the scar, nodding. "He did. And more."

"I need to know about that, too." He pulled a woolen scarf from the pocket of his leather coat and wound it around her face, hiding her nose and mouth. And her throat. "This way if one of them does get a picture, no one will be able to identify you."

Once again she was touched by his thoughtfulness. "Thank you."

He lifted his brows mockingly. "All part of the good-cop service. I see one of the ER nurses up there at the side door, waving us over. Let's go."

Chapter Eight

Eastern Kentucky
Monday, November 3, 9:55 p.m.

Where the hell is the damn road? He hadn't been here for a while, and last time it had been in the daylight in the summertime. The road looked different, with many of the surrounding trees now leafless skeletons.

He'd passed his turnoff, not realizing he'd gone too far until he'd seen the lights of Morehead. He'd had to double back and now drove extra slowly, with his high beams on. What should have taken him two hours had taken nearly three.

Ah. There it is. He turned from the main road onto an unmarked, rutted dirt one, ignoring the painted symbols on the trees indicating that he'd crossed onto private land. Gritting his teeth as the van bounced unmercifully, he rounded the final curve and relaxed.

There it was. The little cabin in the very big woods. He'd wondered why its owner had picked this particular location but had never asked.

He'd already decided that he'd bury the two dead bodies he carried under the cabin's rustic wood floor. The other two . . . He hadn't yet made up his mind. He'd figured on killing them quickly when he arrived and dumping all four bodies in a mass grave. But that seemed like such a waste.

He'd worked hard to obtain Longstreet, having chosen

her carefully. He'd already lost his home because of the Escobar bitch. He didn't want to lose his prize, too. He had plans for the blonde. Fun plans.

And the child? When his temper had cooled, he'd realized that she was worth more to him alive. She was leverage, pure and simple. She always had been. But she'd need to be reconditioned. Somehow she'd grown up a little faster than he'd expected, finding a spine somewhere.

But spines could be broken. He'd get a lot of pleasure teaching the child everything he knew, and in so doing, increase her value. Truly good leverage was damn hard to come by.

The little cabin was isolated, so no one would hear their screams. He could stash the Longstreet woman and the child here and come back for them later. *Over and over again.*

And when he was finished, he'd bury Corinne Longstreet under the floorboards with the power guy and the locksmith. As for the child . . . he'd find a place for her when he was confident that she no longer had a spine.

The more he considered the idea, the more he liked it. He wouldn't have to rush with the females, and it allowed him to get back to the city with all haste. Because he had one more loose end to snip. As long as Faith Frye still breathed, she was a danger.

He slowed the van to a stop in front of the little cabin. Hopefully, the owner had left some food in the pantry, because he was starving to death and there was still significant physical labor to be done before he could leave.

He had to pull up the floor and dig a hole big enough for the power guy. The locksmith was a skinny, bony old man who wouldn't take up much room at all. The power guy was the challenge. He got out of the van, slamming the door in annoyance. Of course the power company couldn't have sent a skinny tech to his house. That would have been too easy.

He'd walked toward the cabin and was a foot from the door when he realized that something was off. He drew a breath through his nose, his stomach growling at the enticing aroma.

Stew. What the hell? Someone was making beef stew.

He slunk around the building, squinting into the surrounding woods. No car. Peering through the window, he saw a dirty backpack and a dirtier young man standing at the stove, stirring a pot.

A trespasser. A squatter. They happened from time to time, even in the best of homes. He'd had a few of them himself, but any who'd been foolish enough to enter the O'Bannion house were buried in his basement.

This trespasser had made himself at home. The trash can in the back was filled with empty cans of soup. At this rate, the pantry would be empty and the gas tank drained.

He slid his gun from his waistband and palmed it. The interloper would have to be dealt with. Cleanly, of course. It wouldn't be wise to leave a mess inside.

He made his way quietly to the gas tank and twisted the knob, cutting off the flow. A few minutes later he was rewarded with an oath from inside the cabin.

"Sonofabitch!" the young man said. "Do not tell me the gas is out."

He pressed his back to the cabin wall, waiting patiently in the shadows, rewarded when the front door slammed and the young man came around the back, his steps loud enough to wake the dead. The kid had his arms wrapped around himself, shivering as he walked up to the gas tank and bent over to read the gauge.

The young man never looked up as he approached. One bullet to the back of the head, and the body crumpled to the ground, blood spilling all over the recently fallen leaves.

Luckily, the guy was skinny, otherwise he'd have to dig an even bigger hole.

Eastern Kentucky
Monday, November 3, 9:55 p.m.

Corinne flinched at the single shot, her heart beating so hard that it hurt. She'd heard the door slam. Then nothing until the gunshot.

He's going to kill us. Her and the girl. *He's going to shoot us and kill us.*

But why hadn't he done that already? Why wait? She didn't know and was too afraid to guess. All she knew was that she hadn't had enough time to cut through the ropes. It had taken her forever just to open the old man's penknife and position it where she could saw the rope around her wrists without hurting herself.

And sawing through rope? A helluva lot harder than she'd thought it would be.

She was covered in sweat and teetering on exhaustion. Even if she managed to free herself, she couldn't fight him. And if she did, she couldn't run. Her legs were too sore, her joints too swollen. *More time,* she thought, sawing the rope across the knife wildly. *Just a little more time.*

Cincinnati, Ohio
Monday, November 3, 10:25 p.m.

"I'm all done in there," the nurse said, closing the door to the small, unoccupied office where she'd taken Faith's personal information. "You can go in now. I'll let Dr. Novak know you're ready for her when she comes in."

Deacon found Faith sitting at a small round table, hands folded in front of her. It was the first time he'd seen her in normal light. Her skin was porcelain with a faint spattering of freckles over her nose. Her eyes were a darker green than they'd appeared in the dim light of his SUV.

Leaning over her, he took a second to check the roots of her hair before sitting next to her, angling his chair so that he could fully see her face. She was frowning, just as he'd expected.

"What were you looking at?"

He hadn't lied yet and decided not to start now. "Your hair. Your coloring is very unique."

She gave his hair a pointed glance. "So is yours."

He inclined his head. "Touché." He took a notepad from his coat pocket and dropped it onto the table. "When did your grandmother die? The exact date?"

She blinked at him. "September twenty-fifth. Why?"

"Because I'm starting from the position that you are a completely innocent bystander and that your finding Arianna was a simple coincidence."

She stilled. "It doesn't sound like you believe either of those things," she said quietly.

He held her gaze. "I don't, but only because Arianna knew your name."

"Because she heard it from her captor. He had to have known that I'd inherited the house."

"How would he know that?"

"If I were squatting in someone's basement, I'd want to know what was going on with the owner. I'd do a property search online. It's easy enough to do. He wouldn't need to have super cyber skills. How long has he been there?"

"Why?"

A muted sound of frustration. "Because if it was longer than two weeks, he would have found my grandmother's name on the deed, not mine."

He thought of the basement's torture room, the well-used cot with its rusted shackles. The office and the kitchen and the little sleeping alcove. "Assume it was longer."

"All right. Then he would have known that my grandmother was the owner. He'd also know that her death was just a matter of time," she added sadly.

"How would he know that?" Deacon asked.

She shrugged. "She was eighty-four. Even if she'd been in the best of health—which she hadn't been in years—she wasn't going to live forever. If I'd been squatting, I'd set up a Google alert to let me know as soon as she died because the house would change hands. There's lots of activity when a house changes hands. Realtors, appraisers, buyers, tax assessors. He would want to be gone before they descended. He'd also want to know about the new owner. My grandmother's attorney transferred the deed into my name two weeks ago. It's public record."

"So you're assuming that whoever assaulted Arianna has a computer and is tech savvy."

"Who doesn't have a computer these days? He might not be young, but he's not old, either. You said there was evidence of a fight behind the house and the power company tech is missing. He has to have moved the body, so he has some strength. He's not eighty-four, that's for damn sure. And even if he weren't tech savvy, there's always the public records office. He could have easily gotten my name any number of ways."

She was right about that. Why Arianna's abductor would have revealed Faith's name to his captive was another question. "When was the will read and who was there?"

"October first. The attorney called us into his office individually. I don't know if he does that all the time, or if he expected one of my uncles to make a scene."

He lifted his brows. "So you *were* here more recently than twenty-three years ago."

"In the city, yes, for the will, and several times over the years to visit my grandmother. But I never went to see the house, not when she was alive and not when she was gone."

He'd suspected as much. "Why not? It was your property."

"Because," she said calmly, "as you so astutely noted earlier, I don't like it. I didn't intend to live in it."

He glanced at the hollow of her throat, where her pulse beat rapidly. She wasn't as calm as she appeared. "What had you intended to do with it?"

"On the day I found out I'd inherited it? Nothing. I was too shocked. I thought she might leave me a few of the paintings she'd hung in the townhouse, but not the house. Never the house."

Every time she referred to the house, she recoiled. It was a subtle reaction, Deacon thought, one that seemed deeply ingrained. He made a mental note of it, planning to dig deeper later. "Did you see either of your uncles when you were here before?"

"I had lunch with Jordan."

Outwardly she was the picture of serenity, but her pulse continued to hammer in the hollow of her throat. Deacon wished he knew if it was his mention of the house that was still agitating her, or her uncle—or both uncles. "You don't trust Jeremy, but what about Jordan?"

She shook her head slightly. "I'm not going there, Agent Novak. I'm not throwing my family under the bus, as Kimble so colorfully put it. Investigate Jeremy for this, by all means. But other than a few childhood memories—which did not seem to have any validity when I checked them out as an adult—I don't know him."

"And Jordan?"

"We were closer when I was a teenager. For the last twelve years or so, I only saw him when I came to visit my grandmother, and then only a few minutes here and there. He took care of her for twenty-three years and never once complained, but he did appreciate when I visited because he got a little break. He'd usually go off and paint."

"How did he feel about you inheriting the house?"

"He was thrilled because it meant he wouldn't have to fight with Jeremy over it."

"Jeremy wanted the house?"

"I don't know that for sure," she said hastily. "I never heard him say so because I haven't talked to him in years. But if Jordan had inherited the house, he told me that he and Jeremy would have probably ended up in court, contesting the will. My grandmother made it clear that she did not want Jeremy to get a penny."

"Just because he was gay?" Deacon asked mildly, although he knew families that had been bitterly divided over the very issue.

She shook her head, making all that dark red hair pool on her shoulders before sliding down her back. *Like silk,* he thought, and wondered how it would feel running through his fingers.

Whoa. He stopped that train of thought in its tracks. *No, no, no. Not like silk. Like hair. It would feel like hair.* Nothing special.

"I think Gran's issue was really that Jeremy wouldn't just hide it. She said that he sent my grandfather to an early grave. Anyway, Jordan said that my inheriting the house saved him a lot of trouble and a fortune in attorney's fees. I need to call him about what's going on."

"I called him while you were asleep in the car. I called both of your uncles. Neither was home, so I left messages on their answering machines asking them to call me back."

"Jordan is never home this time of the night. He's an art dealer and always seems to be at a party. You'll have a better chance of contacting him after eleven in the morning. But . . ." She bit her lip again. "If Jeremy's involved—and I am not saying that he is—but *if* he is, won't leaving him a message just tip him off?"

"You don't need to worry about that right now."

She gave him an annoyed look. "Because you put surveillance on his house."

And outside his office at the medical school as well, Deacon thought, but didn't mention it. Instead, he held her gaze steadily, giving away nothing until she rolled her eyes and muttered in a twangy drawl, " 'You don't need to worry 'bout that right now, little lady.' "

He bit back a grin. "I never called you 'little lady.'"

She arched one eyebrow. "But you thought it."

"I can assure you that I did not," he said firmly. "You said you didn't plan to live in the house when you first inherited it. When *did* you decide to live in it?"

"Friday afternoon."

He let a beat pass, but she said no more. "This past Friday? Three days ago?" The day that Arianna and Corinne disappeared.

He didn't like that at all, but kept his voice mild. "Why?"

"Because I got a job offer."

"At a bank," he remembered, and she nodded. "But you had to have applied for that job before Friday afternoon, so you must have at least considered living in the house before."

"Not really. What I knew was that I needed to leave Miami. I didn't care where I went."

"Because of Peter Combs."

An involuntary swallow. Her pulse had kicked up again. "Yes. I feared for my life."

"When did you decide to leave Miami?"

"A month ago, although I'd been thinking about it for months before that. I wasn't picky about where I went, so I applied for a lot of jobs online, all over the country. The bank job was something of a whim, truthfully. The listing jumped out at me because I'd just come home from Cincinnati after seeing my grandmother's attorney. I met the job's qualifications, and it paid more than any of the other positions I was applying for. They interviewed me over Skype the following week, but I didn't hear back from them again until they called me on Friday afternoon. By then I'd nearly forgotten about them."

"So you loaded up your Jeep and drove up the next day?"

"Something like that."

"Who knew you were leaving on Friday?"

"I already told you. No one except my father and stepmother, and they thought it was only for a few days, to meet with a Realtor and sell the house."

"Why did they think that?"

"Because my dad is recovering from a stroke. He assumed it and I . . . let him."

His brows shot up. "You mean you *lied* to him?" he said mockingly, then immediately regretted it because her eyes filled with sudden tears.

She swiped at them with the back of her bandaged hand. "To protect him. He knows about what Combs did four years ago." She touched the scar on her throat. "My dad never left my side while I was in the hospital. But he doesn't know about the stalking. Combs was paroled a few weeks after my dad had his stroke. I knew it would upset him, so I didn't tell him."

Chastised, Deacon found a packet of tissues in his coat pocket. "They're crumpled, but unused."

"Thank you." She dabbed at her eyes, letting out a teary laugh. "I keep expecting robotic arms to pop out of your coat pockets like Inspector Gadget. What else do you have hidden?"

He grinned, relieved to hear her laugh. "I've been compared to a lot of cartoons, but never Gadget." He leaned back, watching her. "You'll have to tell him you're living here sometime."

"He knows now. I called him while I was driving to the house tonight and told him that I was relocating, but I didn't tell him why. I just said I needed a change. Please don't contact him about any of this. He might not survive it, and I would never forgive myself."

He wished he could tell her what she wanted to hear. "I said I wouldn't lie to you, Faith. You know better than to ask me for that. If I need to talk to him, then I will, but I won't unless I must. It's the best I can do. When was Combs paroled?"

She went still, the fear in her eyes giving way to a fiery rage that took him aback, but at least she wasn't crying anymore. "December first, a year ago, at two fifteen in the afternoon. At six thirty that night, he was shopping for vegetables in my neighborhood Publix."

Sonofabitch. It was all he could do not to snarl. "That wasn't a violation of his parole?"

A muscle in her jaw twitched. "No."

He needed to find out why, but the look on her face told him it would be better to come back to it later. "You must have been scared," he said calmly, hoping to soothe her.

She actually snarled at him. "Y'think? He'd show up outside the dry cleaner's, the bank, doctor's appointments, even my hair salon, for God's sake. He joined my gym, and I'd find him watching me from across the weight room. From the floor when I was climbing the rock wall. He'd come up behind me when I was running on the track and just smile at me. He'd send me *flowers* and *candy*. It went on like that for *months*."

"Did you consider a restraining order?"

"Of *course* I considered a restraining order!" she hissed. "Why the fucking hell do you think I went to all the trouble of filing all those complaints? I'm not *stupid*, Agent Novak."

"I haven't thought that for a single moment, Faith."

She took a deep breath and then continued. "To answer your question, I did get a restraining order. A few weeks later, I'd gone out to dinner with my boss and some people from work. Came out of the restaurant and got in my car, then Combs walked up and got into his—the one parked right next to me. When I filed the complaint that he'd violated the TRO, he told the police that he didn't know I'd be there, that his girlfriend had sent him to the drugstore to pick up her prescription. The girlfriend excuse checked out."

Sonofabitch. "What happened to his wife—the mother of the girl he molested?"

"She found another man while Combs was in prison and divorced him."

"Poor guy. My heart bleeds."

Faith sighed. "She never got her daughter more therapy after the court mandate was no longer in effect. She moved in with someone else the day after Combs was sentenced."

That she knew the family's business struck him as odd, but he pocketed that for later, too. "What kind of car does Combs drive?"

"Nissan Sentra, red. It's registered to his newest girlfriend." She grabbed his pad and wrote down the license plate number. "I know it by heart."

"Give me a minute." Deacon texted the information to Bishop, Adam, and Crandall, then put out a BOLO for the vehicle.

"What are you doing?" she asked warily, leaning over to look at his phone.

Giving him a perfect view of what lay under her sweater.

His heart skipped a beat, then thudded to beat all hell. Rounded breasts swelling above black lace. Creamy white skin. *Soft,* he thought. Her skin would be so soft. And he needed to look away. *Now*.

With an effort he did so, turning his phone so that it captured her attention for the moment it took to get his racing pulse under control. "Putting out a BOLO on Combs's car."

She looked up at him, genuinely confused. "Why?"

"Just in case he followed you, or might follow you later." *Or followed you before.* That Combs was involved in this case was still not out of the realm of possibility. "We'll do our best to keep your name out of the press, but it's going to happen sooner or later."

She returned to her chair, sitting back with a rigid control that clearly broadcasted her fear. "I know. I knew it as soon as I called 911 tonight."

Yet she'd called anyway. She wasn't guilty. Deacon's gut and brain were in complete agreement. "We need to find out how he knew about your schedule. Do you store your calendar on your phone?"

"I did. But my phone was always with me."

Deacon gave her a rueful smile. "These days it doesn't matter. If he hacked into your phone, he'd know everything about you."

"He hacked . . . ? I never even . . ." She paled. "He could have been tracking me, all this time. Dammit. That was so stupid of me. He was a programmer, too. Why didn't I see that?"

"It wasn't stupid," he said firmly. "It wasn't your job to see it. It was the job of the cop who took your statement. You'd been contemplating leaving Miami for months because he was stalking you. What made you finally decide to leave a month ago?"

She looked down at her hands, front and back, as if seeing something he could not. "My boss was murdered. His blood was on my hands."

Deacon frowned. "Literally or figuratively?"

"Both." Her mouth twisted bitterly, and her green eyes filled with self-contempt. "I tried to save him, but he bled out before the EMTs arrived. Gordon was a good man. Decent. He had two kids and a pregnant wife. He didn't deserve to die because of a bullet meant for me."

Deacon sat back in his chair, studying her. There wasn't an iota of melodrama in her eyes. She was coldly, brutally serious. "How do you know it was meant for you?"

"Because a few days later, Combs shot at my car and tried to force me off a bridge."

Hiding his shock, Deacon had to take a moment to decide which question to ask first. He needed to know how and when. He needed to know if she'd been injured in any of the attempts. He needed to know what was wrong with the cops who'd taken her statements that they'd let this go on, but mostly he needed to know *why*.

Because, although his emotions were worrying about the woman, his mind remained rational. Stalking her would have been bad enough. Attempted murder—several times—was unexpected. Being sent to prison wasn't normally enough to motivate such violence. If it were, cops would have a hell of a lot more homicides on their hands—and cops and prosecutors would top the list of victims. Therapists seemed like they'd be at the bottom of the list.

What would drive Combs from stalking to repeated attempted murder? This was . . .

Personal. Deacon's gut did a slow roll as he thought about the accusation Combs had made during his trial—that Faith had been his lover. Looking at her now, he couldn't believe that.

No, he thought. He didn't *want* to believe it because he genuinely liked her. He was letting his feelings take the reins, and this he couldn't allow.

"Maybe we should start further back than your inheriting the house," he said carefully. "Let's go back to Combs. He was your client, right?"

Revulsion flashed across her face for a split second before her expression flattened to that of a statue, every flicker of emotion disappearing from her eyes. The transformation made him want to flinch. He didn't, of course, keeping his own expression passive as he waited for her answer.

She leaned back in her seat, mimicking his pose as she studied his face, and he had a bad feeling he wasn't going to like her answer.

"You think I somehow brought this on myself," she said. "And now you think that Detective Kimble was right, that I may be compromised after all. You might even think

Combs was telling the truth about me." She smiled at him mockingly. Coldly. "Do you know what I think, Agent Novak? I think I should get a lawyer. Now."

Cincinnati, Ohio
Monday, November 3, 10:40 p.m.

Faith was furious. Partly with Novak. Mostly with herself. She'd kept telling herself that she wouldn't fall for a cop's BS again, yet here she was.

"You're not a suspect," Novak said, but she could tell that she'd surprised him. He'd thought she'd just spill her guts because he'd been kind enough not to alert the press to her presence. Because he'd made her feel safer.

"Goody for me," she said sarcastically. "But you also said that you wouldn't tell me when I became one, and I appreciate the warning. I've been on this carousel before. I'm done here."

His eyes flashed, darkening as they narrowed. She'd made him angry. *Good.* "Were those just pretty words, Dr. Corcoran? Are you willing to let a rapist go free? Are you willing to allow Corinne to die? You had a bad experience, and I'm sorry, but that wasn't Corinne's fault."

"It wasn't mine, either," she shot back, slapping her palms on the table, then sucking in a pained breath as she pressed her bandaged hands between her breasts. "Dammit," she breathed quietly. "What happened to not jumping to assumptions based on my background?"

"I hadn't. Yet."

"Yet. But it was coming."

He shook his head. "You don't know that. *I* don't even know that. What I do know is that a young woman will die if we don't figure out who took her and what he's done with her."

"I had nothing to do with what happened to those girls. I don't know who took them. *He got my name off the deed.* Just because I had the bad luck to inherit that damn house doesn't mean I can help you. I don't even know why you're here."

"What if he didn't get your name off the deed?" Novak asked quietly. "What if he does know you? What if he came here because of you?"

Faith's mouth dropped open as his words sank in. "What? What are you saying? That Combs is here? That . . . that he took those girls?"

He braced his forearm on the table, leaned forward. Invading her space. "Is it possible?"

She stared at him, wondering if he could be serious. He stared back, his mesmerizing eyes full of challenge. His lips formed a hard line within the frame of his white goatee. His jaw set like granite. *This is the real Novak,* she thought. He was grim, hard, large, and intimidating. And desperate. He cared about those two women.

"Of course it's possible," she said. "But it's highly unlikely. You've made a connection that doesn't exist. It's like . . ." The connection she sought snapped into her mind. "It's like the wolf beating me to Grandmother's house, for God's sake. You're crazy."

He leaned closer. "I might be crazy, but *you're* a coincidence. I don't like coincidences."

"I can't help what you don't like." Her heart began to race as she considered the possibility of what he was suggesting. *Combs here. In my grandmother's house. Waiting for me.* And torturing two young women as he did. "There isn't a single shred of evidence to back it up."

"You don't know that, Faith. You did the right thing tonight. You stood guard over Arianna and made sure that whoever hurt her couldn't hurt her again. Do that now. At least help me rule Combs out so I can focus on another suspect. Please." He pulled out his phone, tapped the screen, then slid it across the table until it was right in front of her. "Please."

Don't look down. Do not look down. But Faith's eyes did not obey, and a second later she found herself staring at one of the photos taken of Arianna Escobar lying in the road, covered with Faith's wool coat. The girl's face was crisscrossed with shallow cuts and bruised beyond recognition, her mouth bleeding and swollen. She'd been abused so cruelly.

Faith closed her eyes, knowing he'd won. "Goddamn you, Novak," she said wearily.

"Then you'll talk to me?" he asked, his voice deep and quiet. She'd expected to hear elation. Maybe smug pride or victory. But all she heard was grim determination.

"What do you want to know?"

"I need to know why Combs hated you enough to terrorize you, to try to kill you. Maybe enough to follow you here. It's personal, isn't it?"

She opened her eyes to find him only inches away. Watching her. "Yes, but not the way you think. I didn't sleep with him." She hated that her voice trembled. Hated that she needed Novak to believe her. "I despised him. I despised all of them."

His expression softened. "All of who, Faith?"

She clenched her jaw. "Every last sonofabitch pervert who walked into my office."

A frown creased his brow. "But if you hated them, why did you treat them?"

"Because of the victims. The children. I wasn't there to 'cure' the offenders. I don't believe there is a cure, at least not for most of them. I was there to help the victims. Any way I could."

"I don't understand, but I want to. Help me understand."

"Right out of college, I worked in a rape crisis center. I'm good with kids and teens and was getting a lot of referrals. I took my first offender because of the little girl, his daughter. She was only five and so broken. I can still see her face." She could still see all their faces. The memories still broke her heart. "Her eyes were dead, you know?"

He nodded, so close that she could see the striations separating the blue and brown in his irises, like shattered glass. So close that she could see the pain flitter thorough his eyes. "Yeah. I know."

"Her social worker begged me to take her case. I initially refused because it was a court-mandated family therapy. To help the child, I had to take on the father."

"At the same time? The victim had to sit in your office with the offender?"

"Oh no. The appointments were separate, but the court wanted the same therapist working with each individual in the family unit. For continuity. I bit back my distaste for the father and focused all my energy on the little girl. And she made progress. Enough that I got more referrals. Soon those were the only cases I was getting. My boss at the time was thrilled—the contracts he signed with the court system were our practice's bread and butter."

Novak tilted his head a fraction. "But you could have quit."

"I wanted to, but I realized that the kids who came to my office through the court-mandated programs weren't likely to get therapy otherwise. So many of the mothers were in denial or such dependent personalities that they would have allowed their partners to do anything to their children as long as they stayed. Those mothers wouldn't get their children the help they needed."

"Unless they were forced by the court," he murmured. "I understand now."

She nodded, relieved. "I got the rep of being the best sex-offender rehabilitator in the county. It made me want to scream, because I knew I'd become part of the problem. If there were no therapy programs, judges wouldn't have it as a sentencing option. But it's moot. Judges *do* have the option, and they aren't going to give it up easily, especially not with the prisons as overcrowded as they are."

"But if you'd walked away, the victims would have had no one."

She nodded again, feeling the old helplessness rise to choke her. "It's a vicious circle."

"But you counseled dozens of offenders, Faith. What made Combs different? What made him hate you so intensely?"

Faith hesitated, knowing what her honesty would cost her. "They all hated me."

His eyes grew sharp, sensing her evasion. "But only Combs tried to kill you." He leaned forward, closing the distance between them. *"Why?"*

She steeled her spine. "Because I stalked him first."

Chapter Nine

Now I've done it, Faith thought miserably. She'd just given Agent Novak the ammunition to destroy her career. She'd never planned to tell another living soul what she'd done to Peter Combs. That she'd told Novak after knowing him only a few short hours meant he was that good or she was that tired. Or maybe she'd simply been ready to tell.

Novak didn't blink. "You stalked Peter Combs first? How? Tell me exactly."

Faith opened her mouth to answer but was spared a reply by a knock at the door. It opened and a woman peeked in. "Can I come in?"

Novak frowned in frustration. "No. Come back later."

"You're kidding, right?" the woman said. "I came down here for you."

Faith knew it was cowardly, but she welcomed the chance to organize her thoughts before she laid them bare in front of Novak. "Come in," she said.

Novak shot Faith a knowing glare, but waved the woman in. "Sure. Yeah. Come."

"Well, hello to you, too, sunshine," the woman said dryly, closing the door behind her before turning to face Faith. "Dr. Corcoran, I'm Dr. Novak. What seems to be the problem?"

Faith stared, aware that she was gawking but unable to stop herself. In her early thirties, the woman was of average height, but that was the only thing average about her. Her long black hair bore a two-inch streak of bright white that framed both sides of her face. Her skin was the color of café au lait and her mouth curved naturally, as if she smiled without thinking about it. But it was her eyes that were the focal point of her striking face. With a slight upward tilt, one was a vivid blue, the other a dark chocolate brown.

And then what the woman had said sank in. *Dr. Novak.*

Novak had said they went way back. *Well, duh.* That they were siblings was unmistakable. The white hair, the heterochromatic eyes. Novak's were far more interesting than his sister's, though. Her eyes were the more common occurrence, one of each color, while his were that amazing half-and-half.

Faith turned to Novak with a frown, the motivation behind his choice of doctors suddenly clear. "She's your sister," she accused.

Dr. Novak turned to her brother. "You didn't tell her?"

He shook his head, his expression unapologetic. "No."

"Why not?" Dr. Novak asked.

"Because he wanted me to trust him," Faith snapped. "He figured that if he told me he'd called you, I'd suspect he'd get you to reveal my personal information and refuse to come."

The doctor frowned at her brother. "Is that true?"

Novak nodded once, not even trying to hide his duplicity. "Yes."

His sister frowned. "Shame on you, Deacon. Wait outside."

"How long will you be? I need to run to Tam—" He cut himself off. "Out to Norwood."

"Give us thirty. Now go." Dr. Novak closed the door behind him. "I'm sorry, Dr. Corcoran. I didn't know he'd been so stingy with information." Smiling warmly, she pulled out a chair. "He's a good guy, really. But he gets all cloak-and-daggery sometimes. Makes me nuts."

"I suppose that comes with being an FBI agent," Faith said. "I apologize. I was rude after you came in on your night off to help me. Thank you."

"Not a problem. I assure you that I will keep your medical information confidential. He can bribe, beg, and cajole all he wants, but my lips are sealed."

Faith believed her. "Thank you."

The doctor scanned the chart the nurse had filled out. "Dr. Faith Corcoran. May I call you Faith?"

"Sure."

"And you should call me Dani. Deacon said that you were in an accident. What happened?"

Faith recounted the accident as the doctor pulled on a pair of gloves with a snap.

"You're lucky," Dani said when Faith was done. "You walked away from that wreck with barely a scratch. I get so many accident cases who have far more serious injuries than you have." She shone her penlight in Faith's eyes, then probed the back of her skull and neck with gentle hands. "Headaches?"

"Just one named Deacon." Faith liked the name. It fit him somehow.

Dani's lips twitched. "Any headaches *not* named Deacon?"

"Not really. He gave me some pain reliever, and that took care of most of it."

"Did you lose consciousness?"

"For maybe a few seconds. No more."

"How do you know?"

"The radio was on. A song was playing when I saw the girl in the road, and it was still playing when it was all over and the airbag deflated. I may have missed a line of the chorus."

"Which song?" Dani asked.

Faith grimaced. " 'Live Like You Were Dying.' "

Dani snorted. "Sorry. That's just dang ironic."

Faith had to smile. Novak's sister had put her at instant ease. "Ain't it just?"

"I used to cry when I heard that song on the radio. Now, thanks to you, I'll probably laugh and people will think I'm a sociopath." She held up her index finger. "Follow the finger with your eyes," she said, putting Faith through her neurological paces. "I don't think you have a concussion. Just take it easy for the next forty-eight. Get lots of rest. That means no computer, no day at the office, no reading books. Rest."

Faith thought of the army of law enforcement on her grandmother's front lawn. Somehow she didn't think resting was in her immediate future. "Sure. You got it, Doc."

Dani rolled her eyes, then stood to remove the bandage from Faith's forehead. "It's not too bad," she pronounced. "I can close this with some superglue and you'll be good as new." She proceeded to clean the wound. "So are you angry with my brother?" she asked as she closed it.

"I don't know. I'm trying not to make assumptions based on his background."

"His background? What background?"

"That he's a cop," Faith said flatly.

"Ah. Cops are wired differently from the rest of us. You know, seeing bad guys everywhere they turn. And they're so darn bossy."

Faith chuckled. "I know."

"He didn't mean harm, I can promise you that," Dani said quietly. "He's a good man."

"I certainly hope so," Faith murmured. She'd all but confessed to stalking her own client, which could mean the end of her license. What he'd do with that was anyone's guess.

"He called me because he'd already called the ER and found out that the wait time was three hours," Dani said. "He just wanted to get you in and out of here quickly."

"I can accept that." Faith thought of the desperation in his eyes as he'd begged her to help him find Corinne. "He definitely wants to protect the woman who's still missing and get justice for the one I found." The doctor said no more, leaving Faith to study the white streak in her hair as she applied the glue. "May I ask you a personal question?"

"You can ask," Dani said pleasantly.

"Your hair. Is it natural?"

Dani leaned back to wink at her. "Mostly. This is how it looked when I was sixteen. The streak was there at birth but started to spread when I was in my late teens. I liked the streak but didn't want to be all white. So the black's from a bottle." She grinned as she resumed her task. "It allows me to channel my inner Rogue."

"X-Men?" Faith asked, already liking Dani more than her brother.

"Of course. Rogue's my favorite. Absorbing other people's powers for a little while would be seriously useful.

Without draining them to death, of course." She made a face. "Hippocratic conflict and all that."

"Damn ethics," Faith said dryly. "I was always more of a Black Widow fangirl, myself."

"With your red hair, I can see why." Dani paused, her voice becoming cagey. "Or is it perhaps because of her superskills? You know, all that karate and kung fu, the acrobatics and super-marksmanship? Or, uh, maybe even the climbing of sheer rocky embankments?"

"You know your comic-book canon. Except for the rocky embankment part, of course. I don't recall the issue where Black Widow did that. Obviously, you've talked to Agent Novak."

"He texted me the high points, and then I called Sheriff Palmer and the EMT who treated you for the detailed version. That was a pretty impressive climb you made."

Faith shrugged. "I do wall-climbing at the gym. Did, anyway, back in Miami. The embankment wasn't all that difficult."

"I've been considering trying that, but I'm probably too old to learn now."

"Nonsense. I didn't start until a few years ago." Right after she'd recovered from Combs slitting her throat. She'd learned to defend herself and escape various situations.

Dani put the glue away. "Then I might try after all. What about Black Widow's other superskills? Running? Martial arts? Marksmanship? Classical ballet? Can you do those, too?"

"All of the above, except for the being a ballerina part. I grew too tall. Did Agent Novak have dark hair with a white streak, too?" Faith asked, needing to deflect attention away from herself.

"He did. Except he went the other way, letting it all go white. It works for him."

It really did, Faith thought reluctantly. Everything about Novak's appearance worked for him. Which didn't seem quite fair. "And what about your younger brother? The one who's in hot water with the older-than-dirt principal? Does he have the same streak of white?"

Dani laughed. "She *is* older than dirt, but she can still make me shake in my shoes. She never, ever forgets a student or their transgressions. Deacon's in for it." She leaned forward to inspect her work. "Not bad, if I do say so myself. You shouldn't have a scar."

"It's okay if I do," Faith said, noting that the other woman had evaded the question about her younger brother. "I'll just have a matched set." She pulled her sweater away from her throat and watched Dani's mismatched eyes flash hot with surprise.

"That's quite a souvenir," Dani said. "Hopefully, your attacker won't find you here."

But if Novak was right, Combs already had found her, arriving long before she had, lying in wait for his victims.

In Grandmother's house, no less, Faith thought with a mental eye roll. Peter Combs was a beast in his own right. He needed no assistance from a fairy tale.

Novak simply couldn't be right. His theory was ludicrous.

But . . . *What if he* is *right?* Then Kimble was right, too. Faith was involved. *Culpable.* Because if Novak *was* right, it meant that she'd led the beast here. Which meant that Arianna and Corinne had been abducted, tortured . . . *Because of me.*

"If he finds me, I'll be ready. I won't let him hurt me again." *Or anyone else.*

Dani frowned. "I'm all for taking care of yourself but within reason. If the man who did that to you surfaces, I hope you'll contact my brother. I know he ruffled your feathers, but Deacon is *very* good at what he does. And even though he can be a cocky son of a gun, his heart's bigger than any I've ever known. Please, Faith. Don't take Combs on by yourself."

Faith leaned back a fraction, startled. "You know about Combs? You know who I am?"

"I know who you used to be. I Googled you before I came in."

Faith narrowed her eyes. "How did you know who I used to be? Did your brother tell you?"

"No. My cousin called to give me the heads-up that Deacon was bringing you to the ER."

"Kimble," Faith said darkly.

Without commenting, Dani took Faith's hands and with gentle efficiency stripped away the bandages the EMT had applied. "No need for stitches. Just keep them clean and dry. What about your feet? I heard you climbed that embankment without shoes."

Faith hated that people could Google her. She hated that this woman, with whom she'd felt so comfortable, knew everything about her. Knew who she *used to be.* "My feet are fine."

Dani met her eyes again. "You don't like it that I know about Combs and what he said about you when he was on trial."

"That I slept with him? No. Would you?"

Dani's smile was strangely sad. "We all have secrets we'd rather keep buried, so no, I wouldn't. But I wasn't interested in what the press said. Have you ever gone on the loops?"

"Which ones?"

"The online forums where victims can tell their stories, get support from each other."

Faith's irritation dissipated, curiosity taking its place. "I know they're there, of course, but visiting seemed like an invasion of my clients' privacy, so I never did. What did you find?"

"That they talk about you, your clients. I didn't have to search hard to find some incredible stories of the work you did. Real tearjerkers. A few discussions about the accusations Combs hurled at you. Your clients supported you. Recommended you to other victims."

Faith swallowed hard, but the tears came anyway. "I didn't know," she said hoarsely. "Thank you. God. Just . . . thank you."

Dani slid a box of tissues across the table. "You're welcome. Look, right now you're scared. Angry that no one helped you. Maybe even feeling a little sorry for yourself?"

Faith dabbed at her eyes. "Yeah. Pretty much all of the above."

"I'd say you're entitled—to a point. But watch the self-pity. It can eat you alive from the inside out. When you're ready to make a difference again, give me a call." She handed Faith her business card. "When I'm not on shift here—or in the principal's office with my little brother—you'll find me there. We're always looking for people with your skill set."

Faith read the card. *Dr. Danika Novak, MD.* And above her name in a simple, bold font—LORELLE E. MEADOWS CEN-TER, "THE MEADOW." "What is the Meadow?"

"A free clinic in Over-the-Rhine. We have two locations, one for men, one for women and kids. We provide basic medical and counseling services. We get a lot of addicts and runaways. A lot of STDs. And sex-abuse victims who are reluctant to go to a traditional hospital because they don't want the police involved. Some are afraid they'll be thrown out of their homes for accusing stepfathers or fathers or mothers' boyfriends." Dani pulled her pager from her pocket, glanced at the screen. "I have to go. If you need a general practitioner, I can recommend several."

"Thank you. But I thought you'd get to go home now."

"Not yet. I'm on call for hearing-impaired patients since I'm the only doctor who signs. I would have been called in even if you hadn't been here." She pointed to the scrubs she'd placed on the table when she came in. "The nurse said you were still wearing bloody clothes."

Faith's fingers rose to tuck the collar of her sweater more firmly against her throat. "I'll borrow the pants. My sweater is okay."

Dani's smile was understanding. "I'll tell Deacon to knock before he comes back in. Take care, Faith. I hope I see you again, and if you decide to come down to the Meadow, let me know. I'll meet you there and show you around."

"I will." *If I still have a license when Novak is finished with me.* "Thank you."

Cincinnati, Ohio
Monday, November 3, 11:05 p.m.

Deacon parked his SUV behind Aunt Tammy's minivan, swallowing a wince at the sight of the classic Lincoln Continental that was Jim Kimble's pride and joy. He'd hoped his uncle wouldn't be home, but with it being so late, he'd known he would be.

So Deacon had come bearing gifts.

A light was on in Greg's room upstairs, and the television flickered in the darkened living room. Feet in pink fuzzy slippers were visible on the recliner that pointed toward the TV. Deacon tapped lightly on the front door, in case Tammy was asleep. The door opened without a sound, and Deacon found himself eye to eye with the reason he'd never sought an assignment in Cincinnati up until now.

Jim Kimble was the only man Deacon had ever met who could look intimidating while wearing a faded flannel robe and fuzzy pink slippers. Maybe it was his unflinching stare, his square jaw, and the fact that he was built like a six-foot-tall brick. It might have been the fact that he was a tough cop with a reputation for banging heads together to keep the peace.

But it was more likely because Jim had been the only man who'd ever forced Deacon's father to back down, which he'd accomplished by sending Arnie Cavendish flying through a plate-glass window with a single punch. Arnie had had it coming, that was for damn certain. But Deacon had been afraid of Jim for years thereafter. His uncle had never raised a hand to him, but the threat was always there.

Jim still had the power, with a single arched brow, to make Deacon feel like an inadequate, scrawny teenager. He was giving him the look right now.

Without saying a word, Deacon lifted the bags he'd brought. Skyline Coneys in one hand and Graeter's ice cream in the other. The chili dogs were a Cincinnati staple, and the ice cream was his aunt's favorite.

Jim looked the offering over, then stepped back, motioning Deacon inside with a jerk of his head. Deacon followed him into the kitchen, held up two fingers, then watched as Jim took two plates from the cupboard and set them on the table.

In silence, Deacon put two chili dogs on each plate, then held the pint of ice cream out for his uncle to check that it was sugar-free before putting it in the freezer.

"At least you're not trying to kill her anymore," Jim grunted.

Deacon barely kept from rolling his eyes. Tammy's doctor had limited her sugar intake, but the barb was aimed at his and Greg's fight that afternoon. "I wasn't trying to kill her earlier today, either. I lost my temper. I'm sorry."

Jim sat at the table and downed a Coney in three bites. "You eating?"

"No. I can't stay. I have a witness getting worked on in the ER, and I have to go collect her. I just came by to check on Tammy and talk to Greg."

Jim shook his head, lips hard and thin. "That boy is killin' her. Breaking her heart."

"I know." Deacon picked up one of the plates to take up to Greg. "He'll have to stay here tomorrow until his meeting with the principal. I'm sorry. I don't have anywhere else to put him."

"That house of yours almost done?"

"Almost. End of the week, just like I promised. We'll move Greg's stuff on the weekend."

"See that you do."

Gritting his teeth, Deacon walked away from his uncle and went up the stairs, flicking the switch outside Greg's room. If Greg wasn't wearing his hearing aids, he wouldn't hear a knock.

There was no answer so Deacon tried the door, surprised when it was unlocked. Greg was lying on his bed, staring up at the ceiling, throwing a basketball a few feet into the air and catching it. He looked at the Coneys, then back up at Deacon.

"You plugged in?" Deacon asked, touching his own ear.

With a long-suffering sigh, Greg put his aids in his ears and turned them on. "What?"

"Food?" Deacon asked with only a little sarcasm. He put the plate on Greg's nightstand and walked to the window and stared out, his hands deep in his pockets, trying to think of what to say. Behind him he heard the rattle of the Coney's wrapping paper.

"Why do you do that?" Greg asked, his mouth full.

Deacon looked over his shoulder. "Why do I do what?"

"Stand at the window and stare out. You always stand there. Since I was a kid."

Deacon sat on the corner of the bed so that Greg could see his face. "That was my window, over there, across the way." He thumbed at the window behind him. "You know that."

He and Dani had lived in the house next door until Arnie Cavendish had died in a bar brawl. Then Deacon, his mother, and sister had moved into this house with Tammy and Jim and Adam until Bruce Novak had come into their lives. Bruce had been good to his mother and had adopted him and Dani so that they didn't have to say "Cavendish" out loud ever again.

"This was my room for almost four years," Deacon added. "I shared it with Adam. But I always missed my old room. It had glow-in-the-dark stars on the ceiling."

The new tenants had taken them down and thrown them

away. It had been another reminder that he and Dani and his mother were homeless, dependent on the goodwill of others. Specifically, Uncle Jim.

The fact that Jim owned the house next door had made Deacon angry then. Jim still made him angry more than two decades later, but not for the same reasons. Now he understood that Jim and Tammy had not been rich and needed the rent income from the house to pay its mortgage. He understood that they had never planned to be landlords, that they'd only bought the house so that his mother could have a decent place to live because she was pregnant with Deacon, and Arnie had insisted he could only afford subsidized housing. Deacon knew that after Arnie's death, his mother couldn't afford the rent on her salary alone, so Jim had had no choice but to rent it out to strangers.

What made Deacon angry was that Jim had never taken the time to explain the situation to a scrawny, scared little boy so that he knew he wasn't unwanted or a burden. In Jim's mind, Deacon should have been satisfied that he had a roof over his head and food in his belly. Explanations had been unnecessary.

Greg laughed derisively. "Glow-in-the-dark stars. You were such a nerd."

"I still am. Look, I don't have much time. I wanted to apologize to you. Not for confronting you about the suspension, but for the way I did it. I never should have let myself get so angry."

Greg's eyes, one blue and one brown just like Dani's, briefly widened in surprise. But he shrugged. "Whatever, D. It doesn't matter."

"Yeah, it does. I was tempted to use my fists on you today. I'm sorry for that, too."

A shocked flicker, covered by a sneer and another shrug. "I would have hit you back."

"Which is my point. If you'd hit me back, where do you think we would have ended up?"

"You in the hospital," Greg said cockily. "I would have handed you your ass."

Deacon shook his head. "Not now," he said seriously. "Maybe in a year or two when you're fully grown. Right now I'm bigger than you are and my fists are bigger than yours and I've been trained in how to use them. I would have done more damage to you than you could have done to me. That would have been wrong. And I never would have been able to take it back."

"You want me to say I'm sorry, too, for yelling at you? Fuck that."

Deacon winced. "Yelling is a shitty way for us to start off together. Plus, it's a waste of energy on my end when you can just turn off the hearing aids and let me tire myself out."

Greg grinned. "I thought your veins were going to pop right out of your neck."

Deacon's chuckle was rueful. "So did I." He sobered. "We upset Aunt Tammy."

Greg's grin disappeared like mist, his expression going as stony as Jim's had been.

Deacon sighed. *I should have never agreed to let Jim raise you,* he wanted to say, but he didn't. Greg had enough issues with respect without Deacon giving him additional ammunition against their uncle. Jim had allowed Tammy to take Greg in and raise him as her own. He'd made sure Greg was fed and clothed and schooled, that he'd had braces and hearing aids. . . .

The man deserved some respect for that if nothing else.

Deacon wanted to believe that he could have been a better guardian for Greg. He might be now, but as an eighteen-year-old with an infant? It wasn't going to happen. He'd made an attempt to take custody, but Jim had told him in no uncertain terms that he'd squash Deacon in court. *Like a bug* had been his exact phrasing.

"I didn't mean to make her upset," Greg said.

"I know," Deacon murmured, feeling a little hope for the boy. "Did you tell Tammy that?"

Again the sneer. "No. Why should I?"

"Because she loves you and always has. Because you don't have to be a tough guy around her. Because it's the right thing to do. Why did you get into this fight at school, Greg?"

Greg rolled his eyes. "*Now* you ask me?"

"Yeah, because it occurred to me as I was driving away that I hadn't. I just yelled. So why?"

Greg looked away again. "They had it coming. Damn bullies pissed me off."

Deacon frowned. "They bullied you?"

Greg's chin went up, and he visibly braced himself before meeting Deacon's eyes. "Yes."

There was something there, Deacon thought, troubled. His brother was clearly lying. "Why didn't you tell a teacher? Why take it into your own hands?"

"Like the teachers would do jack shit," Greg muttered. "I can take care of myself."

"And that worked out well," Deacon said mildly. "I'll pick you up tomorrow for your appointment with Ms. Pohl. Be ready. I have to go now. You should use tomorrow to start packing your things. Saturday is moving day." He went to the door, stopped with his hand on the knob, then turned to meet Greg's eyes again. "I wouldn't have hit you today. I won't hit you in the future. You have my word. I want you to know that you're safe with me."

Greg unexpectedly launched himself off the bed and walked over to the window, looking out much as Deacon had done. "Fine," he said, arms crossed tightly over his chest.

Deacon felt a spurt of fear. "Greg, what's going on here? Is somebody hitting you?"

"No. I'm fine. You don't have to worry about me. Thanks for the Coneys." Greg pulled his hearing aids out and tossed them on the bed. "I'm tired. I'll see you tomorrow."

Deacon couldn't let it go. He crossed the room to stand beside his brother, so that they could see each other's reflection in the window. "Does Jim hit you?" he asked, enunciating the words so that Greg could read his lips.

Greg's mouth fell open in shock. "No. Where'd you pull that from?"

From too long on the job, Deacon thought. Greg's surprise seemed genuine. Whatever was happening, it wasn't happening here. "Okay. I'll see you tomorrow." He let himself out with a quiet good night to Jim, who grunted in response, then waved to the two old ladies who lived across the street when they peeked at him through their curtains.

Sentries, he thought, and once again he wished someone had been there for Arianna tonight.

Someone had been, though. *Faith Corcoran.* Deacon started his SUV, his mind conjuring a picture of her face. Her troubled green eyes. The hands she'd folded neatly in her lap to hide their tremble when she'd dropped that little bomb. *I stalked him first.*

What the hell had she meant by that? He was going to find out.

Quickly, he checked his phone to see if anything had changed in the time he'd been in Tammy's house with Greg. Nothing much. Tanaka was still processing and Adam was still with Sheriff Palmer, who'd brought in a canine search team. Still no trace of Corinne Longstreet.

He saved the e-mail from Dani, with "Your witness" written in the subject line, for last. Expecting a summary of Faith's injuries, he was surprised to find a set of links to a victim message board. He glanced at the clock on his dash. He'd already used most of the time Dani had given him. He should go back to the hospital. But he was too curious about the links to put his phone down now. He'd read for just a minute. Then he'd go back.

Eastern Kentucky
Monday, November 3, 11:10 p.m.

The buzzing of his phone interrupted his rhythm, making the shovelful of dirt he'd thrown over his shoulder fall short of the pile. It was a notification from his tracking app. Faith's red Jeep was on the move. Away from the house. Back toward the city. At least something was going right tonight.

It was time to deal with the woman, once and for all. Before she went into the house and ruined everything.

Hurry and finish this job. He had to get back to the city, but first he needed to dispose of his cargo. The hole wasn't quite as large as he'd wanted it to be, but it would have to do.

He found a wheelbarrow propped up against the cabin and pushed it to the van. He dragged the power tech's body out first, then used the wheelbarrow to dump the man's body into the hole.

Excellent. Plenty of room left for both the locksmith and the stew-making trespasser.

He made quick work of it, dumping them in, then filling the hole in with the dirt he'd removed. The bodies were hidden beneath eight inches of earth, enough to keep the smell contained and the scavenger animals away. Especially after he replaced the floorboards.

Once he'd done so, he walked across the floor several times, making sure it was even and there was no echo of his footsteps in empty space. He still needed to remove the extra fill dirt, but he could do that once he'd taken care of Roza and Corinne. *And Faith,* he thought with a frown. He'd be back soon enough and he'd clean up the cabin then. Better yet, he'd make that Roza's first task when she finally woke up.

Now to deal with Corinne. Behind the cabin were the double doors leading to the root cellar. It wasn't a large space, nowhere tall enough for him to stand upright, but it would do. Corinne Longstreet would be comfortable enough down there until his return. He'd leave Roza in the cabin, properly restrained, of course. He didn't want her to have anything more to do with his captives ever again. He didn't want to have to kill her, too.

Chapter Ten

Cincinnati, Ohio
Monday, November 3, 11:55 p.m.

>>*SuzyQ253: What he did to you was pure evil. Tell somebody. Get help.*

    >>*Jen1394: You don't understand. I can't tell anyone. I can't tell my teacher. She'll call the cops. I sure as fuck can't tell my mother. She'll throw me out on the street. She already did it to my sister. But he's still there. My mom won't make him leave.*

Deacon frowned when the screen disappeared, interrupted by an incoming call. He'd been engrossed in reading the posts from real victims, pouring out their anguish in a forum of their peers. Real victims who'd been counseled by a therapist named Faith.

He backed out of Tammy's driveway and headed toward the city. "Novak."

"It's Bishop. I'm still at King's College. We finally got their video feed. It's way too grainy, but we found where the girls disappeared. It's on the path between the library and the dorms—a section that's not covered by cameras."

"Of course it wasn't. Deliberate sabotage, normal technical issues, or poor planning?"

"Two and three, I think. I talked to a student who's been blogging about the security concerns—trying to get the school to fix the issues. She's posted a list of all the places where the cameras don't pick up as a warning to the other students."

"Or as a how-to for an abductor."

"Exactly. I've got the area cordoned off and uniforms on watch. Tanaka's got all the spotlights over at Corcoran's place, so we'll have to wait till morning to process it. It's been a few days and it's a public area, so I'm not sure what we're going to find in the way of evidence, but we'll look anyway."

"What about their dorm rooms, their friends?"

"I've searched their rooms and have CSU boxing up their belongings to bring in to the lab. So far nobody seems to know Corinne Longstreet very well. She's older than the other students and keeps to herself. According to Arianna's roommate, neither Corinne nor Arianna were party girls. Corinne is ex-Army, did half a tour in Afghanistan, but was medically discharged. I've requested her records, but it doesn't look like a psych discharge. I found bottles of prescription meds and vitamins—enough for a damn pharmacy."

"Painkillers?"

"No. Hold on, I'll read you the list. There's prednisone, Cytoxan, Rituxan, Trexall, Bactrim, and Fosamax. Plus a huge bottle of folic acid and other OTC vitamins. I hope none of this is for a life-threatening condition."

"Text me the drug names and I'll ask the ER doctor when she's done stitching up Corcoran. She may be able to tell what condition Corinne has. Based on the prednisone alone, it could be an immuno disease or maybe arthritis. Either way, she might not have been strong enough to fight her abductor and escape like Arianna did."

"Or make it as far as Arianna did if they managed to get away together. I thought as much when I saw all the bottles. Kimble says they haven't found any sign of her though."

"What about Arianna? What did her roommate tell you?"

"The roommate is Lauren Goodwin. She and Arianna are freshmen. Lauren said that Arianna and Corinne met in an art class and became BFFs right away. Lauren figured Arianna had gone away with Corinne for the weekend when she didn't come back on Friday night. She didn't get worried until this evening when Arianna still wasn't back.

Lauren's family is also Arianna's foster family, and they've been called to the hospital. Corinne doesn't have any family listed on her university records. I'm hoping her Army records will be more complete. So far that's all I've got. How's our Good Sam?"

"Not what I expected," Deacon said carefully. "Her stalker's name is Peter Combs. In the last year, she's filed thirty complaints against him. I've requested them from Miami PD, but so far, nada. He hated her enough to try to kill her at least twice."

Bishop gave a low whistle. "Shit. Why?"

Because I stalked him first. "I was just getting to that when the doctor came in to stitch her up. But it doesn't seem that she offered Combs or any other offender therapy because she wanted to or believed in them. She says she did it because the victims wouldn't get therapy outside of a court-mandated order."

"I guess that makes some sense in a twisted-logic kind of way, but it's still her word."

He could hear the warning in Bishop's voice. "I know. And her stalker might be in Miami and have nothing to do with Arianna and Corinne, but something tells me they're all connected."

"Your famous gut?" she asked, amused but not scoffing. Novak's gut had more than proven itself in the month they'd been partners. His sense about people was rarely wrong.

"Something like that. Where are you going now?"

"Back to the lab to go through the boxes we took from the dorm rooms, to see if I can find anything to indicate whether these women had boyfriends or planned to meet up with someone. You?"

"When the doc's done stitching up Corcoran, I'll take her to her hotel. I'll have a squad car sit out front, just in case my gut is lying to me, but I don't think she's directly involved. Then I'm going back to the house. Tanaka's had six hours. I want to see what he's found." His phone vibrated. "Hold on. I have a text. I have to find somewhere to pull over."

"I just got a text, too. Is yours from Adam?"

He glanced at his phone long enough to check. "Yeah. You read it," he said, glad that his cousin had texted instead of calling. He wasn't ready to deal with Adam directly. Not yet.

"Nothing on Longstreet, but they did find the road that the abductor used to get away. Dirt road, hidden by brush. Connects to Kellogg Avenue, down by the river."

"Which means he could be anywhere," Deacon said. "Where are the traffic cameras?"

"On that stretch of US 52, there's a gas station near the highway entrance."

"It won't matter until we have a vehicle make and model, but I want to be ready. Hopefully, when Arianna wakes up, she can give us a description of her abductor and his ride."

"Have they checked river access points?" Bishop asked. "As your Good Sam pointed out, he got away with three victims—the power guy, Corinne, and potentially the lock-smith, if he was there. There's a good chance he dumped the bodies in the river. Wait, I have another text," she said, then quietly cursed. "The locksmith was definitely there. Adam just found his car."

"Hell. I'll talk to the locksmith's family on my way back to the O'Bannion house."

"What about a BOLO on Corcoran's stalker?" Bishop asked.

"I posted one already. I haven't talked to any actual MPD detectives. I left a message with their desk for who-ever worked Faith's case to call me."

A beat of silence. "Didn't *Faith* tell you who worked her case?"

Deacon shoved back the instant rise of annoyance. In Bishop's place, he would have asked the same question.

He realized that even though it had only been a few short hours, he no longer thought of Faith Corcoran as a suspect or even a witness. He thought of her as his to protect.

And that was not okay. "No, she didn't. Not yet. When I get the police reports I requested, I'll forward them to you. Call me when you know more."

Eastern Kentucky
Tuesday, November 4, 12:10 a.m.

Please let him be gone. Corinne ached. Every bone, every joint, every inch of her body simply ached. Her shoulders and arms had already hurt from trying to cut the damn rope, but then he'd dragged her out of the van and into that wheelbarrow like she was a sack of potatoes. It had been all she could do not to make a single sound. Not a wince.

She had clenched her teeth against the pain, hoping it was too dark for him to notice. Hoping he'd be in too much of a hurry to see that her ropes were frayed from her attempts to cut them or that the duct tape wasn't on her face exactly as he'd first placed it, because she'd flung it back over her eyes with a quick jerk of her neck that left her feeling like an eighty-five-year-old with whiplash.

But when he'd dumped her out of the wheelbarrow and down a short flight of steps . . . Oh God, that had hurt more than anything. Still, she'd swallowed the cry of fear. Of pain. Most of it, anyway. A little whimper had escaped and she'd prayed he hadn't heard.

Luckily, she'd landed on her face or he would have seen the tears she couldn't control. Within a minute he was gone and she could let the moan out.

It was really cold. She didn't have a coat, but at least she still had her shoes and the sweater she'd been wearing the night she'd been taken. It was bulky and warm—with sleeves loose-fitting enough to hide the penknife she'd taken from the old man's pocket.

The dead old man. *Don't think about him. Not yet. Not till you get out of here.*

She made herself go quiet and listened. Really listened. She could hear nothing. Had heard nothing since he'd driven away . . . how long ago now? Maybe ten minutes, maybe an hour. It was hard to tell. Maybe he was trying to trick her.

But she didn't think so. Besides, if she lay here and did nothing, she'd freeze to death.

Rolling to sit up, Corinne jiggled her arm until the knife slid from her sleeve. All it would take was one good cut. She gritted her teeth, visualized the outcome, and managed one more jab with the knife. And then she was free. *Free.*

Fingers trembling, she peeled the tape from her eyes and brushed the dirt from her face. At the top of the stairs she could make out two doors, sitting at a slant.

Storm cellar, she thought, scenes from Auntie Em's house in *The Wizard of Oz* rolling through her mind. She was in a storm cellar.

Where is the girl? He must have put her elsewhere, because she wasn't here.

A hard shiver shook her body, making her teeth chatter. She shook her arms and rubbed her hands together to get her blood moving. The joints in her fingers were stiff, partly because of the cold, partly because she'd been tied for so long, and partly because of the illness she'd just gotten under control. How many doses of her meds had she missed? How long would it take to reverse the damage this time?

Goddamn asshole. He had to be coming back soon. He couldn't leave her like this for too long and expect to find her alive when he got back. *So move your ass, Corinne.*

She felt for the little knife and grimaced as her now-burning fingers plucked it from the cold dirt. She bent at the waist and began working on the ropes that bound her ankles. She managed about thirty seconds of sawing before looking up to the doors at the top of the stairs, remembering the sound of metal clanging after he'd slammed them closed.

A chain. Sonofabitch had locked her in. "How the hell am I gonna get out of here?" she whispered to the dark, defeated. *I'm going to die here.*

No. You are not *going to die here.* She hadn't survived a war zone in Afghanistan only to come home and die in a dirty storm cellar. *A little at a time, Corinne. You can eat an elephant one bite at a time.* It had become her life's mantra after she'd woken up in the Army infirmary, a shadow of the woman she'd once been. *Do it for the little girl. Do it for Arianna.*

Cincinnati, Ohio
Tuesday, November 4, 12:10 a.m.

Deacon pulled into the ER parking lot, replied to Adam's texts, then went back to reading the remaining post from the victims' forum.

>>*SuzyQ253: Ask for Faith. She really cares and helped a lot.*

>>*Jen1394: And now you're all fixed. :P Yeah, right. What BS.*

>>*SuzyQ253: I'm not fixed. But I'm not broken anymore, either.*

That Faith cared about the victims was clear. *Because I stalked him first.* Deacon had begun to wonder what she had been willing to do to help these young women.

He'd crossed the parking lot when he heard Dani calling his name. She was pacing outside the ER entrance wearing only her lab coat, hugging herself against the cold.

"What are you doing out here? Where is your coat?" he demanded.

"Inside. I'm waiting for an incoming GSW. Faith is downstairs in the room where I left her. Did you get the link I sent you?"

He nodded. "Yeah, I did. Did you tell her what you'd found?"

"I did. I also told her that you were a good man. Don't make me a liar, okay?"

Deacon dropped a kiss on her cheek. "I won't."

Dani closed her eyes, leaning in to him until she was tucked under his chin. "I'm so glad you came home," she whispered. "I've missed you so much. Christmas was never enough."

His heart squeezed with both love and guilt. He'd left her to shoulder far too much responsibility. "Me, too, kid." His phone buzzed. Bishop had texted Corinne's meds. He showed Dani the screen. "Do you know what condition these drugs might treat?"

She scanned the list, then her eyes flicked back up to his. "These were prescribed to the victim that Faith Corcoran found?"

"No, to her friend, who's still missing. What are we dealing with?"

"Definitely a condition of the immune system. Let me check my pharmacopeia app. Ah. Yes, I was right. She could have RA or Wegener's."

"Rheumatoid arthritis I know. What's Wegener's?"

"Wegener's granulomatosis. Usually affects the kidneys or liver or upper respiratory. It can cause restricted blood flow or inflammation that can destroy the organs. Or both."

"Fatal? Infectious?"

"Infectious, no. Fatal, yes, if untreated. Usually renal failure."

"How long can she be off her meds?"

"Depends on how controlled her disease has been. With

all those drugs? I'd say she's not in remission yet, so not long. She'll start to have joint aches and trouble breathing. But if the victim you guys brought in earlier is any indication, her current situation is a greater risk than her disease. Either way, you're working against the clock."

"That's what I needed to know." He dropped another kiss on her cheek. "Thanks, kid. I'll see you tomorrow morning. Not sure when I'll be back tonight."

"Me either."

"Why are you still here? Can't you go home now?"

"The incoming GSW is deaf."

And Dani signed fluently. She and Deacon had both taken classes when Greg was a little boy, but Dani had stayed close to home with Greg when Deacon joined the FBI. Without constant practice, Deacon had forgotten most of what he knew. Luckily, Greg was skilled at speechreading and voicing, but Deacon's project after finishing the house was to retrain himself to sign.

"How bad is it?" he asked.

"They shot him," Dani snapped, exasperated. "That's bad enough. When are the cops going to get trained to recognize disabilities? Here they come now, so you need to go. Oh," she called over her shoulder. "Knock before you go into the office. I left Faith scrubs to change into."

He watched Dani spring into action, impressed and proud of the doctor she'd become, before heading down to the little exam room where Faith Corcoran waited.

Changing her clothes.

Deacon blinked hard to clear the sudden barrage of inappropriate images from his mind. He hit a few buttons on his phone, bringing up the photo of Arianna, beaten and bloody. It was more than the jolt he needed to focus. It had affected Faith as well.

This was the photo that had convinced Faith to spill her secret.

Because I stalked him first. This should be interesting.

Cincinnati, Ohio
Tuesday, November 4, 12:25 a.m.

Deacon's heart squeezed painfully as soon as he saw Faith's tear-streaked face. *She's still beautiful,* he thought. Perhaps even more so since he'd read those heartfelt posts by her former clients. He had to fight the urge to stroke her hair, to give her comfort.

I'm in trouble here. I should have handed her off to Bishop. But he didn't want to. He wanted her story. He needed to understand why a sex offender had hated her so passionately.

"I'm ready to go to the precinct," she said. "Or your field office. Doesn't matter to me."

His gut also told him that he'd get more out of her in a less stressful environment. Her distrust of cops certainly qualified as stressful. And . . . he wanted her to himself for just a little while. "We can stay here if you'd like. You're not a suspect."

"Yet." She waited for him to sit. "I liked being a therapist. I made a difference."

It was an odd segue, he thought. "Then quit the bank and go back to being a therapist."

"I might. Later. Of course, that will ultimately depend on you."

"How so?" But he thought he might know. "What did you do, Faith?"

"What I thought was right." She met his eyes, hers filled with a fierce resolve. "I couldn't stomach the offenders. Couldn't stomach their excuses when they got caught. 'She came on to me. She's a little slut.' One of the 'little sluts' was four years old, Deacon. *Four.*"

Deacon. Not Agent Novak. His pulse kicked up. "I know. I've arrested some of the bastards. Unfortunately, there are a lot more out there."

"The ones you arrested probably didn't serve much time, and many went right back to abusing kids. They just got smarter about how they did it, which made it harder for the cops to catch them the second time around." She drew a deep breath. "So I helped the process along. The only way I could make a bad situation remotely right."

"What did you do, Faith?" he asked again, this time in a murmur.

"I told you. I stalked them. Kept a camera with a zoom lens in my car at all times. Took photos when they went where they weren't supposed to, like the homes of children with whom they had court-supervised visitation only. Or the homes of children belonging to their newest girlfriends. Or when they hung out near playgrounds with a hungry look on their faces when they were supposed to stay a thousand feet away from a school."

"What did you do with the photos?"

"Gave 'em to a cop," she said with grim satisfaction.

"Your ex-husband?" He didn't want to think of her with her ex. He didn't want to think of her with any other man. He shouldn't think of her at all. But he did. How could he not? *Careful, Novak. Be very careful here.*

"No," she said on a soft exhale, as if there were a whole lot of other words she'd chosen not to say. "I knew a detective in Sex Crimes named Deb. I became her confidential informant."

He held her gaze for a long moment as something settled within him. *This* made sense. *This* was the woman who'd scaled a rocky embankment in bare feet to save a girl she didn't know. This was the woman who'd stood watch over Arianna Escobar, armed and ready to defend her.

"And if you'd been exposed?" he asked.

"Hard to say. It's a gray area, to say the least. Some people might think that was my responsibility—to protect the victims—but the reality is that the offenders were my clients, too. Most of them paid for their own therapy, so in invading their privacy, I broke procedure. At the very least, I'd have lost the trust of the agency I worked for, which would have rendered me useless in helping victims or putting reoffenders away. And I probably would have lost my job. The evidence I provided as a CI might have been deemed inadmissible in court, weakening the state's case. At worst, I'd have lost my license to practice entirely. But I never got caught." The look she gave him spoke clearly. *Unless you turn me in.*

Not going to happen was his knee-jerk response. But he didn't say it. Couldn't promise it until he knew all the facts. "Didn't anyone suspect?" *Didn't your ex-husband know?*

"No. I watched the offenders assigned to other therapists as well. Deb and I managed to spread it out. We made it work."

"For how long?"

"For two years. Until Combs."

"Did your husband know?"

Hurt flickered in her eyes. "No. He never suspected a thing."

Deacon left it alone. For now. "What happened with Combs?"

"He'd molested his twelve-year-old stepdaughter, who just 'wouldn't snap out of it,' according to her mother. Sometimes I wanted to hurt the mothers worse than the offenders. They offered their children up like sacrifices, just to get a man." She shook her head. "Anyway, his stepdaughter wasn't sleeping, afraid he'd come to her room again in the night. She waited until Combs and her mother went to work, then went to a friend's house to sleep. Combs followed her one morning, saw her friend as fresh game. He waited until the friend came home from school and his stepdaughter left."

Deacon hated that he knew what was coming. "He molested the friend, too."

"Yes. The friend refused to tell anyone, but I had to do something. I tried all afternoon to call the friend's mother but didn't reach her. My last session was with Combs himself, so I thought both girls were safe. If he was with me, he couldn't be with them, right?"

"He didn't show."

"No. And I *knew*."

"He was molesting the friend when he was supposed to report for a session with you? Doesn't seem smart to take such a chance. Missing his session was a violation of his probation."

"You'd think these guys would make every effort to show up for that one hour a week with their therapist, but so many don't. They believe they can lie their way out of any 'mistake.' It's pathological. They got away with rape, after all. Surely they can get away with missing a little old appointment, and who knows what they're doing during that hour? In Combs's case, though, I think he simply lost track of time. The young girl he'd molested told the police that at one point he looked at his watch and cursed that now he'd be late 'for the bitch.' I think part of his thrill was going to be coming to see me for a session having just raped a child."

"I wish that surprised me, but I've seen similar behavior myself. They get a rush from the crime, but pulling one over on the cops makes it that much sweeter. So what happened next?"

"I drove to the friend's house. Combs's car was in the driveway. He was hurting her, and . . . I couldn't let him do it. Deb had made me promise not to enter any of the houses, to let the cops handle it. But that day, something snapped. I drove up to the house to stop him, but then Combs came out, casually adjusting his tie, like he hadn't just been raping a twelve-year-old."

Deacon's jaw tightened, his eyes dropping to glance at the scar on her throat. "He saw you."

"No. I had some sense of self-preservation, I guess, because I hid behind my car and took a picture of him with my phone. I sent the photo to Deb, who told me that the cops were on their way and for me to go. She didn't want me to get hurt, physically or professionally."

Again he glanced at the scar on her throat. "She was right."

"Yes, she was. I went straight back to my office and called Combs's probation officer. Reported him as having missed his session. That was grounds for dismissal from the program, which would have violated the terms of his probation and sent him to jail. The PO called Combs, and within an hour, Combs showed up at our office with an excuse—he'd had to change a flat and had gone home to shower and change, but now he was ready for his session."

"He washed away the evidence," Deacon said grimly.

"Exactly. I told him to reschedule and figured the police would catch up to him. Deb sent a unit to his house, but his wife called to warn him to hide. The next day he showed up in my office with a knife, put it to my throat, and dragged me away. He blamed me for reporting him to his PO. He was arrested by Miami PD, went to trial, and was sentenced."

There were a whole host of scenes missing here, but he'd let her tell the story her way for now. "What was his sentence?" he asked, because that was where she'd led him.

"Ten years. He served three."

Three of ten? "It's actually more than most judges would give. I know that doesn't help."

"No, it doesn't, because the ten years weren't for what Combs did to us," she said bitterly. "He got three years for me and only two years each for the twelve-year-olds. The ten years was a separate sentence for the arson. All sentences to be served concurrently."

Deacon frowned. "Arson? What arson?"

"He set a fire in one of the restrooms in our office to create a distraction. Everyone evacuated through the front while he dragged me out the back." She closed her eyes. "I sprayed his face with pepper spray. His hand jerked, and he cut me."

"He could have killed you," Deacon said, relieved when his voice didn't shake.

"He planned to after he was done with me. While he was dragging me out, he told me all the things he'd do. I knew that if I let him put me in his car, I'd end up in a shallow grave somewhere and my father would never know what had happened to me. So I did what I had to do."

Deacon had pulled enough bodies from shallow graves to visualize it all too well. "And then?"

"He was shoving me in his trunk when some firefighters saw him. At least the pepper spray had slowed him down enough that they could overpower him. One of the firefighters held him down while the other did first aid on me. They got me to the hospital in time, but it was close."

Another quarter inch to the right would have sliced her carotid, and no amount of first aid would have stopped the bleeding in time. *She would have died. I would have lost her before I ever found her.* The thought left him shocked and shaken.

Mentally, he backed away. It didn't matter how pretty she was or how valiant. She was a witness. Protecting her was not his job.

Finding Corinne was his job. Bringing Arianna's assailant to justice was his job. *So focus on Combs. On whether or not the bastard came here to play his sick games. If not, move on and find out who's responsible for whatever happened in that basement and leave Combs to Miami PD.*

Drawing on every ounce of discipline he possessed, he pressed on. "So Combs went away for three years," he said tersely, "after which he stalked and tried to kill you. Is that correct?"

She stiffened. "Yes, Agent Novak. That is correct."

Deacon hesitated. "Faith . . . You think I don't care about

what you went through, but you're wrong. If I let go with what I'm feeling right now, I'd be stealing time and energy that belong to Corinne and Arianna. For now, know that I understand that you have just relived what I can only hope was the worst day of your life. Know that I appreciate it and I won't abuse your trust."

Her eyes held his as the rigid line of her spine relaxed. "Thank you. I needed to hear that."

"Now, after he shot your boss, he ran you off a bridge. That happened when?"

"October third for Gordon's murder and four days later for the bridge."

Combs had made two attempts on her life less than a week *after* her grandmother's death—after Faith was revealed to be the heir. Deacon wondered if the two attempts were in some way connected to her grandmother's passing. And if so, how?

She stilled. "It's the house, isn't it? I don't know why I didn't put it together before. Combs stepped up the attacks after I inherited the house. He wanted me dead because he didn't want me to take it. Why didn't I see this?"

Deacon wrapped his hand around her upper arm, squeezing gently but firmly. "Faith. I can't have you falling apart on me. Breathe."

"You're right. I'm sorry. I'm all right now."

He let her go, watching her intently. Every time he mentioned the house, she panicked. He needed to know why, but she was fragile at the moment, and he needed information on Combs more than he needed information on the house.

"Was there any evidence to link Combs to these two attacks against you?" he asked.

"No. But no one else hated me that much. And it wasn't two. It was four."

Deacon leaned back in his chair, suddenly drained. "Hell, Faith. He made four attempts on your life? In a single month?"

"Yes," she said calmly. Evenly. "He tried to come into my apartment through the window when I was asleep. That was on October fourteenth, a week after the bridge. The final time was this past Thursday night, when he set my apartment complex on fire."

He'd stopped being surprised. "Like he'd done to your office. Was anyone hurt?"

"No, but fifteen families lost everything they owned."

"Fifteen families including you?"

"I didn't have much to lose. I wasn't even in my apartment at the time. I didn't see it on the news until Friday morning. That's when I hurried through the rest of my new-identity to-do list. I was going to leave Saturday morning. I didn't know where I was going. I didn't care. Enough people had suffered because they'd had the misfortune to be associated with me."

"Okay." He let out a breath, giving himself time to parse through everything she'd told him, one statement rising above the others. "Where were you, if you weren't in your apartment?"

Not with a boyfriend. Don't let her say she was with her boyfriend. The image of her in another man's arms . . . in another man's bed . . .

But then he realized Faith Corcoran was one of the most alone people he'd ever met. It was unlikely she was with a boyfriend through any of this.

"I was staying in a hotel. With good security."

A few hours ago he might have been suspicious that she'd stayed in a hotel the one night her apartment had been torched. Now he simply assumed there would be a good reason. "Why?"

"Because of attempt number three. I was too afraid to stay in my apartment after he broke in, but I wasn't ready to leave the city yet. I had a few more things on my to-do list, like I said. I didn't want to leave, only to have him follow me and start the whole nightmare again."

"What happened the night he tried to enter your apartment?"

"It was three a.m., and I was asleep. I heard a noise and saw a big, bulky shadow coming through the window. I grabbed my gun from under my pillow and fired." She made a disgusted face. "But I didn't have my glasses on or my contacts in, and I missed him. I thought I hit his arm, but there was no sign of any blood when the police came to file the report. There was no sign of the bullet that I'd fired. There wasn't even a sign that he'd been there."

"There was no sign of a break-in?"

Her expression hardened. "Yes, there was, but the cop who came said that I couldn't prove it had been done that night. It could have happened years before. I heard him tell his partner that I was the whack job who thought everyone was out to get me. Humor me and I'd go away."

Deacon's cold blood began to boil. "Because of the thirty complaints you'd filed."

"Exactly. We have a problem in this country when victims of stalking are ridiculed for making reports and denied justice when they don't. It's a vicious catch-22."

"I know." He was learning more and more about why she didn't like cops.

Needing to give himself a moment to bury his rage, Deacon said nothing more about Combs or cops, instead leaning forward to examine Faith's eyes. They were clear now, filled with righteous indignation but free of panic. Deep forest green, unbroken by any other color save the black of her pupils. No sign of contact lenses.

"You should have said you needed your glasses, Faith," he murmured. "I would have had one of the deputies get them from your Jeep."

He'd deliberately encroached on her space, but she didn't back away. Instead, she remained seated, the thrumming pulse in her throat the only sign she was affected by his lack of distance.

"I don't wear glasses or contacts anymore. The day after the break-in, I scheduled Lasik. The next time he comes for me in the night, I'll be ready. I won't miss again."

Respect swelled and with it a rush of desire that stole his breath. "Good," he said, then managed to ease himself back into his chair, uncomfortable as hell and not giving a damn. The mental image of Faith lowering her gun, the satisfaction on her face after ridding the world of a filthy predator ... That was hotter than hell.

And if he let himself, he could imagine a whole helluva lot hotter. *If you* let *yourself?* Who was he kidding? His imagination had already conjured an entire collection of images that would make it very embarrassing were he to need to stand up anytime soon.

Images that, until he closed this case, were completely inappropriate.

She was watching him warily. "Good? That's all? No

'don't take the law into your own hands'? No 'violence isn't the answer'? No 'let the cops do their jobs'?"

"No," he said. "You do whatever it takes to stay alive. And if you need help, call me. How well do you shoot?"

Pride glinted in her eyes. "I hit where I aim. Always."

"Good," he said again, still hard as a rock. *Focus, Novak. The clock's ticking. Corinne is still out there.* The young woman's dire situation was the cold bucket of reality he'd needed.

This . . . infatuation was unacceptable. It was a distraction he could not afford. It wasn't Faith's fault. It was his. All his. So he'd do now what he should have done back at her grandmother's house. He'd hand her over to Bishop.

He stood up while he could, tugging his coat around him. "I need to get back to the precinct now. I'll drop you off at your hotel. Let you get some sleep."

"Thank you. Did I give you anything useful?"

"I don't know. If Combs followed you here, you've given me a helluva lot. If it's someone else, you've given me enough to get started." He gave a nonchalant half shrug. "At least I can cross you off my list." He held the door open for her, drawing a breath as she passed. Allowing himself to tuck away the memory of the scent of her hair, because it would be the last time he let himself get this close to her. He pulled the door closed behind them, forced his voice to be impersonal. Brusque, even. "I'll need the name of the MPD detective who worked your case."

She abruptly stopped in the middle of the hall. "Oh, *shit*. Detective Vega."

"Vega worked your case?"

"No. She worked Gordon's murder. But she was also the only one who listened when I realized that I was the target and not Gordon. I need to use your phone, like, now."

He fell back into his slightly mocking tone, but it was far more difficult than it had ever been before. "Why do you need to talk to her, like, now?"

Her brows crunched in confusion as she searched his face, no doubt looking for the reason for his sudden mood change. "Because she called my stepmother this afternoon looking for me."

He tilted his head. "And you're just remembering this *now*?"

Her cheeks darkened. "I've been a little distracted," she said, clearly irritated.

Good. She was too tempting when she trusted him. Hell, she was tempting when irritated, too, and that made *him* irritated. He pulled his phone from his pocket. "What's the number?"

"I don't know. I was going to search for Miami PD's number online."

"No need. I called their main desk earlier, so it's in my call log." He placed the call, then put it on speaker, holding it between them. "I need to hear what she has to say."

"Fine. She's not going to be there anyway. It's too late," Faith said as the phone rang.

"Leave her a message then. Give her my cell number."

Faith rolled her eyes. "I could give her my own number if you'd give me back my ph—"

"Miami PD," the operator said. "How can I direct your call?"

Giving Deacon an annoyed look, Faith leaned closer to his phone. "The Homicide Division, please. Detective Vega." Faith sighed when she got Vega's voicemail. "Hi, this is Faith Frye. If you're calling about the fire, I'm all right and you don't need to call back. If you're calling because you found Combs or know where he is, please call me back at this number and not at my father's house." She looked up at Deacon. "Tell her your number."

Deacon started to recite his own number, then remembered the resolution he'd so quickly forgotten and gave Bishop's number instead.

And that was that. He walked her to his SUV and touched her only long enough to help her into the seat. "I'll return your jacket tomorrow," she said quietly.

"It's okay. I have others."

His step heavy, he walked around the SUV and climbed behind the wheel. He sat there a moment, the silence between them thick and heavy. She wasn't stupid. She'd detected the change in his demeanor.

But she said nothing, looking straight ahead. "I'm ready when you are, Agent Novak."

He started the engine without a word, welcoming the sudden buzzing of his phone. "Novak," he answered.

"It's Isenberg. I just got a call from a Detective Vega."

Deacon blinked. "That was fast. Dr. Corcoran just called her."

Beside him, Faith turned to stare, questions in her eyes.

"She was returning *your* call, Novak," Isenberg said. "You called the Miami desk looking for anyone who'd worked Faith Frye's stalking complaints. She's been looking for Corcoran all day, although she still knows her as Frye. I told her to call back, that you could be here in ten minutes. She wanted you to bring Dr. Corcoran with you."

"I'm on my way." He hung up, then turned to Faith. "Slight change of plans."

Chapter Eleven

Corinne couldn't move. *So tired.* She'd finally freed herself from the ropes that had bound her ankles. *Just want to sleep. Just a little while.*

But she knew the temperature had continued to drop despite the fact that she was covered in sweat. If she fell asleep, she'd die. Because even if the cold didn't kill her, *he* would. Sleeping would waste valuable time she should use to get away.

She and the girl. There was no way she was leaving without the girl. Assuming he hadn't taken her with him. *And assuming that she's still alive.*

Corinne crawled up the stairs, giving one of the doors an experimental shove. It moved relatively easily—until the chain caught. So at least it wasn't pinned shut with a block of wood. *Better than I hoped. Still sucks.*

She pushed the door again, peeking through the opening, which was too small for anyone to slip through. She could see the chain and the handle on the other door, both rusted metal. She reached through and gave the chain a yank. *Sturdy, dammit.*

But the tug had brought the lock itself into view. It was a simple little lock that took a key. The kind she'd used on her locker back in high school, a million years ago now.

She thought of the old man in the van. His shirt had said Dilman's Lock & Key. He'd probably had very specific tools with him, but all she'd found was his knife. She took it from her pocket, examining it in the thin beam of moonlight that shone through the opening. She let out a careful breath, daring to hope. It was one of those Swiss Army jobs.

"Corinne, your luck might finally be about to change," she murmured, pulling out all the tools. Corkscrew, bottle opener. Good if she wanted to get drunk. But for now, not useful.

She pulled out the scissors, tweezers, and . . . a toothpick. *Yes.*

The toothpick might just work. *I can do this. I have to.*

Cincinnati, Ohio
Tuesday, November 4, 12:55 a.m.

It was like he'd flipped some internal switch, Faith thought, watching Novak sign her in at the Cincinnati PD's front desk. He'd been interested, back at the hospital. When he'd leaned forward to check her eyes for contacts, he'd been close enough . . . to kiss. And that was exactly what she'd considered doing, which had been—and still was—insane. She didn't know him.

But I want to. He'd cared. She'd seen it. He'd cared about the victims. About Arianna and Corinne and about a twelve-year-old victim of child molestation he'd never even met.

And me. He cares about me. About her terror and pain. And he believed her about Combs, about why she'd done what she'd done, which meant even more.

But for a moment he'd more than cared. For that one moment when he'd leaned forward, looked in her eyes . . . he'd wanted. And in that one, ill-timed moment, so had she. She'd wanted to reach out and touch his face. To find out if it was as warm as it looked. If the goatee that framed that mouth was soft or rough.

It had taken every ounce of control she possessed to stay in her chair, to keep her hands folded and on the table. But it looked like she wouldn't have to worry about that from here on out. Novak had decided to back off and that was fine with Faith. Really.

"Why are we here?" she asked, pushing that super-charged memory from her mind.

He glanced up from the ledger in which he was writing her name. "Because my LT said to."

"No, I mean why are we here in Cincinnati PD's head-quarters? You're FBI. Why aren't we in a field office? And why are we meeting your LT? Don't you guys have agents in charge?"

"I'm part of a joint task force," he said lightly, handing her a visitor's badge. "MCES. Major Case Enforcement Squad. I'm the token Fed."

She clipped the badge to the FBI jacket he'd loaned her. "What am I?"

He pointed to her badge. "Visitor." He started walking, clearly expecting her to follow.

She didn't move. "Novak." He kept walking. "Agent Novak? Deacon. *Please*."

He stopped but didn't look back. "Yes, Dr. Corcoran?"

Call me Faith again. Please. "Did I have a choice in coming here tonight?"

His back stiffened, then he turned to meet her eyes. His were serious, all mockery gone. "Yes. Do you want to leave? I'll take you to your hotel."

"No. I want to talk to Vega. I just wanted to be sure I'd be allowed to leave once I have."

He approached her slowly, as if his feet weighed a ton. When his shiny wingtips were less than an inch from her beat-up sneakers, he hunched his broad shoulders, bending his knees until his eyes were level with hers.

"Have you done anything else that I should know about?" he murmured.

For a moment she couldn't breathe. Nor could she look away. He'd flipped the switch again, his expression utterly compelling. Cedar filled her senses as she slowly wagged her head, wondering if the scent came from his coat or his skin. "No."

"Then you should be fine." He straightened, back to being cocky Novak. "I haven't worked for Lieutenant Isen-berg long, but I do know she is a stickler for punctuality. Let's go."

Faith followed him into the elevator. "You don't have to

do that," she said when the doors had closed and they were alone. "Not with me."

He fixed his gaze on the number display. "What don't I have to do, Dr. Corcoran?"

"Act. If you want distance, that's fine." No. No, it wasn't. It really wasn't. "But you don't need this . . . veneer. Not with me."

He tossed her an amused look. "How do you know this is the veneer?"

"Because your sister said that you're a good man, and she had no veneer."

He shrugged dismissively. "Dani sees the good in everyone."

"You say that like it's a bad thing."

"It can be." The doors opened and he gestured her forward. "This is our floor."

He led her to an interview room, where a woman already sat at the table, waiting for them with obvious impatience. She didn't rise when they entered, just pointed to two empty chairs. Faith sat, noting the two-way mirror to her left, returning the woman's assessing stare.

"Dr. Corcoran," Novak said, "this is my boss, Lieutenant Isenberg."

The lieutenant was in her forties. Maybe fifty. Her faded tan was wrinkle free—not a laugh line in sight. Her short, iron gray hair stood on end like she'd shoved her fingers through it.

Just like Novak's did, although Faith hadn't seen him touch it since she'd met him.

Isenberg sat back in her chair. "You're the infamous Dr. Corcoran. You've had a busy day."

"Yeah. I guess I have. Do you know why Vega wants to talk to me, Lieutenant?"

"Yep. She's been calling you all day. What's wrong with your phone?"

Faith sighed. Another cop ignoring her perfectly reasonable question and flinging her own. "Are you asking why didn't I answer her calls?"

"No, I'm asking why they don't show up on your phone to begin with." Isenberg leaned forward, placing a plastic evidence bag on the edge of her desk where Faith could see it. It contained her new prepaid cell. "No calls from Vega in the log. It's not even the same number."

"It's a new phone. I just got it today. That's not a crime," Faith added, pissed off that they'd checked her call log without a warrant. "Nor am I a suspect. Or so I'm told."

"You get a prepaid, untraceable phone," Isenberg said, "on the same day you just happen to discover a woman lying in the road who escaped from the basement of your house, where she'd been tortured. Where her friend—who is still missing—had been shackled to the wall."

Faith beat back the panic that had become a reflexive response to any mention of that damn basement. "Is there a question in there, Lieutenant?"

"Yes. Why the new phone, Doctor?"

"I didn't want anyone to be able to track me. I removed the SIM card from my old one."

"Who does 'anyone' include?" Isenberg asked.

"My stalker, Peter Combs. And the MPD cops. I haven't had the best of relationships with any of them except for Detective Vega. Should we call her?"

"Let's do that." The lieutenant dialed the phone on the table, hitting the speaker button. "It's Isenberg," she said when Vega answered. "With me are Special Agent Novak, FBI, and Faith Corcoran."

"Faith Corcoran?" Vega asked, confusion in her voice. "You mean Frye."

"I'm here, Detective," Faith said. "Alive but far from well."

Vega sighed her relief. "Alive is better than I've been imagining all day. You are a hard woman to track down, Dr. Frye."

At least I did something right, Faith thought. "Why are you calling me?"

"Why are you in Ohio?" Vega asked.

Just answer my goddamned question, Faith wanted to snap, but controlled herself. "Why are you calling me, Vega?" she repeated more forcefully. "What's happened?"

A beat of silence. "Did you try to run away, Faith?"

Faith's shoulders sagged wearily. "Can you blame me?"

"No, I don't suppose I can. I hear you've had an eventful day, so I'll cut to the chase. Your old Prius was in a major accident. It's now a heap of twisted metal."

Faith stared at the speakerphone, trying to make sense

of Vega's words. Why was she telling her this? *It's not even my car anymore and—*

And then she understood. Her breath came out in a shocked rush. "Are you saying it was tampered with?" she whispered, not wanting the answer.

"Unquestionably. Both the brake and steering lines were cut. We need your help."

Faith pressed her fingertips to her temples. *He keeps trying. He won't stop.*

She looked up to see Isenberg watching her, eyes narrowed in speculation.

"What happened? When?" She forced the image of her burned-out apartment building out of her mind as she forced the next question out of her throat. "Was anyone hurt?"

"When did you sell the car, Faith?" Vega asked.

Fury hit her hard, stealing all reason. "Answer my question, dammit!" She started to pound her fist on the table, but Novak caught her arm, his grip gentle but firm.

"Don't hurt yourself," he murmured, then released her. "Detective Vega, was anyone hurt?"

A long, long pause had Faith's gut turning inside out. Finally, Vega sighed. "Yes. The driver was killed. Several more were critically injured, including some children." Another pause, another sigh. "And one of the children died. Later. At the hospital."

The room began to spin, bile rising to burn Faith's throat. "No," she whispered. Hugging herself, she fought the need to rock where she sat. "That can't be true. I tried to make it stop."

"I know you did, Faith," Vega said softly. "I need you to stay calm for me. Strong, okay?"

The tears were coming. She couldn't make them stop. It didn't matter what Isenberg thought. Or even Novak. "How old, Detective?" she asked, her voice hoarse and unfamiliar.

"Faith, you don't need—"

"Goddammit!" Faith shouted. "Don't you *dare* tell me I don't need to know. *How old was the child*, Vega?" She felt a warm palm on her back. Novak. He didn't pat. Didn't rub. Just applied a soft pressure. A human connection. Suddenly overwhelmed, she choked back a sob. "Please. I *do* need to know."

"Tell her, Detective," Novak said quietly.

Vega cleared her throat. "Thirteen. The two children in the backseat received only minor injuries and they'll be fine."

Faith closed her eyes. *They'll be fine? No, they won't. Their mother is dead. They will not be fine. This can't be happening.* But it was. A mother and her child were dead. *Because of me.*

She didn't recognize the keening whimper as her own until Novak began to stroke her hair. Still he said nothing, allowing her to gather her thoughts. But they would not be gathered. She gave in to the need to rock herself, hunching over as the sobs broke free. Still he stroked her hair, silent as she cried. Finally, the wave ebbed and she struggled to breathe.

Novak's hand disappeared and she wanted to beg him to come back, but she did not. Not while Isenberg watched with an eagle eye. A few seconds later, a box of tissues was placed on the table in front of her. She looked up, way up, and found Novak watching her, too. But it was entirely different. Isenberg's gaze was like a hatchet. Novak's was like a blanket.

"It should have been me," she said, and his eyes flashed, blue and brown growing almost black.

"No," he said. "But pull yourself together so that we can make sure no one else is hurt."

She nodded, mopping her face with a tissue. "What do you need from me, Detective Vega?"

"For starters, I need to know when you sold the car and to whom."

"I sold it on Saturday morning to a used-car dealer in Hialeah. Garcia Motors."

"One of the things on your how-to-disappear list?" Novak asked.

Faith nodded miserably. "He'd been following my car. I never dreamed he'd so indiscriminately hurt whoever bought it, but I should have. He'd done it already with the fire."

Isenberg's brows lifted. "What fire?"

Novak answered. "Her stalker, Peter Combs, set fire to her apartment building two days before that. She wasn't home, but a number of families lost everything they owned."

"I had a bad moment this morning," Vega confessed. "I

went to find you, to find out how the victim had ended up with your old car. Then I saw the burned-out building and thought you might have been inside. Your super told me that you weren't, but I looked for you all day."

"I'm sorry," Faith said. "I didn't think that you'd be afraid for me. I should have. I should have thought about all of this. I should have thought that Combs wouldn't simply give up, that he didn't care who got hurt. Why didn't I *think*?"

"You did, but everyone was telling you that you were imagining things," Vega said sharply. "Stow the guilt, Dr. Frye. You shouldn't have thought of it then, but I need you to think now. Why Garcia Motors? I just looked them up. They're tiny. You couldn't have gotten fair market value for the Prius. Why not one of the bigger dealerships?"

"Because I wanted the anonymity, okay?" Faith hated how selfish that sounded. "I only got half of the blue book, but it was worth it to avoid the paperwork." She swallowed hard. "But if I had picked a bigger dealership, they would have done a thorough check and seen that the brake line had been cut. That mother and her son would still be alive." *Hold on.* Faith frowned. Suddenly something didn't seem to fit. "Wait a minute. I sold the Prius on Saturday morning. When did the accident occur?"

"Sunday morning," Vega said.

Faith leaned toward the speakerphone, concentrating. "If he'd cut the brake and steering lines before Saturday morning, wouldn't I have felt some sluggishness or . . . something?"

"Yes," Vega said. "Our lab estimates that the lines were cut Sunday morning, while the victim was at the grocery store. She bought the car Saturday afternoon and drove it enough miles that any damaged lines should have failed before she got home."

"Garcia Motors sure sold it fast," Faith murmured. There was something here. Something important that she was missing.

"Priuses are sought after and yours was well cared for," Vega said. "Plus Garcia bought it off you cheap. He could have sold it at a bargain and still made a profit."

Novak had been listening carefully, his head tilted as he absently stroked his thumb and forefinger down the stark white of his goatee. "How did Combs know where to find

the Prius on Sunday morning, Detective? If he followed
Dr. Corcoran to the used-car lot, he would have known
she'd sold it and he would have sabotaged the Jeep instead.
We wouldn't even be having this conversation, because Dr.
Corcoran would be dead. It doesn't make sense that he'd
sabotage the Prius *after* she'd sold it. What aren't you telling us?"

Faith threw him a grateful glance. He just lifted his eyebrows and shrugged carelessly, as if it was no big deal. But
it was. That was the detail that she'd been unable to grasp.

Vega sighed again. "We found a tracking device tucked
under the front wheel well."

Faith sat back, stunned. "He was tracking me?" She
looked from Novak to Isenberg, both appearing equally
perplexed. "Why would he track my car if he had already
hacked into my phone? He knew where I was going all the
time."

Novak's frown furrowed his brow. "Maybe he didn't
hack your phone after all."

Faith lurched to her feet, walking around the table with
movements jerky from the stiffness in her legs. It hurt to
move, but she could no longer sit still. "But he had to have
access to my calendar. Most of the times he'd just show up, so
he could have followed me then. But not that last time,
when his car was parked next to mine."

"Outside the pharmacy," Novak said, and she nodded.

"I'd had dinner in a restaurant next to the pharmacy. His
girlfriend's doctor had called in a prescription to that *same*
pharmacy *hours earlier*. He *had* to have known ahead of
time."

"You're right," Novak said, giving her a hard nod of approval. "So why plant a tracker?"

"Maybe because you'd become too careful by that point,
Faith," Vega said through the speakerphone. "CSU thinks
he planted it right after the fire in your apartment."

Faith sank into her seat. "Because he knew he hadn't
killed me in the fire. He put the tracker on because he figured I'd come back for the car at some point."

"Why weren't you in your apartment that night?" Isenberg asked.

"I was at a hotel. He'd tried to climb in my bedroom
window two weeks before, and I'd moved to a secure place.

Plus I'd just gotten Lasik on both eyes. I didn't want to be vulnerable."

Isenberg inclined her head. "Reasonable. When did you move your car?"

"Saturday morning. I'd taken a series of cabs from the apartment to my hotel the week before—the morning after he broke in—because I thought he was following my car. I took a cab from my hotel back to the apartment parking lot Saturday morning. The police tape from the fire was gone by then. I just got into the Prius and drove straight to the used-car lot."

"And how did you buy the Jeep?" Isenberg asked.

"Craigslist. I paid cash. They didn't ask any questions." But something still wasn't right. She rubbed at her forehead, trying to work it out. Her gaze landed on the map on the wall, and then she knew. "Your theory that Combs followed me here doesn't hold up logistically. He couldn't have tampered with the Prius on Sunday morning and made it back to my grandmother's house by five o'clock that evening. It's a sixteen-hour trip by car if you don't stop. That means he would have needed to leave Miami before midnight on Saturday."

"How do you know he was in the house at five on Sunday?" Isenberg asked.

"Because I heard a scream." She closed her eyes, remembering it, wishing once again that she'd done something. "I thought I was imagining it, but it had to have been Arianna."

"You said you arrived at five thirty," Novak said, his eyes grown sharp. And perplexed.

"About that, yeah. And he was in Cincinnati on Friday night at eleven, because that's when he abducted Arianna and her friend." She looked over at Novak. "That's thirty-two driving hours over a forty-two-hour time frame. Plus the time to locate the car and do the damage. And sleep somewhere in there. It doesn't look good for your theory."

"Unless he flew," Novak said, his jaw firming.

Faith looked unconvinced. "I suppose he could have."

"You really think Combs is behind your abductions, Agent Novak?" Vega asked doubtfully.

Faith watched Novak exchange a long glance with the lieutenant, who gave him a small nod.

"We don't know," Novak said. "But somebody doesn't want Dr. Corcoran to take possession of that house. It might be Combs, or it might be someone else. If you can locate Combs, we may be able to eliminate him. What have you done to find him?"

"Hell. What haven't I done?" Vega had swung from doubtful to frustrated. "He's gone under. Nobody's seen him or heard from him in weeks. His girlfriend suggested that he'd gone back to his ex, but she and her daughter claim they haven't seen him since his arrest."

"I put a BOLO out for Combs's girlfriend's car," Novak said.

"I know where the girlfriend's car is," Vega said. "Combs doesn't have it."

"How can you be sure he doesn't have access to it?" Isenberg asked.

"Because we have it. I got a warrant for the car after Combs broke into Dr. Frye's bedroom."

Faith stared at the phone. "I didn't know that. I wasn't sure if you even believed me."

"I believed you, but couldn't prove it. Nothing turned up to implicate Combs or point to where he's hiding. However, we did find a half kilo of coke under the seat. I arrested the girlfriend for possession and dealing and impounded the car."

"Will that stick?" Faith asked. "Did the warrant cover the girlfriend?"

"No, and some high-powered attorney will probably get the arrest thrown out, but for now Combs's girlfriend is without wheels. As is Combs."

Novak tilted his head abruptly as if a thought had hit him hard. "Vega, can you send me the ballistics on the shot that killed Faith's old boss?" He gave her his e-mail address. "We recovered a bullet from Faith's house. If the ballistics match, we can tie these crimes together."

A keyboard clacked on Vega's end. "I just sent you guys the whole file."

"Thank you," Isenberg said. "Did Combs always drive his girlfriend's car, Dr. Corcoran?"

"Yes. Except for once. When he tried to run me off the bridge, he was driving a white van. I gave a description to the officer who took my statement. It's in the police report."

"Sending that one to you, too, Novak," Vega said, "along

with the Frye stalker file. Faith, the van you described was white, no windows, had license plates with a sun on them."

"Lots of states have suns on their plates, though," Faith said. "I never saw the state or any of the numbers."

"We might be able to narrow it down after this call," Novak said. "Anything more, Vega?"

"Only that you keep me up to speed with what you find. I have three unsolved homicides hanging on Combs. I'll continue to search for him down here in case he's not involved in your case, and I'll press the girlfriend for his whereabouts."

"We'll keep you up to speed," Novak promised, "if you do the same."

"Then I'll sign off now. Good night, and, Faith, be very careful."

The line went dead. Faith looked Isenberg in the eye. "Am I free to go, Lieutenant?"

"Of course," the lieutenant said mildly. "Did you think yourself a suspect?"

"I wasn't sure."

Isenberg's mouth curved. Not quite a smile, but it did serve to soften her severity. "I'm still not sure either, but I'm willing to give you—and Novak's gut—the benefit of the doubt." She stood. "I'll expedite the ballistics on the bullets pulled at the scene. Novak, narrow down that license plate. And, Dr. Corcoran, don't go out alone. Someone is determined to see you dead."

Cincinnati, Ohio
Tuesday, November 4, 1:10 a.m.

Well, shit. He'd been monitoring the location of Faith's red Jeep as he'd raced back from eastern Kentucky. The Jeep had been stationary for over an hour. Now he knew why.

He glared at the twisted hunk of red metal, still on the flatbed trailer along with the Earl Power and Light truck. And the locksmith's car.

All of which were currently being unloaded into the Cincinnati PD's forensics garage. The cops had Faith. He couldn't be sure why.

But he knew how she felt about cops. So he could count on her refusing to talk to them about anything. *I'm safe. For now.* It was just a matter of time before she went into the house and then . . . Who knew what the bitch would do?

The only action he could reasonably predict was that Faith would return to her hotel at some point. And had she already returned for the evening, she'd come back out again in the morning to go to work. Either way, he'd be waiting.

Cincinnati, Ohio
Tuesday, November 4, 1:25 a.m.

Isenberg had been gone for a full minute, but neither Deacon nor Faith said a word. If he'd had any doubt about her innocence, it was gone now. Her tears hadn't been delicate or pretty. Her grief had been wild and consuming. He'd been unable to stop himself from touching her. Giving her comfort. Even though he'd felt Isenberg's scrutiny the entire time.

Isenberg was no fool. She'd picked up on his attraction to Faith Corcoran. But she'd said nothing, even directing further contact when she might have ordered him to switch places with Bishop, which was what he would have done under the same circumstances.

But she hadn't. So either she trusted him to do the right thing and keep the connection professional, or she was setting him up to take a fall. He doubted the latter. Isenberg seemed too direct to orchestrate something like that. It was possible that she'd set it up as a test, though.

He realized that was probably the smarter thing to do in these circumstances.

"Thank you," Faith murmured, breaking into his thoughts. "You kept me from falling apart."

"Their deaths were not your fault."

"Of course they were. I knew that he knew my car. I should have considered that he'd do something like this. But it's done now, and I can't change what's happened. Only what *will* happen. What can we do to narrow down that license plate?"

We. He was liking the sound of that too much. "I can show you some examples of sun graphics. Use some mild hypnosis to help you remember. You'd have to be open to it, though. It's my soothing voice, which you don't seem to care for."

"I think I was more angry that it worked. You've been trained in hypnosis?"

"Yes. And in facial cues. I don't want you to think I'm using any of it to trap you."

She met his eyes squarely. "I don't think you would. Let's give it a try."

"Give me a few minutes to prepare. Relax."

Her smile was brittle. "Find my happy place?"

"If you can. If you can't, just breathe." He forced his eyes away from her face and down to his tablet, connecting to his e-mail account. True to her word, Vega had already begun to send him e-mail after e-mail with large attachments, each subject line a short description of the incident. He opened the report on the bridge incident and immediately had to fight the need to scowl.

The cops had breathalyzed her. Suggested that the gunshot she'd heard was no more than the van backfiring. Portrayed her as pathetically delusional, possibly mentally ill.

No wonder she hadn't trusted him. But she did now.

Deacon committed the date, her route, and the road conditions to memory, then ran a search on license plates bearing suns. Faith was right—there were a ton of them. "Did the police have you look at any license plates the night on the bridge?" he asked.

"No," she said bitterly. "They didn't seem to take my complaint very seriously."

"But Vega did. And so do I. That'll have to be enough for now."

She drew a breath, shifted her shoulders. "You're right. I'm just agitating myself, and that will block your hypnosis." She opened one eye, peeked at his screen. "I did that same search. I went over each and every license plate a hundred times, but I couldn't remember."

He wasn't surprised that she'd tried. If she'd been even half as tense as she was right now, he wasn't surprised that she'd failed. "We'll try it a different way, together."

She sighed wearily. "You want me to go back to the night of the bridge, don't you?"

"Yes, but first we'll do some breathing. You're still too tense."

He guided her through the breathing exercises that were part of his routine, watched her grow more relaxed. Told her to remember a place where she'd been happy, at peace. And privately wondered which memory she'd chosen. "Where were you going that night, Faith?"

"To my apartment."

Not home. Just her apartment. "Where had you been?"

A sad slump of her shoulders. "The hospital."

He controlled the sudden spear of concern, keeping his voice smooth. "Why?"

"Because of Ivy."

"Who is Ivy?"

"She was one of my clients," she said, her tone still depressed. "She was only thirteen."

Oh no. "Why were you with her?"

Faith's throat worked as she swallowed. "She took every pill in her medicine cabinet. Then she called me to ask for help. But I was in sessions. I let it go to voice mail." Her voice cracked, and so did a piece of Deacon's heart. "I heard her message too late. She died that night." Two tears seeped from beneath her lashes and rolled down her cheeks unchecked.

He wanted to wipe them away, wanted to stroke her hair, but that might break her concentration. "So you left the hospital. Is it day or night?"

"Night. Late. After midnight."

"You're tired," he murmured. "And so sad. Where are you?"

"In my car. Driving. It's hard to see."

"Because it's dark?"

"No. Because it's wet."

"It's raining?" he murmured, knowing otherwise. The report had stated that the night had been clear, the road dry.

"No," she whispered.

"You're crying," he said, and she nodded, a tiny movement. "Where are you now?"

"Still driving." A frown bent her lips as she concentrated.

"Do you see anyone?"

"No. Just me."

Just me. Her aloneness struck him again, hard. "What about the van?"

"It came out of nowhere," she said, her voice tinged with panic.

"It has to be somewhere," he said soothingly. "Think about your rearview mirror."

Another frown, followed by an indrawn breath. "On the shoulder before the bridge. I forgot that before. He was waiting for me."

"So he pulls onto the bridge. How fast is he going?"

"Fast. I was surprised. He came up beside me. I thought he was passing me."

"But he didn't."

"No. He stayed in the left lane. Going the wrong way. I thought it was kids. Stupid kids."

"Can you see in the window?"

"No. The glass was dark. But the window rolled down a little. And there was a gun."

Deacon frowned. That she'd *seen* the gun wasn't in the report. That changed things. "Is it a handgun or a rifle?"

She bit at her lip. "Handgun. I saw the barrel."

"Good." *Very good.* "And then?"

A hard swallow. "He shot at me."

He had to concentrate to keep the rage from his voice. "Did he hit you?"

"No. He missed." Her eyebrows crunched. "He swerved, then he started to come over, wanted to force me over." She was breathing hard now, fresh panic in each word. "I stopped."

"You stopped?"

"Hard. He kept going."

"That was smart, Faith. You're safe now. Not shot. Not hurt. Now look at the van. It's driving away, fast. But for a second you can see, straight ahead. What color is the sun?"

"Red," she said, and went deathly still. "My God," she whispered. "It was red with stripes, yellow stripes. A rising sun."

"You're doing great, Faith," he said soothingly, choosing the rising sun designs from his search results. "Can you see any letters?"

She clenched her closed eyes. "No. I'm sorry."

"You're doing great," he said again, but he could see that she was stressing herself, dragging herself out of that moment. "I want you to take a few deep breaths for me, Faith. Good. Now think about the van. You slam on your brakes and you can see it as it drives away. It's dark outside and the van's taillights are red. Are they rectangles or squares?"

Her brow wrinkled. "Rectangles."

"Are there doors?"

"Yes. Two. Side by side. No windows."

"Where is the van now?"

"Slowing down." Her breath hitched. "He turned around."

He could feel her fear, could visualize her terrified and alone. Focusing on his voice, he calmed her with it. Stroked her with it. "What are you doing now?"

"Crying. My hands are shaking." Clenched in her lap, her hands trembled. Her whole body trembled. "He was coming back, and I wanted to turn around, but it was too late." Her chin lifted along with her shoulders as she drew a deep breath. "So I charged him."

Deacon was fiercely impressed with her courage even though his heart knocked in his chest. She'd played chicken with a killer. "And then?"

"He swerved."

"Left or right?"

"My left. I sped past him." She opened her eyes, met his. "I got away."

"Good for you," he said. "You didn't tell the police that you saw the gun."

She frowned. "I thought I did." Her eyes flickered as she considered it, and he could see the exact moment she realized the importance. She sucked in a breath. "He had a passenger."

"I think so, yes." He slid his tablet across the table so that she could see. "Which of these plate designs best matches your recollection?"

She scanned the screen, then pointed, her mouth firming with grim satisfaction. "This one."

"Good. Give me a minute." Dialing Dispatch, he amended his earlier BOLO. "White Ford cargo van, double doors. Tennessee plates. Tinted glass."

"But even if he is here," Faith said when he'd hung up, "and even if he is involved in your case, do you really think he kept the same license plates? He planned what he did on the bridge. He was careful. He'd be stupid to keep the plates."

"You might be right, but it's worth a try. He keeps coming after you, which shows a growing level of desperation. Desperate people make stupid mistakes."

"Then if he *is* here, I hope he's very stupid," she murmured. "For Corinne's sake."

Not for her own. In that moment Deacon knew he was going to take care of Faith Corcoran. He was going to make damn sure she stayed safe.

The door to the interview room opened. "Novak, you were right," Isenberg said, a triumphant gleam in her eyes.

Faith looked at the mirror uncomfortably. "You were watching?"

"Most of it. I'd heard tell of Novak's interview skills and wanted to observe."

Deacon had suspected she might be watching, but hated that Faith's privacy had been invaded once again. "What do you have?" he asked the lieutenant.

Isenberg's grin was pure shark. "A ballistics match. You were right. The same gun that killed Gordon Shue in Miami was fired at Dr. Corcoran's house yesterday afternoon."

Yes. Deacon grinned back. "It was a long shot."

"Well, it paid off," Isenberg said. "I'm liking your gut more every hour."

"Oh my God," Faith whispered, and Deacon's grin abruptly disappeared. Her mouth had dropped open, her expression horrified. "You were right. I brought him here."

Deacon realized that until that moment she hadn't truly believed it even possible that Combs was to blame for the abduction of Corinne and Arianna. Yet she'd told him everything he'd wanted to know, risking her license. Her livelihood. All for two young women she'd never met.

"He may have followed you here," Isenberg said, "but this is not your fault. Agent Novak, I have a few other points to cover with you. If you'll excuse us, Dr. Corcoran."

Deacon rose, his heart cracking a little more at the sight of Faith's expression. "I'll be back as soon as I can, and then I'll drive you to your hotel." He hesitated, then lightly squeezed her shoulder. "You didn't cause this, Faith. You tried everything you knew to avoid it."

She nodded silently, her eyes bright with new tears as he left her alone at the table.

Chapter Twelve

Corinne had nearly given up. Her bare foot was like a block of ice and her arm was screaming in pain. And her head hurt. She hurt all over.

She'd used her shoe to prop the heavy door open so that she could snake her arm through to get to the lock. It had seemed like such a good idea at the time. She just had to get the little toothpick tool in the lock. That was all. *It shouldn't be this hard.*

Her eyes filled with tears as she sagged against the top step. She was going to die here.

No, you're not. Arianna's out there somewhere and so is that little girl. They need you.

Blindly, she reached through the opening, bending her arm unnaturally to reach the rusted padlock. *Don't skitter away,* she commanded the lock. *Just . . . stay.*

She held her breath when the pick didn't skate off the padlock as it had a thousand times already. It went in. All the way in. *Don't you dare drop the knife now.* She controlled her breathing, then jiggled the pick. And heard the click of the lock giving way. Tears burned her cold cheeks. The chain slid free of the handles. Slowly, carefully, she pushed the door open.

I did it! She wanted to shout it to the sky, bright with the most beautiful stars she'd ever seen. But she held it in. *Be quiet. Just in case he's still here.* She shoved her foot back into her shoe and stepped onto the cold ground.

Her heart sank. *Woods.* They were surrounded by woods. No neighbors. They were miles away from civilization. *Dammit.*

She turned in a circle. And gasped. Blood was spattered all over the back of the house, by the gas tank. The shot she'd heard when they'd first arrived, she thought. Who had he shot?

Afraid to know the answer, she crept around the house, peeking in the side window.

There was a tall mound of dirt on the floor inside the cabin. A shovel had been propped against the wall. And the girl lay on a cot, her wrists and ankles bound. She wore a thin T-shirt and faded jeans. No shoes or socks. No coat. No blanket.

Corinne saw no sign of the monster who'd brought them here, and the front door was locked. The van was nowhere to be seen. He really was gone. For now.

Picking this lock was far easier than the last one. It was a simple lock, probably intended to keep bears out more than to keep people in, she thought.

She slipped into the house, stealing glances at the mound of dirt. He'd buried the two dead men from the van under there. And whoever he'd shot when they'd first arrived. Who was the third person? Whoever it had been, she couldn't help them now.

But the girl was still alive, even though her skin was cold. Getting her warm and waking her up were the priorities. A second cot had a blanket. He could easily have covered her, Corinne thought as she ripped the blanket off the bed and wrapped it around the girl's frozen body. She wondered why he hadn't.

To teach the girl who held the power, she answered herself. The child would wake up and see that there was a blanket and want it. She'd have to depend on him to give it to her.

He's teaching her, the girl had said. *What she needs to know.*

On the stove was a pot of cold stew, fat congealed into a thick layer on top. Her stomach growled, and she suddenly realized how hungry she was.

I need to eat before I fall over. She scraped off the layer of fat with trembling, dirty fingers, hygiene the last thing on her mind. She crammed handfuls of the stew into her mouth, but saved some for the girl. Hopefully, there was more and they could both eat their fill before he returned.

They'd need their strength to escape.

The girl's hair was dark, short. Choppy, as if she'd hacked it off herself. She was petite, her breasts just starting to form. How old was she?

Twelve maybe. Corinne shook her softly. "Wake up. Please." But the girl didn't stir. "I can't carry you. I can't even carry myself. Please wake up."

But the girl continued to take steady, deep breaths. Whatever he'd used to drug them, he'd given the girl way too much of it. Just watching her breathe was making Corinne sway with exhaustion. The girl wasn't waking up anytime soon.

"You need to go for help," Corinne told herself firmly. "But not unarmed."

She didn't know how far she'd have to walk to find help, and they were in the woods. She searched the cabin for a weapon. There was a rifle rack over the fireplace, but it was empty. The kitchen drawer had a few sharp knives and she took those. The only other thing that showed any promise at all was the shovel. She pulled it from the dirt and dragged it to the front door, each step a struggle. She'd reached for the doorknob when her legs gave out.

Shit was all she had time to think before everything went dark.

Cincinnati, Ohio
Tuesday, November 4, 1:50 a.m.

Deacon followed Isenberg into the adjoining observation room, then stopped abruptly. Both Bishop and Adam stood at the glass watching Faith, who'd turned her face away from the mirror.

She's entitled to some privacy, he thought, wishing he could take her away right now. Because even though he couldn't see her face, her slim shoulders were shaking. She was crying again, and it tore him up inside. *She's been through enough.*

With an effort, he turned away from the glass. Adam's expression was unreadable, but Bishop's had softened in sympathy. Isenberg watched them all, assessing.

"What do you have?" Deacon asked again.

Adam spoke first. "We got tire prints from the dirt road across from the house where the victims were held. Treads are consistent with a van. I've got uniforms canvassing Route 52, trying to find any security camera footage available."

Deacon knew that Adam was sharing important information, but at first all he could hear was his cousin saying *walking freak of nature.* Pushing Adam's cruel words aside, Deacon focused. For Corinne and Arianna. And for Faith.

He nodded. "Hopefully, he *is* stupid and it's the same van. He had an accomplice on the bridge. I'll ask Vega to haul the girlfriend's ass in for questioning again."

"Corcoran had a good point," Bishop said, "logistically speaking. Combs would have been hard-pressed to drive back and forth to Miami and still have time to screw with her old car, kidnap Arianna and Corinne, and still be able to inflict all Arianna's wounds. The surgeon said that some of the wounds were days old. Some were from yesterday. Some are only hours old."

"So he was in the house at least part of the time every day," Deacon said.

Bishop nodded. "He *had* to have flown. Nothing else makes sense. We should check passenger manifests at the airports around Miami and Cincinnati."

Deacon finally felt some control over the case. "We can use facial-recognition software to check around the airport gates before and after the flights. I want a timeline for his movements for the past four days. If Combs flew anywhere last weekend, we need to know."

"Crandall can take point," Isenberg said. "I'll call him back in."

"It's a lot of data for one man to sift through," Deacon said doubtfully. "Hours of airport video. I should get a few Bureau resources on it as well."

She nodded, but not happily. "Make the calls."

"Will do," he said, relieved that she'd been reasonable.

He had no desire to get stuck in a turf war. "I'm going back out to the house as soon as I've taken Dr. Corcoran to her hotel. I'll put uniforms in the parking lot."

Adam studied Faith through the glass. "He could have killed her yesterday. He had the perfect opportunity when she was standing at the cemetery fence, alone and unaware of his presence. Why didn't he kill her then?"

"Maybe she surprised him," Deacon said. "Especially since she'd switched vehicles. He might have thought she was still in Miami. He might even have heard about the accident and thought he'd finally succeeded in killing her."

Bishop's dark eyes narrowed. "True, unless he put a tracker under the Jeep, too."

Deacon swore. "I'll have CSU check. But I don't think he knew what she was driving or that she'd left Florida. She drove for thirty-two hours and he didn't try anything."

"Maybe he didn't kill her because he never saw her," Adam said curtly. "He was busy abducting and torturing Arianna and Corinne."

"Good point," Isenberg said. "What's up with Arianna and Corinne? Why take them?"

"It doesn't make sense," Adam said, "unless Faith knows them. If she's not lying and she doesn't know them, then they weren't being used to lure her here."

Deacon considered Adam's words and had to admit he agreed. "But I don't believe he lured Faith here. He doesn't *want* her here—he tried to kill her before she could leave Florida."

"True," Adam allowed grudgingly. "He would have killed her if he could have, so we have to assume she surprised him or he didn't see her there."

"And if he didn't know she was there," Bishop said, "he couldn't have anticipated that she'd call Earl Power. We know Ken Beatty surprised him. They obviously fought."

"We know that he dragged Beatty away," Deacon said. "We found the tracks. At some point the locksmith shows up and Arianna escapes." He grimaced. "Scene missing here."

"Pretty damn big scene," Adam grumbled.

Deacon nodded. "I know. Hopefully, Arianna can fill in the blanks when she wakes up. In the meantime, I want to know why Combs is even here. Why take Faith's house to begin with?"

"The better to see you with, my dear," Bishop said, then looked embarrassed when he and Adam stared at her. She shrugged self-consciously. "Her hair made me think of it."

"I thought of it, too," Isenberg confessed with a wry smile. "Faith was headed to Grandmother's house. Combs beat her there and took up residence."

"The wolf ate Grandma because he was hungry and she was available," Bishop mused. "Combs might have grabbed Arianna and Corinne for the same reason. They were walking along the path from the library to the dorms. According to the student blogger who's been challenging the college administration about safety concerns, it was also in the security cam's blind spot. The path was deserted. It was Halloween night, and there were parties in all of the frat houses. Maybe he got bored waiting for Corcoran or became desperate to feed his perversion. Maybe Corinne and Arianna were simply convenient."

Isenberg shook her head. "That might explain the abductions, but it still doesn't address *why* he took the house to begin with. He didn't try to grab Faith so that he could torture her. He tried to outright kill her. Why go to the trouble to set up in her house if he didn't want her here?"

"*Because* he tried to kill her multiple times," Deacon said, the pieces falling into place. "He kept missing or she thwarted him somehow, but he could see her calendar. He knew she'd come here for the reading of her grandmother's will."

"Most people would visit a house they'd just inherited," Bishop said, giving him a nod. "He didn't know that she hates the house. He expected her to come much sooner."

But there was something wrong with that, too, a hole in their logic that Deacon couldn't put his finger on. He reviewed everything Faith had told him until he realized what he'd missed. "The timeline doesn't work. He wouldn't have known that she'd inherited the house until two weeks ago, when the new deed was filed."

"He's been in that basement more than two weeks," Adam said grimly. "My guess is that it's been months at least. Long before her grandmother died."

"Exactly," Deacon said. "The timeline only works if he knew the contents of the will. He attempted murder after her grandmother's death. So either it's not Combs, or he had inside info about the will. That opens the suspect list up to the grandmother's lawyer, his staff, and the other heirs."

"And the disinherited," Adam said. "They'd know *somebody* got the house, just not them."

"Her uncle Jeremy," Deacon said.

"He's the uncle her father didn't trust when she was a little girl," Adam told Isenberg and Bishop. "He made her uncomfortable enough as a child that she had him checked out when she grew up."

"Where is this uncle?" Isenberg asked, frowning.

"In his 'estate' in Indian Hill," Adam said, a subtle sneer in his tone. "Probably surrounded by a gaggle of lawyers."

"We know his address," Deacon said. "We don't know that he's there. I've contacted both of her uncles, but haven't heard back from either of them. We'll pay both of them and the attorney visits first thing in the morning."

"He still has a captive," Adam said. "First thing in the morning is too long to wait. We should be on their doorsteps right now."

"To say what?" Deacon shook his head. "'Do you have Corinne Longstreet shackled in your basement? No? Oh, sorry to have bothered you.'"

"No, we ask them where they were at eleven p.m. on Friday," Adam said, through clenched teeth.

"We don't have enough to bring them in for questioning. If one of them does have her, all we'll be doing is tipping them off. If Corinne is still alive, he could kill her."

"If she's still alive, he's torturing her," Adam countered.

Deacon searched his cousin's face, saw the flicker of desperation in his eyes. "I know," he said gently. "But until we have a solid lead, I'm not willing to risk her life or anyone else's. Whoever took Corinne and Arianna has already killed three people in Miami while trying to kill Faith and two more tonight—assuming the power tech and the locksmith are dead. He won't hesitate to kill Corinne, too. I put unmarked cars in front of Jeremy's estate hours ago. We'll know if he leaves. Then we can follow him, hopefully to Corinne."

Adam's jaw was tight, but he nodded his head. "All right."

Deacon returned his attention to Faith. "The house itself may tell us what we need to know. Tanaka hasn't finished processing it, and Latent still has yards of surfaces to check for prints."

"What's up with the house, Deacon?" Bishop asked. "Other than being a perfect set for a horror film, of course. When we were there earlier tonight, she looked at it like it was alive."

"It terrifies her," Deacon agreed. "She said it's bad memories, because she was at the house when she learned of her mother's death, but I think there's more to it than that. She said her mother died in a car accident, but the circumstances don't seem proportionate with her reaction. Whenever I mention the house, she has a panic attack. My mother died in a car accident, too. I remember the moment I was told, down to every detail. I don't dread the location, though."

"But she was just a little girl at the time," Bishop said. "How old were you?"

"Eighteen," he and Adam said simultaneously.

"And you went off the straight and narrow when you found out," Adam reminded him.

Deacon remembered the night. Remembered Adam sitting at his side, offering sympathy and strength. It didn't make the cruel words his cousin had spoken a few hours earlier hurt any less, but it did remind Deacon that the man who'd said them had been his closest, most loyal friend. And it made him wonder again what had spurred the rage that Adam was struggling to control.

"Maybe she is just dreading it because of her mother's death," Deacon said. "But the house is the center of all of this. As hard as it will be for her, I think she needs to do the one thing that Combs—or whoever's working with him— tried to prevent. She needs to go into the house."

"I have to agree," Bishop said reluctantly.

Isenberg nodded. "Get her there tomorrow morning. Now, what about the scene at King's College? Where the girls were abducted? What's the status on that?"

"It's too dark to process it now," Bishop said. "It's so heavily wooded that even with spotlights, we could miss something. There's an access road that's used by the maintenance department. It empties out onto West Sixth through a back gate. It wouldn't have taken more than a few minutes for someone to grab both women, toss them in his van, then drive away unseen."

"You secured the scene?" Isenberg asked.

Bishop looked offended. "Of course. I requested all the campus security footage, including any cameras around that back gate. Unfortunately, that gate is a hangout for students indulging in 'extracurricular activities.' So the cameras always get tampered with. I did a walk-through to check for witnesses, but nobody was indulging tonight."

"Let's meet CSU at King's College at dawn to look around," Deacon said. "In the meantime, I'll take Faith to her hotel, then I want another look through the house myself."

Cincinnati, Ohio
Tuesday, November 4, 1:50 a.m.

There was a cruiser parked across the street, in front of Faith's hotel. *Not a good sign,* he thought as he checked the view from his window. It could be a simple coincidence, but he didn't believe in those any more than the police did.

If the cops were watching her, well, that wasn't good. If they were watching *for* her, that was even worse. If they just happened to be there for the free Wi-Fi in the lobby, only slightly better because any way he sliced it, a pair of cops was too much scrutiny for what he was planning.

Not that he had much choice. He needed to silence her permanently, and at the first possible opportunity. It was only one cruiser. By the time they got their shit together, he'd be long gone.

He took off his padded coat and ball cap and laid them on the unmade bed next to the golf bag he'd carried right past the hotel's security cameras. The bag was nothing exceptional, just a plain black bag he'd bought from Goodwill.

What was inside was a different story. He took out the golf clubs and carefully drew out the rifle he'd hidden among them. It wasn't his, which made it even better.

The nine mil he'd been using all this time wasn't his, either. He'd have to throw it into the river soon. He'd used it too many times in too many different places lately—and he'd left both slugs and casings behind. It was only a matter of time before police ballistics connected the dots.

It could never be traced to him, but he wasn't free after

all this time because he took unnecessary chances. He was a careful man.

He pulled a table in front of the window and set up his rifle. He'd learned from his mistakes. He'd missed her before, but he'd been caught off guard when he'd broken into her apartment. He hadn't expected her to have a gun of her own. He would not miss again.

Cincinnati, Ohio
Tuesday, November 4, 2:05 a.m.

This cannot be possible. Face buried in her hands, Faith had said the words to herself over and over, but it didn't change the facts. It was not only possible, it was true. "I am responsible."

"No, you're not," Novak said, his voice low and warm and steady. He'd returned to the interview room a minute ago, shrugging into his leather coat before crouching next to her chair so that he could look up into her face. "Let me take you to your hotel. You need to sleep."

His eyes were so intense, so compelling, that she almost believed him. Too weary to argue, she allowed him to put her arms through the sleeves of her borrowed jacket as if she were a child. Carefully, he pulled her hair free and rested his hand at the center of her back, holding her steady when she swayed.

"I'm so tired," she whispered.

"I know you are," he murmured back. "Things won't necessarily look any better in the morning, but you'll be better able to think them through."

He led her out into the night, his hand never leaving her back. When they were free of the building, she found herself wishing she had the right to lean on him. He was solid and had been kind, but she knew better than to depend on him for any more than that. Holding herself rigid, she stayed upright for a few more steps. Until his hand moved to her shoulder, gently urging her to lean on him.

"It's all right," he said softly. "You've had a long day."

She didn't have the strength or the will to resist. Her head rested against him, and she breathed deeply, the smell of cedar soothing her. She pretended for just a minute that she could do this any time she pleased. That she belonged to him. But she didn't belong to him, and letting her guard down could only end badly. "You stored your coat in a cedar chest."

"My mother's," he said. "Her coats always smelled of cedar because she'd put them in the chest between seasons."

He said it so wistfully. "Your mother is gone?" she asked, and he nodded.

"When I was eighteen. We lost her and my stepfather the same night. Drunk driver."

Her shoulders stiffened. "I'm sorry."

"Thanks. It was a long time ago, but I don't think you ever get past missing your parents."

Swaying red Keds, bright white shoelaces dangling. She hated her mother, had hated her all these years, but she missed her. "I don't suppose you do."

They reached his SUV and she wished they could walk a little more, if only to feel his arm around her. It had been such a long time since she'd been held.

Novak helped her up into the seat, buckled her in, then slid behind the wheel. "You need to get some food and some sleep."

"Both sound wonderful, but I don't know where you can get food this time of night."

"Don't worry. I do." Novak pulled the SUV into sparse traffic. "Are you a vegetarian?"

"Not even remotely," she said.

"Then I know a few all-night burger drive-thrus."

"That's fine, but . . ." She stopped herself. *Don't be rude, Faith.* "A burger is perfectly fine."

"But what?" he asked.

"Well, earlier, when we left the hospital, I could have sworn I smelled Skyline chili in here."

His brows lifted. "You did. I took Coneys to my brother and my uncle. I must admit you surprise me, Faith. I wouldn't have expected you to be familiar with our local delicacies."

"I used to eat Coneys for lunch when I was here in school." Cinnamon-spiced chili and cheese over hot dogs or spaghetti noodles, it was uniquely Cincinnati. "My uncle Jordan and I would sneak out at night for three-ways, because Gran would smell the onions in the four-way and we'd be busted." She laughed out loud, a little stunned that she could when she'd been crying a half hour before. "Only in Cincinnati can you say that phrase in polite conversation."

Novak grinned. "Which phrase? 'We'd be busted' or 'smell the onions'?"

Faith's heart did a little flip. A grinning Agent Novak was a captivating sight, and for a moment she let herself look her fill. "Gran said the name 'three-way' was just vulgar."

"Seriously? She'd really get upset? It's just food."

And delicious food it had been, Faith thought. And one of her happier memories. "Gran got upset about a lot of things. She was very strict, but Jordan would make sure I didn't miss out too much. He'd sneak me to all the places Gran nixed on principle."

Novak gave her an odd look. "Like what?"

"Rock concerts, rated-R movies. Bars. Beer. Cigarettes."

He frowned. "How old were you?"

"Fourteen, fifteen. Jordan shouldn't have allowed me the freedom he did. I could have gotten into a lot of trouble. I'm lucky, actually. I drank . . . a lot then, and there is alcoholism in my family. I could have slid down that slippery slope, but I didn't get too caught up in it."

"What kind of uncles do you have?" he demanded.

"Young ones. Jordan and Jeremy are only twelve years older than me. Jordan was only twenty-six at the time. More like an older brother than an uncle."

"Twenty-six is old enough to know better."

"I know that now. So does he. But back then he was re-living some of his own adolescence. He had cancer when he was seventeen. He lost a few years to chemo and recovery. I was just a little girl, but I remember how sick he was. So maybe he was feeling his oats, too."

Novak nodded reluctantly. "I did some dumb things when my mother and stepfather died. I was eighteen and should have known better. It sounds like you spent a lot of time with your grandmother and uncle back then."

"I lived with them during my sophomore and junior years of high school."

"Why?"

"My dad got sick and couldn't take care of me for a

while." Her father's time in alcohol rehab had been hell on them both. "As soon as he'd recovered, he moved me back in with him, and I finished high school in Savannah."

"Hell of a time to have to switch schools," Novak commented.

"By then Dad had married Lily and was happy." She shrugged. "Now that I'm back, I'll have to see if Cincinnati chili is as good as I remember it. I'll get some at lunch tomorrow."

Novak took a sharp right into a Skyline parking lot. "Or now."

Faith's eyes widened in delighted surprise. "They're open now?"

"Till three. This was where I'd hang out when I was in high school." He went through the drive-thru and ordered more food than she'd eat in a week, then pulled the SUV into a parking place and offered her the bag. "To memory lane."

She smiled at him. "Thank you, Agent Novak. This is lovely. I'm starving."

She dug into the bag and pulled out the three-way he'd gotten her. He waited until she'd taken her first bite. "Well?" he asked.

"The same," she pronounced. "It's good to know that some things don't change."

He methodically demolished almost everything else in the bag. He offered her the last Coney, then turned in his seat to talk to her, all business.

"You have a squad car sitting outside your hotel." He dug into one of the pockets of his coat and produced the prepaid phone she'd purchased the day before. He handed it to her, followed by his business card. "Add my number into your contact list. If you see Combs or even have the feeling you're being followed, call 911 first, me second. Okay?"

She studied his card, then looked up at him, confused. "This isn't the number you gave Vega when I called her from the hospital," she said, and thought she saw his cheeks flush.

"It's not." He hesitated. "That was Bishop's number."

It took her a second, but then she understood. "You're handing me off to Bishop?" It stung, far more than it should have. *Oh, Faith. You're an idiot.* She'd taken a few kind words and some Skyline and blown them all out of proportion.

"I was planning to earlier," he admitted quietly. "I probably still should. But I'm not."

She held her breath. "Why?"

"Because I changed my mind."

Cincinnati, Ohio
Tuesday, November 4, 2:45 a.m.

I changed my mind. Deacon pulled his SUV behind the cruiser parked in front of Faith's hotel, the four words he'd spoken still echoing through his mind. He wasn't sure exactly why he'd told her that. He knew he shouldn't have told her—or changed his mind.

But she fascinated him—her courage, her fears. Her face. And that intriguing glimpse of cleavage he'd caught back in the little office in the hospital sure didn't hurt, either.

Trouble was, she was still a witness. And he still had a job to do. He injected a businesslike brusqueness into his voice that felt like sandpaper in his throat. "Your security detail is already here." He started to get out of the SUV, but she leaned forward, turning on the map lights. *Shit.*

"Why?" she asked, studying his face. "And don't pretend to misunderstand. And please do not hide behind that too-cool-to-care mask. I just want an honest answer. Why did you change your mind about handing me over to Detective Bishop?"

"I don't know," he said quietly.

"Is it because you feel sorry for me?"

"No." He calmed his voice, schooled his features. "I respect the risks you took in order to stand up for the victims back in Miami. I respect what you did for Arianna and Corinne tonight."

"Respect is all well and good, but your job isn't to babysit me, Agent Novak."

Deacon, he wanted to growl. *My name is Deacon.* But he couldn't say that. He'd led her on enough already. "I know my job. I'm not here to babysit you. I'm here to keep you safe."

She attempted a smile. "The officers you've assigned can do that."

No, I'll *keep you safe. It's* my *job.* He gritted his teeth, saying nothing.

Her smile faltered, but she pasted it back on. "Call me if you need any other information. If I see Combs or think he's near, I'll call 911, then you." She reached for the door handle, but he was faster, leaning over the console to grab her wrist.

"Stop. Wait for me to come around and cover you."

"You're right." Her shoulders sagged. "I don't know what I was thinking. I'm sorry."

He knew she wasn't sorry about leaving the SUV. He knew she was sorry that she'd read more into his changing his mind than she should have. Except that she shouldn't be sorry, because she'd understood his words exactly the way he'd meant them.

He knew he should release her wrist, but he couldn't make himself do so. Because the skin he was touching was soft and her pulse raced against his fingertips. Shifting his grip, he stroked the inside of her wrist with his thumb. "I'm not sure what I feel right now, but it sure as hell isn't pity." Her eyes flew up to meet his. "Is that honest enough for you?"

He watched her cheeks grow redder than her hair. "Yes. For now."

He made himself let her go. "Not just for now. Until this case is closed. You're a witness," he said, trying to be firm. "Anything more wouldn't be ethical."

"No, I don't suppose it would be." She held his gaze, hers suddenly challenging. Sexually aware and full of bold invitation. "Then again, I'm not exactly the poster child for ethics, am I?"

For a moment he couldn't breathe. He could only stare. And wish they were alone. Just the two of them. He'd find out if her mouth tasted as good as he hoped. He'd make her forget every terrible nightmare Combs had inflicted. After he caught the sonofabitch.

That Combs was still out there wasn't the cold bucket of water it should have been. That Faith would offer herself up as a "poster child" for bad choices was.

It was as if she considered herself damaged goods, that he'd want her only because he shouldn't have her. Because she wasn't a wise choice. And he wondered who'd put that idea into her head.

"I think you misunderstand me," he said. "What I meant was that there isn't anything wrong with your ethics. But if and when we get together, it will be because I respect you and like you and want you, not because you represent some cheap thrill or forbidden fruit."

Her eyes flickered. "You can't like me. You don't even know me."

But he did like her. That was the problem. "I know enough. I'll figure out the rest as I go," he said, then got out of the SUV before he did something stupid, like taking her up on her offer.

Cincinnati, Ohio
Tuesday, November 4, 3:00 a.m.

She'd finally returned. But she wasn't alone.

He squinted at the dark SUV in his crosshairs. It had parked behind the cruiser, which held two officers. She had a security detail of three. She must have told them something for them to be guarding her. Or the Escobar girl had told them something. *Shit.*

He gave himself a mental shake. *Think positive.* Arianna hadn't seen his face. She could tell them nothing more than the location of the house, which they already knew. His jaw clenched. *And the existence of the child, dammit.* Now they'd be out looking for the kid.

Relax. Roza was locked up with the Longstreet woman in the cabin, both awaiting his return. Eagerly, no doubt. The Longstreet woman would know exactly what was coming, having heard the screams of her friend. He loved it when he could abduct two at a time. The terror of the second one was always so much more gratifying.

He frowned, his eye still focused on the SUV parked under the hotel's overhang. What the hell were they doing in there? Negotiating peace in the Middle East? They'd been sitting there for two minutes now. *Ah. Finally.* The driver's door opened and . . . "Whoa."

The man getting out was good-sized, his leather coat stretched taut between his shoulders. He looked like he'd have muscles on his muscles. More like a Mafia enforcer than a cop.

But it was the man's hair that drew his attention. Snow-white, it rose in jagged peaks all over his head. The guy was old. His reflexes wouldn't be what they ought to be.

The man closed the SUV door, standing for a moment, drawing a deep breath. Then he turned, his face clearly visible in the rifle's sight.

Well, hell. He wasn't old at all. He was quite young. And the expression on his face . . .

Ha. He knew a frustrated, horny man when he saw one. The white-haired man had a thing for little Faith. *Too bad, man. She'll be dead as soon as she gets to the hotel door.*

Chapter Thirteen

Faith watched from the passenger seat as Novak met the two uniforms between their vehicles. He handed the officers copies of Combs's mug shot and then took a stroll around the front and sides of the hotel.

Cheap thrill. Forbidden fruit. Was that what she thought of herself? Maybe. Then again, maybe she'd simply been trying to forget the terror of the last few weeks. Of the last few hours. Maybe she just wanted someone to hold her. That wasn't so wrong, was it?

You would have been using him. You know it. And so did he.

Faith sighed, knowing it was true. She'd gotten swept up in the moment. Tried to be the siren she most definitely was not. *He could have taken me up on it.* But he hadn't.

Part of her was relieved. Part was frustrated. But mostly, she felt ashamed. Novak's sister had sworn that he was a good man, and Faith had seen him demonstrate that so many times over the last few hours. She'd seen it just now. Because even though he'd refused, he'd been tempted. *At least there's that.*

Novak appeared in the SUV's side mirror, having cleared the hotel perimeter. For a moment she let herself just look. And want. He was an impressive man, head to toe.

He opened the door and held out his hand, helping Faith down to the curb. She stumbled when her shoes hit the pavement, her stiff knees stealing any grace she'd had left.

He caught her before she hit the concrete, pulling her against him just as he had in the cemetery. Except this time she was facing him. And this time he held on a few seconds longer than he had before, his chest expanding against her breasts as he breathed her in.

They fit, her head finding a resting place in the curve of his shoulder, her cheek pressing against his pounding heart. And then her good sense returned. She pulled back. "I'm sorry."

Resolutely, he set her on her own two feet. "Are you all right?" he asked, the huskiness of his voice sending another shiver across her skin.

"I didn't mean to . . ." She looked over her shoulder, saw the two cops in the cruiser watching with interest. Her face heated as she looked away. "I didn't mean to lean."

"It's all right." His voice had lost the huskiness, but it was still deep and smooth, tugging at her way down. "It's not every night you climb a rocky embankment in your bare feet to save a girl's life. You're entitled to lean."

He lifted his head, scanning the cars parked along the street. She tried to follow his gaze, but she was too short, the SUV blocking her view.

"Any white vans?" she murmured.

"No."

She hadn't really thought so. If Combs was still here, he had to have ditched the van. "It's late," she said. "I have to get some sleep so I can go to work tomorrow."

Novak's frown was instant and formidable. "You can't go to work, not until we solve this."

She tilted her head, mimicking his habit. "Um, reality-check time? I just started a new job. I can't call in sick on my second day. I'll get fired."

"It's better than calling in dead," he said grimly. "I'll write you a note if you want. 'Dear Banker, please excuse Faith from work today, as she has a large target painted on her ass.'"

"I've been shot at and burned out and all the rest of it. I never once skipped work. Besides, I work in a bank now. Guards with guns everywhere. It's very secure."

He spread his hand across her back, urging her forward. "Let's talk about it inside," he said, guiding her toward the double glass doors. The one on the right was being held open by a bellman whose stare was a little too curious, but she supposed it wasn't every day a guest was escorted in by the likes of Deacon Novak.

Abruptly, the bellman paled and stepped back, letting the door drift closed. Faith looked over her shoulder to find Novak wearing a scowl that might have terrified even her. His eyes bored a hole into the poor bellman, who now stared down at his own feet like a guilty child. When Novak leaned forward to open the door himself, Faith met his scowl with a scolding glare.

"Was that really necessary?" she murmured.

But then the glass door next to her shattered, and with it all semblance of coherent thought, a sense of déjà vu sweeping in to blanket her mind. In the next heartbeat, Novak was moving, grabbing the door and flinging them both inside the hotel lobby and down to the floor.

"Everybody down!" he shouted as they landed hard. He covered her with his body as the adjacent glass door shattered, a second shot showering them with shards of broken glass. He was big and heavy, completely immobilizing her. Barely able to breathe, she began to tremble.

Gordon was all she could think. He'd killed Gordon the same way. *Combs is out there.*

Trapped under Novak's weight, she craned her head to look behind them, sliding her cheek across the rough carpet to glimpse the bellman slumping to the ground in an eerie, slow-motion kind of silence. He didn't get up.

Not again. Please. She struggled to rise, but Novak pushed her back down with a ruthless strength that she couldn't hope to fight.

"Stay down," he hissed.

"He's hit, Deacon." Her voice came out pitched too high. Panicked. "He's going to die. Just like Gordon. Please. We need to help him."

Novak cursed viciously. "That sonofabitch is trying to draw you out, Faith. He knows you'll run to help a victim. *Stay down.* The officers outside are pulling the bellman behind cover. I need you to not move. Are you hurt? Did he hit you?"

"N-no." Beneath him, Faith was trembling violently. Her teeth began to chatter. "Are you?"

"No." His body lifted a hairbreadth, his chin brushing the back of her head as he scanned the lobby. "Anyone else hit?"

"No," a woman said, her voice barely audible. "I called 911."

"Good," he said. "Get everyone behind the desk and stay there until I tell you to come out." His body shifted as he went for his phone. Faith could hear it ringing, Isenberg's voice answering, and then Novak's voice, calm and authoritative. "We have a sniper situation at Faith's hotel. He appears to be set up in the hotel across the street. Send backup and have them cover the exits. We have one hotel employee down here who needs an ambulance." A pause, then a terse reply. "Working on that now. Just get me that backup ASAP. Thanks." He slipped the phone back into his coat pocket, then shifted again, twisting to look behind him.

His voice had calmed her, at least enough that she could think. "What are you working on?"

"Getting us out of the line of fire."

"Oh." That would be good. "Is the bellman still alive?"

"Yes." But he'd answered hesitantly, and Faith's heart sank. "The uniforms got him behind one of those big-ass flower pots outside, but you and I are sitting ducks here with all this glass."

Placing one hand on either side of her head, he pushed his upper body up. An instant later he slammed back down hard, smashing the breath from her lungs. *"Holy fuck,"* he groaned. "Mother*fuckin'* sonofabitch. Dammit, dammit, *dammit.*"

No. Panic was a live thing inside her, clawing at her chest. *He's been shot.* Faith struggled frantically to get out from under him. To help him.

"Faith," he whispered. He was panting above her, struggling for air. "Stop."

"He's not going to give up." She was trapped, her body pressed to the floor. "He'll shoot you again." And then he'd bleed to death and there wouldn't be anything she could do. A sob caught in her throat. "Please *move.* I can't wear your brains. I can't."

His chuckle snapped her out of the panic and back to reality. He wasn't Gordon. He was Deacon Novak and he wasn't dead. His exhale was warm in her ear. "I'm not too keen on that idea myself," he said.

"Where are you hit?" she asked, voice shaking. Hell, her whole body was shaking.

Novak wrapped his arms around her head, enveloping her in a black leather cocoon. She drew the scent of cedar into her lungs, letting it calm her. The sight of the gun in his hand calmed her even more. He wasn't hurt so badly that he couldn't move.

"Left shoulder, but I'm okay. It hit the vest."

A vest. A picture flashed in her mind, the one time Charlie had come home after taking a bullet in his vest. His whole left pec had been black-and-blue. But not bleeding.

"He'll keep shooting," she said. "He kept shooting at Gordon until he was dead."

"He hasn't fired again, so we're probably in his blind spot. Hush. I'm doing math."

Trajectories, she realized. There had been no other shots fired. She considered the layout of the street, of the parked cars. Of the hotel across the street.

"He's not on the roof," she said. "The overhang above the entrance would have obstructed his shots. Something's shielding us. Your SUV?"

He twisted to look behind them. "Up to the doors, anyway. The windows are shot to hell. He's got to be somewhere on the second floor of the other hotel." He rested his forehead on the back of her head. "He can't get to us when we're lying flat and we can't go forward, so we're going to have to move backward on our stomachs. Can you do that?"

"I climbed an embankment barefoot," she said, feigning confidence. "This is a cakewalk."

He squeezed her upper arm. "Good. Just keep your head down. Your hair is like a flare."

"Keep your own head down, Novak," she said, snapping because she was terrified. For him. In that moment she knew that he'd protect her with his life without blinking. "Your head is like a damn spotlight."

He chuckled again. "So it is. Let's go."

Dropping his head down over hers, he scooted backward a few inches at a time, using his forearms as leverage. Beneath him, she did the same, quickly realizing an unintended—and awkward—consequence of his plan.

With every movement backward, her stomach rubbed the floor, but her butt rubbed against his groin, and his body instantly responded. He was growing harder by the second.

Harder and bigger. So much so that there was no way he could hide it from her, like he'd tried to do at the hospital. And just as she had in that little room, she wondered how it would be with him. Uncomfortable at first, maybe, because his size was proportionate to the rest of him.

But worth it. Just once. She scowled at herself. *Stop that right now. You might die. Stop thinking about his ... yeah. That.* Although it was becoming increasingly hard not to.

Thinking about sex when she might die suddenly didn't seem all that foolish. And sex with Novak? She could die happy.

That is enough. No one is going to die. No one else, anyway. Biting her lip, Faith focused on the floor inches from her face and the fact that Combs was out there somewhere trying to kill them. He'd already shot the bellman. *Just like he shot Gordon.*

That memory of Gordon's blood on her hands cleared her mind, but it didn't make her any less aware of Novak's body. Apparently, he felt the same way, because by the time they had moved back to the entrance, his breathing was labored.

"I'm going to straighten up," he said in her ear, making her shiver against him. She heard his breath catch. Heard his quiet curse. "When I tell you to, I want you to get up on all fours and crawl to the left as fast as you can. Do not look back at me. On three."

When he got to three, Faith crawled over broken glass for the second time in twelve hours. When she reached the wall, she collapsed against it, sitting on the floor. She could hear sirens now. His backup had arrived. That they'd catch Combs was a long shot. He'd been too smart to allow himself to be cornered before this. She doubted he'd make a mistake now.

Novak had crawled behind her and now rose fluidly to his full height, gingerly rolling his shoulder while taking in the scene outside. His jaw hardened, his expression growing bleak.

Faith pivoted so that she could see around the wall to the glass entrance, and she understood why. The two officers had dragged the bellman behind their cruiser, their hands and uniforms covered with blood. One of the officers was doing chest compressions, the other trying to stop the bellman's bleeding.

Faith's chest hurt. What if he died? Like Gordon? Or like that mother and her son?

She turned away, looking back up at Novak. His jaw was clamped, his lips pursed so hard that deep lines radiated from the corners of his mouth. He was in serious pain. What if he'd been lying about the vest? She realized it would be like him to try to spare her the worry.

Using the wall at her back as leverage, she forced herself to stand. She tugged at Novak's leather coat on the side that had not been hit by the bullet.

He grabbed her wrists in a gentle hold. "He might still be out there. I need to go."

She pulled her wrists free. "You can't catch him if you're bleeding out."

"You sound like Dani," he grumbled, but allowed her to tug the coat from his shoulders.

That he didn't argue spoke volumes. His grimace when she eased his coat down his arm spoke even louder. She let the coat drop to the floor, unable to ignore the brand-new bullet hole in the leather. "Your coat is ruined."

"It can be repaired. This isn't the first time I've caught a stray bullet."

Was that supposed to make her feel better? Frowning, she hurried to remove his suit coat, relieved that his white shirt was, except for the charred hole in the fabric, unsoiled. "No blood."

"Like I told you," he said. "The vest stopped it."

She ignored him, dropping his suit coat on the pile, yanking the shirt from his trousers, her trembling fingers fumbling as she tried to undo the buttons.

"Faith? *Faith.*" He grabbed her wrists again, still gentle despite the look of affront on his face. "I am *not* bleeding. The bullet never touched my skin."

"You don't know that. You could be bleeding under the vest." She fought back a sudden surge of tears. *Adrenaline crash,* she thought dimly. "I watched Gordon die in front of me," she said hoarsely. "I can't let you die, too. Not because of me."

"I'm not going to die, Faith. Not today, anyway," he
added lightly. Mockingly.

"Don't *do* that. Don't you *dare* joke like that. It's not
funny. Combs tried to kill you."

"No, honey, Combs tried to kill *you*. He shot me and the
bellman on purpose. To draw you out." He pulled his leather
coat back on, wincing as he shoved his arms through the
sleeves.

Faith took a step back, suddenly cold. Exhausted. The
tears she'd fought streaked down her cheeks when she tried
to blink them away. She dropped her chin so that he couldn't
see. "Just . . . don't get shot again, okay? I can't handle any
more blood on my hands."

"You aren't responsible for this, Faith." He slid his forefinger under her chin, urging her to look up at him, wiping
her cheeks with his thumb. "I'm sorry. I shouldn't have
joked. I didn't mean to make you cry. Stay here. Please. I'll
be back for you as soon as I can."

His eyes were intense, both colors darker, the lines
where they merged appearing more jagged than they had
been before. Beautiful. Powerful. Like a storm.

"All right," Faith managed. "I'll wait."

Cincinnati, Ohio
Tuesday, November 4, 3:05 a.m.

He cleared the hotel exit, his body shaking. He'd missed.
He'd had her in his sights and he'd missed. Shooting the
bellman hadn't brought her running outside like he'd hoped.
The white-haired bastard hadn't let her up. Hadn't let her
run to the aid of her fellow man. *I should have blown his
white head to high heaven when I had him in my sight.*

But he hadn't wanted to kill him. Not right away, anyway. He'd only wanted to maim him so that Faith would
stand up and drag him away, like she'd done with her boss
in Miami.

But the bastard hadn't been maimed. He must have been
wearing a vest. And he'd parked his damn SUV in the way.
I couldn't see.

And now he'd tipped his hand. *She knows I'm here.
Dammit.* It was a hell of a lot easier when she'd believed he
was still in Miami. Now she'd be even more careful. Worse

yet, now the cops would believe her. *Shit.* It had been so much simpler when they'd thought her delusional.

He tossed the golf bag into the van and drove away slowly, like the rapidly approaching sirens weren't making his heart beat out of his chest.

The hotel had cameras in the parking lot. He'd worn the ball cap, so they hadn't caught his face, but his vehicle would be the subject of a BOLO within minutes. He needed to ditch the van. Needed to change vehicles before they locked the city down and caught him.

Hands shaking, he gripped the steering wheel so hard his knuckles ached. "Stop this," he hissed aloud. "They will not catch you." Because he was careful. *You planned for an outcome just like this, remember?*

He'd already scoped out the perfect place to swap the van because he'd known about the cameras. He'd even made a secondary plan to buy time to get there.

Calming himself, he pulled into an alley, jumped out of the van, and quickly changed out the Tennessee plates for an Ohio set he'd stolen long ago. For once he was grateful for the gloves he wore, he thought as he screwed on the new license plate. It was cold outside.

It took him thirty seconds more to place magnetic signs bearing the logo of a local roadside-assistance company on both sides of the van, the back doors, and the hood. He'd had the signs made with nighttime getaways in mind. Roadside-assistance vehicles might be called out at any time of the day or night, so no one would question his being out at three a.m.

With his van disguised, he drove to the closest suburb, thinking through what had just happened. The white-haired bastard was a cop. Who was he? Where would he take her?

I have to find her. I have to shut her up before it's too late. That the white-haired bastard had worn the look of a frustrated, lovesick puppy was the key. He wouldn't be able to stay away from Faith. *So I'll find him. I'll follow him. And when he goes to her, I'll kill them both.*

He felt much better now. By the time he passed the all-night grocery he'd scoped out earlier, he was breathing almost normally again. He drove a lap around the parking lot, biding his time. Within minutes a woman came out, pushing an overloaded cart. She looked tired.

A tired woman was exactly what he needed tonight. She

hit a button on her key fob, and the hatch of a silver Nissan minivan in the third row began to rise.

Nothing like a good heads-up. He parked in the slot next to her vehicle seconds before she arrived with her unwieldy cart, piled too high for her to see over or around. She left the cart by the open hatch and came around to the driver's side to put her purse on her seat.

He moved then, staying between the vehicles, out of any camera's range. Covering her mouth with one hand, he pressed his pistol to her head with the other. She surprised him, exploding into motion. He'd thought she'd be too exhausted to put up such a fight.

Yes, he thought as her adrenaline rushed to fire his own. He'd thought he'd needed a tired woman who'd give him no trouble, but he'd needed exactly *this.* A woman's fear had a potency like nothing else. His heart raced, his thoughts cleared, and his strength was renewed.

He yanked her against his chest, shoving the gun against her temple harder in case she'd missed it the first time. "Don't fight and I won't hurt you. I want your minivan. Drop your keys."

She stopped struggling, Her keys landed on the asphalt at her feet. "On your knees."

She dropped to her knees, drawing a huge breath through her nose as she did so, intending to scream as soon as he released her. They always did that. Normally, he used that breath to his own advantage, covering their faces with a sedative-laced rag.

But he hadn't come prepared for that, so he put the barrel of the gun at the base of her skull, pulling his hand from her mouth a split second before he pulled the trigger.

The silencer emitted a pop, but nothing loud enough to draw attention. She slumped to the ground and he kicked her under the white van, then loaded her groceries into the back so that no one would be alerted by the full cart. By the time she was discovered, he'd be long gone.

Cincinnati, Ohio
Tuesday, November 4, 3:15 a.m.

Deacon found Bishop briefing the SWAT team when he arrived in the lobby of the hotel across the street, still breathing hard from his sprint. And from having Faith Corcoran nearly ripping his shirt off. *Good God.* His skin still felt supercharged.

During those moments when they'd crawled backward, her curvy body pressed tight against his . . . He'd thought he would literally combust.

But seeing the bullet hole in the bellman's chest had more than taken care of deflating the very visible evidence of his desire. It could have been Faith lying on the ground in a pool of blood. It had been too damn close, and now an innocent man's life hung by a thread.

Bishop gave him a fast, up-and-down look. "You and the doc okay?"

"Yeah. But the bellman might not make it." The medics had arrived on the scene as Deacon was running across the street. The hotel had brought them in a back way to minimize their exposure to additional gunfire, although it appeared their gunman had ceased firing.

"He was standing next to her?" she asked.

"No. I was standing next to her. The bellman was several feet away."

The cop on Bishop's right nodded, grimly satisfied. "He's not much of a shot then, if he missed by that much. Good to know. I'm Sergeant Rayburn, team leader."

"Special Agent Novak, but you misunderstand me. The first shot he took was aimed at Dr. Corcoran. If she hadn't turned to talk to me at the last moment, she would have been hit instead of the glass door. The bellman wasn't shot until after we were on the floor inside the lobby."

Rayburn frowned. "Then the bellman was deliberately shot."

"Bait," Bishop said with disgust. "Combs wanted to draw the doc out so he could try again." She turned her attention to the older man hurrying toward them, his face pinched and drawn. "That's the hotel manager," she said to Deacon. "Did you get the key, sir?"

"I did. The room is registered to Anthony Brown. He checked in Sunday afternoon."

"We need all hotel guests to stay in their rooms," Deacon said to the manager. "Nobody goes in or out until we give the all-clear. We may evacuate, but for now, everyone stays put."

"This can't be happening," the manager said, his face graying visibly.

"I also need the last eight hours of footage for the hall-ways on the second floor, the elevators, the roof, and all exits," Bishop said. "Can you pull that together?" She waved an officer over, glancing at his badge. "Doyle, stay with him. I want to know who went in or out of that room."

"Yes, ma'am," Doyle said.

"If you're ready, gentlemen," Bishop said. "Let's go."

The SWAT team split up, taking different stairwells up to the second floor. Deacon followed one half, Bishop the other. Everything was quiet as they assembled outside the hotel room door.

"How do you know this is the one?" Deacon asked softly.

"The window was missing one of its panes," Bishop murmured. "Someone cut it out carefully. No jagged edges, nothing to notice unless you were looking, but when I did look, it was obvious." She glanced at Rayburn. "On three."

She slid the key card through the reader and stood back, letting the team enter first. Bishop followed, and Deacon brought up the rear. The bedroom was empty, the bed un-made. A half-drunk cup of coffee sat on the nightstand. A laptop computer sat on the desk, its screen dark. On the dresser were a wallet, a set of car keys, an expensive wrist-watch, and a handful of change.

"Detectives?" Rayburn backed out of the bathroom carefully. "He's in here."

Deacon entered the small bathroom with dread, know-ing what he'd see. But even after more crime scenes than he wanted to count, finding the dead was always worse than he expected.

This was no exception. Deacon crouched by the tub while Bishop stood at his back taking pictures. The man had been in his mid-forties. Wearing only a pair of boxers and a T-shirt, he lay in the tub, a bullet hole in the base of his skull. The tiled wall was covered with splatter. Blood and brains. Combs had made no attempt to wash away the evi-dence.

"Fuck," Deacon whispered, both for Faith and for the newest victim of Combs's evil.

"Execution style," Bishop noted, her voice emotionless.

Deacon knew that Scarlett Bishop was considered a cold-hearted woman by others in the department, but he wasn't fooled. He'd seen the pain in his new partner's eyes many times over the last month. She cared too much.

We all wear our masks, he thought sadly. "He must have a silencer. Somebody would have heard the gunshot." Straightening, he grimaced when pain streaked through his shoulder.

Bishop frowned at him. "What happened to you?"

"I got shot," he said flatly. "He got me in the shoulder. Don't worry. The vest caught it." He left the bathroom and examined the bedroom, looking for anything Combs had left behind. Of course there was nothing. "Status, Sergeant?"

"We're clear here, but he might still be hiding in the hotel. We've got the exits locked down. We can evacuate or do a room-to-room search if need be."

"Let me check on the security tapes first," Bishop said. She made the call to the front desk, then turned back to Deacon and Rayburn, frustration evident on her face. "A man Combs's size left this room at three oh four, with a golf bag over his shoulder. He exited through a side door at three oh five. He drove away in a white van with Tennessee plates. Backup arrived at seven minutes past three."

Deacon hadn't expected Combs to stick around, but . . . *Dammit.* They'd been so close. "I doubt he broke down his rifle. Probably just stowed it in the golf bag until he was able to dismantle it. On the upside, he kept the van *and* the plates. He doesn't know what information we have, or he would have gotten rid of them. Did the camera get his license plate?"

Bishop nodded. "Officer Doyle, the uniform I put downstairs at the desk, already added it to the BOLO and informed Isenberg, who's shut down all major roads out of the city."

"When CSU gets here, show them this." Rayburn pointed at the windowsill. "These gouges in the wood are from the stand he used to set up his rifle. He came prepared. Where were you when you got hit, Agent Novak?"

Deacon joined him at the window and pointed to the lobby, barely visible with all the emergency vehicles now parked in front. "In the shadow of my SUV. When I lifted my head—about two feet off the floor, he fired."

Rayburn whistled softly. "Your guy might be military. If not, he trained somewhere. To make that shot, with it being dark outside and the lights around the overhang making a glare? And considering he'd already missed several times before and had to have figured the cops were on their way? He has a steady hand and a good eye. You're damn lucky, Novak."

"Lucky I had the vest, I think. He didn't want me dead. He wanted Faith Corcoran to jump up and try to save me. I was bait, just like the bellman. I didn't realize how skilled he needed to be to make the shot. Thank you, Sergeant."

"Anytime." Rayburn gave Bishop a little salute. "You know where to call if you need me."

When he was gone, Bishop turned to Deacon. "Go let the EMTs check you out. Bruises turn into blood clots. You could throw a clot and die. Then I'd have to break in somebody new."

He gave her a weary smile. "You haven't broken *me* in yet."

"My point exactly. Go on. Get yourself checked out. Check on the doc. You take the scene at the creepy old house, and I'll process the scene here and write the report." Bishop went to the window, looking at the broken glass and bloody concrete below. "That was a pretty amazing shot. Vega had to have done a background check on Combs. If he was military, it would show up. I don't have her number on me, do you?"

"I do." Deacon dialed Vega's cell, put her on speaker. "It's Novak in Cincinnati."

"What time is it?" Vega yawned. "Hell, Novak, it's after three a.m. What happened?"

"I'm with my partner, Detective Bishop. A gunman fired on Faith Corcoran at her hotel."

Sheets rustled, a bed creaked. "Shit." Vega was alert now. "Was anyone hurt?"

"Corcoran is okay," he said, "but a bellman was shot in the chest, just like her boss. He's on his way to the ER. No word yet on his status. He'd been holding the door for her. Just like Shue."

A slight pause. "Gordon Shue didn't die from the shot to the chest."

Deacon frowned at Bishop. "Then how did he die?"

"Shot to the head. Four shots were fired, two of which hit

Shue. The first hit his chest, but probably wouldn't have been fatal. The second hit the glass in the door a few inches from where Faith was kneeling beside him, so, thinking the gunman was shooting at Shue, she grabbed his feet and had dragged him halfway in when the third shot went over her head. The fourth struck Shue in the head. The first responders said they had to pull her away from Shue. She was trying to stop the bleeding in his chest, but his brains were all over the floor." Another pause, followed by a heavy sigh. "All over her, too. Her clothes, her hands. Her face."

"Oh my God," Bishop murmured. "Poor Faith."

Deacon couldn't say anything at all. Shue's blood on her hands was what she'd described when she'd related the incident earlier that evening. When she'd been safe. But when they'd been on the hotel floor, Deacon's body covering hers . . .

I can't wear your brains. She wasn't being wry. She'd been reliving personal trauma.

"When I got there," Vega finished, "Faith was sitting in a chair, rocking herself. CSU had bagged her hands, and one of the evidence techs was swabbing the brain material from her face. When I asked her what happened, she'd only tell me about his blood on her hands. And then later, when she realized she'd been the real target? No one took her seriously except me."

Someone should have, Deacon thought, furious on her behalf. And then he remembered that someone had known the truth—the cop for whom she was a CI. "She mentioned a friend on the force, a sex-crimes detective named Deb. Ring any bells?"

"Debra Kinnion?" Vega sounded shocked. "Debra hated therapists like Faith."

Deacon frowned. "Hated? As in past tense? What happened to her?"

"She died two years ago. Killed in the line of duty."

Deacon was conscious of Bishop's watchful stare. "Did you know her to be a successful detective?" he asked. "With a good arrest and conviction track record?"

"Hell yeah. Nobody put away more sex offenders than Deb Kinnion and . . ." Vega's voice trailed away, only to return sharply suspicious. "Exactly what are you saying, Novak?"

Standing next to him, Bishop crossed her arms over her chest and gave him a pointed look.

"Nothing," Deacon said easily. "Just asking questions."

Vega snorted. "Seriously, did Faith Frye help Deb Kinnion put offenders away?"

"That would have been incredibly unethical of her," Deacon said quietly, hearing Faith's voice as clearly as if she were standing beside him. *I'm not exactly the poster child for ethics.*

"I suppose that's true," Vega agreed just as quietly. "A therapist who leaks her client's information to the cops risks losing her license. Although that would make a lot of things make sense. But I don't suppose it matters one way or the other now."

Bishop's eyes softened, her expression one of new understanding. "I have a question. How was Faith covered in Shue's brains if she was by his feet when he was shot?"

"After the third shot, people in their building came running to see what was wrong."

"After *three* shots?" Bishop exclaimed. "What the hell?"

"It's a tough neighborhood in Miami, *chica*," Vega chided, purposely thickening her accent. "By the fourth shot, we had witnesses who told us that Faith was standing over Shue, lifting him by his shirt to pull him over the threshold, which put her in Combs's sight."

"Got it," Bishop said. "Did Combs serve in the military?"

"Army," Vega answered promptly, "somewhere in the Gulf."

"Was he a marksman?" Deacon asked.

"Not that I recall. Why?"

"He had to have used a rifle to make the shots he did tonight," Deacon said. "Not the handgun he used on Gordon Shue."

"I don't know that Combs has a rifle, but I don't know that he doesn't, either. I doubt his girlfriend would tell me if he did, but I can ask her. What else do you need?"

"Nothing at the moment, but I'm sure that will change." Deacon ended the call and met Bishop's sharply intelligent stare. "What?" he asked as innocently as he could.

"You knew that she helped cops arrest offenders. When did you plan to tell me that?"

"When it became relevant to the case."

"I might have distrusted her a little less." Bishop's eyes narrowed. "But you trusted her even before you knew the facts."

The smile fell from his lips. "She's a victim in this, Scarlett. Surely you get that by now."

"Oh, I get it. Your feelings for her are no secret. Watching the two of you from behind the glass . . . In my opinion, you're playing with fire. It's too much, too fast."

It *was* too much, too fast, but playing with fire was becoming more attractive with every new piece of Faith's history he added to the puzzle. "So noted."

Bishop sighed. "Just be careful. Mixing business with pleasure rarely ends well."

"I know." The thing was, Deacon no longer cared.

Chapter Fourteen

What is wrong with me? Faith rested her forehead on the edge of the table in the hotel employees' break room. *First I proposition him, then I rip his clothes off.* The woman who currently inhabited her body was a stranger, doing the stupidest things. *What was I thinking?*

She wasn't thinking anymore. She was reacting, her mind protecting itself from the overload of one shock after another. The pressure had been building for months, but she hadn't let down her defenses until tonight. Not until the moment she'd looked into Deacon Novak's eyes, the shields she'd knitted so tightly unraveling in a few hours. She'd told him everything.

Almost everything. She'd kept back the things that would hurt her father, and that was only out of habit. And fear, she admitted. If her father ever found out the lies she'd let him believe ... *Oh God.* He'd be so hurt. *So angry.* So those secrets she'd take to her grave.

Which, if Peter Combs had his way, wouldn't be too long from now.

The door opened, and Faith lifted her head, hoping it was Novak. But the man who walked in didn't have a spiky head of snow-white hair and incredible eyes. He was dark and grim. Angry.

Faith watched warily as Detective Kimble took the chair across from her and placed a spiral notebook on the table. "I apologize for grabbing your arm, Dr. Corcoran. I was out of line."

Faith blew a breath up her forehead. "If I open that notebook, will I find those exact words written inside? Because that was as insincere and forced an apology as I've ever heard."

His jaw tightened. "Just because it's written down doesn't mean it's not sincere."

"Whatever. If you and Isenberg are worried that I'll sue the department, don't be. If you really want to make things right, apologize to Novak. You just made me mad. You *hurt* him. I don't know exactly what you said, but I saw his face after your little testosterone-induced shoving match in my grandmother's front yard. You cut him deeply."

Something shifted in Kimble's eyes. Shame. *Good. He should be ashamed.*

"You're right," he said quietly. "I hurt him. I did apologize, but he didn't want to hear it."

"If your apology was anything like the one I just heard, I'm not surprised," she said tartly.

"Point made, Dr. Corcoran. I still don't like what you did for a living, and I don't like you. But your grief over the family in Miami seemed sincere. Plus, Agent Novak appears to think you're misunderstood and I trust him, so you and I will have to agree to respect his opinion of us."

Faith had to breathe through a wave of fresh grief. She'd managed not to think about that family in Miami for a whole hour. *Because you were too busy escaping Combs. Again.* That sent another wave of guilt hurtling through her.

"Do you know anything about the bellman's status?" she asked him.

"He made it to the ER and is now in surgery. It'll be hours before we know anything more."

"That he's made it this far is better news than I expected. Why are you here, Detective?"

"To take your statement. Yours and the other witnesses'. And to coordinate the efforts of our people with the FBI's forensics team. We had to contract out," he added in disgust. "Your ex-con has wreaked a lot of havoc in a very short time."

Your ex-con. Faith rubbed her aching forehead, sighing when her fingers came away bloody. The superglue Dani had applied to the cut on her head had ripped. *Dammit.* She stood up and grabbed a box of tissues. Dabbing at her forehead, she sat back down, glaring at Kimble.

"*My* ex-con? Do you understand what it means to be a victim? Do you tell the victims of sex crimes that they shouldn't have worn that skirt or walked down that street? He is not *my* ex-con. I didn't ask for *anything* he did to me, and I don't deserve your backhanded insults or half-assed apologies. Just ask your damn questions and leave me alone."

"All right," he said quietly. "Tell me what happened."

In as few words as she could, Faith told him, then pushed away from the table, wobbling on her feet. "I need some air. I assume I'm allowed to leave?"

"Of course. Where do you plan to go?"

"Agent Novak asked me to wait in the lobby. That's where I'll be."

"Stay out of sight if you don't want your picture in the paper. The press is gathering."

"It doesn't matter anymore," she said, finding it hard to stay upright. "I was hiding from Combs. He's obviously found me." She swallowed hard, furious that her eyes were filling with tears. Turning on her heel, she walked away. Her hand was on the doorknob when he spoke again.

"We fought about you, Dr. Corcoran."

She looked back at him with a frown. "Excuse me?"

"Our little testosterone-induced shoving match was about you. I thought he was thinking with the wrong head. I still do. I've known him all of our lives, and only one other time did I see him jettison all common sense because of a pretty face. He fell like a rock that time, too. I warned him that she was a viper, but he wouldn't listen and she nearly destroyed his life."

"Are you suggesting *I'll* destroy his life, Detective Kimble?" she asked, injecting as much haughty incredulity into the question as she could muster.

"You could destroy his career," he said coldly. "For men like Deacon Novak, that's the same thing. While you appear to be a legitimate victim in all this, you are a distraction at best."

Appear? Legitimate? "A distraction?"

"At best. At worst, you're a career killer. He shouldn't be looking at you the way he did in that interview room. He for damn sure shouldn't have touched you, even to comfort you. Even if you *were* sincere in your grief. He's personally involved now, and everyone knows it."

Mortification mixed with fury. "You were watching?"

"Damn straight. We all were. Deacon Novak is new to Isenberg's department. Don't think she's not watching every move he makes. This case could make him, but if you distract him and that missing girl dies, you'll break him. And not just professionally. *So stay away from him.*"

He clearly meant every word he said. And the devil of it was, he was right. She was a distraction, whether she meant to be or not. In the space of several hours, she'd come to depend on Deacon Novak in a way that wasn't healthy—for either of them or for Corinne Longstreet.

I've been alone for a long time. She could be alone again. But she didn't want to be. Nor was she sure that she could let Novak go. And that terrified her.

Shaken, Faith left the break room without another word, closing the door behind her.

The lobby was loud and crowded, a forensics team hard at work, processing the scene. Faith looked around numbly, uncertain of where she should go.

All she knew was that she could not, would not, be a distraction. *I will not risk that girl's life.* No matter how safe Novak made her feel.

Cincinnati, Ohio
Tuesday, November 4, 3:40 a.m.

Deacon pushed past the media gathered on the other side of the crime-scene tape, wishing for the first time in years that he wasn't so noticeable. He was going to draw attention to Faith.

"No comment," he kept saying, gritting his teeth when their flashes popped all around him. He'd be front-page news tomorrow morning. He didn't want Faith plastered there with him.

He saw her as soon as he entered the lobby. She was sitting on a chair next to the front desk, waiting for him, as she'd promised. There was activity all around her as hotel employees dealt with hysterical guests, CPD officers blocked the press from entry, and a forensics unit wearing FBI jackets processed the scene. But Faith sat as still as a statue, her hands folded in her lap.

Alone in a throng of people.

He headed toward her, halting when a thin young man with horn-rimmed glasses stepped in front of him. "Agent Novak, I'm Agent Taylor with the Cincinnati field office."

"CPD called you in?" Deacon asked, and Taylor nodded.

"I'll be processing the scene here and across the street. I understand you were just there?"

"Yeah. Caucasian male in room 245, one bullet in the head. Detective Bishop is still there, waiting for you and the ME." He started to resume his path to Faith, but Taylor shuffled a half step, blocking him again. "Do you need something from me, Agent Taylor?"

Taylor hesitated. "Your coat. As evidence."

Deacon sighed. He'd known this was coming. He shrugged out of his coat, wincing when his shoulder complained. "I want this back. We've been together longer than most marriages."

"I know." Taylor gave him a crooked smile. "Everyone read about the case in West Virginia you worked on with the Baltimore task force. Your coat kind of has a legend of its own."

"A legend, huh. Who knew?" Deacon kept his expression bland even though the mere mention of that case in West Virginia always made him feel like throwing up.

Taylor still stood in front of him. "I'll need your shirt and the vest, too," he said apologetically. "I have a T-shirt in your size. The SWAT team should have an extra vest."

Sighing again, Deacon quickly unbuttoned his shirt, risking a glance across the lobby at Faith. She was watching him. Steadily. He looked away as he stripped down, then re-dressed, feeling far too exposed. "Who's in charge of this scene?" he asked.

"Detective Kimble. He's in the break room, taking statements from the hotel staff."

Shit. "Did he take a statement from Dr. Corcoran?"

"I don't know. You'd have to ask Kimble. She was visibly upset when she came out of the break room. I asked her if

I could call anyone for her, and she said she was waiting for you."

Adam, you are a dead man. "Thanks for looking out for her. Can you call me when you've finished processing the coat? I don't have another, and it's cold outside."

"Of course." Taylor stepped away, nodding. "It might be a few weeks though."

Deacon barely heard him. He was already crossing the lobby to Faith, who rose uncertainly, a host of questions on her face. "You didn't get Combs, did you?" she asked.

"No. We found the room he used. And the body of the man who'd been checked into it."

She lowered herself to the chair, what little color she had draining from her face. "Oh no."

Deacon crouched in front of her, holding her bandaged hands between his. The bandages were now dirty and torn, her fingers icy cold. "Not your fault, Faith," he said softly.

Her throat worked as she struggled to swallow. "I wish I'd killed him when he came into my room that night," she whispered hoarsely. "Too many people have died. How do we stop him?"

We. It was like a fist grabbed his heart and squeezed it bloodless. *We.* Most people would have turned tail and run long, long ago, but Faith kept coming out swinging.

"The attempts on your life started when you inherited the house."

Her green eyes flashed with a virulence that stunned him. "I hate that fucking house."

He leaned in, watching every nuance on her face. "*Why* do you hate it so much?"

It was as if he'd flipped a switch. She blinked once and, when her lashes lifted, the fire had transformed into that calm he found disquieting. She tugged her hands free from his.

"I already told you, Agent Novak, I have bad memories. I learned about my mother's death there. I saw them put her in the ground. I had nightmares for years. I still do."

Deacon didn't blink, holding her gaze in a way that let her know he didn't believe a word. The stare had worked hundreds of times in the past, cracking the wills of everyone from teenaged punks to hardened killers. But Faith Corcoran remained calm, staring back impassively until finally he exhaled his frustration. "You said you wouldn't lie to me, Faith."

Her eyes shifted, grew pained. "I haven't. I never lie. To you or to anyone else."

But she hadn't told the whole truth. "Combs doesn't want you to have the house. Why?"

Confusion clouded her expression. "Because he used it to torture Arianna and her friend. You called the basement his 'torture chamber.' He didn't want anyone to know."

"And an hour ago I believed that, but then he tried to kill you again. We already knew about the house. We had Arianna. It's all over the news. Why would he risk killing you now? He saw the squad car from the window across the street. He saw me escorting you. He got away just minutes before CPD blocked the exits and had that entire hotel under lockdown." He rose a little higher from his crouch, invading her space, and when she backed up, he followed until his nose was only an inch from hers. "Why, Faith? Why would he risk it?"

"I don't know," she blurted out, "and that's the truth. I just don't know." Her shoulders slumped, leaving her looking exhausted and lost. "If I did know, I'd tell you. I promise."

"I want you to come with me to the house."

She closed her eyes on a weary sigh. "I knew you would. When?"

Tomorrow. Next week. Never. "Now."

Her eyes flew open, her terror a tangible thing. But she controlled it quickly, and moments later she appeared detached. *Her mask of choice,* Deacon thought.

"Can I take a shower and change my clothes first?"

Lust slapped him hard, but he kept his expression passive. "Yes."

Her mask slipped, her lips trembling. "Will . . . Will you go with me?"

"To the house? Yes, of course."

She forced a smile. "I didn't doubt that for a moment. I meant upstairs." Her cheeks flushed a dark red, too harsh against her pale skin. "I won't make any advances or try to take your shirt off again. If you could check my room first, then wait outside my door, I'd appreciate it."

Every ounce of blood drained out of his head, straight to

his groin. *The next time she tries to take off my shirt, there is no way in hell I'm going to stop her.* "I'd already planned to clear the room before you went in." He rose, offered his hand. "Come on, let's go."

Cincinnati, Ohio
Tuesday, November 4, 3:30 a.m.

"Who the hell was *that*?" he murmured to the man next to him, a harried reporter who'd been yelling questions at the white-haired bastard.

The man barely spared him a glance. "FBI. Name's Novak. Do your homework, Jack."

He melted back into the crowd, careful to keep his eyes down. He didn't want to call any attention to himself. He just wanted to get away and do a search on Novak.

Who was an FBI agent. Now, that was a surprise. The man looked like he was an actor or an escapee from a comic-book convention. Special Agent Novak with his leather coat and spiky white hair should not be difficult to find. A guy like that must be a field day for reporters.

And Novak had the hots for Faith. He almost felt sorry for the man. Novak would die lonely, because Faith would die first.

Cincinnati, Ohio
Tuesday, November 4, 3:55 a.m.

Faith managed to stay upright for all of a minute and a half—the amount of time it took to get an elevator. When the doors closed them in, she leaned on the wall and looked at Novak, who was leaning against the opposite wall. "Your back is black-and-blue."

He grimaced. "I hoped you wouldn't notice."

"I noticed." Because she'd stared, holding her breath when he'd taken his shirt off. She would have had to be dead not to notice. His back was broad and roped with muscle. He'd rippled when he moved. And he had tattoos—three of them. A large one on his back and one circling the biceps of each arm, all now covered up by the ugly FBI T-shirt and jacket. She wanted a closer look. She wanted a taste.

She needed to stop this hormone-crazed insanity. "My room has a kitchen. The freezer will have enough ice for your back." *And you just invited him inside your room after telling him you wouldn't make another pass.* "I can bring the ice to you. I'm not trying to pick you up. Really."

The elevator door slid open, giving her a small reprieve from her embarrassment. "The manager gave me another key card. The old one was in my purse. Which you guys still have in evidence."

"Your purse can keep my coat company," he said dryly, his hand resting lightly on her back.

It took every ounce of her control not to lean in to him. "That forensics guy, Taylor, he took your suit coat, too. I was going to call you to warn you to stash your leather coat somewhere so that he couldn't take it, too, but my new phone got cracked when we hit the floor. I guess I can go back to my old one now. I'm not exactly incognito anymore." She stopped at her door. "This is it."

"Don't use the old phone until I get it checked for viruses or tracking software," he said. "Give me your key, and do not come in until I tell you to."

She obeyed, leaning against the wall outside her room until the door opened again. Novak looked perturbed. "It's clear now, but it looks like someone went through your things."

Faith rushed in, then stopped, her body sagging in relief. The sitting room was exactly as she'd left it, as were the bedroom and bath. "I was going through my boxes last night," she said, "unpacking a few things. The mess is mine."

He relaxed. "That's good. But just to be certain, check for your valuables."

She complied, opening the safe while he came to stand behind her, warming her with the heat of his body. "My personal papers are still here, including the deed to the house." She passed him an envelope over her shoulder. "Gran's attorney's name is on there, in case you need to contact him." She removed two handguns from the safe and heard him sigh.

"I wondered why you didn't ask for your gun back when you were so insistent we return your phone," he said. "How many more do you have?"

"Just these. I have permits for both." She reached deep,

extracting the small box holding her jewelry and the cell phone she'd disabled the night before. "Did you want this phone?"

"Absolutely. I want to know how he tracked you. Wait," he said as she started to put the contents of the safe back. "There's another envelope in there. What's in it?"

She looked over her shoulder, startled to find him so close that she could see his individual eyelashes. They were white, too. "My comic books."

He arched his brows, looking amused. "*That's* your collection? In that one envelope?"

"No. My collection is in a dozen boxes in Dad's attic. That one envelope holds my best six. Most of them are only worth a few hundred dollars, but the one where Black Widow fights the Avengers is worth almost a thousand. Gran gave it to me when I graduated high school." Faith smiled at the memory. "She thought comic books were 'appropriate fun for kids.'"

"Unlike the R movies, bars, and cigarettes your uncle exposed you to," Novak said dryly.

"Oh, she never found out about any of that stuff. I would have been grounded for the rest of my life. Jordan never told because he would have been in even more trouble for corrupting me."

Faith put everything back in the safe except one of the guns. She popped the magazine, reloaded, and flipped the safety. She looked up to see Novak watching her every move. "I'm not giving this to you. I won't be defenseless."

"I wasn't asking you to. I was making sure you really knew what you were doing."

She lifted her brows. "Did I pass?"

"I'd still like to see you shoot, but yeah. You seem to know your way around a firearm."

"Thank you." She set the gun aside and returned to the sitting area, where she opened a box marked DRAPES and scooped out the pretty yellow curtains Lily had made for her apartment. "Everything's here. My laptop and Xbox don't fit in the safe, so I hid them under my curtains. Most hotel employees are honest, but there's no point tempting fate."

A beat of silence. "You collect comics *and* you're a gamer. Really?"

A delighted grin had transformed his face, making him look young. Lighthearted, even.

It made her smile back, which made him dangerous. The black-leather-clad, larger-than-life Novak had captured her imagination. The Novak who cared about the victims had won her trust. But the Novak standing in front of her now could easily steal her heart.

"Since I was a kid," she told him. "You, too, I take it?"

"Of course." He picked up the game she'd played last night after the nightmare had robbed her of sleep. "You were killing those poor, defenseless zombies?"

"With unadulterated glee."

His laugh warmed her down to her toes. "Me, too. I have that same game. And this one, and these, too," he said as he looked through the other games in the box. But his brows lifted in surprise at *Prison Escape*. "Not this one, though. Have you played it yet?" he asked carefully.

"I finished it. Twice."

He blinked. "Oh. Then I guess I don't need to warn you about the graphic violence."

"I find killing hard-core felons therapeutic. Especially after the sessions with the offenders."

His eyes hardened. "Like Combs."

"And all the others like him." She forced a smile. "But if it makes you feel better, last night I only killed zombies, a few aliens, and a horde of marauding Mongol warriors. It took me all night, but Genghis Khan and his crew will think twice before terrorizing Europe again."

"You played all night? Why? Were you that afraid that Combs would find you?"

"Well, yes, but that's not what had me up," she said, busying herself with removing the soiled bandages from her hands. "I had a nightmare."

"About Combs?"

"No." Tossing the bandages in the trash, she washed her hands at the kitchen sink, scrubbing until she winced. *No blood this time,* she told herself. *There's no blood on your hands.*

He followed her into the kitchen, giving his bruised shoulder an unconscious roll, which reminded Faith why he'd come into her room. She took the ice tray from the freezer and cracked the ice into a plastic shopping bag she found under the sink.

"What did you dream last night, Faith?"

The same thing she'd dreamed for twenty-three years. *Twelve steps and a basement.* She wanted to answer him, to tell him about the nightmare, but the words simply would not come.

"Put this bag of ice on your shoulder. It will help with the bruising." She focused on filling the ice tray with water, the task made difficult given the way her hands were shaking.

"Let me do that," he said, so gently that it made her eyes sting. Reaching around her, he took the ice tray from her hands, filled it, set it aside. He didn't move, didn't step away. Didn't touch her. He just stood at her back, warm and steady.

Calming her with his presence. The seconds became a minute. One minute stretched into several, and still he said nothing. Did nothing. And slowly the realization seeped in that, for the very first time in her memory, she didn't feel so utterly and terrifyingly alone.

"Deacon," she whispered, because she didn't know what else to say.

He moved then, as if he'd been awaiting her permission, leaning closer until his nose brushed her hair. He inhaled deeply, sending everything within her liquid with longing.

She let her head fall back until it rested on his uninjured shoulder, closing her eyes. Wishing he'd touch her. Needing him to.

His hands slid up her arms, covering her shoulders, pulling the rest of her body fully against him. "Don't cry, Faith," he murmured in her ear. "Please."

She touched her cheek, surprised to find it wet. "It's just . . . nice to be held. Thank you."

His hands tightened on her shoulders, the only warning before he turned her around and wrapped his arms around her. One of his hands threaded through her hair, cradling her head against his shoulder. The other hand rubbed her back in long, slow strokes.

Feeling safe, cared for. Being held. Things that so many took for granted. Faith knew how rare they were. Having them now, from this man . . . She'd kept the events of the day boxed in, compartmentalized. It was how she'd coped her whole life. But now the walls crumbled, the grief and fear from the day and all the days that had come before welling up with the force of a flash flood until she was sobbing harder than she had in the police station.

"Sshh," he murmured. "You're here. You're safe. He won't hurt you. I won't let him."

Maybe you should let him. Maybe he'll stop once I'm gone.

No. She immediately smacked the notion down. Combs wouldn't stop once she was dead. He'd go on, hurting other people, more young women like Arianna and Corinne. Like his own stepdaughter and her friend. Like Gordon. And he wouldn't care. Good people's lives would be ruined, and the bastard would not care.

"All those people," she whispered into Novak's chest. "He's killed so many innocent people. How can I live with that, Deacon? How can I make this right?"

He tugged on her hair gently, urging her to look up at him. He wiped her tears with his fingers. "You're innocent, too," he said fiercely. "Don't you ever forget that."

"Would that mother in Miami think so? Could I honestly have expected her to?"

"You can't think like that," he said, his voice husky.

"How do I not think it, Deacon? How do you stop from thinking about it?"

He said nothing for a long moment, his eyes locking with hers. Then he bent his head and brushed his lips against hers, so gently. He kissed the corner of her mouth, her cheeks, her temple, then returned to her mouth for another kiss, harder this time but still careful.

"Like that," he murmured, his mouth curving ever so slightly. "Just like that."

She stared up at him, stunned. Then, like the lash of a whip, the need rose as swiftly as the grief had done. Clutching handfuls of his jacket, she pulled him down as she lifted to her toes to kiss him back. Hard.

He made a low sound of approval and took over, taking it deeper, angling her head to perfect their fit. This was no pity kiss, she thought. His heart was beating so hard she could feel it. Or maybe it was her own heart. It didn't matter. She let herself go and enjoyed being kissed by a beautiful man who totally knew what he was doing.

She slid her hands up his chest, feeling the hard muscle beneath his T-shirt and wanting more. He felt good. So, so good. She wanted the shirt gone. She wanted to touch him. Wanted to know if the rest of his skin was as tanned as his face.

He ended it too soon, dragging a protest from her lips as he pulled back far enough to search her face. His cheeks were dark, his mouth wet. But it was his eyes that grabbed her, always his eyes. They glittered like gems. Aroused, yet contained. Watchful.

He was waiting for her to make the next move. She wasn't sure what that should be.

She lifted a tentative hand, feathering her fingertips along his eyebrows, so white they leapt from his bronzed skin and so bright they made the blue and brown of each iris seem even more brilliant. "You have the most beautiful eyes I have ever seen," she whispered.

His eyes flashed, making her shiver in anticipation as his mouth came down on hers again, voracious this time. His hands tunneled into her hair as he backed her into the counter, his hips pressing against her insistently, dragging another moan from her throat.

The hard ridge that had felt so good against her behind when they'd crawled across the lobby floor felt even better now. Bigger. Impossibly harder. She wrapped her arms around his neck, lifted higher on her toes, trying to position his erection where it would do some good.

His sudden hiss of pain had her freezing, and too late she remembered his shoulder—the very reason he was in her room. She dropped from her toes, pulling her arms from around his neck. "Oh God. I'm sorry, Deacon. I'm sor—"

His mouth swallowed the apology, this kiss soft and tender. "I'm not. I'm not sorry at all." He was breathing hard. Trembling as he released his hold. She'd made this strong man tremble. But she didn't have more than a second to bask in the knowledge before he hissed again.

"What the—" He glared at the blood that covered his palm, then gently brushed the hair from her forehead. "Why didn't you tell me that I was hurting you? Why didn't you stop me?"

"You didn't hurt me. Not just now, anyway. That happened when you tackled me—which saved my life. I thought

I'd taken care of it downstairs." Dabbing her head with a tissue, she stepped aside so that he could wash her blood from his hand.

"I need to take you back to the ER."

She wanted to say yes. She wanted to hide in the ER or anywhere in the world that wasn't the house. But that was cowardly. And selfish.

Selfish. Guilt smacked her like a brick. She'd distracted Novak when he needed to be looking for Corinne, just like Kimble had said she would. *If that missing girl dies, you'll break him. And not just professionally.* "Take me to the house first. Corinne is running out of time."

He studied her face, then nodded grimly. "Change your clothes. But hurry."

Cincinnati, Ohio
Tuesday, November 4, 4:45 a.m.

He powered down his computer, satisfied. Novak hadn't been hard to find at all. The man attracted media attention everywhere he went. He'd already been covered in the Cincinnati papers four times, even though he'd transferred from Baltimore only a month ago. Coverage in Baltimore was even more extensive.

Novak had been part of a joint task force there, just like he was here. He appeared to be something of a wunderkind, with degrees in chemistry, psychology, and computer science. He'd been premed in college, accepted to med school, but turned them down for a career with the FBI.

It had been so kind of him to do a Q&A session with the kids at that Baltimore high school on career day. It had been even kinder for the teacher of those eleventh graders to post their summaries of Novak's visit online.

But what he'd learned from all that was that Novak wouldn't be easy prey. He was pretty damn smart, which was all the better. He'd always loved to take the geniuses down a few pegs. Novak, of course, would go down more than just a few pegs. He hadn't been very smart about keeping a low profile personally. He'd bought a house recently, in his own name.

He was ridiculously easy to find. And if he didn't go to his new house anytime soon, that wasn't a problem, either.

Because he had a sister. Dr. Danika Novak was an ER doctor right here in town. How sweet. Doctors were notoriously careless about their own safety, forgetting everything and everyone around them when they were saving lives. He imagined Novak's sister wouldn't be an exception.

And if the hospital had security, she also volunteered at the Meadow, a haven for the homeless. *I can look homeless. I can look wounded.* He took a long look at the photo he'd pulled up of Danika Novak. She was pretty, also in a comic-book-hero kind of way. He imagined Agent Novak could be convinced to trade Faith for his beautiful sister, if it came to that.

But the first order of business was to silence Faith before she returned to the house. She would tell them things that he did not want them to know. If the cops continued to believe he'd only kept Arianna and Corinne there, they'd collect their evidence and go away. But if Faith remembered how things had once been . . .

They'd start digging. And that was something he wanted to avoid at all costs.

Chapter Fifteen

In a generally foul frame of mind, Deacon parked his loaner sedan in front of the O'Bannion house. Faith had said little since they'd left her hotel, looking more fragile with every mile they drove. Now she stared out the window at the big house, her eyes huge in her pale face.

Deacon muttered a curse, hating that she had to face a nightmare that had haunted her for twenty-three years. But hating himself more. *I should have kept my hands to myself.* He'd known she was vulnerable. But he hadn't been able to stop himself.

She'd been so soft. Fit him so perfectly. Made those little greedy sounds that had him wanting to take her right there in the kitchen. Bishop had been right. It was too much, too soon. He needed to put Faith's kissable mouth out of his mind and concentrate on finding out what it was about this house that made Combs keep trying to kill her.

"Are you all right?" he asked, and she nodded once.

"It's just a house. I keep telling myself that." She unbuckled her seat belt and slid from the sedan before he could come around to help her out.

"Faith, wait." He got a bulletproof vest and slid it over her head. It was way too big, hanging on her slender shoulders, falling past her hips. "I don't have a smaller one."

"At least the target on my ass won't be a problem," she said wryly, and he chuckled, proud of her. She was still pale. Still visibly afraid. But her jaw was set, her mouth determined.

He led her through the gate and to the front porch, glancing at her every few seconds. Her breathing had become shallow and rapid, her teeth sunk into her lower lip. Her hands gripped each other so hard that her knuckles were white. She stopped abruptly at the stairs.

"Just a house," she whispered. "Just a goddamn house."

"Lean on me," Deacon murmured. "You're not here alone, Faith."

She took his arm then in a grip so hard, he sucked in a surprised breath. "I'm sorry," she whispered, but she didn't loosen her hold.

"I can take it." He helped her up the stairs, worried when she stumbled over the threshold. "Breathing is good," he said lightly, aware that they were now the subject of the stares of the two forensics techs who'd set up a mini-office on the living room floor. "You should give it a try."

She shuddered in a breath and blew it out. "Just a house, right?"

"Just a house, honey. Open your eyes. It's just a house with a lot of old furniture. It's dusty and desperately needs a few coats of paint."

She opened her eyes and looked around cautiously. "It's bigger than I remembered. I thought it was supposed to be the other way around." Her gaze landed on the ornate banister that framed the grand, curving staircase. "I used to slide down that banister. Gran would be so angry, but my mother would laugh." She swallowed hard. "I can't tell you if anything's missing, Deacon. I don't remember everything that was here."

"Maybe one of your uncles can help," he suggested, watching her face. She flinched, and something deep within him wanted to roar.

Someone had hurt her in this house. It was plain to see. Deacon didn't care who it was, he'd find them and make them pay. One way or another.

"What do you dream, Faith?"

Her gaze flew up to meet his, panicked. Like a deer ready to flee.

He stroked her hair. "You know you need to tell some-one."

She closed her eyes, and when she opened them, she was in control and wary. "Don't play therapist with me, Deacon. Please."

"Faith, whatever it is, it's eating—"

"Whatever it is, it has nothing to do with any of this," she snapped. "If you can't respect that, I don't know what else to tell you."

He stowed his frustration. "I'm sorry. Let me get you geared up." He took the vest off and gave her gloves, then knelt and slipped protective booties over her shoes. Rising, he helped her put the second glove on because her hands were shaking too hard to do the job herself. "The crime scene is in the basement," he said. "Will you—"

She'd tensed again.

Deacon wanted to scream, but he kept his voice calm. "Will you go down there with me?"

"Of course," she said. "It's through the kitchen."

She walked stiffly, one foot in front of the other. The door was open, and she stood there looking down the stairs, her face frighteningly serene. Like she was gone.

"Faith? Are you all right?"

"I'm doing what I need to do, Agent Novak."

He hid his wince at her return to formalities, realizing that she was coping with whatever it was that she refused to tell him.

She leaned forward, a curious expression coming over her face as she inspected the walls on either side of the basement staircase. "That's not how it was."

Standing behind her, Deacon twisted so that he could see her face. "What do you mean?"

"It was open. No walls."

"Maybe they were added later."

She gave him a long, hard look. "No. I was here on that last day. There were no walls."

"The last day? The day your mother died?"

She nodded. "There were no walls."

Okay. "Will you go down the stairs?"

"Of course." She closed her eyes and took a hard step down, wrapping her gloved fingers around the wooden pole that served as a banister. He followed her as she took one stair at a time, her movements jerky. He stayed ready to catch her if she fell.

She got to the bottom and took a final step, far bigger than she needed to. It caused her to stumble, and Deacon quickly grabbed her shoulders.

"Steady," he murmured. "You're down. You did it."

She froze. "No. I'm not. There are two more steps. Always twelve."

Her eyes were clenched shut. "Faith, open your eyes and look at me."

She swallowed hard and opened her eyes. "There were always twelve steps."

"Maybe you're just remembering it wrong."

Her eyes flashed, and he was relieved. She was still in there. He was a little worried he'd pushed her off some kind of emotional ledge.

"I remember twelve steps. Always twelve. I'd always count."

"Why? Why would you count?"

"Because I wouldn't look." She drew a deep breath, her nose wrinkling. "I smell bleach."

"Yes. Why wouldn't you look?"

She looked side to side, her eyes growing wide. "None of this was here. This was all open."

"He added walls, then." Which surprised him. That was not the behavior of a wolf just biding his time as he waited on Red Riding Hood. Her attacker hadn't just set up shop. He'd set up house. "Why wouldn't you look, Faith?"

"I never liked this basement. It always scared me, even when I was really small." She looked up, squinting at the overhead lights. "None of that was here. It was dark and dank. Gran's cook used to send me down here for canned vegetables. She didn't like it down here, either."

"What do you dream?"

She sighed wearily. "Of the steps. Always twelve. You think I'm misremembering. I'm telling you there were twelve fucking steps."

He blinked at her, surprised not only by the curse, but by the softness with which she'd uttered it. "Okay. I'll tell Tanaka."

"Your forensics guy. He swabbed my hands. He was very kind. Where do I go next?"

"Can you look in each room?"

"Of course." She checked the office first. "I know that desk came from upstairs. It was in my grandfather's study. How did he even get it down here?"

"Good question." The desk was massive. "Maybe he took it apart."

"Maybe. The metal file cabinet wasn't in the house. He must have brought that."

"How do you know?"

"Gran wouldn't tolerate anything that looked so common. Everything was wood." She shrugged. "I guess I remember more than I'd thought."

"I thought you would." He pointed to the small kitchen. "And this?"

"The table came from my grandmother's bedroom. She had a vase on it. A blue vase with clouds. The vase she took with her when she moved to the city. It's Uncle Jordan's now. He got all the furnishings she'd taken from the house. I got everything else. Go me."

"Could there be an item in the house valuable enough that someone would kill you over it? Something one of your family members doesn't want you to have?"

She gave him a level look. "You're suggesting my uncles are involved."

"Maybe."

"That's ridiculous. If there was anything here of value, either of them could have come back at any time over the last twenty-three years to retrieve it. Nobody's lived here, and the alarm system is fairly new. Anybody could have come back and looted." She pointed to the refrigerator, stove, and microwave. "None of those are original to the house." She turned to leave, then noticed the blanket hanging over the dug-in hallway. "What's that?"

"There's a crawl space back there, where someone was sleeping." Except that he'd found a women's small T-shirt in the box and nothing to indicate that a man Combs's size had been down here.

Neither Corinne nor Arianna wore a size small. Who else had he had down here?

He followed her to the room with the cot and the shackles in the wall and heard her small cry of anguish. "He held them here?"

"Probably," Deacon murmured.

She stared at the cot for a moment longer. When she turned, she was pale again, her eyes cool and detached. She brushed past him and opened the door to the final room.

The torture room. Deacon waited for another cry of anguish, but she made no sound. She was staring straight ahead, ignoring the autopsy table where Tanaka was collecting samples.

"Where's the door?" she asked quietly.

"What door?"

"There was a door in that wall. It led to the outside." She turned right, avoiding the autopsy table completely. "And there were windows on this wall. Up near the ceiling. I remember."

"She's right," Tanaka said. "About the windows, anyway. They've been covered up outside. Someone plastered over them and painted to make it look like they were never there, both inside and outside. I think this interior wall is a fake. I ordered X-ray equipment to be brought out here. I want to be sure nothing is being hidden in these walls."

"How long ago were the door and windows covered?" Deacon asked, frowning.

"Hard to say without some analysis. We can look at the kind of paint used, how much it's oxidized, run it through a few aging models. Doesn't look recent, though."

"Like older-than-a-year not recent?"

"Like older-than-ten-years not recent," Tanaka said, and Deacon swallowed a curse.

His timeline was unraveling, he realized. Combs had crossed Faith's path only four years ago. Something else was going on here, and he didn't like any of it.

"She also remembers twelve steps," Deacon said.

Tanaka's brows lifted. "There are only ten."

Faith's jaw clenched. "I know what I remember."

"I believe that you remember it," Tanaka said.

She turned to look at him. "But you don't believe it's true."

"I didn't say that, Dr. Corcoran." Tanaka left the torture room and crouched at the base of the steps, shining his flashlight on the floor seams. Then he straightened and went back into the room with the cot and shackles in the walls.

Faith followed him, Deacon at her back. They stopped in

the doorway, watching Tanaka walk carefully across the floor. The forensics specialist paused, bounced softly on his toes, then took a giant step back. When he turned to face them, his eyes gleamed.

"I thought I felt a slight give in this floor when I came through earlier," he said. "I was going to check it further, but I didn't feel it anywhere else, so I back-burnered it."

Faith had gone very still. "The floor is fake, too? Like the wall?"

Tanaka shrugged. "It's not supported in that one spot. That's all I can tell you."

"Are you saying that someone lifted this entire floor by sixteen inches?" Deacon looked up at the ceiling, the roughed-out beams and exposed pipes. "I'd have thought I'd be bumping my head right now, but there's still six inches of clearance. That would mean the ceilings were very high to begin with."

Faith's breathing had grown rapid and shallow again. "Yes. They were high."

Deacon tipped her chin up so that he could see her eyes. "Why? Why were they high?"

She closed her eyes and shook her head, pulling free of his grip. "It would take someone a long time to raise a floor by sixteen inches, wouldn't it, Detective Tanaka?"

"Sergeant," Tanaka corrected mildly. "Possibly. I heard you telling Agent Novak that the walls were different, too. Were any of these partitioned rooms here when you were a child?"

"Yes. That one." She pointed over her shoulder to the torture room. "But not the way it is now. The door opened into a little alcove, where you could change your clothes if you got muddy. My grandmother didn't let muddy shoes in the house."

"Were your shoes often muddy?" Deacon asked quietly, still trying to get to her dream.

"Yes. I liked to play outside."

Tanaka looked concerned. "Maybe you should sit down, Dr. Corcoran. You look pale."

"I'll sit down when I'm done. I'd really like to get this over with."

"You've seen everything down here," Tanaka said.

"No," she said shortly, tersely. "I would like to see you

remove that piece of flooring. If something is under the floor, I'd like to know."

Tanaka looked at Deacon, who gave him a nod. "Let me get photographs of the floor first, then we'll take up the tile."

"Will you see the rest of the other room while we're waiting?" Deacon asked her.

She swallowed hard. "Of course." She marched herself through the door to the torture room, straight to the corner farthest from the autopsy table. "This is where the little changing room would have been. There were hooks for coats and drying stands for boots."

Deacon took her shoulders and gently turned her so that she faced the metal table and the wall beyond, feeling her body stiffen with dread. "What was there? On that wall?"

"Shelves with jars," she said. "Jams and jellies mostly. My grandmother's cook put up preserves back then." Her forehead wrinkled. "And olives."

He blinked. "Olives? Your grandmother's cook canned her own olives, here in Ohio?"

Her forehead smoothed, and she gave him an odd look. "Of course not. They bought the olives already canned." Voices drifted across the hall, and Faith slipped from his grip again, hurrying back to where Tanaka and one of his techs huddled around the floor tiles in question.

Tanaka looked up when Deacon and Faith entered the small room. "This tile is loose. Just stay where you are. We'll pull it up and see if there's anything under here."

The tech inserted a thin file into the seam between the tiles and raised one, immediately recoiling. He jumped to his feet, dropping the tile as he did so. *"Holy shit."*

Faith's strangled cry pierced Deacon's ears as his own stomach turned inside out, bile bubbling up to burn his throat. *Oh God. Not again.*

Looking up at them from below the floor were the remains of a human face.

Mt. Carmel, Ohio
Tuesday, November 4, 7:15 a.m.

"Update," Isenberg demanded as soon as she walked through the O'Bannions' front door.

Deacon took a quick glance out the front door to be sure

Faith was still all right. She was curled up in the passenger seat of his car, her eyes closed. He hoped she was getting some sleep. "We've only pulled up the floor in that one small room so far. We found three bodies, all female. All blondes who appear to have been in their twenties. None were buried in the earth. All were encased in Plexiglas coffins resting on the original dirt floor. We don't know what we'll find under the remaining floor tiles."

"God." Isenberg looked as worn as he felt. "What's the connection to Corcoran?"

"Her recollection of the number of steps down into the basement led us to check under the floor tiles," Deacon said. "Otherwise, we may have thought that this house had been used only to torture Arianna and Corinne."

"So if Corcoran was dead, you might never have looked for his bodies."

Deacon's stomach twisted again. "It's very possible."

"Except that we found that women's T-shirt, size small," Adam said. "Neither of the victims wears that size. Nor does Corcoran. Someone else was down there."

"Maybe his accomplice." Isenberg looked over her shoulder. "Did Corcoran see the body?"

"Just the face of the first one," Deacon said. "She got sick. I got her out of there."

Isenberg gave him an assessing look tinged with sympathy. "And you?"

Deacon grimaced. Watching the bodies recovered and knowing more could be right under his feet . . . It was way too close to the dozens of unmarked graves he'd uncovered on his last case in West Virginia. "I'm okay."

"Good enough. Do we still like Combs for this?"

Deacon rubbed the back of his neck. "It's looking less likely."

"Whoever did the renovations spent a lot of time down there," Bishop said. "Weeks. Maybe months. Two of the bodies appear to be recently deceased. Combs could be involved."

"But the house was modified perhaps ten years ago," Tanaka said. "And Dr. Corcoran only met Combs four years ago."

"But we know the same gun was used here and in Florida, so we need to figure out what role her ex-con plays in all this," Isenberg said.

Adam's mouth curved, but it wasn't a smile. "I wouldn't use that term with her, Lynda," he said mockingly. "She's pretty damn adamant that he's not *her* ex-con."

"Adam, do you know something about Dr. Corcoran that you'd like to share?" Isenberg asked sharply. "Something that makes you suspect her more than the rest of us do?"

Adam shook his head. "No."

"There is something else, though," Deacon said, shoving his anger at Adam aside. "She's dreamed of this house since she was a child. She would go down the steps and count them."

"Which is how she knew there were two less than there were supposed to be," Isenberg said. "What happened to her in that basement?"

"I don't know, but when she first came down, she wouldn't look behind her. When she finally did, she was shocked to see a wall. She said it hadn't been there back then."

"She also said the ceilings were high," Tanaka said softly. "What trauma would make her remember such a detail, Agent Novak? She was just a child. Why would she even notice how high a ceiling reached?"

Deacon met Tanaka's sympathetic gaze and realized the man had picked up on something he had not. Not until that moment, at least. Now understanding dawned, and he couldn't stop himself from looking at Faith, asleep in his car.

"Oh God," he murmured. "She called it 'that last day.' The day her mother died. She said she died in a car accident. Maybe she didn't. Maybe Faith saw something that day when she came down the stairs. Something so traumatic that she hasn't returned to the house in twenty-three years."

Bishop sighed. "Something that made her look up at the ceiling. Dammit, Deacon. You could always check the death certificate for her mother's cause of death to see if it was suicide."

But Deacon was pretty certain it was. *Oh, baby,* he thought sadly. *No wonder you hate this house.* But why hadn't she just told him? Why keep it a secret?

"It would have been a terrible day for her," Isenberg said, "but we need to focus on identifying the bodies that are down there."

"And on finding Corinne Longstreet," Adam said.

"And the locksmith and the power tech," Deacon added, "who are also still missing."

Bishop sighed again. "And on finding out who shot the bellman and Anthony Brown, the victim in the hotel room."

"Plus the three who died in Miami," Deacon said. "Someone has been actively trying to kill Faith Corcoran during the last month, but if the door and windows of this basement were covered up and hidden ten years ago, it's almost impossible that Combs could have been involved back then. If he wasn't involved then, how could he be involved now?"

"I thought she said she saw him breaking into her apartment in Miami a few weeks ago," Isenberg said, frowning.

Deacon considered what Faith had told him. "She said that she couldn't see him well enough to shoot him because she didn't have her contacts in. She may not have seen his face, only that he was the same size as Combs. That it *was* Combs would have been the natural assumption."

"I still think we should get her uncles in for questioning ASAP," Adam said.

"On that we can agree," Deacon said.

"Who else should we be talking to?" Isenberg asked. "Who else had access to this house? The lawn looks like it's been recently mowed. Who does the maintenance?"

"The historical society takes care of the outside," Deacon said. "They employ a gardener. We'll talk to him this morning. But remember, he has to have access and knowledge of the contents of her grandmother's will."

"Dammit," Isenberg muttered. "Check him out anyway."

"Bishop, can you take the gardener?" Deacon asked, and she nodded. "Thanks. We need information on the bodies downstairs. The ME will take them as soon as you're done, Vince."

"We'll pull up the rest of the tiles," Tanaka said. "I estimate it will take us several hours."

Deacon looked out the side window where the O'Bannion land spread as far as he could see. His stomach gave another vicious twist. Lots of land. Lots of space for bodies. "We need to make sure he didn't bury any bodies outside."

"It'll take us a good deal longer to do an adequate search there," Tanaka said.

"Can you use ground-penetrating radar?" Deacon asked.

"I've had good results with it. I know someone who's nationally known for GPR." He remembered the weeks he'd spent digging up bodies in West Virginia. "She should be able to recommend someone local."

"I'll let you know if I need a name. Now, if you'll excuse me, I have a lot of work to do."

Isenberg looked over her shoulder at Faith, still sleeping in the car. "Corcoran can't go back to her hotel. It's a media circus. She'll have to go to a safe house."

"Absolutely," Deacon said. "I'll take care of it."

Chapter Sixteen

Cincinnati, Ohio
Tuesday, November 4, 8:00 a.m.

Faith woke with a start, then relaxed when she smelled the faint cedar that lingered on Novak's skin. They were moving. She'd fallen asleep in the passenger seat while waiting in front of the house, so far gone that she hadn't woken when he'd started the car and driven away.

"I have to call my father when I get back to the hotel," she murmured. "I have to tell him about what's happening before he hears it on the news and starts to worry. Especially since I'm not answering either of my cell phones now."

"You can use mine to call him, if you'd like."

"What time is it?" she asked, raising her seat upright. "He doesn't usually wake up till after—" She frowned, distracted by their surroundings. They were in the suburbs, not the city. "This isn't the way to my hotel. Where are we going?"

"Safe house." He looked at her from the corner of his eye. "You can't stay in your hotel. Not after last night. Even if he doesn't try for you again there, the media will swarm you."

"What about my stuff?"

"Bishop should have moved it all by now, except for what's in your safe."

Her frown deepened. "I don't like people touching my things."

His mouth tightened. "I don't like people shooting at you."

She sighed, knowing she'd been churlish. "Thank you. For everything you've done for me."

He let a beat of silence pass. "Everything?" he asked softly.

She knew he meant that kiss in the kitchen, and for a moment she let herself remember being held in his arms. How good he'd felt ... all over. "Yes, everything. But we can't do that again."

White brows lifted. "And why would that be?"

"Because I'm still a witness, Deacon. You said yourself that it's not ethical."

"I also said I changed my mind."

"About passing me to Bishop. Maybe you should do that, then you won't get distracted."

"I'm not distracted."

"Yes, you are. You're chauffeuring me again," she pointed out. "Don't tell me that you don't have anywhere else to be. You've got three active crime scenes."

"Five active crime scenes, actually. Yes, I am supposed to be somewhere else. I have an appointment with my brother's principal in a few hours, so I'm killing two birds with one stone. I can get you settled while I shower and change my clothes."

Her eyes narrowed. "Excuse me?"

"I can't meet my brother's principal smelling like a crime scene. Although it might make the meeting shorter," he added thoughtfully. "That's not a bad idea, actually."

"Don't try to be cute, Deacon. Exactly whose 'safe' house is this?"

"Mine."

She stared at him. "You're taking me to your house? Isenberg approved this?"

"Just until we set up something better, which should be later this morning. My place has a good security system. I installed it myself, so I know it works." He angled her a sly grin, waggling his eyebrows. "It also has a sixty-five-inch flat screen you can connect to your Xbox."

She found herself chuckling. "You're nervy, Novak. I'll

give you that. Who's going to guard me while you're off
dealing with your delinquent brother?"

His smile dimmed, and she wanted to kick herself for her
phrasing. "I've requested two agents from the field office.
You'll be in good hands."

Of that she had no doubt. He'd promised he wouldn't let
anything happen to her, and Deacon Novak seemed to be a
man of his word. It was the loss of his smile that worried
her.

"I'm sorry. I shouldn't have talked about your brother
that way."

"No, you're right. He's well on his way to being a delinquent, and I don't know what to do."

"I'm sorry," she said again, giving his forearm a light
squeeze, feeling his muscles flex beneath her palm. And that
fast, she wished they were back in her hotel room, kissing
like there was no tomorrow. Touching him, even platoni-
cally, was dangerous.

She pulled her arm away, but he caught her hand.
Threaded their fingers together and rested their joined
hands on his powerful thigh. All while he kept his eyes focused straight ahead.

"Not yet," he murmured. "Don't pull away yet."

There was a vulnerability in his voice that she hadn't
heard before. It made him even more dangerous because
she didn't want to hurt him.

"Do you change your mind with all your witnesses, Deacon?" she asked, hoping he could hear that she was vulnerable, too.

He released her hand as if she'd burned him. "You
should try to get a little more sleep while I'm gone," he said
tersely. "And should you experience any issues with what
you saw, the department can recommend a counselor."

She folded her hands in her lap, feeling bereft. And
guilty, like she'd kicked his puppy or something. Unsettled,
she lashed out. "With what I *saw*? Which thing, Deacon?
Arianna lying in the road, a bellman gunned down in front
of me, or the remains of that poor woman under the floor
of my grandmother's house? Which thing that I *saw* might
give me 'issues'?"

"All of them," he said angrily. "All of them are going to
give you nightmares. Not like you didn't have enough al-

ready. And no, I've never 'changed my mind' with any other witness."

Her heart skittered. "Thank you for that," she said quietly, then attempted a smile. "But I'll pass on the counselor, if you don't mind. I've managed on my own this long. I'll be all right."

He didn't smile with her. He didn't even answer her. Instead, he turned onto a tree-lined street and hit a button above his head. Faith got only a glimpse of a large, two-story Tudor-style house before closing her eyes in a moment of startled panic when he gunned the engine and took a hard right into a driveway, heading for an open garage door. He braked hard, and when she opened her eyes they were in the garage, the door beginning its descent.

He was out of the car before she caught her breath, looking menacing, furious even, as he helped her from her seat, but she wasn't afraid. And when he hauled her into his arms, she wasn't surprised. She was relieved, welcoming the feel of his arms tight around her, of his mouth hot and hard and demanding.

He needed her. Needed this. Which was good, because she needed it, too.

"You are *not* all right," he whispered fiercely against her lips. "And neither am I."

He lifted his head, staring down at her in the darkness. "You have a serial killer after you, and I don't want to let you out of my sight. But I have to. I have to let someone else keep you safe while I stop him, or you will never be safe again."

Her heart skipped a beat. Then pounded so hard that the room spun. *Serial killer. In my grandmother's house.* "How many are there?" she whispered. "How many bodies?"

"Three in the first room. So far."

"Three? So far?" An awful understanding descended, threatening to choke her. "It's not Combs, is it?" *Someone else is trying to kill me.*

"Not only him, anyway. Not unless he knew you before he was assigned to your program."

"No, he didn't. Sergeant Tanaka said the torture-room windows had been covered ten years ago. Whoever this is has been killing for that long, hasn't he?"

"I don't know, Faith. I truly don't know. We'll know more

when the ME examines the bodies. Didn't any of your family go out there ever? In the last twenty-three years?"

"My father went every few years on the anniversary of my mother's death."

"In a car accident," he said carefully. "Even though it's the basement that frightens you, the stairs you count. The height of the ceiling you remember."

He knew. Of course he did. Of course he'd figured it out. On some level she'd known he would. She went silent, pressing her cheek into his chest as he stroked her hair so tenderly it made her want to cry.

"Why won't you tell me the truth, Faith?" he whispered.

"I can't. Please don't ask me."

"Why not?"

"Because we were more Catholic than the Pope," she whispered bitterly, and felt him sigh.

"And suicide is a sin."

"Not just any sin. It's the big sin."

He kept on stroking her hair, holding her tight. "You saw her?"

She nodded, her throat too thick to speak. It was a nightmare she'd never, ever forget, but she couldn't talk about it. Not to him. Not to anyone. Now or ever.

"All right, honey," he murmured. "I won't ask anymore. But I do need to know if your father noticed the change to the outside of the house—the windows being covered."

"He wouldn't have noticed. The cemetery is on the other side of the house."

"He might have seen it from the road when he was driving up."

"He wouldn't have noticed," she repeated firmly. "He didn't know the house like I did. He didn't come with us when we visited. He dropped us off and picked us up later." The only time she could remember him staying for more than an hour was in the days following her grandfather's death. And her mother's. "He and my grandmother didn't get along too well."

"Why not?"

"Because he left the priesthood to marry my mother," she said, and felt his jerk of surprise.

"Okay," he said slowly. "I can honestly say I did not expect that answer."

Faith sighed. "He was still in the seminary and hadn't taken his vows yet, but Gran didn't think that made a difference. So he didn't know the house," she repeated, rubbing her cheek against Novak's chest. He felt good. Hard. Solid. Safe. "You can't ask him, Deacon. My dad is sick. He had a stroke last year. The worry of all this is going to kill him."

He kissed the top of her head and made her heart melt all over again. "Then call him and tell him you're safe. And then keep yourself out of harm's way as best you can."

"So no going to work for me today," she said with a sigh, knowing he was right.

"Y'think?" he asked dryly, making her smile again.

"I've also got to call my boss, then. What am I allowed to say?"

"That you were in a car accident last night and had some complications," he said blandly.

Faith almost laughed. "Complications?"

"It's not a lie."

"No, it's not." Reluctantly, she stepped out of his arms. "Lead the way to my safe house."

He opened the door into the house, and the smell of fresh paint made her sneeze. "Sorry," he said. "I'm camping out here while I get the place ready for us to move in."

"Us?"

"Dani and Greg and I."

She stopped in the laundry room to look up at him warily. "You're moving in with your sister and brother?"

"More like they're moving in with me. I bought this place last summer and started fixing it up when I moved back a month ago. Dani's moving in at the end of the week. So is Greg. If he keeps himself out of juvie, that is."

Her heart softened. "You moved back here for him, didn't you?"

He nodded. "He's been living with my aunt and uncle most of his life, but he's gotten to be too much for them to control, and my aunt's health is fragile. Greg got thrown out of his last school and Dani couldn't handle him alone, so I decided to come home. I wanted a place in a good school system, big enough that we wouldn't trip over each other. We lived in this same neighborhood after my mother married my stepfather, just a few streets over. I wanted to settle here, and this fixer-upper was all I could afford."

"That's why Greg attends the school you and Dani attended before your mother and stepfather died," she said thoughtfully. "Did both Dani and Greg go to live with your aunt and uncle afterward?"

He nodded once. "They let me finish out the year at our old school because I was a senior, but the school system made Dani change schools because my aunt and uncle live in a different district. It was hard on her, losing Mom and Bruce and her friends all at once. Greg's had to change schools, too, but only because he was thrown out of the last two." He shook his head a little. "Let me give you the nickel tour." He led her into the kitchen, flicking on the lights. "I finished this first. Figured we'd need to eat."

Faith looked around, impressed. "You do good work." The cabinets were new, as were the appliances. And the flooring. She jerked her eyes up from the pretty tile, unwilling to think of the tile in her grandmother's basement.

She found herself looking into his eyes, and her already warm cheeks started to burn. Along with the rest of her body. Because he was looking at her, too. Like he was starving and she was food. Alarmed that she might have the same expression on her face, she took a giant step back, holding up her hand like a traffic cop. "This is crazy, Deacon. No."

He flashed a grin that was both mocking and wicked, making him the sexiest man she'd ever seen. "All right," he said smoothly. "Let me show you where you'll . . . sleep."

Everything inside her clenched, and she swallowed a groan, laughing instead. "You're incorrigible, Agent Novak."

"I know," he said with satisfaction, making her laugh again.

"You said you were camping out." She winced, thinking about all the places her body ached after wrecking her car and surviving a murder attempt. "Do I have to sleep on the floor?"

"Hardly. I believe in creature comforts. Like a big-ass flat screen connected to my Xbox, which you can use," he said, pointing as he walked her through the living room. The television screen dominated the wall, but the rest of the room was bare, save two folding chairs. "Folding chairs is enough camping for me. Most of my furniture's still in storage."

He led her up a flight of stairs to an open, sunlit second

floor. She glanced up, the skylights bringing a smile to her face. It was warm here, even though it was cold outside. He opened the door to a room that was empty except for her boxes and a few unopened paint cans.

"Your stuff. This will be Dani's when it's done."

She followed him down the hall, to the master bedroom. It held a king-sized bed with rumpled sheets, a beat-up chest of drawers, and not much else in the way of furniture. Her suitcase sat next to the bed.

"The sheets are clean," he said, using that same smooth voice that was like velvet over her skin. "I only slept on them once. But I can change them if you want."

"No, it's okay." She wanted to smell him on the pillows, she thought, her heart beating so hard she was surprised he didn't hear it. "I'll only be here till late morning, right?"

He nodded firmly. "Bathroom's in there. Let me pull a few things from my closet, and I'll leave you to rest."

Faith pointed at the master bath. "If you need the shower, I'll wait in the kitchen."

He gave her another wicked grin that said he knew she was thinking of him in the shower, which, of course, she was. "I'll use the one off Dani's room. Oh, and Dani's coming by at some point this morning to reglue your head. I'll ask her to push it until after lunch so that you can sleep a little more."

"It's stopped bleeding, so I think it's okay," Faith said. "She doesn't need to."

"Isenberg's orders." He took another suit, shirt, and tie from his closet, his mouth drooping into a slight pout. "I miss my coat."

Faith laughed. "Don't be such a baby. You'll get it back."

He smiled at her. "I know. I just wanted to hear you laugh. You should do that more often."

All the reasons why she hadn't laughed in the last twenty-three years came rushing in. "I'll try," she said quietly. "When this is all over."

His smile faded. "I'll make that happen. I'll get back to the case as soon as I've changed. I'm going to King's College first to check out the scene of the abduction."

He'd get no rest, she realized. "If you have any food, I can make us some breakfast," she offered. "That way you can use your own shower."

"That would be easier. If you truly don't mind cooking, I just stocked the fridge two days ago. You should find everything you need. I like my eggs over easy." His phone buzzed and he read the text, then looked back up at her. "Don't worry about the sedan that will be pulling up out front in about a minute. That's your security detail, courtesy of the Bureau. Agents Colby and Pope. There's a landline in the kitchen if you want to call your father. And keep the shades drawn, please. I don't want you to be lying to him when you tell him that you're safe."

Faith rolled her eyes. "Over easy, Fed detail, shades drawn. I think I can remember all of that." She left him chuckling as she went back to the kitchen to use his phone.

She dialed with leaden fingers, dreading having to tell her father what was going on, unsurprised when Lily answered on the first ring. "Hi, Lily. It's me."

"I am so mad at you," Lily hissed. "Your hotel is on the news. There was a shooting. Where are you? Why didn't you call us? Your father has worried himself sick."

Faith closed her eyes. "I'm with the FBI agent who's working the case. I'm sorry, Lily. I really am. My new phone got damaged last night in the shooting."

Dead silence. Then, "You were *in* the shooting?"

Faith let out a breath. "Well, yes. Actually, I was the target."

"Oh, dear Lord," Lily wailed quietly. "This is terrible."

"I know. Look, Gran's house seems to be at the center of it. It was the scene of a murder." Or three. So far. "The police think I'm a target because my name is on the deed. Truly, Lily, that's all I know. Last night was insane. Oh, and I wrecked my car."

"Your Prius?" Lily's voice was barely a peep. "Were you hurt?"

Faith sighed again. "Well, no and no. I sold the Prius in Miami. I bought a used Jeep and ran it off the road last night. Right after I hung up with you guys."

"On those curves your father hates so much. Because of what happened to your mother."

Because Faith's mother's body had been found in a burned-out car at the base of an embankment not too far from the one Faith had gone over last night. "Right about there, yes."

"You were driving too fast again, weren't you?"

"No," Faith said patiently. "I saw a girl lying in the road, and I swerved to avoid her."

"You what? And *that's* all you know? Care to add any more?" Lily asked acidly.

Lily was more scared than angry, Faith knew. "Well, I changed my name."

"Back to Sullivan. It's about time you threw away any ties to that Charlie Frye."

"Actually, I changed it to Corcoran."

Silence. "Why?"

"It was Gran's maiden name. I didn't change back to Sullivan because I didn't want to lead anyone to you and Dad." She hesitated. "Because I was being stalked. For the last year."

"Oh my God. That's why you moved? That horrible Peter Combs? *He's* behind this?"

"Possibly. I don't know any more. Dad needs to know that Gran's house may come up in the news. I am fine. I am safe. I can tell him so, so that he doesn't worry himself any sicker."

"I gave him a sedative. He's asleep. I may go to sleep for a while, too. I was up most of the night with him, and I'm beat. You need to call back in a few hours. And give me a number where you'll actually pick up."

"I have to get another new cell phone. But call this number." She recited Novak's cell number. "That's the FBI agent. He'll know how to reach me once they put me in a safe house."

Lily sighed. "You going to a safe house is the best news I've heard. I love you, Faith."

"I love you, too. Go to sleep, Lily. I'll call back as soon as I can."

Cincinnati, Ohio
Tuesday, November 4, 8:10 a.m.

Finally, he thought as Novak's garage door started to open. It was about time the white-haired bastard got back. He'd gotten lucky. This corner was a school bus stop, and loads of soccer moms had lined up in their own minivans, waiting with their kids for the bus. He blended right in. But the bus had come a few minutes before, and all the moms had left. He couldn't have stayed here much longer. He didn't want any of Novak's neighbors to notice the silver minivan loitering on the curb and call a cop.

He climbed out of the driver's seat, over the console to the bench seat in the middle, where he'd thrown the golf bag that held his rifle. Damn vans these days didn't have middle windows that went up and down. Just in and out at an angle, clearing a few inches at most.

But a few inches would be enough. He'd parked in exactly the right place to set his sight on Novak's driveway, just in case the bastard brought Faith home with him.

It was far more likely they'd put her in a safe house, but it always paid to be prepared.

If Faith was with Novak, he'd be able to take out the Fed as he pulled into his driveway. If she leaned over to help the man, he'd be able to get her, too. If she was too wary and stayed down, he had plenty of time before any help could arrive to drive up behind them, get out of his minivan, and shoot her up close and personal. Even if she was smart enough to call for help.

And if Novak hadn't brought her home, he'd go to her eventually.

I can be patient. I have to be. He went still, finger on the trigger of his rifle. *Here he comes.* Driving a sedan. *Because I shot up his SUV,* he thought with a pang of regret. At this angle, the sedan would be a harder target. He squinted, trying to see through the car's windshield into the front seat, but the sun reflected off the glass. *Dammit.*

Was she with him? He didn't want to kill Novak if she wasn't. There would be no one else who'd be predictable enough to lead him to her.

At the last moment, the sedan floored it, rubber burning as it took the turn into the driveway. The car zipped into the garage and the door started down before he could draw a single breath.

"Fuck." He'd expected the man to slow down as he pulled into the garage. Any rational person would slow the fuck down. The white-haired bastard had nearly taken out his own garage door. Novak was insane.

Which was kind of ironic, actually. He was pretty sure Novak felt the same way about him.

Breathe. Calm down. He eased his finger off the trigger. Novak's insanity must have had a purpose. It must mean that he'd brought Faith home with him. She was in the house at this very moment.

His finger itched to shoot in every window in a hail of gunfire. But that wouldn't be wise. They could hunker down and shoot back. Call in hundreds of cops.

But at least he knew where she was. Novak wouldn't stay in the house too long. He had a killer to catch, after all. He might take Faith with him when he left. *If so, I'll be prepared*.

And if Novak left her behind?

He smiled. Even if she was armed, she was a lousy shot. The time he'd climbed through her bedroom window, she'd barely nicked him. It would be like taking candy from a baby.

Cincinnati, Ohio
Tuesday, November 4, 8:15 a.m.

Deacon eyed his bed as he toweled his wet head, tempted to lie down just to close his eyes for a few minutes. *I'm so tired*.

Now, if Faith herself were lying on his rumpled sheets, that would be an entirely different matter. He let himself imagine it, feeling his body grow hard.

She'd considered it, too. He'd seen it in her eyes, in the blush of her cheeks. *Soon*, he thought. Soon they'd be able to explore the chemistry that she'd called "crazy." It scared her a little. It scared him, too.

For the first time in his career, he found himself putting off his duty. He didn't want to leave her here alone. That two perfectly capable federal agents would be guarding her was immaterial. He wanted to be here. He needed to be here.

But he needed her to stay alive even more. So he dragged on his boxers, cracking his bedroom door open so that he could hear if she needed him. *Mmm, bacon*. The aroma wafted upstairs, along with coffee. He would have worshipped her for the coffee alone.

Hurrying now, he reached for his trousers, spinning at the muffled cry behind him. Faith stood in the open doorway, hand over her mouth, her eyes wide.

He crossed the room in two strides, yanking her through the door, pushing her up against the bedroom wall. Covering her body with his, he peered into the hall. "What is it? Who's there?"

"Nobody," she said breathlessly. "It's your back. It looks really bad. I was surprised, that's all. Can you let me breathe? You're squashing me."

He backed up a few inches. "I've had worse," he assured her, cognizant that her gaze had dropped from his face to his body. That he still gripped her arm.

And that his boxers were doing nothing to disguise the fact that he'd grown even harder in the last ten seconds. The room grew warm, the air thick. He let her stare, waiting for her to say something. Do something. *Touch me.*

Cheeks pink, she raised her eyes to his face. She licked her bottom lip, then bit it. He heard a low, rumbling growl. Realized it had come from his throat.

"I shouldn't be here," she whispered huskily. But she didn't move. Didn't make any attempt to pull her arm free. Her eyes dropped again, and he felt the warmth of her slow exhale against his damp chest. Then the tentative brush of her fingertips over the hair on his chest.

He held his breath, hoping she'd do it again. Closing his eyes when she did, cursing silently as she petted his hair so lightly that he thought he'd go insane. Wishing that she'd pet lower. Knowing he'd explode if she did. He captured her exploring hand, flattening it against his chest, bringing the hand he still held to his lips.

"Why are you?" he made himself ask, his voice like gravel.

"Why am I what?" she asked. That she sounded dazed did amazing things for his ego.

He opened his eyes, gritting his teeth when he saw the top of her head. She was still staring down at him. "Here, Faith? Why are you here?"

Her body abruptly stiffened, the moment broken. She laughed shakily as she slipped from his grip and turned her back on him. "Those agents are here. I didn't want to let them in until you said it was okay. I saw your door cracked open and thought . . . I mean, I didn't think that . . . God," she said weakly. "Can you put on some clothes, please?"

He cleared his throat, unable to keep the grin from his

face. "I opened the door so that I could listen for any trouble, but I didn't hear them knock." He pulled on his trousers, wincing as he carefully zipped them.

She turned then, her face beautifully flushed. Her lower lip was plumped from her little bites. Her eyes were dark. Hungry. It was all he could do not to reach for her again.

"They didn't knock. I heard a noise outside the back door. I figured it was them, but peeked through the blinds to be sure."

That brought him back to reality. He chose a clean shirt from his closet, frowning at her. "I thought I asked you to stay away from the windows."

"You didn't ask me. You told me." She crossed the room, stilling his hand when he started to put on the shirt. Her fingertips brushed over his shoulder, lightly probing his bruised back. "I'm not stupid, Deacon. I stood next to the window, not in front of it. Does this shoulder hurt as much as it looks like it does?"

"Hurts more a few feet lower," he muttered, and had the pleasure of watching her eyes flash as she bit her lower lip again. Instinct took over, and he pivoted, lightly gripping her chin, lowering his mouth to hers, intending to nip that lip himself. But she met him partway, lifting onto her toes, surprising him again, and the kiss exploded.

He tightened his grip on her chin and let himself devour her mouth the way he'd wanted to while she'd been staring at his cock with such hunger. A step had her back flat against the closet door. The second step had him shoving himself between her spread thighs, his hands closing over her breasts. She gasped, and he took the advantage, licking into her mouth, his hips rocking into her body, thrusting harder when she made greedy little noises that only wound him tighter.

Her hands flattened on his chest, her fingers furrowing through hair as they dug into his skin, body straining toward his. He let go of her breasts long enough to grab her hips and lift her the few inches he needed to hit the sweet spot between her legs. She moaned deep in her throat, locking her ankles around his calves, sliding her hands up his chest to lock around his neck. She clung to him like a vine, all revving motion, her hips meeting his thrusts, battering at his sanity.

"I need to touch you," he gritted against her lips. "Let me touch you. *Please.*"

"Yes." She peppered hard kisses on his mouth, his cheeks, back to his mouth. "God, yes."

He shoved his hands between their bodies, yanking at the snap on her jeans, his fingers shaking as he pushed the zipper down. He was absurdly happy when he touched lace, then he delved beneath it and couldn't think at all. She was hot. So damn hot.

And so damn wet. As his fingers slid through her folds, she made a little sound, half whimper, half moan, and he needed to get deeper more than he needed to breathe. Cupping her butt with his free hand, he hitched her higher against the door, pinning her with his thigh as he eased one finger up into that tight, wet heat.

She went perfectly still, her head thrown back, her eyes closed. Her mouth opened in a small, silent O. Mesmerized, he could only stare.

He'd never seen anything more beautiful in his life. And then she started to move, slowly riding his hand. Squeezing his finger hard. Any blood that had remained above his neck instantly drained to his cock.

He inserted a second finger less gently than he had the first, pumping as hard and fast as he could with her jeans still on. He wanted them off, he thought wildly. Desperately. Wanted to see her. Wanted to taste her. Wanted to feel her come around him.

He dropped his face to the curve of her neck. Tasted her skin. Kissed his way lower as he pumped harder and faster. He could see her nipples poking against the silk of her shirt, and he wanted them, too. Blindly, he closed his mouth over a hardened peak, sucking hard through the silk, hitching her a little higher against the door, driving his fingers even deeper.

She gasped, her body going taut as a strung bow. On the edge, he realized, but not there. So he bit her, closing his teeth over her nipple just hard enough to shove her over, dragging a strangled cry from her throat as she came in a rush.

Her eyes flew open, and she stared up at him, dazed and sated while he was still so hungry. He glanced at the bed. He could have her there in two steps.

And then he could have her there. He was so hard that he hurt, and she was looking at him like he was a king. He slowly withdrew his hand from her heat, holding her gaze as he brought his fingers to his lips and licked. *So damn good.*

If he didn't have her soon, he was going to die.

"Oh God," she breathed, her hands trembling against the back of his neck. Her pulse knocked at the hollow of her throat. "That was . . ."

Don't say unwise. Don't say it was a mistake. That I was a mistake. Say it was amazing. That I am amazing. Tell me you want me inside you. He closed his eyes. *Please.*

"Beautiful," she whispered, and his eyes flew open. She was staring at him, her green eyes darker yet somehow luminous. "You made it beautiful. You made me feel . . . beautiful."

"Because you are," he whispered back.

He watched her glance guiltily at the bed, then back at him, and for a long moment they hung there, staring at each other, lust warring with indecision.

And then the doorbell rang, jarring them back to reality.

"It's the Feds," she whispered in a disgusted way that made him chuckle, despite the tightness in his groin.

"I'm a Fed, too." He lowered her until her feet touched the floor, then hurriedly shrugged into his shirt. "You stay here. I'll let them in."

She looked down pointedly. "Better not tuck your shirt in for a while."

He laughed, amazed that he could be delighted and sexually frustrated at the same time. "I won't. Should I ask if they want breakfast, too?"

"If they want to take their lives in their hands, sure."

Cincinnati, Ohio
Tuesday, November 4, 8:55 a.m.

If he'd harbored any doubts that Faith was in Novak's house, he harbored them no longer. From his minivan across the street, he watched Novak open the door to two more Feds. Big guys, both wearing black suits. Both looking like they could crush a man's skull with their bare hands.

They were Faith's security detail. She must have told

them something pretty damn important to score federal protection. What had that been?

How nervous he allowed himself to become depended on exactly what she'd revealed. He needed to know. And in the meantime, he needed to make sure she didn't tell them anything else. *Draw her out of that house. If you can't, you'll just have to wait her out.*

He checked his watch with a grimace. The Feds guarding Faith would be looking for anything suspicious. Like a man sitting in a minivan for what had already been too long a period of time. A minivan that was also a liability.

Eventually someone would see the minivan owner's body lying beneath his old van in the grocery store's parking lot. The cops would put out a BOLO on her vehicle.

With me sitting in it, right here in plain sight.

He needed to get another vehicle. He needed a place to hide where he'd have a birds-eye view of Novak's garage and front doors, so he'd know when the Fed left and if Faith was with him. He'd be able to get a few shots off before the others came after him. And if he couldn't get them in his sights, he could follow them without attracting the attention of the security detail.

He knew just which house to choose. At a minimum, he could hide the minivan it its garage. If he was lucky, the garage might hold a car he could steal.

I could get warm. Eat. Sleep a little. He hadn't eaten in hours. Hadn't slept in days.

He wondered if the house's owner was home and, if he was, how hard he'd be to kill.

Chapter Seventeen

Cincinnati, Ohio
Tuesday, November 4, 9:30 a.m.

Deacon looked for a place to park. He was only about a block from Jordan O'Bannion's townhouse, but parking in Mount Adams was hard to come by. Deacon had only been here before as a tourist. It was one of the trendiest areas of the city, with bars, nightlife, and expensive real estate with great views of the river.

Faith's uncle had left a message on Deacon's voice mail at the precinct the night before, sounding frantic, demanding to see his niece and oh, by the way, what the hell was going on around his family's old homestead?

His concern seemed a little odd coming from the man who'd taken Faith to R-rated movies and given her cigarettes when she was only fifteen, but Jordan *had* been younger at the time, Deacon supposed. Only twenty-six, Faith had said.

Although at the same age, Deacon had already joined the Bureau and had petitioned the courts for custody of his brother three times. Every request had been denied, the judge deciding that a married couple in a stable household was in the "best interest of the child."

At the time he'd been devastated, confident that he could raise Greg better than Tammy and Jim. Now he wondered if that was true.

Think about Greg later, like when you're in the principal's office. Focus on Jordan now.

Jordan's townhouse looked to be turn-of-the-century and was painted periwinkle blue. The dormer windows on the third floor probably had a killer view of the park below. Deacon knew he was easily looking at a cool million in real estate. No wonder Jordan hadn't wanted that drafty old house, he thought. Faith's uncle was sitting on a gold mine here.

Deacon walked up to the brightly painted door and knocked. Nobody answered, and he could hear no sounds inside. But he did hear something out back. He had to jog down three houses so that he could hook around behind them. A woman stood in Jordan's backyard, raking leaves.

"Excuse me, miss?"

The woman looked up, startled. She was mid-to-late twenties and wore her dark blond hair in a rather severe bun. She backed up a few steps when she saw him. "Yes?"

"I'm Special Agent Novak with the FBI. I'm looking for Mr. O'Bannion."

"He's not here," the woman said in a hushed tone.

"Do you know where he is? I really need to talk to him. It's about his niece."

"Faith," she said. "How is she?"

"She's fine," Deacon said truthfully. Faith was incredibly fine. "I didn't get your name."

The woman arched dark brows. "I didn't give one," she said, her voice just a hint louder than a whisper. "I'm Mary Jones, Mr. O'Bannion's housekeeper."

"It's nice to meet you, Ms. Jones." He leaned forward. "Why are you whispering?"

She looked startled once again. "I didn't know I was. I guess I'm used to talking softly. Mrs. O'Bannion didn't like loud noises, especially there at the end. God rest her soul."

"You knew her, then?"

"Yes, of course. I was her caregiver for ten years. I miss her."

"I was under the impression that Mr. O'Bannion took care of his mother."

"He did, but he's a man. I was there to take care of her more . . . personal needs."

"I see. Do you know where Mr. O'Bannion is? It's important that I talk to him."

"He's sometimes at the gallery this late, especially if the post-show party went well."

"'This late'? It's not even ten a.m."

"The parties go on all night. Ten a.m. is 'late.' But there wasn't a party last night, so I'm not sure where he went after closing. I'd be happy to give him a message when he gets home."

"Thank you." Deacon gave her a card. "Please have him call my cell number on the back."

"I certainly will." Mary set the rake against the wall. "I have to get to my indoor chores now. Have a nice day, Agent Novak."

"Wait. Where can I find the gallery?"

"It's at the intersection with Hill Street. There's a sign in the yard. You can't miss it."

Deacon turned in the direction she pointed. Hill Street was at the very bottom of the hill, ironically enough. When he turned back toward her, she was gone, the door already closing behind her. She wasn't telling the truth. She knew where her boss was.

Deacon wondered if she was merely discreet or hiding something. She was right, though. He couldn't have missed the gallery or its sign in the yard. O'BANNION'S was all it said, but it was nearly as large as a front door and intricately carved. Deacon got out of his car and walked around it to inspect it more closely before going to the front door.

"He's closed," a woman said from above him, her voice deep and sultry.

Deacon looked up and was glad he had on his wrap-around shades, because his eyes nearly bugged out of his head. The woman sat in the window on the upper floor, balancing on the sill. She hadn't been there when he'd driven down the hill. He would have noticed. Because she was as close to naked as was legally possible.

She was dressed in a tiny genie costume, complete with veil. A tiny pink genie costume.

Halloween, he thought, relieved. She had to be a leftover partier from Halloween. "Ma'am, you could seriously break something if you fall."

She laughed. "I won't fall. I've done backflips off a beam narrower than this."

A gymnast genie, then. "Do you know where Mr. O'Bannion is?"

She smiled and pressed her finger to her lips. "Sshh. He's here, but he's not receiving visitors right now. We partied a little too hard last night, and he's a little unconscious."

Good God. What kind of drugs was Faith's uncle doing? "Should I call an ambulance?"

"Oh, heavens no." She fluttered her hand. "It's just a hangover. We were doing tequila Jell-O shots until dawn. He'll be fine when he wakes up." The genie sounded more than a little inebriated herself. It must have been some party.

"I see," Deacon said, not bothering to hide his annoyance. "When do you expect him to regain consciousness?"

"By dinnertime. Maybe. Can I give him a message?"

"No, I'd like to talk to him. Please wake him up." He started for the front door.

The genie looked back over her shoulder into the room with a frown. "I'll wake him up and have him call you."

"I can wake him up."

"I don't think you can. I know he wouldn't want you to. He . . . he's not presentable."

It was Deacon's turn to frown. "I don't care."

The genie slid from the windowsill back inside the room, then closed the window and pulled the shade. A minute later the front door opened and she stood before him, a cell phone in her hand. "You might not care," she said. "But he will."

She showed him the photo on her phone, and Deacon sighed. A man lay naked, curled almost into a fetal position, empty liquor bottles on his nightstand. He appeared well and truly passed out. She turned off her phone, her expression one of quiet entreaty.

"Let him have his dignity, please. I will wake him, get him cleaned up, pour some coffee into him. As soon as he's lucid, I'll have him call you. Do you have a card?"

Deacon hesitated. Part of him wanted to grab Faith's uncle and shake some answers out of him. Some smaller part, however, considered that Jordan would become part of his life should he and Faith build a relationship. *More like a big brother than an uncle,* she'd said.

"If I say no?" he asked softly.

"Then I'll close the door and tell you to get a warrant," she said. "You may be working an important case, but I won't allow you to bully him."

Deacon hid his annoyance. "I won't bully him. I just want to talk to him." Since he wanted O'Bannion cooperative, not defensive, retreat seemed the wisest action. "He has my number, but here's my card. If I haven't heard from him by noon, I'll be back to wake him up myself."

"I understand. Thank you." She took the card and started to close the door.

"One more question," Deacon said. "What is your name, ma'am?"

"Alda Lane." She closed the door noiselessly.

Faith had told him that she was glad she hadn't developed a drinking problem after Jordan gave her beer when she was only a teenager. *It looks like Jordan wasn't so fortunate,* Deacon thought, texting Bishop as he returned to his car.

Jordan O'B sleeping off a bender, he typed. *Will meet u @ King's soon.*

Bishop had been at the scene of the abduction at King's College for the past hour. Deacon had detoured from meeting her there because of the call from O'Bannion.

Almost done here, Bishop texted back. *Meet at attorney's abt the will?*

Deacon confirmed as two new multi-recipient texts came through. The first was from Isenberg and it was good news: *Bellman from hotel survived surgery. In ICU. Next 24 to tell.*

At least that was one less body on the way to the morgue.

The second text was from Vince Tanaka. Deacon read the message, then simply sat for a moment, his eyes closed and bile rising in his throat. *Fucking hell.*

CSU had finished removing the floor tiles in the O'Bannion basement. They'd found seven more bodies. Ten total. Ten blondes buried in Plexiglas coffins. No wonder this asshole hadn't wanted Faith in the basement. He'd realized she would remember what the place looked like originally and notice how it had changed.

Another text came through from Tanaka, this one sent only to Deacon, asking him to contact the ground-penetrating radar expert for help in mapping the graves.

Tanaka's contact at the university was on sabbatical, and they needed to know if anyone or anything was buried outside. Or inside, in the dirt under the layer of Plexiglas. *Please don't let there be any more.*

Deacon had added Sophie Johannsen-Ciccotelli's phone number to his "favorites" when they'd worked together in West Virginia the previous year. He called her and she answered right away. "Sophie, it's Deacon Novak."

"Deacon! Long time no hear." She hesitated. "I saw you on the news this morning."

"In Philly?" he asked, surprised.

"It's online and top of the hour on CNN. They said you were shot at. Are you okay?"

"Yeah, yeah. Vest caught it. I'm calling because I need your help. I need to find someone with your scanning skills here in Cincinnati."

"Oh no," she murmured. "Not again."

"Yes," he said, knowing that she knew how he felt because she'd gone through it, too. She had, in fact, gone through it more times than he had, because she was the scanning expert everyone called when they found unmarked graves. "Can you recommend someone?"

"Of course. Where is the site?"

"A little town called Mount Carmel, Ohio, on the river near Cincinnati. It's the O'Bannion place. The road doesn't even have a name on the map. I can meet whoever you send and show them the way."

"How many graves do you think you have, Deacon?"

"Ten so far, all aboveground. We don't know what lies beneath."

He heard the sound of an exhale, then the tapping of a computer keyboard. "Send me the GPS coordinates. I'll have someone there by early afternoon."

"Thanks, Sophie. I owe you one."

"Of course you don't," she said warmly. "What are friends for? Take care, Deacon."

He disconnected with a sigh. *Ten so far.* He'd see Faith's attorney with Bishop, then he'd go to the morgue. He needed to see the bodies. Needed to know what had been done to them.

He hoped like hell that the ME would find some way of identifying them. The killer in West Virginia had collected wallets with his victims' IDs, but they'd found nothing like that in the O'Bannion house. Families with missing kids would be coming out of the woodwork as soon as word spread of their grisly discovery.

It had been that way in West Virginia. He'd had to tell grieving parents that he'd identified their missing children, but he'd had to tell more grieving parents that he hadn't. He wasn't sure if he could go through that again, but it looked like he would have to.

If he didn't, who else would? Besides, the victims themselves deserved the courtesy. Someone needed to care about them. Someone needed to get them justice. *That someone is me.*

Cincinnati, Ohio
Tuesday, November 4, 9:45 a.m.

Faith dried and put away the last of the breakfast dishes, surreptitiously watching Special Agent Colby. His arms were crossed over his chest, his finger tapping the biceps of his other arm. He didn't like playing babysitter, and Faith didn't think he liked her. But he'd do his job. Novak wouldn't have left her alone with agents who weren't qualified. She hoped.

"I'm going to try to sleep," she told him.

"We'll keep everything under control out here," he said brusquely.

"Where is Agent Pope?"

"Doing a perimeter check. If you do hear any commotion, stay put in the bedroom. We will come get you when the coast is clear."

"Look for me under the bed," she said with a shaky laugh, grabbing her handbag as she left the kitchen. The weight of it returned some small measure of her confidence. Agent Colby gave no indication that he knew she had a gun in her purse. If Novak hadn't told them she was armed, she wasn't going to mention it. There was no way she'd be unarmed until this was all over.

She paused to check out Novak's TV as she passed through the living room. He'd hooked up a cable tuner and his own Xbox 360. A few of the boxes on top of the console were multiplayer games. That meant he had wireless Internet somewhere, which was good because she needed to

send an e-mail to her boss telling him she'd had a car accident and "complications."

She rolled her eyes as she got her laptop from the empty
bedroom where her things had been stored. " 'Complications' my Aunt Fanny," she muttered, but she knew it was
the best way to deal with the situation. The alternative was
too surreal. *Please excuse Faith from work. Her basement is
flooded with bodies and anyone standing next to her is a
target.*

She opened doors along the upstairs hallway until she
found Novak's home office. Feeling awkward, she checked
his desk, looking for the Internet router. The connection
would be password protected, she was certain. Novak seemed
to be careful about things like that. But passwords were generally noted somewhere on the router, so she should be able
to get in. If not, she knew his cell number and would ask him.
She wasn't going to be able to sleep until she got a message
to her boss.

She didn't find the router on his desk, but the three
framed photos caught her eye. She paused before snooping,
but her hesitation was brief. In a little more than twelve
hours, he'd discovered almost everything about her. It
seemed only fair that she should catch up.

The largest was a photo of a group gathered around a
fancy table set with china and crystal and half-empty flutes
of champagne. Everyone was dressed up, and other tables
could be seen in the background. *A wedding, maybe?*

Novak sat on the far right of the table, looking relaxed—
and amazing—in a black suit and a red tie. His arm rested
casually on the back of the chair beside him, occupied by a
blond, good-looking young man who appeared to be college-
aged. Next to the young man was a woman about Faith's age
with a blond beehive, wearing a lime green strapless gown
and a smile that made Faith smile back. She'd laid her head
on the young man's shoulder in a motherly way while holding the hand of the dark, dangerous-looking man on her left.
The dark man scowled at the camera, one brow lifted in a
warning that seemed more bark than bite.

The young woman standing behind the scowling man,
hands resting on his shoulders, wore a dress identical in
style to the lime green one, but in a more gentle rose. She
was laughing at the camera, undiluted happiness in her

eyes. At the far left was a redhead with an easy smile who'd leaned toward the dark man for the photo but whose arms were folded on the table in a way that said her relationship was not as personal as those shared by the others.

Framed, the photo had been printed on a sheet of paper and signed in the margins. *Thanks for everything, Ford. Our door is always open to you, Love, Daphne. It's been an honor. JC.* And in the same masculine scrawl, as if an afterthought, *You'll be missed.* The redhead had written: *Take care of yourself or you'll answer to me, Kate.* And above the laughing young woman's head, a bubble with the inscription, *Don't forget you promised to come back for my wedding. Who else will keep Joseph from killing Dylan? (jk) LOL. Love, Holly.*

His old work group, Faith thought with a smile. More, actually. She could tell from Novak's relaxed posture that these people were like family. *He must miss them.*

The second photo was a group of five men on the deck of a fishing boat. Faith brought it closer, squinting. The boat was called the *Fiji*. Novak was there, as was the dark, dangerous man from the first photo. It was clear that they were all friends. Novak stood out, his bright white hair a stark contrast to the dark heads of the others. It was a wonder they didn't tip the boat, she thought whimsically. Five men the size of Novak. One was even bigger—he looked like a bodybuilder. But it was Novak who held her attention.

The third photo was of Novak with Dani when they were teenagers. Faith was again struck by the resemblance between them, made so much stronger by their near-identical coloring. Both had black hair with bold white streaks in the front. They sat astride bicycles, laughing, as if they knew a secret joke, just the two of them.

Faith felt a pang of wistfulness. She'd always wanted siblings. At the same time, she would never have subjected anyone else to the pain of her mother's suicide.

Even her father. Especially him. Especially now. Twenty-three years ago her father had grieved so hard when he thought his wife had died in a car accident that Faith had feared she'd lose him, too. Because then she would have been all alone.

But just that fast she heard Novak's voice, soothing her. *You're not alone. I'm here.* He'd gotten her through those moments in the basement. In the hotel lobby. In the police station when she'd thought her heart would break.

He was a good man, one she'd come to depend on shockingly fast.

And a finely built man, too. Her stomach fluttered with the memory of all that bared skin. He was the same bronze color all over. At least everywhere but under his boxers. And maybe there, too. The fluttering in her stomach moved lower as everything within her clenched.

It had been such a long time since she'd looked at any man like that, since she'd wanted to be touched. But this morning, she hadn't just wanted his touch. She'd *needed* it. If the Feds hadn't rung the doorbell, they would have ended up in his bed. They still might.

Might? Honey, it's just a matter of time. Hopefully, not too much time. To have her long fast broken by a man who looked like Deacon Novak was the kind of bright spot she hadn't had in her dismal world for a long time.

Job. E-mail. Focus. Snapping herself back to reality, she returned the photos to his desk and checked the makeshift worktable beside it—a piece of plywood on two sawhorses. There she found the wireless router along with a dozen electronic gadgets and as many power tools. She noted the router's password, then took her laptop to his bedroom.

Which smelled like him. All cedar and . . . delicious. Novak smelled so damn good, it was all she could do not to sniff him like a puppy. Which would be *so* attractive, she told herself with a self-deprecating roll of her eyes. Although somehow she didn't think he'd mind.

She eyed the big bed with its rumpled sheets. That would smell like him, too.

She settled against the headboard, nearly groaning when her butt sank into a soft mattress. Just how she liked them. Not like the hard hotel mattresses she'd been sleeping on for so long. She indulged for a moment by putting her face into one of his pillows and drawing a deep breath.

Yes. It smelled just like him. And imagining him here . . . Her whole body went instantly tight. And wet. *God.* Novak would be an incredible lover, of that she had no doubt.

If he survives. The thought snuck in, leaving her cold. He was out there right now, trying to find the man who had killed so many already. *Who is trying to kill me.* Who'd very nearly killed him last night. *He would have died protecting me. He would have died before I ever got to have him.*

He'd do it again, she knew. He'd risk his life for hers again in a heartbeat, and there would be nothing she could do to stop him. Except keep herself out of the killer's sights as he'd asked.

Faith opened her e-mail, composing a short note to her new boss, just as Novak had suggested. Neither of the numbers the office had on file were functional, so she gave her boss Novak's cell in case he needed to reach her. She sent the message and then checked the news.

And sighed. Both her grandmother's house and her hotel were top of the news on every Web site she checked, including the national outlets. Accompanying both stories were the same photos—aerial shots of the house, photos of the shattered glass at her hotel, and a close-up of the missing windowpane in the hotel the shooter had fired from.

She had no doubt that if she turned on the television, she'd see the same images on the CNN loop. The press had connected the house to Arianna's assault, listing the homeowner as Faith Frye of Miami, who could not be reached for comment. *Well, at least there's that.*

She was extremely surprised that no one had given the press her new name—neither the cops nor the staff at her hotel. But someone would. It was inevitable.

She opened one of the articles and sighed again. Novak's photo was included among the pictures of the hotel devastation. They'd latched on to him like piranhas, making him part of their story, capturing his "bigger-than-life" persona. But not one of the stories included a photo of her—and Faith suddenly understood something that had puzzled her the night before.

She'd wondered why Novak would want to draw attention to himself. Why he'd make himself so *noticeable* when all she'd ever wanted was to become invisible. Now she understood that Deacon Novak drew media attention to himself so that victims like her might be spared.

God. She blinked back the moisture that stung her eyes. Although he still liked the attention, she thought, clicking on a video clip with a teary laugh. He strode through the crowd of reporters like he owned them, his white hair bright in the lights, his leather coat flapping in the night. Even his "no comment" seemed to create a stir.

She scanned the next story, noting that his name was linked to another article. Curious, she clicked it and let out a long, harsh breath.

FEDS FIND TWO DOZEN UNMARKED GRAVES. A shiver ran down her spine. It was dated almost a year ago, the photo of a grim Novak standing in a West Virginia field, surrounded by freshly dug graves as a team wearing protective gear dug a few feet away. It was a candid shot, a little fuzzy, as if taken from far away. Novak wore his black leather coat, yet possessed no swagger. His shoulders were hunched, his face lined with grief.

Faith felt like she was violating Novak's privacy in a way she hadn't while looking at the photos on his desk, even though the story was publicly posted. The news photographer had captured his face unguarded, his weariness palpable.

The text recounted how the team led by FBI Special Agent Joseph Carter had come to find the bodies. *Joseph Carter,* Faith thought. *He's the "JC" from the picture on Novak's desk.* The story went on to describe how Special Agent Deacon Novak had been working with archeologist Dr. Sophie Johannsen for weeks to unearth the bodies, identify the remains, and notify the victims' families.

Two dozen victims. Two dozen graves. *And now he has ten more.* So far.

Oh, Deacon. She wished she were with him, if only to hold him, but she'd promised to stay put. She had to wait until he came home to give him comfort as he'd given her.

His first kiss had been so soft. Sweet. But all the kisses that followed . . . *That's how I'll kiss him when he comes back.* Hard and hot enough to help him forget for a little while.

But he might not be home for hours, and during that time he'd be dealing with victims. And their families. The despair he'd felt a year ago was what he'd be feeling today. Knowing that hurt Faith's heart. She needed to ease him, not at the end of the day when he was hollowed out and weary, but now. She knew she wouldn't be able to rest until she'd at least tried.

She couldn't text him until she got another cell, so she

opened a new e-mail, using the fact that she'd given her boss his number as an excuse for something to say. *Take care, Deacon,* she added at the end. *I'll be waiting.* Then she hit SEND and closed her laptop.

She got into bed, tucking her gun under the pillow, where she could get to it quickly. Then she pulled the rumpled covers over her body, snuggled her head into Novak's pillow, and drew his scent into her lungs. And let exhaustion take her under.

Cincinnati, Ohio
Tuesday, November 4, 10:00 a.m.

"A pink gymnast genie?" Bishop snickered as they walked from the parking lot at the back of the O'Bannion family attorney's building. "You're kidding."

"A half-naked one," Deacon said dryly. "Hearing about Faith's uncles almost makes me glad that Adam's father is my uncle. Almost."

"That bad, huh?"

"More like just not that good. Jim Kimble is very rough around the edges. Serrated, even. What did you find at King's College?"

"A bullet in a tree trunk and a lot of blood," Bishop said. "The bullet was the same caliber you found at the old house and in the body in the hotel room the shooter used. I left the slug with Agent Taylor, the Fed forensics guy who processed the hotels last night."

"Yeah," Deacon grumbled. "The one who took my coat."

"Poor baby," Bishop said, sounding just like Faith, though telling her so would only confirm in *her* mind that Deacon had lost *his*. "What do you know about the attorney?" she asked.

"Herbert Henson, Sr., was Faith's grandmother's attorney for decades, but Faith never met him until he read the will. I asked Crandall to run a check on him and the firm. Established in 1953 by Herbert Senior."

"Wait. The one we're going to see? He's still alive?"

"And practicing. He's eighty-six. It's been Henson and Henson since Herbert Junior got his law degree and joined the practice back in 1978. Junior retired, but it's still Henson and Henson because Herbert's grandson, Herbert the third got his law degree and joined in 2010. They do primarily estate planning, but occasionally handle drunk and disorderly charges against their elite clientele."

"Did Crandall dig up any dirt on the lawyers?"

"Nothing," Deacon said. "Not even a parking ticket. For father, son, or grandson."

"Three generations of squeaky-clean lawyers. What's this world coming to?"

They cut the conversation off when they entered the attorney's office, stopping at a receptionist's desk. "Special Agent Novak and Detective Bishop here to see Mr. Henson, Sr., about the O'Bannion estate," Deacon said, both of them presenting their badges.

The receptionist typed their badge numbers into her computer. For a nonlitigating attorney, Deacon thought, Henson kept careful records. "If you'd like to sit down," she said, "I'll tell Mr. Henson that you are here."

Deacon eyed the waiting room chairs, padded and soft. Only the best for Henson's clientele. "They look too comfortable," he muttered to Bishop. "If I sit down, I'll fall asleep."

"I know." Bishop swallowed a yawn. "Me, too." But she sat anyway, groaning softly. "They're even more comfortable than they look. Don't sit down, Novak. It's a trap."

The woman behind the desk chuckled. "Would you detectives like some coffee?"

"That would be really nice, thank you," Bishop said.

The receptionist disappeared for a few minutes before returning with their coffee. "Mr. Henson's finished his call. He'll see you now."

Herbert Henson, Sr., was seated behind a massive oak desk. He was a tall, spare man with a few curling wisps of gray hair remaining on his otherwise bald head. He wore old-fashioned spectacles and by every outward appearance was a simple country lawyer. But Deacon knew that a man could never hold on to his caliber of clientele without being a shark.

Henson looked them up and down, especially Deacon, who'd removed his shades. The lawyer looked him right in the eye but didn't flinch. He didn't react at all.

He's either color-blind or one hell of a bluffer.

"Sit down," Henson said. "Please." When they had, he steepled his arthritic fingers on his desk. "My office administrator tells me you have questions about the O'Bannion estate. Surely you understand that I'm bound by attorney-client privilege."

"Even when your client is deceased?" Bishop asked.

Sadness flitted across his face. "Barbara O'Bannion may be deceased, but her heirs are still my clients. Ask your questions. I'll answer as best I can."

"Have you seen the news, Mr. Henson?" Deacon asked.

"I did. That house of Barbara's was on the front page, paraded through every news outlet on the television and the Internet, too. I saw the photographs of that hotel, as well. I expected you, Agent Novak." He looked at Bishop. "Not you, ma'am, because you haven't attracted the media's attention like Agent Novak has."

"I never do," Bishop said pleasantly. "If you saw the pictures of the hotel, you also know that a man was shot there last night."

"The bellman, yes. Terrible."

"Did you know that Barbara's granddaughter was the sniper's target?" Deacon asked.

Henson went completely still. "Faith? Or Audrey?"

"Who's Audrey?" Bishop asked.

Henson's jaw clenched, then relaxed. "Faith, then. Why? How do you know?"

"I know because I pushed her out of the way," Deacon said. They'd come back to Audrey later. "She would have been dead."

"But ... I assumed the shooting was part of a manhunt, to find the person who abducted that young girl from King's College." Folded tightly on the desk, Henson's hands trembled.

"No. Faith was the target. The why revolves around her inheritance."

"That house," Henson said flatly. "Because her name is on the deed."

"Her old name," Bishop told him. "She changed it before leaving Miami."

"Back to Sullivan," Henson said. "It's about time. Barbara did not like Faith's ex-husband."

"No, sir," Bishop said. "She changed it to Corcoran. And she didn't change it because she was divorced. She was being stalked."

Henson straightened in his chair. "Faith? Stalked? By whom?"

"By the man who cut her throat four years ago," Deacon said. "She decided to come to Cincinnati after five attempts were made on her life." That he could not say for sure that the same man who'd stalked her was responsible for the latest attempts really pissed him off. "The first attempt was three days after she returned from the reading of her grandmother's will."

Henson paled. "Five times in one month?"

"Plus last night's shooting makes six," Deacon said. Then he waited.

Henson's jaw tensed. "What is in that house?" he demanded, enunciating every word.

"We haven't released that information yet," Deacon said. "But as bad as you're thinking? It's a whole lot worse."

"Someone is trying to kill her over that damn house," Henson spat. "Someone who knew she'd inherited it before I had the deed changed over. That's why you're here, isn't it?"

"Tell us about the will, sir," Bishop said. "Who knew the contents and when?"

"We know Jordan got the townhouse, if that helps you deal with attorney-client privilege," Deacon said when Henson hesitated. "Faith got the house in Mount Carmel plus the land. Jeremy didn't get anything."

"Who's Audrey?" Bishop asked again.

"Audrey is Jeremy's daughter," Henson said. "His biological daughter. He has two stepsons from his ex-wife's previous marriage. He adopted them. Barbara met them only a few times. She never met Audrey."

"Yet you thought we'd come to you about her," Deacon said.

Henson lifted a shoulder. "She's Barbara's granddaughter, too. And if you Google her, you'll find that Audrey gets herself arrested frequently. She's something of a serial protester. There are a lot of people in the world who'd like to take a shot at her. Faith is a model of good manners in comparison."

"Have you known Dr. Corcoran long?" Deacon asked.

Henson blinked for a moment. "I'm so used to knowing her as Faith Frye or Sullivan. I know of her through Barbara. I only met her a month ago, when I read Barbara's will. I don't suppose it would hurt to tell you that none of Jeremy's children inherited."

"Did they know about Faith getting the house?"

"I didn't tell them. I don't suppose Jordan did, either. The only other person who knew the contents of the will was my secretary, Mrs. Lowell, and she's been with me for nearly forty years. Her integrity is unimpeachable."

"What about couriers, copy room attendants?" Bishop pressed.

"No, Detective Bishop. No one."

Bishop pushed on. "Cleaning people, plumbers, locksmiths, the cable company, computer techs, temps when your secretary goes on vacation? You do give her vacation— don't you, sir?"

"Of course I do, but my wife and I take vacation at the same time. I close the office. We've done so for forty years. No one has had access to our files," he insisted, but then faltered. "Computer techs, maybe. We had a new system installed four years ago. Until then Mrs. Lowell stored everything on external hard drives that we kept locked up. It's conceivable that the consultant we brought in saw a file or two while training us on the system."

"It's conceivable that he burned entire copies of your external hard drives," Deacon said, and watched Henson frown. "Who was the consultant?"

"Tierney Phillips. He's my grandson's best friend. I've known Tierney since he was born." Henson exhaled, seeming to have remembered something. "But even if he did steal files—which I do not believe he did—it doesn't matter. Barbara's will predated our first office computer. It had been typed on a typewriter with carbon paper. After we got our new system, we scanned a number of the old documents in. Tierney wouldn't have had access to it."

"Where were the old files kept?" Deacon asked.

"In our basement. We have a vault. I have the combination. Only me."

A man careful enough to record the badge numbers of visiting detectives had a fail-safe, Deacon thought. Someone else had access to that combination. "Okay, so Jordan knew what was in the will, as did Faith. Jeremy and his children knew they weren't in the will. If Faith were to die, what happens to the house?"

"That I'm not at liberty to tell you. I'm sorry."

"Then Jordan gets it," Bishop said reasonably. "He's your only other client who's an heir."

"Don't put words in my mouth, Detective," Henson snapped. "And don't guess. I do not have authority to give you that information."

Deacon managed to keep his tone pleasant, even though he was frustrated as hell. Whoever was next in line for the house had motive. "Who's had access to the house in recent years?"

"Well, I suppose I have. When Barbara moved to the city to live with Jordan, she had the locks changed and gave me the key. I gave that key to Faith when I read her section of the will."

"The lock had been changed," Deacon said quietly.

Henson's jaw tightened. "Which is why Faith called to tell me the key didn't fit. Dammit. Well, at least you have a time frame of reference. The lock was intact three months ago."

Deacon hid his surprise. *It couldn't have been.* The killer they sought had been in that basement far longer than three months. "Why three months ago?"

"Because that's the last time the house was inspected by Maguire and Sons. They make sure the roof isn't leaking, that the foundation is secure. Things like that."

"Do they check inside the house as well?" Deacon asked, and Henson nodded.

"Twice a year, top to bottom. Additionally, after heavy flooding, they check the basement. The house is on high ground, but Barbara was taking no chances with it."

No way in hell had that been happening. Unless Maguire and/or his sons were rapists and murderers. "Twice a year, every year, since when?"

"Maguire's had the contract for ten years. But I've had contractors doing semi-annual maintenance ever since Tobias died and Barbara moved to the city." Henson frowned. "Why?"

Ten years ago was when Tanaka thought the windows and the door in the basement had been covered and hidden. "Who schedules Maguire's visits?" Deacon asked.

"We do. Why?"

"And the key?" Bishop asked. "Do they have their own key?"

"Of course not." Henson's lips thinned. "My grandson meets them out there, then waits for them to finish. He's not here at the moment. I'll have him contact you the moment he arrives. *Why?*" he demanded.

"We can't wait that long, however long that is," Deacon said. "Where is he now?"

Henson's cheeks darkened to a blotchy red. "He is with a client, Special Agent Novak. My grandson's integrity is also unimpeachable."

Deacon leaned back in his chair, a subtle cue for Bishop to grab the baton. She did so smoothly, just one of the things he appreciated about working with her.

"I'm sure that it is, Mr. Henson," she said. "But we have a serious problem here. That thing that Agent Novak said was far worse than your worst imagining? It's going on in the basement and has been for a lot longer than three months. We need to talk to your grandson. If he or Maguire noticed anything while in that basement, we need to know."

Henson grew very still. "I said I would have him contact you when he returns. That's the best I can do for you at the moment."

"Can we have his cell number?" she asked. "We'd be happy to contact him ourselves."

"No. He is with a client and is not to be disturbed. You may reach him here, on his office line. He checks his messages frequently. Our cell phones are for our personal use, therefore we keep that information private."

Deacon didn't hide his irritation. "We have a missing young woman. Every moment we don't talk to your grandson is another moment she comes closer to death. You don't want that stain on your conscience. Or on your sterling reputation."

Henson's jaw clenched. "I will call him on his cell phone and ask him to call you back."

Deacon leaned forward, far enough that Henson caught the movement. "Please make the call now. A young woman's life could hang in the balance."

Henson hit the button on his intercom. "Mrs. Lowell, can you call my grandson's cell phone?" He released the intercom and looked at Deacon.

"Mr. Henson," Mrs. Lowell said through the intercom, "I got his voice mail."

"Leave him a message. Tell him to call me ASAP, that it is urgent." Henson cut off the intercom, smiling thinly. "Now, if there is nothing else, I have an appointment waiting."

Deacon didn't budge. Nor did Bishop. "There is still much you can do for us," Deacon said. "Like telling us when was the last time *you* were at the O'Bannion house."

Henson's eyebrows shot up over his spectacles. "Am I a suspect?"

"Can you answer the question, please?" Deacon countered.

Henson leaned back in his chair, his pleasant facade disintegrating, revealing the iron core beneath. *This* was the man who'd remained a trusted adviser to the wealthy for more than sixty years. "Twenty-three years ago," he answered curtly.

"At Tobias's funeral?" Deacon asked. "Or at Margaret Sullivan's?"

"Margaret's, although I attended Tobias's as well."

"You'd known them that long?" Deacon asked.

"Yes. Anything else?"

"Yes." Deacon was becoming both annoyed and suspicious at Henson's hurry. "I must say I'm a little surprised that an attorney of your stature would take care of such small details as home maintenance for your clients."

"I don't. I did it for Barbara because we were friends. I'd known both Tobias and Barbara since the 1940s. Tobias was the best friend of my older brother. My wife and Barbara were schoolmates. We were Joy's godparents."

"Who was Joy?" Bishop asked.

"Joy was Barbara's firstborn. She died at fifteen. Leukemia."

Deacon frowned. "I thought Jordan was the one who had cancer when he was a teenager."

Henson tilted his head appraisingly. "He was also stricken. How did you know that?"

"Faith told me."

"Interesting. I suppose she would have been old enough to know what was going on at the time," Henson mused.

"The O'Bannions had two children develop cancer?" Bishop asked.

Henson nodded. "The family had more than their share of heartache. At any rate, Barbara and I go back decades. That's why I handled the details of the house for her."

"Why didn't Jordan do that?" Deacon asked.

"He took care of her physically and seemed to do that well. He wasn't so responsible otherwise."

Deacon thought of the photo the genie gymnast had shown him. "In what way?"

"Drinking too much. Carousing with women. Parties. He lives in the art world and, even in a town as conservative as this one, they are rather . . . free-spirited."

"Does he make a good living as an art dealer?" Bishop asked.

Henson frowned, perturbed. "If I knew, I wouldn't tell you. But I don't. Anything *else*?"

"Yes," Deacon said. "Why don't you like the O'Bannion house? You referred to it as 'that damn house.' I know Faith doesn't like it, but why don't you?"

"Because it was a drain on Barbara, emotionally and financially, but she was determined to hold on to it. It was her remaining legacy to leave to her children and grandchildren."

"Remaining legacy?" Bishop asked.

Henson stiffened, as if he'd said too much. "The house was all she had left of her past. The cemetery was there, with Joy's grave. She didn't want to give it up to strangers."

Bishop's black brows rose. "Joy's grave? Not her husband's or Margaret's?"

Henson flushed. "Their graves are there, too. Every O'Bannion for more than a century is buried there. She loved Margaret and Tobias, but Joy died so young. She never quite got over her death."

"One more question," Deacon said. "Where do you keep the combination to the vault written down?"

"I don't," Henson said haughtily. "I have it memorized. I may be old, but my mind is as sharp as ever."

"I don't disagree with that one bit," Deacon said mildly. "But you're also not a fool. You don't have to be old to die unexpectedly. A man as careful as you has backup plans. You keep the combination written down somewhere, or you have a code, or some way to communicate the combo to your successors."

"I said I do *not* have it written down." Henson struggled to his feet, reaching for the walker he kept under his desk. "Now, I have clients waiting. Mrs. Lowell will show you out."

Mrs. Lowell's steps were brisk as she led them to the entrance. Deacon slowed his step when he got to the waiting room and took a moment to study all the photographs and placards on the wall near the door. Henson Senior was shown sitting behind his desk. Henson the third was standing next to his desk, arms crossed casually over a very broad chest.

Henson the third was built just like Peter Combs.

Deacon waited to speak until he and Bishop got to their cars. "Did you see Henson the third's picture?"

"Yeah. Big guy, just like Peter Combs. It also fits with the King's College crime scene. Arianna and Corinne were abducted from the path that led from the library to the dorms. There were signs of a struggle by the path, but then nothing more all the way to the access road. Arianna's a tall girl. He would have needed some height and muscle to carry the women that far. Height and muscle like Combs or Henson's grandson."

"You're sure he used the access road to escape the college?"

"I found one of Arianna's earrings next to tire tracks on the access road's shoulder—the earrings she was wearing in the photo her roommate gave the cops when she filed the missing-persons report."

"Good enough for me," Deacon said. "Henson the third has been in Cincinnati for at least four years, and he's had access to the house and, even though Senior won't admit it, probably to the will as well. He would have known that Faith had inherited the property."

Bishop nodded. "I thought the same thing. He's got the vault combination noted somehow, somewhere. The old man is eighty-six years old. He has to have been handing things off to his grandson. Could Henson the third have been behind the attacks on Faith?" She slanted Deacon a cautious look. "Could it be that this Combs guy isn't involved at all?"

"I've been thinking the same thing," he admitted. "Except that we have the ballistics that link Gordon Shue's murder to the shots fired during the struggle with the Earl Power tech."

"And the bullet that killed Anthony Brown, the hotel guest," Bishop added. "The crimes are connected, but it doesn't mean Combs was the one trying to kill her in Florida or now."

"Or not alone, at least. We could be talking about two killers working together—or at least to the same end, which is keeping Faith away from the house. That's consistent with the fact that Combs only met her four years ago and it's looking like these crimes go back at least ten years."

"When Henson's firm hired a new maintenance company," Bishop said.

"Exactly. Plus, Combs couldn't have known about the will unless someone told him—someone who did know about it. Somebody built like a linebacker tried to climb through Faith's apartment window in Miami. So far, that's Henson the third or Combs. Henson has access to the will, but Combs did try to kill her once before, so his involvement is still conceivable."

"I saw the scar on her throat. Combs did that?"

Deacon nodded, keeping the fury from his voice. "Yeah. He did. Four years ago."

"Because she turned him in to his PO for missing a therapy appointment, or because she was somehow in league with that sex-crimes cop you and Vega were talking about?"

"And if she was?" Deacon asked quietly.

"Then she was directly responsible for him going to prison for three years. She could lose her license. If anyone reported her. Which would so totally not be worth the paperwork."

Deacon smiled at her. "I thought the same thing."

Bishop smiled back, then sobered. "Henson the third has been in Cinci for the last four years. The bios they posted on their foyer wall said that his law degree came from the University of Kentucky, so he was close by during the years before that. But, like you said, we can't dismiss Combs entirely, because he has the history with Faith and we do have a ballistics link to Miami-based crimes. Where was Combs before he got arrested for molesting his stepdaughter?"

"I pulled his record. No previous arrests."

"I mean geographically. Did he come from Ohio? Could

he have known the O'Bannions? Known about the house before he began therapy with Faith?"

Deacon shook his head. "Combs has a steady work history in Florida. There's no mention of any affiliation with anyone or anyplace in Ohio. Plus, a judge ordered him to therapy. That he'd be purposely assigned to Faith is way beyond improbable."

"I agree. Just checking to be sure you hadn't veered off into conspiracy theory territory."

He opened his mouth to protest, then stopped himself. It was fair. They'd been partners for only a month. She couldn't know that he'd never lost his mind over a woman before.

"So," Bishop went on, "let's consider that we're dealing with two different people. What if Combs was sought out by whoever laid claim to that basement years ago *because* he had a history with her? What better person to sic on Faith Corcoran than the man who spent three years behind bars because of her? That way the 'basement-killer' can keep his hands clean then. Nobody would think to look for him because everyone knew Combs had tried to kill Faith before. What if Combs's role is that of a contract killer, whether he's aware of it or not?"

"Good point." Deacon began considering all the possibilities. "If that's the case, it makes sense that the basement-killer made contact with Combs after Faith inherited the house, otherwise the attempts on Faith's life would have started long before now."

"Assuming they didn't. Has she had any other near misses over the years?"

That made Deacon frown. "I don't know. I'll ask her. So we have two suspects—Combs and Henson the third. We need to account for the movements of both of them over the past month."

"We have to find them first," Bishop said pragmatically. "Vega's been looking for Combs for a month. Maybe she couldn't find him because he was here."

"Abducting Corinne and Arianna," he said grimly.

"In the meantime, we still have Maguire and Sons. Let's check them out next. See if they really have been inside that basement. That'll give us more information on Henson the third."

Deacon checked the time. "I have to be at Greg's principal's office soon, and King's College is on the way. Let's split up. You take Maguire, and I'll stop by the college crime scene and see what CSU has found. I'll text you when I'm done with Greg. Then we find Herbie the third."

Bishop gave him a wave as she got into her car. "Good luck with the principal."

"Thanks." Deacon had the feeling he was going to need it.

Chapter Eighteen

Corinne came awake suddenly, her body tensing for a blow. That never came.

She struggled to sit up against the cabin door. She'd passed out, dammit. Somehow she'd slept. But for how long? She forced herself to stand, closing her eyes briefly against a wave of dizziness and nausea. And pain. *Can't forget about the pain*. Every joint in her body hurt.

"Buck up, soldier," she snapped, channeling her boot-camp drill sergeant. "Stop your whining." She opened the door and looked up. The moon had been high in the night sky when she'd escaped from the storm cellar. Now the sun was shining brightly.

She'd slept half the day away. *Dammit*. She'd wanted to be long gone hours ago.

She closed the door and sat down on the bed next to the girl, who'd curled up in a ball. Progress. At least she had moved.

Corinne shook her shoulder. "Please, wake up. We need to run, and I can't carry you."

Her gaze fell on the wheelbarrow, and suddenly she saw herself racing through the woods at a cartoon speed, pushing the girl in the wheelbarrow. She laughed out loud at the notion, then started when the girl's shoulder jerked under her hand. She was waking up.

Corinne rubbed her back. "If I have to push you, I will, but I'd really prefer not to. I know you can hear me. Please open your eyes. I won't hurt you. He's not here."

The girl stiffened. "He'll come back," she whispered.

"Yeah, he will. We need to be gone by then."

The little body began to tremble. "He'll find us. He'll kill us. Or worse."

Arianna's screams echoed in Corinne's mind. "That's why we need to be gone by then," she said, infusing a confidence into her voice that she did not feel. "Can you sit up?"

The girl's eyes slowly opened, and she gasped. "Where are we?"

"I don't know. A cabin, somewhere in the woods. Sit up now."

The girl pushed herself up weakly. "I don't feel good."

"Neither do I. He drugged us."

The girl shook her head. "No, he couldn't have drugged you. I took it all."

Corinne frowned. "What do you mean?"

Large, dark eyes searched the room. "Where is the other girl? Arianna?"

"I don't know. It was just the two of us in the van." And the two dead men.

The girl began to shake. "Then he killed her. I tried to help her, but it didn't work. He won. He always wins. I'm sorry. I'm so sorry. She didn't get away."

Corinne's jaw clenched. "We don't know that. What do you mean, you took it all?"

"He gave me medicine for you and Arianna. To make you sleepy. I wanted her to get away, so I didn't give it to her."

"You took it yourself? All of it? The drug for both of us?"

"I couldn't leave," she said simply.

"Why not?" Had she *wanted* to die there?

The girl's gaze dropped to the blanket. "I couldn't leave Mama."

Mama? Corinne's brows drew together. "Where is your mama, honey?"

"At home. She's dead. I buried her." Her eyes filled with tears. "Please, take me home."

"What do you mean, you buried her?" Corinne asked cautiously.

The girl was staring at her like she was speaking a foreign tongue. "I dug a hole. I put her in it."

Corinne tried not to let her horror show. She'd *buried* her own mother? *Dear God.*

"All right," Corinne soothed, instinct telling her not to try to reason with the girl. Not just yet. "We'll figure out how to get you back. I don't even know your name. I'm Corinne."

"Firoza, but Mama always called me Roza. 'Roza, with a *zed*,'" she whispered, with a nod.

Zed. The British soldiers Corinne had met while she'd been deployed in Afghanistan had said *zed.* Except Roza didn't sound British. Canadian, maybe. They also said *zed.*

If Roza's mother truly was dead, maybe the girl still had family. *If I get us out of here . . . No.* When *I get us out of here, I need to be able to tell the police where to look for her family.*

She made herself smile gently. "All right, Roza with a *zed.* We *are* going to get away from here, and he is *not* going to win. Not this time. But we can't just run through the woods willy-nilly. I need to find you a coat and some shoes. And some food. Do you think you could eat?" Glancing at the stew leftover in the pot, she grimaced. It had been sitting for a long time. The last thing they needed was food poisoning when they were running for their lives. She searched the galley kitchen's cabinets and found them stocked with cans of chicken soup and beef stew. Lots of soup and stew.

She chose a can of soup and turned on the stove, but nothing happened. It was out of gas. She thought about the blood all over the cabin's back wall, by the gas tank.

Whoever had been cooking the beef stew had gone out to check the gas tank because his fire went out. She glanced uneasily over her shoulder at the pile of dirt. He'd shot the stew maker and buried him or her, along with the two dead men from the van. *We need to get out of here.*

"The stove doesn't work, so we'll have to eat it cold," she said briskly. She opened a can and took it and a spoon to where Roza sat on the bed. "Eat as much as you can. We don't have much time, but I don't want either of us collapsing because we're too hungry."

Roza dug in with surprising gusto. "I eat it cold all the

time," she said with her mouth full. "I'm not allowed to use the stove."

Of course she wasn't. That sonofabitch had made this child his slave. Fury simmered in Corinne's gut as she quickly checked every drawer, every cupboard. Cans of soup, a few cans of PET Milk. Bottles of water. Several flannel shirts. The shirts they could use. *We'll layer.*

She found a worn pair of men's boots in the closet, too big for either of them, but closer to Corinne's size than Roza's. *I'll wear these,* she decided. *Roza will have to wear my shoes.*

The boots had been sitting on top of a blanket. She took the blanket, too. No telling how long they'd have to walk before—

"Hello," she murmured. A promising-looking old steamer trunk had been hidden by the blanket. She lifted the lid and found jars. Dozens of mason jars. Canned goods? Fruit? Something besides soup, she hoped. Carefully, she lifted one out of the trunk.

And squinted, at first unsure of what she was looking at. Then realization dawned and she froze, horrified. A thin cry escaped her throat as the jar slipped from her hand and rolled across the floor. It came to rest a few feet away, the contents sloshing back and forth. She stared.

The contents of the jar stared back. *Eyes.* Human eyes.

"Oh my God." Corinne turned her head, gagging. "Oh my God. Oh my God."

There were human eyes in the jars. Dozens of eyes. And other things. Hearts, kidneys, all suspended in a murky liquid.

"They're his," Roza whispered from the bed.

Corinne wrenched her body around to stare at the child. *"What?"*

"He takes them from all the ladies he brings home. Sometimes he lines the jars up on the counter and talks to them."

Corinne slammed the trunk lid down and backed away from the closet, bile burning her mouth. "Oh God," she whimpered. "Did he do that to Arianna?"

"Not if she got away," Roza said, her voice eminently logical, as if all of this made perfect sense. "He always waits until they're dead."

"Oh my God. Oh God." How many had he killed? There were at least a dozen jars. A dozen victims. "We have to get out of here. Now." Corinne lurched to the bed, dragging her shoes off. "Put these on. Fast."

Roza looked at them like they were alive.

"Do it!" Corinne cried. She pulled on the boots and grabbed the blanket. She threw flannel shirts, two bottles of water, and several cans of soup on top, then tied the corners, hobo-style. "Put on the shoes, Roza. We have to run. *Now."*

Roza only stared at the shoes, so Corinne took over, lacing them as tightly as she could.

"Come on. Let's go." She pulled the girl from the bed and wrapped the blanket around her thin little shoulders like a cape. *A weapon. I need a weapon.*

Corinne grabbed the shovel from where it rested against the wall and gathered the knives she'd taken from the kitchen drawer earlier. Then she picked up the blanket holding the supplies and wrenched open the door, half expecting to see *him* looming.

But no one loomed. The sun shone quietly. Corinne stepped outside, but Roza hung back. She hadn't moved from beside the bed, her eyes huge in her small face. She stared at the open door, still as a statue.

Corinne felt desperation clawing at her. She dropped her bundle on the porch, forced herself to reenter the cabin, then grabbed the girl's arm and pulled her toward the door.

"No!" Roza yanked out of her grasp and dropped to the floor, huddling in a small ball.

Corinne grabbed Roza's shoulders. Tried to pull her to her feet. "Roza, please. If he comes back, he will kill us."

Roza shook her head. Curled back into a ball.

Corinne wanted to scream. She wanted to cry. But she did neither, instead calming her voice. The girl was terrified. *More terrified than I am, which says a lot.*

"What's wrong, Roza?" she asked gently. "Why won't you come with me?"

"It's outside," Roza whispered.

Corinne looked over her shoulder. There was nothing there. "What's outside, honey?"

"Outside," Roza repeated in a strangely hollow tone.

"There's nothing out there, honey. Just trees and birds. There's nothing out there that can hurt you, but if we don't leave soon, he'll come back. We need to find help. I want to go home."

Roza seemed to settle. "Me, too. I can't leave Mama there all alone. I'm all she has."

She buried her own mother. Oh God.

Roza was a brainwashed, terrified child. *Do what you must to get her to safety.* "All right," Corinne said softly. "I'll get you back to your mama."

"No, you won't. He'll kill you."

"I'll get help. I'll find someone who can make him go away."

A moment of indecision. Then a nod. "Faith. We have to find Faith."

And hope and charity and love, Corinne thought, fighting the urge to look over her shoulder. "I have faith, Roza."

Her eyes widened. "Here? She's here? Oh no. He got her, too?"

Her? "Faith is a person?"

"Yes. He doesn't like her. He's afraid of her. I told your friend to find her."

"Okay. That's good. Does Faith have a last name?"

"Frye. He made a lot of phone calls, asking for her room. He didn't know I heard him."

Calls to whom? What room? It didn't matter right now. "Okay. Then we'll find Faith Frye. She'll help us. And we'll go to your mama. But we need to get away from here." Corinne held out her hand, praying that Roza would take it. "Please, honey. Before he comes back."

She sighed with relief when the child took her hand. But the relief was short-lived. At the door, Roza yanked her hand free of Corinne's and stood there, staring outside.

Shaking like a leaf.

Oh God. What now? Corinne kept her tone calm. "Roza? What's wrong?"

"It's outside."

They were back to that. "There isn't anything out there that can hurt you, sweetie." *Only if he comes back.* "It's not dark outside. It's daytime. See? The sun is out."

A hard shake of her head. "It was always dark in the basement."

Then Corinne understood. "Are you afraid of going outside?"

Roza shrugged her thin shoulders. Then nodded, ducking her head in shame.

Corinne tipped up her chin, wondering just how long the girl had been held in that basement. "Roza, sweetheart, you remember going outside, right? Before he took you?"

A slow shake of her shaggy, dark head. "No."

Realization dawned and with it a deeper horror. "You've never been outside before?"

Big, dark eyes looked up at her. "No. I was born at home."

Cincinnati, Ohio
Tuesday, November 4, 11:10 a.m.

Deacon had to elbow his way through a crowd of college kids, their cell phone cameras clicking like paparazzi, to get to the crime-scene tape wrapped around the abduction site.

CSU was busy taking samples and photographs, and Deacon carefully picked his way around them to study the ground near the bench on the path. The signs of a struggle started here, ending about ten feet away, just as Bishop had said. Whoever had been sitting on the bench stopped struggling after a few seconds of being dragged. Drugged, probably.

Agent Taylor was attaching colored trajectory string from the tree nearest the path to a point at the edge of the forest. He looked up when Deacon approached.

"What have you found?" Deacon asked.

Taylor indicated a pole near the path. "The camera was stolen weeks ago."

"You think our abductor knew it?"

"If he read that goth girl's blog he did." Taylor pointed at a black-haired, sober-faced young woman standing off to the side of the crowd. "She's on a mission to point out school safety hazards, but it's a users' manual for the pervs. She posted about the stolen camera two weeks ago and the blown light above that bench just last Wednesday."

"And two days later Corinne and Arianna are taken," Deacon said with a sigh. "Bishop mentioned a bullet and a lot of blood."

"Detective Bishop found the bullet embedded in that tree." Taylor indicated the tree to which he'd attached the string. "The blood is the same type as Arianna Escobar's, and the bullet came from a nine mil."

"Same as shot Gordon Shue in Florida and the power company tech," Deacon said.

"And the man you found in the hotel room last night. The slug from the tree is on its way to Ballistics." Taylor walked into the woods. "Trajectory puts him shooting her from around here."

Deacon stood in the spot Taylor pointed to and studied the path. "Corinne and Arianna left the library together on Friday night, right?"

"At eleven o'clock," Taylor confirmed. "The path forks at that bench. To the right is Corinne's dorm. Arianna's is to the left and up the hill. They would have separated there."

"All right. So let's assume he drove up the access road, parked, got out, and hid in these trees, waiting. Corinne's path is closer to him and Arianna's already headed up the hill, so he grabs Corinne. How did he get her to the access road without anyone seeing them?"

Taylor stood beside him, surveying the scene from his point of view. "Maybe Arianna saw her being taken away and ran down the hill after them, trying to save Corinne, but he shot her."

Deacon walked back to where they'd found the blood. "From the amount of blood here, Arianna was stationary for a while. Long enough for him to stow Corinne in his van and come back for her. Yet she didn't call 911. The bullet hadn't hit her femoral artery, so she wasn't gushing blood. Teenagers have phones permanently fixed to their palms. Why didn't she call?" He checked his screen. "I have four bars here. How about you?"

"The same. She had enough signal to call. Maybe her battery had run out of juice. Or maybe she did but didn't stay on long enough for 911 to triangulate her location. Maybe he took her phone away."

"That's most likely. If so, he knows how to disable the GPS. Tanaka tried tracking her phone but got nothing. Bishop also mentioned tire prints."

"Yes. They match the ones Tanaka took from the dirt road near the O'Bannion place. Good possibility it was the same van."

"It connects the dots nicely," Deacon agreed, "but

doesn't give us anything new. We knew he had a white van. We knew he'd taken them. We know he likes blondes. What we don't know is why he came here. Did he pick Corinne specifically? Or would any blonde have sufficed?"

"If he picked Corinne specifically," Taylor said, "did he watch her beforehand, learn her habits? Maybe one of those college kids saw him hanging around."

Deacon eyed the curious crowd gathered behind them. "I've got a few minutes before my next appointment. I'll ask them." He could show them Combs's mug shot, as well, but not Henson the third's picture. Not until they had more evidence. "Hopefully, we can start ID'ing those bodies soon so we can figure out what else they had in common besides being blond and being dead. Then we can see where Corinne fits into all of this, see if this guy has a pattern."

Eastern Kentucky
Tuesday, November 4, 11:20 a.m.

Corinne stared down into Roza's thin face, horrified. "You were born in that basement?"

A small nod. "Mama said so."

Oh God. Could that horrible man have been her father?

Corinne glanced at the jar on the floor and swallowed hard, wondering if any of those eyes had belonged to Roza's mother. Unwilling and unable to consider that Arianna's eyes might have been taken, too. *Or that mine will be if he comes back and we're still here.*

"Step outside with me. Just one step." *And then one more step and another until we're safe.*

"Just go," Roza begged. "Just go and leave me here."

"No. That I will not do. Please, Roza. Just take one step."

"I never had shoes," Roza whispered, still panicked. "They hurt my feet."

Corinne's heart cracked wide open. "I'm sorry. I'm so sorry, baby. I wish I could carry you, but I can't. I'm not strong enough." She used to be. Before she got sick, she could have carried Roza and the bundle of supplies and run for miles without stopping.

Roza's head tilted. "You need my help?"

Was it that simple? Roza had been in that basement her whole life. How many victims had she cared for? Corinne glanced at the jar again. *Too many. Way too many.* Had her mother been forced to care for the others, too?

"Yes, I need your help. I can't make it home by myself. Will you come with me? Help me like you helped Arianna?"

Roza shuddered out a breath. Straightened her spine. Closed her eyes and stepped over the threshold. Then drew a deep breath and burst into tears. "I'm sorry. I can't help you. I can't. Just leave me here and go. Find Faith. She'll know what to do."

"I can't do that. I need your help, remember?"

Corinne put her arms around the girl, rocking her as she watched the road outside. If he came back, she'd have to take him on. She had knives. She had a shovel.

And she had a belly full of rage. *He touches this child over my dead body.*

Cincinnati, Ohio
Tuesday, November 4, 12:30 p.m.

MS. POHL, PRINCIPAL. Deacon stared at the nameplate on the door, summoning his courage. He'd faced killers without breaking a sweat. Surely he could handle one very old woman.

"We could probably take her together," Greg whispered dryly from beside him. He'd been waiting when Deacon picked him up at Jim and Tammy's house, dressed and ready, his hearing aids both in *and* turned on. Deacon had taken it as a good omen.

Now he looked down to see his brother's face pinched and a little pale. "I don't know. She used to scare the heck out of me when she was only vice principal."

Greg's eyes widened. "You knew her then?"

"Better than I should have," Deacon admitted. "I sat in those chairs a lot. Are you sure you don't want an ASL interpreter for this? We can still get one."

"No. I'll manage with my hearing aids. I don't want anyone else to know about this."

Not a good omen. "Okay," Deacon said, and opened the door to Ms. Pohl's office.

She looked up and started to smile, but it died on her lips. "Well, well, well," she said softly. "Deacon Novak. I was expecting your sister."

She looked almost the same, Deacon thought. Older, grayer, more wrinkled than she'd been fifteen years before, but she had the same look of authority that had shamed him into obedience when he'd been no older than Greg.

His brother flopped into one of the chairs in front of her desk and his head immediately went down, arms crossed over his chest. *No, not a good omen at all.*

"Dani's working," Deacon said. "I guess you're stuck with me this time."

"Not at all. Look at you, all grown up and an FBI agent, of all things." She smiled wryly when he stood up straighter. "I've kept up with your career over the years, you know. Through the newspapers, of course, since you haven't come back to see me," she added pointedly.

He winced. "I figured you'd seen enough of me in detention to last you a lifetime."

That made her chuckle. "You were a handful, but you turned out all right. I consider you a success story. Your work seems very exciting, I have to say. Where's that coat of yours?"

Her praise warmed him. *I guess I did turn out pretty well.* "You remember my coat?"

"Of course. You made quite a stir with it back in the day. And I've seen you wear it in the news photos over the years—as recently as in this morning's paper. So where is it?"

Deacon scowled. "Got taken as evidence, I'm afraid. I should get it back. Eventually."

Her eyes sharpened, her glance falling briefly to Greg before looking back up at Deacon. "Will they be able to repair the bullet hole?"

Greg's head jerked up. He spun in the chair to stare up at his brother. "Bullet? What bullet?"

"I got shot at last night, but I was wearing a vest. I always wear a vest, Greg. You don't have to worry about me." Deacon squeezed his shoulder. "I'm careful."

"Fine." Greg pulled away from his grasp, sprawling nonchalantly in the chair. "Can we get this over with? I've got *Breaking Bad* on my Netflix queue. I figure I can get through season two while I'm on suspension."

"Better living through chemistry," Ms. Pohl said sarcastically, and Deacon thought he saw Greg's lips twitch. But the kid pulled his stony face back on so quickly that he couldn't be sure.

"I've blocked that show ten times," Deacon said. "But he always finds a way to get through the parental controls. He's got a good brain in there, when he chooses to use it."

Greg's lip curled in a sneer. "Is there a point to this?"

"Yes," Ms. Pohl said crisply. "You were caught fighting again, Greg. Your aim is getting better. This time you broke the other student's nose. Witnesses say that you started it."

"So?"

Deacon rapped the wooden arm of the chair. "Sit up straight. Show some respect."

Ms. Pohl pursed her lips for a moment, and Deacon thought she was fighting a smile. Then she leveled a harsh look at Greg, waiting until he sat up and met her gaze. "Thank you, Greg. What do you have to say for yourself besides 'So'?"

"Nothing. You can suspend me if you want. I'll just come back and do it again. It would be better if you expelled me. I can work from home. Do my degree online." He shrugged. "Or I could just take my GED now and be done with it."

Deacon opened his mouth to explode in protest, but Ms. Pohl silenced him with a look.

"You could," she said. "But I hope you won't. You could have a bright future. If nothing else, hacking into the databases of enemy governments. Hopefully, you won't consider our own government the enemy."

Greg's mouth dropped open, and Deacon stared. "What the hell, Greg?"

Ms. Pohl frowned at him. "Just because you're grown up and an FBI guy doesn't mean I'll tolerate bad language in my office, Deacon Novak."

Deacon slumped in his chair. "Sorry," he muttered.

Greg was still gaping. "You know about that?"

"I know about everything that goes on at my school. I have cameras everywhere, and I know how to use them. I know that you started the fight a few weeks ago so that another student who was being bullied could walk away unharmed. I'd hoped you'd confide in me then, but you didn't, so I had no choice but to suspend you."

Greg's chin lifted. "Fine. The fight yesterday happened off school grounds."

She tilted her head like a small bird. "Yes, I know."

Greg didn't blink. "So, technically, you have no jurisdiction here at all."

"None," she agreed.

Deacon was gaping at the tiny old woman as well, this time with real respect. "Then why are we here? Is it because of the hacking? And . . . *what hacking?*"

"I could call the police," she said to Greg, ignoring Deacon. "Hacking *is* a crime."

Greg's jaw tightened. He leaned back in his chair, wary. "What do you want from me?"

"I want you to stop trying to hack into my network. I don't care what your reasons are, although I want to know those, too. I want you to tell me why you fought with that hairy ape yesterday, and I want you to stay out of trouble."

"And I want to know what the hell—heck—is going on here," Deacon demanded.

"Greg tests way off the math charts but uses his gift for trouble. Just like you did, Deacon. He also hit a growth spurt about the same time you did. He's got size and strength this year that he didn't have last year, and he's making up for lost time. Just like you did."

"Shi-oot," Deacon muttered. "You're enjoying this."

"Oh yes." Her eyes glimmered. "I've been hoping for this day since you gave me my first gray hairs, more than fifteen years ago."

Deacon smiled at her. "You had gray hair before I met you, so don't be blaming your woes on me." He turned to Greg. "Start with the fight. Why did you break the hairy ape's nose?"

Greg shrugged. "Renzo was talking trash."

"About?"

"Me." Greg looked away. "Said I was a freak of nature."

Deacon flinched, Adam's words coming back with a vengeance. "So you showed him you were just like him."

Another shrug. "Pretty much."

"But you did it off school grounds so you wouldn't get in trouble. Why didn't you tell me?"

Greg hunched his shoulders. "You didn't ask."

Deacon sighed, remembering the shouting. The angry words. "But I did later, and you didn't tell me then. That's not fair." He turned to the old woman with a frown. "You told me he'd gotten in trouble at school. Why did you say that?"

"I *said* he got into a fight after school. I *said* charges might be filed, and that may still be the case. I hadn't reviewed the security tape when I called you yesterday. Now I have. He won't be suspended for the fighting this time. But, Greg, what happens next time? You've made an enemy. What happens when Renzo and his friends jump you in the stairwell? You've put my staff and the other students in a dangerous situation. If fighting breaks out in the hallways, someone else is bound to get hurt."

"I'm sorry," Greg said quietly. "I didn't think about that."

"I know you didn't," she said kindly. "Now we deal with the real issue. The hacking."

Greg narrowed his eyes. "How did you know it was me?"

"I didn't until you admitted it. I knew someone had tried to break into the network. I figured it was you, but I wanted you off guard before I accused you. Yesterday I got the opportunity I'd been waiting for."

Greg's mouth had fallen open again. Deacon had to chuckle. "Well played, Ms. Pohl."

She beamed. "I thought so." She leaned forward. "So, what was the plan, Greg?"

He looked down. "You're going to suspend me for this, aren't you?"

"You bet your bloomers, I am. But we might be able to make some kind of deal. Why were you attempting to break into my teachers' e-mails?"

"I was going to change Renzo's grades. I just wanted him to fail. I just wanted him gone."

Ms. Pohl looked concerned. "Why? Because he called you names?"

"Isn't that enough?" Greg asked petulantly.

"No," she said quietly. "It's not. And I don't buy your story. You know we would have noticed a grade change. What were you really trying to do?"

"Fine. I didn't just *attempt* to access the e-mail server." Greg looked away, but his lip trembled, reminding Deacon of how young he really was. "I did it."

"Why, Greg?" Deacon put his hand gently on his brother's back. "What did you do?"

"I sent e-mails from the nurse's account to all of Renzo's teachers. Told them that one of their students had a health issue. The teachers' student aides see their e-mails. They talk."

"You knew the aides would compare notes," Deacon said, "and then they'd see which other teachers got the same e-mail and figure out which student had all those classes. They'd point the finger at Renzo, and the gossips would do the rest. Not a bad plan, actually."

"Deacon Novak!" Pohl exclaimed, annoyed.

Greg studied his brother, and Deacon knew that how he handled the next few minutes would be pivotal to their relationship for the rest of their lives.

"Well, it is," Deacon said. "Disinformation is very *Mission: Impossible*–esque. What health issue did you give him? Exploding diarrhea?"

Greg cocked his jaw. "HIV."

Deacon exhaled quietly. *Oh God.* "Why?"

Greg swallowed hard. "Because Renzo found out. He was going to put it online." Tears shimmered in his eyes, one blue, one brown, just like Dani's. "I couldn't let him do that."

Now Deacon really understood. "No, I couldn't have, either. How did he find out?"

"I don't know. I didn't tell anyone. Honest. I wouldn't do that. Especially to her."

"I know you wouldn't," Deacon said calmly. "I thought maybe he told you how he found out when he was taunting you with it."

Gratitude flashed in Greg's eyes. "I wanted to hurt him," he whispered, "but mostly I just wanted to make him stop."

"I know." Deacon rubbed Greg's back as he'd done Faith's last night. "I understand."

Pohl was watching them both. "*I* don't understand. Found out what? About whom?"

Greg shook his head again but said no more.

"Dani wouldn't want you to get in trouble for her," Deacon said. "Tell Ms. Pohl. Let her help you stay in school. You deserve more than a GED and a dead-end job."

Pohl went very still, and Deacon could see the moment

she truly understood. "This is about your sister? She's . . . ? Dani has HIV? How?"

"That's her business," Deacon said stiffly. She'd been so young then, barely older than Greg was now. And she'd listened to the boyfriend who'd claimed to love her and claimed to be clean. The bastard had lied on both fronts, and Dani's life was forever changed. All of which was her goddamn business. "Which is the point of this, Ms. Pohl. Somehow Renzo found out about her medical history and was going to use it against her."

"Of course it's her business," Pohl murmured. "I'm sorry I asked. It was just so unexpected. Oh, Greg. What have you done, son?"

"What I had to do. Renzo would have ruined my sister's career, and she worked too hard to become a doctor. She never hurt a soul in her life. He was laughing at her. Telling his friends. Saying she had to be a slut or a junkie to have HIV." Greg looked down at his clenched fists. "He said once a junkie always a junkie and that he'd make her share her stash with him. Even if he had to beat her senseless to make her tell him where it was." He looked back up at Pohl defiantly, tears in his eyes. "But now everyone is saying the same things about him. Now anything he says about Dani or anyone else is being laughed off."

Deacon closed his eyes. *Dear God, this is a mess.* "Why didn't you tell me, Greg?"

"I didn't think you'd believe me. I was in so much trouble, and you left your job to come home." The boy was crying in earnest now, and Deacon's heart broke. He put his arm around his brother's shaking shoulders. "I just wanted to make him stop."

"I understand. Sshh." Deacon looked at Pohl, who looked like she'd aged twenty years in the last few minutes. "Now what?"

"I don't know." She pressed her fingertips to her lips for a long moment, thinking. "Well, the reaction of the other students makes a lot more sense now. Greg hit the other boy in the nose, the kid's blood went spewing, and everyone ran. Greg's made Renzo a pariah."

"Sounds like he deserved it." Deacon wanted to find the hairy ape and hit him all over again.

"I've never had anything like this happen. I don't know what punishment is in order."

"Just expel me for the fight," Greg said, and Pohl gave him a knowing look.

"But not for the hacking? You just don't want anyone to know that you set him up."

"No, I don't. I want him to suffer and I want him to pay."

"What should we do, Ms. Pohl?" Deacon asked. "This kid Renzo threatened to expose the fact that my sister—who never hurt a soul—has HIV, which could damage her career. Then he threatened to beat her up. The threat of violence cannot go unpunished."

"I agree with that." She rubbed her temples. "Take your brother home, Deacon. I'll consult with the school's attorneys and see what the recommended course of action is."

Deacon looked at his brother's young face. "If we can fix this so that you can stay in this school, do you want to?"

Greg's eyes narrowed, his mouth hardening. "Yeah. I'll stay."

"That may not be possible, Greg," Pohl said. "I may not have any choice but to expel you. Tampering with records is a privacy issue. Law enforcement has to be called. This is bad."

"He didn't tamper with anyone's actual medical records. He tampered with e-mail." Deacon squeezed the back of Greg's neck. "We're going to hire an attorney. We'll fight any attempt by the school to expel him."

Pohl stared, astonished. "But . . . surely you can't condone what he did."

Greg looked astonished, too. "*We're* getting me a lawyer?"

"Yes," Deacon said firmly. "*We.* And when Dani finds out about this? She'll help us find the best damn lawyer in town." He looked at Ms. Pohl. "No, ma'am. I don't condone any part of this. What Greg did was wrong, but he did it for the right reasons." He stood up and motioned Greg to follow suit. "Come on, kid. I'm taking you home."

Greg hesitated at the door, wiping his eyes with his sleeves. "To Aunt Tammy's?"

"It has to be Tammy's. Your room's not ready yet. I still have painting to do."

"I don't have anything else to do for a while. I can paint."

Greg looked down at his shoes. "Don't make me go back, D," he whispered. "Tammy's going to have another heart attack over all this, and it'll be my fault. I already caused her enough trouble. Let me go home with you."

But Faith is there. In my bed. Hopefully getting some much-needed rest. He thought about what he'd prefer to be doing with her in his bed. Which was most likely unwise.

Not that he really cared.

Therein lay the problem. He simply did not care what was wise when it came to Faith Corcoran. He sighed silently. Having the kid around might be just the deterrent he needed to keep from taking the too-much-too-fast relationship to the next level. And at least there would be bodyguards on duty in case trouble followed Greg home.

"Okay. The rest of the painting is up to you." He put his arm around Greg's shoulders. "Let's go home. Ms. Pohl, you'll let us know what the school's action will be?"

"As soon as I know," she promised. "Greg, we'll figure this out somehow. And, Deacon, don't get shot anymore, okay?"

Deacon forced a smile. "I'll do my very best."

They said no more until they got to Deacon's car. "You gonna tell Dani?" Greg asked softly.

"Don't you think she has a right to know? Not only what you did, but what might be coming her way? Renzo did tell people. Her secret won't be a secret for too much longer."

Greg typed a text on his phone. "I just asked her to meet us at your house."

"Our house. Give me a second to catch up, and we'll head home." Deacon checked his phone, wearily scanning the voice mails, texts, and e-mails that had accumulated while he was in Pohl's office. Both of Faith's uncles had returned his calls. Alda Lane had kept her word. Jordan sounded like he'd sobered up and was frantically concerned about Faith. Jeremy the med-school professor sounded unmoved. Both said they'd be available to meet with him at any time of the day, and both demanded answers about the activities at their old house.

Deacon would call them back when he could deal with their questions without a fifteen-year-old hanging on his every word.

I'm so tired. He scrolled through the rest of his messages, thinking once again about Faith asleep in his bed, now wishing he could join her there to just sleep. *Must be tired,* he thought. At least when he finally did get to close his eyes, the scent of her would be in his sheets. It wasn't anywhere close to the real thing, but it would have to do until this was over.

And then he found the e-mail she'd written. *Take care. I'll be waiting.* Everything within him settled. For once, someone was waiting for him. Just for him. She might not stay long, but for now he let himself steep in the feeling.

Chapter Nineteen

Scarlett Bishop knocked on the door bearing the sign MA-
GUIRE AND SONS, but there was no answer. The office's exte-
rior was identical to that of its neighbors in the business
complex. Standing outside the door, she called the number
she'd been given for the maintenance business but didn't
hear any phones ringing inside.

That in and of itself wasn't damning. Many people used
cell phones exclusively these days. But that the doorknob
was coated in a layer of dust set off alarms in her mind. No
one had been here for quite some time.

She dialed Crandall next. "Hey, it's Bishop. Can you look
up a company for me in the business registry? Maguire and
Sons. I need to know if it's legit."

"Just a sec." Crandall's keyboard clacked in the background. "It's registered as a general contractor. Business
was created in . . . 2002. President is listed as John Maguire
of Batavia."

Batavia was the next town over. "So it's legit? Because
I'm standing here outside their office on Maple Street, and
it doesn't look like anyone's touched the doorknob in
weeks. Do they have another location?"

"No, Maple Street is listed as their only location. You
think it's a sham business?"

"I think it's convenient that the only people who were supposed to have been in that basement over the last ten years are not here. I'm going to ask around, see if any of their neighbors have seen them. Get back to me with what you find."

Scarlett tried the door to the next office—an accountant's firm. It opened right away, revealing a fiftyish woman sitting behind a receptionist's desk. Her nameplate read CAROLE WINSTON. "Can I help you, ma'am?"

"I hope so, Ms. Winston. I'm Detective Bishop with the Cincinnati Police. Do you happen to know the people in the office next door?"

Winston frowned. "I can't say that I do, Detective. They keep to themselves."

"When did you last see them?"

"A long time ago. Several months, at least."

"Do you remember who you saw?"

"They're criminals, aren't they? I was afraid of this. I thought it was strange that they'd pay the rent and never occupy the space. Well, let's see." Ms. Winston put on her glasses and opened her calendar. "I saw the receptionist the day I was leaving for the doctor. That would have been last August. I remember because I was in such a hurry that I didn't take time to talk to her, which I normally would have, for simple curiosity alone. When I came back from the appointment after lunch, I heard a man next door. He had a deep voice. It boomed."

"Do you remember what he said?"

"No. I couldn't really hear him, just the bass of his voice. He was big. I remember that."

Scarlett fought to keep her expression neutral. "You saw him?"

"Yes, for a minute. I'd gotten up to go next door to introduce myself to the receptionist once he'd gone, but right after that, she left."

"She? The receptionist?"

"Yes. I figured we could do lunch sometime. I went out my door and saw she was locking up. I introduced myself, and she got this look on her face. Like a scared rabbit. She mumbled something under her breath and took off. I thought then that they might be criminals, but I didn't want to seem like a silly old woman by reporting them."

"You may have been smart to suspect them," Scarlett said. She Googled Herbert Henson the third on her phone and chose the photo that hung on Henson's office wall. "Is this the man?"

Ms. Winston took off her glasses to stare at the photo up close. "Yes, but he wasn't dressed that nicely. He wore a polo shirt and khakis." She paused a moment. "And gloves. He had white gloves in his back pocket. And golf shoes."

"Golf shoes?"

"Yes. Black and white. With spikes." Her mouth tipped up sadly. "My late husband used to wear the same pair."

So Henson the third didn't meet Maguire at the house after all. He'd probably dropped off the key and gone to play a few rounds rather than spend his afternoon in a musty old house.

"This is very helpful, Ms. Winston. Can you tell me about the receptionist?"

"She was late twenties, early thirties, maybe. She had dark hair and covered it with a baseball cap. She was average height, maybe five-six. Average weight. I'm sorry, Detective. She was . . . average."

"No, no, don't be sorry. You've been incredibly helpful. Do you remember her eyes?"

"Scared. They may have been brown or dark blue. I didn't get that close."

"Do you think you could describe her to a sketch artist?"

Winston bit her lip. "I could try. She wouldn't have to know it was me who described her?"

"She wouldn't know," Scarlett assured her. "Can I call you when I have the artist lined up? In the meantime, here's my card, just in case you hear or remember anything else."

She handed over her card, then questioned the complex's other tenants. Mrs. Winston had been the only one to ever see anyone coming in or out of the office. The others had varying theories about who Maguire and Sons were, but most agreed they were shady.

On her way back to her car, Scarlett spied the building owner's sign on the office's outer wall, advertising their empty office units for rent or lease. She dialed, crossing her fingers that they'd be helpful without a warrant. Sometimes she got lucky.

"Grice Hill Realty," a woman answered in a nasal voice. "How can I help you?"

"This is Detective Bishop, Cincinnati PD Homicide," Scarlett said. "I'm hoping you can help me with an ongoing investigation. Can you tell me who's leased the property at 2826 Maple Street, unit 2-B? That's in Mount Carmel, Ohio."

"If you'll give me your badge number, I'll be happy to call you back with the information after I've verified your credentials."

Scarlett suppressed a sigh. The woman was within her rights. She gave her badge and cell phone numbers. "Thank you. This is very urgent. I appreciate any expediency you can muster."

Getting in her car, she buckled up and relaxed into the seat. *So tired.* She hated Halloween weekend. A goddamned serial killer would have to pick this week to act. *Just when we're so tired we all just want to sleep.*

Maybe that was it, she thought wearily. Maybe he'd picked this weekend because he'd known the police force would be busy with partying college kids.

She'd started to note it in her log when her cell phone rang. "Bishop."

"It's Carrie Washington."

Now we're cookin'. Washington was the ME, and a damn good one. *Maybe we'll finally get something useful.* "You got something for me? Please say yes."

"Oh, yes. You and your partner need to get down here as quickly as you can."

"I'll let Agent Novak know. We'll be there ASAP."

Cincinnati, Ohio
Tuesday, November 4, 1:20 p.m.

Deacon found Bishop pacing outside the autopsy room. He'd come directly from Greg's school, bringing his brother along and leaving him to scowl in the waiting room. "What's up?"

"Don't know yet." Bishop tossed him goggles and a mask. "It ain't pretty in there."

"I didn't think it would be," he said as he covered his eyes, nose, and mouth. "Not with ten bodies in various stages of decomp. I can smell it from here. Ready?"

She nodded, a little green around the gills. "On three."

Deacon followed her in, grateful that the eggs he'd eaten for breakfast had already digested. Mostly. He hated the morgue almost as much as he hated the thought of more unmarked graves.

Both autopsy tables were occupied. Carrie Washington was examining a body on the table closest to the door. The victim's dirty, tangled blond curls looked familiar. This victim was the third they'd uncovered. She'd been under the floor of the room with the cot.

Washington looked up, her dark eyes unnaturally large behind the magnifying goggles she wore, the white of her mask a stark contrast to her dark brown skin. "We've identified two of the bodies you sent us from the basement. This victim is Roxanne Dupree, twenty-two years old, Caucasian, a senior at the University of Miami. She's his most recent kill of the bodies we've found so far. She's also been—"

"Wait," Bishop cut in. "You mean Miami U, right? Miami of Ohio. The University of Miami is in Florida." She glanced at Deacon. "Miami U is in Oxford, not far from Dayton."

The back of Deacon's neck itched. "I know all about Miami of Ohio," he murmured, studying the face of the victim. "I got my undergrad there." *She can't be from Florida. Can't be from the city of Miami.* That put this killer way too close to Faith. Again.

"I meant what I said, Detective Bishop," Washington said. "This victim was alive and enrolled in school in Miami, *Florida*, as of three weeks ago."

"How did you ID her?" he asked. "And how do you know she was alive three weeks ago?"

"I submitted her fingerprints, and AFIS came back almost immediately with her name. She has a record for shoplifting. She spent a night in a Miami jail three weeks ago."

"She got jail time for shoplifting?" Bishop asked, incredulous.

"We can ask Vega to get us her background," Deacon said. "We need to know if her path crossed Faith's at any point. God, I hope not."

"Vega is a Miami PD detective we've been working with," Bishop explained when Washington's brows lifted in question. "Should we be asking her to check on IDs for the other bodies Tanaka found? Maybe the killer took them together, like he did Corinne and Arianna."

"You can and should try," Washington said. "But I can at least tell you that Ms. Dupree wasn't taken with the others. At least not with this one." She moved to the next table. The next blonde whose life had been brutally stolen. "Susan Simpson went missing two summers ago."

Both Deacon and Bishop stared, first at Washington, then at the body. Decomp looked nowhere near that advanced. "Are you sure?" Deacon asked.

"Maybe she just ran away?" Bishop added. "Maybe she went on a long vacation and crossed paths with Dupree down in Miami?"

Washington carefully lifted the woman's hand and pointed out the faded orange stamp. "She went to the Wild Wave water park, and their season ended on Labor Day, so time of death would have been no later than that. Except that Wild Wave discontinued this ink two years ago."

Deacon frowned at the body. It looked far too good to be that old. "How did you ID her?"

Washington laid the victim's hand down with a gentleness that earned her Deacon's respect. "She was a cop. Had just started with Butler County Sheriff's Department."

"I remember that case," Bishop said. "Her photo was on every TV station, every station wall. . . . But she doesn't look like she's been dead for two years."

"That's why I called you in. These women have something in common."

"Yeah," Deacon said. "They're all blond, in their twenties, and they're all dead."

"They've also all been embalmed and expertly prepared for burial—including a viewing." Washington went back to Dupree's body and pulled the sheet down. "They've all been autopsied as well, but the sutures are small and expertly done."

Bending closer to the body, Deacon could see the tiny stitches that ran up Dupree's torso, forking into a Y on her chest. "Someone knew what they were doing."

"Exactly. Every organ has been removed, including their eyes. Did you find them?"

"No," Bishop said. "We didn't find anything like that. Yet. He's either thrown them away or hidden them somewhere."

"I doubt he threw them away," Washington said. "I don't know if the internal incisions are of the same quality as the external ones, but even if they're half as good, this guy is a pro. If he took so much care in removing his victims' organs, he's unlikely to destroy them."

"Why take them?" Bishop asked. "Why remove them to begin with?"

Washington pulled the sheet up to cover Roxanne Dupree's face. "Because he could? Because he wanted to? Because he liked looking at them? To slow decomp so that he could look at them longer? Take your pick."

Deacon stepped back, stilled his racing mind. "Faith's uncle Jeremy is a surgeon," he said.

Bishop nodded. "I was thinking that. Did he call you back?"

"Left me a voice mail saying that he'd make himself available for a meeting."

"Make himself available? That's cold. Did he ask about Faith?"

"No. I want to see how he lives, then talk to his colleagues and students at the med school. Can you determine cause of death, Dr. Washington?"

"Not yet. Susan Simpson has a scar on her calf. Probably a GSW. It wasn't listed as a finding in the physical she took when she started her job with the sheriff's office. She also has identical scars on the backs of both of her thighs. Deep cuts. None are the cause of death, though."

"He hamstringed her," Deacon murmured. "Maybe shot her to slow her down first, then hamstringed her to keep her from running."

And *this* was the monster who was after Faith, he thought grimly. *Over my dead body.*

"He's taken three college students so far," Deacon said. "Roxanne, Arianna, and Corinne."

"But Arianna isn't blond," Bishop said. "So why her?"

"I think he grabbed Corinne first, but Arianna came after him to help her friend. He shot her, then grabbed her, too. Arianna's abduction may have been unplanned. Circumstance."

"Makes sense," Bishop said. "We know that Corinne was military and has an exemplary record. I found certificates and medals when I went through her things. So Corinne and Susan are law abiders, but Roxanne has a record. The only things the three have in common are that they're all single, blond, and in the same age group. Beyond that, we've got nothing. We need college majors, hobbies, religion."

"And how and where he took them," Deacon said. "There must be a pattern, something connecting these victims."

"I'll inform you as I make identifications," Washington said. "And once I know what caused their deaths."

Deacon nodded. "Thank you. As a heads-up, I've got a ground-scanning expert arriving this afternoon to check the O'Bannion land for more bodies."

"I pray you don't find any more. For the obvious human reasons, of course. But we're running out of room." Washington gestured behind her. "Even the cold room is filling up."

Deacon made himself walk to the cold-room door, his feet protesting every step. His gut protesting even more loudly. He opened the door and stepped inside, barely feeling the chill.

He wanted to close his eyes. Wanted to run away. But he planted his feet and made himself look. Made himself *see*. Let himself feel. And let his heart break for the senseless waste.

Eight more stretchers filled the room. Eight more bodies, all blond, young. Nude. In various stages of decomposition. Eight more young women who'd been robbed of their lives.

He heard the door open and close behind him. "Can I help you with something, Agent Novak?" Carrie Washington asked softly.

"Why aren't they draped?" he asked, immediately wishing the words back. He'd sounded accusatory, which he hadn't meant.

But Washington didn't sound offended. "We haven't prepared these victims. I've called in help from Butler and Warren counties. Butler is eager to help because of Officer Simpson."

"We haven't notified her family," he said hoarsely, taking a few steps farther into the cold room so that he stood in the middle of the stretchers, four on each side of him. He looked at their faces. Committed them to memory. "The MEs can't make any family notifications or public statements until we've cleared them."

"The MEs know to keep confidentiality," she said quietly, still unoffended. Then she earned his total respect with her next words. "Don't worry, Deacon. We'll take good care of them. As soon as they're prepared, they'll be draped. They'll have the dignity that was stolen from them."

"Thank you, Carrie." Deacon's eyes stung, his nose burned, partly because of the stench. But mostly because of the tears he'd allow himself to shed only here and now. Once he left, he'd have to focus on bringing their killer to justice. "You're running out of room, and we're running out of time. If we haven't already."

"You think the Longstreet woman is dead?" Washington asked.

"If he feels threatened with exposure, it's highly likely. My only hope that she's still alive is this." He swept his arm to take in all eight of the bodies. "He's a creature of habit. He'll want his things around him. His tools. He'll want to be able to torture her."

"And prepare her body after she's dead," Washington added in a murmur.

"Exactly. But the reality is that he can't have his things around him right now, and Corinne becomes a liability if he gets stopped, assuming he's still on the run. He may have killed her and dumped her body somewhere, just to get away cleanly."

Part of him hoped so, for Corinne's sake. Which, frankly, scared the shit out of him. That he considered a quick and painless death to be the best of the possible outcomes told Deacon just how tired and emotionally ragged he'd become. He needed to sleep. To recharge.

I'll be waiting. He drew strength from the knowledge that Faith slept safely in his bed. Waiting for him to come home. It was just enough to enable him to step away from the victims. Because they were already sucking him in to their pain. They always did.

"I'm ready to go," he said, then followed Carrie Washington from the cold room. If he wasn't careful, he'd become too overwhelmed to think. And he needed to keep thinking.

"I'll keep in close contact," Washington said. "Don't worry about them, Deacon."

"Thank you." He held the door open for Bishop, both of them stripping masks and goggles off as soon as they were back in the hall. He sniffed the sleeve of his suit jacket and winced. "Dammit. I just had this suit cleaned. I need to go home to shower and change again."

"Same. But there are showers at the precinct. It's a lot closer." She gave him a look that spoke volumes. "I saw a spare suit in your locker. You don't *need* to go home."

But he did. Because he didn't turn off the grief when he walked out of the morgue. He wanted to, but never did. It was pushing at him, a weight on his shoulders, an ache in his chest.

I'll be waiting. He needed to see Faith. Just see her. And he didn't need to justify that to Bishop. Still, he was glad to have an excuse his partner would accept. "Yes, I do, actually. I have to take Greg home. I brought him with me because you said we should hurry."

"He's in the waiting room?" Bishop looked sympathetic. "What happened at school?"

Deacon thought of the mess his brother had gotten himself into. And of the pain he'd tried to save Dani. "Too long to tell right now. Let's meet at the precinct in four hours."

She narrowed her eyes at him suspiciously. "Four? Why?"

"Because, I don't know about you, but I need a few hours' sleep."

She shook her head. "We can't stop. We still haven't interviewed the creepy uncle yet."

"I know. But I also know that I'm not sharp enough right now to truly hear anything he says. I don't want to miss something crucial because my brain's turned to mush."

"I am tired," Bishop admitted grudgingly. "I'll crash at the station for a few hours."

"Good. After that, we'll interview Uncle Jeremy, and then I want to go over the O'Bannion house top to bottom. There are probably a million places he could have stored their body parts. And we still haven't found his souvenirs."

"Are we sure he kept any?" Bishop asked.

"He kept their bodies under glass, Scarlett. He wanted to see them. Relive the experience in between abductions. I have to believe he kept souvenirs."

"What did the serial in West Virginia keep?"

"Wallets. Driver's licenses. Jewelry, clothing. Anything and everything." And Deacon had handled each and every item with care, making sure they were returned to the families. "Nearly all of his victims had some form of ID, which made identification a lot faster."

She stood there for a moment, studying him. "You identified them all, didn't you?"

"With a lot of help, yeah."

"Who talked to the families?"

"I did." He turned on his heel and started for the front entrance, Bishop beside him.

"All by yourself?"

"No, not always. Sometimes one of the other agents worked with me. Sometimes my boss went with me. I think his involvement was more to assess my psychological state, though."

"You liked your boss?"

Some of the tension in his body unwound as his lips curved at the question. "Not at first. He didn't like me, either. But I grew on him."

"I heard Isenberg tell one of the head honchos that your old boss didn't want to let you go. That you were his right hand."

Deacon glanced over at her. "Thanks. Even if it's not true."

Bishop shrugged. "I don't like you well enough yet to try to make you feel better."

His lips curved. "Thanks. I needed that, too."

"You went into the cold room. Why?"

"I needed to see them. I needed to know their faces."

Bishop sighed. "If you let the dead mess with your head, you'll burn out too fast."

"I didn't let them mess with my head at first. Then I realized that I wasn't seeing the dead as people, just victims. One just like all the others. That scared the hell out of me because it put me that much closer to the monster who'd hurt them. He sees them as victims, too. One just like all the others."

"That's not the same at all," she protested. "We don't look at them as objects or as conquests. We don't get off on their pain."

"No, of course we don't. But to keep myself separate from their pain, I had to distance myself from the victims as people. If I burn out, I'll do something else. But I won't do this job by stripping the victims of their humanity. It was stolen by their killer. I won't do the same to them, or to myself."

Cincinnati, Ohio
Tuesday, November 4, 2:55 p.m.

Voices. Someone is here. Instantly awake, Faith lifted her head from Novak's pillow cautiously, her hand sliding beneath the pillow to close over her gun. She heard the louder, agitated voice of a female and the quieter, more muted voice of a male. The male didn't sound like either of the FBI agents. And it wasn't Novak. Of that she was certain.

She crept down the stairs, the hand clutching her gun at her side. A peek into the living room had her eyes growing wide. Dani stood with a tall, burly young man who looked just like her and Novak. The boy's hair was as black as Dani's with a white streak just as wide, but the style was spiky like Novak's.

This would be the troubled Greg. Who was evidently hearing impaired, because he and Dani were signing to one another furiously with loudly spoken cursing interspersed between the hand signals. Whatever Greg had done, it was bad. Tears streamed down Dani's face, her expression a mix of anger and fear. Mostly fear, Faith thought, at a loss for how to help.

Where was Novak? Why wasn't he here to referee?

Finally, Dani threw her hands into the air in frustration, before flinging her arms around Greg, holding on tight. "You stupid idiot," she choked out brokenly. "I love you." She pulled back and held the boy's face in her hands. "Why did you do it? Why would you ruin your future like this? I'd've been all right."

He drew back to sign his reply, making Dani weep harder. Then he pulled his sister into his arms, and the two of them stood there, rocking together, comforting each other.

Faith's eyes stung at the sight. The two were clearly close, leaning on each other for support. They were family. *But where is Deacon?*

Feeling like an intruder—because she was—Faith backed away. *And not just any intruder,* she thought, *but an armed one.* She was sure Novak would be annoyed to find she'd risked his family's safety by sneaking up on them with a gun.

Tiptoeing back up the stairs to her room, she slipped her weapon into her purse.

"I'll get you another holster, if you want," Novak said softly from behind her.

She spun. And gaped. He stood in the master bathroom doorway, wearing nothing but a towel. His hair was wet and spiky and water still clung to the crisp white hairs on his chest.

Hairs she now knew to be soft to the touch.

His legs were every bit as nice as his chest, just as bronzed, his thighs as solid as tree trunks. She thought about the photo of him and Dani as teenagers, both on bicycles, both smiling for the camera. Obviously, it was a sport he'd kept up with.

"I didn't mean to startle you," he said, still quietly, as if he were soothing a feral animal.

She glanced at the bed, knew it would still be warm from her body. She hadn't been gone more than a minute. Two minutes, tops. That he'd been in the room while she slept didn't bother her. That he'd entered undetected bothered her a great deal. "How did you get in here? I was just here. I would have heard you in the shower. I would have woken up."

"I used the shower in Dani's room, but I forgot my boxers." His cheeks darkened. "I was going to ask Dani to get them for me, but then I saw you go downstairs. I figured Dani would introduce you to Greg and you guys would talk a while and that I could get dressed and be gone before you got back." He shrugged awkwardly. *Endearingly,* she thought. "But you came back too fast. And you were armed. I thought it best not to startle you until you put the gun away."

She tried not to stare at his body, especially not at the towel that hung low on his waist. Because she'd felt what it concealed. Up close and very personally. She cleared her throat, but her voice was still husky. "Because getting shot twice in one day would suck."

He didn't smile. "Yes, it would. Why did you leave the room with a gun?"

"I heard voices."

"So you went to investigate even though the agents told you to stay put?"

"Of course," she said lightly, hoping to make him smile. But when she dragged her eyes up to his face, she saw pain in his eyes. She took a step toward him, then stopped herself. If she got too close, she'd be in his arms. And this time, she wasn't sure she'd have the willpower to stop. "What happened, Deacon?"

"At the school or the morgue?"

She drew a careful breath. "You went to the morgue?"

"Yeah." He went to his drawer and pulled out a pair of black silk boxers, these with tiny red flames. "Which is why I had to come home and clean up."

He disappeared into his closet, and Faith carefully lowered herself to sit on the edge of the bed, thinking of the bodies they'd found under the basement floor. Under Plexiglas.

She hadn't envied the MEs their job, but hadn't thought about Deacon having to inspect the bodies up close. She should have. He wouldn't leave that important task to someone else.

The picture of him in that news article flashed into her mind. He would grieve for the victims he'd seen in the morgue, just like he'd grieved for those on that hillside in West Virginia.

He emerged from the closet wearing trousers and a shirt, buttoned to his throat. A tie hung from the index finger of each hand. "Blue or red?"

She came to her feet unsteadily but made herself smile when she approached him. She took the ties and held them up to frame both sides of his face. "The blue. It matches your eyes."

Without a word, he took the tie and started to put it on. He seemed tense. Edgy. Her tiger now paced behind the bars of an invisible cage.

My tiger? Yes. He was _her_ tiger, whether it was wise or not.

She waited until he'd snugged his tie to his collar before reaching for his hand. "I never learned to tie ties, but I do a mean button," she murmured, bending her head over his left cuff. When she'd released the left, he silently gave her the right. "You'd really get me a new holster?" she asked lightly. "You realize you'd only be encouraging me to pack heat."

His lips curved, but there remained a remoteness to his expression that she wanted to erase. "I need to wear a fedora if we're going to speak noir. Nobody says 'pack heat' anymore."

She brushed her lips over his knuckles. "Lily's a classic film fan. She says it. Does it, too."

White brows shot up in surprise. "She packs heat?"

"Since Dad's stroke. She hasn't felt comfortable in the house with him being less mobile. Not since Combs got out."

"I thought you didn't tell them about Combs stalking you."

"I didn't, but I did tell her he was out of prison. I tried to scare her in generalities, to keep her on her guard. I was successful enough that she bought a gun even though my father despises them. But she doesn't know about Gordon's murder or any of the attempts to . . . you know."

"Kill you," he supplied coldly.

"Yeah. That." She sighed. "I'm sorry. I don't seem to be able to lighten things up for you." She tried to let go of his hand, but he held on, threading their fingers together. This time he brought her hand to his lips and, as she stared, transfixed, kissed her fingers one at a time.

"That you even tried is more than I've ever had before," he said.

Her heart broke at the thought of no one trying to lighten the load that this man carried on his shoulders. "What happened at the school, Deacon?"

"Which one?"

It took her a minute to remember that he'd been planning to stop at King's College before meeting with his brother's principal. "I meant Greg's school, but I'll take news on either."

"It looks like Corinne was the original target. Arianna may have been trying to save her."

He needs to tell me about this case, but he doesn't want to. A wave of fresh dread washed over her. "Have they found more bodies, Deacon?"

Grief darkened his eyes, making her think about that picture of him, surrounded by graves. "Yes. Seven more."

She gripped his hand, holding on. "You've found ten bodies in the basement?"

"So far. There could be more. We're going to have to dig up your property."

Just like on his old case. "Oh my God," she whispered. "I'm so sorry."

His brow furrowed slightly. "You didn't put them there, Faith."

"I know, but I'm sorry you had to find them."

His jaw cocked. "What do you mean?"

She hesitated. "One of the articles about the shooting at my hotel linked your name with the case in West Virginia last year. You had to deal with a lot of graves."

"You saw the picture." He swallowed hard. "I really hate the guy who took that picture."

"I know," she said softly. "I hated the guy who took my picture, too, the one that made all the news reports of Combs's trial. It was taken as I was leaving the hospital after Combs slit my throat. I looked haggard and terrified. Each time I saw the photo, it was like Combs was hurting me all over again."

"You looked terrified with good reason. But not haggard."

Faith's cheeks heated. "You saw the photo?" She drew a breath when he nodded cautiously. "But it *is* the same, Deacon. That people saw me like that embarrassed me. I looked awful. And I looked afraid. But that *you* saw me like that . . . I hate that you'll always have that picture of me in your mind, because once it's there, it never goes away. It was the same with the photographer who took that picture of you. He caught you in a moment of grief that should have been private. I hate that you experienced that, but knowing that you were moved by the victims' suffering . . . I felt like I'd glimpsed the real you. I felt privileged."

He was too silent for too long a moment, and Faith thought she'd gone a few sentences too far, but then he spoke, his voice husky. Deep. Velvet on her skin. "I got your e-mail."

I'll be waiting. She dropped her gaze to her feet, suddenly shy. "I'd just seen the picture. I wanted to comfort you. Like you comforted me. You looked so alone."

"Faith, look at me," he whispered. Summoning her guts,

she met his eyes. And slowly exhaled. He was looking at her like she was a lifeboat floating in the sea. "I was alone that day," he admitted, his tone so soft she had to strain to hear him. "I've been alone for years. But this morning . . ." He swallowed. "No one's ever waited for me."

She touched his face, tracing the line of his lips. They were soft. Until he kissed her. Then they were as hard as the rest of him. "How can that be? How can someone like you be alone?"

"I think the same thing about you. I also think that if you don't want me to kiss you again, you need to tell me now. Because it was all I could think of when I was on my way home."

She leaned up on her toes, brushing a kiss over his lips. "Like that?"

"Not even close," he ground out, then his mouth was on hers, hard and hot and more wonderful than it had been any of the other times. His hands dug into her hair, holding so tight it almost hurt. He tilted her head to one side, then the other, kissing her like he was starved. She slid her arms around his neck and kissed him back, aware of him. Everywhere.

He was already erect, the thick ridge in his pants too much temptation. She rocked up on her toes to press against him, needing to feel him against her, wishing she had the courage to grab handfuls of his shirt and yank him down onto the bed.

But if she did that, he might think . . . what? That she wanted him, too? Because she did. Too much. *This is crazy, Faith. Totally crazy.*

"This is insane," she whispered against his lips.

"I know." His mouth took hers again as he walked her backward. Three steps later, the back of her legs hit something solid, and then he was lowering her to the soft mattress. He followed her down, settling his hips between her legs. He dragged his hand down her body, his thumb caressing the side of her breast before continuing down, toying with the hem of her blouse.

She held her breath, her body going rigid as she waited for him to touch her skin. He hesitated, too, then brushed his thumb up under her blouse, fanning her rib cage. He lifted his head, and she murmured a protest against the loss of his warm mouth.

Until she saw the way he was looking down at her, so hungry. But waiting. For permission.

"Yes. Please." The words came out of her mouth on a rush of air, her heart hammering in her chest. He pushed her blouse up an inch at a time, kissing his way as he went, licking each rib as he bared it. Again she held her breath, waiting until he'd pushed the silk past her bra.

"Mmm," he breathed. "So pretty." He licked the swell of each breast, plumped up by the bra. "I knew they would be. I peeked last night."

Her eyes flew open at the admission. "Excuse me?"

"You leaned over. I couldn't resist. I wanted to do this then." He fumbled with the front clasp, managing to pop it open on the third try. His mouth curved sinfully, making her shiver. "I wanted to do this, too." He leaned down, drew her nipple into his mouth and sucked. Hard.

She gasped, her hips lurching against him. "Do that again. Please."

He blew against the wet nipple, making her twist against him as he sucked the other one. He lifted his head, staring at her breasts. "God, what you do to me."

"What?" She arched her back, tugging his head back down, urging his mouth back to her breast. "What do I do to you?"

"Make me lose my mind. I want you so much that I can't think." He cupped one breast in the palm of his hand, testing its weight, rolling her nipple between his thumb and forefinger. Making her lose her mind, too. Her hips bucked, and she rubbed against the hardness of his chest, wishing it was his erection instead.

She wanted him, too. Wanted him inside her. Wanted to know what sex felt like with a man who desired her this much.

"All the way home, I thought of this," he whispered. "Of kissing you. Sucking on your breasts." His voice deepened. "Tasting you again."

Her body clenched, and she arched against him, into him, invitation and plea. "Yes."

His breath caught as he met her eyes. Searching them for truth. He rolled off her, far enough to push the jeans from her hips and down her legs.

"Pretty." He bent lower, rubbed his chin into the lace of her panties. "Are you wet, Faith?"

"Yes," she whispered, making barely a sound. "You make me want you."

His eyes blazed and her hips rocked toward him. And then he stunned her by stripping the panties down her legs and . . . She held her breath for a storm but got a simple little lick that nearly sent her into orbit. He lapped at her sweetly. "You taste so good. I knew you would."

"More. Please."

His control faltered and he tongued her hard. Tugged on her with his teeth. Licked her long and deep until she couldn't think. She didn't want to. He added a finger, sliding it up into her, all while his mouth did the most amazing things. He pulled her clit into his mouth and sucked until she came on a silent rush. Still he lapped, like a cat. Like a giant cat. *My tiger.*

When her shudders stilled, he licked up her torso, sucking one breast and then the other before laying his head on the pillow beside her. His eyes seemed brighter. Seemed to shimmer, the line between blue and brown like a Fourth of July sparkler.

Against her thigh she felt the throb of his erection, and she rolled in to him, her hand seeking, those eyes of his blazing again as she fondled him, learning his length.

"I want you." He closed his eyes. "God, I want you."

She swallowed, turned on by the wetness on his lips. "I want to feel you." She pulled down his zipper, humming her appreciation when he filled her hand. "Too many layers of clothes, Deacon," she whispered.

"If I take them off," he whispered back, "I'll come inside you."

She licked his lips, tasted herself. "Take them off. Please."

He didn't wait for another invitation. Rolling to his feet, he stripped off his clothes and crawled to her, a big, beautiful animal. *Who wants me.* She reached for him, stroking him.

"Do you have a condom? Because I don't."

"I do." He found one in his drawer and quickly sheathed himself, disappointing her a little.

"I wanted to do that. Next time, let me. Now, just . . .

hurry, Deacon." She closed her eyes and waited. He pressed into her, rocking, pushing into her a scant inch at a time.

"You're tight. I don't want to hurt you." He was panting. "Are you sure, Faith?"

She looked up at his handsome face, her muscles tensed. Waiting. "I'm sure. Come—" She gasped when he slammed into her, sending an orgasm rippling through her.

He groaned. "You feel so damn good. I want to go slow."

"Don't want slow. I need fast." She arched off the bed when he complied, plunging hard, over and over, his face a picture of concentration. Her nails digging into his back, she dissolved again, her deep moan swallowed by his mouth. Unbelievably, he picked up the pace, each thrust going deeper, and then he took her mouth in a kiss as he came, shudders racking his body.

He dropped his face into the curve of her shoulder, his body trembling through the aftershocks. "Oh God," he breathed. "I needed that. I needed you."

"I needed you, too." She ran her hands through his hair, scraping her nails over his scalp. Another shudder shook him. And then he stilled. Opened his eyes and stared down at her.

Faith thought she could look into his eyes for hours, watching the colors swirl together. "What makes them like this?"

His body froze, suddenly heavy against hers. "Makes what like what?"

Oh no. He couldn't go all remote when she was lying in his bed, her bare breasts pressed to his chest, his body buried deep inside hers. "I've never seen eyes like yours, not in my whole life."

"Genetic mutation," he said shortly. "Goes with the hair."

She'd triggered something ugly with her question. She traced the seam of his frowning lips with her fingertip. "The white tiger is a mutation, but what makes him different also makes him the most beautiful animal in the jungle."

His frown didn't disappear, but it eased. "To some."

"To me. And who else is here?"

"Just you," he murmured. "Only you. How did this happen?"

"I don't know. I keep thinking this is crazy. That I've never felt this much, this fast."

"It's the same for me." He shuddered again when she

lazily raked her nails across his scalp. "I needed this. Needed you. I can go back out there now. Thank you."

He rolled off her and disappeared into the bathroom. Suddenly awkward, she sat on the edge of the bed and was fastening her bra when he reappeared in the doorway, tall, broad-shouldered, and beautifully nude. Bronze skin ... all over. When he crossed the room toward her, she was transfixed by the roll and ripple of his muscles, her heart fluttering all over again.

Cheeks heating, she adjusted her blouse, aware that he was watching every move she made.

"Are you sorry we did this?" he asked.

"No. Not at all. But ... I don't do this. Don't fall into bed with men I've known not even a day. I don't want you to think that I do."

"Are you worried that I'd think less of you?"

"Of course. But I worry more that this is just my way of avoiding what's happening right now—the house, Combs, the bodies piling up everywhere I look. What if I'm using you as an escape? I don't want to hurt—"

He kissed her. "Hush. For now let's just enjoy the fact that we're not alone. We'll figure this out as we go. Stay here. I need to check in with the agents downstairs. I'll be right back."

He pulled on his pants and shrugged into his shirt, leaving it unbuttoned. He slipped out the door, closing it behind him. A few minutes later he was back, cell phone in one hand and his gun in the other. "I left them in Dani's room," he said. "I actually came home to grab a shower and a few hours' sleep, but I needed to check my messages first."

"Any new victims?" Faith asked.

"No, thank goodness." He put the phone and gun on his nightstand next to her purse. Then he quickly stripped her of her bra and shirt, shucked his own clothes, and tugged her back to bed, wrapping his arms around her. "Sleep with me, Faith."

He murmured the invitation in a husky voice that made her shiver. She snuggled in to him, resting her head on his shoulder, even though she wasn't the least bit tired anymore. But he hadn't slept at all, so she contented herself with petting the hair on his chest as his breathing began to even out and her mind began to quiet.

Until the sight of his gun made her remember drawing her own gun because she'd heard voices downstairs. Dani and Greg. *Who've been downstairs this whole time.*

She winced sharply. "Crap," she mouthed soundlessly.

"What's wrong?" he asked, the words more a rumble in his chest than sounds in his throat.

"Just that your brother and sister were downstairs while we were . . . you know."

"Dani's gone to the ER. She's on shift today. Pope's outside and Colby's in the kitchen. Too far away to have heard anything. Greg's sacked out on the floor in front of the TV." A slight hesitation followed by what sounded like an admission. "He had a rough morning, too."

"What happened in the principal's office, Deacon?" she asked.

He sighed. "Greg did something stupid for a really good reason. I wish he'd trusted me enough to tell me what was happening, but he was scared. He doesn't really know me, not yet."

Faith remembered Greg and Dani's argument. Greg had protected her, which was probably the stupid thing he'd done for a good reason. "Why doesn't he know you?"

"Because my uncle and I have never gotten along well. He's always insisted that I leave the child-rearing to him and Aunt Tammy. I didn't want to. I actually fought Jim for custody of Greg after Mom and Bruce died, but Jim won."

She patted his chest, trying to soothe him. "You were only eighteen years old, Deacon."

"I know. I tried for custody two more times after I joined the Bureau, but the judge considered Jim and Tammy's two-parent household preferable to mine. But when Greg started rebelling in middle school, Jim was all in favor of sending him to live with me in Maryland."

"When Greg became an inconvenience?"

"Jim wouldn't agree, but that's how I saw it. Greg was already out of control. He fell in with a gang and got thrown out of the school in Maryland, so Dani brought him back to Cincinnati and I came home to start over with him. But this . . . He could be in serious trouble, and I don't know what to do."

He sounded as lost as she had been the night before. "What can I do to help you, Deacon?"

"Just be here," he murmured against her hair, and her heart melted all over again.

"That I can do. Go to sleep." She curled in to him, listening to him breathe while she eyed the phone on his nightstand, daring it to ring and disturb him.

He'd started to snore softly when the phone defied her and rang anyway. He came awake in a smooth motion, as if he'd had lots of practice at being jerked out of sleep.

"Novak." He listened. "I'll have her there in thirty. See you there." Hanging up, he reluctantly got out of bed. "Get dressed," he told Faith. "Arianna Escobar is awake and refusing to talk to anyone but you."

Chapter Twenty

Corinne sank down on a tree stump, utterly exhausted. They'd walked about five hundred feet in four hours. Unfortunately, they'd walked the same hundred-foot path five different times. Roza would walk, then stop, then run back, as if tethered to the cabin's front porch.

Corinne was very tempted to knock her out again. It would be for the girl's own good. *It would be for* my *own good*. They could have been far away by now. They could have been safe.

Roza had begged to be left behind, but that had never been an option.

I'm going to save her even if it kills us both. Corinne trudged to the porch where Roza sat on the front step, head hung dejectedly. "Roza, what do I have to do to get you away from here? This isn't your home."

"I don't know!" Roza blurted. "It's too . . . *much*."

It's just trees. The sun. Green grass and the occasional falling leaf. The wind. Actually, it was a lot, Corinne realized. For a girl who'd never been out of that basement, this was a lot to take in in a very short time. She hunkered down, took Roza's hands in hers.

"Do you trust me, Roza?"

"I'm going to get you killed. Just go. Please."

"Not without you."

"Why not?" Roza exploded. "I'm no one. I'm not important. I'm nothing," she finished on a whisper. "I'm not worth it."

Corinne's eyes stung. "You are Firoza. You *are* important. You saved my best friend. You took care of me." She squeezed the thin hands. "You *are* worth it. Do you trust me?"

A dejected nod.

"Do you trust me enough to let me blindfold you?"

Roza's head shot up, eyes wide with alarm. "What?"

"You're experiencing something called sensory overload. Colors, sounds, smells. The wind. It's too much. Of course you're overwhelmed. If you let me blindfold you, it'll be dark again. Maybe you won't be so afraid."

Dark brows crunched. "I'll fall down."

"I'll pick you up. Can we try it? Please?"

Roza hesitated. "Okay."

"Okay. Good." Using one of the knives she'd taken from the kitchen, Corinne sliced away a strip of the blanket and handed it to Roza. "You want to put it on yourself?"

The girl swallowed hard. Nodded. Covered her eyes and tied the strip behind her head.

"Good." Corinne rose, shouldered the supply bundle, slipping the knife up her sleeve where she could reach it easily. "Give me your hand."

Roza extended her hand, then her head jerked up in alarm. Corinne heard it, too. An engine. *Oh no. Oh God, no.*

"He's coming, isn't he?" Roza asked fearfully.

"We need to run. Put your arm around my neck."

"You can't carry me."

"I will not let him have you. *Do it!*" Not waiting for compliance, she grabbed Roza's arm, looped it around her neck, and started to run, heading behind the cabin, into the woods.

Away from the road. She hit a small hill and slid down it, half dragging, half carrying Roza behind her. Her lungs about to explode, she collapsed on the ground, holding Roza down when she tried to get up, clamping her hand over the girl's mouth when she tried to cry out.

"Sshh," Corinne breathed. "He'll hear you and kill us. Quiet. I've got you. You're safe."

She heard the vehicle stop. A car door slam. Corinne

frowned. It didn't sound like a van at all. The motor had revved like a sports car.

The cabin door slammed. He'd gone inside. There was a minute of silence, then the cabin door slammed again.

A shout shattered the silence. *"No!* Goddammit! *No!"* His curse had come from behind the cabin. He knew they were both gone. That the root cellar was empty.

Roza squirmed frantically. Corinne shushed, tried to soothe. But she didn't let her up.

Time passed. Corinne wasn't sure how much. Minutes? Hours? She listened, holding her breath, knife in her hand, waiting for him to come over the hill.

Finally, the car started, the engine roaring as it was gunned once, then twice, driving away in a squeal of tires that sounded like a race car exiting the starting gate. She held her breath as the engine faded away. *He is not driving a van. Why did he change cars?* Maybe he'd dumped the van. Maybe it meant he was worried about getting caught. Either way, she'd have to be on the lookout for both a van and a sports car as she and Roza made their way to find help. She rolled off Roza, exhausted again.

Roza pulled the blindfold off and used it to wipe the tears from her cheeks. "Is he gone?"

"I think so," Corinne whispered. "Are you all right? I didn't want to hurt you."

"I'm okay. You should have let me go. I wouldn't have told him you were here."

Corinne sighed. "I'm tired, Roza. I can't carry you anymore. Will you walk with me? Because if you won't, I can't force you to. I think I'll just curl up and go to sleep because that's all the energy I have."

"But he'll kill you."

Corinne hoped her bluff would fool the girl. "I need your help to get away."

Roza looked at the blindfold crumpled in her hand, then brushed her fingertips over the grass, then patted it with the flat of her palm. She met Corinne's eyes, hers wide with wonder. "It's sharp *and* soft."

She'd never touched grass, Corinne thought. Or trees. Or felt the sunshine on her face. *Be patient.* "Yes, it is."

"My mama liked the snow," Roza said abruptly. "When will we have snow?"

Be patient. But it was hard with her heart beating so hard. He could come back any minute. "Soon. In a few weeks." Corinne made herself smile. "We can build a snowman."

Roza's eyes filled with tears. "Mama said we'd do that someday. If we ever got out." She blinked, sending the tears down her face. "You'll take me to her? To my mama?"

"I will. I promise."

Roza tied the blindfold over her forehead. "If I start to be afraid, I'll pull it over my eyes." She grabbed Corinne's hand and pulled her to her feet. "I'm ready. Let's go."

Cincinnati, Ohio
Tuesday, November 4, 5:20 p.m.

"No more than five minutes," the ICU nurse warned. "I'm serious, Agent Novak. I will throw you out myself if I have to."

Deacon nodded respectfully. "I believe you, ma'am. But we still have one young woman missing, and so far we have very few leads. Arianna's recollections may be our only hope of bringing Corinne Longstreet home alive."

Sympathy flickered in the nurse's eyes, but she held firm. "Arianna is my priority. When you bring Ms. Longstreet in, she'll be equally protected. Five minutes. Follow me, please."

The uniformed officer standing outside Arianna's room checked their IDs against the printed list he'd been given by Isenberg's office. Deacon looked through the small window in the door. An older man and a young woman sat next to Arianna's bed, blocking his view of the patient. "Who are they?"

"Lauren Goodwin and her father," Bishop said. "The Goodwins are Arianna's foster family. Lauren and Arianna room together at King's. They've been friends since high school. She filed the missing-persons report on Arianna yesterday."

"Why didn't she report Arianna missing on Friday when she didn't come back from the library?" Faith asked.

"At first she thought Arianna had gone away for the weekend with Corinne," Bishop answered, "but then she saw Corinne's car parked in the student lot and reported them both missing. King's College security didn't believe her. It was Halloween weekend. They figured that Arianna was partying. Lauren enlisted the help of her father, who finally got the security people to look at the tapes. Arianna and Corinne are seen leaving the library and walking along the path. They enter the area where the camera had been stolen and aren't seen on any cameras anywhere on the campus afterward."

Bishop pushed the door open, and Lauren and her father immediately rose. Mr. Goodwin took one look at Deacon and flinched. "Who the hell are you?" he demanded.

"This is Special Agent Novak, Mr. Goodwin," Bishop said. "He's my partner."

Goodwin glared. "You expect me to believe *he's* FBI?"

Beside him, Faith bristled, but Deacon's surreptitious squeeze of her arm had her clamping her lips shut. Deacon produced his ID calmly. "We need to talk to Arianna alone."

"No," Goodwin said, shaking his head. "You don't talk to her without me."

"I'll stay with her, Mr. Goodwin," a female voice said from behind them. Deacon looked over his shoulder to see a woman with dark auburn hair standing in the doorway.

"Who the hell are *you*?" Goodwin asked belligerently.

"Dr. Meredith Fallon. I'm a child psychologist. I work with adolescent trauma victims. I've been assigned to Arianna's case because she's a minor. Don't worry. I've done this before. I won't let them upset her. But Corinne's still missing. We need to hear what Arianna knows."

"And you've already used up one of our five minutes arguing, sir," Deacon said quietly.

Lauren kissed Arianna's forehead. "I'll be back later. Come on, Dad. Let's get some lunch." She paused in the doorway, giving Faith a long look. "You're Faith Frye, aren't you?"

"Faith Corcoran. Until recently my last name was Frye."

Tears glinted in Lauren's eyes. "You saved her. Thank you. But the doctors said she was unconscious when you found her. How does she know your name?"

"I don't know. I was hoping Arianna could tell us."

"Lauren," Bishop prodded. "You're taking up time we could be talking to Arianna. Please."

When Lauren and her father had left, the psychologist closed the door firmly. Her assessment of Faith was shrewd and not terribly warm. "Please proceed, Agent Novak. I'm a silent observer—unless you ask anything not in Arianna's

best interest. I have authority to stop the interview and will
not hesitate to do so."

Deacon and Bishop took positions on either side of the
bed. Arianna's face was pale, her lips gray. But her dark
eyes were open and clear, the beeping machines indicating
that she was stable.

"Arianna," Deacon said, "this is Faith. You asked to see
her. We need to know what happened to you and Corinne."

"Did you see your abductor?" Bishop asked.

"No. Faith, please." Arianna waved weakly at the chair
next to the bed, and Faith sat down.

"How can I help you, Arianna?" Faith asked softly. "Why
did you ask for me?"

"Because she told me to," Arianna rasped.

Faith bent closer. "Who? Corinne?"

Tears filled Arianna's eyes. "You didn't find Corinne?"

"Not yet," Deacon answered. "But we're still looking.
Who told you to ask for Faith?"

"The girl." Her whisper was barely audible. "In the basement. She helped me get away. She told me to ask for you."

Faith frowned up at Deacon over her shoulder, before
leaning over the bed rail to better hear Arianna. "Do you
know the girl's name?"

"Roza. She said her name was Roza."

"How old was Roza?" Deacon asked.

"Not a little girl, but not a grown-up. Maybe twelve. She
saved me. Helped me get away." Tears welled in Arianna's
dark eyes. "I think he might have killed her for that."

Bishop shot Deacon a look before easing into a crouch
next to the bed. "Did she seem small, size-wise?" she asked
softly.

"Yes. She was thin. Short. Dark hair, ragged. Big, dark
eyes. Middle-Eastern, maybe?"

Deacon thought of the dug-out room, the pallet on the
floor. *A child.* Not what he'd expected to hear. "Was she a
prisoner, too?"

"Not the same as me. He made her work." Arianna
closed her eyes. "Made her clean me. After he . . ." She began to tremble, and the heart monitor started to beep faster.
"He . . ."

Dr. Fallon stepped forward, her mouth opening to protest until Faith brushed Arianna's hair from her face, her

touch gentle. "It's all right," Faith soothed. "You don't have to tell that part. You don't have to tell anyone."

Dr. Fallon stepped back as Arianna's heart rate began to stabilize once more.

"You saw Roza's face?" Bishop asked.

Arianna nodded. "She took off my blindfold at the end. Helped me get away."

"Did you see your captor's face, too?" Bishop asked.

"No. He was gone to the backyard when I got away. I ran."

"How did you get away, Arianna?" Deacon asked. "How did Roza help?"

"Earl came."

"Earl?" Dr. Fallon asked quietly. "Who is Earl?"

"Earl Power and Light," Faith said. "I called them to turn on the electricity. I didn't know you were there, Arianna. I'm so sorry."

"I know," Arianna whispered. "He said nobody could hear us scream."

Faith stiffened but didn't confess that she'd heard Arianna scream on Sunday afternoon, which Deacon thought was best for everyone all around.

"He got mad when Earl came," Arianna continued. "He ran outside. Didn't lock the door at the top of the stairs. Roza helped me get away. Do you know her? Can you find her?"

"I don't know anyone named Roza," Faith said. "Did she say why you should ask for me?"

Arianna opened her eyes, held Faith's gaze. "Because he's afraid of you."

Faith let out a strangled breath. "Do *I* know him, Arianna? Did he say he knew me?"

"No. He didn't say your name to me. Just to Roza."

"How did you get the truck?" Bishop asked.

"He was fighting with the Earl man. He shot him. I didn't wait. I didn't try to help the Earl man. I ran to the truck. I took it." New tears welled, fell. "But I crashed it. I'm sorry."

Faith stroked the girl's forehead. "Nobody's mad at you, Arianna. You did the right thing. You got away. Now we know to look for Corinne and Roza."

"Find her. Please. Corinne needs her medicine."

"We're looking as hard as we can," Bishop assured her. "But we need to ask you something else. Before the night you were . . . taken, did you notice if anyone was following you or Corinne? Were you afraid of anyone?"

"No. He came out of nowhere. He grabbed Corinne and put a cloth on her face. I tried to stop him, but he shot me."

"What was he wearing?" Deacon asked.

"Coat. Sneakers. Mask. Halloween mask."

Deacon bit back a curse. *Goddamn Halloween.* "Did you see anyone else around the path that night? Maybe someone saw you get taken or heard you yell?"

"Nobody was there. Everyone was at the party. I'm sorry. I tried to fight him."

"Sshh." Faith stroked her hair. "You are so brave. You have nothing to be sorry for, honey. Tell me, how did you know about the man from Earl? Did he come in the house?"

"No. Roza saw him on the laptop."

Laptop? Deacon shared a glance with Bishop, saw that she was thinking the same thing.

"Cameras?" Bishop mouthed.

Deacon shook his head. They'd found nothing like that last night. They'd need to look harder. If the cameras had captured the power tech, they might have captured his killer, too.

The nurse pushed her way in. "Time's up. Everyone out. It's time for her evening medication. It will help her sleep, which is what she needs right now."

"Wait." Arianna clutched Faith's arm when she started to stand. "Come back."

"We will," Bishop said. "Don't worry."

"No. Faith. Come back."

"I will. I promise. But I have to go now." Faith carefully pulled Arianna's hand from her sleeve. "Sleep, baby. It's time to sleep."

The four of them left the room, silent until they reached the empty waiting room.

"I promised Arianna I'd come back," Faith said. "I'd like to stay."

Deacon shook his head. "I need to know you're in the safe house."

Dr. Fallon's brows lifted. "I'll stay," she told Faith. "I'll call you when she wakes up."

"Really?" Faith asked. "I was under the impression that you weren't too sure about me."

"I wasn't," Dr. Fallon admitted. "I still may not be. I Googled you and read all the articles about your former clientele. I don't believe sex offenders can be rehabilitated."

"Neither do I," Faith said quietly.

Dr. Fallon regarded her steadily. "Then one day perhaps you'll tell me why you treated them for so many years. For now my job is to judge whether you should be allowed to see Arianna. Today she seemed calmed by your presence. If she asks for you again, I'll call you."

"Fair enough," Faith said. "Give me your card. When I get a new cell phone, I'll text you the number. Until then you can reach me through Agent Novak or Detective Bishop." She turned to Deacon when Dr. Fallon had returned to Arianna's room. "I have to warn you, I've given a few other people your number to reach me—my boss, Lily and my dad, and Detective Vega, of course."

Deacon checked his phone messages. "None of them have called for you. But your uncle Jordan did. He's in Isenberg's office, demanding to see you, so he can know you're all right. I was going to take you back to the safe house, but I'd like you to talk to your uncle first."

"Did Jordan bring his friend with him?" Bishop asked, humor glinting in her dark eyes.

"I don't think so," Deacon said dryly.

"What?" Faith asked. "What did I miss?"

Deacon took her elbow, lightly steering her toward the elevator. "I'll tell you in the car."

Cincinnati, Ohio
Tuesday, November 4, 6:05 p.m.

Jordan O'Bannion was taller and leaner standing up than he'd appeared while curled up in a drunken, fetal ball. His short hair was as red as Faith's with just a hint of gray. His tired eyes and the lines around his mouth were the only indications that he'd been passed-out drunk hours before. That and the tremors in his hands as he paced the inside perimeter of Interview Room 1, having been moved there by Isenberg, who needed the privacy of her office.

He stopped pacing when Deacon and Bishop entered. "Agent Novak?"

Deacon nodded. "And my partner, Detective Bishop. Would you like to sit down?"

"No," the man snapped, but he sat anyway. "I called you before noon, and here it is, six hours later and you're just now talking to me? I've been worried sick about my niece. I heard she was shot at last night. Was she hit? Is she all right? Where is she?"

O'Bannion directed his questions to Bishop, meeting her eyes but avoiding Deacon's. Deacon suspected that he knew exactly what Alda Lane had shared regarding his condition that morning. *If I knew someone had seen me passed-out drunk, I'd be ashamed, too.*

"We're sorry we made you wait," Deacon said, taking the chair to O'Bannion's right. "We've had a busy day. Faith is fine. The bullet never touched her. She sustained only minor injuries while being pushed out of the way."

"Thank God," O'Bannion breathed. "I'm sorry. I've just been beside myself. I've called her cell phone, but she never answered. *Why* was she shot at? By *whom*? What is she even doing here in Cincinnati? Why didn't she tell me she was in town? When did she get here?"

Bishop sat next to Deacon so that O'Bannion was forced to face both of them. "You should probably ask her those last three questions yourself," she said. "As for the *who* and *why* she was shot? We don't know yet, but the FBI and CPD are working together to find out. In the meantime, I'm afraid we have a situation at your family home, Mr. O'Bannion."

O'Bannion frowned. "I saw it on the news when I woke up. I couldn't believe it. They said an abducted girl had been held in the house. That's . . . well, upsetting, of course. I called the police information number but was told the matter was still classified. Playing phone tag with you, Agent Novak, made it even worse. And then I saw news coverage of police removing items of furniture. I want to know what's happening. Those are antiques. Heirlooms."

Tanaka had hoped that draping sheets over the Plexiglas coffins as they were moved to the morgue would make viewers believe it was furniture, buying the department time to make a proper statement.

"How long has it been since you were at the family house, Mr. O'Bannion?" Deacon asked.

"At it? Last month when I buried my mother. In it? More than twenty years. The house was my mother's, but Faith has inherited it."

Bishop had briefed Deacon on her visit to Maguire and Sons. Henson's grandson's behavior was highly suspicious. That the elder Henson had vouched for him put everything the old man said under doubt. Deacon and Bishop wanted Jordan's point of view.

"Who's been caring for the house all this time?" Deacon asked.

"Our attorney hired a service," Jordan said, still directing his answers to Bishop. "They do inspections on the roof, check for termites, rodent infestations, and things like that. Any of the big things that might cause irreparable harm to the structure. I'm sure our attorney can give you the name. Someone from his firm took the contractors into the house periodically and stayed during the inspection to make sure they were doing the work. Henson paid them and sent my mother the receipts. Neither Mother nor I ever dealt with them personally."

"Dr. Corcoran tells us you were your mother's caretaker," Deacon said.

O'Bannion's brows crunched together. "Dr. Corcoran? Who is that?"

"Dr. Corcoran is Faith," Bishop said, her brows lifted. "Your niece."

O'Bannion shook his head. "No, Corcoran's my mother's maiden name. Faith wasn't a Corcoran. Her maiden name is Sullivan, but she still goes by her married name, Frye. She was divorced a few years ago but never changed it back. What's going on here?"

"Faith changed her name last week," Deacon told him. "To Corcoran."

"Why?" O'Bannion asked, genuinely puzzled. "She built her career using Frye. I figured that's why she didn't change it after the divorce." He waved an impatient hand. "I'll ask her myself when I see her. None of that has anything to do with whatever happened in the house. Why did your people take our furniture?"

"Certain items were taken as evidence, sir," Bishop said. "You'll get receipts for the items removed and everything will be returned in due course."

"In due course?" He frowned. "That sounds like you expect this to be long and drawn out. I thought you found the girl. What's really going on here?"

Deacon cut to the chase. "Where were you on Friday night, between eleven and one?"

O'Bannion's eyes widened. They were green, just like Faith's, Deacon noted. A dull red rose on the man's cheekbones, and his jaw clenched for a long moment. "You called me here to question me? Am I a suspect?"

"You have access to the house, sir," Bishop said evenly. "We're asking everyone."

"I do not have access to that house! I haven't had a key in more than twenty years."

Deacon kept his voice mild. "If you could just answer the question, sir, we can cross you off the list."

O'Bannion's nostrils flared. "I was at home."

Something about the statement was off. "Do you have anyone who can verify this?" Deacon asked, expecting O'Bannion to name Mary Jones, the housekeeper he had met behind the Mount Adams townhouse.

O'Bannion swallowed audibly. Then looked away. "Look, I wasn't at my apartment. I was with my lover, who is married. If this gets out, her husband could ruin me."

"We'll be discreet," Bishop promised. "Her name, sir?"

"Alda Lane."

The pink genie gymnast. *Well, that makes a lot of sense.*

Bishop's eyes had widened, surprising Deacon because he didn't remember telling her the name of the pink genie. "Oh," she said. "I see how that could be a problem." She glanced at Deacon. "Very old money. Mr. Lane is a well-known patron of the arts. He's elderly. Alda is quite a bit younger and an artist. A painter, as I recall."

Deacon held his phone under the table and quickly texted Bishop. *Pink Genie.*

"We met when I exhibited Alda's work at my gallery," O'Bannion said. "We've been lovers for some time. Her husband could take me down over this."

Bishop glanced down at her phone and didn't miss a beat at the revelation. "We'll be discreet," she said again. "Where might we contact her?"

O'Bannion's face became even redder. "This is humiliating," he sputtered.

"I can look up her address, if you'd like, sir," Bishop offered. "The Lane mansion shouldn't be too hard to find. Although I imagine I'll have to sign in with security and give my name."

O'Bannion's jaw was trembling, he'd clenched it so tightly. "That won't be necessary. Agent Novak's already been there. She's in the apartment above my gallery. It's rented in her sister's name." He rattled off the address through bared teeth. "It's our place."

"Thank you," Bishop said politely. "Can you think of anyone else we should talk to?"

O'Bannion pulled his temper into check. "Depends on how old the victim is. If she's a teenager?" He hesitated, then shrugged. "My brother likes them young."

"Really?" Deacon was a little surprised O'Bannion had offered his brother up so readily. "How young are we talking?"

"Post-pubescent. If they get much older than sixteen or seventeen, he loses interest. At least he did. I'm told that individuals with those proclivities don't really change their modus operandi." O'Bannion's grimace was self-effacing. "Sorry. I obviously watch too much TV."

He probably did watch too much TV, Deacon thought, but he had a point. College-aged Corinne had been the most recent target. Arianna was by far the youngest victim—and she appeared to have been an accidental acquisition. But Roza was only twelve or so. "When you say 'At least he did,' what did you mean?"

"My brother and I are not close. We haven't spoken in years. He may have changed his ways. I certainly hope so."

"You know that he molested underage girls?" Bishop asked sharply.

"No, not at all. I said he *liked* them young, but he always made do with the 'barely legal' group." He quirked his fingers in air quotes. "And I didn't say 'girls,' either. He prefers boys, but swung both ways as the opportunities presented themselves."

"Do you have names to go with any of these accusations?" Bishop asked.

"No. I kept to myself, he kept to himself. I heard voices in his bedroom, that's all."

Bishop's brows shot up. "He brought them home?"

"Sometimes. When our parents weren't home, of course."

"Your parents wouldn't have approved, I take it," Bishop said dryly.

"Oh no. Our father was very strict. Homosexuality . . . well, that was simply unacceptable. My brother was disowned."

"Your father found out about his sexual orientation?" Deacon said.

Deacon remembered what Faith had told him regarding the rumors around her grandfather's death—that Jeremy had been so flamboyant about his sexuality that the elder O'Bannion had had a fatal heart attack. He made a mental note to share that with Bishop later.

"Yes. It drove my father to his death, but Jeremy didn't care. After that, the family splintered. Maggie died a few days later, and my mother was never the same." He frowned, as if suddenly realizing he'd been sidetracked. "But that's all water under the bridge and nothing to do with what's happening in the house right now."

"You're the one who suggested we talk to your brother," Deacon reminded him.

O'Bannion's mouth opened and closed like a fish out of water. "I didn't mean that I actually thought . . . No. He's perverted, but he'd never abduct a woman and . . ." He shook his head. "The news reports said the girl had been assaulted. Jeremy wouldn't do that."

"How do you know?" Bishop asked. "You haven't spoken to him in years."

"He's my brother. I'd know," O'Bannion insisted. Then he sighed. "God. This would have killed my mother."

"How did you feel about your mother leaving the house to your niece?" Deacon asked.

"I was surprised. But then I thought about why she had done it and I was fine with it."

Deacon tilted his head, watching the man carefully. "Why do you think she did it?"

"Because Faith needed a home. She's been rather lost since her divorce, and Mother wanted her to have a place to call her own. I certainly didn't want the place. I couldn't live way out there." He shuddered. "Not my cup of tea."

Rather lost since her divorce. Deacon had gotten the impression that the divorce had been the least of Faith's stressors over the last few years.

"Did your mother know what Dr. Corcoran does for a living?" Deacon asked curiously.

He frowned. "I can't get used to you calling Faith 'Dr. Corcoran.'"

"That's how she introduced herself to us. Did your mother know what her job was?"

"Yes, Mother knew, and she did *not* approve. Neither did I. We always thought that one of those perverts would attack Faith. Sure enough, one of them did. I kept that from Mother, though. Her heart had begun to fail, even then."

Like Faith had brought the attack on herself, Deacon thought, disgusted. "Where were you this morning between two and four?"

O'Bannion's eyes flashed, furious. "Now, you're accusing me of shooting my own niece? I won't stand for this deliberate humiliation when you know I was with Alda, because she told you so. She told you far too much." His face burned with embarrassment. "Where can I find Faith? I need to see her with my own eyes to know that you're telling the truth. That she is unhurt."

"She's here where we can ensure her safety," Deacon said. "Because she was *shot at* last night. Which is why we are verifying everyone's whereabouts. That my knowing your situation humiliates you is unfortunate, but your niece's safety matters more to me than your dignity, sir."

O'Bannion flinched. "I'm sorry. Keeping Faith safe is the most important thing. You already know that I was with Ms. Lane in our apartment, Agent Novak. If I'd known Faith was in town, I'd have asked her to stay with me and she wouldn't have been in harm's way to begin with." He dropped his gaze to the table. "But I wasn't there for her when she needed me because I was too busy getting drunk. And yes, that humiliates me."

Deacon recognized the shame on the man's face. His biological father had worn that look more times than he could count. It never made a difference. His father would just get drunk again the first chance he got until it had finally killed him.

"Your personal issues are not my business, Mr. O'Bannion. My business is finding out who abducted a young woman and held her in the basement of your family's house, and who wants your niece dead."

For the first time since Deacon had entered the room, O'Bannion met his eyes squarely. "Do you think whoever—" He stuttered to a stop, staring for a moment, then gave one long, slow blink. "Do you think whoever shot at her will do it again?"

"Possibly. We're taking the threat seriously." Deacon's phone buzzed. Isenberg was messaging him and Bishop. "If you'll excuse us, we'll send Faith in so that you two can catch up. Detective Bishop?"

He and Bishop went into the hallway and shut the door.

Bishop held up her phone. "Isenberg wants a team status meeting in an hour."

"I got the same text. Can you go to Jordan and Alda's love nest to verify his alibi? I'll use the hour to run searches on Roza and on Jeremy and his children. I'll bring Faith to the interview room and observe while she chats with Jordan."

"Sounds good. One love nest coming up. God, I hope Alda's still wearing the genie suit."

Cincinnati, Ohio
Tuesday, November 4, 6:35 p.m.

"I didn't tell him about Combs," Novak said, stopping with Faith outside the interview room door. "I thought you might want to handle that."

Faith looked at the door, secretly dreading the conversation with Jordan. She wasn't sure she had the energy—or the patience—for his reaction once he found out she'd been stalked by Combs. If he didn't straight out say *I told you so*, he'd imply it.

He hadn't approved of her work. He'd warned her she'd get hurt. When Combs had attacked her the first time, he'd given her the I-told-you-so look. And every time she'd visited her grandmother, he'd made her wear a scarf so that her scar wouldn't show.

Which she would have done anyway because she hadn't wanted to upset Gran any more than she already had. But to be commanded to do so had really pissed her off.

And then, of course, there was always the house. Jordan had claimed to be relieved when she'd inherited it, but she knew he'd really been hurt. He was the oldest surviving

O'Bannion male and he'd cared for her grandmother for so long, yet Gran hadn't left the house to him.

It had to be especially galling because he knew how much Faith hated the place. And why.

"Got it," she said quietly. "Where will you be?"

"In the observation room. Not observing, but staying close by." Novak hesitated, then sighed. "Faith, do you know who would've inherited the house if . . . ?" He winced. "You know."

"If whoever's trying to kill me had succeeded? If I'd made a will—which I haven't—my father would. If I'd died without a will, the house would go to the Foundation."

"What Foundation?"

Faith could hear her grandmother's voice in her mind as clear as day. *Your birthright, child.*

"The Joy O'Bannion Foundation. It's a charity my grandmother oversaw," she told Novak. "They give financial help, mainly in the form of scholarships, to college students who've had debilitating illnesses. As Gran's heir, I'm expected to manage the details at some point. I've put it off, though. I can barely manage my own life right now, much less a scholarship program."

He tilted his head. "Is Henson the attorney for the Foundation?"

"Yes, he is. Why?"

"Bishop and I talked to him this morning. He wouldn't answer the question about who would get the house, insinuating it was to protect another client's confidentiality."

"You were thinking that whoever got the house had motive to kill me, but nobody really gets it. It would have been added to the Foundation's assets."

"Who has access to those assets?"

"Only the accountant who writes the checks and the investment broker who manages the portfolio. The board has access to the account statements but not to the money itself."

"I see. How much money are we talking about?"

"A lot. Five million maybe? Give or take."

Novak blinked. "That's a chunk of change. Is it a private or public charity?"

"Private. Why?"

"Where can I get a list of the board members, the broker, and the accountant?"

"They're on my laptop, which is at your house. I can send you the list when I go back. But why? They don't have access to the money."

"Not legally, but it's the illegal activities that'd be motive for murder. Brokers skim. Accountants cook books. And private charities don't have the same level of auditing scrutiny. It may be nothing, but it's too many zeroes to ignore when we're still not certain of why someone wants you dead. One other question. What can you tell me about Jeremy's children?"

It was Faith's turn to blink. "Oh dear. They wouldn't know who did inherit, but they'd know they didn't, wouldn't they? I hate to think of any of them as suspects. Jeremy has a daughter named Audrey. She's in her early twenties. I don't know anything about her other than that she lives in Cincinnati and often gets into trouble with the law for being a bit overzealous with her causes. Jeremy has two stepsons— the ex-wife's sons by her previous marriage. He must have adopted them—they go by O'Bannion, not their father's name. I met Stone and his older brother, Marcus, the Christmas before my grandfather died, when Jeremy brought them to the house for Christmas Eve. Stone was my age and Marcus a year older. Jeremy announced his engagement to Della that night. I remember my mother being a bit appalled because Della was at least ten years older than Jeremy, who was only twenty-two—and, even worse, a Protestant."

"Really? Jordan just said your uncle Jeremy 'liked 'em young'—boys and girls. Just this side of legal, even."

"Oh no, I never heard that, but the adults never directly told me anything. Everything I know I overheard by accident. My father was shocked that Jeremy married a woman. I heard him tell my mother that he'd always thought Jeremy 'light in the loafers,' though I had no idea what that meant. Stone is now a famous journalist, kind of bigger than life, and Marcus runs a small newspaper in one of the northern suburbs. That's all I know." She turned toward the interview room door. "I shouldn't keep Jordan waiting any longer."

"Faith, wait." Novak curled his fingers around her arm,

the sweep of his thumb making it a caress. "I didn't tell him about the bodies. Not yet. Not until we verify his alibi."

"But . . ." Faith shook her head. "He wouldn't. He's . . . *No.* Jordan has his faults, but he takes care of people. He doesn't hurt them. He took care of Gran. He took care of me. If he hurts anyone, it's himself with all the drinking."

"I understand that. But until we verify his alibi, I'm keeping my cards close to my vest. And even then, I don't want to tell him any details that we're not putting in press releases. I don't get the impression that his girlfriend would blink twice before talking to anyone who'd listen. If you gave him confidential information and he told her, even a bit, she could compromise our investigation."

"But when the truth comes out, he's going to be hurt that I knew and didn't tell him."

Novak frowned, concentrating. "All right. Tell him we've found one body, and that there could be more. At least we'll know if we can trust him if the information gets out before the press conference."

That was fair, she thought. She'd always believed that Jordan had kept her secrets safe, but the truth was, she didn't know what he told people when he was drunk out of his mind.

He'd always been too wild, too spoiled, too *bohemian*, ever since she could remember. But it seemed he'd only grown wilder over the years. She'd outwardly smiled when Novak had told her about the pink genie gymnast, but inside she'd winced. Still, she understood why Jordan was the way he was. He'd had a sister who'd lost her fight with leukemia. He himself had fought cancer when he was only seventeen. He'd been told that it could come back at any time.

Some people would see that as a call to make every day count for good. Jordan had taken it as a call to see that every day counted for Jordan. *There but for the grace of God go I.*

She'd walked that road with him for a while—the drinking, the parties. She was glad she'd left it before she'd fallen into the same hole that trapped him.

Drawing a deep breath, she pushed the door open and went in, finding her uncle sitting at the table looking . . . old. His hard living was catching up to him. He was only forty-four, but he looked ten years older. "Uncle Jordan."

Jordan jumped to his feet, folding her in his arms and hugging her so tightly that the bruises on her body protested. At her gasp, he dropped his arms and stepped back. "What's wrong?"

"I'm just a bit bruised up."

His face fell. "I'm sorry, Faith. I didn't mean to hurt you."

"It's okay. Don't worry about it." Faith sat at the table and twisted her fingers together. "Jordan, we have a problem with the house."

"That girl was held there. I know."

"There's more than that. The police found a body in the basement."

He went still, horrified. "In our basement? Who? When?"

"I don't know." Which was the truth. "I only got a glimpse of her."

"You *saw* her? Oh, Faith." Then Jordan's eyes changed, filling with a different kind of horror. Gentler. "You went down there? To the basement? Are you all right?"

She shrugged her shoulders fitfully. "I'm fine. Unsettled."

"I guess so." Jordan squeezed her hand. "I would have gone with you."

"I know." She made her lips curve at him. "It's all right. I'm a big girl now, Jordan."

"And obviously a busy one. Dr. Corcoran," he added. "I didn't make a big deal of it with the detectives, but . . . what the hell, Faith? What's with the name change to Mother's maiden name? I mean, I'm happy you finally ditched that asshole Charlie completely, but why not just go back to Sullivan? Or even O'Bannion? Why Corcoran?"

She drew a deep breath. "Because Faith Frye needed to disappear. I was being stalked."

His eyes narrowed dangerously. "By whom?"

She looked away. "Peter Combs."

He leaned back on a furious exhale. "God*dam*mit, Faith. Did you report him?"

"Of course I did. Dozens of times." She forced herself to look her uncle square in the eye. "The cops thought I'd brought it on myself. Just like you did," she added bitterly.

"I never thought you brought it on yourself," he denied, still furious. "Not once. But you have to admit that working with the scum of the earth lifted your odds of being attacked. I worried every day that I'd get that call, and then I did."

"And you came to the hospital," she murmured. "Right away."

"Yeah," he said, quieting down. "I came. Because I had to see for myself that you were okay. Mother needed to know, too, and she wasn't always sure your father told her everything."

That's because her father hadn't, Faith thought. The O'Bannions and the Sullivans were master secret keepers. *Of course I would be, too. I come by it honestly enough.*

Her uncle leaned forward, now intensely earnest. "But, Faith, you weren't okay. You haven't been okay in a long time. That scared look you had when you left the hospital is still there. I can see it. What did the bastard do to you?"

"Stalked me for almost a year. Then tried to kill me."

Stunned, he glanced at her throat, then lifted fearful eyes to hers. "Again? How?"

"He shot at me, tried to run me off a bridge, burned my apartment down."

A muscle twitched in his cheek. "And the Miami police did nothing?" he asked too quietly.

"When they finally believed me? He was gone. Disappeared under the radar somewhere."

Jordan leaned back in his chair, his expression gone dark with anger. "Since someone is shooting at you, he's obviously reappeared. What are the cops doing to try to find him?"

Looking for clues on the bodies of ten dead women, she thought, but she couldn't say so. "BOLOs," she answered, knowing it sounded woefully inadequate.

"BOLOs," he repeated flatly. "What about the body in the basement? Why are the cops asking me who had access to the basement when they know who did it?"

Because the bodies were there long before I met Combs. But of course she couldn't say that, either. "They have to explore all possibilities and eliminate anyone connected to the house."

"What about this body they found? How does she connect to Combs? He had a daughter, right? Is it her? Did he kill her?"

"Stepdaughter, and no, she's alive." Vega had said that she'd spoken with the girl a few weeks before. "I don't know who she was. I don't know if the police have identified her yet."

"I don't like this. None of it. I don't like that you have to be afraid again. I don't like that this guy was using our house for his sick games. I especially don't like that the cops have no idea where he is. I don't like that they're keeping information back." He went still, his eyes narrowing. "What about the furniture they were removing, Faith? What were they really doing?"

Bodies, she realized. The bodies she wasn't supposed to be talking about. But before she could think of a response, there was a knock at the door and Novak entered the room.

"I'm sorry to cut your visit short, but I've had something come up. Mr. O'Bannion, thank you for coming in. I'll have an officer escort you back to the lobby."

"No. I want some answers. What are you removing from my mother's house?"

"Evidence. That's all I can tell you now."

He bristled. "And the body you found in the basement? Who is she?"

"We truly don't know, but even if we did, we couldn't release her name until we'd informed her family. I'm sure you understand that." He gestured to the officer now standing in the doorway. "Again, I'm sorry that I kept you waiting so long, but I do need to go."

Jordan rose but didn't move toward the door. "And my niece?"

"I've located a safe house for her. She'll be protected. Don't worry."

Jordan shot Faith a frown. "I'll worry less if you're with me. Your old room is ready."

"My old room? What happened to your housekeeper?" she asked.

"Mary moved into my room and I'm in Mother's suite." He took her arm protectively. "Faith will come home with me, Agent Novak. She'll be safe there. I promise you."

Faith gently pulled away. "I can't come with you, Jordan. Neither of us would be safe if I did. My hotel was sprayed with bullets last night, and a young man was hurt. My going to a safe house protects both of us—and all of your neighbors, too."

Plus, she'd lose ready access to Deacon Novak, and she wasn't ready for that to happen yet.

Jordan gave her a helpless look. "I don't like that you're in danger and I can't protect you."

"I'll be safer with the police."

He sighed wearily. "All right. But if you need me, you call me. I'll come right away."

"I will," she said. "Don't worry." When her uncle was gone, Novak closed the door, leaving the two of them alone in the room.

"What's happened?" Faith asked. "Please don't tell me they've found more bodies."

"No, they haven't. I needed to stop him from pushing you for an answer on what we were removing from the house."

"The bodies. I wouldn't have told him anything."

"You did, kind of," he said gently. "When you realized what he was talking about, your face gave you away. I know you didn't want to lie to him, so I stopped the conversation."

"No, I didn't want to lie. He did take care of me, Deacon, the best way he knew how. After Combs . . ." She realized she was tugging the collar of her sweater higher and made herself stop. "After he cut me, I woke up in the hospital to find Jordan sitting with me. He'd gotten there even before my dad. Dad and Lily drove down from Savannah, but Jordan dropped everything and caught a flight out of Cincinnati. He brought me comic books and my Game Boy. A portable DVD player and all the X-Men movies. And then, when they let me eat real food, he snuck me in some Skyline." She smiled sadly. "A five-way with extra onions."

"In Miami? Really?"

"There are a few in Florida. Jordan went out of his way to find it. He's always taken care of me. I hate to keep him in the dark. When will you tell him what's going on?"

"Once we've eliminated him as a suspect. Speaking of which, I have to send you home, too. Agent Pope's here to take you to my house."

"Why? Why can't you?"

"Because I have a meeting with Isenberg in a few minutes. If I had time to take you back to my place, I would, but I'd probably be *very* late coming back."

His voice had dipped suggestively and she found herself at a sudden loss for words. "Oh."

His lips quirked up briefly, but then he was sober again. "There is something you need to know. I got an e-mail from the lab while you and your uncle were talking. They found a tracking device on your Jeep identical to the one Vega found on your Prius."

Faith stared up at him. "What? How did it get there? *When* did it get there?"

"I don't know yet. I'll need a list of everywhere you stopped on the way to Cincinnati from Miami and every place you stopped after you arrived."

Faith sank into the chair, her knees a little weak. "He was close enough to me to put a tracker under my Jeep. Why didn't he just kill me then?"

"Maybe there were too many people around."

"He wanted to wait until I was alone somewhere." She took the hand he offered and levered herself to her feet. "Where is Agent Pope?"

"Waiting for you in the lobby. I'll be home as soon as I can."

"I'll be waiting."

Chapter Twenty-one

Cincinnati, Ohio
Tuesday, November 4, 7:30 p.m.

"I have to meet with the commander and the mayor in thirty minutes," Isenberg said, taking her seat at the head of the table. "Where is everyone?"

So far Deacon and Isenberg were the only ones to have shown up for the meeting. "Bishop's on her way up from the parking garage." Deacon turned to the bulletin board, where someone had hung photos of the victims they'd identified so far, alongside a map showing where each abduction had occurred. "Nice case board."

"Crandall's new intern is very thorough, which isn't surprising as she's Crandall's niece."

Bishop burst through the door, trying to catch her breath. "You're here already. Damn, I was hoping you'd be late like usual." She slid in the chair on the other side of Isenberg.

"Where were you?" Isenberg asked with a frown.

"Mount Adams, verifying Jordan O'Bannion's alibi. He and Alda were together every night this past week, including the two nights in question." Bishop grimaced. "Alda was very specific as to the details of the positions they explored on each night. Apparently, they've been reading the *Kama Sutra* and checking off positions as they try them. So, yeah. Alibi is verified."

Momentarily speechless, Isenberg was saved from a response when CSU leader Vince Tanaka entered the room and sat next to Deacon. "Where's Kimble?" she asked.

"He had to take a phone call," Tanaka said. "He said he'd be here in a minute."

"Okay, so the rest of you, give me something that'll keep the brass from breathing down our necks and make the press go away."

Deacon shook his head. "You're not going to make the press go away, Lynda. This case is going to draw media from all over the country before we're done." With mounting dread, he remembered the constant barrage of questions in West Virginia, the photographers with their long-range zooms. "It'll be a madhouse. You need to prepare yourself for that. All of us do."

Isenberg sighed. "I know. At least we'll have good news to go with whatever bad you're about to tell me. The hospital says that the bellman at Faith's hotel will make a full recovery."

Deacon's shoulders relaxed a hair. That would give Faith some small measure of comfort. "That *is* good news. I didn't think he'd make it."

"So where are we?" Isenberg asked. "Please say we're still at ten bodies."

"Yes," Tanaka said. "But that could change. Novak's archeologist arrived, so we'll soon start looking outside. The officer managing security sent me a picture so that I could verify her ID." Tanaka turned his phone so that they could see the photo of a blonde wearing an ancient army jacket. "I wasn't expecting Dr. Johannsen herself."

"Neither was I," Deacon said. "All she said was that she'd find us someone good."

Tanaka's smile was weary. "She's the best out there, so I'd say she kept her promise."

"Who is Johannsen?" Isenberg asked.

"She's the archeologist I worked with in West Virginia."

"Ah. She mapped out all the graves," Isenberg said.

"She's one of the world's leading experts in ground-penetrating radar," Tanaka added. "She assists forensics teams and disaster-recovery efforts all over the world. If she doesn't find anything, we can safely say we've found all the bodies."

"From your mouth to God's ears," Isenberg muttered. "So, what do we know about the ten?"

"All blond, all about the same age," Deacon said. "All autopsied and embalmed, internal organs removed. I got a status update from Carrie Washington just before you came in. She ID'd one more of the women, so we're up to three ID'd. Another college student who disappeared from Ohio State three years ago. Assuming Corinne Longstreet was his intended victim, we can add the common link of college attendance or recently graduated when they were abducted."

"Any commonalities in college majors?" Isenberg asked.

"No. Corinne is an art major. Roxanne Dupree studied interior design, and Susan Simpson had her BA in Criminal Justice. The most recent ID, Wendy Franklin, was a chemistry major. The outliers in terms of both coloring and age appear to be Arianna and Roza, the girl who helped Arianna escape—both are dark and younger. I checked the missing-children database for girls named Roza, but the only matches were either too old, too young, or the wrong race. When Arianna is able, we'll get a sketch artist with her."

Adam let himself into the room, closing the door behind him. "We got a hit on the white van. It was called in by the first responders."

Isenberg's eyes narrowed. "Responders to what?"

"GSW," Adam said. "Attempted homicide."

Everyone perked up. "The victim survived?" Bishop asked.

"Barely. The van was found in the parking lot of a twenty-four-hour grocery store off of Red Bank Road. The victim had been shot in the head and rolled underneath the van. A shopper noticed a hand sticking out from under the vehicle. It appears she may have pulled herself a few feet, but lost consciousness. The first responders recognized the white van from the BOLO, so they called us immediately. The officer on duty said there was an exit wound, so they've secured the scene and cordoned off the area, looking for the slug. Vince, can you send a forensics team?"

"The team that processed the original scene where Arianna was found has had time to rest. I'll send them." Tanaka tapped out a quick text. "They'll be there in twenty minutes."

"The victim had no ID on her person," Adam went on.

"Her purse wasn't in plain view. The van's plates had been changed from the Tennessee plates it had in the hotel's video to an Ohio set, reported stolen five years ago. They were on a car that had broken down on the side of the road. Whoever took the plates left the car alone. That's why it took so long to find the van. We were looking for Tennessee plates. He's not as stupid as we'd hoped."

"But he made a mistake," Deacon said. "He left a potential witness alive."

"What about the location?" Bishop asked. "Red Bank Road is out east, not far from Lunken Airport, which isn't far from Mount Carmel. He passed several places where he might have ditched the van before he got to Red Bank. Maybe it's an area he's familiar with? Comfortable with?"

Isenberg nodded. "Maybe close to home. Or maybe chosen to make us think he was close to home. Suspects?"

"Maguire and Sons," Bishop said. "Whoever they really are. Their office is in Mount Carmel, not far from Red Bank. Twice a year they inspect the O'Bannion house, top to bottom. The way it was supposed to work was that the grandson of the O'Bannion family attorney—Herbert Henson the third—would meet them at the house with the key and wait as they did their inspection and maintenance. However, a witness says that Henson the third, wearing golf clothes, just dropped the key off at Maguire's Mount Carmel office. The business is legit from a paperwork standpoint, but their office is abandoned. Crandall says their mail is being forwarded to a mailbox store in Forest Park."

"That's a fair distance from Mount Carmel," Tanaka said. "Inconvenient for mail pickup."

"Unless it's close to something that *is* convenient," Bishop said. "Crandall's getting the store's security tapes so we can see who's collecting the mail. My bet is that it'll be the same woman who took the house key from Henson the third. I've put in a request for a sketch artist to get a description of the woman from the witness. When we're done here, we'll interview Jeremy O'Bannion. He's a surgeon, so that fits with the way the victims were autopsied, their organs removed. And so far two family members have mentioned his predilection for young women."

"The ten victims weren't minors," Isenberg said. "They were all college age or older."

"We know," Deacon said. "That's why we want to interview Jeremy at work. He might like younger girls, but he's a med-school professor with access to college-aged women. I want to watch him among them. He's publicly gay but was married to an older woman, so his image could be a smoke screen. I hope we can find something during a voluntary interview that'll be enough to get a warrant to search his home."

"So he's on our list of suspects?" Isenberg asked.

"Definitely a person of interest," Deacon said. "Jeremy doesn't meet the physical description of the gunman from the hotel last night, but that could have been Combs."

"Who is still on our list because (a) he's trying to kill Faith," Isenberg said, "and (b) we have a ballistics match on the gun he used last night at both the O'Bannion house and on the dead hotel guest with the gun used to kill Gordon Shue in Miami."

"Yes," Deacon confirmed. "But the gunman from the hotel last night also could have been Jeremy's stepson Stone O'Bannion."

"Since when?" Bishop asked in surprise.

"Since ten minutes before you got here, when I received a report from the agent who's been watching Jeremy's estate. I forwarded the e-mail to you as soon as I got it. Jeremy didn't leave his house last night, but his stepson did. Stone O'Bannion left at eleven p.m. and returned at four fifteen this morning."

"Gives him the perfect window to shoot you at the hotel," Bishop said, "then steal a van from the store parking lot on Red Bank Road and make it back to Jeremy's house."

"Exactly. Add to it that Stone is former Army. Served two tours in the Gulf. Crack shot. Does a lot of hunting. I pulled this photo—his height, weight, and build are the same as that of Peter Combs—which is the same as that of the gunman from the hotel last night and the man who climbed through Faith's bedroom window two weeks ago in Florida."

Isenberg studied the photo. "What does Faith have to say about him?"

"She only met him once, when they were kids. Jeremy's side of the family is estranged. He has one biological daughter and two adopted sons. None of them were included in either of the elder O'Bannions' wills. Could be hard feelings."

"When did Stone finish his last tour overseas?" Tanaka asked.

"Five years ago," Deacon said, "so he would have been stateside during the time frame of the abductions that we've identified so far."

Tanaka shook his head. "But with two tours in the Gulf, he may have been out of the country when the O'Bannion basement windows were covered up."

Deacon sighed, frustrated that he'd missed that. *I need to sleep.* "You're right. No one person's a perfect match to all the evidence. But Stone is still one we need to watch. Google says he's a reporter now, freelance. His work's been published in *Newsweek* and *Time*, but also in *Hot Shots*—an article on sights for long-range shooting. I ran a background on him right after I received the surveillance report. Stone's got no arrest record, but he does have a number of registered weapons, including a nine mil he reported stolen after his return from the Gulf."

"Convenient," Isenberg said. "Report it stolen, then use it to kill . . . how many?"

"Faith's old boss in Florida," Deacon said, "and here in Ohio there was the Earl Power tech, the locksmith, the occupant of the hotel room. That's four. We have a missing slug that hit the woman found under his van. Plus, I assume the bullet we found near the path at King's College was a ballistics match."

"It was," Tanaka confirmed.

"So he also used it to abduct Arianna," Deacon said. "Of course, we don't know if the nine mil involved in all those crimes is the one Stone reported stolen."

"Bring him in anyway," Isenberg said. "We need to have a chat with the man."

"Bishop and I were going to visit Jeremy next," Deacon said. "But after that, we need to crash for a little while. We're running on fumes."

"I got a decent nap between the morgue and interviewing Arianna," Bishop said. "I'll drive to Jeremy's and you can sleep."

"I'll take you up on it," Deacon said, "but we need more support—more agents and detectives. I can request support from SAC Zimmerman if CPD's resources are being stretched too thin." Deacon was part of Isenberg's task force, but Special Agent in Charge Zimmerman, the head of the FBI's Cincinnati Field Office, was his official boss. "We need someone to pick up and interview Stone and to track down Henson the third, who hasn't contacted us yet. Maguire is still an unknown, if he's even a real person. We could use at least three more detectives or agents."

"I'll contact Zimmerman," Isenberg said. "We'll get more bodies. If you're too tired to interview Jeremy, I can send someone else."

Deacon shook his head. "No, he's a key person of interest, and we're the lead investigators. We'll interview him. Then we'll hand off to whoever's second shift and get some sleep."

"I have a question," Adam said. "Did any of the victims found under the floor have GSWs?"

"Just the cop," Bishop said. "But the wound had healed before he killed her. Why?"

"Because what I can't figure is why he keeps using the same gun," Adam said. "He's got to know we can compare ballistics."

"Maybe he doesn't care," Deacon said. "He may be that arrogant. Or he may have figured that he'd have killed Faith by now and we'd never connect the dots. Have we found any usable fingerprints in the basement?"

Tanaka shook his head. "Surprisingly few. Every surface has been cleaned—walls, doors, the autopsy table, all of it. We found several partial prints on the cot, but only one yielded anything through AFIS—those of his most recent victim, Roxanne Dupree."

"The student at Miami University," Isenberg said. "Any word on why he picked her?"

"I asked Detective Vega to check her out," Bishop said. "She said she'd get back with us."

Isenberg checked her notes. "She was going to talk with Combs's girlfriend, too. Did she?"

Bishop grimaced. "The girlfriend and her attorney are playing games with the DA, trying to make a deal on the possession charge. Vega thinks they'll have something tomorrow."

Isenberg's eyes narrowed. "Their DA understands what we're dealing with, doesn't he?"

"Yes, ma'am," Bishop said soberly. "Don't forget, they have three homicides, too—Gordon Shue and the mother and son killed in Faith's old car. They've managed to keep the link between their homicides and ours on the QT, but it's just a matter of time before a reporter connects our Faith with the Faith that was holding Gordon Shue's shirt when his brains got splattered all over her."

"Who's Vega's CO?" Isenberg asked. "I'll give him a call to make sure we're coordinating information before I go in front of the press."

"Lieutenant Neil Davies," Bishop said. "Vega trusts him. So far, I trust her."

"Good." Isenberg turned to Tanaka. "Vince, run me through everything you've found in that basement that isn't a body. Quickly. I'm due upstairs in ten minutes."

"Latent pulled three distinct sets of prints that don't match any of the bodies. One belongs to Arianna Escobar. The second belongs to a child or an adult with very small hands. The last is a single print and very faint. None of the prints match Peter Combs's. The child's prints don't match any in the Missing Children database."

"Can you estimate an age from the print?" Deacon asked.

Tanaka shrugged. "Pre-pubescent? Maybe? It's hard to say."

"In the whole basement you only found three sets of prints? Really?" Isenberg pressed.

"The walls and floors were *exceptionally* clean, Lynda," Tanaka said. "The room with the autopsy table had been hosed down with bleach. The child's prints were found everywhere. She was evidently allowed freedom in the basement. Everywhere but the handle of the door at the top of the stairs, where we found Arianna Escobar's prints."

"When she escaped," Deacon murmured. "Where did you find the faint print?"

"In the little dug-out room," Tanaka said. "It was on the hairbrush we found in the box on the pallet. Everything else in the room had only the girl's prints."

"The brush could have belonged to one of the other victims," Bishop said.

"God, I hope not," Tanaka said fervently. "Because if so, we'd have more than ten victims, because that print doesn't match any of the bodies we've found. I'm hoping that the girl had it with her when she was abducted. In the brush were hairs belonging to two different people. One hair is short and dark, the other long and blond. We'll run DNA on both and let you know." He glanced at his notes. "The blanket found in the dug-out room is a generic camp blanket. It could have been bought anywhere, but it's been down there a while."

"What's a while?" Isenberg asked. "How long has the girl been there? Weeks, months?"

"The blanket could have been down there for years. I can't say how long the girl's been there. We found a number of cameras inside and outside of the house. Unfortunately, they recorded to a DVR which had been removed."

"Damn," Deacon muttered. "That was too good a lead to pan out."

Tanaka shrugged. "Sorry. The only other thing I have is a summary from Agent Taylor's forensics team. The shooter didn't leave anything behind in the hotel room. Oh, and the new crime scene at the grocery store, of course. We'll have the van towed to the garage and go over every square inch ASAP."

"Good work, Vince," Isenberg said with a nod. "Anything else I need to know?"

Deacon's phone buzzed with an incoming e-mail. "It's from Faith—the list of places she parked her Jeep since she bought it Saturday morning. At some point this guy stuck her with another tracking device."

"I'll check it out," Adam offered. "Send me the list."

"Thanks," Deacon said, wondering if Adam was being truly helpful or trying to find another reason to suspect Faith. *He'd accept her if he knew how she'd worked with that Miami PD sex-crimes detective to put offenders back in prison.* Perhaps, but whether he should be told wasn't Deacon's decision to make. It was Faith's.

"What about Combs?" Isenberg asked. "Has our BOLO turned up anything?"

"No," Deacon said, frustrated. "It's like Vega said—he's dropped off the earth. Crandall ran a check for credit card and bank activity, but Combs truly has gone off the grid. The gunman last night met his physical description, but none of the tapes show his face, so we can't even be sure it was Combs. He might not be involved at all. It might have been Stone. Or whoever is posing as Maguire and Sons. Or it might be someone we don't know about yet."

"If Combs *is* involved, it hasn't been for long," Bishop said. "He's only been out of prison about a year. Gordon Shue was shot a month ago, so Combs can be a suspect for his murder, but at least some of the victims in the basement went missing while Combs was serving his sentence. It's possible that he was contacted by the killer of those ten women when he was in prison. I asked Vega to check on his visitors and jailhouse buddies and to pump the girlfriend for information about anyone he met in the last few months. We're not without leads, Lynda."

"What about this newest victim?" Deacon asked. "The one at the grocery store? He shot the woman presumably for her vehicle. Since her purse wasn't found with her, we can only assume he kept it. He'd have her keys and her address from her license. He could be hiding out there— maybe with two live victims."

Isenberg gave him a long look. "You really think Corinne is still alive?"

"Yes," he said firmly, "Until we know otherwise, I have to. And even if he has killed her, there's still the girl. Arianna believes that he'll kill the girl for helping her escape, but until we understand more about the relationship between them, we can't know what he intends to do. We need to find out where our main suspects' hidey-holes are— Jeremy, Stone, Combs, Henson the third, Maguire."

"Have Crandall run a search for all their real estate," Isenberg said, then grimaced when Tanaka tapped his wrist. "I know it's time for me to go. I hate these things. Goddamn vultures."

"What do you plan to disclose?" Deacon asked.

She stood up, gave the coat of her uniform a tug. "That we've found victims buried in the basement, but not how many. That there is a commonality of age, race, coloring, and educational status. But not the Plexiglas, nor that he embalmed them."

"And don't mention the autopsy stitching," Bishop added.

"That, too, will remain undisclosed."

"What about the child?" Adam asked. "Will you disclose her existence?"

"Yes, along with her description and her name. Adam, have Crandall coordinate a call center. We're about to get a flood of calls from desperate parents. I want anyone who is outside or doing any fieldwork wearing vests. Vince, that includes your teams. Go. Track down the leads we have and get some new ones. Keep me up-to-date."

When she was gone, Deacon took out his phone. "Okay, let's divvy up the work here. I'll make the list and e-mail it to all of you. Adam, we need an ID on the grocery store woman ASAP. Her killer could be hiding in her house right now. Also, as soon as she is conscious, find out what she saw."

"Will do. And when I'm done there, I'll find out where Corcoran was when the tracker was placed under her Jeep."

"I'm going back to the O'Bannion house," Tanaka said. "I want to watch Johannsen operate the ground-penetrating radar. Maybe pick up a few tricks. Although I hope to never need them again. We're also going to x-ray the walls. We still haven't found his stash of souvenirs."

"The organs he removed from his victims," Bishop said. "Shit."

"If Faith remembers the layout of the house from before," Adam said, "maybe she can help Vince locate the hidey-holes."

Ask her to go back into that house? No fucking way. "No. She's not able to do that."

Bishop's eyes narrowed. "Says who?"

"Says me. She nearly passed out the last time I forced her to go down there."

Adam and Bishop shared a glance. "Shouldn't we ask her what *she* wants?" Bishop asked.

No, because she'll say yes. But he knew Bishop was right. "Fine. I'll ask her, okay?" He stood up, needing to get his blood moving so he could stay awake. "Scarlett, will you drive us to Jeremy's house? I'll catch some z's on the way." He hesitated as he passed Adam's chair. They couldn't function as a team with the way they'd been behaving. "Thanks."

"I still think you're crazy," Adam said under his breath. "But Dani said I should trust you."

That the two of them had talked about him didn't surprise Deacon a bit. It actually made him feel a little better. "You might stop by later and talk to Greg."

Adam's dark brows went up. "How much trouble is he in?"

"A whole helluva lot. He's at my house. He was afraid to put Tammy under any more stress. She could use a visit from you, too. Scarlett, let's go see Uncle Jeremy."

Cincinnati, Ohio
Tuesday, November 4, 7:35 p.m.

"You can come out now," Agent Pope said, holding out his hand to help her up from the floorboard where she'd been hiding for the last mile of the journey back to Novak's house.

Faith groaned quietly as she climbed out of the car. "This is getting a little old."

"Better old than dead," Pope said soberly. The man had not cracked a smile since his arrival that morning. Not waiting for her reply, he went into the house to check for invaders.

Someone screamed, and Faith rushed inside to see Dani Novak backed up against the dishwasher, a frying pan held tightly in a two-fisted grip.

Pope's hands immediately lifted, palms out. "Easy, Dr. Novak."

"It's okay, Dani," Faith said quickly. "He's a Fed."

Dani relaxed, as did Pope. "I'm sorry, ma'am," he said. "I thought you were expecting us."

"Colby, sure." Dani spread her hand over her heart. "I didn't know about you."

"I was on outside duty when you came in before. I'm going back out there now. As soon as I can hear again," he added in a mutter, making Faith laugh.

"He never jokes," Faith explained to Dani. "I'm surprised to see you here. I thought you were on shift."

"Greg woke up and found he was the only one here except for the Feds. He was nervous with Agent Colby in the house, even though I told him it was to guard you. Between you and me, I think he's still rattled about the trouble at school and just wanted the company, so I got someone to cover the rest of my shift. I made Greg and Colby grilled-cheese sandwiches for supper. Are you hungry? There are a few left."

"Sure." Faith sat at the center island while Dani fixed her

a plate, then leaned in and looked at Faith's forehead with a frown.

"You popped your superglue."

"Last night," Faith admitted. "Deacon tackled me to keep me from getting hit with a bullet. I bandaged it up and figured I'd tend to it later."

"This is later," Dani said. "I'll fix you up, but eat first."

She did, suddenly realizing how hungry she was. "That was delicious," she said, pushing the plate away. "I haven't had grilled cheese in a long time. It was always my go-to comfort food when times got stressful. I haven't had a home-cooked meal in weeks. I've been living on take-out food."

"Sounds like the past several years have been stressful, Faith. And based on what I'm seeing in the news, it doesn't look like it's about to get better anytime soon. I checked on the results of the blood I drew last night in the ER. You're low on iron and vitamin D. You need to eat better and take vitamins."

Faith sighed. "I always mean to take vitamins, but then I forget. I'll add it to the list of all the things I've got to do." On her phone she opened the list she'd composed while waiting to talk to Jordan and typed a few new lines. "Eat better, take vitamins, schedule a physical, get a new phone and a new car. Find someplace to live and get a big dog for protection."

"A dog?" Dani grinned. "I love dogs. I've wanted one forever, but I haven't lived in a house of my own since Mom and Bruce died. I was either in a dorm or an apartment. Where will you go to get one? Maybe I'll go with you and pick one out for us—for me and Greg and Deacon."

"I'll definitely go to the pound." Faith frowned as a thought occurred. "But I won't be able to afford to buy a house for a while. If I get an apartment, I can't get a dog after all."

"Don't you already have a house? That big house on the news—that's yours, isn't it?"

"Yeah but . . . I don't know if I can live in it after all this. I mean, Arianna was tortured there. How can I live there?"

"I don't know the answer to that. But if you don't live there, what will you do with it?"

"Sell it, I guess. I don't know anything anymore."

Dani patted her hand. "Don't worry about it now. We'll still go to the pound together and you can help me pick out my dog." Her gaze became unapologetically curious. "Besides, if you start seeing a lot of Deacon, you'll be here all the time anyway."

Seeing a lot of Deacon. Faith's cheeks superheated as her mind replayed the memory of a boldly nude Deacon Novak striding toward her. Yeah, she'd seen quite a lot of Deacon this afternoon. And she planned to see even more of him later.

Dani cleared her throat. "Okay, that's enough of that. I guess that answers my question. I think my face is turning red just from watching your face turn red. He's my brother. There are some images that simply should not be in a sister's head. No more details, please."

Faith rolled her eyes, embarrassed. "I didn't give you any details."

"You didn't have to. Your face told me plenty."

"My face is saying all kinds of things today," she muttered. "Of course, it's your fault."

Dani's eyes—one brown, one blue—opened wide. "My fault? How?"

"'He's a good man, Faith,'" Faith mimicked. "I was doing all right with being angry with him last night. But then you sang his praises."

Dani's smile was affectionately proud. "He is a good man. He's always been my rock. My mother wasn't home that much after our biological dad died. She had to work two jobs to make ends meet, but Deacon took care of me while she was working, even though he was only ten years old. He made my school lunch, helped me with my homework, fixed dinner. Made sure I had clean clothes and that my hair was brushed. Even took my temperature when I was sick."

No wonder Deacon had been so angry with Jordan. Her uncle had encouraged her to ditch school, giving her beer and cigarettes when she was fourteen. Deacon had had better parenting skills at less than half Jordan's age. "That's quite a load for a little boy to carry."

"It was, but he never complained, not until we were forced to move in with Aunt Tammy and Uncle Jim."

"I thought you and Greg lived with them *after* your mother died."

"We did then, too. Deacon also lived with us then, but for only a few months. He graduated high school and left for college. But when Mom was alive, before she remarried and had Greg, it was Deacon and Mom and me living with them. Mom nearly worked herself to death for a year after our father died, but we still couldn't pay the rent. It was Uncle Jim's house, but he had to move us out so that he could rent to someone else. Tammy later told me that they'd covered Mom's rent for months before he moved us out, but Deacon and I didn't know that then. Deacon hated him for evicting us, for making Mom cry. But most of all, I think because Jim treated him like he couldn't take care of us, like he was just a kid."

"He *was* just a kid."

"I know. Looking back, Jim was trying in his own rough way to give Deacon back his childhood, but Deacon didn't see it that way. I'm still not sure he does."

Deacon's need to take care of Greg now was making even more sense. "How long did you live with them?"

"Four years. Then Mom met Bruce. I think we were all a little afraid she'd jumped into marriage with Bruce because she was desperate to get away from Uncle Jim, but it turned out better than any of us could have imagined."

"Bruce was a good stepfather, then?"

Dani smiled. "The best. He was the dad he didn't have to be, but was. He even adopted us. For the first time, Deacon had a true father figure. I mean, Jim took us in, but we never forgot that it was only because of his kindness that we weren't homeless. Bruce . . . loved us. Wanted us. We were a family. When he and Mom died, it was like . . . well, like your whole life you got old, crusty bread, then someone gives you a steak dinner. But then they take the steak away and you have to go back to eating crusty bread. The bread sustains life, but it's not the same."

"And it's almost worse because now you know what you're missing."

"Yeah. But at least Deacon and I had the time with Mom and Bruce as a loving family. Greg never got that. Tammy's nurturing, but Jim can be . . . well, hard to live with."

"Adam grew up with Jim, too," Faith murmured. "Which may explain a lot."

"Adam's a good man," Dani said loyally. "Although I can

understand how you might think otherwise right now. He called me last night after the two of you talked. He was very worried about Deacon being led astray again."

Again? Who led him astray the first time? Faith was tempted to ask, but knew the answer needed to come from Novak himself.

And Dani had just bitten her lip as if she'd said too much and wished she could take it back. "Adam's been worried about your having counseled offenders," she added hurriedly. "I sent him a link to the victim forums, but I don't know if he read them. Sometimes he cares too much and it gives him tunnel vision. He gets very protective of his family, Deacon especially. But that's his wrong to right. I'll get my bag and fix you up."

"Wait, Dani. Why Deacon especially?" This was a topic she felt more comfortable pushing with Dani than with Deacon.

"Deacon wasn't always the big, strong guy that he is now. When he was young, he was skinny and shorter than the other boys his age. He was nerdy and geeky and way too smart. Plus, we looked different." She tugged at the white streak in her hair. "*Now*, this is cool. *Then*, not so much. It's hard being the different kid."

"And Deacon's eyes made him even more different. He was bullied?"

"Unmercifully. Adam, on the other hand, was big even then, just like Uncle Jim."

"Adam took up for Deacon?"

"Unfailingly. Deacon hated the arrangement, but he hated getting the snot knocked out of him even more. Adam taught him to fight back, but that just made things worse. It was looking pretty bleak until the summer before Deacon went to high school. We moved into Bruce's house, changed to a new school. That same summer, Deacon hit a growth spurt."

"The bullying stopped?

"No, not really. It just changed. He was all long legs and beefy arms and big shoulders, but he was still a geek. He still had different hair and eyes. He just was able to fight back better. He fought a lot. Was in the principal's office a lot. Then he finally found a way to deal."

"The whole coat, hair, sunglasses persona?"

"Exactly. The coat was a gift from Bruce. I think that man understood us better than anyone else ever had. Maybe ever will."

I'm not so sure about that. Faith had wondered why Novak would want to be so visible, but he wasn't. Not really. "Deacon created the person he wants everyone to see. Because if he could manipulate the perception, he could keep people from hurting him."

Dani smiled. "I've always hoped Bruce wouldn't be the only one who understood my big brother. Let's get that gash closed up. And then I want you to lie down and get some of that rest I ordered last night."

Cincinnati, Ohio
Tuesday, November 4, 8:45 p.m.

"Novak, wake up." Bishop tapped Deacon's shoulder. "We're here."

Deacon opened his eyes, needing a second to orient himself. *Here is where? Oh, right.* The mansion in front of him was his first clue. They were sitting in front of Jeremy O'Bannion's estate in Indian Hill, one of the ritziest burbs of Cincinnati. Less than a half hour from downtown, it was an area that Deacon's family had never had cause to visit.

Bishop brought the car to a stop and pointed to the stately old plantation-style home at the end of a driveway holding a Bentley and a Rolls-Royce. "That's it."

Deacon noted the dark sedan parked farther down the street—the agent watching Jeremy's mansion, which was the picture of simple, understated wealth. "Jeremy looks like he's doing just fine, despite being cut out of Granny O'Bannion's will. What little I turned up on him said that his ex-wife is wealthy. Her name is Della Yarborough."

Bishop whistled. "The Yarboroughs are *old* Cincinnati money."

"Like Alda Lane's husband?"

"Take Lane's net worth and add a few zeroes," Bishop said. "I don't know how much of her money Jeremy got in the divorce versus what he earned on his own by being a surgeon, but he's clearly invested well. What else?"

"Faith remembers him 'looking' at her when she was a little girl."

"Oh no," Bishop said softly. "Tell me he didn't do what I'm thinking."

"She said he never touched her. She told her father about the inappropriate looking. Her father had disliked Jeremy before that, and afterward he wouldn't allow her to be alone in the same room with him. She had Jeremy unofficially investigated years ago."

"Hm. Not surprising. I take it she didn't find anything?"

"She said there was no indication that he'd ever had a single complaint. He does charitable work in the city, used to be part of Doctors Without Borders. He started teaching when he was injured in a car accident years ago and lost the use of his right hand."

"Lots of car accidents in this family," Bishop observed.

"True. I confronted Faith about her mother's death, Scarlett. The family made up the accident story because they were 'more Catholic than the Pope,' and suicide wasn't just any sin. It was the *big* sin."

"Suicides weren't given church burials back then," Bishop murmured.

"Exactly. I tried to get more information, but she got so upset that I stopped."

Bishop raised a brow. "You've gone squishy, Novak."

He rolled his eyes. "Let's do this." Despite the fact that the sun had set two hours before, he slid on his shades just in case he needed to throw Jeremy off balance, and he and Bishop walked to the door through an immaculately kept garden.

"There's a guesthouse in back," Bishop murmured. "I saw it on Google Earth. Plenty big enough to store two hostages."

"Maybe we'll go for a stroll when we're done." Deacon rang the bell.

The door was opened by a blonde in her mid-twenties. "May I help you?"

"I'm Special Agent Novak, and this is my partner, Detective Bishop. We'd like to speak with Dr. O'Bannion."

"He's not available." The woman started to close the door.

Bishop flipped out her badge with one hand and held the door open with the other. "He's here," she said flatly. "Please tell him to come to the door."

Panic skittered across the young woman's face. "What is this in reference to?"

"That's between us and Dr. O'Bannion," Bishop said. "May we come in?"

"No," the woman said. "You can't."

"Hailey?" a male voice interrupted. "What's wrong?"

"You've got visitors, Dr. O'Bannion," Hailey said, keeping her chin down but her eyes up.

Deacon ceased paying attention to the woman when the man approached. It was Jordan O'Bannion, but not. Jeremy and Jordan looked alike. Moved alike. Except for the mustache that this man wore, they were the same. *Twins.*

"Did we know they were twins?" Deacon murmured so that only Bishop could hear.

"I didn't," Bishop murmured back. "Faith didn't think to mention it?"

Deacon thought back to that conversation next to the family cemetery. Right before he'd held her against him for the first time. *Twins, actually. Jordan and Jeremy.* "She did, but she didn't say they were identical."

Jeremy stopped in the doorway, his left hand on the young woman's shoulder in a gesture that was more fatherly than romantic. "What seems to be the problem, Detectives?"

Deacon's gaze dropped from the man's face to his hands. *Gloves.* Jeremy wore skin-colored gloves that appeared to be made of thin leather.

"He's a special agent," Hailey said softly, pointing to Deacon.

"I see," Jeremy said in a way that told Deacon he was being actively appreciated. A tactic to throw him off his game, he was certain.

"I called yesterday," Deacon said. "We'd like to talk to you about a situation that's arisen."

"Oh. Well, I have to confess that I didn't get your message myself. My partner gets my voice mail for me. What's happened?"

Deacon wanted to frown but did not. Jeremy had not only received his message, he'd returned it. "May we come in? I'd rather not have this kind of conversation on your doorstep."

"Show them into the parlor, Hailey. Perhaps they'd like some refreshment."

They were escorted through the foyer in which Deacon immediately recognized both the curving staircase in the entryway and the design of the wallpaper. The interior of the house had been modeled after the house in Mount Carmel. A glance at Bishop confirmed that she'd seen the resemblance as well.

Jeremy sat in an overstuffed chair and gestured to the sofa with his left hand. He slipped his right hand—also gloved—into his pocket. "You mentioned a situation?"

"Yes, one that revolves around your family home in Mount Carmel," Deacon said, pasting a pleasant expression on his face as he and Bishop sat.

Jeremy's eyes grew instantly frosty. "You're mistaken. *This* is my family home. Right here."

"Jeremy? Is everything all right?" The question came from a man in his early forties who rushed into the room looking as if he expected to have to save Jeremy, presumably from Deacon and Bishop.

Deacon swallowed his sigh. While this man's face looked nothing like Peter Combs's, he was built like him. Same size and shape. One more bruiser to add to the possible suspect list.

"I'm fine, Keith. Please join us." Jeremy patted the arm of his chair. "These officers have come to ask me questions about the old O'Bannion homestead."

Keith fixed his gaze on Deacon's face. "You're the one who called last night. I expected you to *call* for an *appointment*. Dr. O'Bannion is a busy man."

It was Keith who had left the voice mail, Deacon realized. "*I* expected that my message would have been returned by Dr. O'Bannion himself, as it regarded the safety of his niece."

"Faith? What's happened to her?" Jeremy looked up at Keith. "Why didn't you tell me?"

"Because I don't care about *Faith* or any of that group of bottom-feeders that call themselves your *family*," Keith gritted out. "I didn't realize it was urgent."

"I believe I used the word 'urgent' in my message," Deacon said mildly.

Keith's cheeks turned a dull, angry red. "I'm sorry, Jeremy. I'd hoped I could deal with the detectives for you."

He has a temper, Deacon thought. *Good to know.*

"Well, we're here now," Bishop said, her tone neutral. "I didn't get your name, sir."

Jeremy's chin lifted a fraction. "This is my partner, Keith O'Bannion. He's privy to all my business. He can hear whatever you have to say to me. What's this about Faith's safety?"

"She's *not* your family," Keith hissed, and Jeremy patted his knee.

"I know, I know," he murmured soothingly. "But she was just a child when all of that happened. She had nothing to do with any of it."

"She got the *house*, Jeremy," Keith protested under his breath. "It should have been yours."

Jeremy looked up at Keith, speaking to him as if they were the only two in the room. "Yes, she did. And, yes, it should have been. But if I had gotten it, I just would have had to fight Jordan to keep it, so it's for the best. We don't need the house, Keith. And we don't need the money."

"That's not the point," Keith insisted. "They revile you and mistreat you, but now that your niece needs your help, they come to you."

Interesting, Deacon thought. Faith had mentioned that Jordan had said that he would have to fight Jeremy to keep the house if he'd inherited and now Jeremy was saying the same. Perhaps Granny O'Bannion had left it to Faith to keep her sons from fighting.

"What happened to Faith, Agent Novak?" Jeremy asked. "Does she need my help?"

He sounded like he really cared, but in a way that sounded a little too sincere.

"Last night a young woman was found on the road leading to the old homestead," Deacon said, choosing his words carefully. "She'd been assaulted and barely escaped with her life."

The two men stared at him. "Faith was assaulted?" Jeremy asked, quietly horrified.

"No. Faith found the victim. She was on her way to the house when she saw the woman in the road. She swerved to avoid her, went down an embankment, and hit a tree."

Jeremy paled slightly, a curious response. "Is she hurt badly?"

"No," Deacon said. "Just a few cuts. She managed to climb the embankment and call 911."

"Then why are you here if she's not hurt?" Jeremy asked.

Deacon kept his gaze glued to their faces. "We found evidence that the young woman had been held prisoner in the basement of your old home."

Jeremy's pleasant veneer disappeared to reveal something dark and angry. "Why are you telling *me* this? I walked away from that family and that house almost twenty-five years ago. I never looked back. I've made a new home and a new family."

"I'm telling you because someone has tried to kill your niece six times in the last month."

"The attacks started a week after she inherited the house," Bishop added. "The latest one was early this morning. A sniper shot at her. Missed her, but injured an innocent man in the process. So we need to know where you were between two and four this morning."

"Are you accusing Jeremy?" Keith asked from behind clenched teeth.

"No," Deacon said. "But as you so accurately put it, the house should have been Dr. O'Bannion's. If we didn't put him on our list of suspects, we wouldn't be doing our jobs. Dr. O'Bannion, we're here to get your statement, to eliminate you from the list. May we have your whereabouts?"

"I was home, asleep in my own bed," Jeremy said. "With Keith. And no, we can't prove it."

The agent outside had said the same, but Jeremy and Keith didn't need to know that.

"We've also talked to your brother," Bishop said to Jeremy.

Jeremy clenched his jaw. "I can only imagine what he said."

"He gave us his alibi for last night," Bishop said. "And then he recommended we speak with you." She exaggerated a hesitation, looking up at Deacon. He played along, giving her a facial shrug and a tiny nod. "He suggested," she added, "that you might like young women."

"That is a *lie*!" Keith cried viciously. "A *dirty* lie. Jeremy, call your lawyer."

"I certainly intend to," Jeremy said evenly, but his hand trembled.

Now's the time. When they're both vulnerable and shaking. Deacon slid his sunglasses off and met Jeremy's eyes, allowing his own to communicate the contempt he felt for the man.

Jeremy stiffened and stared, his gaze never flickering away. Beside him, Keith flinched. And then Jeremy surprised Deacon, closing his eyes, his shoulders slumping in weary despair. "What exactly did Faith tell you, Agent Novak?"

"Why do you think she told me anything?" Deacon asked, intrigued by the man's response. It wasn't the color of Deacon's eyes he had flinched from, but the expression in them.

"Because you look at me the way her father did. The way all of them did that day. No one has looked at me like that since. Not until today."

Chapter Twenty-two

Eastern Kentucky
Tuesday, November 4, 8:45 p.m.

Corinne let the pack slide to the ground and collapsed in a heap next to it. Three feet away, Roza was curled into herself, her thin arms pulling her bent knees as close to her body as she could, rocking, rocking.

Roza had been so brave—but it had lasted all of ten minutes. For the next four hours Corinne had had to half drag her through the woods. Every gust of wind terrified her. Ever shriek of a hawk flying overhead had her ducking, hands clamped over her ears. Every time Corinne had loosed her hold, the girl had gone all potato bug on her, rolling up into that damned ball.

Which Corinne totally understood. She'd like to curl up herself, and poor Roza had been through so much more. But there was a limit to what was humanly possible, and Corinne had hit that wall. *I'm done,* she thought. *I'm all used up. If he comes after me now, I won't be able to fight.* She was hungry. And dehydrated. *Poor Roza must be, too.*

She didn't even know where they were. It was dark, and they were in a huge forest. Miles and miles of forest. They hadn't seen a single, solitary person, or a house, or even another road. She'd steered them west, because that was the way she thought his car had gone when it left the cabin earlier. With no compass, she'd been depending on the sun. But it had set hours ago and there were no stars, so now she was afraid they'd been going in circles.

She pawed at the knot she'd tied in the blanket in which she'd packed their supplies, the joints in her fingers now too swollen to move properly. Each tug brought pain that, exhausted as she was, had become too much to bear.

"Roza, honey, I can't drag you any further. I need to eat and so do you. I need your help."

There was no indication that Roza had even heard. Just that horrible rocking, rocking, rocking.

"I'm *serious*," Corinne snapped, letting her frustration come out. "I have only about five good hours that I can use my hands every day before they start to hurt. And that's *with* my medicine. Now I can't even untie this knot. You're going to have to do this or we're going to starve. Roza?" She waited but got no response. *"Roza with a zed!"*

The rocking stopped and Roza lifted her head.

"Thank you. Now come here. Please." Corinne held up her hand, which had locked into a claw long before. "I've helped you. Now I need *your* help."

Slowly, Roza uncurled her body, crossing the distance between them by scooting on her butt, her eyes down. "What's wrong with your hand?" she asked as she picked at the knot.

"I have a disease. It's not catching," Corinne added when Roza's head jerked up in alarm. "It causes my joints to swell—like my knuckles and my knees."

Roza went silent, working on the knot until it came loose. She spread the blanket out. "What do you want to eat? Give me your knife. I watched you open the last can. I can do it."

"The bean soup has protein," Corinne said as she handed over the knife, "so let's eat that. And we need to drink some water. But be careful. Drink only a little and don't spill any. I don't know when we'll find a stream to refill our bottles."

Roza opened a bottle of water. "This is our last one."

"Thank you," Corinne said. "You have some, too, okay?"

Roza obeyed, then picked up a can of soup, squinting at the label. "That says 'bean.'" She opened the can competently, then folded up the knife and gave it back to Corinne.

"You're awfully good at taking care of people," Corinne said softly.

A shrug of those frail shoulders. "I watched Mama do it. It was her job. Then it was mine."

Corinne thought about the jars of eyes and swallowed hard. Roza and her mother had cared for the victims. How many had there been? Dozens at least. "Did your mama tell you how she came to be in that . . . awful place?"

"Home," Roza murmured. "It was home." She handed Corinne the can of soup. "I don't have a spoon. I'm sorry."

"It's all right. I've guzzled it down straight from the can before."

Roza looked up with a slight frown. "Why? Didn't you have a home?"

Corinne noted that the child's trembling decreased as they spoke. "I was in the Army out in the desert. Sometimes we had only a few seconds to slurp our supper down." She rephrased her earlier question. "Did your mama tell you how she came to be in your home?"

"She said she and her sister were walking outside one night and he . . . took them." Roza's dark eyes were wide. "You were really in the Army? In the desert?"

"Before I got sick. Yeah, I was." Corinne looked around at the trees that seemed to go on forever. "I hated the desert because it was hot and dry and there was sand everywhere. At least we have some shade here."

"Did you see a tiger?"

Corinne blinked at her, then smiled. She'd been so busy thinking of Roza as a child victim that she'd forgotten she was still a child. "Not in the desert, no. But I did see camels."

Roza frowned. "Camels?" She shook her head. "I don't know what that is."

"You've never seen a camel? It's this . . . um. Well. How do you know what a tiger is?"

"I saw it in a book. We would take them from the girls' backpacks sometimes when he wasn't looking. Mama would hide the books until he left, and then we'd look at them together."

"Okay. Then do you know what a horse is?"

"Of course," Roza said. "Does a camel look like that?"

"Not exactly. Imagine a horse with really long legs and

instead of the back dipping in, it bumps out." She drew the shape in the air. "They need very little water, which is why they can live in the desert. Because it's really dry there. You said your mother was with her sister when they were taken? Was your aunt in the basement with you?"

"For a while. But he killed her, then put her in a wooden box and buried her." Roza's little face pinched. "My mama cried for a long, long time. He never let her say good-bye."

Corinne had to swallow the lump in her throat. "I'm so sorry, Roza."

The girl shrugged. "I don't remember her very well. I was too little."

"Do you know how old you are?"

Roza looked offended. "Of course. I'm eleven."

"I thought so. What was your mama's name?"

"Amethyst. It's a pretty purple rock. But he called her Amy. Did you kill anyone?"

Once again, Corinne blinked. "Excuse me?"

"When you were a soldier. Did you kill anybody?"

"Yes. But I really would rather not talk about it, if you don't mind."

"Were they bad?"

Corinne sighed. "Some were very bad. All of them wanted to kill me, so I guess that made them bad enough."

"Will you kill *him*?"

Ah. "Do you want me to?"

Roza's dark eyes flashed hatred, raw and virulent. "No . . . *I* want to."

Corinne hesitated, not wanting to say or do the wrong thing, because she believed that Roza was capable of killing the man who'd taken her mother and her aunt, who'd held her as a slave. Who'd killed so many. "Did he kill your mama?"

"Not with his knives. But she got sick and couldn't get warm. We weren't allowed to use the stove except to make things for him, but I did anyway. I heated some water to make her tea, just like I always did for him. But he found out." Her lips quivered. "He hit her. Again and again. She didn't get up. I tried to make her get up. But she wouldn't. I took her to her pallet and tried to take care of her, but she never woke up."

"Oh, Roza. You aren't to blame."

Her chin came up. "I know. He is. That's why I want to kill him."

"We have to get out of here before we even think about that. Can you walk some more?"

A nod of brutal acceptance. "If I'm allowed to kill him, I will walk across the desert."

Cincinnati, Ohio
Tuesday, November 4, 8:45 p.m.

Faith closed her laptop, having checked her e-mail. That there was no reply from her boss to her message about her car accident made her worry. *I should have called him. I shouldn't have e-mailed.* But she'd been so tired and distracted at the time. She'd been shot at and then had seen a dead body under her grandmother's basement floor.

No longer tired, she was now restless, edgy. Sitting cross-legged in Deacon's bed, she wondered if he'd talked to her uncle Jeremy. What he'd found out.

She stretched out on the bed, trying to get the rest Dani had ordered, but a minute later she was up again. She should be exhausted, but she was too wired to sleep. Nerves jangling, she left the quiet of Novak's bedroom and went downstairs to the living room. Greg sat on a folding chair, hands gripping a game controller, his attention focused on the big-screen TV on the wall, where a virtual battle was raging.

All in total silence. Greg had taken off his hearing aids and set them aside and had muted the television. She wondered if he'd done it because Dani had told him that Faith was supposed to be sleeping or whether he preferred the silence. She edged into his peripheral vision, waiting until he spied her there.

He paused his game. "Am I bothering you?" he asked politely, his speech a little thick, but understandable.

"Not at all. Can you read my lips?"

The boy shrugged. "Well enough, I guess."

"Where is Dani?" Faith asked.

"She had an emergency at the shelter. I'm used to the Feds now. They're here because of you, aren't they?"

"Yes. Unfortunately."

"Because you're in trouble or in danger?"

"Mostly the second one." She pointed to the other chair. "Can I join you?"

He gave her a strange look. "Why?"

"Because I'd like to play." She moved her shoulders restlessly. "I'm too wired to sleep."

He frowned, then nodded. "Wired," he repeated. "I thought at first you said 'weird.'"

She grinned at him. The words did look very similar on the lips, she thought. "That too." She pointed to the game, a multiplayer military role-playing game. "You on a team?"

"Nah. I just picked these guys up. You want a different game?"

"I like to kill zombies."

Greg's smile was slow but real. "All right." Then he glanced guiltily toward the stairway to the bedrooms. "Except I'm supposed to be painting the walls. Not playing."

"How about I help you paint, then we'll have more time for play?"

He shook his head. "Deacon won't want you working on his house."

"Deacon doesn't have to know everything. Besides, I've got a lot of nervous energy. I'd normally go running, but I can't leave the house. So let's go paint a wall."

Greg put his controller away, then narrowed his eyes at her. They were like Dani's, one blue and one brown. Other than that, the boy looked just like Deacon in that old picture. They were like twins born eighteen years apart. "I heard that you are a therapist," he said.

"I was. Now I work at a bank." She winced inwardly. *At least I hope so after all this.*

"I don't want you doing therapy on me. Or asking me any questions about my suspension."

"Understood and agreed." She gestured for him to lead the way. Once in his room, she saw that someone had already started the job. One wall was a peaceful, misty green that complemented the other colors in the house. "Who picked the colors?"

"I did. We all picked our own bedroom colors, but Dani picked everything else."

"I like it," Faith said. "It's peaceful without being girlie. Did you paint all this so far?"

"Yeah. I was taking a break for a while downstairs. I'm

taller than you. I can paint the top half, you do the bottom. I won't be able to hear you if I'm not looking at you."

"Don't worry. I'm not looking to talk your ear off."

"That's what girls always say, but then they want to talk anyway."

"Not me. After the past day, I think I'm all talked out."

Cincinnati, Ohio
Tuesday, November 4, 9:05 p.m.

Keith put his arm protectively around Jeremy's shoulders. "I told you to let them go," he said softly. "Don't let them hurt you anymore."

"What day are you talking about, Dr. O'Bannion?" Deacon asked.

"That day twenty-three years ago," Jeremy answered, as if that explained it all.

"The day your father died?"

Jeremy looked up, a mild frown furrowing his brow. "No. It was a few days later."

Deacon felt the hairs on the back of his neck prickle. "The day Faith's mother died."

"No, the day before." Jeremy swallowed hard. "I loved my sister. But she sided with them and not me. It's the last memory I have of her."

"Jeremy," Keith said helplessly. "Don't do this to yourself."

"Do what?" Bishop murmured. "I'm afraid I don't understand."

"Neither did I," Jeremy said. "I still don't."

"They treated him like a . . ." Keith hissed out a breath through his teeth. "Like a pedophile. Just because he'd finally told his father what he was."

"What your father was?" Deacon asked, purposely misunderstanding.

One side of Jeremy's mouth lifted, as if Deacon's ploy had been too terribly transparent. "No, Agent Novak. What *I* was. What I am."

"Homosexual," Deacon supplied neutrally. "Not an easy topic for Catholic families in those days."

"No, it wasn't. It still isn't for many, but it was much worse then." Jeremy drew a deep breath and let it out. "It was the day before Maggie died. When my father's will was read."

"You were cut out," Deacon said.

"Not just me. Everyone. Except my mother, of course, but even she was short-changed." He smiled bitterly. "My father was not a kind man. He was harsh and very much believed in 'spare the rod, spoil the child.'"

"He was physically abusive?" Bishop asked.

"Physically, emotionally. All of it. When I was small, I used to think it was because we were poor and that he was under such strain. That's what my mother would say, after all."

"Poor?" Deacon asked with a frown. "I thought the family had always lived on the estate."

"We did. There had been plenty of money before we were born, but my parents spent millions on Joy's treatments."

"Joy had leukemia," Deacon recalled.

"Yes. My parents were desperate to find her a cure, but nothing they tried worked. After she died, there wasn't enough left for the land and the house and the taxes. It would have been far easier to sell it all, but my father wouldn't hear of that. It was O'Bannion land, the O'Bannion legacy." Jeremy rolled his eyes. "More like a curse."

"How did he save the legacy?" Deacon asked.

"He sold some other family assets and he invested the proceeds well, from what I'm told. I was only five years old when Joy died. And, of course, he wasn't without skills of his own. He was a genius in advertising. He took a hiatus during Joy's illness, but after her death, he made a very good living peddling other people's products. Within ten years, he'd replenished the family coffers. By the time he died, he was considered rich again. Of course, it did help," Jeremy added caustically, "that after Joy died, he never made the mistake of spending any of his money on his children ever again. But that's all water under the bridge, as my mother used to say. You were asking me about the day I realized I'd lost my family."

He's a bitter man, Deacon thought. "The day they read your father's will."

"Yes. When he died, my father left everything to the Foundation."

Bishop's dark brows shot up. "Everything? Nothing to his family?"

"Not a penny. My mother was left the house and the land, of course. He wasn't going to boot her ass to the street, after all, and he'd set up a trust for her living expenses until she died. But the rest of us . . . not a penny. I didn't need it. I was married to Della at the time. But Jordan was most displeased, and Maggie was distraught. I think she'd been counting on the money. Rick—Faith's father—was upset that Maggie was so upset. He had never wanted any of the O'Bannion money. I'd gotten the impression that this was something he and Maggie had argued about before, but they really argued that day and Faith started to cry."

Jeremy's expression grew pained. "I'd always liked Faith. She was a bright, funny kid. I only wanted to comfort her, I swear. I put my arm around her and she turned into a little tornado, clawing at me. Next thing I knew, Rick had me by the throat, threatening to cut off my balls if I touched her again. I fought him at first, thinking Maggie would pull him off me, but I saw her huddled against the wall with Faith in her arms. My own sister was looking at me like . . . well, like she believed it. That's the memory of Maggie that I carry."

Deacon had walked into this interview prepared to believe that Jeremy was twisted, even if he wasn't their killer. He knew that the man could be cleverly turning what had been a vile attempt to touch his own niece into a smoke screen that painted him as the victim.

The very fact that Deacon was having doubts disturbed him intensely.

"What did you do next, Dr. O'Bannion?" Bishop asked.

"I was devastated. I knew Rick had never felt comfortable around me, but he'd never actively hated me. Not like he did that day. And Maggie . . . I thought she loved me, but she looked like she wanted me to die. It was Faith who stopped her father from bashing my face in. She ran over and grabbed his arm, begged him not to hurt me. Rick shoved me out the door, told me never to show my face around his daughter again. Maggie didn't say a word in my defense. That's when I left that house and never looked back."

"What about your mother?" Bishop asked softly.

Jeremy's jaw tightened again. "She'd already stopped speaking to me."

Keith's hold around Jeremy's shoulders tightened. "Jeremy's father hadn't taken his coming out well, shall we say. His mother blamed his father's heart attack a few weeks later on Jeremy, instead of on the fact that the old man ate a fatty diet, smoked like a chimney, and had a trigger temper. The old woman never forgave him, till the day *her* miserable heart gave out."

"Yet you still hoped she'd leave the house to you?" Bishop asked sympathetically.

Jeremy shrugged. "O'Bannions have always owned the homestead. I figured she'd leave it to one of us. She left it to Faith and that was her right. Like I said, I don't need the money the sale of the property would have brought."

"You would have sold it?" Deacon asked.

"I certainly wouldn't have *lived* there." He shuddered. "Drafty old place. Probably has rats."

"What about O'Bannions always owning the homestead?" Bishop asked, one brow raised.

He shrugged. "Selling it would have been my final revenge against my parents. I would have sold the place to developers and slept with a smile on my face, thinking about them spinning in their side-by-side graves like rotisserie chickens. However, I fail to see what all this family history has to do with Faith's safety now."

"Someone doesn't want her to have the house," Deacon said simply. "If you don't want it and Jordan doesn't want it, who does?"

"Who said Jordan didn't want it?" Keith asked belligerently. "That bastard needs the cash."

"Keith, please," Jeremy murmured, but there was a glint in his eye, quickly hidden.

Bishop sat forward, her expression rapt. "Jordan needs money? Really? Why?"

Keith leaned toward Bishop, his tone confidential. "His gallery is always in debt. He has to sleep with rich women to keep it going. Usually they're married rich women."

Pink genie gymnasts. "And you know this how?" Deacon asked.

Keith shrugged. "It's my job to know. I handle Jeremy's security."

Why would a med-school professor need security? Deacon looked over his shoulder at Hailey, who'd been hovering in the doorway. "What is your job, Hailey?"

"Hailey is my housekeeper," Jeremy said. "She is not part of your case. Now, if there is nothing else?"

"As a matter of fact, there is. We'd like to talk to your son Stone. Is he here?"

Jeremy froze for a split second, then smiled sadly. "No. He's not. I haven't seen Stone in months. The last I heard, he was covering a riot in Turkey. Or was that Greece, Keith?"

"Definitely Turkey," Keith said. He came to his feet. "I'll see you out, Detectives."

Turkey, my ass. They were lying for Stone. The agent outside had documented that Stone had left the house at eleven and returned at four fifteen. Why would they think they needed to lie?

Jeremy also rose. "Please give Faith my regards. She was such a pretty little girl. I'm sure she's grown into a lovely woman."

"She has," Deacon said. "I'll be sure to pass on your good wishes." He waited until he was in the parlor doorway before turning back to Jeremy. "I have one more question, sir. Why did you tell your father you were gay when you did? You were married, had two sons. By my calculations, your ex-wife was pregnant with your daughter. What made you decide to come out to your father then?"

Jeremy's lips thinned. "I didn't 'decide.' I was outed by my brother, a preemptive move on his part. He knew I was about to tell our father that he'd misused Foundation funds. When I tried to tell him that Jordan had done this to obfuscate his own crime, he didn't care. He threw me out. Said he never wanted to see me again. And he didn't. The next time I was at the house was the day of his burial. The last time was the day his will was read. My family considered me dead to them long ago. The feeling has been mutual."

"You could have denied it."

Jeremy lifted a shoulder. "I was caught off guard. And I've never been a very good liar."

Which is actually true, Deacon thought. Jeremy had clearly been lying about Stone's whereabouts—a fact that was underscored when Deacon's phone buzzed a moment later, the vibration pattern the one he'd assigned to the agent sitting out front. He glanced at the text and hid his surge of adrenaline. *Stone O'Bannion headed to guesthouse.*

"We have to attend to this," he said. "Thank you for your time. Detective Bishop?"

Bishop had glanced at her own phone and was also nodding her thanks to the two men.

A scowling Keith opened the door and slammed it closed behind them.

Deacon walked into the front garden, pretending to talk on his phone while he and Bishop wandered to the far corner of the house. Just in time to see Stone O'Bannion disappearing into the guesthouse out back. His shoes were muddy, as were the cuffs of his trousers. It hadn't rained recently. There was no mud anywhere in the area.

Where have you been, Stone? Digging graves? You fucking sonofabitch.

"I'll take the left," Bishop murmured.

Deacon nodded grimly. Drawing their weapons, they started after him.

Eastern Kentucky
Tuesday, November 4, 9:35 p.m.

It was a sign. An honest-to-God printed sign, the first manmade thing Corinne had seen since they'd made their escape from the cabin from hell. It was tall and brown and too far away to read in the dark.

She stopped to catch her breath, and Roza sank to her knees, still chanting, "I get to kill him. I get to kill him."

As if I don't have enough problems, Corinne thought miserably. She'd allowed the child her hate because it was the only thing that kept her moving. Corinne figured the bastard deserved it. But she knew what it meant to kill another human being. *Even one trying to kill you.*

It hurt you. Changed you. *It steals a part of your soul.* And Roza had lost so much already. Corinne hated the thought that she'd allowed, even encouraged, that seed of murderous hate to flourish, but if they both died because Roza was rocking away in the woods, it wouldn't matter. She'd get the girl to safety and allow the therapists to sort it out later.

"Roza, I need your help in reading that sign."

"You can read," Roza grumbled.

"And you can walk. I need your help."

Roza pushed to her hands and knees, her head hanging. "I can't walk anymore. I'm tired. My feet hurt." Close to a whine, she sounded so perfectly eleven that Corinne smiled.

"So do mine. I know you're not used to so much walking. But we don't have a choice."

"I get to kill him," Roza muttered, the words sounding more like a march chant than a threat now. She got up, and together they shuffled toward the sign.

"Look!" Corinne cried, excited. The sign marked a trail. "It's a path?"

Corinne laughed, elation making her giddy. "Yes. Go up to the sign and read it." She could read it herself at this distance, but she wanted to keep Roza awake and engaged.

DANIEL BOONE NATIONAL FOREST. The arrow to the left said, MOREHEAD, 24 MI. The arrow to the right, RT. 60, 12 MI.

Morehead is a town, Corinne thought. *They'll have police. Help.* But the path to Route 60 was half the distance. They'd go that way, flag down a passing motorist, and use their phone to call for help.

" 'Twelve mi,' " Roza read. "What's 'mi'?"

"Miles. That's twelve miles. You can walk that. I know you can." But maybe not tonight.

Reality was quickly eroding Corinne's elation. It was dark. And cold. They needed shelter.

"Let's go a little further. I'm looking for a place where we can sleep for the night."

Roza looked up. "Promise?"

"I promise." Corinne glanced toward the sky. "Come on."

Roza tugged on Corinne's shirt, then pointed back into the woods, the way they'd come. "What about that house?"

Corinne squinted in the direction of Roza's finger and her mouth fell open, amazed. It wasn't a house, but it *was* a structure of some kind. The two of them hobbled, but quickly, their energy renewed at the sight of the strange little box built atop four stilts.

"What is it?" Roza asked. "A tree house?"

"No, because it's not up a tree. It's a deer blind." Corinne looked down to see Roza's forehead scrunch in puzzlement. "Hunters hide here and wait for the deer to come along."

"That doesn't sound fair."

Corinne wasn't touching that one with a ten-foot pole. "Let's go up."

Roza went first, tugging on the door. "It's locked."

"I've already picked two locks. Let's make it three."

Cincinnati, Ohio
Tuesday, November 4, 9:35 p.m.

The first wall was done and didn't look bad at all, Faith thought. She and Greg had found a comfortable working rhythm that required no words. At last she was getting tired. Her brain was finally starting to slow down. When she eventually did sleep, maybe she wouldn't dream.

They'd started on the second coat when Faith caught the boy stealing curious glances, his expression saying he wanted to talk. But she kept quiet, swallowing back a smile when he stated that he was going to get some food—and then maybe his hearing aids.

She was loading her roller with more paint when she heard the doorbell. Her first thought was that Greg wouldn't have heard it and that Agent Colby would answer it. Her heart nearly stopped when she heard the door open and Greg asking, "Yes?"

She ran down the stairs to see Greg standing at the open door, talking to a man. "Greg, no!" she shouted, and he wheeled to look at her, startled.

"It's only a delivery guy with a package for Deacon. Chill, Faith. You almost scared me to death."

A louder, male voice intruded. "Put the package on the floor and your hands in the air, sir. Greg, back away and walk over to Faith. Leave the box where it is."

Agent Colby, she thought. He'd somehow come up behind the man. She could see the deliveryman pale. Where was Agent Pope?

Even paler than the deliveryman, Greg did what the agent said, backing away from the box and joining Faith.

"Faith, go back upstairs to the bedroom and close the door," Colby said grimly. "Do not open a window or pull back a shade. Sit on the floor, up against the wall on either side of the window. Do not come out until I tell you to. We're on lockdown until further notice."

Faith took Greg's trembling hand and helped him do as Colby demanded.

"What's going on?" the boy asked, shaking all over.

"I'm not sure. But you weren't supposed to open the door, Greg," she said gently.

"It was only a deliveryman."

"That's what he says. But you don't know who he really is."

He shook his head. "We can't sit against the wall by the window. The paint's wet."

"Then we sit in the closet. Come on." She turned on the closet light and motioned him in first. "We'll leave the door open."

She wished like hell she hadn't left her handbag in Deacon's room. She wanted her gun. Unhappy with her unarmed situation, she saw an X-Acto blade Deacon had used to scrape old paint from the windowpane and grabbed it. Then she stood inside the closet door, waiting.

Cincinnati, Ohio
Tuesday, November 4, 9:35 p.m.

Standing to the right of the guesthouse door with Bishop on the left, Deacon knocked.

"I'm not hungry," Stone called from inside. "I don't need any food."

Deacon knocked again but said nothing. If they had to go in, they'd identify themselves, but right now he was hoping to bring Stone to the door.

A labored sigh came from inside the house. "Fine. Come in. It's unlocked."

Deacon gave Bishop a shrug and a nod. She pushed the door open, took a quick look, and walked inside, Deacon a half step behind her. "Thank you," she said. "We appreciate the invite."

Expression flattened with shock, Stone whirled around, one hand sliding under his jacket.

Bishop raised her gun. "Don't do that, please."

Indignation filled his eyes. "Who are you? What the hell gives you the right to barge in?"

"You told us to come in. I'm Detective Bishop, Cincinnati Homicide. This is my partner, Special Agent Deacon Novak, FBI." She showed him her badge, Deacon following suit. "We just have a few questions for you. If you'd pull your jacket back, please? Then put your gun on the floor. It'll be more comfortable if we can chat without pointing guns at each other."

Stone looked from Bishop to Deacon, then slowly did as Bishop asked. "I didn't invite two cops into my house. I thought you were someone else. You did not identify yourselves."

Bishop blinked at him innocently. "Of course we did. Just now. If you missed it, I can repeat it for you. If you'd have a seat, I'd be ever so grateful."

Stone sat, his mouth curving in a confident smile. "To what do I owe this dubious honor?"

He'd focused on Bishop, almost ignoring Deacon. Which was fine. Bishop could more than handle herself, giving Deacon the opportunity to watch. The fact that he was a suspected killer aside, Stone O'Bannion gave off a vibe that Deacon simply did not like.

"We're investigating a murder in which your name has surfaced," Bishop said. "If you'll indulge us?"

"Can I stop you?"

Bishop smiled. "Not without looking guilty. Could you tell us where you were on Friday night between eleven and one?"

"Would you mind putting your gun away?" Stone asked blandly. "I'm cooperating, as you can see. I'd be much more cooperative without a gun in my face."

Bishop slid her weapon back into its holster but kept her hand on the gun's grip. "Better, I hope. Where were you Friday night? Between eleven and one?"

Deacon's phone buzzed, and it took him a moment to place the assignee of the vibration pattern, but when he did, his whole body stilled. *Agent Colby.* Keeping his own expression as bland as Stone's, he glanced at the messages and his heart stopped. Actually stopped.

Have a situation. Pope stabbed. Will need new safe house for witness. More soon.

Deacon's pulse stumbled into an erratic rhythm. *Faith,* he thought. *And Greg and Dani.*

"Agent Novak?" Stone asked mockingly. "Anything wrong? Perhaps you need to leave?"

Deacon fought back the urge to knock the smirk off the

asshole's face, pasting a bland smile back on his own. "Not at all." *Be all right, Faith. Please be all right.*

And Agent Pope, too, of course. What the fucking hell had happened?

"You were about to tell Detective Bishop where you were on Friday night." Deacon caught the flicker of worry in Bishop's eye. "While I make a quick phone call."

"I wasn't going to tell you," Stone said. "But I was going to ask why you want to know."

Deacon heard Bishop reiterate their titles as he dialed his house, wishing that he'd gotten Faith another cell phone already.

"When I ask where you were on Friday," Bishop was saying, "you need to stop wasting my time and tell me."

"I don't suppose you're terribly worried about my time," Stone flung back. "Or my Fourth Amendment rights. You two can take your questions straight to hell, as far as I'm concerned."

Deacon's home phone went to voice mail, so he hung up and texted Greg's phone. *R u ok?*

A new text came through, this one from Adam. *Just heard abt trouble @ your house. On my way there.* Deacon exhaled quietly as three certainties presented themselves.

First, Adam would take care of things. He might not like Faith, but he loved Greg and Dani. Deacon texted a brief, *Thx. Hurry.*

Second, whoever had threatened Deacon's family would pay. He kind of hoped Stone was involved because he'd really enjoy wiping that damn smirk off the guy's face.

Third, Stone couldn't have stabbed Agent Pope. Colby and Pope checked with each other every fifteen minutes, and it was a forty-minute drive from Deacon's house to this one. That didn't mean Stone was not guilty. It simply meant that there might be two men involved.

But Stone held the position of lead suspect at this point because he was twitchy, his father had covered for him, he'd left the house at the right times, and he had mud on his boots.

And to top it all off, I don't like him.

Deacon's shoulders sagged in relief when a new text popped up from Greg's number. *It's Faith. We're okay. Hid-*

ing in closet. Colby has house on lockdown. Don't know any more. Will call soon. Be careful. Don't worry about us. Just catch this SOB.

That she would tell him to be careful made him smile inside. Her admonition to catch the SOB helped him focus. Pocketing his phone, he looked up to see Bishop watching Stone coldly as Stone stared at them, bored. Or pretending to be.

"So glad you could join us, Special Agent Novak," Stone drawled. "Do you have anything you'd like to share with the class?"

Arrogant sonofabitch. But Deacon only smiled. "I'm sorry I interrupted as you started to tell Detective Bishop where you were on Friday night."

Irritation blazed in Stone's eyes. His gaze rose from Bishop's toes to her face, pausing meaningfully to leer at her breasts. "You show me yours first."

Deacon wanted to blacken those leering eyes, but Bishop didn't blink. "You're a reporter," she said. "I'm surprised you haven't heard about all the brouhaha out at the family manor."

"Not my family," Stone said. "Nothing to do with me, whatever it is."

"You're not even the least bit curious?" Bishop pushed. "What kind of reporter are you?"

"The kind that asks the questions," he answered coolly. "Not the kind that answers them."

Oh yeah, Deacon thought. *It'll be a pleasure to take this guy down.*

Cincinnati, Ohio
Tuesday, November 4, 9:55 p.m.

The door opened, and Faith held her breath, clutching her pathetic little blade.

"Dr. Corcoran?" Colby asked.

She let the breath out. "We're here. In the closet."

Colby came into the room, no smile on his face. "Agent Pope has been stabbed."

"By the deliveryman?" Faith asked, horrified.

"I don't know, but I don't think so. The deliveryman is in the living room in handcuffs."

"Who stabbed Agent Pope?" Faith demanded. "Is he seriously hurt?"

"Don't know who stabbed him. I found him against the side of the house, bleeding pretty badly, but he's conscious. The knife's still in his chest. Someone had dragged him from the back of the house. I've called a forensics team in. For now, the house is on lockdown. I've got a message into Agent Novak asking for a new safe house for both of you."

Greg's eyes were huge. "What kind of knife is it?" he demanded.

Colby didn't answer, deliberately ignoring the question. "I'm going back to Pope," he said loudly in a way that annoyed Faith, like he was talking down to Greg. "I need the two of you to stay put in this closet. Do you understand? Stay put."

He turned for the door, and the next five seconds were a blur. Greg leapt from the closet to clutch a handful of the back of Colby's suit coat. "What kind of knife was it?" he shouted.

Snarling, Colby spun, and, pinning Greg's arm behind his back, shoved him face-first against the freshly painted wall. "Not a wise move, kid. What the hell is wrong with you?"

Greg's face was a contorted mass of pain, fear, and misery. One cheek pressed to the wall, tears ran down the other side of his face. "What kind of knife?" he whispered.

"Agent Colby, let him go! You're hurting him!" Faith snapped. Greg's hearing aids were in, so she assumed he could hear her. She drew a breath, fighting to stay calm. "Let him go. You need to see to Agent Pope. I'll take care of Greg."

Colby stepped back, breathing hard. "Call me if you need me."

Faith nodded grimly, realizing that not only had she left her gun in Novak's bedroom, she'd left the cordless landline in the kitchen. How quickly she'd moved from not trusting cops and taking care of herself to total, mindless complacency.

Because I'm tired. I'm tired of all of this. And now one more person was hurt.

She waited until Colby had left the room before gently turning Greg around. His right side, shoulder to knee, was covered in green paint, as was his cheek. He pulled away, slumping against the ruined wall and sliding to sit on the floor, his chest heaving like a bellows.

He turned his face away. "Leave me alone."

Faith knelt beside him, gripping his chin hard enough to force him to look up at her. "Why did you ask about the knife, Greg? I need to know."

"It doesn't matter," he said thickly.

"It does. I assumed that whoever did that to Agent Pope was here for me, but you panicked about the knife. Why? This is important. If this attack wasn't about killing me, the police need to know. They might miss a lead elsewhere if they're looking for clues here. People have already died, Greg. More might. Please tell me."

Greg closed his eyes. "Some kids at school threatened to hurt Dani."

Faith exhaled heavily. Novak had said that Greg had made a bad decision for the right reasons, and now Dani's reaction when she and Greg had argued earlier made a lot more sense. She squeezed his chin lightly until he opened his eyes. "You got suspended for protecting Dani?"

Greg nodded miserably, biting the inside of his cheek, trying not to cry. "They said they'd make me pay. They said they'd make her pay. I didn't know they'd do this." He dropped his head back against the wall, closing his eyes again. "Everything is so fucked up, and it's all my fault. I fuck up everything I touch."

"I know how you feel."

His eyes opened, one blue and one brown. "You can't."

"Oh, yes, I can. When this is all over, I'll tell you a story that'll turn your hair whiter than Deacon's." She was encouraged by his single chuff of laughter. "I promised you I wouldn't do therapy on you and I won't. But if you want to talk, I can listen very well. Now, let me get something to clean the paint off your face. You've got a 'Hulk-smash' thing going on."

Greg laughed again, two chuffs this time. Then sighed. "I ruined the wall."

"Technically, Agent Colby did that, but he's running on adrenaline right now. As are we all. Do you have any clothes here yet?"

He shook his head. "No, but I can borrow a pair of Deacon's sweats."

"Okay." She smiled up at him. "You've got white and

green streaks in your hair now. You could start a new fashion trend. Let me use your phone so I can call Dani and tell her what happened so that she can take appropriate safety measures."

He handed her his phone and Faith dialed, unsurprised when Dani picked up on the first ring. "Who is this?" she demanded, panic in her voice.

"It's Faith."

"Oh God. That's a relief. Greg only texts. I thought something was wrong."

"Something is. Greg and I are okay. He's worried that you might not be because Agent Pope's been stabbed." Quickly, she filled Dani in. "Do you have security guards at your shelter?"

"Yeah," Dani said shakily. "We have a retired cop who volunteers. Will Pope be all right?"

"I hope so." Faith could hear sirens. "Looks like the cavalry's coming. I'll keep you up to speed. Just be careful. I don't know what happened to Greg or what kind of trouble he's in, but he seems to think this threat was directed toward you, not me."

A weary sigh. "I'll be careful. Tell him I love him."

"I will." Faith hung up and returned the phone to Greg, who had watched her every move. "Dani says she loves you." She got up, suddenly ready to sleep. *Adrenaline crash.* "I'm going to get the phone from the kitchen and a wet cloth to wash the paint from your face. Stay here. I'll be back."

As she hurried through the living room, she spared a pitied glance for the terrified deliveryman still kneeling on the carpet, his hands cuffed behind him.

"I don't know what's happening," she said before he could ask.

Outside she could hear raised voices, but no specific conversations. The windows were thick and extremely well insulated. Novak had wanted his house to be secure.

"I'm just delivering a package," the man said, his voice trembling. "That's all."

"What company are you with?" Faith asked.

"Speedy-24. We do around-the-clock deliveries. I swear I didn't do anything wrong."

Faith crouched next to the box, noting the return address without touching it. *Daphne Montgomery, Hunt Valley, Mary-*

land. A Daphne had signed the group photo on Novak's desk, so this was likely a legit delivery. "I'm afraid that you walked into the wrong place at the wrong time," she said sympathetically. "Hopefully, we can get you out of here quickly."

She grabbed the cordless phone, then ran back to Novak's bedroom for her gun, looping her purse over her shoulder and opening the flap so that she could get to her weapon if she needed to.

Feeling far more confident, she called Novak's cell phone from the landline as she wet a cloth in his bathroom.

He answered immediately, his voice almost a whisper, but his relief as clear as if he'd shouted. "Thank God. Colby says you two are all right. Are you?"

"Yes, but Greg's shaken up. He told me that he thinks Pope was stabbed by whoever threatened Dani."

A beat of silence. "Did you tell Colby?"

"Not yet. Should I?"

"No. Let me do it. Thanks for calling me. My heart stopped when he sent me that text."

"Don't worry. I'll take care of Greg, and I called Dani to tell her to be careful. She says she has security at the shelter where she is."

Another beat of silence. "Thank you."

"I didn't do anything," she said softly.

"You're taking care of my family. That's a lot. Just tell Greg . . . Hell, I don't even know."

"How about that you love him?" Faith supplied.

"Yeah," he said gruffly. "That. Thanks. I'm in an interview now, but I'll call when I can."

"Deacon, wait."

"Yes?" he asked, his whisper going from gruff to . . . intimate.

The one word curled around her, leaving her warm. And missing him fiercely. "Greg answered the door for a delivery. I tried to stop him, but he'd already opened the front door. Anyway, the package needed to be signed for. The return address is Daphne Montgomery in Hunt Valley. If you could verify with her that she sent a package, they could uncuff the poor deliveryman."

"Daphne?" She could hear his smile. "I can't right now, but I can give you her number. You could call her. I'll send her contact info to Greg's phone. I'll call you when I can."

Chapter Twenty-three

Deacon hung up, swallowing his exhale. *They're both okay.* He met Bishop's worried eyes and gave her a small nod, saw her relax.

Stone O'Bannion watched them both warily. "What's going on here?"

Bishop pointed to his shoes. "Where have you been digging, Mr. O'Bannion?"

Stone didn't blink. "Why is that your business, Detective?"

Bishop was annoyed but hid it behind a serene smile. "Please answer my question, Mr. O'Bannion. Unless, of course, you feel it incriminates you in some way."

Stone made a show of rolling his eyes. "I've been interrogated by gorilla-thugs of Third World dictators far scarier than you two, so don't even try to intimidate me." He cast a glance at Deacon. "Although I have to say that none of them have looked like you, Agent Novak." He returned his gaze to Bishop, openly appreciative. "Or you, Detective."

Bishop didn't rise to the bait. "Perhaps you missed part of our introduction. I'm a *homicide* detective. Agent Novak and I are conducting a *murder* investigation. You and your father have come up as persons of interest."

"Oh no," Stone drawled. "The dreaded 'persons of interest.' My heart is pounding in fear."

But his eyes had flickered, Deacon thought. He was rattled, even if he didn't let it show.

"It would save us a lot of time if you just told us where you've been," Deacon said. "So that we can eliminate you as a suspect."

Stone leaned back, purposefully propping one leg on the other knee so that his boots were clearly visible. *Taunting us.* "I don't have to give an account of my whereabouts to you or to anyone else. I regret that you're wasting your time, but frankly, that's not my problem."

Deacon's phone buzzed, an incoming call. He glanced at the number, not recognizing it.

"You've got to be kidding me." Stone rolled his eyes. "Go ahead. Take the call." He gestured widely, like a sultan on his throne. "My time is obviously your time."

Bishop had stiffened at his broad gesture, expecting a physical attack, but when Stone did no more, she gave Deacon a nod. "Go ahead. I've got this."

Deacon stepped back, watching Stone flash a perfect smile that had to have cost Jeremy and his ex-wife thousands in orthodontia bills. "Of course you do, honey," Stone said with just enough sarcasm. "It's what sidekicks do. They watch the store while the boss is away."

Deacon shook his head. Stone was a real prick, but to her credit, Bishop didn't even blink.

"Novak," he murmured into the phone.

"Agent Novak, this is Meredith Fallon. I'm here with Arianna Escobar."

Deacon went still inside but kept his own expression slightly mocking for Stone's benefit, very aware that he could be staring at her abductor. "I'm in an interview, Doctor," he said, hoping Fallon would take the hint and not mention Arianna again.

A slight pause. "Of course. My charge is awake and would like to speak to your charge. I've tried to get my charge to speak to me, but she's very insistent."

Translation: Arianna would speak to no one but Faith. Deacon's mind scrambled as he considered the logistics of Dr. Fallon's request. They needed to get Faith to the hospital before Arianna went back to sleep. With Agent Pope injured and Agent Colby dealing with the scene, he needed someone else he could trust with Faith's safety.

"I can't make that happen right now, but I can text you the name of someone who can."

"You should hurry, Agent Novak. She won't be awake for long."

"Understood." Hanging up, Deacon sent her Adam's number and then texted Adam to expect a call from Fallon. *Please do what she asks. Keep Faith safe.* He hesitated. *For me,* he added, then hit SEND.

He stepped back into Bishop and Stone's cozy little circle. Stone sat with both arms outstretched, resting on the back of the sofa. Bishop stood at attention, her hand resting on the weapon holstered on her belt.

"I trust your business is taken care of?" Stone said. "Your assistant here kept a good watch, but I'm a little short on time. I'd appreciate it if you could get right to the rubber hose, so we can get this little Q and A over with."

"All right," Deacon said affably. As long as Stone was here with them, he couldn't be anywhere else, like terrorizing Faith or Arianna. And if he and Bishop played this right, he might lead them to Corinne and Roza. "You have a cousin. Faith."

Stone shook his head, his expression mockingly helpful. "Sorry. Name doesn't ring a bell."

"That's a shame, because she remembers you. She's the daughter of Jeremy's older sister."

"Ah. Aunt Maggie." Stone smiled, but thinly, his eyes growing hard. "Her name I know. I like family trees, you see. They hold so many secrets. I take it my cousin was murdered? You two being *homicide* detectives after all."

He asked it carelessly, as if speaking about a walk in the park. Or a game.

Deacon's anger bubbled, but he kept his own mask intact. "Your cousin is still alive, but not for lack of trying. Last night was the sixth attempt on her life since your grandmother died."

"She wasn't my grandmother," Stone replied, showing no reaction to the news of the attempts on Faith's life.

Deacon met the man's hard eyes. "Jeremy adopted you legally, isn't that correct?" He watched Stone's wary nod. "Then Faith's grandmother is your grandmother, too."

"She disowned him. Therefore ..." Stone scissored his fingers. "Snip, snip. No relationship. No Aunt Maggie. No Cousin Faith. Please hurry, Agent Novak. I've tried to be hospitable, considering you forced your way into my home, but I do have a schedule to keep."

Deacon looked around. "You live here? Full-time?"

"Only when the cravings call. My father's partner is an amazing chef. His spinach frittata is to die for. I'd offer you some, but I polished off last night's leftovers for breakfast this morning."

Bishop's smile became genuinely amused. "Your dad says he hasn't seen you in months. That you're currently on assignment in Turkey, covering ... what was it, Novak?"

"A riot," Deacon supplied. "We didn't believe him, of course. Because we knew you were here last night. We've had this house under surveillance."

Stone's face hardened, a dark flush spreading on his cheeks. "By whose order?"

"Mine," Deacon said flatly. "You left at eleven last night, returning at four fifteen a.m. That allows sufficient time to get to Cincinnati and back after making an attempt on your cousin's life."

Stone sat up slowly, fury in his eyes. "You are accusing me of this?" he asked quietly.

"We know you're a crack shot," Deacon continued. "And that was some mighty fine shooting last night."

"The man you killed in that hotel room was a month away from retirement," Bishop said quietly. "He was just trying to support his family. Now his family has to go on without him." She clapped her hands twice, the sound echoing hollowly. "Bravo, Mr. O'Bannion."

Stone's chest rose and fell with the deep breaths he took. "You are seriously *accusing* me?"

Deacon pointed to Stone's boots. "You have dirty boots and dirt under your otherwise well-manicured nails."

"Digging," Bishop said grimly. "What were you burying, Stone? Or who?"

Stone's face froze for a split second before he relaxed into a smile that grated on Deacon's nerves. "You said my cousin had an *attempt* made on her life," Stone said. "That means that she's still alive, yes? So who might I have been burying?"

Bishop's eyes flashed in raw rage. "The locksmith maybe? Or the Earl Power tech? Or maybe Corinne Longstreet? Did you have to kill her, Stone? Where did you put their bodies? Their families need to know."

Stone had paled, but barely enough to notice. A beat later his eyes narrowed, calculating. Then his mouth curved and he was back to appearing bored. "I'm afraid you two are barking up the wrong tree. I don't know what you're talking about."

Deacon used Stone's moment of distraction to sit on the sofa and grab his hand before the man could react. "Then may I have the dirt from under your nails, Mr. O'Bannion? The dirt will know exactly what we're talking about."

Stone ripped his hand away, all pretense gone. "Fuck you. No. Arrest me or leave."

They couldn't arrest him. Deacon knew it. They had nothing that wasn't circumstantial. Once they took him into custody, they'd have only seventy-two hours to hold him, at which point they'd either have to arraign him or let him go. Stone seemed to know that, too, which was infuriating.

Still, Deacon had gotten what he wanted—he'd brushed enough of the dirt from Stone's hands to provide a sample to the forensics lab. If they backed off now, Stone might lead them back to where he'd been digging. Rising, Deacon inclined his head. "Next time we'll have a warrant."

Stone came to his feet, fists clenched at his sides, his eyes dark, his stance pure menace. "Get out of this house," he gritted from behind clenched teeth. *"Now."*

In a repeat of Keith's farewell from the main house, he slammed the door as soon as Deacon and Bishop were on the front stoop.

"Evidence bag, please," Deacon said. He brushed the precious grains of dirt on the palm of his hand into the plastic bag she supplied. "His hands were still dirty," he explained. "The dirt under his fingernails would have been more ideal, but he wasn't going to give us that. I only asked for it to distract him. Hopefully, the lab can get something from this. It may not be admissible in court, but at least we can narrow down where he's been."

Bishop looked over her shoulder. "He's watching us."

Stone had been glaring through his front window while Deacon brushed the dirt into the bag. Deacon had hoped he would. "I know. He'll either be more careful from now on or so rattled that he makes a mistake. Let's hope for the second, but turn up the heat just to be certain."

They walked back to the sedan, Deacon pausing to inspect Stone's red Corvette, parked behind the Bentley. It's hood was still warm. "Muddy, like his boots."

Bishop unlocked the sedan and waited until they were both inside. "He's hiding something big. But I don't know that he's our killer. We're looking for a man so careful that he left nothing behind to identify him in that hotel room. He's been killing for years and hasn't been caught. Nobody even suspected he was using that old house until now."

"And only because Faith tried to move in," Deacon said. "He's too smart to leave a scene with dirty hands. Stone wanted us to stay. Wanted us to tell him what we knew."

She shrugged. "He *is* a reporter."

"'The kind that asks the questions. Not the kind that answers them,'" Deacon mimicked. "Asshole."

Bishop laughed. "Agreed. But I did startle him when I asked who he'd been burying." She sobered. "And when I mentioned the locksmith and the Earl Power tech."

"You really got his attention when you mentioned Corinne Longstreet."

"I was hoping to," Bishop said, her eyes narrowing in satisfaction.

Deacon was impressed. She'd performed her role to perfection. *I was too angry and distracted with Faith.*

"We'll bump up surveillance here," he said. "Keep one agent on the house itself and another to tail Stone." He looked back at the house, saw the curtains move, a large shadow behind them. A glance up showed a similar movement on the second floor, the hand on the curtain much smaller. *Hailey.* "I'll make that at least two agents on the house. I'd like to know why a med-school professor needs a bodyguard. And what Hailey's job really is."

"You don't believe Keith and Jeremy are a couple?"

"I don't *dis*believe it," Deacon said. "But there's more there than simple domestic bliss. Why does Keith keep tabs on Jordan?"

"Especially if Jeremy walked away from the family and never looked back. I wonder if Jordan is still dipping into the Foundation for spending money."

Deacon wondered the same thing. "He told Faith he didn't need the money and was glad she'd inherited the house."

"Let me guess," Bishop said. "He figured Jeremy would have fought him for it. One of those boys is lying. Or both. Jeremy never took his right hand out of his pocket. Carrie Washington said that those sutures were done by a real expert."

"He may have lost enough dexterity that he can't perform surgery anymore, but that doesn't mean his hand is useless. If he killed ten women, he'd want to make it look that way. I think he, Keith, and Stone let us see what they wanted us to see and told us what they wanted us to know."

Bishop started the car's engine with a scowl. "Wily rich bastards. So, where to? The university to ask his students if Dr. Jeremy's a perv or back to the city?"

"Back to the city. That call was from Meredith Fallon. Arianna asked for Faith again. I asked Adam to get her to the hospital. We might get there before she drifts back to sleep."

"And the text? The one that had you going as white as your damn hair?"

Deacon told her about the attack on Agent Pope. And, more reluctantly, about Greg's possible connection.

"Shit, Novak. You need to tell Colby," she said when he'd finished.

"I know. I was hoping to keep this quiet until I got a lawyer for Greg, but that's not going to happen now, dammit." His curse had little heat, though. *I'm so damn tired.*

So tired and mentally scattered that he'd forgotten to text Daphne's information to Greg's phone. That poor deliveryman was probably still sitting cuffed on his living room floor. He sent the text and closed his eyes for just a second. "Head back to Cinci," he told Bishop. "I'll call for more surveillance here and update the agent on duty. Then I'll call Colby."

What he wanted was to sleep in his nice, soft bed. He wanted to go home. *To Faith. Preferably also in my nice, soft bed.* She was like an addiction, stuck in his system. All he wanted to do was take her somewhere quiet and make love to her again, slowly this time. But he didn't have that luxury. Not if he wanted to keep her alive.

Cincinnati, Ohio
Tuesday, November 4, 10:40 p.m.

What is taking them so long? But Faith kept the question to herself. No one had given them an all-clear, so she and Greg could do no more than sit on the floor and wait in tense silence.

Greg's phone buzzed, making them both jump. "It's for you from Deacon," he said, handing it to her. "Why don't you have your own phone? Everybody has a phone."

"Mine got busted," she said, reading the message. Deacon had finally texted her the contact information for the sender of the package. Hopefully, this meant that he was finished interviewing Uncle Jeremy. She was afraid to even wonder at the outcome.

Greg eyed her suspiciously. "Taken-by-the-cops busted or broken busted?"

"Both," Faith said dryly as she dialed the number Novak had sent.

"Hello?" a woman answered cautiously, her twang very pronounced.

"I'd like to speak with Daphne Montgomery, please."

"This is Daphne." Her voice hardened. "Who is this? How did you get this number?"

"My name is Faith Corcoran. I'm a friend of Deacon Novak. I'm sorry to call so late, but it's important."

"Where is Deacon?" Daphne demanded. "Is he all right?"

"He's fine." Faith used her most reassuring tone. "He asked me to call."

"Why did he—? Wait. Faith Corcoran? You were with him last night when he got shot."

Faith hesitated, uncomfortable discussing the situation with a stranger. Except that this woman was clearly important to Novak. "Yes," she admitted. "I was there."

"I'd say you were a sight more than *there*, sugar. From what I hear, you were the target."

Faith frowned. None of the newsfeeds had named her as the intended target. At least they hadn't when she'd last looked, but that had been before she and Greg had started painting. "What did you hear and where did you hear it?"

A slight pause. "Do you know who I am, Faith?"

"I know that you're Deacon's friend. Why?" A sliver of doubt injected itself into her mind. "Are you more than that?" Faith winced, hearing the jealousy in her own voice.

A husky laugh. "I'm only his friend, sugar. But my husband is his old boss."

"Ah. He'd be the JC in the picture you signed for him."

"Special Agent Joseph Carter," Daphne confirmed. "I nearly had heart failure when I heard Deacon had been shot, but Joseph said he wasn't hurt. That better be true, or he's in trouble."

Faith wondered who would be in trouble — Joseph or Deacon. "He was wearing Kevlar, so thankfully, all he has is a bad bruise. He pushed me out of the way."

"I'd have expected nothing else from our Deacon. Why are you calling me, Faith?"

Oh, right. "To verify that you sent him a package."

"I did, through Speedy-24 Courier Service. Why?"

"That's good. Now we can let the deliveryman go."

Greg was watching, eyes narrowed. "Told you he really was a legit deliveryman."

"Who was that?" Daphne asked. "What deliveryman? You're not making sense."

"That was Deacon's brother, Greg. He opened the door to the deliveryman, who had the misfortune of arriving with your package at a very bad time. The delivery looked suspicious."

"You're in Deacon's *house*? And he's not there? What kind of friend are you, exactly?"

Faith blushed, suddenly glad Daphne couldn't see her face as everything she and Novak had done in his bedroom came rushing back. "The kind of friend he gives your number to, I suppose," she hedged.

A short pause, then a delighted chuckle. "How long have you known our Deacon?"

Faith checked the time on Greg's phone. "About twenty-nine hours."

"That long, huh?" Daphne sounded amused.

"It's been a very full twenty-nine hours," she said quietly.

"So I've heard," Daphne said, her amusement gone. "Are *you* all right, Faith?"

Sudden tears pricked at Faith's eyelids. "Sure," she said unsteadily. "I will be." *As soon as Deacon comes home.* She cleared her throat. "Is the box you sent him perishable? Because it's likely to be taken as evidence."

"No, don't let them take it as evidence," Daphne protested. "Why?"

"Because one of the two agents guarding me was stabbed less than fifteen minutes before the delivery guy rang the doorbell."

"Hell," Daphne muttered. "Things really are messed up out there. Is the agent all right?"

The voices outside were becoming increasingly loud, but Faith didn't want to scare Greg so she kept a smile on her face. "I don't know. I hope so. What's in the box? I'll try to save it."

"It's a coat. I'd bought a leather coat and sunglasses like Deacon's for Joseph—as kind of a birthday gag. But then I heard Deacon had been shot in the shoulder, and I figured his coat was ruined. So I sent him the one that I had. I know how much he loves that old thing."

Faith's heart melted. "That was very kind of you. He said his coat could be fixed, but it got taken as evidence and I think he's missing it more than he lets on. I'll try to grab the new one before Forensics takes it away. Thank you, Daphne. I know this will mean a lot to him."

"Ah. So you're *that* kind of friend. Good. I'm very, very glad. Tell Deacon we miss him."

"I will." Faith hung up, gave Greg his phone. "Deacon left some good friends in Baltimore."

A shadow passed over Greg's face. "I know. He left them to come back here. For me."

"Because he loves you," Faith said softly. "He told me to tell you so."

A look of pleased shock passed over his face, then he let loose a characteristically teenage roll of the eyes. "Yeah, right."

"Wish me luck," Faith said. "I'm going to try to rescue that package."

"Good lu–" Greg broke off with a frown, the shouting outside becoming so loud, even he could hear it. "What's happening?" he whispered.

Damn good question. "I'll find out. Sit here inside the closet." Where no bullets could come bursting through the window glass. "Promise me," she whispered fiercely.

Her urgency must have made an impact because he did as she asked. Drawing a breath, Faith went into Deacon's room and, kneeling on the bed safely to one side of the window, pulled back the shade.

And was instantly sorry she had, because she saw Agent Pope die.

Pope was lying on a stretcher, his face as white as the pillow that cradled his head. But his face and the pillow were the only things that were white. Everything else was bloodred.

The loud voice belonged to Agent Colby, who stood at his partner's side screaming at him to hold on. For Fran and the kids. And then everything went silent.

Colby stopped yelling as giant silent sobs began to shake his broad shoulders. Because Pope wasn't breathing anymore.

The EMTs looked grim. And so damn sorry.

And then Faith realized she was crying, too, a low, keening wail that she couldn't keep in. She let go of the shade and slid down until she sat against the headboard. Burying her face in Deacon's pillow to muffle her tears, she rocked herself as she cried.

Dammit, dammit, dammit. It didn't matter if the stabbing hadn't been about her. *Pope wouldn't have been out there in the first place were it not for a psychopath trying to kill me.*

But managing only to pick off everyone around her.

The sound of footsteps had her simultaneously lifting her head and reaching into her purse for her gun. She blinked hard to see who was coming. An angry groan rose in her chest when she did. "Oh, wonderful. It's you."

Adam Kimble crossed Deacon's bedroom in a few long strides, his dark eyes intense. "What's wrong? Are you hurt?"

"Does it really matter to you if I am? If you're here to babysit me, fine. Just leave me alone. Greg could use your company." She put her gun back in her purse, brought her knees to her chest, and buried her face in the pillow again.

"Why are you crying, Dr. Corcoran?" he asked carefully.

Faith jerked her head up, glaring at him. "Because he's dead," she shouted. "Pope is dead. He was guarding me and someone stabbed him and now *he is dead.*" She swallowed hard, her tantrum leaving her spent. "Go ahead," she whispered. "Tell me it's my fault. You know you want to. Might as well get it out of your system."

He stood there looking at her while she counted the throbs in her now-pounding head. Finally, he sighed. Shoulders sagging, he propped his fists on his hips and dropped his chin, staring down at the floor. "I don't think it's your fault, Faith."

"It's mine." Greg edged into the room, his steps uncertain. His face as white as chalk. "Adam? Is it true? He's dead? Really dead?"

Adam gave a single, sober nod. "Yeah. It's true."

Greg sank to the floor, the green paint on his clothes streaking the wall, his stare glassy-eyed. "What kind of knife was it, Adam?" he asked numbly.

"Looked like a Bowie. Why?"

"What color was the handle?"

"Redwood. Why?" Adam repeated, but Greg had covered his face with trembling hands. Adam crouched in front of him and pulled his hands from his face. "Greg?"

"He thinks the boys at school who threatened Dani are responsible," Faith said, her heart breaking. She still didn't know what Greg had done, but she realized the repercussions of it could very possibly have left a man dead.

"This was what got you suspended?" Kimble demanded, letting out a harsh breath when Greg only nodded. Kimble looked up at Faith. "Do they know this outside?"

"I told Deacon. He said he'd tell them, but he was in an interview when I called." She rubbed her aching forehead. "This day completely and utterly sucks."

"I can agree with that," Kimble said, abruptly rising to put his hand out to stop her when she started to leave the room. "Whoa. Where are you going?"

"There's a package on the living room floor that belongs to Deacon." She could do nothing to help Pope or his family, but she'd be damned if she let the Feds take Deacon's coat. "I was going to grab what's inside before the Feds take custody of it."

Kimble stared at her. "You're going to tamper with evidence?"

She bared her teeth. "It's not evidence. It's a gift from one of Deacon's Baltimore friends that had the bad luck to be delivered now. Dial the last number in Greg's call log and talk to her yourself. She sent him a replacement coat, for God's sake."

Adam's expression was grim. "Stay here. I'll talk to whoever's in command out there and see what I can do about the coat." He laid a hand on Greg's shoulder and squeezed. "I need details. Names, addresses. How you knew about the knife. What happened to make them willing to kill." He looked over at Faith again. "I'm taking the two of you away from here, so pack what you need for a few days."

Faith's mouth fell open. "What?"

"This safe house isn't safe anymore. You need to move. And hurry up, if you would. I have to take you to the hospital first. Arianna's awake and asking to talk to you."

Feeling as numb as Greg looked, Faith watched Kimble disappear down the stairs. *Move. And quickly. For Arianna. And, please, God, for Corinne and the little girl, too.*

"Greg, you need to change your clothes." She hardened her voice. "Come on. Move it."

He didn't move. Just stayed there, forearms resting on bent knees. Staring straight ahead.

Muttering curses at the universe in general, Faith opened and shut the drawers in Deacon's dresser until she found his stash of sweats and dumped the entire contents of the drawer onto the bed. "Here's a set. Go into the bathroom and change. Leave the paint-covered clothes in the tub. We'll deal with them later." When Greg didn't move, she went over and grabbed his hand, trying to yank him to his feet. "Greg, you have to move. We have things to do. Go, change." He slowly came to his feet, took the clothes she offered, and trudged into the master bathroom, his head down.

The slamming of the front door caught her by surprise. It sounded like it had been thrown open. Seconds later Agent Colby barreled up the stairs and into Deacon's bedroom.

"Where is he?" Colby asked quietly.

"Who?" Faith asked, genuinely confused.

Colby leaned down until he was completely in her space and she felt the old panic return. "Greg. The kid. Deacon Novak's brother." He spat the words into her face.

What the fuck? She moved to block Colby's path. "Why?"

He put both beefy hands on her shoulders and shoved her aside. Faith backed up and blocked his path again, palms out like a traffic cop. "Agent Colby. *Stop.*"

He moved around her, advancing toward the bathroom. Faith ran to the bathroom door, putting her body in front of it. "What are you doing, Agent Colby?"

"He played games at school," Colby said, his fury audible now. "Hacked into teachers' e-mails and made them think some kid had AIDS. Did you know that?" He didn't stop for her reply, just dragged her away from the door.

She shoved him hard enough to send him back a step. "What is wrong with you?" she cried. "Greg, lock the door. Do not come out." But the lock didn't turn and Faith's stomach twisted. *Fine time to take out your hearing aids, kid.* "Kimble!" she shouted. "Help me!"

"He'll come out," Colby gritted, his breath hot on her face, "and he will see what he has done. Kids play on the computer and think they're God." He reached around her and rattled the doorknob. "Come out, you little prick. Come outside and see what you've done."

"I'm coming, Faith," Greg said impatiently through the door. "For God's sake."

He couldn't hear their voices. *He thinks I'm rushing him to hurry.* "Kimble! *Help!*"

The door opened behind her and she heard Greg's gasp. Colby reached over her shoulder and took a handful of the boy's sweatshirt and dragged him forward.

"Kimble!" Faith shouted, wedging herself between Colby and Greg. "Agent Colby, you're upset. You're grieving. Do not do this. Do not throw your career away." She gave another shove, one hand on each of them. Greg managed to wrench himself from Colby's grip and slam the bathroom door, locking himself inside.

Leaving Faith to face the enraged Colby alone. *Oh God.* Wild-eyed with grief, he grabbed her blouse, viciously hauling her to her toes.

"Don't *tell* me what to do," he hissed. "My partner is dead. And it's that kid's fault. And yours." He gave her a shake that rattled her to her bones. "We were stuck here protecting *you.*"

"When I brought this all on myself?" she asked with a calm she didn't feel. "Is that what you want to say?"

"No." His eyes filled with tears. "But he was my partner. My friend. Now he's dead. He didn't deserve this."

"No," she whispered. "He didn't. I'm sorry." Tentatively she reached up, cupped his cheek. "I'm so sorry."

Colby shuddered, the tears falling unchecked. "They gutted him like an animal," he whispered. "Like a goddamned animal."

Faith left one hand on his face and with the other gently covered the fist gripping her blouse. "Agent Colby, you're hurting me," she said softly, pressing on his fist firmly. "I don't think you want to do that. I don't think you're that kind of man." The wild fury that filled his eyes began to dissipate, misery taking its place. Misery, horror, and shame.

He released her blouse, and she eased down until her feet were flat on the floor again. "Thank you, Agent Colby."

"I'm sorry," he rasped. "Oh my God. I'm sorry. I . . . I'm sorry."

She wasn't going to say it was okay, because it wasn't. "I'm not hurt," she said, keeping her voice noncombative. "You're not hurt. Let's leave this room." She took his arm and turned him toward the bedroom door just as Kimble ran through it.

"Tend to Greg," she told Kimble. "I'm going to make Agent Colby some tea."

By the time she got him down into the living room, Colby was trembling. He closed his eyes as they passed the deliveryman, still sitting on the floor but no longer in handcuffs.

Kimble must have freed him. *On my say-so,* Faith thought. *I guess we're making progress.*

She guided Colby into the kitchen and up onto one of the barstools. He buried his head in his hands, his shoulders shaking silently as Faith put the kettle on the stove and prepared his tea.

Kimble brought Greg through the kitchen on his way to the garage. Greg wouldn't meet her eyes as he passed, embarrassed now that it was all over.

Kimble, on the other hand, stopped and held her gaze for a long moment. "Thank you," he murmured fiercely. "I got a few of your things. We need to go. Now."

He had her laptop bag on his shoulder and carried the overnight case she'd left in Deacon's bathroom. The sight of a big, brooding man carrying a Hello Kitty overnight case might have made her smile under any other circumstances.

"Colby's boss is outside. He'll take over," Kimble said. "I just got a call from Meredith Fallon wondering where the hell we are. I explained, but we need to go now. Arianna's already dropped off to sleep once. She's refusing pain meds until you get there, so she can stay awake."

Spent, Faith followed him to the car and climbed down onto the floorboard next to Greg, who still wouldn't look at her. "I might sleep on the way to the hospital," she said as Kimble pulled out of the garage. "So don't worry about me if I don't sit up when the coast is clear."

"I'd say you'd earned a nap, Dr. Corcoran," he said gently. "I'll wake you when we get there."

Exhaustion pulled at her, but she fought it a moment longer. "Did you get Deacon's coat?"

"Yes, I did."

Relief. "How?"

A chuckle. "I signed for it when I uncuffed the delivery guy. It's in the trunk."

"Won't you get into trouble?"

"Probably. I'll open the box in Tanaka's lab, just in case it's a decoy package. But I owe Deacon. If I get into trouble, I'll just be paying my debt."

Cincinnati, Ohio
Tuesday, November 4, 11:15 p.m.

I blew it, he thought in disgust. From the upstairs window of the house three streets away, he watched the sedan pull out of Novak's garage and just knew Faith was in it. *They're removing her. Taking her to a new safe house.*

Gutting the FBI agent had seemed like a good idea at the time, but this was what happened when he acted impulsively. If he'd just been patient, he could have drawn her outside by killing the boy when he opened the door to the deliveryman.

But he'd become impatient from too many hours of waiting for Faith to leave the house. When he'd seen the high school punk approaching the house holding a big-ass Bowie knife, he thought he could make something happen.

Of course, a high school punk with a big-ass knife had

been a wild card on which he hadn't planned, an extra player over whom he had no control. So he'd taken the kid out of the picture. Luring the boy away before the patrolling Fed saw him had been the dicey part.

Killing the punk had been a piece of cake. Sneaking up on the Fed had been only a little challenging. He'd been watching the two men patrol and knew their patterns.

At least killing the Fed had been satisfying. And now he had a new gun. He could throw that old nine mil into the river.

But that was the only good that had come of the whole thing, because the ploy hadn't worked. He'd been so certain that Faith would run outside to help a wounded FBI agent, but she was actually following instructions and staying indoors, the bitch. Now the place was crawling with FBI and CPD and Faith was being taken elsewhere.

This house was now useless as an observation point. He'd killed the old man who lived here for nothing. At least they wouldn't find his body anytime soon, or the body of Greg's classmate for that matter, the two of them stashed in the big freezer in the basement that the old guy had used to keep venison.

Luckily for him, it wasn't deer season yet and the guy had eaten nearly all of last year's hunt. There was plenty of room for both the homeowner and the kid who'd been stupid enough to bring a blade to Novak's house.

Unfortunately, his own plan had backfired as abysmally as the punk's had, with Faith slipping out of his hands once again. On the bright side, the cops would be chasing their tails for a while, trying to figure out who'd killed the Fed.

Giving me time to draw Faith out of wherever they're taking her next.

He'd have to come up with a different approach. She wasn't risking her own hide for random strangers, but if he had the right lure, he could still force her to come to him. The kid would make good bait. Or Novak's sister.

Or Corinne Longstreet. Why hadn't he thought of this before? He'd kept Corinne alive for his own enjoyment, but she might be more useful as the one carrot Faith would respond to. The one death she'd trade herself to avoid.

So go back to the cabin and collect Corinne. He could drive out there and be back in four hours. He took a step

away from the window, alarmed when he stumbled. *Shit.*
How long since he'd slept more than an hour at a time?

He'd been going strong for days, but he had to face facts.
His body would give out soon. He could handle driving the
interstates if he drank a strong cup of coffee, but those
twisting roads through the woods to the cabin were treacherous in the dark.

Getting caught by the cops because he'd wrapped his car
around a tree was not going to happen. Although the irony
would be almost too delicious.

Chapter Twenty-four

"Hell, hell, hell," Deacon muttered as he ended what he prayed would be his last call. He'd been on the phone since they'd left Indian Hill, Bishop at the wheel, her hands tightening on it with every new piece of bad news they'd had, starting with the shock of hearing that Agent Pope was dead.

Deacon still couldn't believe it. The man—an experienced federal agent—had been killed.

Outside my house. Only yards away from Greg and Faith.

"The second-to-the-last call was from Adam. He's just getting Faith to the hospital to see Arianna. He wants you to be there if we can get there in time. Just in case Arianna will give a statement. He thought she might be more comfortable with you."

"What else did he say? What was that about Colby? He lost it?"

"Completely. He tried to grab Greg and drag him outside to see Pope's body—to show him the consequences of his prank."

"He tried to drag your brother out of a safe house?"

"He wasn't thinking of it as a safe house at that point, I guess. I didn't realize he was so unstable when I called him about Greg and the school. I thought he'd redirect resources to look for the kid who'd threatened Dani. I never thought he'd go after Greg."

"Because you're not irrational." She shook her head. "Where is Colby now?"

"In custody." Deacon's mouth tightened, his fury still boiling. "Adam said Colby had grabbed Faith by her blouse and lifted her off her toes." Deacon was glad he hadn't been home to see it. *I might have killed him.*

"But Adam stopped him, right? Colby didn't hurt her?"

"She talked him down herself," he said in disbelief. "Then she made Colby a cup of tea."

Bishop's frown softened. "I'm liking her way more all the time."

Me, too. That she'd put herself in harm's way for Greg shouldn't have surprised him. She'd been doing the same thing for kids for years, just in a different context. As much as her lack of self-preservation terrified him, he was grateful she'd protected his brother.

"Who was the last call?" Bishop asked. "The 'hell, hell, hell' one?"

"Vince," he said. "He received Jeremy's prints from the Ohio Medical Licensing Board and they don't match the print from the hairbrush found in the basement. Not even close."

"Damn," Bishop said, but without much heat. "That would have been too easy, though."

"I wish we could have gotten Stone's prints."

"He was military. They would have taken prints. Can we pull them?"

"If they still exist. Discharged vets can petition their prints be wiped from the database. Stone may have been wily enough to do that." He sent a text to Tanaka. "Asked for them."

"So Jeremy didn't bury ten bodies in the O'Bannion basement and he didn't try to kill Faith. But Stone's still a suspect in both, although not in the murder of Agent Pope. Tell me about this kid who's threatened Greg and Dani."

"Sixteen years old, always in trouble. Big, plays varsity football. Defensive lineman."

"So not terribly light on his feet," Bishop said. "Certainly no sprinter."

"He moved pretty slowly in the school security video

that I saw. Apparently, he was fairly popular, although at least some of that was via intimidation. Not so popular recently."

"Because Greg made everyone think that the kid's HIV positive, which is scary, Deacon. Both that your brother thought up something like that and also that he's got the skill to pull it off."

"Trust me, I know, but right now I'm not thinking about Greg. I'm thinking about the fact that a trained federal agent let a high school kid get the drop on him."

"I was thinking that, too," she said reluctantly. "Not wanting to disrespect Pope's memory, of course. But, wow . . . *that* was the guy they sent to guard Faith?"

"I might have thought that, too, but I checked his background when he was first assigned to Faith. Pope was Special Ops before he joined the Bureau. *Nobody* should have been able to get the drop on him and certainly not with a knife. And certainly not that kid," he added. "So what if Pope's murder wasn't a cosmic coincidence?"

"Meaning that he was killed deliberately by our guy?" Bishop considered it for a moment. "It's possible. Where is this kid now?"

"In the wind. He's skipped the last few days of school, and the agents that went to retrieve him from his house say he wasn't home. His parents claim they don't know where he is, either. The SAC put surveillance on his house and the houses of his friends in case he resurfaces."

The special agent in charge was ready to tear down the town looking for the kid who'd murdered one of his men in cold blood. Deacon knew he needed to have his thoughts in order before presenting an alternate theory at this point.

"And the knife they found in Pope?"

"Adam says it matches the description Greg gave him. The bully had been showing the knife around at school. He'd bragged that he'd stolen it from the sporting goods store."

"That'll be easy enough to verify. If it *is* the boy's knife, but it *wasn't* a coincidence, how did the killer get the knife?"

"Good question. I don't know. Maybe I'm seeing conspiracies that aren't there."

Bishop shook her head. "Except that Pope was Special Ops, and he shouldn't have been taken by surprise. So if it was our killer, how did he do it? How'd he get the drop on Pope?"

"Maybe he shot him first, like the Butler County sheriff's deputy. Or maybe he drugged him." Deacon got out his phone. "I'm texting Washington a request for a tox screen on Pope."

"If it wasn't the kid, we know it couldn't have been Stone, Keith, or Jeremy because they were with us at the time. That just leaves Combs plus whoever was in the basement."

"Who wasn't Jordan because his alibi checks out or Jeremy because his fingerprints don't match, but could still be Stone or Keith." He scowled. "It's like a damn jigsaw puzzle."

"There's still Herbie the third. Or even a Mr. X. And we can't forget about the woman who met Herbie at Maguire's fake offices. Could be a woman who fired on Faith from that van on the bridge in Miami. If our killer has a partner, maybe *he's* a *she*. Regardless, we're looking at someone who squatted in the house for years, has good handyman skills, and is a crack shot."

"And is strong enough to drag the Earl Power guy across the back of the O'Bannion house," Deacon added, "can sew stitches like a trained physician, and embalm like a mortician. And, importantly, had access to that damn will."

Cincinnati, Ohio
Tuesday, November 4, 11:20 p.m.

Faith stood in the doorway to Arianna's hospital room, using the moment it took to unzip her borrowed FBI jacket to center herself before barging in on the teenager. Her mind was still a little hazed from being woken from a deep sleep, her body aching from having taken that sleep while curled up on the floorboard of Kimble's car.

But her discomfort was a drop in the sea compared to Arianna's. Deep lines that hadn't been there that morning radiated from the corners of Arianna's pursed lips. *She looks my age.* The girl had refused her pain meds to stay awake, and this was the result.

Meredith Fallon, seated at Arianna's side, stood as soon as Faith and Kimble entered the room, her eyes widening when she saw Faith. "Dr. Corcoran, what happened to you?"

Faith looked down, astonished to see the front of her blouse streaked with blood. *Oh, right.* Agent Colby had grabbed here there. "It's not my blood." It was Agent Pope's. Colby's hands had been covered in it. "If I can get some scrubs, I'll cover up. And please call me Faith."

"I'm Meredith." Grabbing a clean hospital gown from a shelf near the door, she glared over Faith's shoulder at Kimble. "You didn't even let her change her clothes?"

Kimble opened his mouth, probably to make a smart remark. Or maybe to defend himself, but Meredith was having none of it. "Go," she said, flicking her hands toward the door. "Out."

Meredith had pushed Kimble from the room, closed the door, and was dragging Faith's blouse from her jeans before Faith could form a thought. Making a face, Meredith pulled on a pair of gloves. "Give me your blouse."

Faith stared at her. "What? Why?"

"It's going in the biohazard bin. This is an ICU ward."

"Of course." Faith's mind clicked back into place. "I'm sorry," she said, stripping the blouse off and dropping it in the biohazard bag with a pang of sadness. That was the blouse she'd worn when Novak had . . . *No, Faith. Not going there.* She shook her head hard. "We had a disturbance at my safe house. Kimble rushed me out and straight here and I fell asleep in the back of the car. I'm still a little cobwebby. Give me the gown."

"Um, no." Meredith's nose crinkled. "The bra, too."

Faith sighed. Blood had seeped through her blouse, speckling her bra. Popping the front clasp, she held the gown to her chest while she dropped the bra in the bag along with the blouse. "It was my nicest one, too," she murmured.

"Sorry," Meredith said softly. "Arms in."

Faith obeyed, allowing Meredith to dress her as though she were a child. She caught Arianna struggling to open her eyes and gave the teenager as bright a smile as she could muster. "Hi, honey. I'm sorry I'm late."

"Hold your hair," Dr. Fallon ordered, stepping behind her to tie the gown.

Arianna's dark eyes grew big as saucers. "What happened?" she whispered, horrified.

Too late, Faith realized she'd neglected to cover the scar

on her throat. She dropped her hair, instinctively covering her scar, but kept her voice warm and soothing. "It happened a few years ago. Nothing for you to worry about now." She allowed Meredith to drag her to the sink and scrub her hands, giving Arianna a helpless look that made the girl's pursed lips curve.

"Now you're clean enough to sit in an ICU ward with a patient recovering from surgery," Meredith said crisply, but she put a gentle hand on Faith's shoulder. "Kimble called while he was driving you over here and told me what happened. He said you stepped in front of a grief-stricken, out-of-control federal agent to keep him from abusing Kimble's fifteen-year-old cousin."

Faith wondered why Meredith had taken precious seconds to rehash Agent Colby's meltdown. Until she saw a subtle change in Arianna. Minute relaxation, the lines of pain around her mouth softening.

"You did that?" Arianna asked.

Faith sat in the chair at the girl's bedside. "Yes," she said simply.

"Like you did for me." Arianna's eyes filled with tears. "I thought it was a dream."

"Arianna woke with nightmares," Meredith explained. "By the time I arrived, she was a tad worked up. She's a little unsure of what exactly happened last night."

Faith noted the soft restraints still hanging from the bed rails. A "tad worked up" really meant that Arianna had been thrashing so frantically that she'd been a danger to herself. The hospital never would have restrained her otherwise, knowing what she'd been through.

"Waking up from nightmares is always disconcerting," Faith said. "But the fog you're experiencing is normal. You're not losing your mind." She watched Arianna's gaze flick up at Meredith, who smiled and nodded as if she'd said the exact same thing.

"I'm so damn scared," Arianna whispered. "I always kept clear before. I can't go crazy."

"Before?" Faith asked carefully.

"Before Lauren's family took me in." She closed her eyes. "I had a lot of uncles back then."

Faith's heart broke, but she kept her tone strong. "But you could always count on your mind to tell you what was real and today you haven't been able to do that. Well, don't worry. Some of your confusion is shock from your injuries, and some is a side effect from the anesthesia. It happened to me, too, but at least I woke up to see my dad and step-mother and uncle, not two redheaded strangers."

Dark eyes opened to lock on Faith's face. "I remember that you covered me with your coat. Then you stood over me. You had a gun. I thought maybe you were going to shoot me. But then you said that no one would hurt me. That they'd have to go through you. Did that happen?"

Faith held Arianna's hands. "Yes. I didn't know if who-ever hurt you would come back."

Arianna's brows knit together. "Why didn't you *run*?"

"I wouldn't have left you. How did you get in the road? I mean, one second it was empty, then all of a sudden, there you were."

"Dragged myself."

Just like Deacon had thought. "From the power compa-ny's truck?"

"Yes." Her eyes shadowed. "I saw the man from the power company get shot, but I left him there. I left Corinne there." A sob broke from her throat. *"I ran away."*

"You ran to get help." Faith wiped the tears from Arian-na's face. "I was the one who called the power company and asked them to send the man out. Do you think I'm to blame?"

A slight frown, as if trying to make sure it wasn't a trick question. "No."

"Then how can you possibly be? And a lot of people are looking for Corinne because you got help." Faith brushed dark hair from Arianna's damp forehead. "Don't lose hope."

Arianna's face tightened on a spasm of pain, shuddering out a breath as the pain ebbed.

"The nurse is going to make you take that medication now that Faith is here," Meredith said. "You should make good use of the time you have before you go back to sleep."

"Okay. I'm ready to talk about what happened now." Ar-ianna dropped her gaze to the scar on Faith's throat. "But first, tell me how you got that."

"All right. I used to counsel victims of sexual assault. Usually incest. But I also had to work with the people— mostly men—who'd hurt them."

A frown bent dark eyebrows. "Why?"

Faith could feel Meredith also watching, waiting for an answer. "Because many times a judge would order it that way to try to rehabilitate the offender," she said. "And fix the family."

Arianna's face turned to stone. "You can't fix them. They don't change. They do it again and again. And it's not the family's fault. They don't need *fixing*."

"You're right," Faith said. "But the victims, the kids—they need help. The mothers that *truly* didn't know it was going on—they need help, too. The mothers that allow it to happen . . . Well, I didn't think they needed fixing. I thought they needed jail. But I wasn't a judge."

"My mother knew."

Faith's heart broke a little more. "Did she take you to therapy?"

Dark eyes rolled. "She wouldn't even take me to school. She was usually too high."

"Many of my girls had moms like yours. They wouldn't have gotten therapy, not unless the court ordered it. And usually those mothers only complied to keep the offender out of jail. If I wanted to help those girls, I had to work with evil to do good."

"You did it for the kids," Arianna murmured.

Meredith relaxed, and Faith felt like she'd passed a critical test. "Anyway, one of the abusers got angry with me and did this." She pointed to her throat. "I was terrified, I have to admit."

"I'm sorry. I shouldn't have asked. Shouldn't have made you remember."

This, too, was a test, because even as Arianna whispered her consolation, her eyes remained watchful. "You didn't make me remember. I've never forgotten. I just push it aside when I have to deal with whatever life's throwing me at the moment. You won't truly forget what's happened to you. You'll have to find your own way to deal. And to go on. I think you know this already."

Arianna nodded grimly. "Yeah. I do. And I will."

"Good. It's my turn to ask a question. The police can't find a record of Roza. Who is she, and why didn't she leave with you?"

"I don't know who she is, but I *begged* her to come with

me." Arianna's eyes were haunted. "She said she wouldn't leave her mother. That her mother was there."

Faith blinked, startled. "Her mother was also being held prisoner in the basement?"

"I don't know, but she said she couldn't leave her. Find her mother. Please."

"I'll do everything I personally can. But it's the police who are searching. You can help them by answering their questions. Detective Kimble is waiting outside."

Faith wished it was any cop but Kimble, but she sensed that Arianna was ready to talk.

"I don't know him."

"He works with Agent Novak and Detective Bishop. You met them here last time."

"The man with the white hair? And strange eyes? I thought I might have dreamed him, too."

That made Faith smile. "Agent Novak is very real. Will you talk to Detective Kimble?"

"What happened to the lady detective? Where is she?"

"She's with Agent Novak, looking for Corinne. Kimble brought me to see you."

Doubt flickered in Arianna's eyes. "What will he ask me?"

"Details of your abduction and assault. About the man who hurt you. And what he did."

Doubt became accusation, childlike and shrill. "You said I didn't have to tell! You *said*!"

"Arianna. Listen to me. You don't have to talk about anything you don't want to. It's *your* right to talk when *you're* ready, and I will protect that."

Meredith Fallon smoothed her hand down Arianna's arm. "We both will, Arianna. I've told you that. You have our word. Now, settle down or you'll pull out your stitches."

Arianna stopped struggling, slumping into the mattress. "I'll have scars, too, won't I?"

"Probably. But none of your cuts were deep enough to leave a scar like mine. And this scar used to be a lot worse. It's faded. So yours will fade even more."

A long silence. Faith might have thought Arianna had fallen asleep, but for the continued iron grip on her hand. The girl's eyelids fluttered open. "If I talk to the cop, will you stay?"

Tears stung Faith's eyes. "Let them try to make me leave."

"Then tell him to come in."

Cincinnati, Ohio
Tuesday, November 4, 11:35 p.m.

Deacon let out the breath he'd been holding, as did Adam and Bishop. He and Bishop had arrived in time to hear Arianna refusing to talk to Kimble. He'd been disappointed, but hoped Faith could bring her around.

Along with Bishop and Kimball, he'd been mentally urging Faith to push Arianna, but instead Faith had backed away. And it turned out that she'd understood the girl better than they'd hoped. Arianna had agreed to help them of her own accord.

The door opened and the three of them jumped back like guilty eavesdroppers. Dr. Fallon emerged from Arianna's room. She pulled the door firmly shut.

"Let me guess," she said dryly, looking up at Adam. "The wind opened it."

Adam's cheeks darkened. "I'm good with that explanation."

"Well, are you going in there or not?" Dr. Fallon demanded. "She might change her mind."

Adam shook his head. "She'll be more comfortable with Bishop. I think Faith will be, too."

Bishop gave Adam a nod, then followed Dr. Fallon back into the room.

There was silence between Deacon and Adam, heavy and awkward.

Deacon cleared his throat. "Where is Greg?"

"I couldn't leave him at your house, so I brought him with me. I sent him to the hospital cafeteria with the cop who was guarding Arianna's room, just in case the punk from his school finds out where he is and tries to make more trouble. What the hell happened? Greg wouldn't tell me. How was Dani threatened?"

Deacon gave him the quick version, feeling more helpless every time he told it.

Adam shook his head. "Why didn't Greg come to me first? I could have helped him."

Deacon shrugged. "You haven't exactly been around for

the past month." He hadn't meant it to come out sounding like an accusation. *Did I?* Honestly, he was too weary to know for sure.

Adam's eyes flashed with anger. "Now you know how we've felt for the past fifteen years."

Deacon flinched. "That's not fair and you know it. I tried to get custody of Greg before and Jim always fought me. Should I have just kidnapped him?" He shook his head, unwilling to go on. "Never mind. I'm here now, and I'm trying to do the right thing."

"You're right. You did try. I'm sorry. What *is* the right thing for Greg?"

"I truly don't know. He did it for the right reasons, but he knowingly broke the rules."

"And now Agent Pope's family has to live with the consequences."

"That I'm not so sure about." Deacon told him what he and Bishop had discussed.

Adam's expression became openly cynical. "Are you saying that you think Pope was stabbed by the killer we're looking for, with the same knife the high school kid just happened to have shown half of Greg's school? The killer who has *shot* every other victim thus far?"

Deacon's defenses rose, but he kept his cool. "It's what I'm suggesting. If Combs is involved, he used a knife on Faith. And this killer did slice at least one victim's hamstrings. Plus, Arianna is proof that he cuts his victims. You don't agree that it's at least a possibility?"

"I think it might be a little convenient. And detrimental to Greg. He needs to own up to the consequences of his actions, not have you trying to get him off the hook."

The accusation stunned Deacon. "Buy into the possibility of this killer stabbing Pope or don't, but do *not* question my integrity." The breath he drew filled his mouth with the taste of disinfectant, reminding him that he was standing outside a victim's room in the ICU ward. *Stick to business. Sort through all the personal shit later.* Brusquely, he flipped through the to-do list he'd stored on his phone. "Have you determined when the tracker was placed on Faith's Jeep?"

"I was in the middle of that when I got the call about Agent Pope," Adam replied, also tensely businesslike. "I'll go finish it now."

"Thank you. I'll see you in Isenberg's office for the debriefing."

"Yes, sir," Adam said, and walked away without another word.

Deacon flagged down a nurse. "May I use a landline, please?"

She pointed to an empty room. "That one is unoccupied, but that could change on a dime."

Closing himself into the small room, Deacon called Isenberg to give her a heads-up on his theory about Pope's murder. He didn't want to blindside her, and he certainly didn't want her to react like Adam just had. Although if she did, it wouldn't hurt nearly so much.

Cincinnati, Ohio
Tuesday, November 4, 11:45 p.m.

He went straight to bed. *So damn tired.* He'd spread himself too thin this time. He never should have grabbed Corinne, not until he'd been sure that Faith was dead. But he'd been so frustrated that morning after the fire in Miami. Everyone had poured out of that building like rats from a sinking ship. Except for Faith. Because she hadn't been there.

He felt a twinge of pain in his jaw and realized he was grinding his teeth again. Faith should be dead already. Years ago. *But she just wouldn't die.* He'd returned home so agitated, his temper raging almost past his ability to cage it. He couldn't lose it. When he did, he did stupid things. So he'd grabbed Corinne. Just to take the pressure off.

Which had turned out to be just as stupid. He should never have taken her. And when things got crazy, he should have just killed her and buried her with the Earl Power guy and that damn locksmith.

He frowned. And the boy. A trespasser. A squatter. *That's right.* He'd shot him and buried him with the other two. He shouldn't have forgotten about the boy that quickly.

I'm just tired. A few hours of sleep would resharpen his mind. It was good that he hadn't killed Corinne, he reminded himself. She was going to be his bait for Faith. And once he'd drawn Faith out into the open, he'd kill both women, snipping off the worst of his loose ends.

That left Roza. He eyed his bedroom, kept neat as a pin

by Jade for ten years now. But Jade had become too old for him. Roza would soon be old enough to take over Jade's responsibilities. When that time came, he'd dispose of Jade and bring Roza here to serve his needs.

"Jade!" he thundered. "Come here!"

She appeared a minute later, stumbling and sleepy-eyed. "I'm sorry. I fell asleep."

"Have I had any calls?"

"No. None."

"Good. I need to get some rest. If anyone calls, tell them I'm not here. If anyone knocks, do not open the door. If it's the police, you are still not to open the door, but come and wake me immediately. Are we clear?"

She nodded. "Yes, sir. But . . . what if the police have a warrant? And guns?"

"They can't get a warrant. They have nothing on which to base it. I will sleep now. When I wake, I expect steak and eggs." He needed the protein to give him energy. "That is all."

"I'll keep everything quiet so that you can rest."

"See that you do." After she'd left, he got up and double bolted the door. Then he stripped out of his clothes and added them to the garbage bag that held what he'd worn as he'd dealt with the man whose home he'd borrowed.

And that kid, too. The punk. *See, memory's good. No worries.* He could remember every moment of killing that boy. No quick shot in the head for that punk. *Au contraire.*

What. A. High. That was his drug of choice. When this was over and he'd found somewhere to begin again, he'd include a few punks like the one he'd butchered today. He enjoyed the women, but there had been something satisfying about showing that kid who was boss.

He set his alarm, stretched out on his bed, and let himself drift into sleep.

Chapter Twenty-five

Cincinnati, Ohio
Wednesday, November 5, 12:35 a.m.

"This is your desk?" Greg asked, disappointed. "It's ... boring."

"That's because most of our work is boring," Deacon said, pulling out his desk chair for Faith. "The past few days have been unique."

"That's for sure," Faith murmured as she sat down.

They'd come straight from the hospital, the interview with Arianna taking so long that Deacon had had to rush to get to Isenberg's debriefing without dropping off Greg and Faith first. Not that he knew where he would have taken them. His house was still a crime scene.

He needed a safe place for them to stay tonight. He wanted a soft bed for Faith and he wanted to sleep in it with her. He'd gotten a short catnap while Bishop and Faith had been in with Arianna, but it hadn't been long enough to blunt the edge of his exhaustion. Had they not just interviewed their only witness, he would have called it a night already. But Arianna had given Bishop information that needed to be disseminated to the team.

He needed to stay upright and lucid a little bit longer.

"Just sit tight," he said. "I'll get this debriefing done as quickly as possible. And, Greg, if you think about touching a computer, I'll ..." He shook his head. "Just don't go there."

Greg ducked his head. "I won't," he said sullenly. "Jeez, D."

Deacon squeezed his brother's shoulder before turning for the conference room, where Isenberg, Tanaka, and ME Carrie Washington were already waiting, all three looking as tired as he did.

"You got the victim's statement?" Isenberg asked as he and Bishop sat down.

"I did," Bishop said. "Where's Kimble?"

"I don't know. He called me to talk about your theory, Novak."

"And?"

"I told him what I told you: It bears looking into. He wasn't exactly pleased."

Bishop's expression went dark. "What am I missing here?"

"Adam didn't agree with my take on Pope's murder," Deacon said. "He thinks I'm trying to get Greg off the hook."

Bishop's mouth fell open. "That boy needs help. And I'm not talking about Greg."

Isenberg tapped the table. "We'll get started without him."

Deacon nodded at Bishop. "Scarlett, you first. What did Arianna tell you?"

"She was blindfolded and tied to a metal table until the girl, Roza, released her. She said that he always wore gloves, which is probably why we haven't found any usable prints. He had a lot of knives and he used them on her. Inside and out. He raped her at least twice. It might have been more, but she could have been too drugged to remember. He'd tell her that he'd killed Corinne and he'd tell her how. He'd play her tapes of screaming. And then he'd tell her that he'd lied. That Corinne was alive and that how much torture she endured would depend on how much Arianna fought him. He went back and forth several times."

"He was trying to break her," Deacon said.

"Exactly. Dr. Fallon agreed. She was quite good in the interview, actually. We should consider using her in the future. She pulled things from Arianna's memory that I might not have been able to get on my own, because Arianna's had bad experiences with cops. He's local, we're pretty sure. He's a baritone and slightly nasal, about six feet tall and broad-chested. But soft."

Deacon frowned. "Soft?"

"'Not buff.'" Bishop used air quotes. "She said that after he shot her, he threw her over his shoulder and carried her to the van. She was fighting him at that point. The drug hadn't completely kicked in. She said she hit him with her fists and he didn't have muscles. Which, unfortunately, crosses all of our big guys—Combs, Keith, and Stone—off the list."

"How reliable is that sensory memory, though?" Washington asked. "She was drugged."

"I know and I agree. I'm just telling you what she said. She said there was some kind of flashing light toward the end and he got very freaked out. She heard what she thought was him putting his knives in a toolbox. She also heard him moving glass jars and muttering, 'No one will get my things.' She said he'd been confident and cruel up until then, but just before he left he sounded like a 'homeless crazy guy.'"

"'My things' could be his collections—his souvenirs," Carrie said. "Have you found them?"

"No," Tanaka said. "We've been looking for bodies. Luckily, we've found none outside."

"Well, that's something, at least," Deacon said. "What about inside?"

"Dr. Johannsen and her assistant wanted to check the outside of the property first. They'll come back tomorrow for the basement floor."

Isenberg gave Tanaka a nod. "Good news there. Anything else from the victim, Scarlett?"

Bishop's reply was interrupted by the door opening. Adam came in carrying a box under one arm. He gave Isenberg a nod and sat down at the far end of the table. "Sorry I'm late."

Isenberg gave him a long, long stare before turning back to Bishop. "You were saying?"

"That Arianna was most worried that he'd sexually assaulted her and didn't use a condom. She didn't want a pregnancy or STD to follow her for the rest of her life as a constant reminder."

"How did she know he didn't use a condom?" Isenberg asked.

Bishop scowled. "Because at one point he untied one of

her hands, held a knife to her throat, and made her put him in. He told her that she wanted it. That she liked it."

Deacon kept a lid on his temper. "Sonofabitch. If he kept his victims long enough and did that often enough, he'd have them believing it. He knows victim psychology very well."

"He must, because he gagged her so that she couldn't bite him and bound her fingers so that she couldn't scratch or grab. He kept telling her she was a fighter, but that he'd break her. That he hadn't enjoyed himself so much since he 'did the cop.'"

"Deputy Simpson," Isenberg said, her jaw hard.

Bishop nodded. "Arianna wasn't sure if he'd really abducted a cop or if he was just trying to prove how macho he was. Being tough seemed to be important to him. She considered the fact that he seemed threatened by her to be a compliment. It's how she got through that particular assault."

"Gutsy," Isenberg said. "It'll help her make it. Anything else?"

Bishop checked her notes. "Yes. He was hairless in his groin, chest, and legs. Smooth as a baby's butt. She wasn't sure if he was hairless on his head, because he didn't force her to touch him there. She thought he must have waxed."

"Makes sense," Deacon said. "He might not have worried about dropping hair of his own in the basement, but he wouldn't want to drop any for Forensics to find while he's grabbing his victims. What else?"

"Wait," Carrie said with a puzzled frown. "Let's go back to the sexual assault. Was the live victim's rape kit positive for semen? Because none of the deceased victims' kits have so far."

"No, it wasn't." Bishop rubbed her forehead. "It was positive for sexual assault, but not for fluids. *Dammit.* Now her story doesn't hold together."

"Maybe he didn't ejaculate," Deacon said.

"According to her, he did, or he was an amazing actor."

"He might orgasm and still not ejaculate," Carrie said. "It's something else to note."

"What are the causes of that?" Deacon asked. "It could be a lead."

"Certain illnesses. Certain drugs. Certain kinds of surgeries, because they damage the nerve pathways that control flow. I can make you a list."

"Do that," Bishop murmured. "Imagine the freedom that would allow him, if he could rape women without a condom and still have no chance of DNA being linked back to him."

Carrie nodded. "Not ejaculating semen could be quite a perk, but also a curse. Just like women can feel incomplete if they can't conceive, the inability to impregnate can make men feel incomplete. My old roommate from med school is an infertility specialist," she added when they all stared at her, the men wincing. "Shoptalk over wine."

"I don't want to have wine with you," Tanaka muttered.

Carrie's lips twitched. "One thing you should consider is that just because he doesn't ejaculate doesn't mean that he doesn't produce sperm. It might mean simply that his body just doesn't have a way to get it out. Every so often, a few will escape. And there are some drugs that help this along. Like pseudoephedrine."

"Allergy medicine?" Isenberg asked. "Seriously?"

"Seriously," Carrie said. "The other MEs and I only did standard swabs on the first six victims we examined. Now that I know this, we'll go back and look more closely at those six and pay special attention to the remaining four. We may get lucky. Or he could have just been a good actor and wanted Arianna to believe he was finishing."

"Which means he's an impotent little prick," Bishop said. "But at least that eliminates Arianna's fears about pregnancy for now." She sighed. "He was trying to get her to scream, especially at the beginning, but nothing worked, so he tried an electrical probe. She was ashamed, but we couldn't believe she held out as long as she did. After she screamed the first time, he went back to the knives, which he seemed to prefer. Importantly, he cut that torture session short, because something—or someone—disturbed him enough that he left a little while later."

"Faith," Deacon said. "He must have seen her at the cemetery with his cameras." He frowned, something nagging him. Something was missing. "You said he left 'a little while later.' How much later?"

"Maybe fifteen minutes? Arianna said that he was slicing into her skin, and she thought she saw a flashing light at the edge of her blindfold. Then she didn't feel or hear him at all for a minute, and she thought he left because she heard the door close. He came back a few minutes later, and that's when he packed what she thought were knives into his toolbox. After that she slept. She doesn't have an idea of times, but he came back and bellowed for Roza. After that, he didn't come back for a long time."

Deacon realized what he'd missed. "He didn't follow Faith. He went back down to the basement. We assumed that's how he knew which hotel she was in, but he didn't follow her. So how did he know where she went?"

"He had to have already put the tracker on," Bishop said. "But that doesn't make sense, either. If he was tracking her, how did she surprise him like that? She'd been driving for two days. Surely he would have seen her coming."

Adam spoke up. "He had to have found her sometime before nine a.m. Monday morning, because he didn't attach the tracker to her Jeep until then."

Cincinnati, Ohio
Wednesday, November 5, 12:55 a.m.

Faith fired up her laptop, eyeing the door to the conference room uncertainly. Wondering what was going on in there, because Deacon and Bishop had been gone for a while. Wondering what the hell to make of Adam Kimble, who was broody one moment, then decent the next.

"What?" Greg asked. "What's wrong?"

"Nothing. It's just that your cousin confuses me a little."

Greg's bicolored eyes darted to the office door. "He's been like that since D came back, almost like he's jealous, but he got Deacon the job. So I don't get it, either."

"Adam got Deacon the job here? With Lieutenant Isenberg?" Elbows on Deacon's desk, she propped her chin on her fists. "Tell me all," she said conspiratorially.

Greg laughed. "What's it worth to you?"

"I've got *All-Night Zombie Buffet* in one of my boxes back at your house. You can have it."

His eyes grew wide. "That's on my Christmas list. Seriously?"

"It's played already, but sure. Spill."

He moved his chair closer, making her lips twitch. "Well,"

he said, "Aunt Tammy told me that Adam was getting burned out on Homicide so he changed jobs."

He got burned out on Homicide and then moved to Personal Crimes? Really? Usually the sex-crimes unit burned up everyone it touched. "So Adam worked for Isenberg first," she said.

"Yep, when she was just Homicide. Aunt Tammy said that Adam told her that Isenberg was building a joint task force." His expression shadowed. "Adam knew Deacon had been looking to transfer here, so he recommended him."

"That was nice of him," Faith said.

"Yeah, Adam's always been a nice guy. I don't know what's wrong with him lately."

"Him, too," Faith said. "But I meant Deacon. Why did your brother transfer here?"

Greg's eyes narrowed suspiciously. "He didn't tell you what happened at school today?"

"He said that you'd done something wrong, but for the right reasons. I guessed that you were protecting Dani because I overheard you two in the living room this morning. She loves you very much. So does Deacon. That makes you really lucky, Greg."

His eyes flashed unexpectedly, his mouth taking on the mocking cant she'd seen on Deacon's face too many times already. "Yeah, real lucky. So lucky that I've been kicked out of three schools in two years and I've just gotten a Fed killed. Real lucky."

Deacon had pulled her aside to tell her that Pope's murderer might not be the high school bully, but she couldn't share that with Greg. That needed to come from Deacon when the time was right. Although, even if that bully had come for Greg, the murder of Agent Pope was not his fault.

But she didn't think he'd accept her word for it, and why should he?

I haven't accepted the same kind of assurances and I'm twice his age and trained as a therapist. She couldn't assuage Greg's guilt, but she also couldn't ignore his torment. She simply wasn't built that way. So she picked around his primary angst, zeroing in on the secondary. *Kicked out of three schools? Why?* Greg was not an evil kid. So what had happened?

"Three schools?" She leaned forward a little more, not allowing the sympathy she felt to show, keeping her expression avidly curious. "Care to share the details?"

He stared for a moment, then huffed a laugh. "You're really not horrified by me, are you?"

"Horrified? What an odd word to use." *A desperately sad word.* "Why would I be?"

He shrugged. "I could be a time bomb, just waiting to explode."

Now *that* sounded like something an adult had said to him. "I hardly think so, Greg." She studied his face, his growing apprehension. "I'm not doing therapy on you, honest. I just wanted to know because I'm curious. We can talk about something else if you want."

"Like?"

She searched her mind for another topic. "Can I ask about your eyes? They're remarkable."

He shrugged. "D's are cooler."

Mesmerizing, she thought. "I agree. Deacon said it was genetic."

A single chilly nod. Not wanting to talk about their eyes was obviously a family thing.

Okay. "So that's not a good topic either, huh?" she asked.

He grimaced. "It's just that if I tell you, you'll look it up on Wikipedia, and the first photo you'll see is one of some person who lived back in the fifties that . . . doesn't look like me." He lifted his chin, his blue and brown eyes defiant as a pair. But under the defiance was a brittle shame, as if he was just waiting for her to laugh at him. Because someone obviously had.

Dani had said that she and Deacon had been laughed at, bullied, too. Which boggled Faith's mind. They were beautiful people, all of them.

Deacon Novak turned heads. *And not only mine.* She'd seen it happen several times. Nurses, the woman at the hotel desk, even the young woman at the Skyline Chili drive-thru window the night before. His hair and coat captured their startled attention, but the stares that followed had been openly admiring or blatantly lustful. Or both. And how could Faith blame them? He was a gorgeous man who looked amazing in a leather coat or a suit. *Or out of them.*

None of which she planned to tell his fifteen-year-old brother.

"You know you've only whetted my curiosity," she said matter-of-factly. "I'll find it on my own and eventually I'll see that photo. Which I bet bothers you a lot more than it will bother me, so here's the deal: I'll show you my worst photo first, to level the embarrassment factor." She pulled up the photo—the one taken as she'd left the hospital after Combs's attack. The one that made her look haunted and gaunt. And afraid. The one that made her look like a victim.

Greg studied it for several seconds before giving her a bored look. "Bad hair day, Faith."

Faith choked on an unexpected laugh. Her hair had truly been a mess that day, limp and dingy, pulled back from her face in a severe bun. "Yeah. But it was a bad day all around."

"For what it's worth, I saw it already." He showed her his phone when she looked at him in surprise. Sure enough, there was the photo. "I Googled you. It's the first thing that comes up."

"Well, isn't that good to hear?" she asked dryly. "I showed you my photo. Let's have it."

His smile faded. "Why? Why is so important for you to know?"

"Because my family had a lot of secrets and it . . . damaged me." She pressed her hand to her heart. "I'm tired of tiptoeing around topics. Does that answer your question?"

He nodded, grimly, she thought. "Waardenburg," he said. "Two *a*'s."

She typed it in and skimmed the article. A genetic syndrome that affected the pigmentation of hair, skin, and eyes and often caused varying degrees of deafness. And the picture, which, as she suspected, wasn't nearly as bad as he thought.

"Bad hair day," she said, intentionally mimicking him, and his lips tilted. "This photo doesn't give the person decent light or makeup or anything. It was taken clinically, to support medical documentation."

"It's the photo that all the doctors see in their books," he agreed.

"And the one all the kids at school see when they go online."

"Pretty much. It's just names, but . . ."

"Names can hurt. All I can tell you is that the moment I saw your brother, I couldn't look away. Like he came from a movie where he's a hero who doesn't always follow the rules."

Something settled in the boy's eyes. "You like him, then."

"Yes, very much. But I've only known him a day. It might work out and it might not."

"I hope it does. That case in West Virginia was hell on D. He was . . . different when he came back. Sad and far away even when he was with us. And then last year, I got myself kicked out of school again and Aunt Tammy had a heart attack. . . . I didn't mean to make it worse for him. For either of them. But I did it again today. I only make him mad."

Faith's heart twisted. "Tell him that. Just like you told me. He wants you to be happy."

"Whatever," he mumbled, and dropped his gaze to his phone, their conversation over.

Which was okay. She'd gotten him to say more than she'd expected. He'd talk more when he was ready. She just hoped she'd be around then. She and Deacon had started something that felt good. Felt right. But whether it would last past this case was another matter.

If it didn't last? She'd go on, because that was what she did. But if it did last, she'd finally have all she'd ever really wanted. A home. A family. A man who made her want to lick him head to toe. A man who made her feel wanted, desired. Just like a woman ought to feel.

A man who made her feel safe.

But most importantly, a man who seemed to see the real her more clearly within a single day than any other man she'd met. Certainly more than the man she'd been married to.

Maybe even more than my own father. The thought came from nowhere, stealing her breath.

No, not from nowhere. It had always been there, lurking beneath her consciousness.

Her mother had committed suicide. She'd found the body. Deacon had known her less than a day when he'd figured it out. Her father had known her for thirty-two years. But had he really known her? If he had, could she have kept such an enormous secret from him? Or had he known she was lying all these years and simply chosen to allow the lie because it was easier than the truth?

God, I hope not. Because keeping that secret had cost her dearly. Her peace of mind. Her childhood. But to even think it felt like a betrayal, so she shoved the thought away.

Because despite everything, her father loved her. She needed to let him know she was okay. It was much too late to call. Except that they might be up worrying, waiting for her to call. *Text first.* If they were waiting by the phone, they'd have their cell phones out, too.

She tapped Greg's shoulder to get his attention. "Can I use your phone?"

He handed it over with a roll of his eyes and a shake of his head. "Get your own."

"I will, as soon as it's safe for me to go out shopping." She texted both her father and Lily: *You up? It's Faith. I'm okay. I can talk if you can.*

Greg's phone rang, Lily's number on the ID. "Are you all right?" Lily demanded.

"I'm fine. I'm sorry I'm calling so late, though. Is Dad awake?"

"He is. He slept most of the day because of the sedative, so he's still wide-awake."

Her father came on the extension. "Faith? Baby."

Faith closed her eyes, suddenly choked up. "Hi, Dad. I'm okay."

A shuddering exhale. "Good. Just for the record, I know what's happening at your grandmother's house. Lily tried to keep me from the television, so I knew something was up. You do not have to keep these things from me. I'm not as fragile as you seem to think."

"What do you know?" she asked cautiously.

"That an 'undisclosed number of bodies' was found in the basement." A pause. "And that you were shot at. And that some federal agent is watching over you."

Faith's eyes widened. "*That* was on television?"

"No. I called your uncle Jordan and asked him what was going on. Said the guy's name was Novak, so Lily and I looked him up online."

Faith's cheeks heated. "You did?"

"Of course we did." Her father sounded a bit tentative. "But he's . . . not what I expected."

"He's a good cop, Dad," Faith said quietly. "He protected

me. Threw himself over me so that I didn't get shot. I'm alive because of him."

"Then I owe him a debt I can never repay. When can I thank him in person?"

"When he's closed the case, I expect. Look, I'm using someone else's phone here at the police station. I just wanted to hear your voice and let you know that I'm all right. And to tell you that I love you."

"I love you, too, Faith. You *will* be careful?"

"I promise. Good night." She returned Greg's phone to him. "Tomorrow I have to get a phone, even if it's a rental," she said. "I'll have to find someone to go to the phone store for me."

"Ask Dani. She'll go for you."

"That's a good idea. I will." Taking her laptop from its case, Faith did a quick check of her e-mail and frowned. Her boss still had not replied to the message she'd sent about her accident. She had expected a "Take care and call me tomorrow" reply. At least an acknowledgment. But there was nothing. Had he not gotten the message? Had he thought she just didn't want to come to work? Or was he just plain rude?

There was an e-mail from the Realtor who'd been referred by her grandmother's attorney, saying that she'd be delighted to discuss the sale of the property. Faith had nearly forgotten about her in all the chaos surrounding the house. She wondered what impact the news stories would have on the property value. Would gawkers rush in to buy? Or would it become a white elephant no one wanted to touch?

"What are you doing?" Greg asked as she stared at Novak's desk.

"I'm looking for a pencil and paper, but I don't want to touch anything. I need to write down a phone number so that when I finally get a phone—please, God, tomorrow—I'll remember my Realtor's name."

"A Realtor? You're buying a house?"

"Not yet. I'm going to sell . . ." Her focus scattered as Greg came to his feet, his expression suddenly grim. She followed his gaze to the bullpen entrance, where a big, hulking man stood next to a thin woman with a worried face.

The man looked just like an older Adam Kimble, their

dark scowls nearly identical. This, then, would be Uncle Jim and Aunt Tammy. Faith looked up at Greg, tugged on his shirtsleeve. "Should I get Deacon?"

Greg nodded. "I think so. Jim looks unhappy. They probably want me to go home with them, but I don't want to."

Faith stepped in front of Greg with her back to the approaching couple. "Do they hurt you?"

Greg shook his head. "No, but I hurt them, even though I don't mean to. I can't make Aunt Tammy have another heart attack. It'll kill her."

Faith started to deny his claim to the blame for his aunt's poor health, then realized she felt the same way about her own father. She started for the conference room door, only to be stopped by a big, booming voice.

"You," the big man said. "Therapist."

This isn't going to end well, she thought. But she turned to face Deacon's uncle anyway. "My name is Faith Corcoran," she said levelly.

Jim Kimble's gaze raked over her in contempt. "I know your real name. I want you to stay away from my nephew."

Which one? was on the tip of Faith's tongue, but she bit it back. She glanced at Greg, whose hands were clenched into fists at his sides, his mouth opening to protest. "Don't," she said to the boy. "It's all right. I'll see you later."

"No, you won't," Jim said, standing so close that Faith would have had to crane her neck to see his face. "I know what you are. I don't want you around him. Ever. Stay away from Adam, too. The last thing he needs is the likes of you."

O-kay. Faith took a large step back. Glanced at Tammy Kimble, saw her biting her lip. But her focus was on Greg, not Faith and not her husband.

Faith felt like standing on a chair so that she could yell in the older Kimble's face, but that would solve nothing. "If you'll excuse me, I have to go." She packed up her computer bag, reacting to Jim Kimble only when he moved to take it from her arms. "Don't touch me."

"I want to be sure you haven't taken anything you shouldn't have."

"Jim," his wife said. "Leave her be. Deacon can search her bag."

Jim Kimble rolled his eyes. "Deacon's not rational about this woman."

"She saved my life today," Greg said loudly, and both Jim and Tammy looked at him like he had three heads, giving Faith the seconds she needed to step out of Jim Kimble's reach.

She gave Greg a nod. "This makes us square, okay?"

"Do I still get *All-Night Zombie Buffet*?"

Faith continued to walk backward toward the conference room. "I never welch on a deal."

Chapter Twenty-six

Adam held up a DVD. "He planted the tracker in Corcoran's Jeep while it was parked in the garage near her office," he said. "You need to see it." He slipped the DVD into Isenberg's machine, hit PLAY, and stepped back so they could see the screen.

"There's Corcoran's Jeep, arriving at eight forty-five yesterday morning." Thirty seconds later the white van entered the garage. Adam switched views. "This is the fourth floor of the garage."

The Jeep parked, and Faith got out wearing the green suit she'd had on Monday night, the black coat with which she'd covered Arianna draped over her arm. Seconds later the white van came into camera range.

"The van was waiting on the ramp, just out of sight. I checked the other floors, and the van followed the same pattern, giving her Jeep a head start at every floor, then following."

"What's on the door?" Isenberg asked, leaning closer to see. "A sign, but for what?"

"It reads 'John's Emergency Auto Service,'" Adam said. "Magnetic sign, probably a fictitious company or a sign stolen from a legit business."

"She might have been suspicious of a plain white van

after the bridge incident," Bishop said, "but she wouldn't have thought twice about a van for an auto service in a garage. Slick."

But Deacon wasn't looking at the van or its signs. His eyes were on Faith, who'd dropped her car keys. She looked both ways, then stooped down to retrieve them before hurrying to the elevator. All while the white van idled thirty feet away. Once again he'd come close to losing her before he'd even met her.

Bishop's exhale was audible. "She was a sitting duck and didn't even know."

Deacon's heart was beating unevenly. "When did he put on the tracker?"

"After she got into the elevator." Adam changed views again. "The van went one floor up and parked. The driver got out, dressed like an old man." They watched as he walked hunched over with a cane. He wore a trenchcoat and a hat, so the camera couldn't see his face. He stopped next to Faith's Jeep, pretended to drop a pen. "You have to slow the video down to see him slap the tracker under her engine, because he does it so fast. Then he picked up the pen he'd dropped, went back to the van, and was gone. The white van exited at nine ten a.m."

"He could have killed Dr. Corcoran there in the garage," Tanaka said. "Why didn't he?"

"He must have thought the risk was too high," Deacon said, his heart racing. "He might not have been able to get away—he could have been stopped at any of the exits. Plus, we'd have film of it. He clearly expected the garage to have cameras."

"He might have grabbed her and dragged her into the van, but that would have been captured on video, too," Bishop added. "He didn't want any link to her."

"He probably figured he'd know if she came close to the house again." *But how had the bastard found her?* "He was going to be ready for her."

"But by the time Faith approached," Bishop said, "our guy had chaos everywhere. The Earl Power tech had surprised him, they fought, and Arianna escaped. The locksmith must have arrived at about the same time that Faith found Arianna. The killer had to cut and run."

"Wait a second." Deacon looked through his notes,

frowning. "Adam, you called Earl Power. Didn't the tech's supervisor say that he texted when he got there?"

"He did." Adam checked his notes. "It was at three fifteen. But that leaves a gap. If the locksmith arrived at five, what was the killer doing all that time? Why didn't he go searching for Arianna?"

"Because the Earl Power tech drugged him," Deacon said. "You found the dart, Adam."

"We need to know how he knew where Faith was," Bishop said. "If he followed her to the bank, he had to know she worked there. So that makes her boss a suspect, plus anyone who saw an organizational announcement that she was joining the company." She groaned. "Does anybody know how big the bank is?"

"Three hundred people," Adam said. "It's their headquarters." He looked at Deacon. "I called her boss and told him she was involved in an investigation, that I needed to confirm her employment. He confirmed that she did work there, that she'd started Monday morning."

Deacon stared at him. "You informed her boss? Why would you do that?"

"Because I didn't trust her. I wanted to be sure she was who she said she was." And he didn't appear sorry in the least. "You weren't asking the right questions. Somebody needed to."

"And so you decided to take that on yourself." Deacon dropped his gaze to the table for a long moment, arranging his thoughts and trying very, very hard not to lose his temper. "She wasn't a suspect, Adam." He managed to say it evenly, conscious of everyone at the table watching his response. "How long do you think it will take for rumors to start that she is?"

"We question people's alibis all the time," Adam said, no fluctuation in his tone. "We probably start rumors that impact people's lives. It's part of the job."

Part of the job. But it wasn't the job. It was Faith.

Deacon listened to himself, to what he'd just thought. Okay, maybe—in the absence of data—Adam had a point. He hadn't treated Faith like a suspect when he probably should have.

Because he'd known she hadn't done anything wrong. *No, you hoped.* But he knew that wasn't true. He'd *known*.

From the moment he'd laid eyes on Faith Corcoran, he'd *known*.

But Adam hadn't known. Like Greg, Adam's reasons were good. But Adam had made a choice to act off-script and that couldn't be ignored. *Put this confrontation off till later. Then decide what to do.* And when he did act, he'd be doing so because Adam wasn't respecting the chain of command. Not because he'd threatened Faith. Deacon only hoped Adam's query hadn't caused her to lose her job.

"You supervised the crime scene in the grocery store parking lot, correct?" he asked Adam. "What did you find there?"

Surprise crackled through Adam's eyes as if he'd expected to be rebuked. "What we knew. Caucasian woman, thirty-five. No purse or other ID found around the body. No security tapes. The cams in that area weren't working."

"Just like the cameras at King's College. And the lights," Bishop said. "He might have found out about the college security issues from the blog run by that student, but how did he know about the parking lot?"

"It was common knowledge," Adam said. "Several of the cashiers said they'd complained about it in the past."

"They complained to the newspaper," Tanaka said. "One of my guys did a search for other crimes in that same parking lot and came up with two, both within the last three months. Both articles quote the cashiers as saying the store had 'shoddy security' and broken cameras. It wouldn't have been hard for him to know it was a safe place for him to go."

"Were either of those earlier crimes against blondes who went to college?" Deacon asked.

"No," Tanaka said. "Common muggings, nobody injured. Unrelated to this crime."

"The white van," Adam said, "was found with several bags of dog food in the back. We figured he put her purchases in the van, then stole her vehicle. I questioned the cashiers who were on duty last night, and one of them remembers her, but said she paid cash."

Deacon sighed. "Of course she did. No cameras in the store, I take it."

"Yes, but they don't show anything that could tell us who she is."

"Of course they don't. Did you get the bullet?"

"We did," Tanaka said. "Nine mil, ballistics match for all the others."

"As of thirty minutes ago, no missing-persons report had been filed in the entire tristate area," Adam added. "By the amount of dog food in the van, she either has a houseful of normal-sized dogs or a few St. Bernards. I sent her photo to some of the local vets asking if she was a client. So far, no replies."

"The vet angle is a good idea," Deacon said. "Hopefully someone will either recognize her or will have missed her by tomorrow. Carrie, what can you tell us about Agent Pope?"

"I personally examined Agent Pope's body when it was first brought in. The damage done by the knife was extensive. The knife wounds might have been enough to cover the bullet entry wound if the bullet hadn't ricocheted off one of Agent Pope's ribs."

Someone shot at Pope. That was news, and strengthened Deacon's argument that the serial and not the high school student had done the killing. "Did you find the bullet?" he asked tightly.

"Not yet. But there's no exit wound, so if it's still in there, we'll find it."

"So he shot him first," Bishop said. "That's how he got the drop on a former Special Ops soldier. Then he used the knife to try to hide what he'd done."

"He was attempting to draw Faith out into the open. Just like with the bellman." Deacon set his teeth against a sudden wave of rage at the callous disregard for life and for the guilt Faith was going to feel when she found out.

Adam's cheeks had gone dark, whether from fury or embarrassment Deacon wasn't sure. "Still, how did he get the knife from that kid?" he asked. "How would he know to? How would he know this one high school kid was a threat to our family?"

"I don't know yet." Deacon rubbed his forehead. "The kid is a loudmouth, a bully. He's got a posse who heard him threaten Dani before. If they knew, the whole school knew. Maybe this killer overheard them trash-talking. We can question the kids tomorrow, but first we need to find the gunman. He's driving whatever he stole from the parking lot victim—or at least he drove it for a little while. Lynda, can we get photos of this victim to the squad cars and have them visit all the veterinarians in the area?"

Isenberg nodded. "I've freed up personnel. They can start when the offices open."

"Thanks. Are you done with the basement, Vince?" Deacon asked Tanaka.

"Not yet. Dr. Johannsen still has to examine the basement floor. I've borrowed X-ray equipment to see inside the walls, but it won't be here until tomorrow morning."

"Corinne could be dead by morning, dammit," Adam said, his jaw tense.

"I know," Deacon said quietly. "We all know, Adam."

Adam jerked a nod, slouching in his chair. "Sorry, Vince."

Tanaka's nod was weary. "It's okay. We're all running on fumes."

That was God's truth. "We'll start ripping out walls when we get the go-ahead from Vince. Carrie, anything else?" Deacon asked.

"That was it. If you don't need me anymore, I'm going home." Carrie gathered her things and reached for the door, only to step back when it opened on its own. "Oh."

Faith came through the door, and Deacon automatically came to his feet. "What's wrong?"

"Excuse me," Faith said, "but you have visitors, Agent Novak. Your family is here."

Cincinnati, Ohio
Wednesday, November 5, 1:20 a.m.

Faith stepped farther into the conference room, giving Deacon room to pass. He surprised her by stopping in the doorway.

"Fucking hell," he muttered.

Tammy stood in front of Jim, his big hands covering her shoulders with a gentleness that was at odds with his scowl. On the other side of Deacon's desk was Greg, fists still clenched.

Isenberg frowned. "Get this little family circus out of my bullpen, Agent Novak," she snapped. *"Now."* She went into her office, closing the door with a small slam.

"Excuse me, Faith," Deacon said wearily, and crossed to his desk, his stride so long that she had to almost skip to keep up with him. *There is no way I'm missing a word of this,* she thought. Not considering how grim Greg had become. She wasn't sure that she believed the boy when he'd said he wasn't being hurt by his uncle.

Adam brought up the rear, surprising Faith by standing shoulder to shoulder with Deacon.

"What's this all about?" Deacon asked quietly.

"We came to get Greg," the uncle said, his voice booming. His scowl deepened.

Greg shook his head. "I said no. I want to stay with you, Deacon. I'm not going back."

"You can't say with Deacon," the aunt implored. "Please, Greg, come with us."

Somehow that was the last thing Faith had expected them to say. She thought they'd thrown Greg out of their house because of the trouble he'd gotten into at school.

"You can't stay with Deacon," the uncle reiterated. "His house isn't safe." He aimed a cool glance at Deacon. "We'll have to take him back until you fix this problem."

"Please, D. Let me stay with you. I won't be any trouble. I promise."

Deacon straightened his spine and turned to his aunt. "Please sit down, Aunt Tammy. You can use Bishop's chair. How did you know Greg was here?" He looked at Adam when he asked the question. Adam just shook his head.

"Dani told us," Tammy said, slumping into the chair. "But we had to call her first." Her eyes were red and swollen when she lifted them to Deacon. "We saw your house on the news. There was a murder there. And you didn't tell us." Her voice broke. "You didn't even think to tell us Greg was all right."

Deacon rubbed his forehead. "I'm sorry. You're right. I should have called you."

"He's been a little busy, Mom," Adam said quietly, coming to Deacon's defense.

Tammy whipped a furious gaze at her son. "Don't you talk to me right now, Adam," she whispered fiercely. "You haven't called or come by in a month. I've gone whole weeks worrying if you were alive or dead. You don't get to talk to me right now."

Adam nodded, stoically taking her temper. The twitch of

the muscle in his jaw was the only sign that he was affected at all. "I'm sorry, too, Mom. I didn't mean for you to worry."

"Well, I did." Tears now streaked down her cheeks, her nearly transparent hands coming up to cover her mouth. "I did. I do. I have every night for forty-five years. I worried every night that your father wouldn't come home, that I'd have to bury him in his uniform. And now you two boys." She glared at Deacon. "I had to hear that you got shot on the news. So yes, I called Dani. Thank God she has more common sense than the lot of you put together. She told us that Greg would need a place to stay until you get your house back."

Greg's panicked eyes shot to Deacon's face. "I can't stay there," he pleaded. "You know what will happen," he added through clenched teeth. "They don't *know*."

Faith suddenly understood Greg's predicament, but it didn't look like Deacon did yet. She tapped him on the shoulder. "Can I talk to you for a minute?" she whispered. "It's important."

"This is a family matter," Jim said loudly when Deacon turned to walk with her.

Deacon sighed. "Jim, nobody wants a fight tonight. Just be patient." He took Faith into the conference room where Tanaka and Bishop looked uncomfortable. Faith knew how they felt.

He closed the door and leaned against it. "What?" he said wearily, suddenly looking just like a man who hadn't slept in two days.

"Your aunt and uncle don't know what happened at Greg's school, do they?" He shook his head and she pressed forward. "Then they don't know that Dani had been threatened. Greg still thinks he drew Pope's murderer to your house—which he also can't tell them about because then he'd have to tell them about the threat to Dani. He thinks he's going to get them killed if he goes with them. If you know for sure that Pope was killed because of me, you have to take Greg aside and tell him the truth. Don't let him suffer another minute, please."

"You're right. Thank you." He scrubbed his palms over his face. "I think I hit the wall the minute I saw Jim standing there. I wasn't thinking clearly." Deacon returned to Greg, and Faith's heart sank. *Then it was me, not Greg. Pope was killed to draw me out.*

From the open doorway, she watched Deacon take Greg aside, his hands on the boy's shoulders. He leaned forward until their remarkable eyes were locked together—and so that Greg could watch his mouth. Because Deacon wasn't making any audible sound. He was mouthing the words so that Greg could read his lips.

Greg's face went slack with shock, and he began to cry. Deacon put his arms around the boy and held on. *Just like he's done with me.* Her heart cracked a little more.

Suddenly feeling like an interloper, Faith shut the conference room door and joined Bishop and Tanaka at the table. Sinking into a hard plastic chair, she rested her eyes, her head pillowed on her folded arms. She must have dozed off, because the sound of the door opening had her head jerking up.

Disoriented, she blinked, bringing Isenberg into focus. "Oh, Lieutenant. I'm sorry. I'll leave." She started to stand, but Isenberg waved her back down.

"They seem to be wrapping up the family meeting out there," she said dryly. "It's probably better for you to stay here until Jim Kimble's gone."

"Yeah, he didn't like me very much."

Isenberg put a folder on the table and began sorting through photos. "Jim Kimble is an old-school cop."

Bishop rolled her eyes. "Which is code for 'Neanderthal.'"

"But his views are commonly shared," Isenberg said. "I have to admit that I've thought the same way as Adam and his father at points during my career."

"So have I," Faith said quietly.

"I believe that." Isenberg tilted her head. "I've always been curious about something. Did you ever treat sex offenders that you thought really wouldn't reoffend?"

"Yes. I did meet a few that I thought would be able to stay straight. Most people in this country think that reoffending is a fait accompli. I don't necessarily believe that. The statistics say it's fifteen percent, twelve with counseling."

"You can set up a test to give you any numbers you want," Tanaka said derisively.

"I agree," Faith said. "Those stats assume that successive crimes are reported and only take into account the reoffenders who get caught. The truth lies somewhere between fifteen and a hundred percent. I worked with offenders for years and I can count on two hands how many I was confident wouldn't hurt another child, and a few of those were simply too old. If they'd been young and healthy, they would have been back out there, hunting the helpless."

"Just like the man we're looking for." Isenberg pinned one of the photos in her stack to the left-hand side of the bulletin board, labeled VICTIMS. The photo was Agent Pope's, and it filled Faith with a sense of despair. *No one is safe around me. Not until the bastard is dead.*

Deacon and Adam filed back into the room and took their seats tiredly. "Sorry, Lynda," Deacon said. "We all agreed it was best for Jim and Tammy to take Greg home. If he stays with me, he could draw the killer's attention."

Because Deacon will be with me. And I have the killer's attention. Lucky me.

Faith looked up, her eyes darting away from the victims' side of the bulletin board to focus on the right, where the card read SUSPECTS, unsurprised to see a photo of her uncle Jeremy. She'd led them right to him, after all. But her eyes narrowed at the photo below Jeremy's. "You suspect my cousin Stone?"

"He looks a lot like Combs," Deacon said. "Similar size, weight, and coloring. You could have mistaken him coming through your window. And his behavior has been suspicious."

"Details of which you're not going to tell me," Faith muttered, then sat back, shocked to recognize the photo of Herbert Henson the third that she'd seen on the attorney's lobby wall. "You think the attorney's grandson could be involved?" But when she thought about it, it made a sick kind of sense. "He could have known I'd inherit the house even before Grandmother died," she said quietly. "And he would have had access to the house. For years. Has his behavior been suspicious, too?"

"And how," Bishop said dryly.

"Why haven't we brought the lawyer in yet?" Adam demanded.

"Because we can't find him," Bishop said glumly. "Not at

home or the office. He could have skipped the country by now. Did Crandall have any luck finding video of the mystery woman who got the key from Herbie Three?"

"What mystery woman?" Faith asked.

"She showed up at the firm your lawyer hired to do the maintenance on your house and took the key from Herbie Three," Bishop answered. "I'm getting the witness in with a sketch artist tomorrow."

Mystery woman. Roza's mother. Dammit. "Deacon, had any of the victims given birth?" Faith asked. "Because Arianna said that Roza wouldn't leave with her because her mother was there, that she couldn't leave her. I just remembered it now. It was one of the things Arianna said before Detective Bishop came in the room. Either her mother was taken away alive, or she's dead. Were any of the victims old enough to have a twelve-year-old daughter?"

"Only if they'd been twelve-year-old mothers themselves," Bishop said.

"When does Sophie start scanning the basement floor?" Deacon asked Tanaka.

"In the morning," Tanaka said. "I'll tell her that we may be missing a victim."

Deacon turned to his to-do list. "All right, guys. Let's get this done so we can all go home and get some sleep. On my list: find out how he got the kid's knife, find Henson the third, and get sketches of the mystery lady and Roza." He looked through his notes. "Did Crandall run a list of properties owned by Jeremy O'Bannion?"

"He did," Isenberg said. "Jeremy's listed as owning only the house in Indian Hill."

"Damn," he muttered. "The other loose end we had was checking to see how our killer got from Cincinnati to Miami and back on Saturday to tamper with Faith's old car. Combs's face isn't showing up in any of the Bureau's facial-recognition checks. I'm adding Jeremy, Stone, and Herbie Three to the list of faces to search for." He sighed heavily. "And we need to begin notifying the victims' families."

"I'll make a plan for this," Isenberg said. "We'll share the burden."

"Thank you," Deacon said quietly.

Adam cleared his throat. "I'll take care of finding Faith a new safe house."

Everyone around the table was clearly stunned. *You will?* seemed to be the unspoken consensus. The tangible apprehension pouring off of Deacon didn't help. "You don't have to do that," he said. "I'll take care of it."

"I've worked Homicide for years," Adam said mildly. "I can locate safe shelter for one person. I already have a place in mind. I just have to make sure that it's not currently in use."

"All right," Deacon said. "Go home and sleep. Everyone work their to-do items in the morning, and we'll reconvene at oh nine hundred."

"Lynda, how are you going to notify Roxanne Dupree's family?" Bishop asked as she rose and gathered her things. "We could ask Vega to—"

Faith's heart stuttered. "*Wait.* Did you say Roxanne Dupree? From Miami?"

"Yes," Bishop said, sharing an uncertain glance with Deacon. "Do you know her?"

No, no. Don't let it be her. Her hands shaking, Faith ran to the bulletin board and took down the photo of Roxanne Dupree. Her eyes stared out from the photo taken from her driver's license. *She's dead.*

"She's mine," she whispered, her knees buckling. *Oh God. No. No.* "She's one of mine."

Cincinnati, Ohio
Wednesday, November 5, 1:50 a.m.

Deacon rushed to catch Faith as she crumpled, but wasn't in time. Her knees hit the floor with a sickening thud, but she didn't seem to notice as she stared at the photo she clutched in her shaking hands.

Gently, he pulled her to her feet, guided her back to her chair. "What do you mean, she's yours? Faith?" He went down on one knee beside her, looked up into her devastated face.

"Goddamn you, you sonofabitch," she whispered brokenly, her eyes still frozen on the picture. "She was making it. She was going to be all right. Now she's dead. Because of me."

Deacon took the photo from her hands and gave it to Isenberg, who looked as helpless as he felt. Her hands now empty, Faith wrapped her arms around her middle, hugging herself as she rocked in place. No tears flowed. Her eyes were completely dry. But empty.

Which was somehow far worse than wrenching sobs. Alarmed, Deacon rubbed her back gently. "No, not because of you."

"Then who?" she whispered, sounding so lost. Slowly, she turned her head to meet his gaze. "Who, Deacon? If not me, then who?"

Her eyes were dry, but Deacon's stung. "He's evil, Faith. You know that evil exists."

"When does this stop? How do I make him stop?"

"*You* don't," Deacon said. "*We* do."

She shook her head as if he hadn't said a word. "How many more people have to die? Maybe I should just . . ." She closed her eyes. "I don't want to die. But I can't live with this."

Fear sliced through his heart. "No way. You are not giving yourself up."

"I know. But I just want him to stop." Her eyes opened, still dry. Now haunted. "How did he know she was mine?"

"That's a damn good question," he said.

Bishop knelt on the other side of Faith's chair. "Who was she? How was she yours?"

"She came to me when she was seventeen, and so damn brave. She'd been molested by her father for four years. Her mother accused her of lying and threatened to throw her out if she told anyone else. But Roxie was going away to college, leaving her eleven-year-old sister behind. She couldn't let her father start up with her sister, so she reported him. Her father was convicted, but not jailed like she'd hoped. Because it was his first offense," she added bitterly.

Deacon exhaled wearily. "Probation only. And court-ordered therapy with you."

"Yes. Roxie was devastated. Her sister was still in danger. Her father was just biding his time until Roxie was out of the house. Her mother was in denial so deep . . . and blaming Roxie because he wasn't allowed to live with them during the time he was in counseling."

"What did you do, Faith?" Bishop asked softly.

"I gave her a micro camera. Told her where to plant it in

her sister's room, then to pretend to spend the night with a friend but instead hide in her sister's closet. To text me when her father came into her sister's room, then call 911 and break out of the closet to stop him—with the operator still on the line so she could hear what was happening."

"Where were you?" Isenberg asked.

"In my car, right across the street with my telephoto lens. And my gun. Roxie did everything I said, but her father grabbed her phone, hung up on 911, and ran. I got his picture as he was running out the front door, zipping his pants. When the cops came for him, he claimed the girls were lying. But Roxie had video from the hidden camera. My friend Deb was the arresting officer. I sent her the photo of him leaving the house—anonymously, but she figured out what I'd done. It was the first case we worked on together. He got three years."

"And when he got out?" Isenberg asked.

"Wife still in denial. Younger daughter sleeping with a butcher knife under her pillow. First night home, Dad sneaks into her room and ends up dead." Now her eyes filled. Spilled. Quiet tears. "Roxie had a lot of lingering issues—drinking, indiscriminate sex. Shoplifting trinkets. But she was working on them in therapy."

"You were her therapist?" Bishop asked.

"Before her father went to jail. She was seeing a counselor at the college. I was just her friend. She always called me when she got in trouble and I'd go bail her out."

"You paid her bail?" Adam asked in disbelief. "With your own money?"

Deacon blinked, startled. He'd all but forgotten that Adam was there.

Faith shrugged again. "Used my alimony. Knew it would piss Charlie off. Double bonus."

Deacon had also all but forgotten she'd been married. What kind of man had her ex been that he'd let her get away? Luckily for Deacon, Charlie Frye was apparently a stupid man.

And then a thought occurred, making him ill. Roxanne Dupree had just been released from jail when she'd disappeared. "When was the last time you bailed her out?" he asked.

"It was the day after the white van tried to run me off the bridge, so three weeks ago."

Bishop closed her eyes for a moment, then sighed. "Where did you drop her off?"

Faith's hands froze, then slowly lowered to her lap, her eyes wide. Horrified anew. "No. No." She shook her head. "Tell me I did not lead him to her. *Tell me.*" When they said nothing, a spasm of pain contorted her face. She dropped her chin to her chest and wept silently.

Breaking Deacon's heart. He rose slowly, feeling five hundred years old. He stroked her hair as he looked around the room and saw understanding in the eyes of the team. They knew what she'd done. And why.

In Adam's eyes he also saw shame. And respect. "You worked both sides of the fence, didn't you?" he said quietly. "You helped put Combs away. That's why he hates you so much."

"*If* she did, she might lose her license," Deacon said, his voice sharp.

Adam shook his head. "Don't worry. I won't tell."

Isenberg blew out an unsteady breath. "None of this leaves this room."

Tanaka blinked several times. "None of what, Lynda?"

Isenberg nodded. "Get her out of here, Deacon. And figure out who's behind this before she does something stupid, like give herself up." Drawing a deep breath, she left the room.

"I will," Deacon promised, still stroking Faith's hair. She continued to weep, still silently.

Adam hung back when the others had left. "When did she tell you, D?" he asked.

"Late last night, when I took her to the ER."

"But somehow you knew earlier. I'm sorry, Deacon." He turned to Faith and put his hand gently on her shoulder. "And, Faith, I . . . Forgive me. I didn't know."

She didn't lift her head, but managed a small nod.

Adam gathered her laptop case and overnight bag along with the box he'd brought with him earlier. "I have a safe place for her to stay. I'll text you the address and meet you there."

Deacon looked his cousin in the eye, daring Adam to say he planned to stay the night with them. Adam lifted one black brow. "I'll meet you there to give you the key and show you the security system," he clarified.

"Thank you," Deacon said, and waited for Adam to leave. Then he pulled Faith to her feet and into his arms, holding her tight as she wept for a young woman who'd escaped one monster only to be killed by another.

Chapter Twenty-seven

"Wow." Deacon looked out the floor-to-ceiling windows at the view of the city below. Adam's "safe place" was a penthouse on the top floor of a high-rise on the river. Apparently, it belonged to a corporate bigwig who was currently on assignment in Southeast Asia. The man's daughter had been kidnapped and Adam had been the one to bring her home safely and bring her kidnapper to justice. Grateful for his daughter's safe return, he'd offered his condo for the department's use while he was away if they should ever need it. Adam had contacted the man, who had agreed to let Faith stay there.

Deacon turned from the city lights to Faith, who sat on a sofa, her shoulders pitched forward, her head hanging low, her grief-ravaged face hidden by a waterfall of thick red hair. Her hands neatly folded in her lap, she hadn't moved a muscle since he'd put her there ten minutes before.

She was hiding from him, there in plain sight.

"The fridge is stocked," Adam said, coming out of the kitchen. "Toiletries in each bathroom. Anything that isn't in a locked cabinet is yours for the taking." He handed a set of keys to Deacon. "The elevator is keyed only to come straight to this floor from the parking garage in the basement. No one should bother you. Isenberg's got a uniform by the elevator in the garage and one by the stairwell door, just in case."

"Thank you." Deacon tore his attention from Faith to meet his cousin's dark eyes. "Are we okay, Adam? You and me?"

Adam swallowed hard. "Yeah. I've been a dick and I'm sorry. I don't know what to say."

"It's forgotten." Deacon pulled him close for a hard hug, slapping him on the back. "Go home. See your mother. And if you want to tell me what happened, I'll be around."

"I'm glad. We've missed you, Dani and I. See you tomorrow morning." Adam looked at Faith, then lowered his voice. "There are ice packs in the freezer if she wants one for her face." Without waiting for a reply, he jogged to the door and let himself out.

For a moment, there was only silence, heavy and tense.

"An ice pack would be nice," Faith murmured from behind her hair. "I must look a fright."

Deacon brought her one, then, before she could protest, lifted her in his arms and settled them both into the corner of the sofa, her body tucked up against him, his hand curving over her round bottom to keep her close. His body immediately responded, but she didn't pull away.

He tipped her chin up, but she covered her face with the ice pack. Undeterred, he kissed the top of her head. "You cried because you care. How can I see you as anything but beautiful?"

She rested her head against his shoulder. "My head hurts. My heart, too."

"I know." He tugged the ice pack away from her face. "You'll get freezer burn," he teased, and was rewarded with a hiccupped laugh. "You are the prettiest woman I've ever seen, so please don't hide from me."

She searched his face. "What are we going to do, Deacon?"

"Right now, we're going to sleep. I'm so tired I can't think straight, and I know you are, too. Come with me." He stood, letting her slide down his body until her feet hit the floor. He wasn't so selfish that he'd expect sex after what she'd been through, but he wanted her to know exactly what she did to him. Wrapping his arm around her shoulders, he took her to the bedroom, where Adam had placed her Hello Kitty overnight bag.

"Arms up," he said brusquely, and proceeded to undress her down to her panties. Biting back his lust, he pulled the blanket aside. "Get in."

He tucked her in, unable to resist stroking the silky skin of her back before he drew the covers up to her neck, determined to walk away and sleep in the next bedroom. Otherwise he'd never be able to keep his hands off her.

A little moan escaped her throat. "That felt good. Can you do it again?"

"Sure." *I am a goddamned saint,* he thought, gritting his teeth as he toed off his shoes. He climbed onto the bed, torturing himself by straddling her so that her bottom brushed against his now painfully hard erection. He tugged the blanket down to bare her back and massaged her with long deep strokes that had her sighing.

Her sighs grew quieter, her body still as she finally fell asleep. Gritting his teeth, he pulled the blanket up to her neck and climbed off the bed, taking care not to wake her.

"Where are you going?" she mumbled just as he got to the door.

He didn't turn around. "To sleep in my own room."

"Why? Don't go. Please stay." He heard the sheets rustle and couldn't help but picture all that beautiful, creamy, bare skin. "Sleep here. With me."

"I can't. I can't be that close to you and not touch you."

"I know. Come to bed with me, Deacon."

His pants hit the floor in a jingle of change. He didn't even remember lowering the zipper, but he was climbing into bed beside her wearing only the black silk boxers with little red flames that he'd pulled on earlier that day. When he'd taken the comfort she'd offered. He pulled her back against his chest, wrapping one arm around her waist.

And forgot how to breathe when she moved his hand up to cover her breast. His heart was beating so hard it was all he could hear. He leaned up to look at her face on the pillow. Her lips were parted, her breathing deep and even. She was nearly asleep already, so he took the opportunity to simply look at her. *So damn pretty.*

He didn't know how many seconds ticked by as he watched her sleep. *She's finally calm. Finally unafraid.* Her brow was smooth, unfurrowed with worry and guilt. He wanted this for her waking hours, wanted her to be completely unafraid. He had to stop this monster. Before she did something stupid, like give herself up. Isenberg was right. Too many more victims on her conscience and Faith would give herself up, just to make it stop.

Not on my watch. He'd figure it out. He had to. He'd just found her. *I won't lose you now.* Pressing a kiss to her shoulder, he snuggled behind her and let his mind disconnect.

Eastern Kentucky
Wednesday, November 5, 6:45 a.m.

He took the S curves at a decent clip, appreciating the way the pickup truck grabbed the roads. He'd never been the pickup type and would never have chosen the vehicle. It was the owner he'd targeted as she'd come out of the hospital. She'd been in her fifties, wearing a designer suit that had probably cost more than the truck. And she was a lightweight. She couldn't have weighed more than a hundred pounds.

Light enough to pick up and toss in the backseat after he'd come up behind her, clamped one hand over her mouth and slit her throat with the other.

But even though she'd been wealthy, she'd been too greedy to pay for parking in a lighted area, and that had been her downfall. When he'd first followed her, he'd expected her to drive a classy sedan or an SUV. He hadn't expected her to walk up to the big king cab truck.

According to the Facebook profile she'd left open on her phone, she owned a barn full of fancy horses and had just become a grandmother, which was why she'd been at the hospital all night. The truck was deluxe, with all the bells and whistles. He'd have liked to keep it, but a vehicle like this would be noticed, especially in his neighborhood. So he'd get the job done and ditch it.

He stopped in front of the cabin, almost sorry he'd already arrived. He got out . . . and went still. The door was open. He'd closed it. He'd locked it. He was sure he had.

Leaving the truck door open in case he needed a quick escape, he pulled the gun from his waistband and approached carefully. He opened the door. And felt his heart stop.

The floorboards had been pulled up and tossed in a pile.

The bodies had been discovered. He crept inside, listening for any sound of a trap. But there was only silence, deep and oppressive. He aimed the beam of his flashlight into the ground. The bodies had been unearthed, head to waist. The Earl Power logo was clearly visible on the power tech's jacket.

I should have stripped them nude. He always stripped them nude. *Why didn't I do that?*

Because he'd been in a hurry to get back to the city and kill Faith. *Damn her to hell.* Why wouldn't she just die already?

Relax. Nobody's reported them. The bodies were still here and there were no police around. The Earl Power guy was a known missing person. Some curious passerby probably saw the mound of fill dirt he'd left on the floor and—

Shit. The girl. *Roza is gone.*

He ran around the back, and his stomach started to heave. The doors to the storm shelter had been thrown wide open. He shone his light down into the cellar, fighting back sheer panic.

Because Corinne Longstreet was gone, too.

He stumbled down the stairs, swinging the beam of his flashlight around the storm cellar, dazed. His mind reeling. He'd left her here for a day. Only a day. He'd expected to find Corinne half-frozen or maybe even dead. But not gone.

His light hit two small piles of rope. His rope. He picked up the pieces and studied the ends. They'd been sawn with a very dull knife. The Longstreet bitch had had a knife.

Where had she gotten it? He'd searched her thoroughly when he'd shackled her to the cot. She'd been carrying a can of pepper spray in her backpack, but he'd found that right away.

I should never have taken her. If he hadn't, he never would have had to take Arianna. Who wouldn't have gotten away, and no one would have invaded his home and taken his things.

He drew a deep breath through his nose, determined to stay calm. *Do not think about it. Do not think about them in my house, touching my things.*

Think about getting Corinne back and making her pay.

Hell, think about getting Roza back before she told the world what he looked like.

He took the stairs in a few leaps, running back into the cabin. *She'd* uncovered the bodies. The Longstreet woman. The pile of dirt and the shovel he'd left behind had piqued her curiosity, no doubt. *Well, all right, then.* That wasn't so bad. It wasn't like anyone else knew. This could still be contained—if he found her. How hard could that be?

Considering she'd hidden a knife and managed to free herself and the girl? *Maybe hard.*

Still, she was one woman and a sick one at that. She'd be needing her medicine soon. And she'd be slowed down by the child. How far could she have gotten?

He swung his flashlight around the room, noting the open drawers and cabinets. She *was* smart, he thought reluctantly. She'd taken supplies. But it was also extra weight she had to carry that would slow her down.

The beam of his flashlight landed on the closet and his gut twisted. *My things.* He'd put the trunk in there the night before. Slowly he approached, almost afraid to look. Then he let out a relieved breath. The old steamer trunk was still there.

He lifted the lid, scanned the contents anxiously. The jars on top had rolled around in the trunk as he'd moved them into the closet, but none had been broken. And in the smaller box next to the jars, his collection of their things— the items each victim had carried on the day he'd taken her—credit cards, cash, jewelry . . . and now cell phones, of course.

Briefly he weighed the danger of keeping the box and trunk with him in a stolen truck versus leaving them in the closet while he looked for Corinne and the child. If they had managed to find help, the cops would storm this place. He was not going to allow his belongings to be taken, especially by the police.

He grabbed the wheelbarrow, loaded the trunk into it, then moved his collection to the floorboard of the dead equestrian's truck. Then he loaded the woman into the wheelbarrow for the trip back into the cabin so he could bury her with the others.

He looked around for the shovel, but it was gone, too. *The Longstreet bitch again,* he thought angrily. *She's stolen my shovel.*

With his hands, he pushed the soil away, once again glad

that he'd picked a skinny victim. Once he'd stripped her
naked, she slid right between the Earl Power tech and the
locksmith. He pushed the dirt back over them and replaced
the floorboards. This time he got rid of the dirt, dumping it
in the storm cellar and closing the cellar doors.

When he got back to the truck, he looked both ways,
shining his flashlight in the dirt along the road. And there
was a footprint. She'd gone back the way he'd just come.
Depending on how long she'd been free and how heavy her
pack was . . . she might have made it ten miles. Which was
just fine because there was no civilization for at least that
far.

But why hadn't he seen her? Maybe she'd hidden. *And I
was driving faster than normal.*

Damn truck. He'd had too much fun driving it. He'd have
to slow down. He got into the vehicle and headed back
toward town, searching for Corinne.

Cincinnati, Ohio
Wednesday, November 5, 7:45 a.m.

Faith woke to feathers tickling her nose. No, she realized.
Not feathers. The soft hair that covered Deacon Novak's
chest. At some point she'd rolled over and now lay sprawled
across him, her legs tangled with his, his chest her pillow.

Lightly, she petted him. His chest hair was solid white,
too. She wondered how far down the white went. Her fingers followed the trail down his chest, over his very nice abs.
The backs of her fingers brushed silk. And then steel. He
was hard.

Her body clenched, wanting him. Wanting him now. For
her own. She slipped her hand under his waistband and
curled her fingers around him, his erection jerking in her
hand.

A hum vibrated through his chest. "Don't stop," he whispered. "Don't ever stop."

Stroking him softly with one hand, she lifted up on the
opposite elbow. "You were awake."

"Just now." He arched, his eyes closed. "I want you. I
want to be inside you."

A shiver rippled over her skin. "Then what are you waiting for?" His eyes snapped open, and Faith was lost. Brown and blue clashed and swirled. "So beautiful," she whispered.

He exploded into action, yanking her panties down her legs, pushing his boxers out of the way, rolling her to her back. He straddled her again, but this time the view was much better. On his knees, he towered over her, jutting out, begging to be touched.

She traced a finger down the trail of hair, over his abs, petting the hair around his cock, making it jump and throb. All while those eyes of his remained fixed on her hands. He met her eyes and she felt scorched.

"I wondered," she whispered, "if your hair was white all over."

"Not all. There are still a few black ones in there." His eyes glinted wickedly. "You'd have to get very close to find them though."

She licked her lips and he groaned. "But not now," he said gruffly. "I need to be inside you now." He leaned to one side, opening the nightstand drawer, heaving a sigh of relief. "There's only one," he said, handing her the square packet. "You said you wanted to do it next time. Hurry or I'll do it myself."

Faith ripped open the condom and slowly slid it down the length of him. "All dressed," she said, her voice coming out strangely deep and husky. "Got someplace to go?"

"Yes." He slid down the bed until his mouth was level with her breasts and took his time, laving each with his tongue, teasing with his teeth until she was bucking beneath him. He sucked and nipped and made her go crazy.

"Deacon, please." She gripped his shoulders, digging in with her nails. "Please."

He slid lower. "Just a little taste. Just a little." And then his mouth was on her, his tongue doing wicked, wonderful things. She squirmed, working herself against his mouth, almost there.

And then he pulled his mouth away, replacing it with the smooth slide of his erection, filling her up. He held himself still, his eyes drifting closed.

"So good. You feel so good." His eyes opened, holding her gaze as he started to move, long, sumptuous strokes that had her trembling beneath him. "Do you like this?"

"Yes. But faster. Harder."

He went still, then pulled all the way out, sitting back on his haunches. "On your knees. Please." She scrambled up, obeying him, sucking in a breath when his hands spanned her waist and turned her so that her back pressed against his chest and she was sitting in his lap. Then he drew her close, sliding her down, impaling her, his hands sweeping up her rib cage to close over her breasts. "Ride, fast and hard."

She did, hoarding the pleasure, his and her own, not even realizing he'd turned them to face the opposite wall until he whispered, "Open your eyes, Faith."

She did and gasped. He'd turned them to face the mirror. "Watch us," he said in her ear, his breath hot against her skin. She shivered again and watched them. Watched herself riding him, her face flushed, her breasts bouncing. He lifted her arms around his neck, arching her back, displaying her breasts for him to see and touch. He filled his hands with them, plucking at her nipples, his face growing more intensely focused.

"Faster," he growled, "or I'll do it myself."

She picked up the pace, her heart beating hard, until with a low roar he came, taking her with him. They knelt together as the seconds turned to minutes, catching their breath, trembles subsiding. Deacon kissed her shoulder. "I have to be the luckiest man alive right now."

Faith laughed breathlessly. "I can't move. Ever again. We have to stay here."

"If only we could. Someday we will. When this is over, we're going away, just the two of us, and we'll stay in bed for a week, doing this."

Reality intruded and with it, the sadness with which she'd gone to sleep. Roxie Dupree. *I'm so sorry, baby.* "I can't believe she's gone. Roxie and all the others, dead because he wants me."

Deacon's arms tightened around her waist, and he kissed her temple. "We'll stop him."

"I know you will." The alarm clock on the nightstand began to ring, and Deacon silenced it. "I guess it's time to get at it," she said, and reluctantly slid off the bed, turning to kiss his mouth softly. "When do we need to leave?"

"I have a team meeting at nine, so eight thirty at the latest. We have plenty of time."

from the foam peanuts and chuckled. "It's another Kevlar vest. The note says, 'Don't get shot again.'"

Deacon's grin softened to a wistful smile. "That's Joseph's handwriting."

"His way of saying you scared him to death because he cares?"

"Yeah." He cleared his throat and put on the coat. "A little tight in the shoulders." Another grin, this one cheeky. "I'll have to let Joseph know."

Utterly charmed, Faith fastened the coat's buttons. "I was going to hide the box from the Feds because I didn't want you to lose another coat, but Adam insisted he'd handle it. I told him he'd get in trouble, but he said he owed you a debt. I hope he keeps the peace between you."

"I hope so, too." But then Deacon frowned. "I can forget about all the things he said to me, but one of the things he did might impact you. He called your boss yesterday morning to verify your employment and told him that you were a person of interest in an investigation. I had no idea he was going to do that. I never expected him to make that kind of decision on his own."

Faith's initial shock was obliterated by a flash of anger. But then years of training kicked in, providing her insight into Adam Kimble, whether she wanted it or not. "He thought he knew me. What I was. He didn't have the benefit of knowing the truth. Neither did you, but you still treated me with respect. Your behavior must have rattled him."

"What if you lose your job? Will you be so understanding then?"

She shrugged. "It wouldn't be the first time a boss fired me on the basis of an allegation. But they haven't fired me yet." At least the lack of reply to the e-mail she'd sent yesterday made more sense. "And if they do, even after I'm cleared, I wouldn't want to work there anyway."

Unease rippled across his face. "You'd leave Ohio?"

"I never said that. At this moment in time, standing here with you? Not on your life."

His smile made her knees go rubbery. "Good. Come on, let's go meet your uncle."

Eastern Kentucky
Wednesday, November 5, 7:45 a.m.

Corinne woke with a start, her heart racing, her breathing hard and heavy. Where the hell—? *Oh. Right.* Deer blind in the woods, running from a madman. *Jars of eyes.*

She blinked, bringing the ceiling into focus. The little room was no longer pitch-dark, but it wasn't quite light yet. *Sunrise.* She'd slept for nearly twelve hours. *I needed it.* She turned her head to the empty space beside her. *Roza.* Corinne sat up like a shot.

And pressed her hand to her pounding heart in relief. Roza sat in the corner of the small shelter, drinking cold soup broth from a can. A second empty can sat next to her foot. Warily, the child watched Corinne's every move.

"I thought you were gone," Corinne said, her voice rusty, her throat dry as the desert wind.

Roza looked at her like she was crazy. "Where would I go?"

"Good point." Corinne looked at the pile of supplies. "We don't have much left."

"I didn't eat all the soup," Roza said defensively. "I saved you two cans."

"That's fine, honey. I was more marveling that a pile that small weighed so much when I was carrying it. How are your feet?"

"I have sores." Roza had taken off her shoes, revealing nasty blisters that oozed.

"Me, too. I hate to tell you to put your shoes back on, but we have to walk some more."

"No," Roza moaned. "Please, no."

"You know he's looking for us. And *you* know what he looks like."

Fear filled Roza's eyes. "He'll kill me for helping your friend."

"I won't let that happen. But you'll have to walk, even with hurt feet. All good soldiers do."

Roza grew grim. "And I get to kill him."

Corinne sighed. "Just put on your shoes, sweetie." She struggled to her knees, every joint in her body aching. *Suck it up, soldier.* She shuffled to the window on her knees. *All clear.*

As shelters went, it was primo. Good visibility. Dry. Six

feet off the ground, it protected them from the critters that were almost certainly out there. *If I had a rifle, I'd stay here and shoot his sorry head off.* But she didn't. She had a few kitchen knives and a shovel.

And she had to pee. "I'm going to go down first. You stay here until I call you. If anything happens to me, you run, understand? You go back to the sign and you run the way that points to Route 60." She waited until Roza nodded before gripping the windowsill and pulling herself to her feet. She gritted her teeth, let the agony pass, then grabbed the shovel and the knives, just in case the critters came too close. "Take this," she said to Roza, handing her a knife. "Just in case. Hold on to it. We might need it."

Roza took the knife solemnly. "I won't lose it, 'Rin."

"Good girl." Corinne made it down the ladder and found a little privacy behind a tree. She was just about to step back in the open when she heard the footsteps behind her. She whirled, her pounding heart in her throat.

And was horrified to see him standing there.

It's him. He found us. She backed away, stumbling when her too-big boot tripped over a tree root. "No," she whispered. "No."

"I'm not going to hurt you," he said soothingly, coming closer. "I've been searching for you."

I'll bet you have. Corinne studied his face, catalogued every feature. Tightened her grip on the knife, turning her arm so that the blade wasn't visible to him.

He kept coming closer, palms out, like he really meant no harm.

She waited . . . waited . . . And when his hand started to move, she struck, arcing her arm up and plunging the knife into his gut, slashing as far as she could.

His face went flat with shock, and he stared down at the knife stuck in his gut. "You fucking stabbed me!" He took another staggering step forward and pulled out the knife.

Corinne feigned left, then darted right to grab her shovel. He was moving more slowly now, one hand clamped over his wound, but he was still moving. Gathering her strength, she ran at his back, holding the shovel with the handle straight out like a bayonet. She hit him hard, then jumped to the side, letting momentum carry her away as he went down on one knee.

"Roza!" she yelled. "Run! *Run!*"

Roza ran out the door, took one look at Corinne, and obeyed, running down the stairs and back the way they'd come.

"Stop!" he cried. "Don't do this. I came to—"

Corinne shifted her hold on the shovel, holding it like a baseball bat, and swung, hitting him squarely in the back of the head.

He went down. He finally went down. He was lying still, facedown.

Corinne bent over, bracing her hands on her thighs, panting, sweating. Shaking like a damn leaf. "I know what you came to do, you sick sonofabitch," she spat.

Get his keys, she thought. *And his phone. And don't forget his gun.* She edged close to the man, bending down to his pants pocket.

He moved like lightning, his hand grabbing her ankle like a vise. *Or a shackle.* Without hesitation, she brought the shovel down on his head again. Then she ran like hell and didn't look back until she'd caught up with Roza at the sign.

"Is he dead? Did you kill him?" Roza asked, panting.

"I don't know. I think I knocked him out, but he kept getting up." She grabbed Roza's hand. "Come on. Let's go before he finds us. *Run.*"

Cincinnati, Ohio
Wednesday, November 5, 9:03 a.m.

"Uncle Jordan!" Faith stood up when her uncle approached, waving him to their table.

"He doesn't look terribly impressed with our hospitality," Deacon murmured. Cincinnati PD's cafeteria was really a glorified break room with a few tables and a lot of vending machines. Too many cops ran on caffeine and sugar, and most mornings, Deacon was one of them. This morning, however, he'd woken to Faith, and his blood was still rushing through his veins.

Jordan O'Bannion, on the other hand, looked as if he'd swallowed a prune.

"Jordan likes fine china and silver teapots," Faith said with a smile. "He's always said that his idea of 'roughing it' is a Holiday Inn without room service." She waited until Jordan reached them before leaning up to kiss his cheek.

Jordan eyed the duct-taped vinyl bench seat with apprehension, making Faith laugh. "I wiped it down before you got here," she said. "It's clean."

Her uncle sat across from Deacon, the way he'd planned it. He'd arranged the chair so that the only place the man could sit was farthest away from Faith. He planned to take no chances, even within the police station's walls.

Jordan's eyes were less puffy today than they'd been the day before, and he appeared to be sober. That was promising. But his face was flushed and sweat beaded on his upper lip and his brow. There was a general edginess to him that Deacon recognized from the few times his own father had tried to kick the habit. *He must really need a drink.*

"Mr. O'Bannion, thank you for being willing to see us here," he said. "It's easier to keep Faith safe here."

"Of course. I completely understand." O'Bannion took a moment to study Faith's face. "You're looking much better today than you did yesterday. I hope you've gotten some rest."

"I did, thank you. Agent Novak said you might have some information for us."

"Maybe. I'm not sure what it is you're looking for and, in many cases, what I was looking at. But first I want to give you this." He pushed an older-model cell phone across the table. "I'd like to be able to reach you myself, without going through Agent Novak. It's not a new phone with fancy features, but you can receive calls and send texts." He gave her a chiding look. "Your father asked me to get you a phone because he was worried. I had an old one in my desk drawer that still had some minutes on it."

Deacon took the phone and looked it over, feeling a sudden prickle of unease. "Why did you have a prepaid phone in your desk drawer, Mr. O'Bannion?" he asked.

"It was my housekeeper's. Mary's never been able to afford a smartphone, so I gave her Mother's." His shrug was rueful. "Mother's not using it anymore."

It was a reasonable explanation, Deacon thought, and Faith's uncle had an alibi for all the times anyone had been attacked. Still, his unease persisted. He hoped it was only

Jordan's edginess rubbing off on him. "Thank you for the phone. I was going to pick one up for Faith today, so you've saved me a trip. Okay, now, what is your information?"

"I spent the evening going through Mother's papers, and I found the name of the company you asked me about yesterday, the company that maintains the estate. It's Maguire and Sons, and they have an office in Mount Carmel." He handed Faith an invoice. "She paid them every six months. Paid them pretty well, too. I was surprised to see how well. Had I known, I would have put a stop to it long ago."

Faith handed the invoice to Deacon. "Can I have all the receipts, Jordan? If I end up keeping the house, I'll want them for reference."

Deacon hid his surprise. Either she'd drastically changed her mind about the house, or she was putting on a show for her uncle.

Jordan didn't hide his surprise at all. "Are you seriously thinking of keeping that house, Faith? It's a huge responsibility. It cost Mother far too much to keep up when it was empty. Living in it would cost a small fortune."

"I was planning to keep it when I came up here. Now I don't know, but I'm thinking that even if I decide to sell, it may be a while before anyone buys it. I'll have to maintain it in the meantime. Maybe I'll find out if the historical society can help defray the cost."

Jordan frowned. "They'll want to put the house on the national registry, and Mother wouldn't have wanted that."

"Why?" Deacon asked. "I'd think she'd want the house to be protected and enjoyed."

"She did—by O'Bannions. She didn't want to share it with the public. She wanted Faith to have it, hoping she'd get remarried and have lots of children to fill it up." He smiled at Faith affectionately. "You know how she was. She kept holding out hope."

Faith rolled her eyes. "I know."

"Why did she allow the cemetery to be registered, then?" Deacon asked.

"It was outside, and she knew she couldn't keep Civil War buffs from visiting it. She figured if the historical society was protecting it, it would be less likely that anyone would vandalize it. She loved that old pile of bones, all the way back to Colonel Zeke—"

"O'Bannion of the 6th Ohio Infantry," Faith finished. "I know. I heard all the stories, if not from Gran, then from my mother."

Jordan's eyes grew sad. "Maggie loved that old place, too. But seriously, I think you need to reconsider the historical society. I found this letter that Mother wrote to them that made me contact you this morning. She never sent it." He handed it to Deacon. "I don't know why she didn't."

Printed on computer paper, it was dated the previous year and signed "Barbara O'Bannion."

Faith leaned over Deacon's arm to read along with him. "She was unhappy with the gardener who was taking care of the cemetery," she murmured, then frowned. "She saw him coming out of the house? How? She never went out there, did she, Jordan?"

Deacon reread the letter, his prickle of unease having just grown. A signed, unsent letter from Jordan's dead mother turning up, giving them a new suspect . . . It could be real, but Deacon's gut found it terribly convenient. It felt . . . wrong.

"This was why I asked you to meet me," Jordan said. "I never took her out there. She had brittle hips. One fall and she would have been in traction. Did you?"

"No! For the same reason."

"I didn't think so, but I wanted to check. I was never quite sure what you two did together when you visited and I went to my studio to paint. So I thought maybe she'd talked you into it."

"She tried, but I always said no. I could never have gotten her down those narrow stairs in your townhouse to begin with. Really, Jordan," Faith added, perturbed, "how irresponsible do you think I am?"

"I'm sorry," Jordan said. "I didn't mean to offend you. The only other person who might have taken her was Henson Senior. She had him wrapped around her little finger."

"He said he hadn't been out there since your mother was buried, Faith," Deacon said quietly.

Faith picked up the letter, troubled. "This is my grandmother's signature. Maybe she just thought she'd been out to the cemetery. I didn't think her mind had grown muddy, but maybe it had."

"I thought the same thing," Jordan admitted. "But he

was there the day we buried her. The gardener, I mean. He stood by the gate, his hat in his hand. I was surprised because it wasn't his day to mow, but I figured he was curious or maybe planned to lock up the gate afterward. At any rate, I thought you should know. If the gardener had access to the house . . ."

Deacon dropped the letter in an evidence envelope. Bishop had checked out the gardener, who was almost as old as Henson Senior and had an alibi. As did Henson Senior. Then, again, so did Jordan, so why would he lie?

The letter could be a perfectly legitimate piece of evidence. Deacon hoped it was. It still felt wrong. "We'll check it out," he said politely. "Thank you, Mr. O'Bannion."

Jordan leaned across the table to peck Faith's cheek. "Be careful, kiddo. You and I are the only ones left. Call me when you get a chance today. I need to know you're safe."

"I will. Thank you." Still troubled, she watched him go, then turned to Deacon. "I didn't think my Gran had developed dementia, but she *was* eighty-four."

"Before you go down that road, let's see what the gardener has to say." He took the phone from her hand and dropped it in the pocket of his new leather coat, making a mental note to call Daphne to thank her. "What?" he asked Faith, who glared at him.

"Why did you take *this* phone?" she demanded. "It's not broken or compromised."

Deacon hoped that was true, but he was going to pay attention to his gut. "Because I'm a paranoid man who's witnessed two attempts on your life."

Her eyes widened. "You think Jordan is the murderer? He's got an alibi. You said so yourself. And don't you think I'd know? Good God, Deacon."

She sounded so flabbergasted that Deacon almost gave her back the phone. The truth was he didn't think Jordan O'Bannion would get his shiny Ferragamos scuffed, much less rip the organs from the dead victims' bodies.

"He does have an alibi, and no, I don't put him anywhere near Stone and the others in terms of suspicion. But let Tanaka check the phone, okay? For my peace of mind."

"All right." She sighed dramatically. "I almost think you want me to be phoneless. Then I'm more dependent on you."

He waggled his brows. "You caught me."

She rolled her eyes again. "You better be glad you're charming, Novak."

Deacon threw back his head and laughed. "Charming? Nobody has ever called me that before. Usually I'm just a pain in the ass."

"That's because they don't see you like I do," she said smugly.

He dropped his voice, gratified when she shivered. "Or like you did two hours ago."

Her cheeks pinked up prettily. "And how I hope to see you again very soon. So hurry up and solve this case, Deacon," she said lightly, but then her smile dimmed. "Please," she added in a whisper. "We need to make him stop."

Chapter Twenty-eight

Cincinnati, Ohio
Wednesday, November 5, 9:45 a.m.

Faith sat in Deacon's chair, staring at nothing. How messed up was this situation that he felt like he had to prove a gift from her uncle wasn't a Trojan horse meant to ensnare her?

How messed up when two of the photographs in the SUSPECTS column of their bulletin board were her own kin?

And what about Combs? Where was he? How did he fit in to any of this?

She dropped her gaze to her laptop on Deacon's desk. And why hadn't she heard back from her new boss? Resolutely, she picked up Deacon's office phone and dialed her boss's number.

"Mr. Burns, this is Faith Corcoran." She'd filled out all her paperwork with the new name, telling them the change was due to her divorce. "I sent you an e-mail yesterday advising you of an auto accident that prevented me from coming into the office. Did you receive it?"

"Yes, Dr. Corcoran, I did."

This is bad, she thought when he said no more. "I'd hoped the situation would have resolved itself by now, but it has not. What is the company policy in situations like this?"

An awkward silence on his end. "We have reconsidered your employment. I'm sorry to tell you that we've chosen to separate ourselves from you." More awkward silence from her boss.

A furious silence from her. Because as positive as she'd been with Deacon about Kimble's rogue inquiry, she really didn't want to lose her job. *At least I have a house to live in,* she thought sarcastically. "Based upon what, exactly?"

"Based on a call we received from a homicide detective yesterday, citing you as a suspect in a murder case."

I'm not the suspect, you holier-than-thou asshole. I'm the goddamned intended victim.

"I'm afraid you were given inaccurate information. I am not a suspect. Did you even consider that it might not be true?"

"We don't have the luxury of taking the chance. We are an old institution and have shareholders to protect, none of whom will accept this kind of taint."

Taint? "Very well. I would like your decision in writing."

A slight pause. "For what purpose?"

"For my records, of course. And because most reporters want documentation."

"Reporters?"

"Yes," she said simply. "Good-bye, Mr. Burns." She hung up and stared at the phone.

And realized that she wasn't trembling. Her stomach wasn't churning. There was no bone-chilling fear about how she'd pay her bills. Other than a mild annoyance at Kimble's interference and a ton of fury for the how-does-this-affect me attitude of the bank, she really didn't feel upset.

She wasn't worried. Wasn't fretting. It was liberating, actually. When this nightmare was over, she could go back to doing what she did well—helping victims.

She owned fifty acres of primo property. She could sell it and live quite comfortably. And if the notoriety made the property hard to sell, she'd hold on to it until the furor quieted.

She might not sell all the land in any case. She might leave some around the house itself for a memorial to the ten women who'd died there.

She did a quick search on her computer and chose a real estate agency local to the area, bypassing the Realtor Mr. Henson, Sr., had recommended. The whole situation with Maguire and Sons showed her that, best case, he was blind to the dealings of his firm, particularly those involving his grandson. Worst case, he was dishonest. Either way, she'd choose her own service providers from here on out.

Normally, she'd add the Realtor to the contact list *on her phone* or file a memo to herself *on her phone*. "It's a sad day when a modern woman has to resort to pencil and paper," she muttered. Deacon's desk was completely clear.

Bishop, however, had a University of Cincinnati Bearcat mug filled with pens. Faith borrowed one and looked for something to write on. The only other thing on Bishop's desk was a thick folder with a rubber band around it. The sticky note on the folder read: *Det. Bishop—a copy of the papers you requested from C. Longstreet's dorm.*

Faith searched around it, trying not to pry, but one of the pages in the folder caught her eye. Legal size, it stuck out of the top, the sender's logo barely visible but very familiar.

She leaned in to get a closer look at the logo and immediately knew why it was familiar. She'd seen it only the night before when she'd taken the deed from her safe to give to Deacon. It belonged to her grandmother's attorney's firm—Henson and Henson.

Why would a college student possess correspondence from a firm hired by the over-seventy set? A firm whose junior partner's photo was on the SUSPECT side of the team's bulletin board.

She reached out to take the legal-sized page from the stack, then yanked her hand back. These were Bishop's papers. Part of an investigation. *That's going on in my damn house.*

Carefully, she slid the page out of the folder. It was a letter to Corinne Longstreet, dated two years before, awarding her a financial scholarship on the basis of her essay and in gratitude for her service in the US Army.

Faith stared at the signature as her heart pounded heavily in her ears. She sank into Bishop's chair, her knees gone weak. *No, no, no.* It wasn't possible. But there it was, in black and white.

"That's how this is all connected," she whispered.

She pushed herself to her feet, ignoring her weak knees as she walked to the conference room and knocked on the door. She didn't wait for an invitation to enter. "Excuse me. I need to show you something. It's important."

Deacon was standing at the bulletin board, where he'd pinned the letter Jordan had just given them, but he immediately pulled out a chair at the table. "Sit down. You're white as a ghost."

Faith took the seat he offered and put the paper she'd found on the table. "I saw this on your desk, Detective Bishop. I recognized the logo on the letterhead and ... I took it from the folder with Corinne's papers. You can yell at me later if you want," she added when Bishop opened her mouth, probably to do exactly that. "This is a letter to Corinne from Herbert Henson, Sr, informing Corinne that she's the recipient of a scholarship. The scholarship was provided by the Joy O'Bannion Foundation. The letter is signed by Barbara O'Bannion." Faith exhaled quietly. "My grandmother."

Cincinnati, Ohio
Wednesday, November 5, 10:30 a.m.

Faith thought that Deacon and Bishop would be shocked. Instead, they seemed almost grim.

"Ah. The famous Joy O'Bannion Foundation strikes again," Bishop murmured.

"The house reverts to the Foundation if Faith dies without a will or heirs," Deacon said.

"And," Bishop added, "Jeremy said that Jordan had been skimming from Foundation money twenty-three years ago."

Faith's mouth fell open. "I never knew that."

Bishop shrugged. "Jeremy said that was why Jordan outed him to their father—to distract his father from listening to Jeremy's accusations. This was shortly before your grandfather died."

"And Jeremy was disowned," Faith added. "Jeremy's accusation against Jordan was probably lost in the turmoil." *But Jordan's accusation against Jeremy stuck.*

"The team has mentioned the Foundation, but I'd appreciate a description," Isenberg said.

"Well, my grandparents had eight children, but only four survived infancy—Joy, my mother, and then Jeremy and Jordan. Joy became ill as a child, and her care depleted the family savings."

"Jeremy says they were poor," Deacon said.

"That may be a relative term," Faith said. "According to my father, the family could have still lived very comfortably in a normal house, but Tobias—my grandfather—was determined to keep the estate intact. Dad could never respect him for that. When Joy died, they'd spent a lot on doctors, and there wasn't enough left to keep up the house and pay the taxes. So . . . Tobias did something that I'm not sure Gran ever forgave him for. I know my mother never did. Gran's family had a sizable property north of the city, up by Liberty Township. She was the last of the Corcorans and it all belonged to her—thousands of acres."

"That's all Westchester now," Isenberg said. "McHouses as far as the eye can see."

"Only because Tobias sold her land without asking her. Gran told me about it once. I'd never seen her cry, not even when my mother died, but when she told me about her husband selling her family land, she broke down. She'd been grief-stricken over Joy's death at the time and her doctor had her on sedatives. Tobias got her to sign over power of attorney and he sold the land. He never told any of them what he'd done. I don't think Gran or my mother knew how much they'd spent on Joy's treatments, and Jordan and Jeremy were too young to understand. They were only five when she died."

Faith took a deep breath and continued. "That land of Gran's had been meant for my mother, as the surviving female child. My mother found out on her twenty-first birthday that her birthright had been sold. She and Dad were newly married. I was on the way. She was supposed to come into some property and had planned to build there. But she found out that there was no land. It had been sold, part of the money going to pay back taxes on the O'Bannion land, part of it invested to restore the family fortune, and the rest used to establish the Foundation in Joy's memory, to help other kids."

"So he sold your mother's birthright to help other children?" Bishop asked. "Why?"

"He liked being seen as a philanthropist. Maybe he did it out of a real need to remember Joy. I don't know. My mother said Joy's death destroyed them all in different ways. My mother was sometimes proud, but mostly resentful of the Foundation. She knew the sick kids were important, but she wanted some of the money. Tobias didn't spoil his surviving kids. Even though they were more than flush, they had to pay their own way the day they turned eighteen. Mother got a job in the office at Mount St. Mary's—that's where she met my dad. He was a seminarian. He eventually chose not to take his vows and to marry her. A few years later, Jeremy married a rich woman who put him through med school."

"Della Yarborough," Deacon said. "Stone and Marcus were hers from a previous marriage."

"And then she and Jeremy had Audrey. Jordan got into law school, but after Tobias died, he dropped out and started painting—and taking care of Gran. Jordan was never a solid student and partied way too hard, but I have a hard time believing he filched from the Foundation."

Deacon lifted a brow in challenge. "Because he wouldn't do that?"

Faith smiled. "No. Because it's very tightly managed by a group outside the family."

"By Herbert Henson?" Deacon asked.

"Obviously some aspects, like giving it away," Faith said, tapping the letter to Corinne. "But the Foundation has a board and its own accountant. Tobias ran the show, but when he died, the reins were passed to one of the board members, who's also dead. The chairman of the board is a voted position. Gran never held a voting position, but she had full control over who got the money in that she signed the checks." She tapped the letter again. "And the correspondence to recipients. I have a nonvoting position on the board as a family member and at some point will be expected to take up Gran's duties of check signing and correspondence, I guess."

"Why you?" Bishop asked. "Why not Jordan?"

"Gran stipulated it in her will. I think she worried about Jordan. His drinking, especially."

"Do Jordan and Jeremy have positions on the board?" Isenberg asked.

"Jordan has a nonvoting position, like mine. Jeremy was barred even from that."

Bishop looked thoughtful. "What's the net worth of the Foundation?"

"Five million, sometimes a little more. Depends on performance of the stock portfolio. Anyway, when he died, Tobias caused a big stir by leaving all the family money that wasn't already in the Foundation—"

"To the Foundation," Deacon finished. "Jeremy told us that Jordan was pretty irked."

"So was my mother. She and Dad fought about it. I can remember lying in bed and hearing them through the wall between our bedrooms in Gran's house. They were saying terrible things. It's my last real memory of my parents together." She frowned and pushed it from her mind. "At any rate, nobody got nothin' out of Tobias. Not even my grandmother, really. Tobias had set up a trust for her, which paid her a generous monthly allowance until the day she died. At that time, any money left in the trust went back into the Foundation. My grandmother told me that she tried to contest the will a few times, but Henson Senior wasn't able to help her. She hated being given an allowance like she was a child, especially since the money came from the sale of *her* land."

"So you have no access to the actual money in the Foundation?" Isenberg said. "Then that can't be why someone's trying to kill you."

"True," Faith said. "I have no access to the money, but I have access to something better—the list of recipients. I hope Corinne was the only victim with a connection, but in the event she's not, the recipient list might identify some of the other victims."

Isenberg nodded, respect in her eyes. "Smart. How soon can you get the list?"

"As soon as someone can take me to Henson's office."

"If one of the Hensons is involved, they aren't going to just hand over a victim list," Bishop said. "And if we go in half-cocked, we could scare him into running."

Faith shook her head. "Any move to bar me from the list would attract the attention of the board. If you go in with a warrant, it'll just get everyone all heated up. Let me ask."

Deacon sat back. "All right, we ask. But we'll also start the DA's office drafting a warrant, just in case they give you the runaround. I'll take you to Henson's as soon as we're finished here. Scarlett, you're working with the sketch artist today—getting Roza's face from Arianna and the Maguire mystery lady's face from the woman in the office next door to theirs. Adam?"

"The victim in the grocery store parking lot survived the night, but she's in a coma. No one's reported her missing yet. I've got copies of her photo and a list of every veterinary office in the tristate area for the uniforms to canvass. I'm also looking at dog parks, kennels, and feed stores. ID'ing her will give us her vehicle make and home address, in case he's hiding there."

"Good," Deacon said. "Vince, you're with Sophie today?"

"Not till noon. I have a ton of stuff to do in the lab. I'll run some tests on your letter, too. See if the inks and paper match with the uncle's story."

Deacon ignored Faith's surprise. "And also this." He gave Tanaka the cell phone that Jordan had given to Faith. "Make sure this is clean."

Faith frowned. "And maybe give me back my iPhone that you took on Monday night?"

"I'll do my best," Tanaka promised.

Faith looked up at the bulletin board. "You've got Peter Combs's picture up there, but do you still consider him a suspect?"

"Yes," Deacon said. "Certainly not the mastermind, since the crimes go back too far. But he could be a hired thug. Scarlett, where is Detective Vega's investigation? She have any luck with Combs's girlfriend?"

"Not yet. The girlfriend's lawyer wants to deal her down on the possession charges, and now the DA is involved and everyone is posturing. She knows we're growing desperate."

"I'll give her LT another call and reiterate our level of desperation," Isenberg said icily.

"We also still need his souvenirs," Adam said. "He's got them there. You know he does. Faith's recipient list may help us ID victims, but finding their belongings might, too. Their families deserve to know what happened to them."

"I remember a few hiding places," Faith said. "If you want me to go to the house and try."

"I don't," Deacon said. "Not unless we don't have another choice. You are a target everywhere you go, and unfortunately, everyone around you is, too." Her wince made

him feel lower than dirt. He sighed. "Vince, aren't you planning to X-ray the walls?"

"Yes, though the X-ray equipment works differently—
and more slowly—than Sophie's ground-penetrating radar.
It could take us all day to do one wall. If Faith can remember anything specific, we might cut that time considerably."

"You could just knock down the damn walls," Deacon
said curtly.

"We could—tomorrow," Vince said. "But not until Sophie finishes scanning the floor."

Deacon scowled. "Fine, but, Vince, if Faith goes out to
that house, any of your people on-site must wear vests and
helmets. And I want to be there."

"Everyone should have been wearing vests and helmets
already," Isenberg said. "I'll begin the family notifications of
the dead we've identified. The brass agrees with me that we
can't keep the names back any longer. The families deserve
to know."

Deacon hadn't realized how much he'd dreaded telling
the families until Isenberg took the burden. "Thank you,
Lynda. So we all have our orders. Faith, let's visit Henson."

Miami, Florida
Wednesday, November 5, 11:15 a.m.

"*Vega!* Get in here."

Detective Catalina Vega winced. The shout had come
from her LT's office. She gathered the files she'd been reading and took them with her into Davies's office. "I'm here."

Davies pointed to a chair in front of his desk. "I just hung
up with Lieutenant Isenberg in Cincinnati, who just tore me
a new one. Can you guess why?"

Cat wanted to scream. "Because I haven't interviewed
Peter Combs's girlfriend yet."

"Right on one. Care to tell me why not?"

"Because the girlfriend's attorney figures that if I want
to talk to her, she's got to have something I want. He's told
her not to cooperate until the DA drops her possession
charge. She was found with almost a half kilo of coke in her
car, so of course the DA said no. I can't get anything out of
her until the DA gives me something to work with."

"Isenberg thinks that if Combs is involved in this—and

she's not certain that he is—it's as a stooge or hired muscle. She wants to know if she can eliminate him entirely." Davies leaned back in his chair. "So tell me what you know."

"I know that the car was tampered with by a guy driving a white van early Sunday morning. Same style van that tried to run Faith off the road three weeks before that."

"And shot at her?"

"Yes. And now I know something more from looking through these prison-visitation logs." She held up the folder she'd been reading. "Combs was visited in prison by Charlie Frye—Faith's husband at the time—shortly after Combs claimed that Faith was having an affair with him. I don't think Charlie believed him, but the accusation was handy for him in the divorce."

"When did Combs shack up with the girlfriend he has right now?"

"He met her in prison—she was his pen pal."

Davies rolled his eyes. "For the love of . . . Who's the DA who's gumming up your works?"

"John Scheiderman."

"Call him right now, tell him you're arresting the girlfriend for conspiracy to murder Faith. Don't ask the girlfriend for any favors. People like her and her lawyer smell blood in the water and circle. Put her on the defensive." He pushed the phone across his desk. "Call. Get the DA to officially charge her with attempted murder. She'll talk."

Cincinnati, Ohio
Wednesday, November 5, 11:30 a.m.

"Thank you for seeing us on such short notice," Faith said as she and Deacon were admitted into Herbert Henson, Sr.'s office by his secretary.

Henson studied them from behind his desk, gesturing for them to sit. "The unmarked car outside my house was unnecessary, Agent Novak. If you'd wanted to talk to me, you should have come up and rung the damn bell. You frightened my wife."

"I'm sorry, sir. That was certainly not my intent. My intent was to find your grandson. I expected that he'd call me back yesterday, but he hasn't. He is back from his client, is he not?"

Henson looked uncomfortable. "No, he has not returned."

That doesn't look too good for Herbert Henson the third,
Faith thought.

"We have evidence that he *was not* personally oversee-
ing the semiannual maintenance of the O'Bannion house,"
Deacon said. "A witness says that he dropped off the key at
Maguire and Sons and went to play golf. I don't think that
behavior is considered 'beyond unimpeachable.'"

Henson's lips thinned. "I'll call him again, Agent Novak.
Is there anything else?"

"Yes," Faith said. "We've come about something else. I'd
like a list of all the recipients of Foundation scholarship
funds from the very beginning."

"Why?"

"You've heard about the local college student who was
found near the house? She'd been held there. Her friend is
still missing. The missing woman's name is Corinne Longstreet, and she was a recipient of a scholarship from the Joy
O'Bannion Foundation."

Henson's face blanched. "Surely you can't be suggesting
that Ms. Longstreet was abducted because of her connection to the Joy Foundation? Or that I am a suspect? Is that
why you had an unmarked car in front of my house?"

"Agent Novak has a car outside your house because he
is erring on the side of caution. If Ms. Longstreet were your
daughter, you'd want him to do the same for her, wouldn't
you?"

"Yes, I suppose I would." Henson swallowed hard. "Of
course I would."

"I thought so. May we have the list?"

"Yes, of course. I'll print it up for you."

Faith squeezed Deacon's knee as they waited for Henson to find the file in his computer.

"You're right," Henson said heavily, as if he'd hoped she
was wrong. "Ms. Longstreet is a Joy Foundation recipient."
A printer whirred to life.

"Who else has access to this list?" Deacon asked as
pages printed.

"Only my secretary. The board approves applications
without seeing the applicants' names. They read only their
essays to minimize any bias."

"I know Gran signed the checks to the applicants, but who mailed the checks?" Faith asked. "They'd have to have their names, too."

"Mrs. Lowell mails the checks herself, but I suppose anyone auditing the account would see them as well. And anyone they told, of course. Here is the list."

Faith's heart sank. It was pages and pages long.

"How many names are on it?" Deacon asked grimly.

She leafed through the pages, her heart sinking further. "Hundreds."

Cincinnati, Ohio
Wednesday, November 5, 11:45 a.m.

"Thank you for coming in, Mrs. Winston." Scarlett led the woman who'd seen the Maguire and Sons mystery woman into an interview room where the CPD sketch artist waited. "This is Sergeant D'Amico. She'll be working with you today."

D'Amico was a sweet-faced woman who didn't look like she'd ever said a cross word. Based on the two years they'd spent on patrol together, Scarlett knew that to be untrue. Lana D'Amico was a damn fine cop and a brilliant sketch artist, and her sweet face put the witnesses at ease. Scarlett had been specifically thinking of Arianna when she'd requested D'Amico. But she was as tough as any other cop, and had a mouth on her to match it.

"I'll wait outside. Thank you again, Mrs. Winston. You're in good hands here."

Scarlett stepped into the hall just as her phone started to buzz in her pocket. For a moment she frowned at the caller ID. It was her own cell number. Her phone had been "spoofed." Companies that would reroute a call and relabel its caller ID could be found in five seconds on the Internet. *Careful here, Scar.*

"This is Detective Bishop," she answered. "How can I help you?"

"I'm helping you."

Scarlett controlled what would have been a sharp intake of air. The man's voice was deep and . . . like music. The saddest music she'd ever heard in her life. "I'm listening."

"I'm going to send a set of GPS coordinates to your

phone. It's a cabin in the Daniel Boone National Forest. Under the floor are four bodies. I believe three of them are yours."

Three bodies. Oh God. Not Corinne. Don't let her be one of them. "How do you know they're mine?"

"One is wearing an Earl Power and Light uniform. I saw him on the news. There is also an old man and a woman."

Scarlett's heart sank. "And the fourth body?"

"He belongs to me. I have to go now."

The call disconnected, and seconds later a text was delivered to her phone, also from her own cell phone. GPS coordinates, just like he'd said. Had she just spoken to the killer? She didn't think so. If it had been the killer, he would have insisted Faith accompany her. No, this wasn't the killer. But then, who?

Scarlett started for the elevator, dialing Novak's number as she jogged, scowling when she got his voice mail. "It's Bishop. Call me ASAP. I just got an interesting phone call."

Her next call was to Isenberg, and she quickly updated her boss. "Can you have someone escort Mrs. Winston out and tell D'Amico to go to Arianna's room by herself? I already cleared her with the uniform on guard duty outside Arianna's room, and the kid shrink, Meredith Fallon, will be there while D'Amico sketches. The coordinates are about two hours from here, but I'll shave some time off that."

"I'll get a trace placed on the call," Isenberg said.

"You can try, but I wouldn't bother. He used a spoofing service to make it look like he was calling from my number. Spoofed calls get wired through a dozen different servers before they hit the recipient's phone. I'm going to ask Novak to contact the closest Fed office to the coordinates for backup before we alert the locals. I don't want my crime scene demolished by a well-meaning deputy. Can you have Crandall find the owner of the cabin at the coordinates?"

"Will do. Drive carefully, Scarlett. Keep me apprised."

Eastern Kentucky
Wednesday, November 5, 11:45 a.m.

He was becoming very irritated by the Longstreet bitch, but at least she hadn't known how to cover her tracks. Disgusted, he stood behind the cabin, staring at the trail that was so obvious that it was probably visible from space. She'd run into the woods. Not down the road as he'd thought. The footprints he'd been following were a decoy. A damn ruse.

From the look of the trail, it appeared that Longstreet had dragged Roza kicking and screaming every step of the way. There might be some hope for the child yet. Which was good, because he had plans for her.

Cincinnati, Ohio
Wednesday, November 5, 12:05 p.m.

Sitting at Deacon's desk, Faith looked up from the long list of Foundation recipients she'd been reviewing when Deacon returned from Isenberg's office. He sat on the edge of his desk, his muscular legs stretched out, his arms crossed over his chest. His grim expression told Faith what she needed to know about the phone call he and Isenberg had just had with Bishop.

"It's Corinne, isn't it?" she asked. "The dead woman?"

"I would have to assume so," Deacon said quietly. "No one's gotten to the cabin yet. I have to leave now and catch up to Bishop."

"I'm so sorry," Faith whispered. "For the locksmith and the power company man. For Corinne and for Arianna, too. She'll be heartbroken."

He took her hand, squeezed it hard. "I know. There's something else, though. The cabin belongs to a business registered to Della Yarborough."

"Jeremy's ex-wife." Disappointment and fury mixed with her sorrow. "Dammit. I can't believe it's Jeremy. I just can't accept it." She watched his jaw grow taut. "There's more?"

"Yeah. Jeremy and Stone are gone. As in 'in the wind,' not dead."

"But . . . How can they be *gone*?" she asked. "I thought they were being watched."

"I had three Feds watching—one each for Jeremy, Keith, and Stone. One followed Stone to a bar last night, then followed him back shortly thereafter. When I told the agents to pick them all up, the house was empty. The agents found a dirt road in the trees well behind the mansion. It had recently been driven over by a large vehicle. Range Rover size—which happens to be the kind of vehicle registered to Keith."

"So they escaped. Which means they're out there somewhere, maybe waiting for me."

"Most likely. I need you to stay safe. I can't be worried about you and do my job, too. Understand?"

"Yes. Go, now. I'll be fine here, surrounded by cops."

Deacon nodded, then fixed his gaze on the far wall, lowering his voice to a murmur. "I'd kiss you good-bye, but there's no privacy here."

"Later you can kiss me hello. Go. Bring Corinne home."

He left with a hard nod. "Stay here. Be safe."

Faith watched him go, his leather coat tails flapping behind him. Then she closed her eyes.

"Are you all right?" Isenberg asked quietly from behind her.

"No," Faith whispered without opening her eyes. "How will I tell Arianna that Corinne is dead? And that my uncle did it? How can I tell Arianna that my uncle was the monster who tortured her and would've killed her, too?"

"And that your uncle is also trying to kill you?"

Faith nodded, tears burning her throat, stinging her eyes. "He's killed all of these people, Lieutenant. There's no way I can make amends." She angrily dashed away the tears that blurred her vision. "But at least I have this list. I can help identify the seven other women who were buried in that basement, whose names we don't yet know."

Isenberg squeezed her shoulder, the gesture unexpected but welcome. "Good girl. How had you planned to do that?"

"By going through each name." Faith thumbed at the edge of the stack, riffling the pages. "There are more than eighteen hundred names on this list."

"Wow. Your family has been very generous."

"I know." One side of her mouth lifted. "So we're not all bad. Tobias established the Foundation thirty-eight years ago, the year after Joy died. The same year he stole my grandmother's land and sold it. I figure we don't have to go back more than ten years. That's how long Sergeant Tanaka thought the basement windows and doors had been boarded up. Going back only ten years cuts the number to just under five hundred names. The board had decided to give out fewer small grants and more large ones, so that works in our favor. If we could separate out the blond females, we could further reduce the list, but these are just names. I'm sure Henson kept files on the recipients. I can ask for them."

"And I'll send over uniforms to bring them here. I started a warrant for the list this morning, just in case he didn't give it to you. I can amend that to the boxes of files." Isenberg made a face. "And then it's just old-fashioned tedious examination of each name to see if they're still alive. Or have been reported missing. I'll get a team of clerks up here to do the analysis."

"I'd like to help," Faith said. "I need to help. I need to do something."

"And we want your help," Isenberg said. She motioned to Kimble, who was sitting at his desk. "Detective Kimble is going to take you to the house to look for souvenirs."

"But Deacon said he wanted to be there," Faith said.

Isenberg shrugged. "That was before Bishop got the call about the cabin. Any of my clerks can crunch through the names on that list, but only you know about the house, and we do need those souvenirs, if they exist. We'll clear the area of all nonessential CSU personnel and alert the uniforms on the scene to be alert for a sniper attack."

"You're wearing Kevlar, aren't you, Detective Kimble?" Faith asked lightly.

"Always," Kimble said. "And so will you."

Chapter Twenty-nine

"Just a little further, Roza," Corinne coaxed. "Please. Just a little bit further."

"I can't." Tears streamed down the child's face. "I can't, 'Rin. My feet are bleeding."

"I know. So are mine. But we should get to the main road soon."

"You said that already. Lots of times."

"I know, but—" Corinne cut herself off. "Wait. Did you hear that?" After what seemed like an eternity in the woods, she'd heard a car. "Come on, Roza! Hurry!"

She caught the girl's hand, yanked her to her feet, and dragged her toward the sound—then yelped when her feet slipped on the dew-covered grass and encountered only air. She was falling, rolling, sliding down a huge hill, hitting rocks and brush all the way down.

When she finally came to a stop, she rolled to her back with a groan. She'd hurt before. She was in agony now. "Roza?" she called, gritting her teeth.

"Over here." Roza's voice was thin. Weak. "I think . . . My head's bleeding."

Corinne's pounding heart skipped a beat. "*No.* I didn't drag you all this way to lose you to a damn hill." She shoved herself to her hands and knees, lifting her head to squint around, looking for Roza's dark head. She dragged herself to Roza's side.

The girl was bleeding profusely from a cut over her eye. "It's not good, but it could be worse," Corinne said matter-of-factly. "Head wounds bleed like a bitch. Trouble is, every inch of me is filthy. I need to find something clean to put over your wound. Wait here."

"Okay," Roza said sleepily.

"And don't go to sleep," Corinne ordered. "You might have a concussion."

"I don't know what that means."

"It means don't go to sleep." Corinne staggered to her feet and took a moment to let her dizziness fade. When it didn't, she squinted and did a three-sixty, taking in the land-scape.

It really was a road. At the base of the hill was a small parking lot, big enough for four or five vehicles. Eventually someone would come by here, but how long would that take?

He could still come. He could still find them. *I should have killed him. I should have stabbed him in the back.* Or hit him with the shovel again and again until he was dead.

She'd allowed her fear to overwhelm her reason. She looked up the hill, half expecting him to be standing there, then heard the low rumble of another vehicle. Frantically, she searched for cover, but there was none. The road ran through a vale, hills sloping up on both sides.

Be friendly strangers, please. Drawing a breath, Corinne stood her ground and waited, prepared to throw herself into the road to stop them, if need be.

A rugged-looking Subaru came around the bend, look-ing like it had spent most of its time in the forest off-road. It slowed when it saw her. Slowed and pulled over. A man got out, walking toward her carefully, his face in the shadow of the far hill.

"Are you all right, miss?" he asked, his deep voice a smooth rumble over her ears.

"No. I need help. My . . . my sister is hurt and needs med-ical attention."

He came a step closer, hands up, palms out. "I've got first-aid training. Maybe I can help."

Corinne took a step back. He wasn't the man she'd

stabbed. This one was just as tall and was still a big guy, but not nearly as massive as the man who'd tried to grab her at the deer blind. He wore a weathered brown leather jacket where the other guy had worn a black Windbreaker over a black hoodie. But their hair looked the same—same color, same style. Her heart began to pound in fear.

He stepped into the light, and her instincts screamed for her to run. His body wasn't the same, but his face was. *Run! Run!* But Roza couldn't run. *I can't carry her.*

She'd used one of the knives on the big guy and had lost the others when she fell. She slipped her hand in her pocket, felt the Swiss Army knife she'd taken from the dead man in the van, but she knew she'd never be able to pry the blade out. Her fingers were too stiff and swollen. It was useless, except to maybe throw at him.

She didn't even have the shovel anymore. She'd dropped it long ago.

She took another step back. "Maybe you could just call 911."

"Fine. I can do that. Just . . . relax."

Relax? I don't think so. Fighting the hysteria she could feel rising, Corinne edged back toward Roza. His hand slid into his coat pocket, and an instant later white-hot pain exploded in her thigh. She heard the gunshot as her knee buckled, taking her down.

Facedown in the dirt, she screamed, the pain consuming. *"You sonofabitch!"*

Roza. Corinne pushed up on her elbows, tears streaming down her face. And then she couldn't breathe, all the air shoved from her lungs when she was tackled from behind. She fought hard, thrashing, bucking, trying to throw him off.

"Stay down!" The man rolled sideways, barely giving her room to draw a breath.

He had a gun, but he was aiming up the hill, not at her. He fired, the recoil jerking down his arm and into his body. No, not the recoil, she thought a split second later when he collapsed on top of her. He'd been shot.

Shot protecting me. What the fuck? She lay there, trembling. Everything was quiet. Then another shot cracked the air. The man's body jerked again, and she felt a burning in her side.

Shot again. Both of us. The bullet had first hit the man

who shielded her. *Then me.* She heard footsteps, then someone sliding down the hill. *He's coming. He'll kill Roza.*

She looked to the side, saw the gun loosely clutched in her rescuer's hand. She didn't know who he was or why he'd shielded her, but she did know that if those footsteps got any closer, she and her mystery rescuer would both be dead.

The bastard who'd shot them had a rifle. He'd been up on the hill when he fired the first shot. She had to move fast or he'd shoot her again.

He'd shoot her again anyway.

Sucking in a breath, she shoved at the man on top of her until she could roll out from beneath him. She grabbed his pistol and swung up her arms, aiming straight up. *Fingers, work. Work, dammit.* She curled one finger over the trigger and squeezed. All she saw was the look of surprise in eyes peeking out from a ski mask before she started firing.

The man with the ski mask had fired at them from the top of the hill she and Roza had slid down, but now he was less than ten feet away, his rifle up against his shoulder, aimed straight at her. Corinne's first shot hit him squarely in the chest, and she felt sick as the recoil sent new pain up her arm. He staggered back but didn't fall, so she shot him again.

What. The. Fuck? He was wearing body armor.

He lifted the rifle, and she fired once more, hitting his arm this time. A wave of curses flowed out of him, but he backed up to aim again.

I'm dead. That's it. And then an engine roared behind her. The Subaru rushed past her, going straight for the masked gunman. The gunman sprayed bullets into the windshield and the tires, then turned and ran. The Subaru did a crazy turn, coming to a stop in a spray of dirt and leaves about fifty feet away.

Corinne stared at the vehicle, air sawing in and out of her lungs. Who was driving? She couldn't see anyone in the front seat.

And then she saw the gunman again. He was running away from them, around the bend and out of sight, something small and dark draped over his shoulder.

"*Roza! No!*" Corinne tried to stand, but her leg wouldn't support her. She sank to the ground, her side burning like liquid fire, watching as the man disappeared. *He has Roza.*

Utterly spent, she sat on the ground and sobbed. "He took her."

"Girl." The deep voice was gravelly. Broken. "You there."

Corinne looked at the man who'd taken a bullet for her. Two, actually. "What?"

"My phone. In my pocket." His breathing was labored. "Call 911."

Still sobbing, she pulled his phone from his pocket just as the ground trembled. The Subaru's driver's door had opened and a man tumbled from its front seat. A huge man.

Corinne gasped. It was the man she'd hit with the shovel near the deer blind. He'd been driving the Subaru, hunkered down. He'd scared the gunman away. Now he stretched out his arm. "Don't hurt him," he begged. "Please. My brother was trying to help you."

"I won't hurt him," she promised. Hands shaking, she dialed 911 and nearly cried when she heard the operator's voice.

"What is the nature of your emergency?"

"Three of us hurt. Two of us shot. One got stabbed, but that was an accident, I swear."

"Where are you?"

"I don't know." She looked at her protector. "Where are we?"

"Daniel Boone National Forest. Route 60. Just out of Morehead. Tell them to hurry."

"I heard him," the operator said. "What is your name?"

"Corinne. Corinne Longstreet. Please, the man who did this to us . . . he took my . . . the little girl who was with me. Her name is Roza. We were kidnapped and held in a house, then a cabin. He shot me and he took her. Please. He'll kill her."

"Can you describe him?"

"Tall, not big, not skinny. Wearing a ski mask. I'm sorry. Please hurry, she's only eleven."

"I'm informing the police right now. Did you see what he was driving?"

"No. He came here on foot. He shot us from up on the hill, then came down and took Roza. I shot his arm. I shot his chest, too, but he didn't go down. He was wearing body armor. And he had a rifle. With a scope. Looked like an M24. But then he ran away on the shoulder of the road, around the curve. He drove a van once, then a car once, but I didn't see which one he had this time."

"Who is with you?"

"I don't know. Who are you?" she asked the man beside her.

"Marcus O'Bannion," he wheezed. "That big guy is my brother Stone."

Stone? Corinne wanted to laugh, knowing it was hysteria. *His head was like one.* She told the operator their names. "The girl's name is Firoza, but she goes by Roza."

"All right, honey. Help is on the way. Sit tight."

Like I have a choice? She couldn't do anything but sit. Except that the man who'd saved her life looked in even worse shape than she was. "How badly are you hit?" she asked him.

"Pretty bad."

She could hear the wheezing sound of his lungs. She'd heard that sound once before. One of the bullets had punctured his lung. "Do you have any first-aid supplies in your vehicle?"

"In the back," Marcus whispered. "A kit."

"He says to look in the back," she ordered Stone, who still lay next to the Subaru. "Can you throw the kit? I can't walk to get it. Hurry or he'll die."

She was watching Stone crawl over with the first-aid kit when their last names clicked. "O'Bannion? The people who gave me a scholarship?"

Marcus's eyes glinted with interest despite his obvious pain. "You're a Joy kid? No shit?"

"Not a kid," she snapped as she opened the first-aid kit. "Are you one of those O'Bannions?"

"Other side of the family," he wheezed. "Small world, huh?"

"Yeah," Corinne said flatly. "Small as hell."

Mt. Carmel, Ohio
Wednesday, November 5, 1:05 p.m.

"It's just a house," Faith murmured as she walked into her grandmother's living room, where CSU had been busy. All the sheets that had covered the furniture had been removed, revealing the massive mahogany pieces she remembered from her childhood. Black fingerprint powder covered the walls and almost every other surface.

All of this is mine, she thought, but there was no joy in it. Only the rapidly growing sense of suffocating, impending doom. *At least this stuff should bring some money at auction.* Her father could definitely use the funds. But so could Gordon Shue's wife and kids. And Agent Pope's. *So many lives irrevocably changed.*

"Dr. Corcoran?" Kimble asked quietly, and Faith's eyes jerked to his.

"I'm sorry. I was thinking about the victims' families. There aren't enough assets in this house to compensate them all, even if I sold everything."

His eyes flickered in surprise. "That you'd even think about it is something. Most wouldn't."

"I hope I'm not most people." *I'm going to have to be stronger than most people.*

This nightmare was only beginning. Her life, her family, the link to the Joy Foundation . . . everything was about to become front-page news. The press knew bodies had been found here, but they didn't know how many. They knew about Roza but not about the girl's mother.

Who might still be buried downstairs. Faith gritted her teeth against the overwhelming need to run away as fast as she could. "Let's do this before I chicken out."

She marched herself through the kitchen, coming to a stop at the door to the basement. The steps grew wavy as she stared. She stifled a yelp when a hand grabbed her shoulder.

"Breathe," Kimble said from behind her. "You have to breathe or you'll pass out."

"Right." She'd done this before. *I can do it again.* But her feet would not move. Deacon had been here last time. He'd made it easier. Suddenly, she wished she'd waited until he could have come with her. But there was work to be done. She closed her eyes, imagined Deacon stood behind her, his soothing voice in her ear, and took the first step. *One. That was one!*

She had the insane urge to laugh, but sucked it back and, eyes still screwed shut, forced her feet down the remaining nine steps. *That's it. There are only ten now.* She took a step straight out but encountered nothing but air. Startled, she found herself falling forward.

She scrabbled for balance, instinctively throwing out her hands to break her fall. Kimble's hands grabbed her upper arms to yank her back, but he was too late. Her hands hit the wall and her knees hit the ground. Pain stole her breath, and for a moment she knelt there, waiting for the initial throbbing to subside.

"Are you all right?" Kimble asked with what sounded like real concern.

"What the—," Tanaka exclaimed, the floor vibrating under Faith's knees as he ran up to her. "Dr. Corcoran, what happened?"

She let the two men help her to her feet because it was easier than telling them no. Also because her hands and knees burned like hellfire. *Because you were in a car accident two days ago, you idiot.* After which she'd climbed an embankment.

She'd actually forgotten. "Just a miscalculation." She glared at the floor, now sixteen inches lower than it had been the night before. "You uncovered the other two stairs. I wasn't expecting that. I should have. I'm sorry."

"Do you need to leave?" Kimble asked. "I can take you back."

Faith straightened her spine. "No. The stairs are always the worst part." Which wasn't true, but it sounded good, and at this point, she'd lie like a damn rug to get through this.

"Um," Tanaka said, looking from her to Kimble. "Why are you here, Dr. Corcoran? I thought Agent Novak wanted you to wait until he got here."

"I asked her to help us find any hiding places where he might be keeping souvenirs," Kimble said.

Tanaka's brows shot up. "O-kay. Well, then, be careful where you step. We've stuck markers in the floor at various intervals, and I wouldn't want you to . . . well, you know."

"Trip," Faith muttered, her cheeks heating at his well-meaning tone. "Because I'm so graceful. I'll be careful." She took a moment to check out the changes made since her last visit. The floor under her bootie-covered shoes was no longer linoleum tile, but wood plank.

She thought about what had filled the space between these planks and the old tile and had to swallow hard. Ten bodies. Ten women who'd had their lives stolen away.

"Is this planking what you found when you removed

the . . . bodies? Or did you put it down to protect what's beneath?"

"It's what we found," Tanaka said. "What was it before, when you were a child?"

"Cement. Have you pulled up any of the planking?"

He nodded. "There's only dirt beneath."

"Then he dug up the cement." A shiver ran down Faith's back as she considered why he would have done so. She forced herself to turn until her eyes met the wall to the right of the stairs and then had to clear her throat. "This wall wasn't here. Do you know what's behind it?"

"Not yet," Tanaka said, then seemed to hesitate. "Do you?"

Yes. Shoes, swinging. Red sneakers with white shoelaces swaying lazily back and forth. Back and forth. Like nothing was wrong at all. "No," she said quietly. "Not anymore."

Tanaka's expression gentled. "He may have things hidden there, but he didn't put them there when he fled on Monday, because the plaster is untouched and we don't detect any seams."

"So it's probably not the jars Arianna heard him packing away," Faith said.

"Correct. Still, that's the first wall we're bringing down, as soon as we finish the scan."

The scan for bodies. Faith couldn't bring herself to ask him what he'd found. "Can't you scan the walls, too?"

"Not yet. The X-ray equipment I requested won't be here until tomorrow."

"Sergeant?" A woman with a long blond ponytail emerged from the room in which they'd found the first body buried in Plexiglas. She wore a Philadelphia Flyers sweatshirt and cargo pants, the pockets of which were stuffed to capacity with tools and . . . Faith squinted. Long sticks of beef jerky. *How very odd.*

The woman stopped short when she saw Faith and Kimble. "I'm sorry to interrupt, Sergeant Tanaka, but I heard you talking about an X-ray scanner. I brought one with me, so if you find a wall you need scanned, I can do that for you."

Tanaka's eyes lit up at the offer. "I didn't realize you had one with you."

"It's part of our gear." The woman spoke to Tanaka, but

her eyes were squarely on Faith as she moved closer. "I'm Sophie Johannsen. I'm a forensic archeologist."

Ah, yes. She'd been in that photo of Deacon staring at the freshly dug graves haphazardly spread across that hillside in West Virginia.

"I'm Faith Corcoran. This is my grandmother's house. This is Detective Kimble. We're here to search for places where the killer may have hidden his souvenirs. How does your wall X-ray work? I mean, how specific an area do I need to identify?"

"We work in pie-plate-sized increments. Each takes a long time and a lot of power. A whole wall would tax CSU's generator. Did you have a space in mind, Dr. Corcoran?"

"Call me Faith," Faith murmured, looking at the ceiling. "The kitchen is above our heads, but it was added in the late 1970s. The original 1859 kitchen was in the back of the house. Almost directly over the room where the autopsy table is."

She gathered her courage and walked into that room. A quick glance from the corner of her eye revealed that the autopsy table was gone, the room now big and bare, except for the cabinets built into the wall to the far left. The doors had been left open, every cabinet empty. To the right was where the door to the outside had once been. Now there was a wall, but she saw no sign of any magic opening—no seams, no missing plaster here, either.

"My mother used to tell me stories about this house," she said, aware that Kimble, Tanaka, and Sophie Johannsen had joined her in the room. "She was the oldest surviving child after Joy died, and the house would have been left to her. She told me to listen to the stories, that they were my birthright. My legacy. Now the only legacy will be what a monster did to his victims."

Severe unease gripped her, making it hard for her to look left at the wall with the cabinets, and she did not know why. It had been like this before, when Deacon was with her. She'd barely been able to look at that wall without being sick.

She looked straight up again, trying to orient herself spatially with the way the house had been before. Trying to remember her mother's stories. It had been a long time since she'd actively tried to remember a word her mother had said.

Because she also said she loved me, but she lied. She left me. On purpose. The adult therapist within her understood that her mother's suicide wasn't so simple, but the child still hurt.

"My mother used to tell me about getting stuck once inside the wall when she tried to ride the old kitchen's dumbwaiter. My grandmother scolded her for lying to me and told me the story wasn't true, but my mother said that was because my grandmother didn't want me trying to ride it."

"Would you have?" Sophie asked, amused.

"Only totally." Faith dropped her eyes to the floor so that she didn't have to look at the wall as she approached it, focusing on the markers Tanaka had cautioned her about. There were more than a dozen of them, placed in groups of two, separated by wide spaces.

It took her a moment to realize that they'd been placed not in twos, but in fours, each marking off a space roughly three feet by six feet. And then she understood.

"Oh God," she whispered. *Graves. Four more graves.* Four more victims buried beneath her feet. "I'm walking on them, aren't I?" Hysteria geysered up. "I can't just walk on them."

"Faith." Sophie Johannsen moved to her side, her tone pragmatic. "They are dead and have been for some time. They don't know—or care—that you're walking over them. But they have families who have been waiting for news all this time."

"Waiting for them to come home." Faith drew on the other woman's calm. "Okay. I'm not good at estimating distances, but the dumbwaiter should be on the other side of those cabinets."

"The space between the walls is too narrow for a dumbwaiter," Sophie said. "Are you sure?"

"I think so. I saw the door to it, but never the actual dumbwaiter. My mother tried to show it to me when I was older. She said that someday the house would be mine and I needed to know everything about it. She showed me the door, but it had a padlock on it. She figured her mother had told someone to lock it so that I wouldn't get hurt."

She looked down at the plank floor again, staying in the narrow aisle between the graves, putting one foot in front of the other, looking up when she came to the cabinets. "This room was different then. There were only wood shelves, not cabinets. But I think it was here."

Kimble inspected the cabinets, giving the right corner an experimental tug. "Solidly fastened to the wall." He repeated the action on the left, with the same result. But when he grabbed the middle section, he stumbled back, pulling one entire cabinet partway from the wall.

"Well, hello," Sophie said.

"It's not made of the same material as the other two," Kimble said. "Much lighter." He pulled it completely from the wall to reveal large steel rods on each corner of the back that had fit into corresponding holes in the wall. "Clever."

And effective. Because in the cleared space was a door in the wall.

"That's it," Faith said. "Padlock and all."

"I'll go get my bolt cutters," Tanaka said.

Eastern Kentucky
Wednesday, November 5, 1:35 p.m.

Deacon hung up with Dispatch and immediately dialed Bishop, his heart pounding hard. Corinne was alive. So who was the third body Bishop's anonymous caller had reported? And the fourth? "Where are you?"

"Ten minutes north of Morehead," Bishop said. "About two minutes from the road that leads to the cabin's GPS coordinates."

"I'm a minute behind you, then." They'd made good time, his a little better since she'd had a twenty-minute head start. "Don't turn onto the road to the cabin. Stay on Route 60. I just got a call from Dispatch. Corinne called 911 while we were on the way up here. She's been shot, along with the O'Bannion brothers, Stone and Marcus."

"You're kidding. She's alive?"

"She's alive," Deacon confirmed, intense relief rippling through him. "She and the O'Bannion brothers are on the side of Route 60, just ahead of your location. Look for a parking area and an entrance to one of the hiking trails."

"What about the little girl, Roza?"

His relief was short-lived. "Roza was taken by the shooter. We've issued a BOLO, but there's not much in the way of a description because he wore a ski mask. He got away, but no one saw what he was driving."

"Then who is the woman buried at the cabin? Who is the fourth person buried up there? And what is the O'Bannions' role in this?"

"Good questions. I keep thinking about the dirt on Stone's hands and boots yesterday."

"Me, too," Bishop said. "He either buried them or found them. Okay, I see the squad cars. They're on the right side of the road."

He rounded a curve and saw Bishop pulling in a few feet ahead of the squad cars. He parked his car, then ran to join her with the gathered first responders, his badge out and ready.

"I'm Detective Bishop, CPD. This is Special Agent Novak, FBI. Who's lead officer here?"

"I am. Trooper Williamson." The man gave Deacon the once-over, frowning at his hair. "Can I see your badge again?"

Impatiently, Deacon showed it to him. "Make sure everyone on the scene is wearing a vest. This guy has killed a federal agent, plus a lot of other people. Where is Corinne Longstreet?"

Trooper Williamson led them to a young blonde who lay on a stretcher, looking battered and exhausted. One paramedic was applying pressure to a leg wound while another set up an IV. The two O'Bannion brothers were also being tended by the medics. Stone was farther away, lying about five feet from a shot-up Subaru. Marcus's stretcher was closer to Corinne's.

What the hell happened here? A million other questions flooded Deacon's mind, but those questions would need to wait a few minutes more.

He and Bishop crouched beside Corinne, Deacon keeping his shades on. No need to startle the girl. She'd been through enough. "We are very happy to see you alive, Ms. Longstreet," he said. "I'm Special Agent Novak. This is Detective Bishop. We've been searching for you."

Her gaze locked on his face. She reached for his lapel and missed. Her swollen hands were drawn into a claw. "Are you real?"

He smiled at her. "I am very real. You're not losing your mind. I just look odd."

"I think you look wonderful. Everyone here looks wonderful." She closed her eyes and let out a long breath. "I'm so grateful to you all. I can't believe I'm here. But he took her. Roza. I tried to save her. I tried so hard."

Deacon gently sandwiched her icy hand between his own, sharing his body heat. "We know. We heard. Can you tell us what happened?"

Haltingly, she told them the tale of their escape from the cabin. Their few hours' respite in the deer blind. Her run-in with Stone O'Bannion and how she and Roza had fled, then fallen down the hill. How the gunman had opened fire.

"Wait. You hit Stone O'Bannion with a *shovel*?" Bishop asked.

"I didn't mean to hurt him. Well, I did, but I thought he was the one who'd taken us."

"Understandable," Bishop said. "Mr. O'Bannion has some explaining of his own to do, too, so don't worry about that. I was just surprised that you used a shovel."

"It was all I had. That and a few kitchen knives."

And she'd survived, Deacon thought, incredibly impressed.

Corinne struggled to see the stretcher behind her. "How is Marcus? Nobody will tell me. He got shot protecting me. He shielded me. Then Stone drove the Subaru at the gunman to keep him from shooting us anymore, but he ran away. The gunman, not Stone. He ran away and took Roza with him."

Deacon and Bishop looked at each other in surprise. "Could Marcus be your anonymous caller?" Deacon asked, and Bishop nodded, her frown a troubled one.

"I suppose it's possible. It didn't sound like Stone, I know that much. I'd say both O'Bannion brothers have some explaining to do." She bent back to Corinne. "Tell us about the man who abducted you."

"I never saw his face. He was maybe six feet tall. He wore a ski mask. I'm sorry."

"It's okay," Deacon said when Corinne became agitated. "You've told us how tall he was. How big was he? Stone O'Bannion's size?"

She frowned. "No. He was . . . normal. I shot him, though. With Marcus's gun. I hit him three times, but the first two shots hit body armor. The third hit him in the arm. It slowed him down for a few seconds—long enough for Stone to rush him with the Subaru."

Deacon felt a thrill of excitement. *She'd shot him.* The killer who left nothing of himself behind might just have left them a gift. "We could have DNA."

Bishop's eyes were bright. "I know. We'll have CSU check for a blood trail. Corinne, tell us about Roza."

Tears filled Corinne's eyes. "She's only eleven. She was born in that place."

Deacon stared. "She was born in the basement? Is that what you're saying?"

"That's what she said. She'd never been outside. She was so scared. But brave. She let me drag her all the way." A sob caught in the young woman's throat. "Her mother died there. Roza buried her. She buried her own mother."

"Oh no," Bishop murmured. "Arianna told us about Roza. We hoped her mother was alive."

"Arianna? You talked to her? She's alive?"

"She's alive and safe," Bishop assured her. "She's been so worried about you."

Corinne started crying, overcome. "I thought she was dead."

Deacon stroked Corinne's hair. "Arianna escaped. She went to find help, but you were gone by the time we got there. She's in the hospital, recovering."

"Is she . . . ? Did he . . . ?" she asked, her tears overwhelming her.

"She's safe now," Deacon murmured. "So are you."

"Oh God. He did. That bastard." She struck out, weakly hitting his shoulder. "He hurt her. She was just starting over and he hurt her."

"She's strong. And she's got support. I think that knowing you're alive will be exactly what she needs to hold on."

Corinne fought visibly to control her emotions. "Roza said he killed so many. Oh, dammit. The eyes. He had a collection of . . . jars. Filled with parts. Eyes. I saw them in the cabin."

"His souvenirs," Bishop said. "Do you remember anything else about Roza? Did she tell you her mother's name?"

"Yes. It was Amy. Short for Amethyst, she said. Amethyst Johnson. She and her aunt were taken at the same time. He killed the aunt and buried her. She said he didn't let her mother say good-bye. He beat her mother to death because they used the oven to make tea."

"That's a huge help," Bishop said. "Anything else? Any other details you can recall?"

"She said *zed*. Roza with a *zed*. Her name is Firoza."

"Very, very good," Deacon praised. "Is she British?"

"She didn't have any accent and I assumed she would have picked up something from her mother, living alone in the basement with her all those years. I was thinking Canadian."

The young woman was sharp. "You have helped us so much," Deacon said. "Is there anything we can do for you? Anyone we can call?"

"No family. Just tell Arianna I'm all right and I'll see her soon. Tell her to hold on for me."

"Absolutely. If you need us, you have someone call us. I'm Deacon Novak and she's Scarlett Bishop. And if you forget our names, just ask for the guy with white hair."

"Okay. Oh, wait. Wait. There were others. Two men, in the van he brought us in. I think they were both dead already. I think he buried them in the cabin."

"We know about the cabin," Bishop explained. "We're going to talk to Marcus and Stone, then the cabin is next on our list."

"I took his knife. The old man who was dead. It's in my pocket. His family might want it."

Deacon found himself swallowing hard. Most uninjured people wouldn't have cared. She'd been through hell and still thought of others. "Would you like us to take it to them?"

She nodded. "Tell them thank you. Tell them it saved our lives."

Bishop gently took the Swiss Army knife from Corinne's pocket. "We'll make sure they get it. I'm sure they'll be glad that you were able to use it to escape."

"For Roza. I did it for her. Please find her. I'll take her if nobody can take care of her."

Again Deacon's throat grew tight. "You are a very kind woman, Ms. Longstreet." He turned his attention to the paramedics, who seemed as emotionally affected as he and Bishop were. "Where are you taking her?"

"To Arianna," Corinne insisted. "Take me to the hospital where she is."

"County General Hospital in Cincinnati," he told the medics.

"Lexington's closer," one of them pointed out.

"Lexington's socked in," the other said. "Fog. We can do Cinci, if that's her wish."

"It is," Deacon said. "Corinne, you're going to where Arianna is, so you'll get to see her. My sister is one of the ER docs on duty there. Her name is Novak, too. She'll take good care of you. We'll keep searching for Roza, and we'll keep you updated. I promise."

Together he and Bishop went to the O'Bannion brother they hadn't yet met. "His status?" Deacon asked the medic.

"Probably a collapsed lung. He lost a lot of blood. We have the bleeding stopped for now. The Longstreet woman actually did first aid on him first, before stopping her own GSW from bleeding. Amazing woman. Did I hear you say she's going to Cincinnati?"

"Yes. County General. Can these two, as well?"

"Yeah. We'll put this guy, Marcus, on the first transport with Ms. Longstreet. The other guy, Stone, he's bleeding, too and may have a skull fracture, but he's more stable. He can wait for the second chopper."

Again Deacon crouched on one side of the stretcher, Bishop on the other. "What's your name?" Bishop asked, leaning in close to hear the answer.

"Marcus O'Bannion," he rasped out in a deep bass.

Bishop nodded. "It's the same voice. You called me," she said to Marcus. "Why?"

"Right thing to do."

"Why didn't you tell me your name?"

Marcus blew out a weak sigh. "Should have. Trying to protect family."

"Do you know where your father is?" Bishop asked.

"With Mother," Marcus whispered.

Deacon frowned. "Why did he sneak out of his house to go see her? Why go to all the trouble to escape surveillance?"

"I can answer your questions," Stone called, voice slurred. "Leave him alone."

"And Marcus really shouldn't be talking," the medic cautioned.

"Okay. Two more questions," Bishop said. "Who is the fourth body in the cabin? The one you said belonged to you. Is he your son?"

"I can answer that, too," Stone said belligerently. "Leave him alone."

"You'll get your turn," Deacon said, wishing he could hit Stone with a shovel, too. If Stone had told the truth yesterday, so much trouble and heartache might have been avoided. "Marcus? Who is the fourth body?"

A tear leaked from Marcus's eye. "Mikhail. Our brother. Only seventeen."

"Your brother?" Deacon swiveled to look at Stone. Gone was the confident, arrogant asshole they'd talked to the day before. His belligerence stripped away, Stone looked haunted.

Deacon met Bishop's eyes, saw that she was as surprised as he was.

"All right," Bishop said gently. "Last one. Why did you shield Corinne?" She and Deacon leaned forward to hear Marcus's answer.

"She might know who killed Mikhail. Needed to know. Plus, right thing to do."

At the roar of the descending helicopter, Deacon and Bishop rose and stepped back. The helicopter landed and the medics sprang into action, loading Corinne and Marcus. Within a few short minutes they were gone, stirring fallen leaves in their wake.

"Wait one," Bishop said when Deacon started toward Stone. "I want to update Isenberg. *Jeremy at ex-wife's house*," she spoke aloud as she typed. *"Corinne en route to County in Cinci, medevac. Third body is an O'B brother, Mikhail, age seventeen. No info on fourth body. Pls confirm Jeremy is there asap."*

She hit SEND, then turned to Deacon. "If we can confirm that Jeremy really is with his ex-wife right now, he can't have done this. There's no way he could have shot Corinne and Marcus, grabbed the child, and made it back to Cincinnati in that short amount of time."

"I know. But given that his cabin was used to hide the newest bodies and that the bodies in the basement are sutured with surgical precision . . . Hell. Someone wanted us looking at him."

"The question would be who," Bishop said. "Not Stone, because he's here. Could be Henson the third or even Combs, but they didn't take Roza. Wrong body type. This guy was 'normal.'" She bit her lip. "Are you thinking what I'm thinking?"

Deacon scowled. "I'm thinking now that I wish I'd gone upstairs with the pink genie gymnast to see if Jordan really was in there. We've based a lot on what he has told us and dismissed him as a suspect immediately because of Alda Lane's alibi."

"I'm thinking that, too. We need to put Jordan back on the suspect list—at least until we can establish where he's been for the last hour."

"I'm having surveillance put on his gallery and his townhouse." Deacon texted the request to Isenberg. "Now let's have a conversation with Stone."

Eastern Kentucky
Wednesday, November 5, 1:35 p.m.

He was shaking. *Shaking. Dammit.* It was the second time in a month that a bitch had put a bullet in him. Faith had shot him in the arm when he'd climbed through her window in Miami. Luckily, it had only been a nick and the coat he'd worn had absorbed the blood, but only because he'd run before any of it spilled on the windowsill or fire escape.

He never left DNA behind. *Never.*

Except that this time he had. *Damn that Longstreet bitch.* He snarled. The bullet had been a through-and-through, but it still hurt. And fuck those two clowns that came to her rescue. *Dammit.* Driving that Subaru straight at him . . . They'd almost killed him. *What the fuck were they doing there, anyway? They'd ruined everything.*

Luckily he'd been smart enough to figure out the direction Longstreet and Roza had taken. After tracking them to the main trail, he'd known where they'd emerge. Then it had been only a matter of driving to the main road, parking the truck out of sight, and following the trail from its end to intercept them.

Except Longstreet had been smart. She and the child

had hiked parallel to the trail, and in his hurry, he'd passed them. He'd heard them running for the road and had come upon them just in time.

His escape had been just as close. He'd passed law enforcement vehicles going toward Longstreet and her saviors as he'd been driving away.

He glanced into the backseat. At least he had the child. Although he was afraid he'd end up having to kill her, too. She'd hit her head hard on the way down that hill and was now unresponsive. If she didn't come to soon, she was as much a liability as Longstreet had been.

And it wasn't like he could waltz into a hospital with her. He could do her stitches, but with a head injury, she needed different skills than his.

His fingers tapped a beat on the dead equestrian's steering wheel, a smile bending his lips. On the other hand, he could bring a doctor to her. He knew of just the one.

Unfortunately, the cops would find the cabin now. They'd find the dead equestrian's body. She was the kind that people reported missing. They'd be looking for her fancy red truck.

So he'd have to switch vehicles again. As he drove down the country road, he saw the perfect choice—a tan Chevy Suburban with darkened windows, parked in front of a double-wide trailer. And the engine had been left running. He wouldn't even have to kill anyone for it.

Quickly, he made the switch, laying the child on the backseat and transferring his guns and, importantly, his collection of jars and souvenirs into the back of the vehicle.

Then he started for Cincinnati. Longstreet had never seen his face, so she couldn't ID him. He'd retrieved the only person who could ID him. And he hadn't lost *that* much blood on the ground. It had been so dry, it probably got soaked up. All in all, things could be much worse.

Chapter Thirty

That Stone O'Bannion was the least hurt of the three victims said quite a lot, Deacon thought. His face was gray, his eyes bloodshot. His black Windbreaker and hoodie had been removed, exposing a jagged tear in his T-shirt, which was crusted with dried blood.

"You look like shit, O'Bannion," Bishop said without preamble. "Before we get into how you got to looking that way, can you describe the man who shot Marcus and took the child? Sounds like you got the closest to him with your Subaru."

"Couldn't see his face. Ski mask. About six feet, maybe one ninety. Built more like Marcus than me. Dark eyes. I think. The woman shot him. Winged his right arm. He couldn't lift the rifle too fast after. She shot him in the chest first, but he must have been wearing Kevlar. He didn't go down and her shots would have been kill shots. Woman's a damn good shot."

"Where was he standing when he got shot?" Deacon asked so he could tell CSU where to search for blood samples.

"Probably just in front of where the Subaru is now," Stone said. "I was trying to run him down when he shot out the windshield and the tires. Stopped me. He ran after that."

"Okay. Start from the beginning," Deacon said. "You had dirt on your hands because you were at the cabin yesterday. Did you find the bodies then?"

Stone closed his eyes. "Yes. I was here looking for Mickey. Mikhail." He swallowed hard as tears seeped from beneath his closed eyelids. "He was only seventeen."

"I'm sorry for your loss," Bishop said kindly. "He was your brother? Your mother's son?"

"And Jeremy's. This is going to kill him. Mom . . . My God. I don't know how to tell her."

Deacon frowned. "I thought Jeremy and your mother had only one child together. Audrey."

"That's what Mom wanted everyone to think. Mom and Jeremy were already divorced when Mickey was . . . made," he finished awkwardly. "It was apparently a last fling."

"And you didn't think to tell us when we questioned you yesterday?" Bishop asked coldly.

"I thought about it. I decided not to. I was looking out for my family. I . . . fucked up."

"Y'think?" Bishop asked furiously. "You have caused so much—" She drew a breath, calmed her voice. "Okay. You were looking for your brother Mikhail? Why?"

"Because he'd run away, because he found out that Jeremy was his bio dad. He wigged out. Disappeared. I decided to check the cabin, 'cause I'd looked everywhere else." New tears ran down his face. "I got there yesterday about four in the afternoon. The door was open and I saw an empty Monster Energy Drink can on the front porch. Kid chugs that shit, so I figured, yeah, he's here. But he wasn't. There was a pile of dirt on the floor, and the bed was unmade. Somebody had made some stew, but they'd left the remnants in a pot on the stove. And the wheelbarrow was inside, next to the bed. I couldn't figure out why the dirt was there and then I saw the loose floorboard. I had this . . . horrible feeling in my gut. Y'know?"

Deacon nodded. "We know too well. So you looked under the floor. Dug with your hands?"

"Yeah. Shovel was gone. Turned out the woman had taken it." He winced, as if remembering the blows he'd taken to the head. "But I didn't dig at first. I thought, maybe he's out back. But the back wall was covered in dried blood. So was the gas tank. The gas was shut off. I think Mickey was lured out back to check the tank and then . . ." The big man's chest rose and shuddered as it fell. "I found him, under the floor. There was a bullet hole in his head."

"What did you do?" Bishop asked.

"Freaked out. Drove home to tell Jeremy, but . . . you guys were there."

"And then you lied to us," Bishop said coldly.

"No. No I did not," Stone said firmly. "I just didn't tell you what you wanted to know."

"Why?" Deacon asked. "Your brother was dead. Why not call 911 when you found him? Or ask for our help when you saw us at your house? I can't understand this."

Stone sighed. "Because my family's fucked up, that's why. My mother divorced my biological father when Marcus and I were kids because he cheated and was an all-around worthless piece of shit. She married Jeremy and everything was great. He adopted us and they had Audrey, and then they divorced because Jeremy was cheating with a man. She'd put him through med school and set him up in his practice, but *he* left *her*. I nearly tore him apart, but Mom stopped me. She knew all along that Jeremy was gay. She didn't mind if he had lovers, as long as they weren't female. She didn't divorce him because he was cheating. She let him go because she wanted him to be happy."

"That's nice," Bishop said, "but it doesn't explain why you didn't ask for our help when you discovered your brother had been murdered."

Stone blew out a breath. "I'm *trying* to explain. Mom wanted a family. Wanted the illusion. Jeremy gave that to her, but then his lover pressured him to come out, to leave Mom for him. Mom said she agreed. She'd gotten Audrey and had had ten good years of marriage. Jeremy was a good man, she always said. Which he is. After I got over my being mad and hurt, I forgave him. I even liked his last partner. He made Jeremy so damn happy."

"His last partner?" Deacon asked. "Not Keith?"

"No. Jeremy's last partner was Sammy. Keith had known Jeremy longer—since high school, but it was Sammy that Jeremy loved. Keith was friends with Sammy, too, but I got the sense he was a third wheel. Even as a kid, I understood the three's-a-crowd concept."

"You think Keith was jealous?" Deacon asked.

"I know he was. He still is. And he has a temper. After Sammy was killed in the accident that ruined Jeremy's hand, Keith helped him through the grief and then they became partners. I've see Keith give men black eyes if they look at Jeremy too closely. I've seen him beat up a guy who called Jeremy a fag. Put the guy in the hospital."

"He wasn't charged," Bishop said. "We ran checks on all of you."

"Jeremy paid the homophobe and made it go away."

"I repeat," Bishop said. "You're still not explaining."

"Be patient," Stone snapped. "I have a concussion. Mom always passed off Mickey as the son of a Russian business-man she'd lived with for a short time after Jeremy left. But last week, Mickey did one of those genetic grids in biology class and figured out that the Russian couldn't be his father. Mom had to tell him the truth—that Jeremy was his father."

Now Deacon understood. "Keith wasn't the only one comforting Jeremy after Sammy died."

"Exactly," Stone said. "Keith was furious. He had never liked Mickey and none of us really knew why. When the truth came out, my sister, Audrey, and I thought that maybe Keith had always had a subconscious feeling that Jeremy was Mick's dad. When I found Mickey's body . . ." Stone shuddered out a breath. "I thought that Keith had . . ." He let the thought trail.

"You thought Keith had killed Mickey," Deacon finished.

"Understandable," Bishop said. "But it still doesn't explain why you didn't tell us about the damn bodies. Nor does it explain why you didn't report Keith. I mean, you believed he'd killed your brother. Why wouldn't you warn Jeremy that you thought that Keith was a killer?"

"Keith wouldn't hurt a hair on Jeremy's head," Stone said. "But it would have killed Jeremy to know that his son was dead because his own lover had murdered him. I hadn't even had a chance to breathe when I got home yesterday before the two of you busted in. And then you told me that an Earl Power guy was dead and I knew I'd seen his body. Keith might kill in fury, but not like how you were talking, not all planned and calm. And he wouldn't abduct women or girls. I figured someone else had killed them and maybe the missing woman you told me about would know who it was. So I didn't suspect Keith anymore, which would spare Jeremy pain, and I could find out who the hell killed my baby brother. I tried to find Corinne Longstreet. I found her trail near the deer blind. I tried to talk to her, to help her, but she went ballistic like a crazy woman and beat the hell out of me."

Bishop rolled her eyes. "She went 'ballistic' because she'd heard her best friend being tortured for days. She thought *you* were the one who'd done it. But none of this explains why you didn't tell us the goddamn *truth*. If you suspected someone else, why didn't you say something? You could have saved us time. Spared Corinne hell. We could have gotten to Roza before a psycho killer did. He's killed a lot of people in the hours since we last talked. Their blood is on *your* hands, Stone. *Yours*." She got in his face, more furious than Deacon had ever seen her. "Why didn't you tell us the truth?" she shouted.

"Because I knew you'd blame Jeremy!" Stone spat out. "As soon as you said Cousin Faith's name, I knew. Because I knew the lies his family told about him. I knew because I was there the day he came home from the reading of his father's goddamn will. He was devastated."

"Because he was cut out of the will," Bishop said.

"No. Because his family thought he could actually molest his own niece. He came home and cried. I'd never seen a grown man cry, and I remembered that. I didn't understand why he was so upset at the time, but I do now. He was heartbroken—to be accused to begin with and because his own sister didn't defend him. She stood there and let her husband beat him up. So, yeah, I didn't tell you any of this. Somehow you'd find a way to pin it on Jeremy. Does that satisfy your need for an explanation, Detective?"

Bishop slowly straightened. "Yes. Yes, it does. Finally." She looked away for a minute, then turned back to him. "You say you saw him come home that day from the reading of his father's will. Do you happen to remember when that was?"

Stone blinked at her. "Around three. It was a Friday and we'd just come home from school."

"You seem to remember it well," Deacon said thoughtfully. "Why?"

"Because the next day was Saturday. Mom wanted to

cheer us up, so we went to Kings Island and rode the Beast all day. It's a roller coaster."

"I know," Deacon and Bishop said together.

"All day?" Bishop asked.

"Yes," Stone insisted. "Why?"

"Just establishing a timeline," Deacon said quietly. "Your cousin Faith remembers things a little differently that day."

"Well, she's wrong. Ask Marcus. Ask my mother. They'll tell you the same thing."

"We will," Deacon said. "Speaking of Marcus, how does he fit into this picture?"

Stone sighed. "I needed to get out of the house to look for Corinne Longstreet, but your people were watching, so I called Marcus and asked him to meet me at a bar downtown. Your Fed tailed me all the way into town. I met with Marcus and asked if he'd take my car back to Jeremy's and sleep in the guesthouse for the night. I told him I had a story lead to follow. Which wasn't exactly a lie. This will make one helluva byline."

"He believed you?" Bishop asked.

"Of course."

"Why did he think he was leading the Feds away from you?" Deacon asked, frowning.

"Because some of my stories are controversial. I've been tailed by Feds before."

"You didn't tell him about Mickey?"

"No. I didn't tell him any of it, because he would have called you. He's just wired that way. I wanted to buy some time. And I wanted him near Jeremy, just in case he found out about Mickey. Marcus is better with him than I am." Stone's body sagged. "Marcus is better with everyone than I am. He led your Fed back to Jeremy's in my 'Vette and I drove Marcus's Subaru to the cabin."

"How did he fool my Fed?" Deacon asked. "You two look nothing alike."

"Not lying down and bleeding and shit," Stone muttered. "But standing up, if Marcus is wearing my coat and we pad it a little, and it's dark? Yeah, he can pass as me. We've done it before, when we needed to fool Mom. I texted him when I came to after that woman coldcocked me with the shovel. Told him to follow the trail the woman and girl had left behind. He was so pissed when he found me. He'd been watching the news. He knew what was going on and why the woman had stabbed me. Said I got what I deserved for lying to the cops and for leaving poor Corinne to wander around the woods. Pretty much word for word what you said, Detective."

"Okay, so that's how you got out," Deacon said. "How did Jeremy sneak out the back way—and why? Why did he go to so much trouble to evade the agents out front?"

"Marcus got Jeremy and Keith out in the Range Rover," Stone said. "Keith had left it in the woods behind the house because he was gathering firewood. Marcus said that Mom came home from a trip last night and realized that Mickey was missing. Audrey and I hoped we could find him and bring him home before Mom got back, but ... Anyway, Mom called Jeremy, and he went to sit with her. He went out the back way partially because he didn't want to arrive at Mom's being followed by the cops and partially because none of them knew that Mickey had run. Mom immediately thought he'd been kidnapped and she didn't want the cops involved." His cheek twitched as he clenched his jaw. "She asked Jeremy not to involve the police."

"Didn't Audrey tell them Mickey had run away?" Bishop asked.

"Yes, and Marcus went out looking for him, not realizing I knew where he was because I, like a fool, hadn't told him. Marcus told them that we'd find him. He's angry with me for keeping this from him. He gave Mom and Jeremy false hope."

"Agent Novak? Detective Bishop?" State Trooper Williamson was pointing to the sky. "Chopper's here. And we need to talk."

"All right," Deacon said. "One more question. Do you know who killed your brother?"

"No. That's why I wanted to find Corinne Longstreet. I figured she knew. That's the truth."

"We'll talk more when you're patched up," Deacon said, and backed away.

"What's going on?" Bishop asked the trooper when Stone O'Bannion had been loaded into the helicopter.

"State police sent a forensics unit to the cabin," Williamson said.

"What?" Deacon exploded. "That cabin is under federal jurisdiction."

Williamson put his hands up. "The Feds are there, too. They're duking it out." He shook his head. "They found four bodies, just like your caller told you, Detective Bishop."

"The caller was Marcus O'Bannion," she told him. "He went in the first helicopter. Who's the fourth victim?"

"A woman who meets the description of Elise Lasker, who disappeared—along with her red truck—from a hospital in Cincinnati early this morning. The Fed up there asked me to tell you that the truck's been added to the BOLO. He said that other than removing the floorboards, they've touched nothing and are in communication with . . ." He pulled out a notepad. "Sergeant Tanaka and Agent Taylor. Those names sound right?"

"Yeah." Deacon nodded, relieved. "Good to see everyone playing well in the sandbox."

"I wouldn't go that far. Anyway, they're waiting for you two. We've got the scene secured here. I'll make sure whoever processes this scene checks for the shooter's blood."

"Tell them to check around the front of the Subaru," Deacon said. "Can you tell us the fastest way up to the cabin?"

Williamson pulled a folded map from his pocket. "You can pick up the road that'll take you there about a mile north. I marked it here." He gave them the map, then tipped his hat to Bishop. "Let me know if you need anything."

"Ready to play peacemaker in the sandbox?" Deacon asked Bishop.

Bishop shook her head. "No. I'm tired and hungry, and if they behave badly, I might just take a shovel to them."

"I almost wish I could see that. Meet you there."

Mt. Carmel, Ohio
Wednesday, November 5, 2:15 p.m.

Faith watched nervously as Tanaka took photos of the dumbwaiter door and the faux cabinet that had covered it. She didn't *want* to know what was back there. But she *needed* to know. For every woman who'd died here, she needed to know.

"Are there any other spaces like this?" Kimble asked.

"Not this big, no, but there are other dumbwaiters in the fireplace mantels all over the house. The side opens up. My mother said they used to bring up firewood that way in the old days—and coal, too— until my grandfather installed central heating. I know there was a laundry chute. A safe in my grandfather's office. And a crawl space in Gran's sewing room. Family legend has it that there was a tunnel, too, because this house was part of the Underground Railroad, but my mother thought that wasn't true."

"I can't comment on the Underground Railroad part, but the tunnel is probably there," Sophie said. "Our GPR scan showed the remnants of what looked like an old tunnel outside. It appeared to have a cave-in about ten feet away from the house, so I don't think it's usable anymore. It'll be in my report. I was focusing on any readings that might be bodies first."

"Exactly what we needed you to do," Tanaka said as he cut through the lock on the dumbwaiter door.

"Let's see what's in here, and then we'll check the other places," Kimble said. "Vince, hurry up. The suspense is killing me."

Tanaka pulled the door open, revealing nothing but black, empty space.

Faith almost cried with disappointment until Kimble said, "Clever," once again.

Kimble reached into the empty space and pulled out a densely woven chain, painted black. He tugged on it experimentally, then nodded. "He keeps it oiled." He pulled more chain, raising a tray into the empty space. It was bigger than a cafeteria tray, but empty.

He continued to pull and a second tray rose up, also empty. It nested with the first, a few inches above the upper border of the doorway, like collapsing window blinds. A third empty tray followed. And a fourth, which was not empty. Not at all.

"Oh God," Kimble said quietly. "Looks like we've found his collection."

Faith refused to look away even though every instinct she had was screaming for her to *run*. The fourth tray was filled with jars. The jars had big dark . . . *things* floating in them.

"They're labeled," Tanaka said heavily. He aimed a beam

of light at one of them. "This one says 'Heart of Simpson.' She's one of the victims the ME has already identified."

He resumed pulling on the chain until the tops of the jars on the fourth tray met the underside of the third. Seconds later, a fifth tray appeared and then a sixth.

"More jars," Faith whispered. *Dozens of them.* Labeled with the likes of "Heart of Parker," "Lips of Smith," "Thumbs of Dreyfus," and "Brain of McCall."

"How many trays are down there?" Sophie asked softly.

Tanaka shook his head. "I don't know. But I think there are some above, too."

And then he pulled up a new tray, loaded with jars. The ink on the labels was dark black. They looked brand-new. "Heart of Dupree." "Tongue of Dupree." Roxanne Dupree. *Roxie.*

"Oh God." Faith backed away, her stomach roiling like an angry sea, her throat burning from bile. Her eyes stinging with tears. "I need some air." She made it to the hall and sat heavily on the third stair from the bottom, scooting over when Sophie followed her out.

Sophie took the stair below and dropped her chin to her chest. "Don't feel bad," she said, her voice muffled. "I've been digging up the dead for years and this is hard for me, too." She pulled her cell phone from her pocket and started flipping through photos, all centering around one blond preschooler and a black-haired toddler who looked about a year old.

Faith found herself drawn to the comfort of those photos. "Your kids?" she whispered.

"Yes. Anna is four, and Michael will be a year old on Christmas Eve."

"They're gorgeous," Faith said. "You're lucky."

"I know. I look at them when I get overwhelmed with all the death. There was a mudslide in Central America last summer. . . . These faces were all that kept me going. And this one, of course." She flipped to a man with dark, good looks and a naughty gleam in his eye. "My Vito."

"He's very handsome. But maybe a little uncontrollable. Like a rogue pirate."

Sophie's laugh was unsteady. "That's him to a T. Do you mind music?"

Faith blinked. "Excuse me?"

"Do you mind if I play a little music? I've got earbuds in my coat pocket if you'd rather."

"As long as it's not hip-hop," Faith said, and Sophie laughed again.

"No." She chose a song from her playlist, and a second later the air was filled with the most beautiful baritone Faith had ever heard.

"Oh." Closing her eyes, she let the music in, let it soothe her. And when the final notes faded, she found her cheeks were wet. "I need to buy that song."

"You can't buy it, but I'll send it to you. My husband sang that at Anna's christening."

"You are very lucky, indeed."

"I know. Deacon and I listened to this song a lot last year when we were digging up graves in West Virginia. It helped him, too."

Faith met her gaze. "He's going to be upset with me. I wasn't supposed to come here without him. He's worried I'll get shot—or get the person standing next to me shot."

"Then why did you come?"

"Because Lieutenant Isenberg asked me to, and Detective Kimble was willing to take the risk. It gave me a chance to *do* something. I've felt so helpless. It's not only the ten victims but their families, too. So many destroyed lives."

Sophie hesitated. "Not ten, Faith. I'd just finished scanning the last of the interior when you all came down the stairs. I found seven more bodies in all."

Seven more. "Seventeen bodies," Faith whispered. *Here. In my grandmother's house.* "Roza's mother could be one of them."

"Or maybe Roza's mother is still alive and with Roza and Corinne."

"If *they're* still alive. I'm starting to lose hope."

"Don't lose hope!" A smiling Tanaka ran from the torture room, nearly skidding to a stop at the stairs. "We just got the call from Isenberg. Corinne is alive!"

Faith pressed her fingers to her mouth, tears of relieved joy springing to her eyes. "Where?" she whispered. "How? Who found them?"

Tanaka's smile dimmed. "Not them. Just Corinne."

The air slammed out of Faith's lungs, leaving her reeling. "Roza's dead?"

"She was recaptured. Corinne managed to get her from your uncle's cabin to the main road, through nearly twenty miles of forest, but a man in a ski mask showed up at the same time as two would-be rescuers—your cousins Stone and Marcus. Ski Mask shot Marcus and Corinne and got away with Roza."

"What about the other cousin?" Sophie asked.

"Stone was already injured. I'm a little fuzzy on those details."

"What were Stone and Marcus even doing there?" Faith demanded. "Did Corinne identify her abductor?"

"No. She never saw him," Tanaka said. "She and your cousins are en route to Cincinnati General by helicopter. That's all I know so far." He turned to get back to work.

Faith took a moment to let her mind process the news. "Poor Roza.... He'll kill her. She knew he would when she helped Arianna escape, but she did it anyway."

"Pretty brave for eleven years old," Sophie said softly.

"Pretty brave for any age." Faith pushed herself to her feet. "If Arianna was here, she'd want to take a look at the dug-out room, so I'll do that for her." *And maybe say a prayer for little Roza.* "And then I'll ask Kimble to take me back. It was nice to meet you, Sophie."

"Likewise, but what's this about a dug-out room?"

"It's at the end of the passageway. Didn't Tanaka tell you?"

"Yes, but I didn't understand that it was an actual room. I thought it was just a crawl space, so I haven't scanned it yet. I'll take a look with you."

A minute later, Sophie was hunched down and grimacing. "It *is* just a crawl space, Faith."

Faith followed her into the little room, swallowing back new tears as she took it in. "It's where she lived with her mother. Deacon told me that there was a blanket here, with a thin pillow. Roza slept there." In the cold darkness.

God, please. If nothing else, please help this child. She deserves a life.

"Deacon found a box here," Kimble said from the doorway, startling Faith. Kimble didn't try to enter. He was too tall, and there wasn't enough room. "Inside was a ratty old hairbrush, a battery-powered light, and a T-shirt. It was either all she had or all she had time to pack."

Sophie swept the beam of her flashlight over the floor, studying it with a critical eye. "Or maybe all she wanted to admit she had. There's something buried here, under where her blanket was. The ground is slightly curved. Same over here, next to where she slept. Let me do a scan and see what's here before we start digging."

Kimble backed out, and Faith and Sophie followed. In the hall, Sophie stretched with a groan. "I'm glad I'm not claustrophobic. That was a tight fit." She held out her hand. "A pleasure, Faith. Don't be a stranger."

"Are you leaving?" Kimble asked Sophie.

"No, I am," Faith said. "You wanted me to help you find the hidey-holes."

"I do. We found one. We may need your help again. Can you stay for a little while?"

Faith shrugged. "I suppose so. You have Internet here, right?"

"A satellite hookup, yes," Kimble said. "Why?"

"I brought my laptop, so I can work here. I recognized at least two of the names on the jars as scholarship recipients. I'll write down the others and start checking against the list."

"What is this about?" Sophie asked. Quickly, Faith explained, and Sophie's eyes grew wide. "He's hunting from the scholarship pool. Sonofabitch. You go do your job and I'll do mine. I'll let you know if I find anything back in that room."

Faith straightened her spine before going back to the room with all the jars. She'd return their identities to them, so that Deacon could get them justice.

Eastern Kentucky
Wednesday, November 5, 3:00 p.m.

There were enough law-enforcement personnel at Jeremy's ex-wife's cabin to run a small country, Deacon thought as he and Bishop walked along the long line of parked vehicles. A few of the state troopers had gathered around the car parked closest to the house—a sleek silver Porsche.

"Marcus must have driven it up here," Bishop said. "He and Stone switched cars at the bar last night and Stone's Corvette is still parked in front of Jeremy's estate, right?"

"Right. The agents said none of the cars moved from the driveway after Marcus got back with the Corvette last night. Who owns the Porsche?"

"It's registered to Audrey O'Bannion," one of the troopers volunteered.

"Marcus borrowed his sister's car after sneaking Jeremy and Keith out in the Range Rover," Bishop said. "Ever think about driving one of these, Novak?"

"Only once," Deacon admitted dryly. "They had to pry me out with a crowbar."

Bishop chuckled, but quickly sobered as a balding man in a black suit and tie met them at the door. "Bishop and Novak," she said briskly.

"Special Agent Hudgins," he said, holding the door wide open. "My office was closest to the scene, so I got tapped to secure it for you Cincinnati guys. But I have to tell you, this wasn't what I expected when I got the call to come out here."

"What did you expect?" Deacon asked, sliding his wraparounds off his face so that he could do a visual check of the cabin interior. The place was a mess—the contents of drawers lay strewn on the floor and dirt was piled next to an open grave. Four faces stared out of the shallow hole, three older and one who was far too young. Mikhail Yarborough, Jeremy's son.

"When I saw the Porsche parked in front of the house? A meth lab or mountains of oxy pills, even a field of pot. Not four bodies under the floorboards and a jar of eyes." Hudgins blinked once when Deacon turned to look at him. "But . . . regular eyes. Not like yours."

Bishop coughed, but her expression remained serious. "Corinne mentioned them."

"Where are these 'regular eyes'?" Deacon asked.

"Look under the bed. We haven't moved anything yet."

Deacon swept the tails of his coat aside as he went into a crouch, Bishop right beside him.

Shining his Maglite under the bed, he saw the jar lying on its side. At least a dozen opaque eyes floated in a dark fluid.

"Looks like a cheesy prop from a cheesier haunted house," Bishop muttered, but Deacon only half heard her, his mind resurrecting a snippet of conversation from Monday night.

Shelves with jars, Faith had said, her tone faraway. *Jams and jellies mostly. My grandmother's cook put up preserves back then.* Her forehead had wrinkled. *And olives.*

Deacon had been surprised. *Your grandmother's cook canned her own olives?*

Of course not, she'd replied as if he'd been silly. *They bought the olives already canned.*

"Faith saw this jar," he said softly. "Or one like it, probably from behind the half wall that hooked around the old basement door. She said that's where she took off her boots when it was muddy." He barely managed to control the shudder at the thought of what might have happened had the killer seen her looking. "She remembered seeing jars of olives."

"I can see how she thought that. Sometimes the mind won't allow you to process what you see, especially if you're very young and it's very traumatic. How old was she?"

"I don't know. Younger than nine, because by the time her mother died, she already had a fear of the basement. It's why she counted the steps. She'd go down them with her eyes closed." New dread filled him. "This means he's been killing for a lot longer than we thought."

"Her mother died twenty-three years ago," Bishop murmured. "This changes things." She turned to Hudgins. "Is this the only jar?" she asked.

"Only one we've found so far. Something was stored in the closet. The dust on the floor has been disturbed. Looks like it was about three feet by four."

"The rest of his collection," Deacon murmured, rising to his full height. "Latent?" he called, and a woman turned from brushing powder on a closet doorknob.

"Yes, Agent Novak?"

"Can you get prints off this jar right now? Thank you." He turned to Bishop. "Let's see if we can make sense of this. The killer brought the two dead adult males and two live females to this cabin on Monday night." He glanced at Hudgins. "He was escaping his playground—a house in Mount Carmel, Ohio."

"I thought this might be related to that case. We got the BOLO on the Earl Power and Light tech and the locksmith. The boy?"

"Son of the cabin owner, Della Yarborough," Bishop

said. "He'd run away from home, was staying here. Probably surprised the killer. I understand the back wall is covered with blood?"

"Yeah. Right by the gas tank. The gas was turned off."

"To lure him out," Deacon said grimly. "Our killer's specialty. So he buries the boy with the two men." Deacon shined the Maglite on the unmade bed. Several dark hairs were on the pillow, and two lengths of rope lay on the tangled sheets. The ropes had been sawed with a small knife. "Roza was here. Where was Corinne?"

"There's a storm cellar in the back," one of the other forensics techs offered. "We found a few blond hairs and some ropes that had been cut, just like those on the bed."

"Okay." Deacon thought it through, reconstructing the events in his mind. "He dumped Corinne in the storm cellar and left Roza here, tied to the bed. Corinne escapes with a Swiss Army knife." He was growing more impressed with the young woman with every new discovery. "Comes into the cabin and frees Roza."

"According to Arianna," Bishop said, "Roza knew she'd be punished for helping her escape the basement, maybe even killed, so she drugged herself."

"Brave little girl," Hudgins commented.

"You have no idea," Bishop said. "Corinne must have then gathered up supplies. She told us she had a few kitchen knives and a shovel for defense. Maybe she goes to the closet, sees a box, opens it, and takes out one of the jars. Realizes what she's holding and drops it and the jar rolls under the bed."

Hudgins blew out a breath. "Makes sense. I might've dropped it, too."

Deacon pointed his light on an empty soup can on the floor. "They must have eaten a little, and then Corinne got Roza out of here. We think the next person who showed up at this cabin was Stone O'Bannion, also a son of the cabin's owner. He was looking for Mikhail, his little brother. He told us he found this mess, saw the pile of dirt inside and the blood outside, and started digging in here."

"He saw Mikhail's body and panicked, drove home to Cincinnati to tell Jeremy, and ran into us because we were at his house questioning his father," Bishop said. "Stone told us nothing, because he didn't want us to accuse Jeremy.

Instead, he came back here to find out from the girl what really happened so that he could protect Jeremy, but Corinne and Roza were gone. He tracked them through the woods, but Corinne assumed he was the one who kidnapped her and tortured Arianna, so she stabbed him with the kitchen knife and hit him with the shovel."

"Good for her," Hudgins said, and both Deacon and Bishop gave hard nods.

"I agree," Bishop said. "Stone passed out, woke up, and contacted his brother Marcus, who'd already snuck Jeremy and Keith out the back entrance right out from under the noses of three federal agents on surveillance."

"Don't keep rubbing it in," Deacon protested, but without much heat. The Feds had royally fucked up the surveillance.

"Hey, I calls 'em like I sees 'em," she said. "Marcus was with his mother and Jeremy, who had by then realized that Mikhail was missing and started getting worried. Marcus went looking for Mickey, then got the text from Stone, borrowed his sister's Porsche, and drove out here to find four bodies. That's when he called me, anonymously."

Deacon frowned. "Wait. That's important. Stone only saw three bodies. Marcus saw four, so the killer came back in between to bury Elise Lasker."

"When did the Lasker woman go missing?" Hudgins asked.

"She was last seen a little before five a.m.," Bishop said. "She was killed for her truck, most likely. If the killer grabbed her at five, he would have been here by seven. He finds Corinne and Roza gone. He must have buried the Lasker woman and covered the bodies back up with the floorboards, then gone searching for Corinne and Roza. Marcus arrives in the forest, finds Stone hurt in the woods, and puts him in his Subaru. Then he comes here, uncovers the bodies again, and calls me."

"While the killer is wandering around, looking for Corinne and Roza," Deacon said. "Does it make sense that Marcus could find them in an hour while the killer wandered around for six?"

Bishop shrugged. "It's a big forest. It's conceivable that he and Marcus passed each other, especially if they were both in stealth mode on foot, although you'd have thought they'd hear each other's car engines. We'll need to figure that one out once we establish where everyone on the suspect board was between four a.m. and noon."

"Assuming he stayed here the whole time," Deacon said.

"What are you thinking?" Bishop asked.

He was thinking what he didn't want to be thinking. "That the killer has been killing for at least twenty-three years. And that Jordan was very insistent on seeing Faith this morning."

"You're thinking that maybe he wanted to establish an alibi?"

"Maybe. I hope he simply wanted to give us information on the gardener from the historical society, but I have to be sure. Faith trusts him."

"Got it. I talked to Isenberg on the way over here. She said that they've picked up the gardener and he's waiting in an interview room. She also said that Keith was waiting outside Jeremy's ex-wife's house in the Range Rover looking 'coldly furious,' because Jeremy was inside with his ex. Isenberg notified them of Mikhail's death, then brought both Jeremy and Keith into the station for questioning. She said Keith's fury disappeared as soon as Jeremy could see him."

"So Keith's still on the leaderboard in terms of suspicious behavior, but he didn't shoot Marcus and Corinne, either. He's the wrong body type, and he has Isenberg for his alibi."

"We need to regroup with the others," Bishop said, then pulled her phone from her pocket when it began to ring. "Speaking of . . ." She held up the phone so that Deacon could see Isenberg's name on the caller ID. "What's up?" she answered, then blinked. "Yes, I'll hold."

A few seconds later Deacon's cell began to ring, also Isenberg. She was conferencing them in, meaning she wanted to say what she was going to say only once. "I'm here," he answered, dread settling on his shoulders. "Tell me Faith is all right and that Corinne is still alive. Please."

"Faith is fine," Isenberg said. "Corinne is still in surgery. This isn't about them. I've also got Adam, Vince, and Carrie Washington conferenced in. Carrie? Go ahead."

"We found the slug in Agent Pope's body," Carrie said. "It wasn't from a nine mil. It was a rifle slug, same as we pulled out of the hotel bellman on Monday night."

Deacon sucked in a quiet breath. "He didn't come up

behind Pope, then. He had a vantage point somewhere in my neighborhood." His stomach turned over at the possibilities—and probabilities. "We need to do a door-to-door search. I doubt he was courteous enough to pick an empty house, and he never lets his victims live."

"I agree," Isenberg said, "and so does your SAC. I've been in contact with Special Agent in Charge Zimmerman, who already had the neighborhood locked down, searching for Antonio Renzo, the kid who bullied your brother and sister."

"Pope was one of ours," Deacon said. "The field office switched gears when I told them that he was shot first. Since then, they've been looking for the shooter, not the kid. But they still have several agents hunting for Renzo, hoping the kid can lead them to . . . Oh, hell." He heard his own words. *He never lets his victims live.* "If Renzo got close enough to the shooter for the shooter to take his knife, then we have to assume he's dead, too."

"Zimmerman said the same thing," Isenberg said. "Next piece of news. Adam, your veterinarian angle paid off. We have an ID on the woman found in the grocery store parking lot—Delores Kaminsky. She ran a shelter for dogs. I sent a squad car to her home address and put out a BOLO for her vehicle. Nissan minivan, silver."

A silver minivan? *Shit.* Deacon's pulse started to race. "I saw it. The silver minivan. It was parked in front of my house Tuesday morning. It didn't register at the time. That's a school bus stop. Parents park there to wait for the bus with their kids."

"And most of the moms drive minivans," Isenberg said grimly. "We were so close to him."

"Dammit," Deacon hissed. "Why didn't I check it out?"

"Why didn't Pope and Colby?" Bishop asked reasonably. "They probably thought the same thing—that it was a mom with kids waiting for the bus."

"And now Pope's dead," Deacon said grimly. "Thanks, but that doesn't make me feel any better. We have news of our own, Lynda. We've got part of his collection—a jar full of eyes that had rolled under a bed. It appears he took a bigger box with him."

"Latent is pulling prints off the jar now," Bishop added, "so you should expect them soon."

"We found a lot more jars at the house," Adam said. "More than four dozen, filled with eyes and tongues and hearts and more. A lot of them were labeled with the victims' names."

"You found his stash?" Deacon asked, feeling relieved. Now there would be no need for Faith to go out there. She could stay put in the police station until he arrived to take her home.

"One of them anyway," Adam said. "Now we can begin identifying some of the victims."

"We have other news," Tanaka said. "None of it good. Sophie found seven more bodies."

"I'll prepare the morgue for more incoming," Carrie said with a sigh.

Deacon's relief drained away. *Seven more. Plus the Lasker woman.* He started for the cabin door. "I'm going to my neighborhood and help with the search. I owe my neighbors that much."

"I figured you would," Isenberg said. "SAC Zimmerman is expecting you."

Chapter Thirty-one

"Dr. Corcoran? *Faith?*"

Faith looked up, jerking away from her laptop screen to find Isenberg standing in the open doorway of her grandmother's living room. "Yes, Lieutenant? What can I do for you?"

"I've been calling your name. Are you all right? You looked like you were in a trance."

"Just concentrating." Looking around, Faith realized that she was alone in the room. "What happened to the forensics guys?" Two of them had been camped out, cataloguing everything they found on their top-to-bottom search of the house.

"On break. Maybe you should take one, too, Faith. Why are you on the floor?"

Faith rubbed her eyes, sore from staring both at her computer screen and at the fine print of the Foundation's recipient list. "It's easier to spread my papers around me."

"Have you found anything?"

"Yes." And it frightened her. "We—"

"Wait. Before you go on, I have a few updates for you. Corinne is out of surgery and stable. Same with your cousin Stone. Marcus is still in surgery and it's less positive. He was shot in the lung protecting Corinne."

"What were my cousins doing there?"

"Did Tanaka tell you that we have your uncle Jeremy in a room for questioning?" Isenberg went on, ignoring her.

"No." Her heart sank. "You still think he's guilty?"

"I don't know. I do know he didn't re-abduct Roza because I was with him no more than a half hour after it happened, and it's a two-hour drive from the cabin to his ex-wife's home. But we've thought he was working with a partner, so that doesn't prove his innocence."

"Why were Stone and Marcus there?" Faith repeated firmly. "Don't ignore me, Lieutenant."

Isenberg sighed. "Stone was there looking for their brother—Mikhail—who is Jeremy's son, too. Mikhail was found in a grave with the locksmith and the Earl Power tech. We think he surprised the killer, who wanted to hide in the cabin. Marcus was there because Stone texted him for help after Corinne stabbed him with a kitchen knife and then beaned him with a shovel. She thought he was her abductor. I still don't know whether she was wrong. Stone fits the description of the man who came through your bedroom window in Miami, Doctor."

Faith pressed her fingers to her temples. "Wait a minute. You've got Jeremy in an interview room while two of his sons are in the hospital and one is in the morgue? Really?"

"Really. And he'll stay there until we're satisfied he's not the killer of the seventeen women in your basement."

"Plus a dozen other people," Faith said, chastised.

"We'll hold him until we can get Bishop and Novak together in the interview room, and then we'll see. Now, tell me what you've found."

"Okay. Dr. Washington had identified three of the seventeen victims—two of which were scholarship recipients from the Foundation—Susan Simpson and Wendy Franklin. We got another seven names from the jars and five of them were on this list. So far I've found five more names on the Foundation list of women who have been reported missing. Three are blondes. That's his MO, yes?"

"Yes." Isenberg sat on the floor beside Faith. "But I heard you muttering, 'no, no, no' as I was walking up to the front door. Why?"

"Because I'm seeing a pattern. I wanted to look at more names before I brought this to you." Faith tilted the page on which she'd been making notes so that Isenberg could see. "The victim he kidnapped in Miami, Roxanne Dupree, wasn't a scholarship recipient. She went missing the day after the van tried to run me off the bridge. Corinne and Arianna were taken the day after he burned my old apartment building down."

Isenberg's brows lifted. "Go on."

"This victim, Katie Badgett, was taken the day my grandmother's will was read."

"Okay," Isenberg breathed. "Very interesting pattern."

"It goes on." Faith pointed to another name in her handwritten notes. "Virginia Dreyfus was reported missing the week after I had a really bad car accident."

"You had a car accident?"

She nodded. "Three years ago, I lost control of the wheel. At the time, I thought I'd fallen asleep, but now I'm wondering if that's not too coincidental, what with all the other car accidents in this case—my uncle Jeremy, the woman who bought my Prius."

"Now you're wondering if all these women were taken because your would-be killer was frustrated when you didn't die."

"Yes. I don't know why anyone would have wanted me dead three years ago, though. It's after my first run-in with Combs. He was in prison at the time. I've been racking my brain as to anything else that happened, but I can't think of a reason."

"Let it go for a little while," Isenberg advised.

Easier said than done. "Does Jeremy know about his son?"

"Yes. I told him myself. About all of his sons."

"I feel like I should say or do something to help him."

"I'd like you to talk to him, but wait until Deacon and Bishop get back so they can observe."

Faith sighed. "But what if he's not guilty? You know he didn't take Roza. What if Marcus dies while you have Jeremy waiting in an interview room? Can't you let him go to the hospital to be with his sons and just keep him under guard?"

"He may have tried to kill you, Faith. He may have killed dozens of people."

"He may not have."

"Your marshmallow heart is going to get you killed someday."

Faith shrugged. "Maybe. But I'd rather stay open and risk being hurt than close myself off the way I have been for the last . . . well, almost forever. Please consider it."

Isenberg rolled her eyes. "Okay. I'll consider it."

"Then I'll keep on task with the list to see if there are any more possible matches between the Joy scholarship recipients."

"I can help with that. The team of clerks I mentioned when you were at Novak's desk? They've been crunching through this list all day. I can have them compile a list of the dates that any of the missing women disappeared and you can look them over."

"That would be helpful, thank you. This is tedious work."

"Well, it's not out of the goodness of my heart. I want this case solved. To that end, Corinne gave us some valuable information on Roza and her mother. Roza was likely born in the basement, which is why we haven't found anything in the missing-children database."

"Oh my God. That poor child. And her mother died here? Oh my God, Lieutenant."

"I know. Roza told Corinne that her mother named her father as Eric Johnson."

"Common name."

"I know," Isenberg said again. "She also said that her mother and aunt were taken at the same time. Her mother's name was Amethyst Johnson. She was known as Amy. To make it even more complex, Amethyst may have been from Canada. She used to call her daughter 'Roza with a *zed*.' Oh, and Roza's full name is Firoza. But according to my team of clerks, there is no Amethyst Johnson on the list, so she might not have been a Foundation recipient. But I still want everyone to have the information, in case there's a name that could be a variation or misspelling of 'Amy.' "

"Or . . . Amy might not be the Foundation recipient. Her sister might have been. He took Arianna because she tried to save Corinne. Maybe he took Amy because she was with her sister or tried to stop her sister's abduction. Amethyst is not a common name. Did you ask your clerks to look for other names that had to do with colors or purple specifically?"

"No, I didn't, but I will. That's very good thinking."

"Now 'Firoza' . . . is also a very uncommon name," Faith said. She typed it into her laptop's search screen and felt a spurt of excitement. "And it connects. Firoza is a kind of turquoise."

"And Amethyst is a gemstone," Isenberg said with satisfaction. "Nice."

"Arianna thought Roza was eleven or twelve," Faith said. "If she really was born in the basement, he would have taken Amy and her sister at least eleven or twelve years ago." She ran her finger down the list until she got to the scholarship recipients from that time period. "No Amethysts, but we do have a Jade. Jade Kendrick," she said, typing the name into the national missing-persons database.

"Not listed," Isenberg said, leaning over to look at Faith's screen.

"Let's see if she's out and about on social media." Faith did another search and came up with nothing. "Her mailing address was Chicago when she was sent her scholarship letter. Her application would likely list her parents' names. I've already asked Henson for the files, but his secretary said they had to search for them in the vault. I'll call again, but they may need someone to push them."

"You try first," Isenberg said. "If they do any dancing, I'll cut in. Put it on speaker."

Faith dialed Henson's number, and Mrs. Lowell answered. "Is Mr. Henson Senior in?"

"No," his secretary said. "If you're calling about the files, we are still working on it. You can recall the policeman who's been standing in front of the office all day frightening our clients. Calming everyone down is taking time I could be using to get your files."

"Oh, I didn't realize there was a policeman waiting." Faith looked at Isenberg, who only shrugged and grinned. "Can you give him what you have so far? I can send him back for the rest. That way I get my files and you get a break from soothing the frightened clients."

"Well, there are several boxes," Lowell said tartly. "I hope you have storage room."

"I'm sure the police can make room at the station. Thank you, Mrs. Lowell. Getting those files could mean life or death for a young girl still being held hostage."

"Oh no." Lowell's irritation disappeared. "Oh my. I had no idea. I'll get the policeman what I've pulled together so far, and you'll have the rest of the files by morning."

"Thank you."

Miami, Florida
Wednesday, November 5, 4:30 p.m.

Detective Catalina Vega looked away from the two-way mirror as her LT entered the observation room, closing the door behind him.

"Is Combs's girlfriend ready to talk?" Davies asked.

"I think so," Cat answered. "Charging her with accessory to murder did the trick. The problem is, I haven't found a single noncircumstantial piece of evidence to tie Peter Combs to our homicides. I can't even find anyone who's seen him in over a month. So unless Paula Boza gives me something, I got nothin'. And her slimy shyster lawyer knows it."

"The team in Ohio said that Combs might not even be involved in the mess they've got up there," Davies said. "Maybe he's not involved in the mess we've got down here, either. Maybe you haven't found any evidence simply because there isn't any evidence to find."

Cat shook her head. "They haven't ruled him out at all. What they said was that if he is involved, it's as a recent accomplice to a killer who'd been at it for a longer period of time. A killer who might have used Combs's hatred of Faith Corcoran to his own benefit. I need to know who that might have been."

"Okay, so what do you have?"

"I've got an eye witness who saw a white van in the parking lot of the grocery store where the Prius was parked. It had a sign for an auto-repair business, just like the van the Cincinnati team found putting a tracker on Corcoran's new vehicle. It doesn't link the van to Combs, but now we have ties to the Cincinnati crimes from both the murder of Gordon Shue and Sunday's vehicular homicide. There's no question that they're connected."

"Does he know that?" Davies asked, pointing to the slimy shyster.

"I don't know. He might know it connects to Faith on

some level. He's slimy but smart. Corcoran's name has been in the news as the owner of the house where 'an undisclosed number of bodies were found.' The articles name her as Faith Frye, because that's how she's listed on the deed. This guy was Combs's trial attorney, too, four years ago. If he does know, he'll ask for a dismissal of Paula's possession charge in exchange for information, but the DA won't budge."

Davies was studying Paula Boza closely. "What does she do for a living, Cat?"

"She's a nail tech."

"Hm. How does a nail tech get her hands on a half kilo of coke to begin with?"

"I had the same question. It may be the only opening we have. She says it's Combs's, but also denied that he's had any access to her car since the attacks on Faith Corcoran began. Her prints were found on the bag, though. She says she must have touched it when she was feeling around for her phone that she'd dropped." Cat rolled her eyes. "I mean, really."

"Go shake something out of her. That Cincinnati lieutenant has been calling me every hour. We've got two in the morgue, one a child. They've got six, plus seventeen buried in a basement. Every time Isenberg calls, the number goes up. Get the girlfriend to talk."

"No pressure," Cat murmured, taking a deep breath before strolling into the interview room and sitting down across from Peter Combs's girlfriend. A second-generation Cuban American, Paula Boza might have been a model, but hard living had aged her. Jail hadn't helped.

Her WASP lawyer leaned back in his chair, bored. "What's this about, Detective?"

"Well, Mr. Green, I'm looking for something, and I think your client knows where it is."

Paula's nostrils flared, but she smiled back sweetly. "What are you looking for, Detective?"

"The rest of the coke," Cat lied. From the corner of her eye she caught Green's surprise. Paula didn't react at all. "I have it on good authority that there was a whole kilo, not half."

"Somebody's lying to you then, *chica*," Paula said with a

shoulder swagger. "I didn't even have half a kilo. Those drugs did not belong to me."

"Damn," Cat said. "I always thought Peter was a liar. So . . . no other drugs?"

Paula's lips curved with genuine humor. "No, Detective," she said.

She knows I haven't talked to Combs. Because she knows where he is? Cat leaned forward. "He warned me you'd say that."

"And why would he tell you that, Detective Vega?" Paula asked, amused.

"Because he was flipping on you," Cat said, using her "duh" tone. "In exchange for leniency on his own charges."

"She's lying to you, Paula," the attorney said. "Peter wouldn't do that, even if they were charging him with anything. Which they're not. He would've called me."

"Of course she's lying," Paula said, irritated now. "She hasn't even talked to Peter."

Okay. "You sound so sure, Paula," Cat said softly. "How can you be so sure?"

Paula pursed her lips. Looked away. *Busted.*

"Well, it doesn't really matter. Whether it's half or a whole kilo, possession charges are gonna make the attempted murder charge that much more believable to a jury."

Paula rolled her eyes. "That's ridiculous. I never tried to kill anyone."

"He said you'd say that, too. He's gonna have some pretty hefty charges against him, and he's saying you were with him all the way. Three counts of murder, four counts of attempted murder. And then there's the arson." Cat made a face. "You know what they say—once a firebug, always a firebug. Um, then there's the vehicle tampering, the B and E, and . . . no, that's it."

"I don't know what you're talking about," Paula insisted. "You're insane."

"No," Cat said soberly, "but the *abuelita* who lost her daughter and her grandson is probably feeling pretty insane with grief at the moment."

"Wait," Green said. "You're talking about that car that crashed on Sunday. The one that was tampered with. You can't put that on my client. She was *here* at the time. In custody."

Cat snapped her fingers. "You know, you're right. But she was out for all the others."

"What others?" Paula cried, managing to sound both furious and bewildered.

"All the attempts on the life of a woman named Faith Frye."

"That *puta*?" Paula's face mottled, red with temper. "The one that turned him in for raping that kid he never even met? *She's* your source? She's a bigger liar than you are. *Dios*," she spat. "*She* was stalking *him*! She *framed* him with that picture! The picture that *she took*! He lost three years of his life and that bitch walked away, scot-free."

Cat's heart skipped a beat. There had been no picture mentioned in the trial transcripts. Everyone had assumed that Peter Combs had been angry because Faith had reported him AWOL from his session. Cat herself had until Agent Novak had hinted otherwise the night before.

She hesitated for a split second. Should she push Paula on the photo or the murder charge? She decided on door number two and sent up a prayer.

"You must love him very much," she observed quietly. "Everyone else deserted him."

"I did," Paula said, breathing hard. She blinked three times, in rapid staccato. "I do."

I did. Cat was officially on mental tiptoes. "And yet here he is," she said pityingly, "throwing you under a bus for attempted murder. Some men just don't appreciate a good woman. I almost hate to see you go down for this, Paula, but Dr. Frye's accusations are very convincing."

Paula's eyes were smoldering fury. "Specifically what murder is that *puta* claiming that Peter and I attempted?"

"In early October, Dr. Frye was nearly run off a bridge by a white van. The passenger opened her window and fired at Dr. Frye's car. She said the gun was held by a woman. With really nice nails, all decorated. Like yours, Paula."

That last part wasn't true, but it could have been. And it worked.

Paula's eyes grew wide and furious. "She's lying!" she exploded.

"Paula," Green cautioned.

"And then," Cat continued calmly, "that same white van was seen near a Toyota Prius belonging to a young mother of three, hours before she lost control on the interstate, killing herself and her little boy. The Prius belonged to Faith Frye up until just the day before. She'd sold it on the down-low, hoping Peter would finally stop following her." Cat ambled around the table, stopping behind Paula's chair, leaning in to whisper in her ear, "So you see, I can tie you to the same van that had a hand in killing that mother and her precious son."

"We've already established that my client was here at the time the woman's car was tampered with," Green said harshly. "What are you really after, Detective Vega?"

"The truth. Combs tried to kill Dr. Frye four years ago. He set fire to her workplace in order to do so. Those are facts. After his release, he blatantly and persistently stalked Dr. Frye. And then someone shot at Frye, killing her boss. Someone tried to break into her apartment, then later tried to burn her out of it. A van tries to run her off the road and a woman shoots at her. It doesn't take a genius to connect the dots. Peter Combs wanted Faith Frye dead. Paula loves Peter. She'd do anything for him." Cat shrugged. "I'm sure even Paula is seeing where I'm going with this."

"I'm not stupid," Paula fumed. "And she's a dirty liar. We did not try to kill her. I was not in that van. Peter was not in that van. He couldn't have tried to run that bitch off a bridge, therefore I couldn't have been his passenger. Therefore I cannot be guilty!"

"Why couldn't he have run Frye off the road?" Cat demanded. "Because you say so? Woman, you're defending a man who raped little girls. Why would anyone believe you?"

"Because he's dead, that's why!" Paula shouted. She drew breath. Shuddered it out. Began to weep. "He's dead. Okay? Are you happy now? That bitch had him killed. And now she has the nerve to accuse him?"

Aw, fucking hell. Keeping the frustration from her expression, Cat casually leaned in to the table, blocking Paula's view of her attorney. "How do you know that, Paula?"

"Paula," Green said urgently, "be—"

Cat threw up her hand, interrupting him. "Mr. Green, the best thing you can do for your client here is to let her answer. If Combs is dead, Paula's off the hook and Faith

Frye is exposed as a liar." Which Cat didn't believe for a
moment. But if Combs was dead, it meant that nobody had
any suspects for a number of homicides in Florida and possibly in Ohio, too. "Tell me, Paula. How do you know Peter's dead?"

"Because *I saw him die*." Paula looked at her with haggard eyes. "Okay? *I saw him die a month ago*." She lifted
her hands, stared at them. "And then I buried him."

Aw, motherfucking hell. Cat dropped a notepad on the
table. "Details, Paula."

Green leaned forward to get past Cat's body, putting his
hand over Paula's as she reached for the pad. "Not so fast.
What does she get if she tells you?"

"She absolves herself from suspicion of attempted murder," Cat snapped. She walked around the table so that she
could look Paula in the eye. "And she absolves Peter, too. If
someone killed him, he's innocent of these murders. He was
framed. But if I can't prove he's dead, he'll be paraded
through the press again. 'Convicted sex offender kills *niño
y mama*.' The pictures of that crashed car will be shown on
every news show and every Internet site. And every head-
line will call him a sex offender again and again and again."
Cat leaned closer with every *again*, until she was nose to
nose with the sobbing Paula. "You know how I know this?
Because I will make sure of it. And I'm not lying. I will *cru-
cify* him. You have my word."

"Stop," Paula cried. "Just stop it. He never hurt those
little girls. He was just trying to make a new life, but *Faith
Frye* wouldn't leave him alone. She kept making complaints.
The cops kept coming to our place. Everyone knew. The
neighbors knew. They whispered terrible lies."

Wow, Cat thought. Denial must be Paula's middle name.
"You said she had him killed. That's a serious charge. Can
you prove it?"

"Yes. I saw the man kill him. He got a call—"

"Paula," Green said. "For the last time, say no more. I
can get the drug charges dropped."

"Like you got Peter's sex charges dropped? You let him
go to prison for something he didn't do. You don't care
about him."

"She doesn't either," Green flung back, pointing at Cat.

"Yeah, but I'll be damned before I let her run his name

through the dirt again." Paula turned back to Cat. "He got a call a month ago. He promised to meet someone at a bar, later that night. I thought maybe he was having an affair, because he'd been acting strangely. Like going to the bank the day before and withdrawing money. Lots of money. I found the receipt in his wallet. He'd taken out all the money he had left after his divorce in cash. I thought, what if he is leaving me, running off with someone else? So I followed him and saw him meet a man and get in the car with him. Peter was driving. And then I thought, God, what if he's gay? What if he's been lying to me all this time? So I followed the man's car, up Alligator Alley. I needed to know. It wasn't till they stopped that I saw the gun."

"Peter had a gun?"

"No, the man did. He made Peter get out of the car and kneel down. And then he shot him in the head. And pushed him down a hill. Then he drove away."

"No body was found along Alligator Alley last month."

"Because I buried him. I didn't want the animals to get him."

She couldn't have buried him deep enough. That stretch of I-75 ran through the wild swamp. Even if she was telling the truth, they'd be lucky to find Combs's pinky bone. "He didn't see you?"

"No. He pulled off the road, into the preserve. I turned off my lights."

The Big Cyprus National Preserve covered more than three-quarters of a million acres of swamp, which made finding a body harder than finding a needle in a haystack. "Okay. Why didn't you call the cops?"

"Oh, right. And then Peter's killer would know I'd seen him and he'd kill me, too. I may not have college, but I'm not stupid, Detective."

"Who did you think had killed him?"

"I figured it was one of those crazy vigilantes. He got hate mail all the time. Because he was a sex offender. It never stopped."

"But why would he have met with a crazy vigilante in the first place?"

"I don't know. That's why I followed him."

"Where did you bury him?"

"I'd have to show you."

"Of course you would," Cat murmured. "What about the money?"

Paula looked startled. "What about it?"

"You said he'd taken out a lot of money from the bank. Where is it?"

"You found it, Detective." A sly sparkle slid through Paula's eyes so quickly that Cat would have missed it had she not been watching her so closely. "Under my car seat. Peter must have turned it into something he could sell later. After he was dead, I figured he might have intended to run away. When you found the coke, I figured he'd planned to sell it so that we'd have money to live on."

"I see." Cat had to smile. The woman had spun a very nice web. If Cat believed one part of the story, it would be harder to negate the other part. If she bought the stranger-killing-Combs murder angle, it would be harder to argue that the coke was Paula's. "I underestimated you, Paula. You're pretty good."

"I told you I wasn't stupid," Paula said mildly.

"Yes, you did. Can you describe this man who killed Peter?"

"He was tall, about Peter's height. Not bad-looking. Big, the same size as Peter, but he moved funny. Like he was robotic or something. He was bald. His head shone like the surface of the moon."

"Let me arrange transport. I'd like you to show me where you buried Peter."

Cincinnati, Ohio
Wednesday, November 5, 5:00 p.m.

By the time Deacon got to his neighborhood, the Bureau agents had narrowed the killer's choice of vantage points from fifty houses down to three. As soon as he heard the street name over his radio, he knew which of the three it would be.

Dread mounting, he parked his car in front of a three-story Victorian that was all too familiar. SAC Zimmerman was waiting out front to meet him. "What made you pick this house of the three?" Zimmerman called out when Deacon got out of his car.

"Two things. It's got a bird's-eye view of my front porch. And I used to live here."

Zimmerman's eyes widened. "You lived here?"

"When I was in high school. Best damn years of my childhood. My stepfather owned this home, and we were very happy here. When Bruce and my mother died, he left the house to my sister and brother and me, but we had to sell it. Did you find evidence of forced entry?"

Zimmerman nodded. "Broken glass panel in the back door. I didn't realize you'd lived here. That changes everything."

"Yeah," Deacon said grimly. "It's a giant eff-you to the Fed who robbed him of his kill the other night. I imagine he thought this was very funny."

"It also means that he's targeted you, too. It's a lot more personal."

"Let him come," Deacon said quietly, meaning every word.

"How did he know you lived here?"

"Not too hard to find. Bruce Novak's name was on the deed, so it's in the tax record."

"Searchable online now," Zimmerman said.

"Yep. Plus I ran track in high school, and there were a few articles in the newspaper the year we went to the state finals. And then Dani, Greg, and I were listed in Bruce and my mother's obituary." He shrugged. "We live life and leave little pieces of information as we go."

"True enough. When did you sell the house?"

"Right after we inherited it. I'm the oldest and I was only eighteen. I couldn't afford the mortgage or the taxes. So we sold it to Noel and Kay Lazar. He was an engineer, she was a nurse. She died a few years ago, but he still lives here. He's retired. If he's still alive."

"We cleared every room," Zimmerman said. "No sign of the homeowner or the shooter. But there is evidence of a struggle. Come in, I'll show you."

Deacon followed Zimmerman into the house he'd called home. *Surreal,* he thought. *Like walking in a dream.* The SAC went up the stairs, pausing outside the retired engineer's study, which appeared to have hosted a barroom brawl—furniture overturned, an open laptop, screen cracked, discarded on the floor, drapes pulled down from their rods. Picture frames had fallen from their hooks and lay broken on the floor.

"I think he surprised the homeowner here," Zimmerman said. "Lazar put up a helluva fight."

"He was in surprisingly good shape for his age," Deacon murmured. "He was seventy, but he jogged five miles a day. I've run with him a few times since I bought our place."

"I'm sorry," Zimmerman said quietly. "I didn't realize you were also his friend."

Deacon was beginning to understand how Faith felt. He'd brought this evil to his neighborhood and an innocent man had suffered. "What about the silver minivan?"

"In the garage. I've got a team combing it for anything this guy left behind—a print, a hair, blood. Lazar's Toyota Camry is gone. BOLO's been updated. There are a few knives and a cleaver missing from the knife block. Not good."

No, it wasn't good at all. Plus the top floor of the house reeked of bleach. *This is bad.*

"Sir?" Agent Taylor stepped out of the bathroom. "Oh, Agent Novak. I didn't know you'd arrived." He noticed Deacon's coat and narrowed his eyes. "Did you get that out of evidence?"

"No," Deacon said tersely. "What do you have, Agent Taylor?"

"Sorry. Come in, please." Taylor flicked off the lights and the entire room glowed, annihilating any hope that Lazar had survived. "Luminol shows blood on the tile, in the tub, and on the floor, and spatter on the ceiling and all the walls. Looks like the victim fought."

"Oh my God," Deacon whispered, hating this. Hating everything about it. Hating that Lazar was dead because Deacon had bought a house three streets over.

No. He stopped himself midrant. Lazar was dead because a monster was determined that no one would disturb his play. Zimmerman was right. *This is personal.*

Zimmerman sighed. "I'll have the teams spread out, search other garages in the neighborhood for the Camry, just in case he's taken over another home."

"Go ahead and search, but I think he's gone. He's got to know that Faith isn't here anymore." The knowledge that she was at the precinct, surrounded by armed cops, was the only thing keeping Deacon from running to her right now. That, and the respect he owed the man who'd lived here. "We found the man he shot in the hotel lying in the tub. No blood like this. He's hidden this body *and* cleaned up. Why?"

"He changed tactics," Zimmerman said. "He didn't want Lazar found. I wonder if the old man scratched him."

"I sure as hell hope so," Deacon said darkly. "It could also be that he didn't want them found *quickly*. Unless someone missed Lazar, nobody would look for the shooter here, but if he'd left the body here in the tub and it started to stink ..." He exhaled wearily. "Did anyone check the freezer?"

"We looked in the kitchen freezer when we found the cleaver missing," Taylor said. "There wasn't a freezer in the garage."

Deacon backed away from the bathroom, stomach churning. "What about the basement?"

"Shit," Zimmerman muttered. "Let's go."

Mt. Carmel, Ohio
Wednesday, November 5, 5:30 p.m.

Faith looked up from her computer screen, her attention snagged by a snippet of music she instantly recognized. She stood up and stretched her shoulders, needing a break.

The music grew louder when she reached the kitchen. Sophie was sitting on the floor, her back to a cabinet door, knees pulled to her chest, listening to her husband, Vito, sing.

"What's wrong, Sophie?"

"We found Roza's mother in the dug-out room."

Faith considered the room's size and understood Sophie's distress. She sat down next to her with a sigh. "She slept next to her mother's grave?"

Sophie swallowed audibly. "She arranged her mother so that she was lying on her side, like she was asleep, her hands tucked under her head. And she put a doll in her mother's arms. I just ... I just couldn't stand looking at that doll for another second."

"*Sad* is such a paltry word," Faith murmured, "for such a devastating feeling." She put her arm around Sophie's shoulders and sat in silence, listening to Sophie's husband sing. Midway through the song, Sophie laid her head on Faith's shoulder, her tears quiet ones.

When the music was over, Sophie wiped her wet cheeks. "It was the doll that did it to me. It was Roza's doll. Her name was written on one of the feet, like Andy's toys in *Toy Story*. I had a doll like it when I was a little girl. When you tipped her over, she said, 'Mama.'"

"My mother had one of those dolls. I got to play with her when I was really little, but I was too rough and tore her arm. I tried to fix it, but I did a horrible job. My mother took the doll, told me I could have it back when I was older. I never saw it again, but I bet it's upstairs in a closet some . . ."

Sophie was giving her an odd look. "Was the doll's name Maggie?" she asked.

"No, that was my mother's name. Why?"

"Because that was the name written on the label of the doll's dress."

Faith's heart eased a tiny fraction. "Whoever held Roza and her mother must have found it. At least he was kind enough to give her a doll. That makes me feel a little better about her being retaken. If he gave her a doll, maybe he won't kill her."

Sophie squeezed Faith's hand. "It's a good hope. We also found a box buried where her sleeping pallet was. Tanaka is bringing it up now. You want to see what's inside?"

"Of course."

Tanaka came up the stairs, carrying the box, followed by Kimble and Isenberg. Tanaka put the box on the living room floor, and everyone stopped what they were doing to see what was inside. "It's heavy," Tanaka said. "Feels like books."

And it was. There were at least twenty books inside the box, and many of them had names written inside. "They belonged to the victims," Isenberg said. "Now we have another mode of identification."

Tanaka picked one up gingerly and flipped through the pages. "Lots of notes in the margins." He picked up an old textbook and smiled. "Roza's mother was teaching her to read using these books."

Faith found a loose sheet of paper in one of the books, a writing lesson this time. An adult hand had written *I LOVE*

YOU lightly on the page, and a childish hand had traced over it.

"At least her mother loved her," Faith said wistfully. "That's a gift some kids don't get."

"I know," Sophie murmured, loud enough for only Faith to hear. "I'm going downstairs. We have to uncover the bodies so that identification can begin." She gave Faith a quick hug. "Thank you for giving me hope for Roza."

"How's the list coming?" Isenberg asked. "Any more connections to family events?"

"Not yet," Faith said. "Has your team of clerks back at the station found anything?"

"Yeah," Isenberg said. "A number of the names have no birth certificates, and a few of them have social security numbers that have been linked to past identity theft."

"Oh," Faith said when the significance dawned. "So someone is making up fake applicants and taking the money they're given."

"Looks like it," Isenberg said. " 'Follow the money' is a well-worn adage for a reason."

Chapter Thirty-two

Cincinnati, Ohio
Wednesday, November 5, 5:45 p.m.

Deacon was not only beginning to understand Faith's feelings of guilt, he was also developing quite an aversion to basements. He had, in fact, found himself counting the steps as he descended into the engineer's basement. *Thirteen, fourteen, fifteen.*

He exhaled when he reached the bottom. Two large chest freezers sat up against the wall.

"What would anyone need with two huge freezers?" Zimmerman muttered behind him.

"He was a hunter," Deacon said. "He mentioned that deer season was coming up. He promised me some of his venison stew." He forced himself to lift the first lid.

Several large black trash bags had been dumped inside. Most appeared filled, but the bag on top was smaller. Bowling-ball sized. *Aw, hell.*

Deacon's hands were steady as he reached for the bag on top, but his heart ached, knowing what he was going to find. How many more would have to die before they caught this SOB?

The bag wasn't tied. He pulled the edges apart and glanced inside, then quickly looked away, not bothering to control his flinch. "Yes," he said hoarsely. "That's him. Just his head."

Most of it. The retired engineer had been shot point blank with a rifle or a handgun with a caliber large enough to take out the back of his skull.

"Oh, hell," Zimmerman said as he lifted the lid of the second freezer. "We've got a second victim." He looked inside the bag on top and flinched much as Deacon had, then spread the sides of the bag wider to reveal the contents.

It took Deacon a few seconds to realize what he was looking at. "Fucking hell."

"That pretty well sums it up," Zimmerman said as he dialed his cell phone. "Gonzalez? You can call off the search for the Renzo kid. We just found him. Looks like he was tortured, maybe with his own knife. His nose is gone. Ears, too. Looks pre-mortem."

"How the hell did he end up in the freezer?" Deacon demanded.

"Just my theory," Zimmerman said, "but Renzo's friends said he was coming to your house to teach your brother a lesson. The serial must have seen him creeping around your place. Pope brought Faith back from the precinct at seven thirty-five last night."

"After she talked to her uncle Jordan," Deacon murmured.

"Right. But Pope wasn't killed until nine twenty-five. The shooter waited for her to pass a window or come outside or even be visible in the car, but she was lying on the floor and he couldn't get to her. And then the kid skulks up to the house, maybe with his knife already out. One of your neighbors saw the boy. He walked the length of the street several times, probably summoning his gumption. Your brother's a big enough guy and Renzo was all by himself. But I'd think this killer would want the kid to try to break in and distract Pope. It might make the woman come to the door to see what was happening."

Deacon frowned. "Maybe he was afraid the kid would trigger a red alert and make it even harder for him to get to Faith. Plus, it would have to be a big deal for her to disregard security and come outside. He's tried to lure her many times already and he knows she's become very careful. He might have figured killing Pope would be enough."

"So he leaves the safety of his hideout to grab the kid to keep him from spoiling everything? Maybe. I would have thought the kid would have spilled his guts without all *that*, though." He pointed to the mutilated head.

"Maybe that wasn't torture. Maybe he did it for fun. And souvenirs."

"Wonderful. We'll wrap things up here." Zimmerman sighed. "At least your sister's safe."

"I didn't want it to be like this," Deacon protested. "Not like this."

"I know, but the result's the same. Renzo's no longer a threat."

"True, but like you said, this killer has made it personal. I need to alert my family and make sure they're kept safe. When can we have our house back?"

"Should be tomorrow. I'll call you when you can go home."

"Thanks." Although Deacon wondered if they'd ever be able to live there in peace or if there would be a constant reminder of the death that had occurred there.

He took my house, he thought. Both his current house and the house of his youth. Neither would feel like home again. Both were now tainted.

I took away his house, too, Deacon realized. Yeah. This had become very personal.

Cincinnati, Ohio
Wednesday, November 5, 5:45 p.m.

"Just a few minutes, Detective Bishop," the charge nurse said. Which was what they always said, Scarlett thought. She nodded as she always did. And then proceeded to ignore them, just as she always did.

Marcus O'Bannion looked better than he had when she'd first seen him, but that wasn't saying much. "How is he?" she murmured to Jeremy, who sat at his side, holding Marcus's hand with his left. Which was bare, Scarlett noticed. Jeremy had removed the glove he'd been wearing the day before, revealing heavily scarred skin. His right hand, she noted, remained gloved and stayed in his pocket.

Keith stood with his back to the wall, ever on guard.

"He'll live," Jeremy said, and Scarlett felt a weight roll off her chest.

It had become increasingly harder to breathe as she'd

come closer to Marcus's room, the sense of dread a palpable force. She had been worrying over his condition since they'd put him in the medevac chopper, but she'd had to put him from her mind and do her job.

Now she could draw an easier breath, so she did. "I'm glad," she said simply.

"Why are you here?" Keith asked.

"I have a few questions for all of you."

"Marcus can't answer your questions," Keith said. "And Jeremy won't. So go away."

"No." Marcus opened his eyes, waving two fingers, gesturing for Scarlett to come closer.

She leaned over his bed, giving him a visual once-over. He was pale and sweat beaded on his forehead, but he was still a very handsome man. "You look better."

"Feel like shit."

One corner of her mouth lifted. "No shock, considering the punctured lung." She looked over at Jeremy. "I need to know when you left your property via the back road and when you arrived at your ex-wife's house."

"Why is it important?" Keith demanded.

She met Keith's eyes over Marcus's bed. "Because I'm trying to catch a killer," she said sharply. "Who is currently holding an eleven-year-old girl hostage."

"He took her away," Marcus whispered. "We tried to stop him."

"I know," Scarlett said, softening her tone. "Thank you. You saved Corinne's life."

"Right thing to do. Does she know the man?" A deep, rasping breath. "Who killed Mickey?"

"She never saw his face. But we have an excellent therapist on our team who can dig details out that a witness doesn't ever realize they know. She'll work with Corinne. We want to find the man who killed Mikhail. We want to put him away."

Marcus's dark brows crunched together. "You put Jeremy in an interview room. Left him there for hours." Another deep breath. "And now we have a guard. Why?"

Scarlett glanced over at Jeremy. "Because we've found more bodies than we've shared with the media. So far all of them have been autopsied, with neat, surgical-style stiches. And the bodies today were found in your cabin, Dr. O'Ban-

nion. And you evaded federal surveillance, making it look
like you had something to hide and invalidating any alibi
you might offer."

"Circumstantial bullshit," Keith growled. "Your LT let
him go because she knew that."

"My LT let him go because Faith begged her to. Faith
didn't feel it was right to keep Jeremy apart from Marcus,
especially after losing Mikhail. She's got a soft heart. I hope
it doesn't get her killed, because somebody is still trying
very hard to do just that. Somebody who knew the contents
of Barbara O'Bannion's will."

"That person is not me," Jeremy said firmly. "But tell
Faith thank you. And to be careful."

"I will. And don't think I didn't notice that nobody answered my question. When did you leave your home in
Indian Hill and when did you arrive at the Yarborough
house?"

Marcus's lips twitched in an almost smile. "You're quick."

"Thank you. A real answer would be nice. Before the
nurse kicks me out."

"I met Stone at a bar at eleven last night," Marcus
rasped. "Came prepared to do a switch."

"Prepared?" Scarlett asked. "What does that mean?"

"Padded coat and baseball cap. In the dark, I look like
him. He had a big lead on a story, but the Feds were on his
tail. Done this before. Lots of times. Water, please."

Jeremy sprang to it, placing an ice chip on Marcus's
tongue. "Marcus got to my house at about one a.m., driving
Stone's car and wearing the padded coat. I knew right away
it wasn't Stone. I always knew, even when you were boys."

"You didn't," Marcus protested weakly, his lips curving
in a smile that Scarlett somehow knew was meant to ease
Jeremy's worry.

Jeremy blotted the sweat from Marcus's brow with a ten-
derness she found hard to disbelieve. "I was an identical
twin, boy. I know about switching places. You two were sad
amateurs." He lifted his eyes to Scarlett, intensely green.
"Marcus has done nothing wrong."

"I believe that. He saved Corinne's life when he didn't
have to. *His* actions speak for him. Perhaps you'd like to
follow suit by answering my damn question. It's not a hard
one, Doctor."

"Della called me at about two in the morning. She'd returned from a trip and found Mickey wasn't at home. She didn't know he'd run away." His jaw tightened. "Audrey knew two days ago, but she didn't want to frighten her mother—or hurt me—so she told Stone instead. Stone had been searching for Mickey. That's why he came in and out of my house Monday night. He was hoping Mickey was with me, that Audrey was wrong. I didn't know that until after we learned he was . . . gone."

"Why would Audrey and Stone think that Mickey's running away would hurt you?" Scarlett asked, wanting to compare Jeremy's answer with the reason Stone had given earlier that day.

Pain flashed across Jeremy's face. "Because Mickey was angry with me. He thought I knew that I was his father all along, that I'd been lying to cover up my . . . indiscretion with his mother. That wasn't true. I loved that boy like my own, even when I thought he belonged to a Russian businessman. I would have proudly given him my name, for what little it's worth."

"It's a good name," Marcus whispered. "Dad."

Jeremy clasped Marcus's hand tightly. "I *loved* him. I always wished he was mine. I wish Della had *told* me, but she didn't want to risk—" He cut himself off.

"Don't stop now," Scarlett said dryly. "Della didn't want to risk what?" She glanced at Keith, who wore an expression of rigid control. "What—or who—was she afraid of?"

"Me," Keith said flatly. "She was afraid of me. Della never trusted me."

"And why might that be, sir?" Scarlett asked softly.

Keith averted his eyes. "Because she thought I was the one who caused Jeremy's car accident. Because I was jealous of his old partner and wanted Jeremy for myself."

Jeremy's head whipped around to stare at Keith. "She didn't! She never thought that."

"Yeah, Dad," Marcus said weakly. "She did."

Scarlett lifted her brows. *This is getting better and better.* "And *were* you jealous, Keith?"

"Yes, but I never would have risked Jeremy. He almost died in that wreck."

That I can believe, she thought. "Why would Della think the 'accident' wasn't an accident?"

More jaw tightening and teeth grinding from Keith. "Because she suspected that the car had been tampered with. I checked the wreckage. She was right."

"Keith!" Jeremy exclaimed. "Why didn't you tell me this? Why didn't you tell the police?"

"Because I thought you'd believe I'd done it, too."

Jeremy's shoulders sagged. "I wouldn't have. I know you wouldn't hurt me."

"That's why you're his bodyguard," Scarlett said, and Keith nodded. "Because someone did try to kill him. Do you have proof that the car was tampered with?"

"No, but I'm a decent enough mechanic to know. Why?"

"Just being thorough," Scarlett said. "So Della was afraid of your wrath and didn't tell anyone that Mickey was Jeremy's son. Do I have that right?"

"Yes," Keith said flatly. "I didn't like the boy. That was no secret. He didn't give Jeremy the proper respect because he was gay. And when Mickey found out that Jeremy was his father, he threw a fit." He looked Jeremy in the eye. "He was ashamed of you."

"No, he thought I was ashamed of him," Jeremy insisted.

"He thought both," Marcus said, starting to wheeze. "He was confused. He was seventeen."

Jeremy's body seemed to deflate before her eyes. "And now he's dead."

Scarlett's heart squeezed, but she kept her expression neutral. "I'm sorry for your loss, Dr. O'Bannion, but I have to know when you arrived at Della's house."

He gritted his teeth, ruthlessly controlling his emotion. "A little before three."

"And why did you find it necessary to slip past the agents?"

"Because Della was frightened. She thought Mickey had been kidnapped at first. So did I. It happens when you're wealthy. I wanted to call the police and she insisted that we shouldn't. So I slipped out of my own house like a thief in the night," he finished bitterly. "We didn't know Mickey was dead until your lieutenant came to tell us. And then she took me away. I couldn't even stay to comfort my wife. Ex-wife," he corrected. "I'm sorry, Keith. I can't pretend I don't love her, because I do. Just not the way I love you. You have to understand that. That Mickey was killed running away because of me . . ." His shoulders sagged, and he covered his face with his left hand. "How can she forgive me for this?"

"She loves you, too," Marcus whispered. "She won't blame you. Go to her now, Dad. I'll be all right. I need to sleep anyway, and Mom needs you."

"I'll take you," Keith said. "Come on."

"The officer will have to follow you," Scarlett said gently. "I'm sorry."

"What about Marcus?" Jeremy asked. "That killer might come back for him."

"I'll get a guard posted, and I'll stay with him until that happens. Okay?"

"Thank you, Detective." Jeremy stood up, supported by Keith's strong arm around his waist. "Find the man who killed my son. Please."

"We will. We have to."

Scarlett watched them go, Jeremy leaning on Keith, the officer discreetly trailing behind.

"Thank you." The words had come from behind her.

Scarlett turned back to the bed. Marcus suddenly looked a thousand times worse, and she realized he'd been holding it together for Jeremy's benefit. "For what?"

His lips quirked. "For getting him out of here before I collapsed. That would have worried him." He closed his eyes on a quiet moan. "And for treating him with respect. He's a good man. Better than he believes."

Scarlett took the seat Jeremy had vacated. "I want to believe that."

"*It's true.* He treated us like sons even when he was so young himself. You don't know how many people he's helped. He treats everyone he takes in like his own children. Ask Hailey."

"His housekeeper. We wondered about her. Who is she?"

"She's Audrey's friend. She came from a bad home, got thrown out when she was still in school. Nowhere to go. Jeremy took her in. Now she runs his house. Fiercely loyal to him, just like the rest of us. *He is a good man.* He could not have done these terrible things." Marcus's face had grown even more strained, his breathing more labored.

"Sshh. Relax. Then someone wants him to look bad. Any ideas?"

He seemed to settle. "If his mother were still alive, I'd look at her. Since she's dead, I'd follow the family tree."

"You mean your uncle Jordan."

"He's the only one left."

"Except for Faith," Scarlett said, watching his reaction.

His eyes still closed, he shook his head. "She's a target. Nothing to gain."

"True enough. What time did you get the text from Stone?"

"You have our phones, Detective. You know this. But it was at nine this morning. It just said, 'Come to blind.'"

She'd seen the text. "I assume a deer blind?"

"Stone has a permanent one in the woods, but it's pretty far from the cabin. I figured he'd gone out to the cabin to look for Mickey and something had happened. Idiots hunting out of season. I was already out looking for Mickey. Jeremy and Mom were so upset, I didn't tell them about the text. I just drove. Got there about eleven, but I didn't go into the cabin because Stone said to come to the blind. We'd switched cars at the bar, so Stone had my Subaru. I'd left his 'Vette in Jeremy's driveway, so I was in Audrey's car, which wouldn't go more than three feet off-road. I had to leave it by the cabin and hike to the blind."

"I saw it. Silver Porsche. Corvettes, Porsches. Your brother and sister have some serious style."

Another quirk of Marcus's lips. *Really nice lips, actually,* Scarlett thought. "Audrey's a speed demon and Stone's a force all unto himself," he said. "Hard to keep up with them, so I don't even try." He sobered, his body sagging in exhaustion. "I found Stone near the blind, weak from loss of blood. He had a fist-sized goose egg on the back of his head—and your card in his pocket, Detective. It took me a while to find where he'd left my Subaru—in the woods behind the cabin. That's when I saw the blood on the back wall and knew something had happened." He paused, licking his dry lips. "Ice, please."

She ran an ice chip over his lips and slipped it into his mouth. "So you called me," she said.

"After I saw what was inside the cabin. I figured Stone had a reason for not calling the cops, so I didn't give you my name. I should have. I was . . . I saw Mickey and I couldn't think."

"Didn't matter," she said. "I think I would know your voice anywhere."

A tiny, sad curve of his lips this time. "Thank you, Detective," he said, then he began to cough. "Dammit," he wheezed.

She gave him another ice chip. "When you're ready, tell me the rest."

"Not much more. I drove the Subaru to the blind and managed to get Stone into the passenger seat." Another small smile. "He needs to lose a few pounds. Don't tell him I said that."

"Your secret is safe with me."

"I think it would be," he murmured. "He came to after I got him in the car, of course. Started going on about a 'scary broad with a shovel.'"

Scarlett's lips twitched. "Line drive to the outfield!" she said in a baseball announcer's voice. "You round those bases, girl."

Marcus huffed a chuckle, then moaned. "Don't make me laugh. He told me he'd scared her, that she thought he was the one who'd kidnapped her. That he should have told you about the bodies he'd found when you came to Jeremy's house, but he was afraid."

"He didn't look afraid to me," she said mildly.

"Well, we all wear our outside faces. I wanted to take him straight to the ER, but he insisted we look for them. He's not a bad guy. He just . . . thinks differently. I told him we'd look for an hour and then I was taking him to the hospital. I'd given up and was on the main road when I saw Corinne on the side of the road. I guess I'm lucky she lost the shovel somewhere along the way."

Scarlett didn't smile. "Corinne has a debilitating disease, Marcus. She went a whole additional day without her medication because Stone was 'afraid.' She was in terrible pain and still walked all those miles to protect the little girl. If we'd been able to get to her before the guy in the ski mask, we'd have them both back safe and sound. Now that child is with a monster. Because Stone was 'afraid.'"

Marcus's eyes flew open, and Scarlett was surprised to see molten fury in his gaze. "He'd seen his *brother* in a *grave* with his *brains* blown out," he hissed. "You have no idea what that did to him. I am *sorry* that Corinne suffered. I am beyond sorry that the little girl was taken. I tried to stop it. But until you've walked a mile in Stone's shoes, don't you *dare* criticize him."

He started to cough, and a nurse came running. "You have to leave, Detective," she said.

"No," Marcus said, gasping for breath. "Let her stay."

Unsettled by his outburst, Scarlett moved out of the nurse's way.

"Don't leave," Marcus commanded her. "Don't leave."

"Sshh," she said. "Don't worry. I won't leave until I know you're safe."

Cincinnati, Ohio
Wednesday, November 5, 6:45 p.m.

Deacon flicked the switch that controlled the light on the outside of Greg's bedroom door, the only way to get his attention if his hearing aids weren't on.

"I'm not hungry," Greg called. "Please go away."

Deacon opened the door. "It's only me. No food tonight."

Greg sat on his bed, engrossed in a video game on his laptop. "What is it?" he asked without looking up. At least that meant he had his hearing aids turned on.

"I have news for you. It's important. Please look at me." He waited until he had Greg's full attention. "Renzo is dead."

Greg's eyes went wide with shock, then alarm. "How? When? I didn't do it!"

"I know you didn't do it. Nobody thinks so. I need you to keep this quiet until after my lieutenant makes a statement, but Renzo was killed by the man who's been after Faith. It looks like he was on his way to challenge you to a knife fight, but the killer saw him, waylaid him somehow, then killed him. It had nothing to do with you."

Greg's face had drained of color. "Yes, it does. If I hadn't made it look like he had HIV, he never would have come here. He'd still be alive. I wanted to make him unpopular. I wanted people to think he was a liar. I didn't want him dead."

"I know," Deacon said again. "I feel the same way. But, Greg, you didn't make him come after you with a knife. He'd bragged to his friends that he was going to teach you a lesson and then he'd teach Dani one, too. None of his friends would come with him, and a few told the FBI agents that they tried to talk him out of it. Now, I'm sorry he was murdered, but to tell you the truth, I'm relieved that he can't hurt either of you anymore."

Greg nodded numbly. "Yeah, but . . . whatever."

Deacon put his arm around Greg's shoulders and gave him a hard hug. "I have to go now, but I want you to stay here. Please don't go anywhere."

"But Renzo is dead. He can't hurt me now."

"No, but the guy who killed him can. He's made this personal against me. I don't want him able to touch you or Dani. Okay?"

Greg bobbed a nod. "Okay. Fine. How is Faith?"

Safe at the station. Surrounded by cops with guns. "She's okay, but I know she'll be glad to see all this over, too. Keep your phone close by. If you see *anything* out of the ordinary, text me. I don't care if you're being paranoid. I'd rather have a false alarm than lose you. Got it?"

Another nod. "Got it."

Deacon hesitated, his cheeks heated. "I love you. I don't say it enough, but it's true."

Greg looked away. "Dammit, D," he huffed, exasperated. "Me, too," he mumbled.

It was exactly what Deacon had needed to hear. "Stay here," he said fiercely. "Stay safe."

He found Jim in the kitchen and told him about Renzo's death. They'd had to tell Jim and Tammy about the situation at Greg's school when they'd shown up at the station last night to collect the boy. "I didn't tell Greg the details. I don't want to put those pictures in his head. But this killer has just upped the ante."

Jim nodded grimly. "Killing in your old house, killing outside your new one. He's coming after you and yours. I'll watch over Greg. Who's going to watch over Dani?"

"I'm going to request a protection detail for all of you."

"We don't need one." Jim patted his hip where his service revolver stayed holstered. Deacon thought he might disarm to shower, but he wasn't sure. "I got Greg. You watch over yourself. Don't get yourself killed."

Deacon's brows lifted in surprise. That might have been the warmest thing Jim had ever said to him. "Thanks, Jim."

Jim gave him a crusty look, as if daring him to smile. "Your aunt would be sad."

"Nobody wants that. I'll be careful. Thanks."

He walked to his car, his heart a little bit lighter. He was going back to the station now. Back to Faith.

He buckled himself in and dialed Isenberg's phone again. He'd tried reaching her on the way from the Lazar crime scene to update her and request the protection detail, but he'd gotten her voice mail. He dialed again now, with the same result.

He dialed Bishop, but she cut off his call after a single ring. A text came through a second later. *In hospital w/O'B boys. Call u later.*

Frustrated, he called Adam's cell, but once again was sent straight to voice mail.

Tanaka was next on his call list. To his relief, the forensics leader answered. "I was just about to call you," Tanaka said. "You want the good news or the bad news?"

"Bad first," Deacon said. "I wanna end on good news. I could use some right now."

"What happened?" Tanaka asked, concerned.

"We found the shooter's hiding place near my house, but he was gone. We also found the remains of my neighbor and the Renzo kid in the basement freezers. Your turn."

"Sophie found a body we believe to be Roza's mother buried in the dug-out room. She slept in the same room where her mother was buried."

Deacon sighed. "What's the good news?"

"It's kind of a relative term. Faith helped us find an old dumbwaiter he'd retrofitted to hold layers of trays. That's where we found his stash of souvenirs."

"Good, that's—" Deacon froze. "*Faith* helped you? She's *there*? In that *house*?"

"Um . . . yes, she's here. With me and Adam."

Adam. Deacon closed his eyes, seeing the two severed heads with terrifying clarity, and fury bubbled up within him, cleansing and revitalizing and, at this moment, more necessary than drawing his next breath. *Sonofafuckingbitch. I told him not to take her out there without me.*

"Is Detective Kimble still there?" he asked softly.

"Um, yes. Look, if you're gonna yell, don't yell at me. Yell at Kimble. But Faith's fine. I think helping us helped her, too."

Deacon started up his car. "I'm on my way."

Cincinnati, Ohio
Wednesday, November 5, 7:00 p.m.

Scarlett was a little relieved to find Stone O'Bannion asleep when she got to his hospital room. She wasn't sure if she could take any new O'Bannion family drama and was still wrestling over Marcus's heated words.

Until you've walked a mile in Stone's shoes, don't you dare criticize him.

She'd watched over the sedated Marcus for nearly an hour, waiting for the uniform who'd been assigned to guard his room. Isenberg hadn't been happy about taking an additional uniform off patrol, but Marcus was the only patient still in Intensive Care. Stone, Corinne, and Arianna were all on a regular ward now, a single uniform watching all three rooms.

So it was just a short walk from Stone's room to Corinne's, where Scarlett heard the happiness before she pushed open the door. For a moment she stood there in the doorway, taking it in, her throat suddenly too thick to swallow. Arianna lay on a hospital bed next to Corinne's, the beds placed only a few feet apart. Arianna's roommate, Lauren, sat on the foot of Arianna's bed, an iPad in her hand. The room was filled with flowers and balloons and the television murmured quietly in the background.

Meredith Fallon got up from her chair in the corner, crossing to Scarlett when she saw her standing there. "When it works out, it gets you right here," she said, tapping her heart.

"Yeah," Scarlett managed, and cleared her throat. "I wish Novak was here to see this. Faith, too. We needed an infusion of happy."

"As you wish!" the three women chorused.

Scarlett laughed. "Nothing like *The Princess Bride* to take your mind off your troubles."

"Detective Bishop," Meredith teased, "I wouldn't have taken you for a fan of romance."

Scarlett shot her a look. "Romance? Pffft. Not this girl. I only watched for the fencing, fighting, torture, revenge, giants, monsters, chases, and escapes."

"And 'true love,' of course," Meredith said, continuing the quote from the movie.

"'And miracles,' most of all," Scarlett whispered, finishing it. "I've always been a sucker for the miracles." She studied Arianna's smile. "She's gonna come down hard when this euphoria wears off, isn't she?"

"Yes, but that's not this moment. We'll take the happiness when we can get it and deal with the trauma when we must. Do you have any news on Roza?"

"Not on her whereabouts, but the team did find her mother's body. Roza had been sleeping next to her grave. She'd buried her mother posed like she was asleep, holding Roza's only doll."

Her eyes suddenly bright with tears, Meredith pursed her lips, drawing a deep breath and blowing it out unsteadily. "Sometimes this job really sucks, you know, Detective?"

"Call me Scarlett, and yes, I do know. So let's soak in some of this happy while we can."

Meredith gestured her welcome. "Come in. I think the girls would like to see you."

"Detective Bishop!" Arianna called when Scarlett stepped through the door. "Come in. We're watching a movie."

"I heard. Look at all these flowers. Balloons and stuffed animals, too. Quite a haul."

"And candy," Arianna said. "Although Lauren's the only one who can eat it right now."

"I'm live tweeting," Lauren said. "Corinne and Arianna: The reunion. You want to make a statement?"

"I'm happy to see them safe," Scarlett said simply. She noticed Corinne searching her face in question, and shook her head. "Not yet, honey. But we will find her."

Corinne gave a hard nod. "Watch the movie with us, Detective. Feel free to quote along."

"For a little while. Sure."

Cincinnati, Ohio
Wednesday, November 5, 8:45 p.m.

He'd sewn up so many bodies, alive and dead, and had taught himself to suture with either hand, but he simply was not able to reach the bullet wound in his arm. Hours later, it was still bleeding steadily, and if he didn't get help soon, he might pass out.

And wouldn't that be lovely?

He looked at the child, still semi-unconscious in the backseat. He didn't think she was faking it. If she was, she was a far better actress than her mother or her aunt.

It was past time to get a doctor. *For both of us.* He'd been waiting all day for Dr. Dani Novak to get off shift, but she hadn't left the ER. He'd grown tired of waiting in his stolen vehicle. He'd wait for her in a much more comfortable location.

Not willing to take any more chances, he'd already tied Roza's wrists and ankles securely. And then he'd gagged her. He'd never gagged her before, but he couldn't be certain what bad habits she'd picked up during her day of freedom.

He made sure the blanket was covering Roza completely before locking her in the Suburban and taking the stairs up to Dr. Novak's third-floor apartment. He twisted the doorknob for kicks, shocked when the door opened. Dr. Dani didn't lock her front door? *Shame on her.*

He'd expected to have to wait in the shadows, forcing her into her apartment at knifepoint. He normally liked to play with his prey, but tonight he was grateful he wouldn't have to fight too hard. He slipped into the apartment and stopped short. *Well, hello.* A young man slept on the sofa, his hair black save a wide streak of white in the front.

Ah. Little brother, Greg, who'd made so much trouble for everyone, had come to visit. His hearing aids, a bus pass, and a single key lay on the coffee table. An unzipped backpack was propped against the sofa, a laptop and a balled-up T-shirt and undershorts visible. Little brother had come to spend the night.

Excellent. The more the merrier, especially when it came to brokering a trade for Faith.

He crept across the floor, being extra-quiet until he remembered the boy couldn't hear. He didn't take prisoners of Greg Novak's size very often, but he was prepared. From his pocket he drew a handkerchief and on it he sprinkled a liberal dose of ketamine. Then he positioned himself behind the sleeping teenager, crouching so that his arms were level with the arm of the sofa. In one movement he set the blade of his knife to Greg's throat with his right hand and pressed the hankie to the boy's mouth with his stronger left hand.

As expected, the kid took a big gulp of air before starting to struggle, but went dead still when he felt the bite of the blade. *Ten, nine, eight . . .* He started to slump and gave a characteristic final burst of panicked energy that was again nipped by the bite of the blade. *Four, three, two, one.*

And the kid was out like a light. *Like taking candy from a baby.* Coming to his feet, he pulled two zip-tie restraints from his pockets and, rolling the kid over, bound his hands behind him. Then his feet.

He sank to the floor, exhausted. Hopefully, Dr. Dani would take her time getting home. He wasn't sure he had the strength to put a gun to anyone's head at the moment, because that was what he planned to do. When Dr. Dani came home, she'd find his gun pressed to her brother's head. It would ensure her cooperation in tending to his wound and then in getting them the hell out of here before anyone came looking for them.

He'd take them all to his own turf and hold them there until he got what he wanted. Faith. Once he had her where he wanted her, he'd kill her without fuss. And then go back to his life.

Cincinnati, Ohio
Wednesday, November 5, 9:30 p.m.

Faith bit her lip as Deacon punched the elevator button for the top floor of the safe house. He hadn't looked at her once, not the whole way from the house back to the city. He'd been professional and polite when he'd arrived to pick her up. He'd even been downright cordial to Sophie, who'd hugged him warmly.

But he hadn't said a word to Adam. She could tell he wasn't simply angry. He was filled with quietly restrained rage. He was the tiger—predatory, powerful, and ready to spring.

"Are you planning to say anything to me?" she asked softly.

"Not yet."

"Okay." She exhaled carefully. "Are you planning to tell me what happened to put you in this mood? Because I have to say that you're scaring me, Deacon."

A muscle twitched in his cheek. "Not yet."

Okay. Whatever had happened had been very serious indeed.

Well, that's just too damn bad. I've had a pretty sucky day, too. Seven more dead. Jars of human organs hidden in the dumbwaiter shaft. Foundation scholarship recipients missing. Fake scholarship applicants invented so that someone could collect their awards. Then there was Roza's box, filled with books. *And Roza's mother, buried with my mother's doll.*

The elevator opened and Deacon held an arm out to keep her from darting into the hall while he looked right and left. He must have been satisfied because he gestured for her to proceed.

Bishop was waiting for them at the condo's dining room table. So was Adam.

Adam came slowly to his feet. "Deacon," he started with a sigh. "This is cr—"

"Don't," Deacon snapped. "Just don't. You knew I was worried. You knew I didn't want her to be there, yet you took her there without me. Did you think to tell me where she was? About how I'd feel when she wasn't where she was supposed to be? Did you even wait until I was out of the station this afternoon before removing her?"

Faith had had enough. "Stop it! I'm right here, so don't talk about me like I'm a piece of furniture. If you're looking for an apology from me, then fine. I'm sorry I've made you angry. But I'm *not* sorry I went to the house. I thought I could help. And I did. I'm not a child, and you are not my keeper. If you expect blind obedience, you will be very disappointed."

He spun to face her so quickly that the tails of his leather coat flared out, following his motion. His eyes were wild, turbulent. He seemed bigger, his shoulders broader. His presence filled the room. He looked . . . absolutely magnificent.

"You think that's what this is about?" he demanded.
"That I want your blind obedience? Goddammit, Faith, I
wanted you to use the brain God put in your head. I *wanted*
you to be safe."

"She *was* safe," Adam said, clearly offended. "She was
with me. She is fine. She doesn't need you hovering over
her. She was helpful."

"Hovering," Deacon repeated so softly that Faith
cringed.

Bishop opened her mouth to intervene, then quickly
closed it, shaking her head with a weariness Faith understood all too well.

"You do realize," Deacon continued in that same low
tone that dripped with sarcastic contempt, "that a serial
killer—whose killing spree has escalated beyond anything
I've ever seen—wants to kill her? You do realize that?"

Adam's expression grew dark. "You are no closer to
finding him right now than you were last night or the night
before. Each hour you've wasted is another hour that Roza
has suffered."

Deacon flinched. "You think I don't know that? You
think I don't hear every one of those hours chiming in my
head like a goddamned funeral bell? I hear every damn
second that ticks by, but the answer is not to endanger more
lives. This man will stop at nothing to kill *her*." He threw an
arm out, pointing at Faith. "He will kill anyone who is
around her to get to her. And you know what? You're right.
I've been chasing this guy for two days and I don't know
where he is or who he is. But I'm not willing to put innocent
lives in jeopardy to find out a few seconds faster."

A muscle in Adam's cheek twitched. "Roza—"

"*—is not the only factor here!*" Deacon exploded, his
control visibly shattering. He slammed his hands on the
chair in front of him. "He kills people for a front-row seat
to wherever Faith is going to be. You know how he knew
about that Renzo punk's knife? Because he invaded the
home of my neighbor and used his house as a sniper post.
And you want to know how he knew which house to pick?
He looked for the one that once had *my name* on the deed."

Adam faltered, confused. "What?"

"He chose my old house. The one I inherited after Bruce
and my mother died."

"Oh God," Bishop murmured. "Deacon, he targeted you."

"He already targeted me the night he tried to put a bullet in my shoulder. This time he targeted a man whose only crime was to buy my old house fifteen years ago. His name was Mr. Lazar, and he was a nice man. But now he's dead. He killed him, Adam, brutally. Then he watched from his window until that punk walked by my new house one too many times. And then he killed that boy. But not before he took a few more souvenirs. That's what he does. That's what he'll do to Faith and anyone around her."

Faith sank into a chair, the blood draining from her head. Two more dead. *Brutally.*

"What do you think he's doing to Roza?" Adam countered quietly. Accusingly.

"I *know* what he's doing to her. I *saw* what he did to the others. I stood in the cold room and I looked at them *all.*"

He hadn't just looked at them, Faith knew. He'd let their suffering into his mind, and it had destroyed a piece of his heart. She'd seen the aftereffects of that herself.

Adam shook his head. "No, you don't. You don't know. You've never seen."

The table jolted as Deacon shoved the chair he'd been holding in a death grip and leaned forward, gripping both sides of the table. His body vibrated in anger and fear and hurt. "He cut them apart! Both Lazar and Renzo. He cut them into pieces and dumped them into garbage bags. He used Lazar's own cleaver to do it." His voice broke. "He cut off his head, Adam," he whispered. "He cut off both their heads and stuffed them in the freezer."

Faith's stomach heaved even as her heart ached for him. His neighbor. He'd known him. Liked him. And then to have found him . . . like that. *Oh, Deacon.*

Adam shuddered out a breath. "I'm sorry, Deacon. I'm sorry that happened to your neighbor, but his ordeal lasted a few hours. Arianna's lasted *days*. He's had Roza for *years*. *Years.* Do you have any idea what he could be doing to her right now?"

"Yes," Deacon said, quietly now. As if he had no strength to say more. He still gripped the table, but his head fell forward, his pose no longer one of menace, but of defeat. "I know."

"No, you don't." Adam took a step back, his breathing too shallow and too fast. "You only see them after. After it's over. You haven't seen. *I've seen*."

Deacon lifted his head. Exhaustion had etched lines into his cheeks, around his mouth and eyes. "What have you seen?" he asked with a gentle sadness that brought tears to Faith's eyes.

"No. I can't do this. I won't do this. I won't one-up you. I am sorry you found your neighbor dead and . . . mutilated. I am sorry that you probably saw Faith that way, in your mind. I am sorry if you think I put her in danger, but I can assure you that she was never in any peril. And I'm especially sorry if you think I'd deliberately put her in harm's way. Because I couldn't. I wouldn't. I—" He let out a breath. "I'll see you tomorrow."

Adam closed the door quietly behind him, leaving them in silence. Faith thought Deacon would face her then, but he shuddered out a breath and turned for an open bedroom door.

"I'm going to sleep," he said woodenly. "Faith, try to rest. We'll figure out your situation in the morning."

"Your" situation. Not "our." Faith could only stare at him as he disappeared into the bedroom and closed the door.

"He'll come around," Bishop said. "He was scared for you."

"I know. I should have listened to him."

Bishop pushed herself to her feet. "I didn't say that. He did expect blind obedience, but only because he wanted to keep you safe. I'd planned to go home tonight, but I find I'm too tired as well. I think I'll stay, just to help cover you if something were to go wrong."

"Thank you, Detective."

"Go to sleep, Faith. It'll all look different in the morning."

"You didn't say 'better,'" Faith murmured.

"No, I didn't. Because I can't ensure that it will be, and I never make promises I can't keep." She grabbed her gym bag and set the condo's security alarm. "Good night, Faith."

"Good night, Scarlett." Faith waited until Bishop had closed the door to the bedroom she'd chosen before going into her own room—the one that shared a bath with the room she and Deacon had slept in the night before.

I need to fix my part in this. Squaring her shoulders, she went through the bathroom and knocked on Deacon's door. "It's me," she said softly. "Can I talk to you?"

The silence stretched so long that Faith thought he wouldn't answer. Then she heard his voice, muffled and defeated. "Sure. Come in."

North of Cincinnati, Ohio
Wednesday, November 5, 10:00 p.m.

He sat the bag of first-aid supplies on the card table he'd set up in the basement of his house.

His house. No one else lived here. No one else knew about it other than Jade, and she knew better than to tell. She didn't know where it was, anyway. No one would search here. No one would find his captives until he was ready for them to be found.

Dr. Dani Novak stared mutinously at the bag of supplies as he slipped off his jacket. "You really expect me to put you back together after you fucking kidnapped me?"

He'd allowed her to do only a temporary dressing while they were in her apartment because he'd been antsy to get away. She'd been much later than he'd expected— apparently having visited all his victims who'd ended up in the hospital instead of the morgue. It had given him a chance to rest, although he hadn't actually slept while he'd waited. He didn't want her coming home to find her brother bound and gagged on the sofa and himself sawing z's on the floor.

He was tired, far too tired to take her lip. "Yes," he said. "I expect you to put me back together, or I start shooting children. Who should die first? Your brother or Roza?"

"Roza might die anyway," Dr. Novak said. "She's not responding. She needed to be in a hospital, not the backseat of your SUV all day. Especially the way you drive."

He backhanded her, knocking her to the floor. She sat there for a moment, seething, then licked her bleeding lip. "You killed the Renzo kid, didn't you?"

"I did," he said with a smile.

"I assume you tortured him for information."

He grinned, pleased at the memory. "I did."

"Then you know you shouldn't be making me bleed."

His grin disappeared. He threw her a box of latex gloves. "Suit up, Doc. Fix the bullet wound and be gentle about it."

He gritted his teeth as she cleaned the wound and packed it with gauze. "You need actual stitches," she said, "but you didn't get the supplies for that. This superglue will have to do."

He moved his arm experimentally. "I guess it could be worse. Sit down and keep your mouth shut or I'll have to drug you. I don't want to have to drug you."

"Will you let me clean Roza's head wound?"

"Just don't use up all my supplies."

She rolled eyes that made him look twice. "Your eyes are different from your brother's."

She said nothing, just bent over the still form of the child and began to work.

As quiet enveloped his house, he started to feel the overwhelming need to sleep. He couldn't do that until he'd tied up the doctor and the child. With his bum arm, he couldn't hold the gun and tie them at the same time. Dani Novak was the kind to fight dirty.

Finally, she finished working on the kid.

"Tie her up with the zip-ties."

"No. I will not restrain this child."

Furious and exhausted, he aimed his gun at Greg, trussed up on the floor. The kid stared up at him, terror in his mismatched eyes. *Good. At least one of them has the sense to be scared.*

"Don't push me," he snarled. "Tie up the girl. And make it tight. If she escapes, I am holding you personally responsible. When you're done, tie your own feet." Glaring at him, Dr. Novak complied. "Now, on the floor on your stomach, hands behind your back."

He secured her wrists with another zip-tie and gave a good tug to make sure she wouldn't be able to slip free. Finally, he slapped a strip of duct tape over her mouth to shut her up.

He backed out of the basement, locking them in. His basement was secure—no doors or windows to the outside. This door was the only way in or out. He set the alarm panel and then lay down on his living room sofa to sleep.

Chapter Thirty-three

Cincinnati, Ohio
Wednesday, November 5, 10:00 p.m.

Faith found Deacon standing with one hand planted on the dresser, his bare back bowed. The mirror reflected the white peaks of his hair as his head hung low. His phone was buzzing on the dresser as he conversed with someone by text. Faith gathered her courage, crossing the room to brush her fingertips against his warm, bronze skin.

He shuddered once but didn't tell her to stop, so she stepped closer and began rubbing his back in firm, wide circles. His phone buzzed again, a new text popping up. "Do you need to answer that?" she asked.

"No. It's Dani. I was going to send a security detail to her apartment tonight, but she's been at the shelter all evening. She's just going to stay there. She's got a couple of off-duty CPD officers with her. She just said that she's fine."

He'd spoken with a bone-deep weariness that made her feel even worse. "I'm sorry."

"For what?" he asked on a sigh.

"For the loss of your neighbor. That you were the one to find him. That now you feel responsible for leading a killer to your neighborhood, just like I felt responsible for all the people who died because of me." She stroked up and down his spine, feeling him shudder again, his back rounding up to meet her touch, just like the great cat she thought he resembled.

"Thank you. But none of those things are your fault."

"I didn't apologize, Deacon. I can be sorrowful without apologizing." He stiffened under her hands. "But I do apologize for hurting you by going to the house. I never meant to hurt you."

"I know," he murmured. "I'm sorry I shouted. I ... I guess I hit my limit tonight. I just wish you'd waited for me or at least that someone had told me where you were."

"I'm sorry for that, too." She found a tight muscle just under the shoulder bruise he'd gotten saving her life and focused her attention on loosening it. "But I *did* help."

"So I heard. Vince showed me the cabinet that hid the dumbwaiter and the jars. You found his souvenirs. Unfortunately, they don't bring us a single step closer to knowing who this guy is. And for that you might have been killed. I'm sorry, Faith. I don't consider it a fair trade."

"More than just souvenirs. Each jar was labeled with a name. We're using the names to identify the victims. And matching them to the Foundation's scholarship list."

"Tanaka would have found that cabinet. He's good at his job."

Her hands stilled, and she swallowed the sudden lump of hurt that was stuck in her throat at his flat dismissal of her contribution. "I needed to *do* something," she whispered fiercely as she stepped back, letting her hands fall to her sides. "Surely you can understand that."

"I understand the need to do something." He straightened slowly, the muscles in his back flexing and flowing. But when he turned, the stark bleakness in his eyes shattered her hurt and her pride. "But I need you to understand that the only thing that kept me going tonight as I held my neighbor's severed head in my hands was the belief that you were safe."

The picture he'd painted with his quiet words was more devastating than if he'd shouted. He'd been afraid. *For me.* "I *was* safe," she said softly. "I *am* safe."

He was unmoved. "This time. What about next time, Faith?"

"What next time?"

"The next time you make a sex offender angry enough to

slit your throat. The next time you climb an embankment in your bare feet after hitting a tree. The next time you step between an out-of-control two-hundred-pound federal agent and a fifteen-year-old boy who outweighs you by fifty pounds." He glared. "The next time someone asks you to help them solve a crime."

She considered her answer, trying to see it from his point of view, then finally settled on the truth, even though it wasn't what he wanted to hear. "That's who I am, Deacon. I promise to be careful, but I can't promise to sit still if someone needs me. Nor would I expect it of you."

"But I'm a trained federal agent. The level of danger isn't even close to being the same."

"No, it's not," she agreed soberly, all too aware that his life might be taken at any time. "But for me this is a special circumstance. You face danger every single day."

Which was all the more reason to resolve this. Life was far too short.

Tentatively, she laid her palm on his chest, feeling his muscles clench. His gaze flicked down to her hand, then slowly rose, his eyes instantly heating, arousal driving his fear far away.

She let herself stare at his eyes for just a few seconds, watching the brown and blue grow darker, the colors blending together until she no longer saw the colors at all, only his hunger, wild and intense and urgent.

Her body responded, her pulse kicking up its tempo as her breasts grew heavy, her skin too tight. Her panties were already moist. And he'd only looked at her.

She pressed her other palm to his heart, feeling his pulse accelerate. "I'm sorry that I scared you," she whispered. "I didn't mean to. I'll try very hard not to again."

He covered her hands with his, holding them in place on his chest. "If you'd waited, I would have gone with you. You didn't have to face that basement again alone."

Her heart turned over. "But I wasn't alone. I imagined you with me every step of the way. It's the only way I got down the stairs."

His chest expanded on a sudden swell. He freed her hands, inspecting her palms before lightly kissing each one. Then he leisurely lifted them to his neck, running his fingers down her arms, flattening his own hands on her back. Pulling her so close that she could feel his erection against her abdomen. His eyes never left hers. "You're tired."

"So are you."

His lips curved, drawing her gaze to his mouth. "I'll never be that tired," he murmured in that black velvet voice, sending a shiver across her skin and a bolt of lust straight to her core. She lifted on her toes to press against him, wriggling to ease the pressure between her thighs.

He huffed a low laugh and a quiet groan. "I need a shower."

"Is that an invitation?" she asked.

The fingers of one hand clenched, digging into her butt, her only warning before he ... pounced. The fingers of his other hand shoved through her hair, cupping the back of her head in the same moment that he took her mouth with a ravenous voracity that left her stunned. Swept away. He pushed his leg between hers, pulling her higher and rocking her hips so that she rode his powerful thigh, all while he ate at her mouth like he could never get enough.

This. This was what she'd waited for all day long. This was what had kept her going. To be in his arms and ... feel. She threaded her fingers through his hair and cradled his head in her hands, pressing her aching breasts against that beautiful bare chest that was hers. All hers.

He pulled back far enough to draw a breath. His fingers kneaded her butt, and his thigh kept just enough pressure between her legs to tease. His eyes glittered with desire, fanning to life every fantasy she'd ever dreamed. "What do you want tonight, Faith? Decide quickly because I'm on fire here."

"Do you have condoms?" she asked calmly, even though her heart was beating through her chest. "Because there are no more in the drawers."

Balancing her astride his thigh, he reached into his pants pocket and drew out a strip of at least six, holding them up for her inspection. He tilted his head, his white brows lifting. Waiting.

Faith laughed breathlessly. "Then let's get clean, Agent Novak."

Cincinnati, Ohio
Wednesday, November 5, 10:30 p.m.

Deacon wasn't sure how he'd made it to the shower, he was so hard. He ran the hot water, then turned to Faith. "I want you. Now." He grasped the hem of her blouse and pulled it over her head, leaving her bared to his eyes. "You are so damn pretty."

She was. Her breasts were the perfect size for his hands. For his mouth. Supple and firm. He tugged her forward, taking a step to meet her halfway.

Slow and gentle. Not like the other times. But his heart was pounding so hard it was all he could hear. He brushed a kiss across her lips and heard her sigh.

"You are a very good kisser, Deacon. Kiss me again."

He obeyed, trying to keep it light, but she licked at his lip, seriously damaging his resolve. His hands were actually trembling as he smoothed her hair away from her face. Gently, he kissed her forehead, then hooked a finger under her chin, lifting her face. She smiled at him.

"I won't break, Deacon."

No, she wouldn't. She might bend and she might find ways to make the best of situations that less adaptable people might find unacceptable. But she would not break.

"I know," he said, and could see that she understood what he meant.

"Thank you," she whispered, then fanned her hands across his chest, setting him on fire once again. Her fingers petted the dense hair that covered his pecs—the last of his body hair to turn white. But she didn't look bothered. She looked intrigued. Aroused. "Touch me, please," she begged. "It feels like I've been waiting forever for you to touch me again."

He drew a breath and prayed for control. "Then take off your jeans and get in the shower, because once I touch you, I won't be able to stop."

She had her jeans and panties shucked off and tossed through the doorway to her room before he could blink. "Last one in . . ." she said, and jumped into the hot shower, her expression becoming almost spiritual. "God, this feels good," she moaned, turning her face into the spray.

He stood there frozen, unable to take his eyes off her.

She was all curves and gorgeous long, toned legs. He'd been so crazy to get inside her before that he hadn't looked his fill, so he made up for it now, savoring every square inch of her body.

She turned to face him, her hair now soaking wet. Water ran down her body in rivulets that streaked across her skin, over those pretty breasts, down her stomach, and into the thatch of dark red curls that tasted so damn good. *That's where I'll start,* he decided.

"Change your mind?" she teased.

"Not a chance." Deacon loosened his belt, took the condoms from his pocket, and let his pants and boxers drop to the floor. Not taking his eyes off of her, he tore one of the condoms from the strip and put it on the edge of the tub. "Just planning my strategy."

She laughed up at him. "I warrant a strategy? I'm not that complex."

Deacon's chest squeezed so hard that he had to inhale to give his heart room to beat. "You're beautiful when you laugh." But it was far more than that. Seeing her laugh, knowing he'd made her happy in the midst of such chaos and pain . . .

He had the ridiculous urge to shout, "King of the world!," which he was not going to give in to. She was already watching him warily as he squirted into his hand about ten times more shampoo than he'd ever need. He reached for her hair and she looked surprised.

"You're going to wash my hair?" she asked.

"Of course." He leaned close to whisper in her ear, "I'm going to wash you everywhere."

She shuddered hard. "Why does that sound so naughty?"

He chuckled, massaging her scalp and making her moan again. "Because the way I plan to do it, it will be. I like your hair, Faith."

She closed her eyes. "I like yours, too. It's like Lake Erie." Surprised, his hands stilled. Shampoo suds ran down her face, making her sputter. "Deacon," she protested.

He resumed his task. "How is my hair like Lake Erie?"

"Ummm, that feels so nice." She smiled a dreamy smile, and he decided he would always wash her hair from now on, just to see that expression of bliss. "One winter, my father and Lily and I went to see her family in Buffalo. We drove by the lake and it was frozen, but not flat like glass. The waves had frozen in place. It looked like Iceman had been there." She opened one eye. "You know Iceman, right?"

"I have *Iceman*," he told her. "Volume one. Christmas present from Dani. Only worth a few bucks, but she was just a kid when she got it for me, so it means a lot. She was Rogue and I was Iceman. It was just a joke, but it got us through a hard patch."

Faith closed her eyes again as he rinsed the lather from her hair. "Dani told me that you had to live with your uncle for a while after your father died. Was it then?"

"Yes." Thinking of those days always made him bitter, but tonight he had a beautiful naked woman in his shower. Bitterness was not welcome here, so he shoved the memories right out of his mind. "Lake Erie?" he prompted.

"I thought the lake looked magical all whipped and frozen like that. Dad said that it was because the waves kept coming and building up the frozen parts, but I like magic better. I thought of that lake when I saw you at Arianna's crime scene Monday night."

His heart clenched again. "You thought I was magic?"

"I thought you looked like a superhero." She slicked her hair from her face and opened her eyes, suddenly very serious. She stroked a finger across his upper lip. "I wasn't too far off."

Emotion barreled through him with the force of an avalanche. He grabbed her face and kissed her hard, skirting the edge of pain, but she held on to him, kissing him back. His hands ran over her body, cupping her breasts, his thumbs teasing her nipples, lightly twisting until she gasped against his mouth. He jerked back, an apology on his lips, but she didn't look hurt.

She looked hungry. "Hurry, Deacon. I need you."

He soaped up his hands, washing her skin, working his way down her body as she watched him, her eyes heavy-lidded. Impatient. He gave special attention to her knees and feet, still scratched and battered from climbing an embankment to save a girl she didn't know. He dragged a quiet moan from her throat when he hit a sensitive place on her foot.

"Deacon, please." She grasped his shoulders, trying to pull him to his feet. "Hurry."

"I don't want to hurry this time." Gently, he pushed her hands away, washing up her legs, hearing her whimper when his thumbs toyed with her inner thighs. He ran his soap-slicked fingers through her slicker folds, not giving her any of the pressure she needed to come. He rinsed her as her legs started to tremble.

"Please," she whispered. "Or I'll do it myself."

Lust slammed into him at the thought. "Next time," he said. "I want to watch you."

She laughed weakly, grabbing his hair and tugging. "Cover your mouth," he cautioned her. "Don't make a sound. Bishop has ears like a bat." And then he set his mouth on her, her muffled scream the most erotic thing he'd ever heard. She tasted like soap and herself and he licked and lapped until her knees gave out. He gripped her hips, pressing her into the tile, keeping her upright.

She was close. He could feel it. Looking up to see her, he plunged his tongue into her. Her body arched like a bow, her shoulders pressing in the tile, her head thrown back, biting down on her hand to control her scream. Then she collapsed, boneless. Dazed and blinking slowly.

He rose, blindly reaching for the condom he'd left outside the shower. He was trembling now, his hands unable to tear the packet. She took over, her movements slow but steady.

"I should do the same thing to you," she muttered. "But I want you inside me too much." She slid the condom over his cock, her hand continuing down to stroke his balls.

"No. I'm too close," he rasped. "If you touch me, it'll be all over."

She jerked her hands away, raising them as if she were being robbed. "Hurry, Deacon."

"I don't want to hurry." He lifted her, winding her legs around his hips. "I want this to last forever."

"I will hurt you," she threatened. "I swear I will hurt you if you don't—" She ended on a strangled moan when he started to enter her. "Yes. Please." She arched her back, forcing more of him in. "You feel so good. So good. More. Give me more."

He was easing his way in when she grabbed his hips and yanked, shattering his control. He growled and thrust the rest of the way in a single stroke, covering her mouth with his to swallow her gasp. He began to move, wanting to go slowly but unable to muster the control. He found himself pounding into her, his thrusts keeping time with her chanted pleas for more.

Her *more, more, more* changed to *please, please, please*, then pants of *almost, almost.* She was so beautiful, a sensual, green-eyed goddess. *Who wants me. Just the way that I am.*

His orgasm broke free, slamming up his spine, exploding in his body as he buried his face in the curve of her shoulder to silence his shout. His release set off hers, and she bit her lip to keep from crying out as her hips bucked and jerked against him.

Deacon was shaking, his limbs like rubber. "Oh God. I can't stand up." He braced his foot against the side of the tub, leaning into the wall so he didn't end up on his ass, dragging Faith down with him.

One hand against the tile, the other keeping Faith upright. He pulled out of her body, feeling bereft as he did so. He lowered her to sit on the edge of the tub, then disposed of the condom and turned off the water.

Her gaze dropped to his groin and she licked her lips. His cock twitched hopefully, but she shook her head. "I'll have to get my revenge another time," she said. "I got nothin' left. I don't even think I can make it to the bed."

He helped her from the tub and dried her as slowly as he'd washed her. Minutes later, she was spooned against him, his arms wrapped around her, fast asleep. Deacon took a moment to capture the moment to his memory. He was happy. And at peace.

Tomorrow would be another day of identifying victims. But until then, he was going to let his mind and body rest and savor the feeling of holding a kind, courageous, beautiful woman who thought he was a superhero.

Cincinnati, Ohio
Thursday, November 6, 4:30 a.m.

The light knocking woke Deacon up. He'd been dreaming that he was holding Faith in his arms. And then realized it had been no dream. At some point they'd changed positions. No longer spooned, he lay on his back with her draped over his body like a soft, redheaded blanket.

Again he heard the knocking. "Deacon? It's Scarlett. I need to talk to you. It's important."

He slid out from under Faith's warmth, murmuring in her ear to send her back to sleep.

"Just a second," he said to Bishop. He pulled on a pair of sweats and a T-shirt, then slipped through the door, making sure Bishop didn't see inside. Her expression said she wasn't fooled.

"This isn't camp bed check. I don't want to know," she said, then held up her phone. "Just got a call from Vega in Miami. She finally talked to Combs's girlfriend today, but the conversation didn't go as she'd expected. Combs is dead and probably has been for a month."

Deacon did a double take. "What? How?"

"The girlfriend claims he met a man who forced him to drive out to the Everglades at gunpoint. The man shot him and left him there. The girlfriend witnessed this and didn't want to be a target, so she didn't tell anyone, burying Combs herself."

"Vega found his body?"

"Yep. An hour ago. We both got texts, but I didn't wake up until she actually called. She said they found a bullet in his head. Ballistics matched the gun that killed Gordon Shue."

Deacon slumped into the nearest chair. "You're kidding. Shit. So Combs was never any part of this at all?"

Bishop took the chair next to him. "Nope. Vega checked his cell records. He got a call from a Miami area code the night before Gordon Shue's murder. She thinks this mystery guy may have tried to get Combs to kill Faith and for some reason he said no."

"That makes no sense given that he'd tried to kill her before."

"She also said that Combs seemed afraid of him, because he'd taken out all of his money from his bank account like he was getting ready to run. Oh, and this is important, too. She said the girlfriend claimed that Faith took the picture that got Combs arrested in the first place."

Deacon blinked. "Really. Who told her that?"

Bishop narrowed her eyes. "I'm tired and cranky, so cut the shit, Novak, and be my *partner*. Did Faith take the damn picture?"

"Yes," Faith said from behind them. "She did."

Deacon whipped his head toward the sound of her voice. She stood in the doorway to her own room, dressed much as he was. "How much did you hear?" he asked soberly.

"All of it." She sat on the sofa closest to him. "So he's dead? All of this, all of my trying to outrun him, change my name, it was all for nothing? He was already dead?"

"Looks that way," Bishop said. "The Miami ME said that the level of decomp was consistent with a month in the ground. I have photos if you want proof."

She grimaced. "That's all right. I believe you. Was the girl-friend able to give a description of the man who killed him?"

"Yeah, but it doesn't make sense. She said he was as big as Combs, but walked like a robot and that he was bald, like shiny bald."

Deacon frowned. "Some killers shave their heads and remove all their hair to prevent leaving DNA behind."

Faith crossed her arms, hugging herself. "I suppose you could go up to all of the suspects and pull their hair to see if they're wearing a wig. Only half kidding there. So, if Combs wasn't involved at all, where does that leave us?"

Bishop rubbed her forehead. "The suspects left are Jer-emy, Herbie Three, and Stone."

"And Jordan," Deacon said. "Let's add Jordan back in the mix for now. I still need to check Alda Lane's alibi. Un-til I confirm it, let's consider him a possibility."

Faith looked uncomfortable, like there was something she wanted to say but did not.

"Okay," Bishop said, "Jordan's back on the leaderboard. The motive is still the damn house because the attacks started after the will was read."

"Unless they didn't," Faith said quietly.

Deacon and Bishop stared at her. "Somebody tried to kill you before this?" Deacon asked.

"Maybe. One of the things I was trying to tell you last night was what we found when we started looking at the Foundation scholarship recipients. Two major patterns emerged. One was that several of the recipients don't ap-pear to have ever existed. They were fake."

"Someone was skimming," Bishop said.

"Jeremy accused Jordan of skimming twenty-three years ago," Deacon said.

"To my knowledge that was never proven," Faith protested. She sighed. "But you have to consider it. The other pattern that emerged was the timing of some of the abductions. Corinne and Arianna were taken the day after my old apartment burned. Roxie Dupree, the day after I was almost run off that bridge."

"Oh, wow," Bishop breathed. "This is huge. Does Isenberg know this?"

"Yes. She was at the house most of the time I was there yesterday." She gave Deacon a gently chiding look. "So I really was very safe."

"Point made," he acknowledged. "What other abductions connect to you?"

"One happened the day after my grandmother's will was read, one a week before my grandfather died, another the day after my grandfather's will was read. And then a woman was abducted three years ago, a few days after I had a very bad car accident."

"A week before your *grandfather* died?" Deacon blinked, losing the thought as her last four words sank in. "Wait. *You* had a car accident, too? Three years ago?"

"I did. So did my dad, about ten years ago. We've had a lot of car accidents in our family. I'd never really thought about it before."

"What happened in your accident?" he asked.

"I lost control of the brakes and went across the median, but I steered out of oncoming traffic and hit a tree. At the time, no one looked for tampering. The police thought I'd fallen asleep at the wheel, and I thought it was possible, because I was having trouble sleeping. I'd had my throat slit by Combs and was divorcing Charlie because he'd been cheating on me. I didn't make a fuss because I didn't want my dad to know. He thought my mother had died in a car wreck, and I didn't want to worry him."

Bishop frowned, puzzled. "Wait. I've had this question for days now and have to ask it. How could your father not know the truth about your mother? Wasn't there an autopsy?"

"No." Faith shook her head, her eyes going vacant. Her defense mechanism, Deacon knew.

"Fuck this," Bishop said briskly. She got up and grabbed Faith's chin and gave her a little shake. "Deacon's not going to make you talk about this because he's gone soft over you.

I have not. So snap out of the trance, Faith, and answer my questions. Was there really a car accident? Or was that just what the family told people?"

Faith recoiled, but her eyes focused, then narrowed angrily as she jerked her chin free. "Yes, Detective. There was an accident. I saw the pictures of the crashed car. It burned up. I saw the pictures of her charred body. And don't put your hands on me again."

She saw the pictures? Deacon stared at her, horrified. *Why? Who in God's name would have shown her pictures?* And then, once again her words sank in: "Wait. I thought your mother killed herself."

"She did," Faith said flatly. "The car accident was just a cover-up."

"Was there an autopsy?" Bishop asked again, not apologetic in the least.

"No. The coroner said there wasn't much of her left and no one wanted an autopsy. My grandfather had just died, and then my mother, and they just wanted to bury her and move on." But as she said it, Faith looked away and her words came out with a slight, singsonginess, like they'd been repeated in her mind for a long time.

Bishop gripped her chin again. "Did you find your mother hanging from the ceiling in your grandmother's basement?"

Faith lurched to her feet and, fists clenched, rocked up on her toes, nose to nose with Bishop. "Yes!" Faith shouted. "I found her, dammit! *I found her.*"

"How?" Bishop pressed, holding her ground. "From a rope or a scarf?"

"From a *rope*. She was hanging from a *rope* and she was *dead*. Are you happy now? My mother committed suicide and I found her."

"How high off the ground were her feet?" Bishop asked, her tone unforgiving.

Still on her toes, Faith clenched her teeth and blinked hard once, sending tears down her cheeks. "This far," she spat defiantly, spreading her hands about five inches. *"Why?"*

"Had she kicked over a chair?"

Faith blinked again and slowly took a step back, looking at Bishop like she'd suddenly spoken a foreign language. "What?"

"Had she kicked over a chair?"

Uncertainty clouded her eyes, and she wiped away more tears. "I . . . I don't know. Why?"

Bishop sat down. "All right. How did she end up in the car? This is important because there *have* been a lot of car accidents. Yours, your mother's, your uncle Jeremy's. The mother in Miami. So how, Faith?"

"I don't know." Still standing, Faith suddenly looked sick. "My uncle took care of it."

Deacon's jaw dropped. "How?"

"I don't know." The exasperated words shot from her mouth. "I was only nine years old. He just told me he'd handle it."

"What happened that day, Faith?" Bishop asked calmly. "Start from the beginning."

Faith took another step back, then another, shaking her head as she blindly backed into the table. "I . . . I . . ." She shot Deacon a look of panicked desperation. "I'm—"

She turned and ran for the little powder room and slammed the door. Deacon closed his eyes, exhaling at the sound of Faith retching. He dragged his palms down his face, unable to remember a moment he'd felt this helpless. Except the night his own mother had died.

"Fuck," he whispered.

"She needs to tell us," Bishop whispered back thickly.

Deacon opened his eyes to find tears in Bishop's dark eyes. But his partner stood and tugged at the hem of her sweatshirt like she might a uniform.

They heard the sound of running water, then quiet. Bishop had lifted her fist to knock when the door opened and Faith came out. Her chin was down, enough that her hair partially hid her face. Her arms hugged her torso and her back was slightly hunched. She trudged to the window with the million-dollar view and looked out, her face carefully blank.

Unsure of what to say or do, Deacon crossed the room to stand behind her, rubbing her back as she'd done his earlier. She swallowed a sob. "I'm sorry. It's . . ." She sighed. "I think it started the day before, at the reading of the will. My parents had an awful fight that night."

"About?" he asked when her voice trailed away.

"My mother was mad at *her* father for not leaving them

any money, and she was mad at *my* father for hitting Uncle Jeremy and calling him bad names." She leaned a little, stiffly, barely touching her head to his shoulder. "Dad was mad because she wouldn't see that her brother was a pervert who should be locked up. And he was disgusted that money meant so much to her."

She drew a breath and hugged herself tighter, tucking her fists under her armpits. Deacon kept rubbing her back, waiting. In the window he could see Bishop's reflection as she stood behind them.

"Why?" Bishop asked softly. "Why didn't he want the money?"

She shrugged. "He was going to be a priest. He didn't care about things. But my mother did. She liked heavy draperies and silver teapots. The next morning we had breakfast and everyone was awkward. Everyone had heard them yelling at each other. I just remember making myself as small as I could."

"Invisible," Deacon murmured, and she nodded.

"After breakfast he took our car, saying he needed to get away from the 'mausoleum' and would be back later. My grandmother took some pills to sleep and my mother was . . . looking for something. It may have been a ring or a brooch. I don't even remember what. She kept muttering about her birthright. Losing her birthright. She was scaring me, so I backed away and went to my room to read. I knew Dad would be back soon and we were supposed to be ready to leave, but my mother hadn't even started packing. So I went to find her. To remind her that she needed to hurry. I looked everywhere, but she wasn't anywhere. The only place I hadn't looked was the basement, so that's where I went, counting the steps like I always did."

She stopped and took a deep breath, than another, each exhale shakier than the one before.

"You went down the steps?" Deacon murmured.

She nodded. "When I got to the bottom, I turned around . . ." She stopped again, pursed her lips, and swallowed hard. "And I saw her shoes," she whispered.

Deacon rested his cheek atop her head and stood with her, waiting for her to be ready to continue. "Red Keds," she added, her voice nearly soundless.

"Excuse me?" Bishop said softly.

Faith cleared her throat. "Red Keds shoes. That's what she was wearing. The laces were dragging on the ground."

"What did you do when you saw her?" Bishop asked, still behind them.

"I stared," she said quietly. "I couldn't even scream at first. Then Jeremy turned around and saw me."

Deacon's brows shot up. "*Jeremy* was there when you found her?" He'd been expecting her to say Jordan. Because Jeremy should have been gone by then. He'd told them he'd left after the reading of the will and had never come back.

A slow nod. "He was cutting her down. I started to scream then, and he covered my mouth with his hand. My mother's body just . . ." She shrugged. "Just fell to the floor in a heap. He told me that my grandmother couldn't know that my mother had hanged herself. Neither could my father. That it would kill them. That suicide was a mortal sin."

"And your family was more Catholic than the Pope," Deacon said grimly.

"I knew that suicide meant my mother couldn't be buried with her family. I knew it meant she was in hell. But most of all, I knew that my father would be devastated. He'd decided not to take his vows when he met my mother. I knew it would kill him if he ever found out. And I love my father. So I never told anyone. Until now."

"How did Jeremy stage the car accident?" Deacon asked.

She moved her shoulders restlessly. "I don't know exactly. He told me that he and Jordan would take care of everything. To go up to my room and wait for one of them to come and talk to me, but not to talk to anyone else."

"Jeremy didn't mention that," Bishop murmured. "Did they come to talk to you?"

"Jordan did, because Jeremy was afraid my father would see him in my room and hit him again. They'd fought at the will reading because he put his arm around me."

"He did mention that," Deacon said. "What did Jordan say when he came to your room?"

Faith's lips trembled. "That I shouldn't blame myself. I hadn't really, not until he said that. He said my mother had confided to him that she was unhappy with my father. Suffocating. That she wanted to leave him but was afraid."

"Was she?" Bishop asked.

"She was unhappy. She didn't like being poor. I know that. I once heard her tell my father that she thought she'd been poor when Joy died but that she'd been rich then compared to living with him. Jordan said my mother couldn't deal with the guilt of leaving my father, but she couldn't keep living with him, either."

"She was unhappy," Bishop said, "but was she depressed?"

"Looking back, I think so. After she had me, she tried to have other children, but she kept losing them. I know of at least three miscarriages. She cried a lot. I used to think about her and try to see a sign or some indication that she was going to do this thing. To kill herself. I used to think that if I'd paid more attention I could have stopped it. Now I know that's not true. I was just a child." She shrugged. "I don't know if anyone really could have seen it coming. All I really knew for sure was that I'd lost one parent that day. I couldn't lose another."

"Were you afraid your father would kill himself, too?" Bishop asked.

"Oh no. No. Suicide is a mortal sin." Faith shook her head. "But his heart wasn't strong even then. He'd already had one heart attack. I couldn't risk it."

"You said your father took the family car when he left that morning," Deacon said. "Whose car was wrecked with your mother inside it?"

"My grandfather's. Everyone knew my parents had been fighting, and they figured my mother was so distraught she lost control of the car." She swiped at her eyes with her fingertips. "She went off the road not too far from where I did on Monday night. Hell of an irony, ain't it?"

Indeed. It was a wonder she'd functioned at all that night, but she'd more than done so. Deacon hadn't thought she could impress him any more, but he'd been wrong.

"So both Jeremy and Jordan might be capable of faking an auto accident," Bishop said thoughtfully. "What happened to the car you were driving three years ago?"

"I'm sure it was junked. It was totaled. The first responders were amazed—both that I'd avoided killing anyone else and that I'd walked away with only minor injuries."

"You did some fancy driving Monday night, too," Deacon remembered, "positioning the passenger side to take the brunt of the impact."

"I took some driving classes to make my father more comfortable. Because of my mother, you know. Guess they paid off."

"I'm very glad they did," Deacon said, keeping his tone gentle, because she seemed so very fragile. "Faith, all the connections you've found so far have been either to recent attempts on your life because of your grandmother's will or to the reading of the wills themselves. What was special about the timing of the accident three years ago?"

"I don't know. I've tried, but I can't think of anything." She rubbed her forehead fretfully. "I'm tired. I'm going to try to get a little more sleep."

Deacon waited until Faith had closed herself back in her room. "She may have tried to remember, but I don't think she really wants to know."

"That the abductions of the Foundation recipients goes back to the reading of her *grandfather's* will is very significant. She dropped that little bomb and skipped right to the next thing. I'm pretty sure Isenberg would have caught that had Faith mentioned it to her."

"I know. Faith doesn't want to admit to herself that the killer is one of her uncles, but I'm pretty much there. Trouble is, I don't know if it's only Jordan, or Jeremy with a helper, or whether the twins are working in cahoots despite their claims to hate each other. I don't know if Stone and Marcus were lying about Jeremy being with them the day Maggie died or if they were mistaken. Or if they were telling the truth." He sighed, new dread layering in his gut. "She's also obviously not considering the implications of the fact that there was an abduction the day after her grandfather died. Because that was *the* day her mother died."

Bishop nodded. "That's why I kept pushing her about the chair."

"I figured that. If you're thinking that Maggie Sullivan walked into the basement while the killer was either killing or putting his souvenirs in jars, then, yeah, I thought the same."

"If Maggie saw him, it would give him a reason to murder her and fake a suicide. Especially since the shoelaces were dragging on the ground. She wasn't hanging that high, Deacon."

"I thought that, too. We need to exhume the body, but I hate to ask Faith to go through that."

"I think she'll want to know, once she's able to grasp all this. It might be hard to accept that her mother was murdered, but easier than thinking she killed herself."

"I know. This would also explain the killer's growing urgency to see her dead. If his motivation had been to keep intruders from the house, he would have stopped on Monday, as soon as we went inside. When he shot at Faith at the hotel, I thought it was to keep her from going into the basement to discover the changes he'd made—that he'd raised the floor sixteen inches—but then later he killed Pope to get to her. Now I'm thinking that he knew it was only a matter of time before we got her to talk about this secret that she's kept all these years."

"Other than her uncles," Bishop said, "Faith would be the only one who'd know that the car accident had been a ruse. As soon as we found the bodies, it became more and more likely that she would start wondering about the circumstances of her mother's death. I mean, what a coincidence that her mother would hang herself in a place where seventeen women were murdered and buried. Like you said, the question is, which uncle? One or both of them is lying. Or they're in it together."

"And we don't have any hard evidence linking either of them to anything." Deacon huffed in frustration. "Dammit."

Bishop looked at Faith's bedroom door, troubled. "I didn't want to be so rough on her, Deacon. I didn't want to make her relive it. I didn't mean to make her cry."

"I know. But you got out of her what I wasn't able to, and that could save her life. We have to find something concrete to nail one or both of the uncles, but right now I'm too worn out to think of what that could be. I'm going to catch a little more sleep. You should, too."

He turned for his own bedroom door, wondering where he'd find Faith. Hoping it would be back in his bed. He just wanted to hold her.

Cincinnati, Ohio
Thursday, November 6, 5:25 a.m.

Deacon found her in his bed, curled up in a ball, her face buried in a pillow. Crying like her heart was broken, but silently. His own heart broke for her as he scooped her into his arms and settled them both in the overstuffed rocking chair tucked away in the corner of the room. Her fingers clutched at his shirt as she tried to stifle the sound of her sobs.

Bishop had pried from Faith the truth she hadn't wanted to tell. It had been necessary, a critical piece of the puzzle that might prove to be the key to this case. But it had been more than a puzzle piece for Faith. It had been the most traumatic day of her life cracked open. Exposed.

"You've never told anyone, Faith?" he asked softly. "No one?"

"No," she whispered. "I couldn't. They'd tell my father. Please don't tell him now."

He couldn't promise not to, because he wasn't sure how much of this might become public knowledge, especially if one of her uncles was responsible for all the killings.

But mostly he didn't promise because he could see that keeping this secret had hurt her, scarred her. And a part of him wanted her father to know that.

He kissed the top of her head. "Sshh, now. You're going to make yourself sick."

Her body shuddered as she attempted to stop without success. Finally, Deacon gripped her chin, tilted her face up, and kissed her. Hard, giving her no quarter. After a few seconds, she started kissing him back with the same intensity, opening to him when he licked at her lips. No carnal exploration, this was a duel of tongues and teeth, her nails digging into his chest as she worked through a flood of fury. He felt the power of it blasting through her and didn't try to calm her. He let her embrace it. Battle it.

Containing his body's whiplash response, he ignored the need to possess her, to throw her on the bed, sink into the heat of her body. Instead, he let her take what she needed.

Abruptly, she released him, her head falling back to his shoulder. Like the fire within her had used up all the available oxygen and simply burned out.

She moaned quietly. "I have an awful headache."

"I'm not surprised." He massaged the back of her skull, gratified when she sighed and cuddled closer. He set the chair in motion, the gentle rocking at odds with the war now raging in his body. It was impossible to hide the fact that he was hard as a rock, but she wasn't flinching away. He touched his tongue to his lip. That she'd actually drawn blood shouldn't have been such a turn-on. "Better now?" he murmured.

"Much." Her fingertips petted his chest where she'd clawed him. "I hurt you. I'm sorry."

He had to take a moment to control his voice, because her gentle caress was driving him wild. "I'm fine. I'm more worried about you."

"She left me, Deacon. She was unhappy with my father, but she'd always acted like she loved me. But she didn't. Not enough to stay with me."

He almost told her what he and Bishop suspected—that her mother hadn't committed suicide—but he held his tongue. If it wasn't true, he would have upended her world yet again for no good reason. "I'm sorry, honey. I'm sorry you've borne the weight of this secret for so long. I'm sorry we had to rip it out of you that way."

"I'm not sure there was another way to make me tell it. A lot of therapists have tried over the years. They should take classes from Scarlett Bishop."

"Which therapists?" He jostled her lightly when she didn't answer. "Faith?"

She sighed. "My dad and I were spiraling down big-time after my mother died. He felt guilty for upsetting her so much that she lost control of the car, and I felt guilty for keeping the truth a secret. He started drinking and it got bad. I took care of the house and kept things up so that no one would know. I kept hoping he'd snap out of it, but things kept getting worse and . . . I kind of snapped under the pressure. I had a breakdown and got sent to a hospital for a while."

Deacon's chest tightened. "Did you try to kill yourself, Faith?" he asked hesitantly.

"No. I went kind of catatonic. Just sat there and rocked. I still do that sometimes when I'm under a lot of pressure."

"I know. I've seen it." She'd rocked herself the night Vega had told her that the mother and child had died in her car. "What happened?"

"I got therapy. Everyone I talked to knew something was wrong, but it almost became a compulsion not to tell. Like the anorexic who finds a sense of control in refusing food."

That explained a lot. "That's why you had such a tough time tonight."

She nodded. "Old habits die hard. It turned out to be a good thing, though. Dad finally snapped out of it and went into alcohol rehab, which is why I lived with Gran for two years. She refused to let me go back to him until he'd proven his sobriety. He's been sober ever since."

"And you kept the secret."

"Until tonight. I'm glad that was my only iceberg lurking under the surface. I don't think I could go through this night again anytime soon."

He kissed her forehead and rocked her a little more. "There is one bright spot in all of this. That bastard Combs can never hurt you again. I only wish he'd never been able to put his hands on you in the first place."

"Me, too." Another pat. "But in a way it worked out."

"How do you mean?"

"Well, it brought things between me and Charlie to a head. After Combs cut my throat, the cops tried to find Charlie to tell him, but he wasn't answering his phone. Finally, Charlie's partner told them that he was at his girl-friend's house."

"Ouch," he said mildly.

"His pregnant barely eighteen-year-old girlfriend."

"What a douche."

She laughed softly. "Yes, he was. He was using me as an excuse to not have to marry this girl. You know, the whole 'my wife won't give me a divorce' thing. I would have. I only stayed with him because of my dad."

"Because divorce is a sin, too?" Deacon asked acidly, liking Faith's father less and less all the time.

"Yes. Although to be fair to my father, he never liked Charlie. When I told him that Charlie had been unfaithful, he supported my decision a hundred percent. I hate to admit this, but Charlie wasn't the only one making excuses. I think I used worry over hurting my father to justify my inaction. I don't like change. I like things orderly. Getting a divorce was scary. And inconvenient, as long as I'm being honest. If Combs hadn't put me in the hospital, I might never have found out that Charlie was cheating. Cheating and physical abuse were probably the only two things that would have gotten me up off my keister and into a lawyer's office."

Deacon couldn't keep his question contained. "Did you love him?"

"No, I hadn't loved him in years, maybe never. At the beginning I loved the man I thought he was. He may have even loved the woman he thought I was."

"Who did you think he was?"

"A good man who took care of other people. A hero. Not a superhero, of course. He didn't have a leather coat or the cool shades."

Deacon's heart warmed. "Who did he think you were?"

"Obedient and biddable."

He snorted. "Then your ex was not only a douche, but a stupid douche."

She chuckled. "True, but I was more timid in those days. I'd just started grad school and was so young. At the beginning we were happy. At least I was. When someone cheats, you're never sure that anything they said or did before was true."

Deacon thought of Brandi, the girl she'd been. And the boy he'd been. "I know."

Her petting fingers stilled. "Who?" she asked simply.

After all she'd shared, he'd be selfish not to give a little quid pro quo. Still, he hesitated. "Brandi," he finally said. "My ex-wife."

She drew back, staring up at him. "You were married?"

"For about six months, back when I was eighteen."

"Oh." She bit her lip. "Deacon, is Greg your son?"

He nearly dropped her, catching her as she started to slide down his legs. "No," he said firmly. "No, no, no. God, no." He shook his head as he settled her back on his lap. "No."

"Okay, okay," she said. "I get that the answer is no. So what happened with Brandi?"

"Just a really bad string of choices on my part. But it nearly killed Greg, so it's not a time—or a *me*—that I like to remember. When my mother and Bruce died, I kind of went off the deep end, and Brandi was there for me. But she was what you'd now call a 'troubled teen.' My uncle Jim called her a whole lot worse. He hated her. Said he knew her 'type' and to stay away from her. Said that as long as I lived under his roof, I had to obey his rules."

"Fightin' words for a teenager," she said.

"Yeah. Jim hated Brandi, but I *really* hated Jim. We'd lived with him before when my father died. We'd been liv-

ing in the house next door to theirs, which he owned and
rented. But when my father died, my mother couldn't pay
the rent, so Jim evicted us."

"I know. Dani told me about it. She said it was especially
hard on you."

"Dani slept with Mom. I bunked with Adam, and his window looked into my old room. It was hard looking out and
seeing someone else in the bedroom that had been mine.
Jim said it was 'just a house.' But for me, it had been home
for my whole life. I forgot about that until Monday night
when I went to see Greg. He's in Adam's old room, and he
asked me why I always looked out the window when I came
to see him. I hadn't thought about that time in years."

"Lots of that going on," she said wryly. "And? *Brandi?*"

"I'm getting there. My contempt for Jim skyrocketed after Bruce and my mom died, because he didn't really want
to take Greg in. He . . ." Deacon paused. Sighed. "Jim didn't
approve of my mother having children in the first place. You
said that Greg told you about our syndrome?"

"Waardenburg with two *a*'s. What about it?"

"Well, it's genetic. Hereditary. In our family, it's passed
down through the women. Some kids in the family get it
and some are completely passed over. My mother had it,
but Tammy didn't. So Adam was fine and Dani and I . . .
weren't."

She stiffened, her hands clenching into fists. "You are
more than fine, Deacon Novak."

"I wish you'd been there to defend me then," he teased,
more than touched. "Anyway, Jim didn't approve of Mom
having more kids, and told her so when she got pregnant
with Greg. So when Bruce and Mom died and Aunt Tammy
insisted on taking Greg in, Jim got on his high horse about
how he'd already taken us in once and now he was having
to clean up my mother's 'mistakes' again."

Faith frowned. "He really thought of Greg as a 'mistake'?"

"He said he did. It's hard to know with Jim how much is
bluster. The other thing he was upset about was that they'd
left the house to us. He decreed that we had to move in with
him and sell the house. I fought him. It was our house, and
he'd booted me out of my home once before already. I
didn't have a sense of mortgages or taxes, but I wanted Dani

and Greg to have Bruce's house. That we had to live with Jim and Tammy again after Mom died, I saw as temporary. In my mind I'd planned to graduate high school, get a job to pay the bills, and have me and Dani and Greg live in *our* house. Looking back, I was embarrassingly unrealistic."

"You wanted your family all together. That's a lovely dream. You were just too young."

Deacon smiled at her. "And I think if Jim had said it that way, I might have listened. But he didn't, and so we were arguing all the time . . . and then there was Brandi. I was eighteen and she was hot. And she was really into the *me* I'd created."

"The leather coat and the hair and glasses."

"Yeah. Having a girl like that want me when my world had just imploded was more than I could resist at that age. But like I said, Jim really hated her type. So when he also decreed that Brandi wasn't welcome under his roof, I figured, *Hell, I have a roof of my own.* I married Brandi in a fit of defiance and we moved into my house."

"I thought Jim made you sell the house."

Deacon winced. "Well, all of this happened in the course of a few weeks. The estate wasn't settled yet. I thought if I got married and set up housekeeping, they couldn't make me leave. So I did. Like I said, I made a string of bad choices after Mom died. Jim ranted that I was an idiot, but Tammy said they should let my little fantasy run its course, that as soon as the mortgage came due and I didn't have the money, I'd realize Jim was right and I'd give up on this whole setting-up-house idea and go to college like she wanted me to."

"And your marriage?"

He shrugged. "I don't think she really took it seriously. It was just paper and easily dealt with later. I wanted to prove them both wrong."

"So how did all of this almost kill Greg?"

"Tammy let me have him for a few hours after school one day. Brandi had done some drugs in high school, but she said she was clean. I foolishly believed her." He sighed. "She also said she loved me, and I foolishly believed that, too."

"Maybe 'foolishly' is too harsh," Faith said gently. "Maybe you were a young man missing your mother and Bruce and wanted to create a home like the one you'd lost."

Something tight in Deacon's heart loosened. Yes, that was exactly what it had been. That she'd seen it so effortlessly . . . *I could love this woman*. Maybe he was already well on his way.

"Maybe," he said gruffly. "But that was a bad day. A horrible day. Greg got into Brandi's purse. Luckily, she'd already snorted all the coke she'd hidden in there. There was just dust, but it was enough to put a one-year-old in critical condition for days. Jim blamed me, told me Brandi had to go, and he was right on both counts. I lashed out at her, but she cried, so repentant, so I let her stay one more day. The next day I came home from visiting Greg in the hospital to find Brandi and her dealer in my mother and Bruce's bed, doing lines of coke. That was it. I called the cops. Of course Jim was on patrol and he showed up to make the bust. Made a big deal of how stupid I was in front of everyone. I gave up. Let him have Greg. Let him sell the house. I went to college and moved out."

"I don't think I like your uncle very much."

"I don't like yours much, either," he said wryly. "But Jim's not a bad man. He just thinks he's right and he is often enough to make him insufferable. I went away to school, but I was still close enough that I could visit Greg and Dani on the weekends. And then I got recruited into the Bureau and was able to visit less often. Greg did come live with me in Maryland for a few years, when he hit middle school. Everything was great for a while, but then he got belligerent and was expelled from the school for the deaf there. Jim said my experiment had failed, and since he still had custody, he took Greg back. Dani was here, but she was doing her internship and she didn't have the time to spend with him. That's when I put in for a transfer. It was so frustrating because I knew Greg was unhappy, but the wheels turn slowly in the Bureau. Greg kept getting into trouble, mostly for fighting. Then Tammy had a heart attack and Jim blamed Greg, even if he never said a word. When Greg got thrown out of the local school for the deaf here, too, I was so desperate to come home that I was ready to quit the Bureau and find another job. I needed to get Greg into a new school and be here when he started."

"He was mainstreamed, then?"

"Yes. And I didn't want him starting a new high school filled with hearing kids on his own."

"He does very well."

"One on one. Not in the classroom. And in the cafeteria at lunch? You might as well put him at a table for one with a big ol' spotlight on it. I needed to be here. Adam helped me get this transfer, and now I'm here and determined to be to Greg what Bruce was to me. The best male role model I can be. I'm not giving up on him."

"You're saying that the two of you are a package deal," Faith said quietly.

"Yes," he answered, and held his breath.

"That's not a deal breaker for me. I like Greg," she said, then smiled when his breath came out in a rush. "So we've made it through day two. What excitement do you have planned for day three?"

"Finding the bastard who wants to kill you," he said soberly.

Her smile disappeared. "Please let me help you. Let me finish going through the Foundation names. At least I can do that much."

"Only if you stay where I know you're safe. That's all I ask, Faith."

"I promise. I'll go to the precinct and I'll stay there all day." She kissed the corner of his mouth tenderly, taking care not to touch the cut on his lip. "Did I do that?"

Just that quickly, his body responded. "Yes. But I kind of liked seeing you all wild."

Her eyes widened as his erection swelled, pressing against her thigh. "We should go back to sleep. But I'm suddenly not very tired."

He smiled down at her. "How might we get tired, then?"

She'd straddled him before he could blink. "I've got an idea or two."

"I was hoping you'd say that."

Chapter Thirty-four

"Good morning, Faith," Isenberg said with a scowl. "Where is Agent Novak?"

Her heart sinking, Faith set her laptop case on Deacon's desk. "He went downstairs to get coffee and Danish." Because when they'd woken up again, they'd forgone breakfast for "just once more" in the warmth of their borrowed bed in the safe house. But now Faith was debating the wisdom of having taken the time for themselves. "What's happened? Is it bad news on Roza?"

Isenberg's scowl relaxed into a slight frown. "No. It's nothing like that. Come with me."

Faith followed her into the conference room and abruptly stopped. The table was completely covered with boxes, three high. More boxes were stacked against the wall, floor to ceiling.

"These were delivered this morning," Isenberg said. "From Henson and Henson."

Faith did a visual count. "These are the Foundation files. Mrs. Lowell said there were a lot, but ... wow. They're labeled by date and ... Mercy, she's indexed all the applications in each box. She must have been up all night with this."

"You gotta love an organized woman like that," Bishop said from behind them. She went straight to the bulletin board, a large folder under one arm. "Or this. Somebody's been busy."

Isenberg shrugged. "I couldn't sleep last night. I have another press conference today, and I wanted a visual that viewers would remember."

Curious, Faith walked up behind them to see the board for herself. "Oh," she said softly. Isenberg had posted photographs of every one of the victims they'd identified to date—and most were happy, smiling, candid shots, not driver's license photos. "How did you get the pictures?"

"From their missing-persons files. Sometimes the families include informal photos."

"So Mrs. Lowell wasn't the only one searching through dusty files all night," Faith said. "It's a lovely memorial, Lieutenant. It shows what he took away. Not just names, but people."

"That's what I thought." Isenberg cleared her throat. "I need a few more photos, Scarlett. Specifically one of Roza. Did you get anything from that sketch artist yesterday?"

Bishop held up the folder. "I did. I went by the hospital this morning to get Corinne's opinion on the sketch since she'd had so much more time with Roza. She said it was 'spot-on.' I also got a sketch of the mystery lady from Maguire and Sons. It's a good bit more vague. The receptionist in the office next door only got a glimpse of her, several months ago."

"If it's all we've got, I'll go with it."

Bishop posted Roza's sketch, and Faith was unprepared for the emotion that hit her like a brick. The child had a gaunt face and big, dark eyes filled with desperation.

"She's terrified," Faith whispered. "And why wouldn't she be? She lived in my basement her whole damn life and I never did anything about it."

Bishop met Faith's eyes, her own stern. "If you'd known, you would have saved her. Roza was brave in that basement. She saved Arianna's life. She was brave in the forest, even though she'd never been outside. She'll hold on until we find her. Don't discount her."

Faith nodded. She turned to the boxes, knowing exactly which file she needed first. Jade Kendrick, Roza's aunt. Thanks to Mrs. Lowell's efforts, she located the box in less than a minute. Another minute later, she had Jade's file in her hand.

"This is the application file for Roza's aunt," she said, walking it over to the bulletin board. She opened the folder and blinked in surprise. "Twins. They were twins."

Cincinnati, Ohio
Thursday, November 6, 8:45 a.m.

"Who were twins?" Deacon asked, walking into the conference room with a tray filled with cups of coffee and pastries. "What happened to the table?"

"Foundation scholarship application files," Bishop said. She shoved a stack of boxes over far enough for Deacon to put his tray down.

"This must be Roza," he said, looking up at the board.

Bishop's smile was sadly lopsided. "With a *zed*."

"Because her mother was from Vancouver," Faith said, her tone odd.

"What do you have, Faith?" Bishop asked.

She didn't look up, continuing to stare at the page before her. "The lieutenant told me yesterday that Roza's real name is Firoza, that her mother was Amethyst Johnson, that her mother and aunt were taken at the same time, and that both were now dead. We didn't find any Amethysts on the list, but we did find a Jade."

"'Firoza' is a kind of turquoise," Isenberg explained. "Faith looked at gemstone names."

"Smart," Bishop said, taking a bite of Danish. "So that's Jade's file?"

"Yes," Faith said. "The Foundation awarded Jade Kendrick a full scholarship to an art college in Chicago."

"Crandall tracked down Jade's missing-persons report yesterday," Isenberg explained. "She disappeared from the college, along with her pregnant sister, Amethyst, who was visiting her from Vancouver."

"The Foundation's file says that Jade was diagnosed with a rare leukemia," Faith said, "the same type that killed Joy, but that Jade underwent treatment and was considered cured."

"All that only to be killed by a sadist," Deacon muttered.

"Maybe not," Faith said, taking out the photograph that was paper-clipped to the file. "The back says 'Jade and Amy, 2001.' Look familiar, Detective Bishop?"

"Holy shit!" Bishop set down her coffee and grabbed the photo. "It's her. Maguire's Mystery Lady." She held the photo next to the artist's sketch. "I think that'll do you better in your press conference, Lynda. Let's get the BOLO out right now."

Deacon froze. *No way. No fucking way.* He snatched the photo from Bishop's hands. "We don't need a BOLO. I've seen this woman. Tuesday morning. She called herself Mary." He caught Faith's gaze, held it. "This is Jordan's housekeeper."

The color drained from her face. "No."

Deacon pulled out a chair and gently pushed her into it. "I'm sorry, honey."

She shook her head. "This is not possible. He couldn't have killed all those women. He couldn't have tried to kill me. He's not even the right size. The man who came through my window was big. The size of Combs. And the man who shot at us from the hotel room across the street was big, too. He was on the camera. You said so. This can't be right."

He crouched beside her chair. "But the man who took Roza matched your uncle's build."

"Stone and Marcus switched places to fool Stone's Fed tail," Bishop added. "Marcus is probably forty pounds lighter but wore a padded coat. From a distance he passed for Stone. Your uncle might have done the same."

Deacon let Faith recover from the initial shock, knowing her denial would be short-lived in the face of facts. It took her less time that he'd expected, confirming that she'd suspected this herself. She was just unable to believe it to be true.

"Arianna said he was soft when she tried to hit him," Faith whispered.

"You're right," he said softly. "I'd forgotten that."

"And if he was wearing a padded suit, he might move stiffly. Like a Michelin Man. Or a robot like Combs's girlfriend said." Tears filled her green eyes, streaked down her pale face. "Why didn't Jade tell my grandmother? She was alone with Gran a lot of the time, taking care of her. Gran would have helped her."

"He had Roza," Deacon said. "Jordan kept Jade in line with threats to Roza."

"That's why he never let Roza's mother say good-bye to

her 'dead sister,'" Bishop said angrily. "He didn't kill her. He's been holding her hostage in plain sight."

"You've never seen her, Faith?" Isenberg asked. "Not in all your visits?"

"No. Whenever I came to visit, Jordan gave her time off. I used her bedroom."

"Then where did he put Jade?" Deacon asked.

Faith shook her head, bewildered. "In the basement?"

"Then Roza might have seen her," Deacon said. He thought of the pink genie. "Maybe he kept her in the apartment over the art gallery. Maybe he has Roza there right now. We've got plenty enough for a warrant."

"I'll get it moving," Bishop said. "We'll turn his place upside down until we find some sign of where he's holding Roza."

"We put unmarked cars outside both his townhouse and gallery yesterday," Deacon said, coming to his feet to join Bishop in the planning. "Jade is still inside the townhouse, and Jordan didn't come home last night. He didn't go to work, either, but add the gallery to the warrant."

They took a few minutes to set up the logistics, and when Deacon turned back to Faith, she was standing in front of the bulletin board, frowning. "What is this list?" she asked.

"A list of diseases that can cause a man not to ejaculate sperm," he said. "Arianna's rape kit was negative for fluids even though he didn't use a condom."

"I remember," she murmured. "Arianna was worried by that." She pointed to the second item on the list. "Testicular cancer. That's what Jordan had when he was seventeen."

"I assumed he had leukemia," Deacon said.

"That was Joy. Jordan's was different." She frowned. "I remember a conversation between my parents, how my mother was complaining about Jordan, that her mother spoiled him so much. Which she did. Gran never held Jordan accountable for anything, but if the rest of us screwed up . . . watch out. Anyway, my dad said Gran felt guilty for causing Jordan's cancer."

"How?" Bishop asked. "That's not a cancer that's caused by anything, is it?"

"I don't know. I can call my father and ask." She turned to the victims' photographs, one arm pressed against her stomach like it hurt. With the other hand, she pointed to the photo of a smiling blonde. "Melinda Hooper was reported missing the day after Tobias's will was read."

Deacon glanced at Bishop. "The day your mother died," he said carefully.

"Yes." She drew a breath. "To answer your question, Detective Bishop, there wasn't a chair. But my mother's toes didn't touch the floor when she was swinging. How did she do that without a chair?"

"What do you think, Faith?" Bishop asked softly.

Deacon held his breath as Faith continued to stare at Melinda Hooper's photo. "I think that it's one hell of a coincidence that Melinda was in the basement being tortured on the same day that my mother hanged herself from the ceiling." She looked from Deacon to Bishop. "You already thought of this, didn't you?"

"Yes," Deacon said. "You'd covered a lot of memories last night. We figured this could wait until you'd had some rest and time to process."

"I'm processing now," she murmured. "Jeremy was standing there, holding the rope. When I started to scream, he let the rope go and grabbed me. Covered my mouth and nose with his hand. What if my mother saw him killing this woman? What if he killed her to keep her from telling anyone?"

"We don't think you're wrong," Bishop said. "Someone keeps trying to kill you. Like he wants to silence you before you remember or before you connect all the dots."

"Well, they are well and truly connected now," she said, a hint of hysteria in her voice. "What can I do? How can I know?"

Deacon smoothed his hand down her hair, hoping to calm her. To take the sting out of what he was going to say. "We can exhume your mother's body. We'd need your permission. But we can probably confirm how she died."

She looked up at him, her eyes suddenly those of a child. "She didn't leave me," she whispered, his suggestion of an exhumation ignored. She was nine years old again and had to process twenty-three years of life seen through a faulty lens. They'd come back to the present soon enough.

"No, I don't think she did," he whispered back.

"Oh my God." The words were nearly inaudible, her breath coming in shallow huffs. Her voice breaking. "All these years I've hated her. But she didn't leave me. She was the victim. All these years, I didn't say a word and he got away with it." She looked away as a quiet sob broke free. "He stole my mother from me. He broke my father's heart and he got away with it." Her chin jerked up, and she met Deacon's eyes, hers fierce with fury. "*He got away with it. And then he killed so many more.*" Angry tears rolled down her cheeks.

Bishop put a tissue in Faith's hand. "We need your help now, Faith. As hard as it is, you're going to have to focus for us for a little while. Can you do that?"

Faith dried her cheeks, nodding unsteadily. "Yes." Carefully, she lowered herself into a chair. "You want to exhume my mother's body. Can I do that without telling my father?"

"Do you have his power of attorney?" Bishop asked.

"I do, since his stroke. So does Lily. But . . ." She hesitated. "Can they even tell anything at this point? The body was . . . badly burned. I saw the photos. I'll never forget it."

Deacon gritted his teeth. "Who showed you the photo of the accident, Faith?"

Her shoulders sagged further. "Jordan. He wanted me to see that no one would ever know that she'd killed herself. He lied to me. Of course he lied to me. He's a killer. Deacon, I let them do that to her. I let them take her away and put her in a car and burn her up."

"You were a child, Faith. Nine years old. You didn't let him do anything."

She shook her head hard. "*Them.* It was *both* of them that day. Jeremy *and* Jordan."

Deacon sighed. "I don't think so, honey. Stone said he remembered the day of the reading of your grandfather's will. He remembered Jeremy coming home devastated because he'd been accused of molesting you by your father, and your mother let it happen. Stone said that the next day they went to Kings Island all day—the four of them: Jeremy, his ex-wife, Stone, and Marcus."

"Stone's lying. Or mistaken. I saw Jeremy in the basement. I *saw* him. I'm not crazy."

"Of course you're not crazy," Bishop said firmly. "But Stone was not lying or mistaken. I went to see Jeremy's ex-wife early this morning, after the three of us finished talking. I asked Della Yarborough about that day at Kings Island."

"You did?" Deacon asked, surprised.

Bishop shrugged. "I wanted to believe Marcus. He behaved like a hero and his story was the same as Stone's. So I went to see his mother. I figured I'd wait until she woke up to see her since it was so early, but she wasn't asleep. Her housekeeper took me up to Mickey's room, where Della was just sitting on his bed, looking lost. When I asked her about Jeremy, she said the same thing that Stone and Marcus did—that Jeremy is a good man. She told me the same story her sons had but added a detail. She was pregnant with Audrey at the time and walked so much that day that she went into labor the next morning. They took a video, Faith. She gave me the cassette. She's as big as a house in the video. Jeremy is in it, too. He even has a black eye from your father hitting him."

"It could have been manipulated," she said stubbornly.

"Possibly," Bishop allowed. "How do you know it was Jeremy you saw in the basement?"

"He had a mustache and parted his hair . . ." Faith let the thought trail. "You think Jordan was pretending to be Jeremy? Why would he do that?"

"To create a scapegoat?" Deacon suggested. "You said Jeremy looked at you in a way that made you uncomfortable. How did you know it was him then?"

"Same way. Oh my God." New tears filled her eyes. "I could have been wrong. All these years he's been estranged from the family because of something I said."

"You were a child," Deacon said insistently. "I'm not saying Jeremy's innocent, but you can't know what you saw when it comes to those two. How often did you see them?"

"Not often. Just when we visited Gran." She dragged her hands down her face, wiping the tears away. She gave herself a little shake. "All right. First things first. Let's exhume my mother's body. I need to know."

"I've got the form ready," Bishop said. "I just need your signature."

"Fine. I'd like to talk to Jeremy."

"Why?" Deacon asked. "What do you hope to accomplish?"

"I want to see his face when I tell him my mother was murdered. And if he's innocent of all the things I've thought all these years, I want to apologize."

Deacon shook his head. "Just because he wasn't there the day of your mother's death doesn't necessarily prove he's innocent of everything else. He and Jordan could still be working together."

"And how can I hope to see guilt or innocence when Jordan has snowed me for so long?"

Deacon swallowed his wince. "Yes," he said simply. "You're not objective."

She nodded once. "I accept that. But don't you want to be watching his face from the other side of the glass when I ask him about my mother?" she challenged.

Deacon let out a breath. "Hell yeah. But you're not leaving this building."

"I'll ask him to come here," Bishop said. "He was touched that you went to bat for him yesterday with Isenberg so that he could be with Marcus. I'll tell him that coming here is for your safety, so he won't feel like he's being interrogated."

Deacon caught Faith's gaze, held it. "We're going to search Jordan's properties now. Do not talk to Jeremy until I get back."

"All right. I promise."

Cincinnati, Ohio
Thursday, November 6, 9:30 a.m.

Faith waited until they were gone, then sank into a chair, trembling. *Jordan wants me dead. He killed all these people. He tortured Arianna. Tortured them all. Every victim on the bulletin board. All the victims in the basement. In Florida.*

And Jeremy? Had he killed? Did he want to kill her, too? Would she even see it in his face if he did? How could she possibly have been so blind?

She closed her eyes as a wave of grief stole her breath. *Mama.* All these years she'd hated her mother. *All these years.* She hunched in on herself, covering her mouth to muffle a whimper, desperately trying to hold it together.

I'm sorry, Mama. I'm sorry. She let herself cry silently for all the times she'd missed her mother. For all the nights her father had drunk himself to sleep alone.

And then she saw Jordan, all those years. Laughing with her. Partying with her. Rock concerts and beer. *Why?* Why would he do that? But when she looked back at those years through the filter of truth, she understood.

He hadn't been laughing with her. He'd been laughing *at* her. And all the partying . . . God. He'd encouraged her to do so many unsafe things. To go with unsafe people. To indulge in a lifestyle that could have easily resulted in her becoming an addict or a drunk. Or dead. Then his problems would have been solved. His dead niece couldn't tell his secret. Couldn't expose him.

And had she tried to tell? Who would have believed her? She'd had a nervous breakdown. She'd snuck out to parties and concerts and into bars on fake IDs. Her grandmother would never have believed her. Jordan had covered all his bases, hadn't he?

Fury suddenly burst within her, burning her up, leaving her cold and focused. And needing revenge. Justice. And answers.

"Why?" she demanded of the empty room. Nervous energy had her surging to her feet, pacing. A clean whiteboard was mounted next to the bulletin board, an irresistible invitation to make a list.

In bold capitals she wrote, *WHY???* And beneath it, she listed her questions. *What made Jordan this way?* She'd slept in the townhouse countless times, oblivious to the danger. *Why didn't he kill me while I slept? What's up with the fake applicants? Who's getting their money? Why didn't an audit pick it up? Why* these *victims?*

She looked at the faces of the victims. *All blond,* she wrote. *All young. All connected to moments of rage.*

All connected to moments when Jordan had lost what he thought should have been his inheritance.

"They got your money," she said quietly. "They got scholarship funds, and that money should have been yours." She shook her head, even as she noted it on the whiteboard. "But it's more than that." Deeper than that. "There's too much rage for it just to be about money."

Of the four O'Bannion children, Joy was the only blonde. The others were redheads. She wrote this down, then stepped back.

"You hate Joy," she said. "You keep killing Joy. She took your money." Her gaze swept over the victims' photographs. "And then all of you took his money."

"I agree."

Faith wheeled around to see Isenberg in a chair behind her, calmly munching a Danish. "When did you get here?" Faith demanded, her hand pressed to her pounding heart.

"I've been here all along," Isenberg said, "sitting behind your boxes. Novak and Bishop had everything under control, so I did my e-mail. But when you started pacing, I wanted to see what you'd do. What you wrote makes sense. And I imagine he didn't kill you in your sleep for the same reason he didn't shoot you when you were at the cemetery on Sunday afternoon. He didn't want to give the police any reason to investigate him."

"He wanted to lure me away and kill me in private. Like maybe in a car accident like the one I had three years ago." Faith turned back to the whiteboard. *What happened three years ago?* she wrote. "It's been nagging at me."

"It should. It's a glaringly missing piece."

"I got a divorce that year. And moved from the house I had with Charlie into this tiny apartment in a bad Miami neighborhood that made Dad nervous." Her heart sank. "And Gran, too. Gran said I needed to leave Miami, that it was too dangerous. That . . ." She swallowed hard. "She said that I should come home." And then Faith knew what she needed to do. Reluctantly, she dialed Henson and Henson.

"Did you get the files?" Mrs. Lowell asked.

Faith put her on speaker. "I did, thank you. Your indexing of the box contents allowed me to find the family of the missing eleven-year-old very quickly. But this morning, I have another question. Can you tell me if my grandmother made any revisions to her will in the last few years?"

"I can check the computer for the change history. . . . Here we are. . . . Barbara filed the original will a few months after her husband died and updated it four times over the years. The last time was three years ago on July twenty-fourth."

Faith drew a breath, struggled to keep her voice calm. Her car accident had been three days later. A week after that, a victim had been taken, tortured, and buried in her basement. "What was the nature of that change?"

"She did a complete overhaul and made you her heir."

Faith had known she'd say that, but still it hurt to hear. "Who was the heir before me?"

"I can't tell you that."

Faith nearly snarled. "Mrs. Lowell, someone has tried repeatedly to kill me since I inherited the house. Someone also tried to kill me on July twenty-seventh, three days after Gran changed her will."

"Oh my goodness," Mrs. Lowell said on a rush. "But . . . I can't tell you, Faith. I'm sorry."

"Was it Jordan? *Please,* Mrs. Lowell. Not only has someone tried to kill me since I inherited the house, they have killed *twelve people* in the last month, trying to get to me. I can't go on like this, wondering who is going to be next. *Was it Jordan?*"

An exhale. "Faith. I can't tell you that it was. But I won't tell you that it wasn't."

Faith shuddered out a breath, her suspicion confirmed. "All right. Can you tell me who managed the books for the Foundation and whether we've been audited? As I'll be taking on my grandmother's place on the board, I need to know."

Mrs. Lowell's answer was wary. "The board hired Michelle Vance as its accountant. We haven't been audited in some time, actually. Not since Mr. Henson Junior was here. Why?"

"I'm familiarizing myself with the financial aspects of the Foundation. How might I reach Mr. Henson Junior?"

Dead silence. "Y-you can't."

"Is he deceased? I thought I saw a plaque on the wall saying he'd retired."

"He did retire, but not really. He's been hospitalized for fifteen years. He is, um, in a permanent vegetative state."

Faith closed her eyes. "Did he have a car accident, Mrs. Lowell?"

"Yes, he did," she said, surprised. "How did you know that?"

"The attempt on my life three years ago was also a car accident. Last week my old car was tampered with and the person who bought it died. Along with her son."

A long, long pause followed by a shaky reply. "Since Mr. Henson Junior was hospitalized, his affairs have been handled by his wife, Michelle Vance."

Faith's mouth fell open. "The Foundation's accountant? I . . . I see. Thank you, Mrs. Lowell." She disconnected the call and met Isenberg's level gaze. "You're not surprised."

"Follow the money. Especially big, fat pots of it being administered by little old ladies."

"True enough. So how about this . . . Somebody creates fake applicants, the board considers them without seeing their names because they don't want to be biased. Some will be approved, others will not, but the people writing the fake apps will know how to best influence the board."

"Makes sense."

Faith stood to pace off some of her pent-up energy. "The checks for fake applicants are prepared, brought by Jordan to my grandmother to be signed, because he managed all of her mail. Mrs. Lowell enters the name, date, and amount, and she mails the checks and is none the wiser. Jordan finds out because *he's* looking for Foundation recipients to murder but, lo and behold, some of them don't exist."

"The very nerve of them," Isenberg said dryly.

"Henson Junior's wife must have known. As the accountant, she'd have to report the social security numbers of the recipients, and the Foundation hasn't been audited by the IRS. She must be submitting fraudulent tax statements. Maybe Jordan knew all along, maybe he even made up the scam, but he's known about this for at least fifteen years, because Junior was hurt in a car accident. Henson the third's involvement is unclear, but he's generally dodgy, so my bet is, he's in on it. Is this enough for a forensic audit of their books?"

"It is if you're on the board and you request it."

"Oh yeah." Startled, Faith grinned at her. "I forgot I have power."

Isenberg smiled. "Power and guts. And intelligence. If you ever get tired of working at the bank, you might consider working for the police department."

The bank. "Oh crap." Faith rolled her eyes. "I totally forgot that I got fired yesterday."

Isenberg's smile disappeared. "Why?"

"Detective Kimble's inquiry to my boss made him believe that I was a suspect."

Isenberg's lips thinned. "I'm sorry."

"It's okay. I don't want to work for a company that is so quick to judge me. I may go back to therapy. For now I'm going back to work on the victim lists. It's keeping me sane, I think."

Chapter Thirty-five

Cincinnati, Ohio
Thursday, November 6, 11:30 a.m.

Deacon stood in the conference room doorway, taking a moment to simply look at Faith, who sat at the table surrounded by stacks of paper, staring at her laptop. She was sexy when she concentrated, he thought. Of course, she was sexier when they were having sex, but that was not a topic he should be thinking about standing out in the open like this.

"You might try not to look so besotted," Isenberg said behind him.

He huffed a chuckle. "I'll try. What's she doing?"

"She and the clerks are still working the list we got from that lawyer Henson. Things got a little interesting while you were gone." She told him about Faith's conversation with Mrs. Lowell, and Deacon's pride for her grew.

"She mapped the whole thing out, huh?"

Isenberg pointed to the whiteboard, covered in questions and lists and boxes with arrows pointing to other boxes. "The DA's drafting the warrants for the Foundation financials."

"Do we know where Herbie Three and his mother the accountant are?"

"Oh yes. I know where they are precisely. An hour after Mrs. Lowell talked to Faith, she called back. She'd pulled copies of the tax returns and showed them to Henson Senior, who then called both his daughter-in-law and his grandson into his office under the pretense of giving them performance bonuses. He held them there for us. They are now in Central Booking. Now for the big question—do we know where Jordan is? I assume not, or you would have led with that."

"We know where he's not. He's not in his townhouse or his art gallery or the apartment above it. We have Jade in custody, but she's going to be a hard nut to crack."

Faith looked up from her computer, eyes wide. "She doesn't want to help Roza?" she asked, and he realized she'd been listening to his update while continuing her task.

"She does," he said, "and that's the problem. She is terrified that Jordan will find out she's talked. She keeps going on about cameras everywhere, and she's right. We found cameras in every room of that house. He can watch her anywhere at any time. She has no privacy."

Faith paled a little. "I lived there for two years when I was in high school. I stayed there when I visited Gran. Was he watching me, too?"

Deacon's jaw tightened. "Maybe not during the two years because that was long before he abducted Jade and Amethyst. But during the last ten years when you visited? Probably."

Faith pressed her lips together. "That is extremely disturbing, but I won't think about it now. What did you find in his townhouse?"

"Nothing indicating where he might go. There was no sign that Roza had been there, but we did find Alda Lane in the bed, high on heroin and still wearing the genie costume from Tuesday. She's pretty ripe."

Isenberg shook her head. "Lovely. Where is she now?"

"Also in Central Booking. She admitted that Jordan was supplying her habit and, in return, she was his alibi. The photo she showed me of him passed-out drunk had been taken over a week ago. He'd instructed her to tell people he was asleep if they came asking for him." Deacon shook his head. "I should have questioned her further on Tuesday. I just figured she was eccentric and a little drunk."

"I should have followed the money earlier," Isenberg said. "We didn't have anything to hold Jordan on at the time. We do now, so we need to find him. For little Roza and all the other victims on the bulletin board. I have a press conference at two, and I'm going to prepare. Update me at quarter till two with whatever you know."

"Will do. Lynda, wait. Where is Adam? I haven't seen him all morning."

Isenberg became abruptly administrative. "He's on leave. That's all I can say."

"What?" Deacon took a step after her when she walked away. "His idea or the department's?"

"His. Talk to him if you want any more than that."

"I will." Frustrated, Deacon sat at the table next to Faith.

"He should've been on leave all week," she said softly. "He's been a powder keg, ready to blow. That he realized it and took leave himself is positive."

"I know, but . . ." He shook off his concern. Adam was an adult. He'd have to deal. "I have something for you." From his pocket he drew both her original iPhone and the non-traceable phone she'd purchased only to have it damaged in the hotel shooting. "The lab has fully checked your iPhone. No bugs, no tracking devices. But to be sure, they completely wiped it and replaced the SIM card. You still have the same number, but everything else is gone. Combs never had access to your phone."

"Then how did he know where to find me during all the months he stalked me?"

"You said yourself that you don't like change. Did you have a routine?"

She nodded. "It would have to be simple," she grumbled. "Thank you for my phone, though. I feel like a real person again." She held up the broken phone. "Why did you give this back? It's broken."

"Just the screen. You still have some minutes on it. And some people like to keep souvenirs of items they were holding during a near miss. That's one of the reasons I keep my old coat. I've repaired a lot of bullet holes and I keep on going."

"I do not like to hear that," she said darkly. "What about the phone Jordan gave me?"

"It's got tracking software installed. He would have known that you were going to the house yesterday. He might have followed and shot you somewhere along the way. Or worse."

"Which was what you were afraid of," she said softly.

He nodded. "I had a bad moment or two when Vince told me that. But we're going to find him and then you'll be free again."

"Until then, I'll be careful." She put the broken phone in her pocket and checked the iPhone. "I have a missed call already. From Vega. An hour ago."

Deacon checked his own phone. "She called me, too, just five minutes ago. I must have been in the elevator because I didn't hear it. Call her back."

Faith dialed, putting Vega on speaker. "Detective, it's Faith. I'm sorry I missed your call."

"I'm sorry, too. I thought we'd use FaceTime so that you could see his expression when he apologized to you, but he's gone now."

"Who?"

"Oh, your ex. I don't like loose ends, and I kept thinking about Combs's girlfriend knowing about the picture you took of Combs leaving that little girl's house. I brought Charlie Frye into my LT's office, and the three of us had a chat. Did you know that Charlie visited Combs in jail?"

"No. I had no idea. Why did he do that?"

"To find out if Combs was lying about you having an affair with him. Charlie had seen the photo of Combs on your phone while you were in the hospital. When Combs accused you in court, Charlie went to see him. He showed Combs the picture that he'd gotten from your phone, said that it proved his guilt. But he said that Combs had a perfectly logical explanation, that he'd been at the house to see the girl's *mother*, not the girl, and that you'd been stalking him out of jealousy. Because Charlie was cheating on you, he found it plausible that you were cheating on him. Still, he said he didn't believe Combs until he started talking about a birthmark you have in a very intimate place. Charlie was a believer then. Any idea how Combs would know that?"

"Yeah," Deacon said tightly. "I do, actually. Faith's uncle had cameras in the room where she stayed when she visited." And in the bathroom, but he wasn't going to make this worse for Faith by telling her that.

"Agent Novak, didn't know you were there, too. You've spoiled my grand finale."

Deacon frowned. "What?"

"Charlie didn't look at Faith's phone on his own. Guess who showed him the photo?"

"Jordan," Faith said. "He got to my bedside even before my dad and Lily did. Gran chartered a flight for Jordan, and my folks had to drive from Savannah. Jordan had my phone."

"Your uncle also continued to call Charlie for updates on you, even after your divorce. He knew Combs had been stalking you for nine months because Charlie told him so."

"So he knew that Combs would be blamed for the attempts on my life."

"He had a ready-made scapegoat," Vega agreed. "We think your uncle killed Combs to keep him from getting caught. If Combs ended up having an alibi for any of the murder attempts, we might have broadened the investigation. *If* we'd investigated," she added with disgust. "I have one other thing for you, Novak. I tried to call you. My sketch artist just uploaded the sketch she did of Combs's shooter based on the girlfriend's description. I sent it to your e-mail as soon as I got it."

Deacon opened his e-mail on his phone and showed the photo to Faith, who swallowed hard. It was Jordan with a big coat and a bald head. "It's her uncle Jordan, but we never knew he was bald. His wig must be high quality. I wonder why he took it off."

"I wondered the same. I checked the weather, and we'd had a hellacious storm that evening. Tropical storm winds. His wig may have gotten wet, or he may have taken it off to keep it from being blown away. So I take it you already knew who we were looking for? A call might have been nice."

"I'm sorry," Deacon said. "We only knew for sure two hours ago ourselves. We believe he's here in Cincinnati. Our one ace in the hole is that he doesn't know we're looking for him. He's been setting up his brother to take the fall. Or they might be working together. We're not sure yet. We're just hoping he makes a mistake soon."

"I hope he does, too. Be careful. Call if you need anything."

Faith disconnected the call. "I think I'd like to see Jeremy now. I have too many questions and not enough answers."

Cincinnati, Ohio
Thursday, November 6, 12:00 p.m.

Finally. He'd been waiting hours for the pair to leave the hospital, and Dr. Dani's ancient car was damn uncomfortable. He had his binoculars ready, focused on the keypad on the Range Rover's driver's-side door.

1-4-3-6-1. The driver's door opened, and Keith got in, leaned over, and opened the door for Jeremy. The two of them pulled out of their parking place and headed out of the parking garage, a squad car following at a discreet distance.

That was a problem. He'd have to figure out what to do about the tail. He fell into line, following the cop who was following his target. Worst case, he'd shoot him.

What was one more at this point?

He followed the little convoy to . . . the police station. Not good. He hoped they wouldn't keep the pair too long. He had plans for the afternoon.

He drove past them when they parked in a spot in front of the police station, watching from his rearview as the pair entered the building, followed by their uniformed tail. If they were aware they were being followed by a cop, they gave no indication.

They had to know. Which meant the cop was a guard, not a tail. That made a difference. He drove around the block, parking a fair distance away, filling the meter with coins. Nobody would notice Dr. Dani's car for some time, and when they did, they'd chase their tails for a while, running the stolen license plates he'd switched with the ones that had been on her car. Every little delay gave him time to get his ducks in a row.

He checked his reflection in the mirror. Mustache, check. Gloved right hand in pocket, check. Sagging shoulders and bags under his eyes, check. He got out of Dani's car and ambled to the Range Rover, tapped in the key code, and got into the backseat. Any street cams would capture the car's owner getting into his own car. No worries.

He'd learned long ago how to hide in plain sight. Just act naturally and everyone assumed you were supposed to be doing whatever it was you were doing. It was when a person got nervous that they raised suspicion.

And he never got nervous.

Cincinnati, Ohio
Thursday, November 6, 12:30 p.m.

"He looks so old," Faith said, watching Jeremy through the glass in the observation area.

"His car accident aged him, I think," Deacon said. "He lost his career and his lover in one fell swoop."

"More car accidents," she murmured. "Is the big guy his partner?"

"Yes. He's Keith O'Bannion. Husband, assistant, and bodyguard."

"Did Crandall get a list of Jeremy's ex-wife's properties?"

"He did. I'll forward the list to you. Are you ready to talk to him?"

"I think so. It's only been twenty-three years."

She was nervous, he realized. He squeezed her hand briefly. "You'll be fine."

Both men at the table jumped to their feet when they entered the interview room. Faith hung back for a moment, her eyes locked with Jeremy's.

"Uncle Jeremy? I'm Faith. Maggie's daughter." She held out her hand, and Deacon could see it tremble.

Jeremy searched her face, his expression wistful and sad, before taking her right hand in his left. "I would know you anywhere, Faith. You look just like your mother."

Faith's swallow was audible. "I'm so sorry for the loss of your son."

"Thank you," Jeremy whispered.

"Thank you for coming here to talk to me. I'm limited as to where I can go without someone getting hurt. Can we sit down?"

Deacon stood where he could see Jeremy's face and also monitor Keith. He still wasn't sure about the two men. He wasn't going to let anything else happen to Faith.

Jeremy sat beside her, then assessed the cut on her head. "How did this happen?"

"I swerved to avoid a person in the road on Monday night. She'd been held in the basement of the old house. Arianna Escobar. She was kidnapped along with Corinne, the woman whose life Marcus saved. We're very grateful."

"The Longstreet woman's also responsible for Stone being in the hospital," Keith grumbled.

Jeremy sighed. "He kind of deserved it. Stone doesn't think. What can I do for you, Faith?"

She drew a breath. "I think the man who killed your son also killed my mother."

Jeremy frowned, worried. As if she were crazy. "Your mother died in a car accident, Faith."

Her smile was sad. "I need to tell you a story. I'll keep it short, but please let me finish."

She told him about the family arguments, about her father driving away, about finding her mother swinging from the rope. His eyes had widened, but he said nothing until she told him that he was the one she'd witnessed cutting her mother's body down.

"That's ludicrous!" he burst out. "I wasn't even there."

"I know that now. But . . . the man holding the rope looked like you. He had his hair combed like yours. He had a mustache. Even his clothes . . . they were your style."

"It was Jordan," he said slowly. "Had to have been."

"I think so, too. Now. But for twenty-three years, whenever I had a nightmare about that moment, it was you holding the rope. It was Jordan who came to me later to tell me that the two of you had faked her car accident. And that her body was burned."

"Jordan was even kind enough to show her photos of her mother's charred corpse," Deacon added sarcastically.

Jeremy looked horrified. "He *showed* you? Why?"

"I guess he wanted me to see that nobody would question that she'd died in a crash. That her suicide would remain our little secret." He opened his mouth, but Faith held up her hand. "One more thing. The fight the day before, after the will was read? Between you and my father?"

"Your father broke my nose," he said bitterly.

"And my mother broke your heart because she didn't defend you."

"Your father was such a fanatic. They knew I was gay by then. It had all come out the week before." He shook his head. "Because of Jordan. Anyway, your father thought that all gays were perverts. I couldn't believe your mother believed such a horrible thing about me."

"She believed it because of me," Faith said, her brow crunched and worried. "Because I told her and my father that you'd made me very uncomfortable with the way you'd looked at me and touched me. When you tried to comfort me that day they read Tobias's will, both of my parents saw it through the lens of what I'd told them about the 'last time' you'd touched me."

Again the horror. "But I didn't."

"Someone with a mustache, hair, and clothes like yours did."

His face went slack with shock. "Oh my God. Faith. All these years?"

Her lips trembled. "I'm sorry. I'm sorry that I made the family hate you."

Jeremy patted her hand absently. Using his left hand, Deacon noted. His right remained in his pocket. If he was faking his injury, he was very careful. "I appreciate you making it clear."

"Wait," Keith said. "What about your mother being murdered? You said it was suicide."

"I thought it was. It might still be, but . . ." She told Jeremy about the scholarship recipients and the dates they'd gone missing. Then let him put it together.

"All those bodies. In the basement. You're sure?"

"Eighteen so far," Faith said. "Many more in the last month as he tried to kill me."

"Because you'd inherited the house?"

"It made sense before we knew what lay beneath the floor. Afterward, someone kept trying to kill me, and that didn't make sense. Why kill me now? Maybe revenge for messing with his stuff, but in that case he could wait until I'm out of a safe house and walking the street. He's taken very big risks to take me out. The cover-up of my mother's 'suicide' is the only thing that's left. It's not enough to kill me over."

"But the murder of your mother is," Jeremy said. "Because she saw the victim who'd gone missing that day and was probably in the basement?"

"Maybe. We're exhuming her body to know for sure. I need to know for sure."

"I understand. I'd like to know as well." He patted her hand again. "I have to get back to Marcus and Stone now."

Faith blew out a breath. "I'm sorry, I'm not doing this well. Not only were you implicated twenty-three years ago, you're being implicated now."

"I know. Detective Bishop told me yesterday that the victims had been stitched by a professional. And, of course, I know that my cabin was used."

"It looks like Jordan is involved, but he doesn't have surgery skills. You do. So either you are also involved or he's figured out how to make you appear involved. Based on what I know, the second one makes more sense. Haven't you wondered why your son was killed?"

"Wrong place, wrong time. He ran away because he found out his father wasn't a rich Russian businessman but a 'broken-down homo.' His words. Not mine."

"It was not the wrong place. He had every right to be there. His killer didn't."

"I can't believe Jordan killed my son. Mickey was his nephew. He wouldn't kill his own flesh and blood."

"I'm his niece and he's tried to kill me . . . how many times, Agent Novak?"

"Eight. Seven in the last month. He's killed twelve people, including a child and a federal agent, trying to get to Faith. Your son got in his way. I'm sorry, sir."

"And Jordan didn't know Mickey was yours," Keith reminded him softly.

Jeremy's jaw grew rigid. "Where is he?"

"We don't know," Faith said. "But wherever he is, he's got a hostage."

"The eleven-year-old Detective Bishop mentioned yesterday," Jeremy said.

"Roza," she said. "If he runs to pattern, he'll try to pin this on you. He chose your ex-wife's cabin to bury some of his bodies. He might choose one of her other properties to hide. We want to find him before it's too late. I know you want to get back to Stone and Marcus, but can you take a look at this list of your ex-wife's holdings and tell us which ones he's most likely to choose?"

Jeremy's cheek muscles flexed as he ground his teeth. "Sonofabitch," he whispered. "He kills my son and then tries to pin his crimes on me? Let me see that list."

It took him only a minute. "The one near Woodland Mound, down on the river. The entrance to 275 is only five minutes away. It has sensors to let him know you're coming. It's also up high on a hill, so he'll see you long before you see him. What else do you need?"

"Give me just a minute." Deacon texted Isenberg with the house's location so that a tactical squad could be mobilized but used only if the way was clear. If Jordan was keeping Roza there, they didn't want to storm in and get her killed. "Since Jordan seems to have posed as you several times, can you give us any identifying marks that set the two of you apart?"

"I have a scar above my lip. Got it when we were kids. That's why I have the mustache." Jeremy hesitated. "Jordan has only . . ."

"Only one ball," Keith finished bluntly.

"He had cancer when we were seventeen," Jeremy said. "He's infertile."

Faith tilted her head, puzzled. "How did you know that, Keith?"

He shrugged. "It's my business to know everything that threatens Jeremy."

"Keith is very conscientious and his memory is long. We've known each other since high school, when Jordan was not kind to either of us. The trouble with my family came to a head two weeks before my father died."

"Because Jordan outed you," Deacon said. "Because you were going to tell your father he was skimming Foundation funds."

"I did tell my father, and Jordan's strategy backfired. It appears that our father could hate me for being gay and listen to my accusations about Jordan's embezzlement at the same time. He investigated and found out I was right. He told Jordan that he would never work for the Foundation again. Jordan was livid. Blamed it on me, vowed retribution."

"What kind of retribution?" Faith asked.

"The usual. He'd ruin me. Make me sorry I was ever born. That kind of thing." Jeremy's eyes dropped to the desk. "He's done that now. My son is dead."

"Twenty-three years later," Faith said softly. "What did he do twenty-three years ago?"

"Went to Della, told her what I was. He hoped she'd throw me out. Humiliate me."

"But your ex already knew," Deacon said. "Stone told us that she knew all along."

A weary nod. "Della and I met when I was working my

way through undergrad. She was thirty, lonely, had just divorced a gold-digger—Stone and Marcus's father. She was wary of being wanted for her money. I was wary of family only wanting me for parts. We hit it off."

Faith blinked at him. "That's a strange thing to say, Uncle Jeremy. For *parts*?"

Jeremy studied her face. "How much do you know about Joy, Faith?"

"Obviously not enough."

"Joy had leukemia. This was the late sixties, and there were limited treatments then. Bone marrow transplants had only been done with identical twins. Then, in 'sixty-eight, a transplant was done with siblings, and everyone was so excited. But your mother wasn't a match for Joy."

"No way," Faith said. "Are you going to say that Gran had you for your bone marrow?"

"Yes. I didn't know until I was about eight. Jordan had done something bad and Father was furious, as he always was. He blurted it out in a rant, how worthless we were. That Joy should still be alive. That was hard to understand at eight. It's hard to understand at forty-four."

"Was Jordan angry about being conceived for his marrow?"

"Oh yes," he said with a nod. "Especially when he got cancer himself. Do you know what DES is?"

"No."

"It's a drug that was given to pregnant women to prevent miscarriages. It's now banned. My mother was older and nearly miscarried three times. She was desperate to hold on to us."

"Because of Joy," Faith murmured. "She needed your bone marrow."

"Exactly. The doctor put Mother on DES to save the pregnancy. DES is linked to many kinds of cancers in the daughters exposed in utero. In the sons, there is a tentative link to testicular cancer. I don't believe for a moment either the doctor or Mother knew the possible side effects at the time, but when Jordan got cancer . . . Mother felt guilty that she'd given it to him, especially since having us didn't even help Joy."

"That's terrible on every level," Faith said.

"I know. Jordan hated Joy. He hated me because I wasn't

angry and because I didn't get sick. We were twins, and in his mind we were supposed to do everything the same way. He hated Maggie because she and I were close. He hated Mother and Father and the staff. Jordan was a difficult person to live with. He'd get into these rages and then you'd see him a few hours later and he'd be fine. Inevitably we'd find something broken. Or dead. A bird, the cat. My dog. We could never prove it, and Mother would never believe it. Father didn't care. He kind of closed up shop when Joy died. Now I realize he suffered from depression, but then it just hurt that his grief over Joy was bigger than any love for us."

"I knew Jordan didn't like you, but I never got that he hated your mother or mine."

"Because he's very good at hiding it. He'd lash out when you'd least expect it and in ways that could never point to him. When I realized he was siphoning off Foundation money, I didn't say a word until I had incontrovertible proof."

"Which was?"

"Copies of his bank statements—a secret account. He kept the papers hidden. I wouldn't have known had I not watched where he'd filed them. I made copies of them and of the Foundation statements. That's what I gave to our father two weeks before he died. A week later Jordan was kicked out of the Foundation."

"A week?" Faith asked, and Deacon knew she was thinking of the victim who'd been taken then and the one taken a week later, when Jordan had realized he was getting nothing.

"Almost exactly. When my father disowned me, I was actually relieved. Ours was a desperately unhappy family that I couldn't wait to leave. I've made my own family with Della and now with Keith. I love my children like my parents never loved me. And now I've lost one." Pain slashed across his features. "I used to hate my mother for having me only for parts, but now I know how she felt, what it's like to lose a child. I would do almost anything to give Mickey back his life. I suppose I can't hate my mother too much for wanting to save Joy." He stood unsteadily. "I need to get back to my children and to Della. She's not doing well."

"I can't imagine what she's going through right now."

"You can, a little," Jeremy said. "You lost your mother."

Faith swallowed hard. "Twenty-three years ago."

"But you didn't know the truth until now. The pain is fresh and you have to grieve. Just like we will over Mickey." He clasped her shoulder with his left hand. "You're all I have left of my sister, and the time is right to put the past behind us. Do you have my number?"

"No, so let me enter it into my phone." When she finished, she gave him a sad smile. "Take care, Jeremy."

Deacon had the two men escorted to the lobby by an officer, then turned to Faith. "I'm going out to the property he mentioned. I've got the SWAT team closing in, securing all the exits."

"Do you still think he's involved?"

"I don't want to. I want to like him. Bishop thinks he genuinely cares for his sons. If that's the case, he could never hurt Mickey. And if he ever had been working with Jordan? I don't think he is now."

"How can I be sure?"

"I don't know yet, but we'll figure it out. Stay—"

"Stay here, stay safe. Yeah, yeah." She pulled his head down for a quick kiss on the mouth. "Go. Find Roza. And you stay safe, too. He's focused on you now, as well."

Cincinnati, Ohio
Thursday, November 6, 1:20 p.m.

God, what are they doing in there? He'd been curled up on the floorboard in the back of the Range Rover for nearly an hour. Maybe they weren't coming back. Maybe they had been arrested.

That would be most inconven— *Ah. Voices. Coming this way.* He stayed down, waiting.

The driver's door opened first, and the gorilla got in, leaned over, and opened the door for his twin, who slid into his seat, a hangdog expression on his face.

"I'm tired, Keith."

"You want me to take you home? I can make you some soup."

"No. Take me to Della's. I'm afraid she'll do something to herself, and then the boys and Audrey will have to deal with the grief of that, too."

Keith started the car. "She's stronger than you give her credit for. She doesn't need you."

Jeremy turned to Keith, anger heating his face. "You need to lay off. I had a life with Della, and she was good to me when I needed a friend. She needs me now."

"She shielded you and you hid behind her."

"So what if I did?" A huff of irritation. "Take me to Della's or get the hell out and let me drive myself."

I like that better. Get out. Get out.

"No, I'll drive you. I just don't have to like it."

And then they were off. The pair were silent until they'd left downtown.

"Where's the cop?" the gorilla asked.

"I don't know," came the weary reply. "Maybe we passed a test."

That's music to my ears. He really hated killing cops. It was usually more trouble than it was worth. Except for Susan Simpson. She'd been completely worth it.

But Susan was gone now. In the hands of the cops. They'd taken all of his things. He was going to have to start over. But he would manage it. *I'm far stronger than anyone gives me credit for, too.*

He stayed in position until the Range Rover got on the highway. Then he eased up, pushing the barrel of his pistol against the temple of his twin, who gasped. "Keith!"

"Both hands on the wheel where I can see them, Keith," he said calmly. "If you take one pinky off that wheel, I'll blow his fucking head off. And you know that I will." He shoved his pistol harder against his twin's temple. "Both hands on the dash, Jeremy, even the gimpy one."

"What do you want, Jordan?" Jeremy asked, furious but obedient.

"What I've always wanted. Everything."

Cincinnati, Ohio
Thursday, November 6, 1:20 p.m.

"Is she stable?" Faith asked Bishop as they stood on the observation side of the glass. On the other side was Jade Kendrick, hunched into as small a space as she could manage.

Bishop shrugged. "I'm going to try to talk to her. Do you think you can keep her calm?"

"I can try. Are you asking me for a consult?"

She shrugged again. "I heard you're back to therapy. Isenberg said you got canned."

"Like a tuna. Come on. Let's try to talk to Jade."

Jade didn't look up when they came in, her gaze steadfastly pointed to her feet.

"Hi, Jade. I'm Faith."

Jade's head jerked up, her eyes wide. "You're Barbara's granddaughter."

"Yes. And you're Roza's aunt. Can I sit down?"

Jade nodded. "I can't tell you anything. He'll kill her. He'll kill me."

"I don't think he'll kill her," Faith said. "She's too valuable as leverage. He wants me."

"Why?"

"Because I'm a threat to him. I know his secrets. He tricked me into keeping them when I was only nine years old." She told Jade about her mother, about how Jordan had manipulated her. "He wants me dead. He will trade Roza for me. I hope we can find him before it comes down to that. Jade, why didn't you tell my grandmother? I know she liked you."

"She wouldn't have believed me. She doted on Jordan. Let him get away with just about everything. I think, in a way, she was a little afraid of him, too. She was dependent on him. If she complained, he'd find out."

"The cameras. I know."

"There was never any privacy for either of us. She put on a happy face because she knew he was watching."

"Did he hurt her? My grandmother?"

"No, not like that. But he hurt me, and I think she knew that. That's why I couldn't tell her about Amy or Roza. She couldn't even defend herself. He always knew what I was doing. And then he'd disappear for days and I'd know what he was doing to some poor woman." Her eyes filled with tears. "I'd hate him, but I'd be a little relieved, too, because he wasn't doing it to me."

"That's human," Faith said softly. "You can't be angry with yourself over that. It will have to come with time. When he sent you 'on vacation' when I came to visit, where did you go?"

"To his house."

Bishop leaned forward. "You mean his apartment over the studio?"

"No. It's an actual house. I don't know where it is, though. He always tied, blindfolded, and gagged me. Put plugs in my ears so I couldn't hear anything. He'd park in the garage and take me out of the van, so I never saw the neighborhood. He'd take me straight to the basement. Sometimes he'd stay with me, but if he had a woman in the other basement where he kept Amy and Roza, then he'd go there."

"Did you know where he was keeping Amy and Roza?" Faith asked carefully.

"No." Jade looked away. "For a long time I thought it was Mrs. O'Bannion's old place, but when she described the basement, it was nothing like the place where we were kept. That's when I first learned he had cameras all over the townhouse. He played back a tape of me talking to his mother. And then he took me to the other basement—the one in his other house. He told his mother that he'd given me two weeks' vacation, because that's how long it took for the bruises to fade. Then he showed me a photo of Amy. Her bruises were much worse. He said he'd do that to Roza if I asked again."

"We understand," Faith said. "In the other house, was there anything you noticed in particular?"

"Only on the inside. He had a portrait of Joy on the wall in the basement, but he'd slashed the face. It wasn't the same one your grandmother had in her bedroom. I think he did the portrait himself, just to give himself something to destroy."

"Did you ever go anywhere with him?" Bishop asked, and she nodded, dropping her chin.

"We went to Miami once. We took his van, and he drove the whole way. He shot your friend, the man."

"Gordon Shue?"

"Yes. And then we tried to push you off the bridge. He made me shoot at you. I missed on purpose. I couldn't kill you, even to save Roza. God help me, I hope he's not hurting her now."

"Thank you for not killing me," Faith said gently. "I'll do my best to bring Roza back to you. She has a father, right? Eric Johnson?"

She nodded. "He and Amy got married while they were at college, and they were so happy." She stopped abruptly, then asked, "My parents? Are they still alive?"

"Yes," Faith said. "They've been contacted and they're on their way."

Jade's shoulders shook as she started to cry. "Thank you. Thank you."

Faith touched Jade's shoulder gently, swallowing her wince when she felt only sharp bone beneath the thin T-shirt she wore. "We have to go now, but we'll come back. And as soon as we find Roza, we'll let you know. At least we know who we're dealing with now."

Out in the hall, Bishop leaned against the wall, frustration etched deep into her face. "Any idea where this house could be?"

"No, not one. Has Deacon had success at Jeremy's ex's estate?"

"I haven't heard anything. I don't know."

"Then I guess we brainstorm how we can track him to this mystery house."

Chapter Thirty-six

He put down his garage door before opening the back of the van. He smiled at the snarling pair. "Welcome to my home. Don't worry, you won't be here long."

He'd parked the Range Rover not far from the small airport he'd scoped out as his plan B should he fail to get Faith this afternoon. If he absolutely had to, he could run. But he didn't want to run. He wanted to fight for who he was and what he'd built.

He'd forced the gorilla to restrain his twin's hands with zip-ties, then restrain his own. He'd marched them to a white panel van that he'd stolen a few years ago but had been keeping for a rainy day. This qualified, he thought. Once they were in the van, he zipped their ankles.

Now he rolled them out of the van, keeping them restrained. He dropped them from the van to the cement floor of his garage. Not a huge drop, but enough to make his weakling brother grunt in pain. Always a bonus.

The gorilla was so damn stoic and powerful, he thought he needed to even the odds. Making sure his silencer was on tight, he fired two shots at him, one in each knee. The gag stifled his cries. A strip of duct tape silenced him further.

Satisfied, he crouched down and pulled the gag from his twin's mouth, keeping his gun trained on his groin. "One question, and if you scream I will shoot your balls off. What were you doing in the police station today?"

"Talking to Faith," Jeremy said through clenched teeth.

"About?"

"I wanted to buy the house from her."

Jordan laughed. "Why?"

"So I could burn it down. I have plenty of money. I can afford it."

That actually made sense. "Okay."

"Wait. I have a question."

"This ain't quid pro quo, Jeremy." He sighed. "Fine. One question."

"Did you kill my son?"

He blinked at him. "No. Wounded him. Didn't kill him. Tried to."

"No, my other son. The boy they found in the grave with the Earl Power employee."

His mouth fell open. "That was *your* son?" He laughed. "That squatter was really lord of the manor? Now, *that's* irony. Yeah, I killed him. Now, I have to go. When I get back, I'll let you go."

"Right," Jeremy said grimly. "You'll let me go."

He cut a piece of duct tape and pressed it over Jeremy's mouth, making sure to cover his mustache. Whoever removed it would rip the mustache right off his skin. Then he stood up and dusted his hands. "I have to reload my van. You can stay here." He covered both men with a blanket. "Sweet dreams."

Woodland Mound, Ohio
Thursday, November 6, 3:30 p.m.

"There's nothing here, Agent Novak."

Deacon leaned against his SUV, looking through his binoculars at the land belonging to Jeremy's ex-wife. There wasn't a ripple of dust, not a speck of dirt out of place.

"You're right," he said to the SWAT leader. "This was a wild-goose chase."

"You think we were led here on purpose?"

"I don't know. I wanted to believe Jeremy. Jordan's obviously gone somewhere else. I'll leave a squad car here to watch for him in case he comes, but we're wasting our time now." He was starting to make the call when Bishop called him. "What do you have?"

"According to Jade, he has another house," Bishop said. "Where?"

"She doesn't know. We're bringing in the team to brainstorm."

"I'm on my way." As he got into his car, his phone rang again. "Novak."

"It's Jim." And he sounded scared.

Deacon paused, his hand on the ignition. "What's wrong? Is it Tammy?"

"No, it's Greg. He's gone. We let him sleep in this morning, but when he didn't come out of his room, we went in. He left a note that he'd gone to Dani's, but Deacon, she's not here. I'm in her apartment and she's not here."

"She texted me from the Meadow last night. She was staying at the shelter and had a couple of off-duty CPD cops to watch over her."

"No, we checked there. She didn't go in last night. We've been checking all the places both Greg and Dani go. All morning." Jim's voice cracked and broke. "She's gone, Deacon."

Deacon's heart jumped into his throat. "Maybe she's at work."

"No. I called. She texted that she was sick and that she wasn't coming in."

No, no, no. His stomach lurched and he nearly threw up.

"And, Deacon? There's blood on her carpet. It's soaked through. Still tacky to the touch."

No. Not Dani. Not Greg. He couldn't have them. But Deacon's gut told him that Jordan had taken them. "I'll be there in twenty."

He started his engine and raced down the long driveway, calling Bishop back. "It's Deacon. Jordan has Dani and Greg."

"Oh my God. We need to find his damn house."

"Do it fast. He's had them since last night. I'm going to Dani's apartment."

"You want me to send a CSU team?"

"Yeah, that'd be good. Tell Isenberg. Tell Faith to stay put."

He hit the main road in a spray of gravel and put his light

on the roof. *Get out of my way, people,* he thought. *You do not want to be slowing me down today. Hold on, Dani. I'm coming.*

Cincinnati, Ohio
Thursday, November 6, 4:15 p.m.

Faith paced the perimeter of the conference room, her hands shoved into her pockets to keep from wringing them together. Bishop, Tanaka, and Isenberg had their heads bent over a map, trying to determine where the house could be. Crandall was at his computer, running searches on property records. If Jordan had another house, he had it in another name, and that was what they needed to find.

Jordan had Dani and Greg. *He wants me. He'll try to trade for me.* But he didn't let witnesses live. So even if she traded herself, he was going to kill them. *Where did he take them?*

Everyone else was busy, and Faith was pacing. *I'm panicking. Not thinking.*

So think, Faith. Abruptly, she stopped and sat on a box of Foundation files. She closed her eyes and thought about Jordan, about all she'd learned about the O'Bannion family and their many issues. Jordan hated Joy. He hated Jeremy and Maggie. He hated his mother. But he may have hated his father most of all.

Why? Because Tobias had beaten him and ridiculed him and told him he was worthless. He'd sired him for parts. He'd kicked him out of the Foundation. He'd favored Joy over all of them.

She went still. "He stole from them. He stole from all of them."

Bishop, Isenberg, and Tanaka stared at her. "Jordan stole from who?" Bishop asked.

"No. Tobias. He stole from my grandmother. He took her land. He took her birthright so that he could keep up appearances with his peers. Jeremy said that Tobias's grief for Joy was bigger than his love for any of them. Out of either desperation or plain selfishness, he stole Barbara's family land. That land would have gone to my mother when she was twenty-one."

"But Tobias used it to fund the Foundation," Tanaka said.

"Wait." Isenberg held up a hand. "Why would Jordan want his mother's land? Land that should have gone to your mother? It wasn't his birthright that was stolen. It was your mother's."

"True." Faith looked at the whiteboard for inspiration — and found it. Nearly every box connected to Joy. "The land was Joy's first, but she died. Then . . ." Fury blew through her again as she thought about her mother. "Then he killed my mother. That would have been his land had his father not sold it. He and Jeremy would have split the O'Bannion land, but Jeremy had been disowned. And he had the O'Bannion property already claimed."

"He wanted it all," Isenberg said. "All right. You said it was the land up near Liberty Township. That land is all houses now. Maybe Jordan bought one of them."

"It was a lot of land," Faith said. "Thousands of acres. At least five or six square miles."

Tanaka did a calculation using his phone, and his shoulders sagged. "Assuming the average house is on a quarter-acre plot, that's at least ten thousand houses."

"And he didn't buy one in his own name," Crandall added.

"What else do we know?" Isenberg urged.

"We know he made Jade pose as his receptionist at Maguire and Sons," Bishop said. "The company lists John Maguire as the owner. Try that."

Crandall ran the search. "No, nothing."

"He wouldn't use Maguire and Sons," Faith said. "That company was going to be the fall guy if the bodies were ever discovered. He tried to lead Deacon and me in that direction when we had breakfast with him. Mr. Crandall, can you project a map of the land north of Millikin Road? Thank you," she said when the map appeared on the wall. "This is the area. My mother took me there once and showed me a brand-new house. She said it was where the old house had once stood. It got knocked down in the early eighties, when the land was cleared for construction, but I can't remember where it was. Can you look for land under the name of Corcoran?"

"Nothing," Crandall said. "That much land would be noted in a census at some point, wouldn't it?"

"Maybe." Faith bit at her lip. "My father might know. Excuse me. I'll call him now." She dialed her father's number and tapped her foot until he answered.

"Faith? Are you all right?"

"Oh, I'm fine," she lied. "Dad, I'm doing a search of the old homesteads, and I was trying to find where Gran's family lived before she married. Do you remember the place?"

"Oh, yes. I remember it well. It was north of the city, just farmland and rolling fields and trees. Your mother and I went up there for the first time on her twenty-first birthday." The sad smile in his voice made her own grief swell, and she dreaded having to tell him the truth. Dreaded having to admit the secret she'd kept so long. He sounded so tired. "That was the night she found out it wasn't hers anymore. Your mother was full of plans because you were on the way. She knew I didn't have much, but she had this house, so we'd have a place to raise our child. She hadn't been out there in a long time. She tried her key and it didn't work."

Faith thought of Sunday afternoon. She'd been so relieved when the key hadn't fit the door. "That's how she found out her father had sold the place?"

"Actually, the new owner told her when he came to the door with a shotgun. He said he was calling the cops if we didn't get off his property. She said there was a mistake, and he offered to show her the deed—that he'd bought the land from Tobias O'Bannion." His voice trembled. "I think the look of shock on her face got his attention. He put the gun down and invited us in. He'd bought the land from your grandfather, then sold it to a developer. A lot of money changed hands. I was so angry that night. Your mother was beyond devastated. So betrayed."

"Where was the house?"

"It's not there anymore," he said, his words coming more slowly. He was getting tired. She needed to get to what he remembered before he became too worn-out. "You can't visit it."

"I know, but I'm doing some genealogical stuff," she improvised. Not entirely untrue. "I really want the location of the old house."

"That's nice, dear, but I can't remember exactly where it was," her father said, mildly exasperated. "I remember that a creek ran near it. And you could see the old one-room schoolhouse from the front yard. Your mother liked that. She said it was being restored to be a historic landmark, so it should still be there."

"Near a creek and an old schoolhouse," Faith repeated for the benefit of Crandall and the others. "Do you remember the name of the guy who bought the house from Tobias?"

"Heavens, no. That was more than thirty years ago, Faith."

"Okay. Well, thanks, Dad. You're sounding tired. I've kept you too long. I'll let you go."

"Wait," he said with a sharpness that surprised her. "Are you going to tell me what's really going on here?"

"Um, sorry?" she asked as if clueless.

Her father blew out a breath. "Your grandmother's old house is all over the news, Faith. The reporters are all saying they've found bodies in the basement. Do you really expect me to believe you're doing genealogical studies in the midst of all that? Give me a little credit, honey."

She sighed. "Can I promise to tell you later? Things are a little hectic right now."

"Are you safe?"

"I am very safe. I'm in the police station."

"Well, all right. Did your uncle Jordan get you a phone? I asked him to."

She bit back her anger at her uncle. "I got my old number back today. You can use that."

"Good. I hate to keep going through him to contact you."

She frowned. "When else have you contacted him?"

"Sunday night," he admitted. "You said you'd call when you got back to your hotel room, but you didn't and I got worried. That road leading away from your grandmother's place is treacherous in the dark. I called your hotel, but they said you weren't registered."

"Because I'd checked in under Corcoran," she said. It seemed like a million years ago.

"And I was looking for Frye. That makes sense now, but by midnight I'd worked myself into a lather waiting by the phone and worrying, so I called Jordan and asked if he'd go over there and make sure you were okay."

She had dual pangs of guilt and sadness, picturing her father waiting by the phone. Until she realized what he'd said. "So Jordan knew which hotel I was staying in?"

Isenberg, Bishop, and Tanaka looked over at her expectantly.

"Sure. I thought you'd told him. You two were thick as thieves at one time."

"Yeah," she said calmly. "We were. I'll call you as soon as I can, Dad. I love you."

"Love you, too, baby. Be careful."

She hung up. "Jordan found my hotel because my father told him. That's how he knew to stake out that one room. He probably waited for me to leave Monday morning, then followed me into work."

"Where he put the tracker on your Jeep," Bishop said. "You might not want your dad to know that."

"I'm not so sure how well that'll work," Faith said. "Did that information help you at all, Mr. Crandall?"

"Yes and no. I have the creek and I have the schoolhouse, but there are still hundreds of houses to sort through and Novak's family may not have that much time."

"I don't think he's killed them yet," Faith said, needing to believe it was true. "He'll want to trade them for me."

"He can't have you," Isenberg said. "We don't trade, Faith."

She only nodded. She wasn't going to argue the point right now. "Can you find a record of the sale of the actual house?" she asked Crandall. "Dad said the person who bought the land kept the house. Joy died in 'seventy-five and the Foundation was formed in 'seventy-six, so it would have to be somewhere in between."

"Okay. It's not an easy search. Property records are by address or name or parcel, and I don't have any of those. And many of the old records haven't been uploaded to the Web site."

"The seller would have been Barbara O'Bannion."

Crandall tried it. "No, nothing."

Faith sat down hard in a chair, frustrated. "We know he had this new house as of ten years ago, because he took Jade there early on and beat her after she tried to pump Gran for information on the Mount Carmel house. The earliest instances of fake scholarship applicants were fifteen years ago. That's when Henson, Jr.'s, wife started to skim. If Jordan was skimming, too, he would have had a bump in income. He could have bought the house then."

"That narrows it down," Crandall said. "Fifty home sales in the area between the creek and the old schoolhouse." He moved back to let them see his computer screen.

"Phillip Smith," Bishop murmured as she read. "Alan Robinson, Theodore Davidson, Edward Saugh, David Florentino, Victor Shafer, Nathaniel Molyneaux, Shannon Bodine . . . Any of these names ringing a bell?"

"Oh my God," Faith said. "I think my Catholic-school education just paid off. There. Edward Saugh. E. Saugh."

"Esau," Crandall said, rolling his eyes. "Esau in the Bible had his birthright stolen." He clicked on the name, and the address popped up. "There you go, Lieutenant."

"Bishop, you go ahead," Isenberg said. "I'll direct the SWAT team up there, and then I'll call Novak. He can meet us there. Faith—"

"I know. Stay here. Stay safe. I got it. Go, go!"

Cincinnati, Ohio
Thursday, November 6, 4:15 p.m.

Deacon pulled up into the parking lot in front of Dani's apartment, too many pictures in his mind. Noel Lazar's head in a bag. Arianna, covered in slices and bruises. Jars filled with eyes. And the bodies. All the bodies.

He jumped out of the car, breathing too fast, he knew. But there wasn't a way to slow down. That monster had his family. *Please. Please don't let him hurt them.*

Adam was waiting for him at the front door. "CSU is up there. So is Dad. He's kicking himself for not taking your protective detail."

"I'm kicking myself for not calling Dani to hear her voice. Jordan must have used her phone to text me after he took her."

"Jordan?" Adam frowned. "I thought we were looking at Jeremy."

Deacon's mind blanked for a moment, overwhelmed with everything that had happened. But before he could say a word, his cell phone buzzed, Isenberg on the caller ID.

"We have a location for Jordan's house."

Deacon's chest compressed, leaving him breathless. "Where?"

"I just texted the address to your phone. I sent Bishop and the SWAT team that was with you earlier up ahead. I'm going there now. Hurry, Deacon."

"On my way," Deacon said, getting back in his car.

"I'm coming with you," Adam said. "Please. They're my family, too."

Deacon gave him a nod. "Get in and clear it with Isenberg on the way. Let's go."

Cincinnati, Ohio
Thursday, November 6, 4:45 p.m.

Faith looked at her phone for the fiftieth time in as many minutes. Everyone had blasted out of the police station, headed up to Jordan's house on the property that had once belonged to Gran. Deacon was racing to meet them up there.

She'd done what she could. Now there was nothing to do but wait. And watch her phone.

Which began to ring. Faith had to smile. It was the theme from *X-Men*. Deacon had downloaded it before giving her phone back. Caller ID was Jeremy. "Hello?"

"Faith, it's Uncle Jeremy. I was hoping we could continue our negotiations on the sale of the house from earlier."

Negotiations? An alarm bell started to ring in her mind. "Of course. What, when, and where did you have in mind?"

"Now would be good. I want to settle on a price. I've got to go out of town tomorrow afternoon and would like to get this taken care of between now and then. Can we meet in the hospital's cafeteria? I don't want to go too far from Marcus's side."

What the hell? This was not Jeremy speaking of his own volition. He was talking nonsense, and he knew the police wanted her to stay at the station for her own safety.

Someone must be forcing him to try to draw her out. *Jordan.* "That's fine. I'll meet you there. I'll have to hail a cab and we're heading into rush hour, so it might take me a while. Be patient. I'll be there."

She hung up, her heart pounding. She needed to call

Deacon and Bishop, but they were focused on Jordan's house right now. But if Jordan was trying to lure her out, he would be close to the police station or the hospital. Either way, she'd promised Deacon she wouldn't leave.

Jeremy had said he was going to Della's. She didn't have that number, but she knew who would. She dialed the hospital. "Hello, can I have Stone O'Bannion's room?" Stone was not in ICU. More botherable than his brother Marcus.

"Yes?" a husky voice snapped.

"Stone, this is Faith. Your cousin. Is Jeremy there?"

"No, why?"

God, I hope I'm doing the right thing. "Because he just called me. He asked me to meet him at the hospital to discuss buying Gran's house. He acted like it was a continued conversation, but we never discussed any such thing."

"Because he doesn't want your damn house."

"I know. That's why I'm looking for him. I'm afraid someone was with him, making him say those things. I think it was Jordan and, if it was, Jeremy's in trouble."

"The guy in the ski mask," Stone murmured. "He was Jeremy's size. I'll call you back." He hung up, and Faith tapped her foot impatiently until her phone rang again. "He's not with Audrey and Mom or with Marcus. Call the police, then keep me informed," he said as autocratically as if she'd been his servant.

"Of course," she said, determined not to be offended. "Stand by."

She hung up and had started to dial Deacon when Jeremy's number came through again. Steeling her spine, she picked up. "Hello," she half sang, as if she hadn't a care in the world.

"Where are you, Faith?" It was the same voice as before, or sounded like it. Except now the tone was menacing. "You haven't come to meet me."

It could be Jeremy. Or it could be Jordan using Jeremy's phone, pretending to be Jeremy.

"I told you it would take me a while. Really, Jeremy, if you're going to be like this, maybe I won't sell you my house at all."

"Where are you, Faith?"

"On my way. I told you I'd have to catch a cab."

A dark chuckle. "Don't play games with me. You're stalling me so that you can tell your boyfriend that I've called. Here's a new invitation: Get your ass out here in five minutes, or I start shooting your new friends."

A text came through and she fought the dread, forcing herself to look. What she saw was a photo of Dani, a gun to her head, her expression grim and determined. *"No,"* she cried, the word slipping out before she could control it. "No," she said more firmly. "Of course I don't want that. But what about the others? Greg and the child, Roza. How do I know they're alive?"

"You try my patience."

"You insult my intelligence," she fired back. "I want proof you haven't killed them all before I climb up on the sacrificial altar."

"Very well. You now have three minutes, fifteen seconds." He hung up and immediately called back using Face-Time. Live video streaming. But it wasn't his own face. It was Greg's terrified one that filled her phone's screen, the noise of the street the accompanying sound.

He knows I haven't come out. He must be right outside.

"Okay, okay," she said quietly. "I'm coming. Don't hurt him."

"Come out of the building, then wait for my instructions. I'll text this number."

The phone call ended, leaving Faith trembling. *Get a grip. Get a plan. Call Deacon.* She opened the texted photo again. And leaned in closer. Above Dani's head was the portrait of Joy, the face slashed, just like Jade had said. *He has them at his house on Gran's family's old property. Or at least he did.*

She dialed Deacon, and he picked up before the first ring was completed. "Faith?"

She shuddered out a breath. "He's here, Deacon. Outside the police station. He said if I don't come out in three minutes, he'll start shooting."

"No! You do *not* leave the station. He will kill you."

"He may have Jeremy, but I know he's got Greg with him. I think Dani is at his house."

"Fuck. You do not leave the station. There are cops all around you. Tell one of them."

"Can you get a sniper in position in under three minutes? Because if you can't, he is going to kill an innocent

boy. He has a gun to Greg's head. Now, listen to me. I'm not
stupid, nor do I have a death wish, but I cannot allow anyone else to die in my place. Especially not someone you
love. So this is what I'm going to do."

Cincinnati, Ohio
Thursday, November 6, 5:05 p.m.

"Hurry, hurry." Faith glanced up at the elevator panel, her
fingers fumbling with the settings on her iPhone. *Forward,
forward, where is it? Oh, okay.* She forwarded all calls to the
prepaid cell with the broken screen and stepped off the elevator. Using her iPhone, she dialed Deacon's number and
waited until he picked up before turning on the speaker and
sliding the phone into her pocket.

"Faith, do not do this!" Deacon snapped, his voice coming from the phone in her pocket.

"No more talking," she said without moving her lips.
"I'm going outside now."

She looked up and down the street and saw the white
van. Greg stood in front of the slightly open middle door,
his expression grim. He took a little stumbling step, like he
was pushed, then climbed into the passenger seat.

She wished she had her gun. She'd brought it with her
that morning but had left it locked in the trunk of Deacon's
car since she couldn't bring it into the PD building.

Her prepaid cell phone dinged, and she checked the text
that had been forwarded from her iPhone number. Barely
visible through the cracked screen, it said: *Get behind the
wheel.*

Faith obeyed. Once she was in the car, she saw that Jordan was sitting directly behind the center console, his gun
trained on Greg. At first glance he could have passed for
Jeremy with his mustache, crisp tailored shirt, and tie, but
Faith had seen Jeremy up close just hours before. Jeremy's
face was gaunt, his eyes had bags beneath them. The man
who sat behind her was a little pale but otherwise seemed
healthy.

He's got Jeremy, or at least his phone. Faith knew better
than to hope for the second one.

"See, we can all get along if you obey," Jordan said. "Toss
your cell phone."

"But—" Faith cut off the protest she'd made just for appearance's sake and dropped the broken prepaid phone to the pavement.

"Put your hands on the wheel and drive."

Faith obeyed. "Where am I going?"

"Always a bossy bitch. Just go straight."

She tried to remember to breathe as she moved into traffic. "Pretty bold, Jeremy. You pulled a kidnapping in front of hundreds of people and nobody's the wiser."

"I did, didn't I?"

"Can I ask you a question?"

"No. Just shut up and drive."

"You're going to kill me, so it costs you nothing. Did you kill my mother?"

"Obviously you think I did, or you wouldn't have asked it."

She smacked the steering wheel, furious. "Answer my question."

"Yes, I did. I had to. She saw something she shouldn't have seen."

"You murdering Melinda Hooper," she said, naming the victim he'd abducted that day.

He huffed a mirthless laugh. "Melinda Hooper. You've been busy."

"She was a Foundation recipient."

"Yes, she was. You always were too smart. I should've killed you that day, too, but that would have been harder to explain."

"Why didn't you kill me when I lived with you? Why draw it out like this?"

"I figured it would be easier and more fun to bring you into my web of sin." He said it mockingly. "If you were ever tempted—" He stopped abruptly, then yanked her hair, making her cry out and jerk the wheel so hard they went into the next lane.

Faith righted the van's path. "Trying to cause another car accident, Jeremy?"

His grip on her hair tightened until her eyes watered. "Cut the shit. You knew I wasn't Jeremy. How?"

"He never uses his right hand, and at the moment, your right hand is clutching a gun. Plus, he's been grieving for his son, so his face is a little less pretty than yours at the moment."

"Who else knows?"

"I don't know. Why didn't you kill me when I lived with you?"

"Because once you'd jumped in the fast party lane, nobody would have believed you even if you had broken our little secret pact. Especially my sainted mother."

"Did you kill Gran?"

"No. Killing my *mother* would have been stupid. She was my gravy train."

Something in his voice gave her pause. "Your father? You killed him?"

"He had it coming."

"How?"

"Drive, Faith."

She held on to the wheel and prayed that Deacon was still behind her somewhere. A movement in her rearview had her flicking her eyes up to the mirror, and her heart sank. Dani and Roza were back there. *God, this is a mess. Please help me. Please help Deacon if I fail. He'll have no one left.*

I'm so glad I told my dad that I loved him today.

Cincinnati, Ohio
Thursday, November 6, 5:20 p.m.

"Left at the corner," Adam said, his grip on Deacon's phone iron tight.

Deacon was grateful Adam had come. His cousin had taken over tracking Faith's phone, leaving Deacon free to drive. And to worry, because he could hear every word between Jordan and Faith. He had muted his end so Jordan wouldn't know that Faith still had an open phone connection.

They could track her even if the connection was broken, but this way they could hear everything Jordan said.

Jordan knew that Faith knew the truth. Somewhere he was still holding Dani and Roza. Jeremy was missing, too, having not arrived at his ex-wife's house, where he'd been expected.

They'd driven out of the city and were heading east on Kellogg Avenue, along the river. They were going toward the O'Bannion mansion in Mount Carmel. Or Jordan might plan to shoot all of his captives and throw them in the river.

Deacon's gut turned to water and his blood to ice. *Don't think like that. Stay focused.*

Faith's voice came through the phone's speaker again. "How did you kill your father?" she asked Jordan.

"He was on heart medication," Jordan replied. "I just forced him to take a few extra doses."

"Because he'd fired you from the Foundation for stealing."

"You seem to know a lot, kiddo," Jordan said mockingly.

"How did you learn to stitch like a surgeon?"

"Practice, practice, practice," Jordan drawled. "My guests accommodated me by allowing me to use their skin. It's not so hard."

"And the embalming?"

"Bought a machine, bought a book. Turn left up ahead, Faith."

"What are you going to do with me?" she asked.

"You know the answer to that."

Oh God, Deacon thought. "Where's our backup?" he asked Adam.

"We have two unmarked cars behind us. The left turn Faith took puts them on Wilmer. He's headed to Lunken Airport. I have three units a half mile away from the airport."

The turnoff Faith had taken was now in sight, and Deacon increased his speed. "How did you know he'd go there?"

"I didn't. Isenberg and I put together a plan while you've been driving. We have backup stationed all over town, just in case."

Faith's voice rose from the speakers once again. "It was you in my apartment in Miami, wasn't it?"

Jordan made an impatient noise. "You know it was."

"How did you make yourself look like Combs?"

"Not too difficult. I wore a padded coat. Old theater prop."

"Which was why they never found the bullet or your blood. The padding of your sleeves caught it all, so you left no DNA behind. Clever."

"So happy you approve," he said sarcastically.

"What will you do to the others?" she asked.

"They've served their purpose," Jordan said.

"Even Roza?"

"I'll keep her," Jordan answered. "Her aunt's gotten a bit long in the tooth. Roza will be a good 'housekeeper.'"

"At least he doesn't know we've got Jade," Deacon said. "He must not have been back to his townhouse or the studio all day."

"He's been busy kidnapping people," Adam grunted.

"Novak won't let you go," Faith said. "You kill his brother and sister and he will hunt you down to the ends of the earth."

"He has Dani with him, too," Deacon said. "Tell Bishop."

"Not worried, kiddo," Jordan was saying. "He'll be chasing the wrong brother. Even if he suspects, he'll have nothing on me and everything on Jeremy. Including your body in the back of Jeremy's lover's Range Rover."

"Okay," Adam said. "They're slowing down. Turning right . . . into the playfields. Smart. Sun's going down. No night games scheduled. It'll be deserted. Okay, it's that white van. The one that's stopping next to the parked Range Rover. Must be Jeremy's."

"It's Keith's," Deacon said, slowing down so he didn't give away their position. "They used it to dodge our surveillance."

"New text from Bishop," Adam said. "They have Jeremy and Keith. Jordan shot out Keith's knees so he couldn't fight him."

"Where's the SWAT team?"

"On their way to us. Isenberg, too. We've got squad-car backup minutes away."

Deacon killed his headlights and prayed that Jordan wouldn't notice them until it was too late.

"I know these playfields," Adam said. "Keep going another hundred feet. There's a shaded lot, plenty of trees. We leave the car and double back through the woods. It'll take us another thirty seconds, but it could save their lives."

Every instinct Deacon possessed screamed at him to turn *now*, to get to them *now*. But he kept going, following Adam's instructions. As soon as he stopped the sedan, he was out and running, Adam at his side. They were fifty feet from the van when the driver's door opened.

Faith got out, walking stiffly, her face pale. She stopped next to the sliding door on the van's passenger side.

"Greg's in the front passenger seat," Adam said. "Dani and Roza must be in the back."

Deacon and Adam crept forward as the van's side door slid open and Jordan got out, a nine mil in his hand. He took off his suit coat and laid it in the van, then lifted the hatch of Jeremy's Range Rover. Wrapping Faith's hair around his fist, he dragged her to the vehicle and shoved her halfway in, his gun pressed to the back of her head. He seemed to be making her pick something up.

Faith straightened, her face stricken with horror. She held a gas can in her arms.

Deacon's blood froze in his veins. "He's going to set her on fire, like he did to her mother. *Let's go. Go. Go.*"

Gun in hand, Deacon charged, unaware that he was screaming until his throat started to burn.

Jordan spun around, his jaw going slack with shock, but he recovered quickly, shoving the barrel of his pistol against Faith's temple. "I will kill her," he shouted. "I will drop her like a rock. So freeze, Novak."

"You won't leave here alive," Deacon said, slowing to a walk. Adam had made it around the other side of the van and was inching closer.

Dragging Faith with him, Jordan backed up toward the van, its side door still open. "I said freeze, Novak."

"She's not the only one who knows, Jordan. We all heard you confess. Her phone was in her pocket, connected to mine the whole time. You're not walking away."

"I think I will. I'm going to get back into my van and we're all going to drive away, pretty Faith at the wheel." Jordan pulled his arm across Faith's throat, taking the final step backward so that his back was up against the van's open side. All he had to do was take one step up and he'd be able to pull Faith back into the van, just as he'd said he'd do. "So, Agent Novak, if you want your family to survive this day, you will get back in your car and drive—"

Jordan's mouth gaped open like a fish as he gasped. One knee bent, then he went crashing to the ground, dragging Faith with him. The slim hilt of a kitchen knife stuck out of his back.

And an eleven-year-old girl with big, dark eyes and ratty, tangled hair stood in the van's open doorway, looking down at him with contempt. *Roza.*

"Holy shit," Deacon whispered, then started running again, Adam at his side.

Jordan staggered to his knees, waving his gun around like a drunkard. He pointed the gun at Roza and pulled the trigger, his shot going wide. The van's passenger door flew open and Greg jumped out. Grabbing Roza in his arms, he dove for cover.

Another shot split the air, followed by a yelp of pain. *Greg.*

And Faith . . . She wasn't moving. She lay on the ground, her hair still wound around Jordan's wrist. He jerked her up by her hair, arching her back, his gun to her temple again. She blinked, her eyes moving dizzily.

"Put the guns down, gentlemen," Jordan wheezed. "Now."

He was losing blood. Deacon could see it. They just needed to wait him out. Faith was regaining her composure, her eyes growing clearer as Deacon watched.

"I *said* put the *damn* guns *down*." With every emphasized word, Jordan ground the gun into Faith's head, making her wince. Making her pissed off.

Deacon slowly crouched, placing his gun on the ground, hearing Adam behind him doing the same. *Watch her face,* he thought. She was getting ready to do something.

In one motion, Faith twisted, bringing her left fist up to Jordan's right shoulder—where Corinne's bullet had pierced him the day before—then closed her hand over his arm in a claw grip and hung on. With a howl, Jordan dropped the gun and tried to pull her off him, but she clung, digging her fingers in deep.

She pushed him to his stomach, straddling him, grabbing the gun he'd dropped. Gun in one hand, she yanked the wig off his head with her other, then smacked the back of his head with the gun, and Jordan went limp. "You're not getting away with it," she snarled, raising the weapon and hitting him again. "I won't let you. I won't, I won't, I won't."

Her breaths came hard and fast as she lifted the butt of the gun to hit Jordan a third time.

"Faith, no," Deacon cried, rushing up to scoop his own gun from the ground, then pulling Faith off Jordan's back. "He's down. You can stop now. He's down."

Jordan lay on the ground, unconscious, the hilt of the knife still sticking up out of his back.

"He didn't get away with it," Faith said quietly, staring down at her uncle.

"No, honey, you didn't let him." Deacon pulled her into his arms as Adam ran to Greg, turning him over.

"Greg's been hit," Adam said. "He needs an ambulance."

New panic engulfed Deacon. "Where's Dani?" he demanded.

"In the back of the van," Faith said. "She's tied up."

Adam jumped into the van to release Dani so that she could help Greg.

The scene became surreally quiet, the sound of Adam's voice calling 911 fading away so that the beat of his own heart was all Deacon could hear. He let Faith go and took a step toward Greg's still body, but then training kicked in, reminding him of what still needed to be done.

Restrain the bastard and see to the injured.

Deacon dropped to one knee so that he could handcuff the still-unconscious Jordan. He pulled the cuffs from his belt, his hands feeling slow and clumsy. He looked over at Greg, who hadn't moved.

He glanced toward the main road, where three squad cars approached, lights flashing.

It's about time, he thought irritably, until he realized that they had been only a few minutes behind them. Everything had happened so damn fast.

And then, from the corner of his eye, he saw a flash of silver as Jordan rolled to his side and aimed a long, thin blade at his throat.

The bastard was playing possum, Deacon thought as fire seared his throat. He could feel the knife pulling free as he slumped backward, his eyes locked on Jordan O'Bannion's crazed face.

Jordan came to his knees and, hand shaking, raised the blade again. *Lift your arms and block it,* Deacon told himself, but his arms seemed so heavy. His gaze shifted from Jordan's face to the blade as, in his mind, he braced for the blow.

It never came. A shot cracked the air, and Jordan's green eyes widened briefly in shock before he crumpled to the ground.

Faith ran over, Jordan's gun in her hand. Deacon could see her face. Could hear her screaming his name. But he couldn't breathe. Weakly, he touched his throat and felt the warmth of his own blood. *Shit.*

Cincinnati, Ohio
Thursday, November 6, 5:26 p.m.

"Deacon!" Faith shouted his name. She fell to her knees beside him as blood spurted up from the wound in his throat. Dropping the gun she'd used to shoot Jordan, she pressed her hands to Deacon's throat, trying to stop the flow. "Dani! Help me!"

Uniformed officers from the three squad cars rushed the scene as Dani stumbled out of the van. She looked from Greg to Deacon and a split second later was at Faith's side.

"What do I do?" Faith asked, fighting the panic.

"Go to Greg. Use whatever you can to stop his bleeding. Leave Deacon to me. *Go!*"

Faith scrambled across the asphalt to where Greg lay, pale and blinking slowly. "D?" he asked. "What happened?"

"Dani's got him," Faith said, trying to keep her voice positive. "Where are you hit?"

"Leg," Greg said. "Hurts like a bitch."

It didn't look too bad though, Faith thought. It wasn't gushing like Deacon's throat was. She pulled off her sweatshirt and pressed the fabric to the wound. Then she looked at the little girl sitting on the pavement, watching it all with large, dark eyes.

"You're Roza," she said. "I'm Faith."

"Faith Frye," Roza said. "He was afraid of you."

"Good," Faith said with a fierce nod. "He should have been."

Roza's gaze locked with hers. "He killed my mother," she said.

Faith nodded soberly. "He killed mine, too."

"Then it's good we both got to kill him," she said tonelessly. "Where is Corinne?"

"In the hospital. She's okay. She's worried about you."

"I'm okay," the child said, still tonelessly.

Oh no, sweetheart, Faith thought. *You are not okay. None of us are.* "Where did you get the knife?"

"From Corinne, back in the woods."

"How did you free yourself?"

"She gave me the knife," Dani said from behind her. "I cut her free. She was supposed to free me next, but she stabbed him instead."

Bracing herself, Faith turned around to look at Deacon and her heart stopped. His face was nearly as white as his hair. But Dani's hands moved quickly and competently. Dani met her eyes for a split second and gave her a hard nod, and Faith's heart began to beat a little more normally.

"Is he gonna die?" Greg asked, and Faith returned her attention to the boy.

"No," she said firmly. "He won't. He can't. Dani won't let him. Neither will we."

One of the officers ran up to Greg with a first-aid kit. "I can take over here, ma'am," he said.

Faith nodded, scooting back on her butt to get out of the way. She didn't have the energy to stand. And then a pair of strong arms lifted her, and she found herself face-to-face with a very pale, very shaken Adam Kimble.

"You saved his life," Adam said hoarsely. "Look."

Faith swallowed back the tears as they both turned to look at Deacon. His amazing eyes were open and they were watching her. His chest rose and fell with shallow but even breaths. His throat no longer spurted blood, Dani's field dressing holding firm. He lifted his arm an inch off the ground, holding out his hand.

On rubber legs she walked over to him, Kimble keeping her upright until she was at Deacon's side. She fell to her knees a second time and, grasping his hand, brought it to her lips.

"Thank you." He mouthed the words.

She smiled down at him. "I told you that I hit what I aim at," she said, and his lips curved. An ambulance pulled into the lot behind the three squad cars. "Your ride is here. They're gonna have to patch you up, but I'll be there when you open your eyes."

Cincinnati, Ohio
Tuesday, November 11, 10:00 a.m.

"You look like little Red Riding Hood," Deacon said from the hospital bed, his laugh as rusty as an old gate. "Your basket's almost bigger than you are."

"Hardly," Faith said, relieved to see him looking so good. He'd lost a lot of blood when Jordan had stabbed him in the throat. Luckily, his throat was covered in layers of hard muscle, which slowed Jordan's blade down. A fraction of an inch deeper or to the side and he might have bled out. Still, he'd been intubated and sedated for two whole days. His voice was raspy and might not ever sound the same as it had before, but he could still make her shiver when he said her name.

"I have lots of people to see, so my basket is full of goodies," she told him. "But since you're special, you get first pick. I have books and flowers and toys. . . ."

"I want Red Riding Hood," he said, his grin more than a little naughty. He reached out the arm that wasn't connected to tubes. "Everyone else can have what's in the basket."

She put the basket on a chair and walked into his arms, the first time she'd been able to do so since everything went down the week before. "You scared me," she whispered.

His arm tightened around her. "You scared me, too. Promise me you will never, ever get in a car with a maniacal, serial-killing uncle again."

"I won't. I promise."

"Thank you." He kissed her mouth before letting her go and patting the side of the bed. "Tell me what's happening."

She settled next to him and took his hand. "Well, Jordan is still dead."

"That's good. Maniacal, serial-killing zombie uncles are damn hard to kill again."

She chuckled, then sobered. "I never killed anyone before, but I'm not sorry. I feel like I should feel something, but . . . I'm totally okay with what I did."

"If you hadn't shot him, I wouldn't be here. So I'm okay with it, too. What other news?"

"Bishop found Jordan's souvenirs. They were in a box in the house where he held Dani and the others. Driver's licenses, jewelry, phones . . ." Just like his case in West Virginia.

"I know," he said quietly. "Bishop told me. She and Lynda are organizing all the victims' belongings to give to their families when the case is closed. I have to admit I'm glad I don't have to do that again. But Scarlett's looking like I did last year. I hate that."

Faith patted his hand. "She has a partner who she can talk to when the burden gets too heavy." She sighed. "But the good news is that Jeremy's been officially cleared. It turns out that he keeps a very detailed calendar. He was able to account for his whereabouts for all of the seventeen abductions. He offered the information voluntarily. He doesn't want anyone to wonder if he's the other half of an unholy duo. He thinks Jordan took him and Keith so that they wouldn't have an alibi for my death. And Dani's and Greg's. Jordan was going to leave us in Keith's Range Rover and then put Jeremy at the wheel and cause another accident. A big, fiery one."

"I'm so glad you killed that sonofabitch," Deacon said mildly, but his eyes were hard.

"Physically, Jeremy's fine, but Keith's in bad shape. The ortho guys are working on his knees and talking about steel plates. Marcus is out of ICU, and Stone's been released. Mickey's funeral is tomorrow, and of course I'll go." She drew a deep breath. "On a happy note, Arianna and Corinne have a Facebook page and currently have twenty-five thousand likes."

"Wow."

"Meredith is worried that all the publicity may make it harder for Arianna to cope with the sexual assault, but Arianna says she's not hiding from life and I say good for her. Both Meredith and I will be here if she decides she needs us." She tapped her lip. "Greg is uncomfortable, but okay. He likes that the girls from school come and fuss over him. That he got shot in the leg saving Roza's life has earned him major hero points."

"What about me? Do I get hero points?"

She threaded their fingers together. "You were already a superhero. How do you get better than that?"

"I don't have an answer for that," he murmured.

She leaned forward and kissed him gently. "You looked so good coming across that field, screaming like a crazy man, your coat flowing out behind you. If I hadn't been terrified for my life, I would have jumped your bones right there."

He snorted a laugh. "Right there?"

"Well, I would have pitched a tent or something. Privacy and public nudity concerns."

He chuckled. "I'm so glad you're here."

"Me, too. Literally. We have to thank Roza most of all."

"How is she?"

"Well . . . fine and totally not fine, depending on the moment. Meredith is working with her, too. Jade's not being charged with anything, and the Kendricks are here from Vancouver. They want to take both Roza and Jade, but Roza is super-attached to Corinne. Poor Corinne can barely take a bathroom break, but she doesn't seem to mind. It'll be years before Roza even approaches normal. Her father is here. He is so happy to have her in his life that he might transfer here so she can stay near Corinne."

"He came by, actually. Roza's father. He was so grateful that he cried." Deacon cleared his throat. "And then Bishop came by. She's pissed that she missed all the excitement."

"That's what she claimed when you were in surgery. But I think she was a little worried about you. Let's see. . . . The bellman is going to make a full recovery and the woman from the grocery store is conscious. She'll have a more difficult recovery, but that she survived at all was a miracle. Turns out she runs a no-kill shelter for dogs. She's got friends who are caring for the dogs until she's able to go back to work. Dani and I thought we'd go out there to get a dog once you and Greg are out of the hospital."

He smiled at her. "I like that idea. Dani's always wanted a dog. Greg has, too. But it needs to be a big dog. A manly dog. No little froufrou dogs with ribbons in their hair."

"We'll make sure it's a manly dog," she promised. "Oh, we figured out how Jordan got to Miami and back that weekend. The FBI was checking commercial aircraft. I got to thinking about how he got to Miami so fast when I was injured by Combs."

"You said he was there even before your dad and Lily."

"Because he chartered a flight. I asked Crandall to check with the charter services that fly out of Lunken. Jordan used his Edward Saugh ID to charter a flight to Miami that weekend and he rented a white van. What else . . . ? Oh, yeah. Henson's grandson and daughter-in-law broke down and admitted to fraud but not murder. They didn't know that Jordan had planned the car accident that hospitalized Henson Junior. Both Henson Senior and Mrs. Lowell are retiring, but I think I'd be hiring new lawyers anyway."

"And your job? Did you get your job back from the bank?"

"No, I don't want to work for them." She lifted her brows. "I got an offer from CPD."

His mouth fell open. "You're kidding. Really?"

"Really. Isenberg wants me as a department psychologist. I also got one from a counseling center. I'd be working with Meredith Fallon. I'm probably going to pick door number two."

"Damn," Deacon said mildly. "I had fantasies about you with a billy club."

She grinned at him. "Me, too."

He traced a pattern on her arm. "What about your mother?"

Her grin faded. "I asked Carrie Washington not to exhume her. Jordan told me what I needed to know. I still have to tell my dad about the murder."

"I'll go with you as soon as they clear me to travel."

"Thank you. Hopefully, they'll clear you soon. Isenberg's kept the murder of my mother undisclosed for now, but I'm afraid somebody's going to run with the story. I don't want Dad to hear about it on the news."

"I'll get better as fast as I can," Deacon promised. "I want him to hear the story about how his daughter saved my life."

Faith smiled at him. "You saved mine. In more ways than one." She leaned in to kiss his mouth, then slid from the bed. "I've got goodies to deliver. But if you're good, I'll let you play wolf later."

His eyes sparkled. "Then I promise to be very, very good."

Don't miss the books in Karen Rose's Baltimore series:

Watch Your Back
Did You Miss Me?
No One Left to Tell
You Belong to Me

And look for her next Cincinnati novel,
coming from Signet in Winter 2016.